The Annotated Baseball Stories of Ring W. Lardner, 1914-1919

The Annotated

EDITED BY George W. Hilton

Baseball Stories of RING W. LARDNER

• 1914-1919 •

STANFORD UNIVERSITY PRESS / Stanford, California / 1995

Stanford University Press
Stanford, California

Printed in the United States of America

CIP data are at the end of the book

Stanford University Press publications are
distributed exclusively by Stanford University Press
within the United States, Canada, and Mexico; they
are distributed exclusively by Cambridge University Press
throughout the rest of the world

To the Fair Constance,
because the decision to propose to her
was made in Comiskey Park

—upper deck, left field

Preface

At risk of understatement, this volume has had a long history. I discovered Ring Lardner's baseball fiction in 1940, when I came upon a copy of his "Round Up" in the Woodlawn branch of the Chicago Public Library. The first paragraph of "Alibi Ike" is the only piece of literature I can remember that reduced me to uncontrollable laughter in a library reading room. Because that story has no empirical content—does not deal with real ballplayers or teams—it did not immediately addict me to Lardner's baseball fiction. When I read *You Know Me Al* in college a few years later, I was impressed with its literary quality, but what captivated me was its setting—on my own team, the Chicago White Sox. I immediately recognized that a great number of the ballplayers and other characters were actual figures, but wondered how many were, and how many were simply fictional.

As it proved, many years were to pass before I began to inquire systematically into Lardner's use of real, as opposed to fictional, characters. When I married in 1970 I sought a project for work in short periods at home in the evenings, and began that process of identification and interpretation—an effort that was greatly facilitated by the first edition of Macmillan's *The Baseball Encyclopedia*, which had been published the year before. The founding of the Society for American Baseball Research at the National Baseball Museum and Hall of Fame at Cooperstown on August 10, 1971, also greatly advanced the research. By one of the remarkable coincidences with which my life appears filled, I discovered the Society's founding on the following day, in the copy of the New York *Times* I brought along to read on the bus from New York to Cooperstown for my initial research on this project.

From the outset I recognized that it was impractical to attempt the publication of an edition at that time. The policy pursued by Lardner's heirs did not allow the reprinting of stories that had not been collected in book form in Ring's lifetime, on grounds that Ring had considered such stories inferior. They continued that policy, with the exception of two stories, "Call for Mr. Keefe!" and "Along Came Ruth," which were published in *Some Champions* in 1976, until authorizing the publication of *Ring Around the Bases: The Complete Baseball Stories of Ring Lardner* in 1992. Accordingly, I decided to pursue the project on a more leisurely basis, updating my manuscript as the remaining living players mentioned in the stories died, drawing on biographies of the players as they appeared, and aiming at publication as the copyrights expired. A further complication was that the American copyright law was in limbo at the time; pending revision, the copyrights on literature were being extended on a year-to-year basis. Congress finally resolved the problem in 1976 by providing for the expiration of copyrights 50 years after the death of the author, or 75 years after the first publication of the work, whichever came later. This set my target date for completion of a manuscript at 1994.

But that this book would be so long delayed in preparation proved an almost unmixed advantage. Jonathan Yardley's biography, *Ring*, the various publications of the Society for American Baseball Research, the *Biographical Dictionary of American Sports*, *The Ballplayers*, learned biographies of Ban Johnson, Ty Cobb, John McGraw, and Babe Ruth, and several other works have all appeared in the interim, to the great benefit of the documentation both of Lardner and of American baseball. The identification of actual figures by years of birth and death could be rendered complete, for no one mentioned in the stories remains alive today. Publication of Matthew J. Bruccoli and Richard Layman's *Ring W. Lardner: A Descriptive Bibliography* also greatly facilitated this book, as it would any other edition of Lardner. (In the present volume, a Bibliography of General Works on Lardner precedes the Index.)

Necessarily, my obligations are many. L. Robert Davids, William J. Weiss, Robert Hoie, Ray Nemec, Bob McConnell, Bill Haber, Jack Smalling, and many other members of SABR assisted me with identifications. The late Paul C. Frisz drew on his extensive collection on the Central League and on Terre Haute baseball generally to help document Jack Keefe's professional origins. A generation of historians and librarians at the National Baseball Museum and Hall of Fame in Cooperstown have been most helpful. Professors Walton R. Patrick of Auburn University and Howard W. Webb of Southern Illinois University, both of them leading Lardner scholars, were very encouraging at the outset of the project, and Professor Webb was kind enough to read the final draft of the Introduction, as were Jonathan Yardley, L. Robert Davids, Barry M. Schutz, and Professor Leonard H. Frey of San Diego State University. I had hoped to impose such duties upon Professor Patrick, as well, but, sadly, he died in 1986; I trust that my debt to his *Ring Lardner* is apparent, however. L. Robert Davids read the footnotes for accuracy, but I retain responsibility for any remaining errors. Eric C. Gabler provided invaluable computer assistance. Phyllis B. Hilton thought the project worth undertaking, and Constance M. Hilton considered it worth completing.

In the annotations, presented as footnotes, my method has been to identify each actual person on his or her—there *are* two women—first occurrence in the stories, and in each case to provide a suitable amount of biographical detail at that point (see the headnote to the Index). My note scheme thus necessarily concentrates the notes in the earlier stories, and that problem is exacerbated by the fact that in the stories beginning with "Alibi Ike" Lardner used fictional characters where the earlier stories had used actual persons. It is not, as the later paucity of notes might suggest, that my enthusiasm for documentation declined as the project advanced. And unlike the earlier stories, where I have placed a number of old photos, there is little to illustrate in the later stories.

I have assembled lifetime records and other data on players' performances from the Fourth Edition of *The Baseball Encyclopedia* (1977), which Organized Baseball accepted as official after the earlier editions were seen to have presented problems in reconciling scoring practices, as between the methods in use at the time these stories were written and those employed at present. Assertions of all-time major league records, which every new baseball season threatens to erase, are valid as of the close of the 1989 season. On the recommendation of Thomas R. Heitz, librarian of the National Baseball Library at Cooperstown, I accepted the names of players as given in John Thorn and Pete Palmer, *Total Baseball* (New York: Warner Books, Inc., 1989), except in a few cases where I used the name shown on a player's death certificate.

It should be noted explicitly that there is no reason to believe that I have exhausted the empirical content of these stories, or indeed that it *can* be exhausted. It would be presumptuous, after all, for any editor to believe either that he knew precisely and exhaustively what was in Lardner's mind when he wrote these works or that today's marvelous panoply of baseball historiography has omitted or got wrong nothing of consequence.

Finally, it will be noted that my father, Lucius W. Hilton, enters into the footnotes at two points, on one occasion identifying the location of a saloon frequented by White Sox fans and, on another, clarifying what had been to me an incomprehensible reference to a poker pot. What I have no doubt my mother would have wanted said is that he was a considerably more respectable figure than those two references might lead the reader to believe. He was, however, very much a part of the era of these stories, and of their subject matter. In 1914 he was a student at the University of Chicago, and by 1919 he was a bright young graduate rising in the city's financial community. He was also a baseball fan, from his childhood to his death at the age of 87. He attended the 1906 World Series, saw Ed Walsh's no-hit game in 1911, and saw the 1919 White Sox frequently. He took me to my first game in Comiskey Park in 1936, and I took him to a game there on his 80th birthday in 1973. He died during the baseball strike of 1981. Given the old gentleman's taste for gallows humor in his later years, I have no question that his posthumous evaluation would be that he had survived a stroke, a heart attack, and various malignancies, but he could not have survived that! He richly deserves being in these pages.

G. W. H.

Contents

Introduction 1

◆ The Jack Keefe Stories, 1914–1919

The six stories subsequently collected in the volume You Know Me Al

A Busher's Letters Home 33
The Busher Comes Back 72
The Busher's Honeymoon 100
A New Busher Breaks In 120
The Busher's Kid 144
The Busher Beats It Hence 168

Later Jack Keefe Stories

Call for Mr. Keefe! 192
The Busher Reenlists 216
The Battle of Texas 236
Along Came Ruth 256
The Courtship of T. Dorgan 280
The Busher Pulls a Mays 302

◆ The Individual Short Stories, 1914–1917

My Roomy 331
Sick 'Em 362

Horseshoes 394
Back to Baltimore 423
Alibi Ike 448
Harmony 466
The Poor Simp 485
Where Do You Get That Noise? 504
Good for the Soul 525
The Crook 549
The Hold-out 573
The Yellow Kid 593

Bibliography of General Works on Lardner 615
Index 619

The Annotated Baseball Stories of Ring W. Lardner, 1914-1919

Introduction

As deeply as baseball permeates American culture, it is inevitable that the sport should have brought forth a literary masterpiece. That masterpiece, collectively, is the baseball fiction of Ring Lardner. Baseball allowed Lardner to move from journalism to fiction, afforded him the perfect vehicle for developing his mastery of the speech of semiliterates, and allowed him to develop his characters in a context that was almost universally familiar. Presented in this volume are 24 short stories published between 1914 and 1919, approximately the period between Lardner's ceasing to be a working baseball writer in Chicago and his removal to New York. Thus, for Lardner they are analogous to Dickens's *Pickwick Papers*, or Gilbert and Sullivan's "Trial by Jury"—early efforts embodying the style that their creator would come to master, but works of considerable individual merit in their own right.

Lardner's Early Years

Lardner was born on March 6, 1885, in Niles, Michigan, just over the border from Indiana, a state that would prove important alike in his development as a journalist, in the setting of his first major work of fiction, and in the publishing history of his books. His family was a prosperous and ordinarily happy one. The name his parents gave him, Ringgold Wilmer Lardner, combined the surname of a Union admiral in the Civil War, Cadwallader Ringgold, and the maiden name of an aunt in the family. Lardner never liked the name, but it served him well, for it lent itself to the enigmatic contraction "Ring," and allowed him to revert to his full name for comic effect, as he did in signing a letter to his future sister-in-law, "Yours in absolute sanity, Ringgold Wilmer."[1] His childhood was unexceptional. Baseball was prominent in his life, but probably no more so than in the childhoods of most Americans.[2] His father took him to Central League games and to ballgames at the University of Notre Dame, in South Bend, but also to major league games in Chicago. More important, as it proved, life in Niles acquainted him with many of the small-town boys of the sort who went off to the minor leagues to play for the chance—in those days about one in a hundred—to make the majors.

Up until he was twelve, Lardner's education was provided privately by his mother and by a tutor. He expressed no great respect for the formal education he received subsequently. The title of his article "What I Ought to of Learnt in High School"[3] renders unnecessary any summary of its contents. His university education amounted to a term at Armour Institute in Chicago, now the Illinois Institute of Technology. He passed only Rhetoric, but claimed to have mastered mechanical engineering in a semester and "was in accord with the dean when he told me I had progressed as far as I could in the subject."[4]

His early vocational experience was little better. He claimed to have been canned as office boy by McCormick, the harvester firm, and by a real estate company in Chicago. A job as freight handler for the Michigan Central turned out no better. In 1904 and 1905, he worked as meter reader and bookkeeper for the Niles Gas Company, an experience that brought him to detest routine or repetitive employment. No less than positive incentives, that experience helped drive him into journalism. In 1917 he characterized his early employment:[5]

1. Letter to Ruby Abbott, August 22, 1910, reproduced in Donald Elder, *Ring Lardner* (Garden City, NY: Doubleday & Co., 1956), pp. 79–80.

2. For biographical detail on Lardner, see Elder, *Ring Lardner*; Jonathan Yardley, *Ring* (New York: Random House, 1977).

3. *American Magazine*, LXXXXVI (November 1923), 10–11, 78, 80, 82.

4. Ring Lardner, Jr., *The Lardners* (New York: Harper & Row, 1976), p. 20.

5. "Ring Lardner Himself," *Saturday Evening Post*, CLXXXIX (April 28, 1917), 37, 45.

Jobs	W.	L.	Pct.
13	8	5	.616

Ring's entry into journalism came about as a consequence of an offer made to his brother, Rex Lardner, a reporter for the Niles *Daily Sun* and Niles correspondent for both the Kalamazoo *Gazette* and the South Bend *Tribune*. In 1906 Edgar Stoll, editor of the South Bend *Times*, endeavored to hire Rex away from the rival *Tribune*, but found him tied to a firm contract. Ring, who had concluded that journalism was preferable to contending with rats for views of Niles gas meters, volunteered for the job and was accepted. For $12 per week, from which he had to deduct interurban fare, he found himself social reporter, drama critic, and sports reporter for a respectable daily in a medium-sized midwestern city. His afternoon duties in summers entailed reporting on the South Bend team, known variously as the Wagonmakers and the Green Sox, in the Central League.

Lardner covered Central League baseball for two years, 1906 and 1907. Although the *Times* has not survived as an operating newspaper, a run of it is preserved on microfilm in the South Bend Public Library. Lardner's accounts, though not identified with a by-line, show steady development in both his writing style and his command of baseball. The leagues soon hired him as official scorer for a dollar a game. The minor leagues were then, as now, classified essentially on the basis of population. The Central League, a Class B circuit, united South Bend with a series of other secondary midwestern cities: Terre Haute and Evansville in Indiana, Dayton and Springfield in Ohio, and various others as franchises shifted from season to season. The experience was seminal in Lardner's development, and he held the league and the people he knew there in exaggerated esteem. In 1931, during one of the golden ages of the game, he manifested his nostalgia for the baseball of his youth by writing that the Class B ball of the Central League of 1906–07 was fully as strong as modern AA ball.[6] References to the Central League and to the people he had met there were to recur in his stories and in his articles throughout his life.

Lardner was to reach the major leagues' press boxes sooner than most of the Central League's players were to reach the big league diamonds. In the fall of 1907 he returned to Chicago, introduced

6. "Meet Mr. Howley," *Saturday Evening Post*, CCIV (November 14, 1931), 12, 115.

himself to Hugh S. Fullerton,[7] the city's leading baseball writer, and accompanied Fullerton to the games of the 1907 World Series in the old West Side National League park. Fullerton, who was then working for the Chicago *Examiner*, recommended Lardner to Duke Hutchinson, sports editor of the *Inter-Ocean*, an excellent newspaper though not a very successful one. Lardner was to write there for only some four months, but the *Inter-Ocean* was the first paper to see the by-line "R. W. Lardner," which was to become familiar to ordinary Chicagoans—some of whom may never have noted his later literary achievements.

In February 1908 Lardner followed Fullerton to the *Examiner*, just as Fullerton was leaving. The intense rivalry among the Chicago newspapers, later celebrated in Hecht and MacArthur's masterful play "The Front Page," produced savage competition for the city's major sports writers, and a revolving-door character to their by-lines. Charles Dryden, who wrote mainly for the *Examiner*, had pioneered humorous sports writing among them.[8] Lardner covered the Cubs and the White Sox for the *Examiner* in 1908 and then moved to the *Tribune*, the traditionally dominant newspaper of Chicago, for the 1909 and 1910 seasons. His accounts of games were competent and informative, but gentle and rather uncritical. Evidently because of his closeness to the players on road trips, he avoided harsh judgments of their work on the field. Fullerton late in life evaluated Lardner as good on the strategy of baseball, but interested not so much in the play as in the players.[9] It was inevitable that he should shift from day-to-day sportswriting to some medium in which he could delineate the players' personalities and problems.

The conversion began inconspicuously in 1911. Lardner left the *Tribune* at the beginning of the year to become editor of baseball's trade journal, *The Sporting News* of St. Louis. He held the position only some three months, but during that brief tenure he wrote a series of renditions of club-car conversations of the Chicago players he had known during his three years of following the two Chicago teams. In

7. See George W. Hilton, "Hugh Stuart Fullerton," in David L. Porter, ed., *Biographical Dictionary of American Sports* (Westport, Conn.: Greenwood Press, 1992), 1989–92 Supplement, pp. 345–46.

8. See George W. Hilton, "Charles Dryden," *ibid.*, pp. 341–42.

9. *The Sporting News*, November 27, 1941, p. 5.

the course of the series, which he called "Pullman Pastimes,"[10] Lardner created funny and penetrating character sketches of Jimmy Sheckard, Lew Richie, Frank Schulte, Solly Hofman, and Ed Ruelbach of the Cubs, and Jiggs Donahue, Jake Atz, and George Davis of the White Sox, with some incidental treatment of their teammates. Suddenly, professional athletes had been converted from objects of veneration to extremely genuine human beings, with senses of humor, educational shortcomings, and very real personality flaws. At 25, Lardner had found the art form to which he was to devote much of his life.

The development was unexpected. Ben Hecht, who began his career as a reporter for the Chicago *Journal* in 1910, stated that Lardner in that period appeared a gloomy-eyed, copper-skinned, inarticulate young man who sat, stared, and seemed to be aware of nothing. Hecht, writing near the end of his life, reported that a talent for humor was nowhere visible in Lardner's person or in his journalistic work.[11]

For the 1911 season, Lardner joined the sports staff of the Boston *American*, rising to sports editor by mid-season. He spent most of the season following an atrocious Boston team that finished last in the National League with a 44–107 record. He clearly relished the experience of reporting on a team this bad, and he allowed himself more humor than he had in his accounts of the Cubs and White Sox. That year on the road afforded him the incidental advantage of an extended honeymoon with his bride, the former Ellis Abbott of Goshen, Indiana. Still, it is difficult to envision Lardner making a career in Boston, where he must surely have been treated as an outlander. His most lasting identification was with the Braves' pitcher Hub Perdue, who had ended his education with the third grade in Gallatin, Tennessee. If Lardner was at all consistent in these feelings, Boston's intellectual distinction had to have been lost on him, and he must have loathed the city's rigid social stratification.

In any case, Ring returned to Chicago in 1912 to follow the White Sox for the *Examiner*, and in 1913 he accompanied the team on its spring-training trip to Paso Robles, California. There, he began regular coverage of the team for the *Examiner*, from opening day. When

10. *The Sporting News*, December 15, 1910, p. 2; December 21, 1910, p. 2; December 28, 1910, p.2; January 5, 1911, p. 3; January 12, 1911, p. 6; January 19, 1911, p. 2; January 26, 1911, p. 3; February 2, 1911, p. 2; February 9, 1911, p. 2; February 16, 1911, p. 2.

11. Ben Hecht, *Gaily, Gaily* (Garden City, N.Y.: Doubleday & Co., 1963), p. 191.

Hugh E. Keough, who conducted the *Tribune*'s sports-page humor column, "In the Wake of the News," died early in the year, Fullerton tried unsuccessfully to run the column himself, and once again recommended Lardner for the appointment. The *Tribune*'s managing editor, James Keeley, responded enthusiastically, and on June 3, 1913, Ring became master of the *Tribune*'s famous "Wake." The column was a mixture of its conductor's observations and its readers' contributions, with a strong dose of doggerel and whimsy.

This appointment, which Ring held for over six years, was a good one for him: he had been made professionally responsible for humor, but he remained in the environment of a sports department. More generally, the situation put him in contact with Bert Leston Taylor, who conducted the more elevated "A Line o' Type or Two" on the paper's editorial page, and with the *Tribune*'s other resident intellectuals. Perhaps most important, assignment to the "Wake" freed Lardner's time—which had previously been taken up following the two ball teams—for his own literary pursuits.

Lardner's humor in the "Wake" is benign and unpredictable, but in the end disappointing, relative to what we now know to have been his genius. Along the way, he produced some excellent lines, notably one that encapsulated his dislike of automobile racing: "The Del Rey motordrome at Los Angeles burned to the ground with a great saving of life."[12] He also expanded his rendition of ballplayers' language from the prior sketches of "Pullman Pastimes" to a series of about two years' duration, in the letters of Bill to Steve. They have little plot, but in the random perceptions of a semiliterate ballplayer they offer an excellent characterization of small-town youths playing the game, the people Ring had observed for so many years. "Where Do You Get That Noise?" in the present volume, though written a good deal later, is an example of that genre.

The Jack Keefe Stories

It was in the device of a series of letters from a ballplayer to his hometown pal that Ring Lardner found his first great success in fiction, and his most popular work on baseball, the sequence of stories now known as the short novel *You Know Me Al*. Lardner wrote the first

12. Quoted in Elder, *Ring Lardner*, p. 106.

set of letters in response to an offer of $50 from Guy Lee, Sunday editor of the *Tribune*, who was seeking a feature. Believing that his readers would not accept Lardner's slang, Lee rejected the piece, and the work was rejected by other Chicago editors as well. Lardner then sent it to *The Saturday Evening Post*, which rejected it so fast that he suspected the magazine had an agent in Cleveland to intercept unsolicited manuscripts; he could not conceive of the piece having had time for the round trip to Philadelphia. Once again, Hugh Fullerton was the agent of Lardner's progress. Fullerton introduced Ring to Charles Van Loan, a former New York sportswriter then on the staff of the *Post*. Upon reading the manuscript, Van Loan concluded that George Horace Lorimer, editor of the *Post*, would accept the story if it were submitted to him personally. Lorimer did, paid Lardner $250, and asked for more.

The story appeared in *The Saturday Evening Post* of March 7, 1914, under the title, "A Busher's Letters Home." In Jack Keefe, Lardner had brought forth a major figure in American humor, a young man whose singularly nonheroic personality Lardner was to develop in 26 stories over the course of six years. All of the stories take the form of letters from Keefe to his friend Al Blanchard, in his hometown of Bedford, Indiana.[13] The device was not a new one, of course, but Lardner produced possibly the most distinguished example of the art form in delineating a character utterly oblivious to his own personality.[14] Keefe is immature, semiliterate, arrogant, unstable, miserly, and vain, but he manages to carry a self-image of shrewdness and great ability through all his experiences. Withal, Lardner managed to make Keefe a likeable character. In part, Keefe's charm is that which W. H. Auden attributed to James Boswell in his journals: here, one feels, is

---

13. The authority for Al's last name being Blanchard is a subheading that appeared only on the initial publication of "A Busher's Letters Home," in the *Saturday Evening Post* of March 7, 1914, p. 6: "Incidents Following a Call to the Big Show as Told in Some Letters from Jack Keefe, Pitcher, to His Pal, Al Blanchard, in Bedford, Indiana."

14. A precursor was Thackeray's treatment of his character the footman James Plush, who after making a small fortune in speculation on railway shares, styled himself C. Jeames de la Pluche, and embarked upon a career of social climbing. William Makepeace Thackeray, "The Diary of C. Jeames de la Pluche, Esq., with His Letters," *Burlesques* (London: Smith, Elder & Co., 1869), pp. 101–65. The character might also be taken as the model for Mr. Gullible and some of Lardner's later social climbers, but there is no evidence that Lardner was familiar with the stories.

a genuine human being with whom one can empathize, but a human being one might judge, on the strength of his behavior, a greater fool than oneself.[15] One recognizes from the outset that Keefe's shortcomings are those of limited education and some basic personality flaws, for neither of which he is responsible. The character is so vivid, and the surroundings through which he moves so true, that readers from the outset presumed Keefe to be the objectification of some actual player. Ring, tiring of efforts to identify the actual Keefe and too careful of the sensibilities of the players he knew to delineate an actual figure as unsympathetically as Keefe, finally said in 1925 that the prototype was the distinguished social worker Jane Addams, whom he identified as a Follies girl.[16] Hugh Fullerton wrote in 1941 that Keefe was drawn from Frank Smith, Jacques Fournier, Ping Bodie, Solly Hofman, Jimmy Sheckard, Frank Schulte, Lew Richie, and Heinie Zimmerman.[17] This is to say simply that Ring drew the character from ballplayers whom he knew and liked. In one sense, he did them a disservice, for although Keefe was widely taken to be representative of the players Lardner knew, the actual players who populate the Keefe stories typically treat the hero with amusement bordering on contempt, and frequently look upon him as a behavior problem for the team.

The 26 stories concerning Jack Keefe span his entire career as a pitcher with the Chicago White Sox. The first, "A Busher's Letters Home," opens in the fall of 1912 with the owner of the Terre Haute club of the Central League telling Keefe that he has been sold to the White Sox, and the last, "The Busher Pulls a Mays," ends with his trade to the Philadelphia Athletics late in the season of 1919. Probably Lardner chose the White Sox rather than the Cubs, for whom he seems to have had somewhat greater affection, because he realized that the celebrated penuriousness of the team's owner, Charles A. Comiskey, would afford his hero an ideal stimulus. Alternatively, one might argue that Lardner chose the White Sox because he had spent quite a bit more time with them, making several spring-training trips with the team. In fact, he produced his first book, a collaboration with Edward C. Heeman, on the White Sox and Giants' world tour of 1913–

15. See "Young Boswell," Auden's review of *Boswell's London Journal*, in *The New Yorker*, XXVI (November 25, 1950), 146–48.

16. Preface to the reprinting of *You Know Me Al* (New York: Scribners, 1925), pp. v–vi.

17. *The Sporting News*, November 13, 1941, p. 5.

14.[18] The choice was in any event a good one, for Comiskey was building toward the world-championship team of 1917. Fortuitously, the choice would also put Keefe, at career's end, on the 1919 White Sox, several members of which were to throw the World Series in the infamous "Black Sox" scandal.

The Keefe stories appeared in five sequence sets, only the first and last of which, along with "Call for Mr. Keefe!" are properly considered baseball stories. The six stories of 1914, which were published as *You Know Me Al* in 1916, take Keefe through 1913 spring training and the seasons of 1913 and 1914, ending anachronistically as he departs with the White Sox on the world tour in late 1913. One of Lardner's most impressive achievements in these stories is building character development into a figure whose principal trait is to be oblivious to himself. Lardner had seen that the life of a major league ballplayer was, in fact, an educating experience. Keefe is not the "Li'l Abner" of Al Capp's world who through decades learned nothing and never moved intellectually beyond his Appalachian origins. From the outset on the spring-training trip of 1913, Keefe learned and developed. From Yuma, he wrote back to Bedford:

> This place is full of Indians and I wish
> you could see them Al. They don't look nothing
> like the Indians we seen in that show last summer.

You Know Me Al also documents what Lardner had abundant opportunity to observe—the negative aspects of adaptation to major league life. Keefe proves unable either to organize his finances or to control his weight. He moves from beer to whiskey and begins drifting unmistakably toward alcoholism. After a series of bungled romances, he marries a woman with whom he is most unlikely to be happy, but he fathers a child, Little Al, for whom he develops genuine affection. The set ends as Keefe characteristically goes off on a world voyage contrary to his original intentions. Keefe had been drawn so well, and his path so clearly set, that sequels were inevitable.

Unfortunately, Lardner's initial attempts at further development of Keefe were generally unsuccessful. In a series of four stories that appeared serially in the *Post* in 1915 under the title "The Busher Abroad," plus one entitled "The Busher's Welcome Home," he followed

18. Ring W. Lardner and Edward C. Heeman, *March 6: The Home Coming of Charles A. Comiskey, John J. McGraw and James J. Callahan* (Chicago: The Blakely Printing Co., 1914).

Keefe on the White Sox–Giants world tour. The stories have their moments, but the presentation this time is much closer to Li'l Abner. The games are meaningless exhibitions that contribute little to the atmosphere, and the series consists mainly of a set of practical jokes played by teammates on Keefe, who in the insecurity of an unfamiliar environment proves unable to cope with them. He retreats below deck when warned of a predatory bird, the Great Australian Bight, and even his illiterate locutions sink below the plausible, as when he writes of his visit to "Honk Honk." Lardner here violated one of his rules of illiterate language: words that were totally out of Keefe's context he would spell correctly, because he would look them up. Although Lardner had been familiar with the White Sox–Giants world tour from his collaboration with Heeman, he had not been part of it, and thus could not bring to these stories the vividness of his treatment of the 1913 spring-training trip in *You Know Me Al.*[19] Keefe retained nothing from the world tour, and never referred to it in his later letters.

The next ten Keefe stories, divided into two sets, are accounts of the hero's wartime services in 1917 and 1918. The first story, "Call for Mr. Keefe!"[20] is an excellent account of Keefe's unsuccessful effort to avoid the draft. The draft board, upon learning that Keefe's wife, Florrie, has established a prosperous beauty shop, refuses to grant him his head-of-family deferment. No doubt this was an experience to cause Americans by the millions to identify with him—however furtively. Keefe characteristically suppresses the facts of his entry into the army, boasting loudly that he had enlisted.

Unfortunately, Lardner's publisher, Bobbs-Merrill, also suppressed this information, and excluded "Call for Mr. Keefe!" from *Treat 'Em Rough*,[21] the volume that reprinted the next three Keefe stories, covering the hero's experiences in basic training at Camp Grant, Illinois. "Call for Mr. Keefe!" is reprinted in the present volume partly because of its omission from *Treat 'Em Rough*, but mainly because it is an

19. See the excellent evaluation of "The Busher Abroad" set of stories in Walton R. Patrick, *Ring Lardner* (New York: Twayne Publishers, 1963), pp. 49–51. This entire volume is highly recommended.

20. *Saturday Evening Post*, CXC (March 9, 1918), pp. 3–4, 78, 80, 82. The story has been reprinted in Matthew J. Bruccoli and Richard Layman, eds., *Some Champions: Sketches and Fiction by Ring Lardner* (New York: Charles Scribner's Sons, 1976), pp. 99–116.

21. *Treat 'Em Rough: Letters from Jack the Kaiser Killer* (Indianapolis: The Bobbs-Merrill Co., 1918).

integral part of Keefe's history with the White Sox. *Treat 'Em Rough* employs some of the elements of "The Busher Abroad" in portraying Keefe as the butt of practical jokes, but its background of fellow-soldiers, officers, their wives and girfriends, and other supporting figures offers greater variety than the baseball stories provided. This circumstance gave Lardner a fine opportunity to delineate characters, and to provide comic situations. Keefe also shows some of his uneducated shrewdness in responding to what is inflicted on him, as he had in *You Know Me Al*. The volume suffers from the exclusion of "Call for Mr. Keefe!" for much of the humor depends on the hypocrisy of Keefe's insistence on his enlistment.

Such plot as *Treat 'Em Rough* sustains in its daily passages is concerned with Keefe's fears of a fellow soldier described to him as "Nick, the Blade." The soldier's intent watching of Keefe proves to be only the hero-worship of a baseball fan—to Keefe's great relief. In the course of his basic training, Keefe receives a pair of socks knit by a woman in Texas, with a note inviting the recipient to correspond with her. In a process entirely parallel to his leaving on the world tour, Keefe blunders into a pen-pal romance, which finally becomes an opportunity to meet in the lobby of the Rice Hotel in Houston when Keefe's company is assigned to duty in Texas. The donor of the socks proves to be an unattractive middle-aged woman, and Keefe, true to form, seeks to escape once he identifies her. A minor-league lefthanded pitcher—the breed for whom Keefe has unbounded contempt—identifies him before he can break away, but Keefe's wife Florrie arives with Little Al as the deus ex machina of escape. The woman is left with the lefthander, and Keefe goes off for a brief reunion with Florrie and Little Al before embarking for Europe.

The set of stories concerning Keefe's experiences in France, published as *The Real Dope*,[22] is much the stronger of the two wartime volumes. Because Lardner had drawn upon a short stay in the war zone in 1918 for his book *My Four Weeks in France*,[23] Keefe's environment at the front proved to be far more realistic than the familiar Midwestern reaches of Camp Grant had been. Some of Keefe's perceptions of European life are extremely well done, notably his view of the French language:

22. *The Real Dope* (Indianapolis: The Bobbs-Merrill Co., 1919).
23. *My Four Weeks in France* (Indianapolis: The Bobbs-Merrill Co., 1918).

Well Al jokeing to one side if I half to go back home without a meddle it will be because they are playing favorites but I guess I wouldn't be left out at that because I stand ace high with most of the Frenchmens around here because they like a man that's always got a smile or a kind word for them and they would like me still better yet if they could understand more English and get my stuff better but it don't seem like they even try to learn and I suppose its because they figure the war is in their country so everybody should ought to talk their language but when you get down to cases they's a big job on both our hands and if one of us has got to talk the others language why and the he--ll should they pick on the one that's hard to learn it and besides its 2 to 1 you might say because U.S. and the English uses the same language and they's nobody only the French that talks like they do because they couldn't nobody else talk that way so why wouldn't it be the square thing for them to forget theirs and tackle ours and it would prolongate their lifes to do it because most of their words can't be said without straining yourself and no matter what kind of a physic you got its bound to wear you down in time.[24]

From the relatively simple sentence structures of his earlier letters to the grandiose constructions of this character, Keefe's style was changing. As Walton R. Patrick observed, that Lardner could carry meaning through such grammatical structures is really remarkable.[25] Perhaps Lardner wanted us to see in Keefe an increasing confidence in his own ability as a correspondent. Isaac E. Clark, in an excellent study of Lardner's use of language, notes that Keefe began with language not far different from the colloquial speech of educated people, but moved to successively more unorthodox spelling and syntax, as if Lardner were conditioning his readers for the more bizarre locutions to come.[26]

The Real Dope further delineates Keefe's extramarital philandering, and by this time Lardner had mastered the pattern: Keefe would set forth clearly the undesirable consequences of the course of action he was contemplating, but then, as if inevitably, proceed to the action. In these stories Keefe conceives the idea of sending a valentine to a Red Cross girl whom he knows as Miss Moselle, but who proves to be an heiress from New York named Ruth Palmer. After writing Al about how unwise it would be to send a valentine, he sends one anyway. The

---

24. *The Real Dope*, pp. 65–66.

25. See Patrick's subsection "Style, Structure and Significance," *Ring Lardner*, pp. 59–64.

26. Isaac Edgar Clark, "An Analysis of Ring Lardner's American Language, or Who Learnt You Grammar Bud?" unpublished M.A. thesis, University of Texas, 1944.

valentine consists of a poem in the sort of doggerel that Lardner had concocted to fill "In the Wake of the News":

To Miss Moselle
(Private)

A soldier don't have much time
To set down and write up a valentine
but please bear in mind
That I think about you many a time
And I wished I could call you mine
And I hope they will come a time
When I will have more time
And then everything will be fine
And if you will be my valentine
I will try and show you a good time.[27]

Shortly after St. Valentine's Day, Keefe has an opportunity to make a speech at a camp show. He devotes the talk to an analogy between baseball and war:

"Gentlemen and friends. I am no speech maker and I guess if I had to make speeches for a liveing I am afraid I couldn't do it but the boys is anxious I should say a few words about baseball and I didn't want to disappoint them. They may be some of you boys that has not followed the great American game very close and maybe don't know who Jack Keefe is. Well gentlemen I was boughten from Terre Haute in the Central League by that grand old Roman Charley Comiskey owner of the Chicago White Sox in 1913 and I been in the big league every since except one year I was with Frisco and I stood that league on their head and Mr. Comiskey called me back and I was still starring with the Chicago White Sox when Uncle Sam sent out the call for men and I quit the great American game to enlist in the greatest game of all the game we are playing against the Kaiser and we will win this game like I have win many a game of baseball because I was to fast for them and used my brains and it will be the same with the Kaiser and America will fight to the drop of the hat and make the world safe for democracy."

Well Al I had to stop 2 or 3 minutes while they give me a hand and they clapped and hollered at pretty near everything I said. So I said "This war reminds me a good deal like a incident that happened once when I was pitching against the Detroit club. No doubt you gentlemen and officers has heard of the famous Hughey Jennings and his eeyah and on the Detroit club is also the famous Tyrus Cobb the Georgia Peach as he is called and I want to pay him a tribute right here and say he is one of the best ball players in the American League and a great hitter if you don't pitch just right to him. One time we was in Detroit for a serious of games and we had loose the first two games do to bad pitching and the first game Eddie Cicotte didn't have nothing

27. *The Real Dope*, p. 52.

and the second game Faber was in the same boat so on this morning I refer to Manager Rowland come up to me in the lobby of the Tuller hotel and said how do you feel Jack and I said O. K. Clarence why do you ask? And he said well we have loose 2 games here and we have got to grab this one this p.m. and if you feel O. K. I will work you because I know you have got them licked as soon as you walk out there. So I said all right Clarence you can rely on me. And that P.M. I give them 3 hits and shut them out and Cobb come up in the ninth innings with two men on bases and two men out and Ray Schalk our catcher signed me for a curve ball but I shook my head and give him my floater and the mighty Cobb hit that ball on a line to our right fielder Eddie Murphy and the game was over.

"This war is a good deal like baseball gentlemen because it is stratejy that wins and no matter how many soldiers a gen. has got he won't get nowheres without he uses his brains and its the same in baseball and the boys that stays in the big league is the boys that can think and when this war is over I hope to go back and begin where I left off and win a pennant for Charley Comiskey the old Roman in the American Leauge."[28]

Once the riotous reception of the speech finally dies down, Keefe's sergeant reads the valentine, to Keefe's acute embarrassment. The episode precipitates a pair of practical jokes, apparently perpetrated by a fellow soldier, Johnny Alcock. Keefe receives a letter from General Black Jack Pershing, with the return address of the Folies Bergère, Paris, seeking advice on strategy, and another from Marie Antoinette in Cologne, suggesting a liaison.

Keefe's responses to both lead to further embarrassment, but by the end of "Sammy Boy," the fifth of the six stories of *The Real Dope*, he comes to see that Alcock and his friends are taking advantage of his naive nature, and the realization induces some maturing. In the final story, "Simple Simon," Lardner introduced Jack Simon, a character even more guileless than Keefe, and Simon immediately becomes the butt of the company's practical jokes. Alcock tells Simon, who is an indefatigable souvenir collector, that the shell holes in no-man's land, beyond the trenches, are a fine source of German artifacts. Keefe, though well aware how lethal the suggestion is, does nothing to discourage Simon from venturing out. When Simon disappears, and a man is seen crawling through no-man's land, Keefe presumes that it is Simon, and goes out to bring him back. The crawling man is actually Alcock, who is on a similar mission to undo the deadly joke. Not recognizing each other in the dark, Keefe and Alcock wrestle, and Keefe is wounded in the left arm by American fire. Simon, for

28. *Ibid.*, pp. 55–58.

his part, returns to the trenches safely, unaware of the rescue attempt. Happily, Keefe's wounds are slight, and the left arm, after all, is that portion of the human anatomy for which he has the least respect. Moreover, the wounds render him, in his own eyes, forever after a war hero. A letter from Florrie, notifying him that he has a daughter, sends him into euphoria, but not sufficiently to curb his flirtation with the nurse who tends him. The army repatriates him for a liberty bond drive, and when he suggests naming the daughter Charlotte, Florrie correctly concludes that that was the name of the nurse.

Lardner had had Keefe drafted in mid-September, 1917, thereby depriving his character of the chance to play in the World Series that year with the world-champion White Sox. He had also brought Keefe home from France at the end of the 1918 season. An offer from *The Saturday Evening Post* of $1,250 for a sequence set of Keefe's return to the 1919 White Sox thus proved to be ideal timing: Keefe would again be in his natural habitat—baseball, the arena in which the ultimate logic of his development could be played out. With only two dependable pitchers, Eddie Cicotte and Claude Williams, the team was a fading version of the 1917 champions, and Keefe's personality disintegration could be realistically portrayed as a serious problem for the club. Lardner provided us with only a single instance of his statistical record: on August 17, 1914, Keefe wrote Al that his record was 10–6—though he inevitably found reasons why it might easily have been 16–0. The context of the stories is thus consistent with Keefe's having had the ability to be a consistent 15-game winner. If so, he would undoubtedly have been the third-best pitcher on the 1919 White Sox.

Lardner was fortunate in that Kid Gleason, the actual figure he delineates at greatest length in *You Know Me Al*, was chosen manager of the 1919 White Sox. This permitted him not only to give greater prominence to Gleason, whom he admired, but also to enhance the continuity from the earliest of Keefe's major league experiences. In a more important way—which Lardner above all men would not have considered fortunate—the return of Keefe to the 1919 White Sox was ideal: the team's throwing the 1919 World Series gave it a permanent claim on American attention, about equally with the *Titanic* disaster, Lizzie Borden, and the assassination of Abraham Lincoln.[29] Although

29. An excellent factual account of the scandal is to be found in Eliot Asinof, *Eight Men Out: The Black Sox and the 1919 World Series* (New York: Holt, Rinehart and Winston, 1963). On the metaphorical level, it is treated in W. P. Kinsella's novel *Shoeless Joe* (Boston: Houghton Mifflin, 1982), from which the motion picture "Field of Dreams" was adapted.

the final Keefe stories were written before the World Series began, Lardner was astute enough to recognize the stresses on the team, and to see that they could lead the players to want to lose. On August 12, 1919, Keefe writes to Al:

> Well when Gleason 1st. told me to go in there I had a notion to go in there and dink the ball up there and let the Washington boys get their name in the averages for once in their life and show Gleason I didn't give a dam but then I thought of the rest of the boys and it wasn't square to them to not give them the best I got so I cut loose and you see what happened.

It is inconceivable that Chick Gandil, architect of the plot to throw the Series, would have approached Keefe, who was not going well enough to be worth including in the conspiracy. In any case Keefe could not have been counted on to keep his mouth shut. There is little question that Keefe would have been receptive, however. Consistently, he would have written Al about the dangers of getting mixed up with the plot, and the inevitability of punishment, but would then have joined it and accelerated the exposure. By the end of August, the issue was moot: Keefe's flaws had driven him from the team, about a month before the fateful World Series.

The 1919 set opens with the story "The Busher Reenlists." Again, the plot and even the title depend upon Keefe's having been drafted in "Call for Mr. Keefe!" He had not enlisted, and neither was his return to the White Sox voluntary. Rather, he makes some characteristically unsuccessful efforts to find other employment, demonstrating—as usual, to all but himself—that he had nothing to offer but athletic ability. Similarly, in hiring him the White Sox were demonstrating, more than anything else, their desperation for pitching. The team had already attempted to peddle him to the Senators in "Call for Mr. Keefe!" in 1917, and had been prevented from doing so only by his army draft status. Keefe begins the season well, but quickly descends into the usual morass of alcoholism, philandering, and hypocritical jealousy of his wife. At one point, even while he is sitting next to Florrie, he is holding hands with Miss Mulvihill, the object of his current dalliance. To Lardner, so puritanical that he thought the song "Tea for Two" immoral, such a transgression was the worst offense he could be expected to put in print.

Keefe's disintegration in the 1919 set is accompanied by a drift to a more cynical or jaded style, an outlook first evident in "Simple Simon" and one more conspicuous in Lardner's "wise boob" characters of

Gullible's Travels[30] and *The Big Town*.[31] The busher of 1913 would never have written what Keefe had to say about the acquisition of Erskine Mayer in 1919:

Well they didn't score off of Cicotte and we got 1 run in the 11th. off of Page and Beat them 1 to 0 but I might of shut them out just the way Cicotte done if he had of left me in there but he has went cuckoo Al and to show you how bad he is he has signed Mayer that has been in the National League 20 or 30 yrs, and the next thing you know he will be sending for Geo. Van Haltren or somebody.

By the final 1919 story, "The Busher Pulls a Mays," Lardner has reduced Keefe to a man almost bereft of resources. Florrie has given up the beauty shop for an unsuccessful partnership, and the family's finances are down to $200. Since early in the season, Keefe has had only one successful relief appearance. His battle with alcohol finally leads him to hit a batter, Yankee outfielder Sam Vick, in the head. He then plots to emulate pitcher Carl Mays, who alone among major league players (until recent times) was able to break free of management's collusion, initiate bidding for his services, and play with the team of his choice. Lardner, after delineating this remarkable character through the equivalent of five short novels, managed to save Keefe's greatest self-delusion for his last: attempting ineptly to interest the Detroit Tigers in his services, he fantasizes that he will be traded for Bobby Veach, who was, in the 1919 season, the second-best player in the American League. Instead, the White Sox dispose of Keefe as a throw-in with cash to the Athletics, in their fifth year of a seven-year tenancy of last place, to make room on the roster for a promising fictional pitcher.[32]

It is difficult to see Jack Keefe as the tragic hero, but no less than Macbeth or Captain Ahab, he has been done in by his own personality

30. *Gullible's Travels* (Indianapolis: The Bobbs-Merrill Co., 1917).

31. *The Big Town* (Indianapolis: The Bobbs-Merrill Co., 1921).

32. Keefe was to return in 1922 in the form of the hero of a comic strip, this time with a wife named Edna, but again as a pitcher for the White Sox. Lardner wrote the continuity for the strip, which was drawn by Will B. Johnstone and Dick Dorgan, brother of the better-known Tad. The strip was discontinued in 1925. Extensive selections from it have been reprinted in Richard Layman, ed., *Ring Lardner's You Know Me Al: The Comic Strip Adventures of Jack Keefe* (New York: Harcourt Brace Jovanovich/Bruccoli Clark, 1979).

flaws. He ends neither beheaded nor affixed to a whale, but his ultimate fate is easy to foresee. At best, Connie Mack could not have been expected to tolerate Keefe's wayward personality, and he was in any case attempting to rebuild the Athletics with younger players for the 1920's. Keefe's marriage never gives the impression of viability, and one or another of his philanderings will very likely terminate it. "The Busher Reenlists" demonstrates Keefe's lack of alternatives to baseball. His alcoholism is apparently irreversible, and one pictures him as the town drunk—worse, the town bore—of Bedford, sitting in the public square giving all who will listen an inaccurate account of such glories as he had had in the major leagues. Al, so brilliantly delineated by Lardner as the uncritical source of support, will likely be Keefe's only reliance, but no doubt that, too, will be withheld in time as Keefe's celebrity status recedes into the past. Better players than Keefe, more admirable personalities than Keefe, wound up as derelicts.

The Individual Short Stories, 1914–1917

The great success of the first of the Keefe stories in 1914 had inevitably brought Lardner encouragement from Lorimer to produce additional stories for *The Saturday Evening Post*,[33] but it also provoked a quick flurry of offers from rival editors.[34] Cameron MacKenzie of *McClure's* wrote offering 7 1/2 cents per word for three or four stories, with a prospect of advancing the rate to 10 cents if the first group proved successful.[35] C. B. De Kamp of *Metropolitan* solicited short stories explicitly on the basis of the Keefe series: "They are the best thing to appear in a long while and I would like to congratulate you on them."[36] Albert A. Boyden of the *American* wrote, "Your 'Bush League Letters' are perfect wonders. I would have given a good deal to have had them in our magazine."[37] He solicited work from Lardner, but was not specific as to type. Lardner responded to all this attention, first, by expanding beyond *The Saturday Evening Post* into the other major magazines of the day, and second, by extending his subject matter

33. Lardner's letters from his editors in this period are preserved in the manuscript room of the Newberry Library in Chicago. Lorimer's letters are in file Lar Sa–Sz.

34. *Ibid.*, file Lar M–Z.

35. Letter of Cameron MacKenzie, June 23, 1914, *ibid.*

36. Letter of C. B. De Kamp, July 17, 1914, *ibid.*

37. Letter of Albert A. Boyden, April 6, 1914, *ibid.*

beyond baseball. For *Metropolitan*, which paid him $600, he wrote one of his most highly regarded pieces, "Champion," a grim delineation of a brutal, amoral boxer.[38] For *Red Book* he brought forth a series of semiliterate letters of an aptly named Fred Gross that later became the book *Own Your Own Home*.[39] Lardner was launched into his career as the premier humorous short-story writer of his time.

Between 1914 and 1919 Lardner produced 27 independent short stories—that is, stories unrelated to the Keefe saga or to the sequence sets that were collected into *Own Your Own Home* and *Gullible's Travels*.[40] Of the 27, twelve concerned baseball, and of those, ten were published in *The Saturday Evening Post*, one in *Red Book*, and one in *McClure's*. Lardner responded to *American*'s solicitation only with a series of short nonfiction pieces on baseball.[41]

Writers as distinguished as Thackeray have manifested the failing of establishing a set of stock characters, then presenting them in different guises in various later works. Having developed a successful character in the person of Jack Keefe, and having presented a consistent style of illiterate English in the form of Keefe's monstrous sentences and virtual absence of commas, Lardner might have been more than ordinarily likely to modify Keefe slightly for his other short stories. Moreover, Lardner treated his early fiction as ephemeral journalistic contributions, not even bothering to preserve his manuscripts. In the short stories that appeared while Keefe's saga was running, he developed highly dissimilar characters, and presented a considerable variety of illiterate English.

Four of the individual baseball stories appeared in 1914, three of them in *The Saturday Evening Post* and one in *Red Book*. The first of the stories in the *Post*, "My Roomy," is a stark delineation of a psychopathic ballplayer named Elliott, told through the barely perceptive account of his Chicago Cubs roommate. Always considered one of

---

38. "Champion," *Metropolitan*, XL (October 1916), 14–16, 62–64.

39. "Own Your Own Home," *Red Book*, XXIV (January 1915), 488–500; "Welcome to Our City," XXV (May 1915), 29–40; "The Last Laugh," XXV (July 1915), 540–50; "Uncivil War," XXV (September 1915), 938–49. *Own Your Own Home* (Indianapolis: The Bobbs-Merrill Co., 1919).

40. *Gullible's Travels* (Indianapolis: The Bobbs-Merrill Co., 1917). The set, which concerns the unsuccessful social climbing of one Gullible and his wife, ran serially in the *Post*.

41. "Braves is Right," *American*, LXXIX (March 1915), 19–23, 66–70; "Some Team," LXXIX (April 1915), 20–24, 80–85; "Tyrus," LXXIX (June 1915), 19–23, 78; "Matty," LXXX (August 1915), 26–29.

Lardner's best stories, "My Roomy" is in retrospect especially impressive for its remarkable foreshadowing of the psychiatric problems of the American League batting champion of 1970, Alex Johnson.[42]

The second of the *Post* stories is "Sick 'Em," an account of two pitchers whose mutual loathing is so intense that they are effective only in daily rivalry on the same team. It is set on the Phillies of 1914, a team with which Lardner had no close associations, but one that was undoubtedly attractive to the *Post*'s editorial staff in Philadelphia. The story offers Lardner's best incursion into his days in the Central League. On mixed grounds of cleverness of plot and freshness of baseball environment, it is difficult to explain why Lardner did not choose the story for reprinting in one of his books; its very quality is one of several indications that his choices included a highly random element.

"Horseshoes," the third of the *Post* stories, is a monologue on a train by an amiable ballplayer whose phenomenal run of misfortunes would challenge the probability theory taught in elementary statistics courses. Lardner set the story on the Philadelphia Athletics, again a choice that was presumably agreeable to the *Post*, but in this instance a team that was the best in baseball, with personnel who would have been immediately familiar to most of his readership.

"Back to Baltimore," Lardner's contribution of 1914 to *Red Book*, was the first of ten stories that he published there, but the only one on baseball. It is an implausible account of a woman's mismanagement of the Boston Braves, focusing on the overdrawn responses of ordinary ballplayers to the introduction of a Yale man, admittedly of no talent, onto the team. Lardner's characteristic device of illiterate English inevitably gave the impression that low educational levels were the norm, but college-educated men were actually common in the baseball of the time. Connie Mack positively sought out college players, and even the shady Hal Chase had attended the University of Santa Clara. The alma maters of many of the college-educated players are cited in the notes to these stories—along with Eppa Rixey's M.A. The story is of interest, however, as one of the few uses Lardner made of his season in Boston in 1911.

All of the stories that appeared in 1914 used the device, so well honed in *You Know Me Al*, of a fictional hero, plus a few fictional supporting characters, on an actual team with actual contemporary

42. See Dick Miller, "Johnson Center of Celestial Storm," *Official Baseball Guide for 1972* (St. Louis: The Sporting News, 1972), pp. 157–59.

players. The realistic background thus concocted heightened the humor of Lardner's situations, afforded him the opportunity to delineate actual personalities familiar to his readers, and allowed him some jokes that would be immediately apparent to ordinary baseball fans.

Beginning with "Alibi Ike," in 1915, Lardner shifted to teams with fictional personnel. He never offered a reason for the change, nor, apparently, has the change been noted in the literature. Ring Lardner, Jr., speculates that the conversion reflects no more than a shift in Lardner's interests, from baseball to fiction.[43] The change in any case gave Lardner somewhat more freedom in drawing characters, and certainly freedom from the prospect of suit brought by a player outraged by his treatment. One may speculate that there was a logical connection between the determination not to reprint "Sick 'Em," a story particularly rich in actual figures, and the decision to move entirely to fictional characters. For most of these stories, Lardner used a fictional version of the Chicago Cubs, with a manager called "Cap." This tactic initially served him well, for "Alibi Ike" proved one of his funniest stories, with one of his most sympathetically drawn heroes. Frank X. Farrell's chronic apologizing is clearly a compulsive state requiring psychotherapy, but as with the more severe psychiatric problems of "My Roomy," teammates were generally unable to see it for what it was.

Thereafter, however, the quality of the baseball stories in fictional settings is mixed, but generally much lower. The best is "The Crook," an excellent study of the consequences of honorable behavior among umpires. Both "The Poor Simp" and "The Yellow Kid" enjoy good characterization and clever turns of plot. "Where Do You Get That Noise?" is a breezy rendition of ballplayers' banter. "Good for the Soul" is Lardner's farewell to the dying Federal League, and "The Hold-Out" delineates avarice within the business of baseball. All of these appeared in *The Saturday Evening Post*, and none of them was collected into any of Lardner's books in his lifetime. The one story of this period widely reprinted is "Harmony," which appeared in *McClure's* in August 1915. In accepting the manuscript, Charles Hanson Towne, *McClure's* managing editor, wrote Ring: "When I tell you that I am not a baseball fan, but that I enjoyed it more than any yarn that I have read for months, I think you will know what I mean. . . ."[44] The

43. Letter of Ring Lardner, Jr., to George W. Hilton, May 24, 1972.

44. Letter of Charles Hanson Towne to Ring W. Lardner, May 20, 1915, Lardner papers, Newberry Library, Chicago, file Lar M–N.

story is apparently based loosely on Lardner's observation of a vocal quartet managed by Lew Richie of the Cubs in 1910. Although the story has considerable merit, it has not met great critical esteem; one suspects that its popularity for reprinting stems in part from its having been allowed to pass out of copyright relatively early.

On the whole, the individual baseball stories published after "Alibi Ike" in July 1915 show a decline in inventiveness. Lardner may already have reaped such benefit as he could from using baseball as a fairly universal medium for communicating with the American public, which Virginia Woolf noted in her evaluation of Lardner in 1925,[45] and may now have been feeling the constriction to "the diameter of Frank Chance's diamond" pointed out by F. Scott Fitzgerald in his famous memorial article of 1933.[46] The loss of novelty in his baseball stories after mid-1915 was probably as instrumental in Lardner's turning to a broader variety of subjects as were the more widely publicized events of 1919–20. As is well known, Ring was greatly shaken by the Black Sox scandal, and especially by Eddie Cicotte's involvement. He had identified himself with the hard-fought low-scoring baseball of the dead-ball era and disliked the power game introduced with the lively ball in 1920. He was particularly repelled by the worship of Babe Ruth as the hero of the new era.[47]

Fortunately, his interest in baseball revived. After the period of this volume, Lardner produced three more short stories and one more sequence set concerned with baseball. Two of the stories—"Women," in *Liberty* in 1925, and "Hurry Kane," in *Hearst's International-Cosmopolitan* in 1927—date from his peak years of short-story writing

45. "[Baseball] has given him a clue, a centre, a meeting place for the diverse activities of a people whom a vast continent isolates, whom no tradition controls. Games give him what society gives his English brother." "American Fiction," *The Moment and Other Essays* (New York: Harcourt, Brace & Co., 1948), p. 123.

46. "Ring moved in the company of a few dozen illiterates playing a boy's game. A boy's game, with no more possibilities in it than a boy could master, a game bounded by walls which kept out novelty or danger, change or adventure. This material, the observation of it under such circumstances, was the text of Ring's schooling during the most formative period of the mind. A writer can spin on about his adventures after thirty, after forty, after fifty, but the criteria by which these adventures are weighed and valued are irrevocably settled at the age of twenty-five. However deeply Ring might cut into it, his cake had exactly the diameter of Frank Chance's diamond." (*New Republic*, October 11, 1933, p. 254.)

47. On Lardner's turning away from baseball after 1919, see Leverett T. Smith, "'The Diameter of Frank Chance's Diamond': Ring Lardner and Professional Sports," *Journal of Popular Culture*, VI (1972), 133–56.

in the mid-1920's. Both are widely reprinted in anthologies of Lardner's work. The third, "Take a Walk," a very good study of an umpire, reminiscent of "The Crook," was published in the *American* of October 1933, almost simultaneously with Lardner's death on September 25, 1933. All three use fictional characters. For the final sequence set, *Lose with a Smile* of 1932–33, Lardner reverted to the use of actual teammates on a real team, in this case the Brooklyn Dodgers. Here, Lardner also returned to the technique of the Keefe stories of presenting the hero in his own letters, but the set is a wan portrayal of a habitual loser, with none of Keefe's brash qualities. Presumably, Lardner reverted to genuine teammates out of a desire to delineate Casey Stengel, whose colorful speech habits were almost ideally suited to Lardner's style. T. B. Costain of *The Saturday Evening Post*, in a letter concerning the first episode of *Lose with a Smile*, expressed the hope that the set would duplicate the success of the original "Busher" series, but it never did.[48] In part, Lardner's ingenuity and especially his health were not what they had been, but more significantly, the time had passed when an author could achieve the importance of Lardner's earlier stories by working in the milieu of baseball.

The Empirical Content of the Stories

The period 1914–19 was the ideal one for the treatment Lardner gave the stories. By almost any standards, it is the pivotal period in professional baseball's history. The era opened with the founding of the Federal League, which, though it lasted but two years, badly disrupted the noncompetitive organization of baseball. Lardner made excellent use of the Federal League in providing Keefe with an alternative to

---

48. Letter of T. B. Costain to Ring W. Lardner, March 11, 1932, in Lardner papers, Newberry Library, Chicago, file Lar Sa–Sz.

Professor Howard Webb interprets the *Lose with a Smile* set as an uneasy reconciliation of Lardner with American society. Webb divides Lardner's career into three periods. The first, which encompasses all of the stories reprinted in the present volume, was devoted to pure humor. The Black Sox scandal and Lardner's move to New York in October 1919, immediately after the World Series, ended this period, and initiated one of satire of middle class values and behavior in which baseball, necessarily, played a small role. After 1929, Webb argues, as Lardner approached his early death, he became reconciled to American society. Baseball returned to his work, but in a melancholy and depressing vein. See Howard William Webb, Jr., "Ring Lardner's Conflict and Reconciliation with American Society," unpublished Ph.D. dissertation, State University of Iowa, 1953.

the White Sox. Similarly, the Federal League gave the narrator of "Back to Baltimore" a way out of the horrors of matriarchy that had, fictionally, beset the Boston Braves.

The period ends not only with the Black Sox scandal and the rise of Babe Ruth, but also with the Carl Mays case, which would prove to be even more important for baseball, in consequence of the changes it produced in the hierarchy of the game. The Mays case nearly caused the American League to break up and was mainly responsible for the decision, in 1920, to empower a despotic commissioner, Kenesaw Mountain Landis, in place of the triumvirate that had ruled the game. The Black Sox scandal, which has usually been cited as the impetus for landmark change, basically provided only a broadly acceptable explanation for a move that was intended to shore up the game's noncompetitive structure.[49]

All three of these forces are clearly evident in the 1919 Keefe stories. For this set Lardner had no alternative but to revert to the use of an actual team with real teammates; continuity with the earlier Jack Keefe stories demanded it. As we have seen, Keefe had developed the desire to lose that had driven the Black Sox conspirators. In "Along Came Ruth" one of the Babe's home runs initiates the hero's decline, and the White Sox finally give up on him when he attempts to emulate Mays in "The Busher Pulls a Mays."

The empirical content of these stories is important on several levels. Like Keefe's desire to lose, it is part of the historical documentation of the baseball of the era. Much of the humor, possibly one-fourth, is dependent on the day-to-day acquaintance with baseball that a fan of the time brought to the stories. Even the titles of the stories demonstrate how fully this acquaintance has been lost: to how many outside the Society for American Baseball Research is "The Busher Pulls a Mays" meaningful without explanation? Finally, the empirical content is an integral part of Lardner's literary craftsmanship. Apart from his use of genuine teams and teammates, he used actual games, real train schedules, and even existing saloons. The effect is to create a world that mixes reality and fantasy, rather like the clerical and political societies of Victorian Britain in the novels of Anthony Trollope.

Lardner's chronology is variable. He adhered most accurately to the actual sequence of events in the spring-training trip of 1913, in "Call

49. See Harold Seymour, *Baseball: The Golden Age* (New York: Oxford University Press, 1971), chapter 13, "Downfall of the National Commission," pp. 259–73.

for Mr. Keefe!" and in the 1919 sequence set. For the last of these, because his commission specified that he write as the season proceeded, his integration of the fictional Keefe into the actual events of the 1919 season is quite adept. He had Keefe variously pitch on days when the White Sox were rained out (May 3), when they were not scheduled (May 19 and 21), and when they played a doubleheader (July 4). He had Keefe relieve Williams in what was actually a complete game by Williams (August 11), and start in place of Williams in a game that Williams in fact pitched (August 24). He substituted Keefe in a relief appearance actually made by Dave Danforth (May 25) and sent Keefe to the Athletics on the day Danforth was released to Columbus (August 31). Lardner recognized, one suspects, that Danforth was doing as poorly as he wanted Keefe to do.

At the other extreme is the chronology of "Sick 'Em," which is an impossible mishmash of the 1913 and 1914 seasons. In this story Lardner made frequent errors in chronology, such as placing Hal Chase with the White Sox during spring training in 1913, even though Chase did not join the club until the season was in progress. Similarly, in "Back to Baltimore" he put Hub Perdue on the Braves of 1914 after he had in fact been traded away. Some of Lardner's deviations from actual chronology must have been intentional, or at least conscious; for example, when placing the White Sox–Giants world trip of 1913 at the end of the 1914 season, he adhered entirely to the actual dates of 1913. He also produced some anachronisms on the basis of his own earlier experience, as when he had the owner of the Terre Haute club of 1906 and 1907 as the current owner in 1912, or the secretary of the Braves of 1911 as the secretary in 1914.

The use of actual players served chiefly to provide a realistic background for the action, but in some instances Lardner attempted actual characterization of the players he knew, and to whose personalities he had warmed. The actual figure most fully delineated is Kid Gleason, the White Sox coach of 1913–14 and manager of 1919. Gleason's sea-captain manner served admirably for the requisite role of someone deputed by the management to shepherd Keefe about. Elsewhere, Lardner presented vignettes of Hub Perdue in "Back to Baltimore" and Frank Schulte in "Sick 'Em." Buck Weaver's enthusiasm shines through in the 1919 set, but Eddie Cicotte's quiet personality would not have lent itself to Lardner's style. In general, Jack Keefe evoked the same response from all who met him, denying Lardner much delineation beyond Gleason.

One of the most conspicuous elements of the empirical content of the stories is the residuum of Lardner's two years in the Central League. His texts abound in people he had known there: umpire Cy Rigler, outfielder Dode Paskert, infielder Donie Bush, and the Terre Haute club owner, Louis D. Smith. In his reporting for the South Bend *Times*, Lardner expressed a high opinion of Smith, and it is probably in consequence of that that he chose Terre Haute as Jack Keefe's minor league club. Like Comiskey, Smith was a tight-fisted operator, and between them they accorded Lardner a continuity in the character of Keefe's employment, from his first letter to Al to his eventual departure from the White Sox. Finally, the Terre Haute Brewing Company's light lager, Champagne Velvet, was an ideal starting point for a demonstration of Keefe's descent into alcoholism.

Lardner's most remarkable use of the Central League, and probably the best single demonstration of his use of actual figures, is to be found in a passage in "Sick 'Em." The passage is the critical one on which the development of the plot depends. The Phillies have a rookie pitcher named Smith, from Fort Wayne in the Central League, who is ineffective in spite of an excellent minor league record. They retain him only because "Alexander strained his souper and Rixey got a pair o' busted fingers, all in the same serious." The team discovers what is wrong with Smith as a result of the following:

> Well, it was the second week in June when Red sent me from Cincy to Dayton to look at a big spitter.
>
> "I ain't strong for the Central League after what they handed me," he says; "but maybe this guy's better'n most o' them, and you can see where we're up agin it. We got to get somebody or we'll go to the bottom so fast they'll pinch us for speedin'. If he's got anything at all and looks like as if he was alive we can use him; but if he's a dope, like this other boob, we don't need him. I don't want to run no lodgin' house for vagrants."
>
> So I beat it over there and seen a double-header between the home club and Evansville. The guy I was sent after worked one game and had about as much action as a soft drink. I voted No! before he'd went two innin's. Evansville had a lefthander who knowed how to pitch, but they told him he'd been in the league six years; and, besides, he was a little feller.
>
> Well, I spotted old Jack Barnett on the Evansville bench, so I waited to shake hands with him when the game was over. You know him and me broke in together at Utica. I found out while we rode downtown that he'd been with the Fort Wayne Club the last year and was traded to Evansville durin' the winter. I'd sort o' lost track of old Jack 'cause he hadn't been playin' enough in recent years to get his name in the book.
>
> "I see your club's still lucky," he says. "We all thought you had a grand chancet till them two fellers got hurt."
>
> "Yes," I says, "but we're gone now. The young guys we got ought to of been

dressmakers instead o' pitchers." Then I happened to think o' Smitty. "Maybe you can tell me somethin'," says I. "How did this here Smitty ever win all them games for you?"

Barnett started to laugh.

"What's the matter?" he ast. "Ain't the big wop worth five thousand?"

"He ain't worth a cigar coupon," I says. "He's a big, lazy tramp."

Barnett kept on laughin'.

"I knowed what'd come off," he says. "I told the fellers what'd happen. I bet Punch Knoll fifty bucks that Smitty wouldn't last the season. You guys can talk about McGraw and Mack, and them other big-league managers, all you want to, but it's us fellers down here in the sticks that knows how to get the work out of a man."

Barnett proceeds to explain that Smith is effective only in rivalry with a pitcher named Fogarty, now doing just as badly with the Chicago Cubs. The Phillies acquire Fogarty, and the two former Central Leaguers pitch them to the pennant.

In the passage quoted, the narrator is, of course, fictional. "Red" is the actual manager of the 1914 Phillies, Charles Dooin. The "big spitter" and the "lefthander who knowed how to pitch," though not named, are readily identifiable as Evansville's two leading pitchers of the 1914 season, Jake Fromholtz and Paul Fittery. Fromholtz was a big righthanded spitballer with a chronic weight problem, and Fittery, a lefthander, stood just 5′8½″ and weighed 156 pounds. The only inaccuracy in the description of them is Fittery's record: he had, as stated, been in the minor leagues (including leagues outside of Organized Baseball) for six years, but not entirely in the Central League. More surprising, the passage is a perfectly accurate scouting report. Fromholtz never rose above Class B minor league ball, and Fittery failed in two tries in the major leagues, winning a single game in two seasons.

The Jack Barnett who figures in the passage is fictional, though there is no obvious reason why an actual character should not have been used. Lardner certainly knew enough career minor leaguers that one of them would have had the requisite experience in 1913 and 1914. Punch Knoll, the actual manager of Evansville, was probably the best-known manager in the Central League.

"The Busher Reenlists" contains a similarly mystifying use of an apparently fictional character where a real one would be expected:

Well after I left Rowland I bumped in to Hy Pond that I was with him down in the Central League and he asked me to come in and have a drink so I went with him and histed a couple beers but it was a mad house and besides wile we was over there takeing the fight out of the Germans the people that stayed home done the same thing to the beer and the way they have got it fixed now you could drink all they have got left without feeling like shock stoops so finely I told Hy to make my excuses to the boys and I come along home.

Rowland, here, was the manager of the 1917 White Sox, but no one named Hy Pond appears either in Central League records or in Lardner's baseball reporting for the South Bend *Times*. It may have been Lardner's puritanical streak that prevented a man's having a drink with Keefe from being attributed to any actual player. Alternatively, Lardner may have used the names of various friends for such characters. He had great difficulty finding names for fictional characters, and according to Ring Lardner, Jr., occasionally adapted the names of friends to his purposes.[50] One example is conspicuous: in "The Courtship of T. Dorgan" of the 1919 set he gave fictional catcher Tom Dorgan the name of a close friend, the gifted cartoonist "Tad" Dorgan. Similarly, in *The Real Dope*, Lardner gave Keefe's fellow soldier Johnny Alcock the name of a colleague in the sports department of the *Tribune*, John J. Alcock.[51] No doubt there are other examples. Accordingly, footnotes reading "Apparently a fictional character" should be accepted as such; Jack Barnett, Hy Pond, and others may well be identified in the course of further inquiry into Lardner's life and times.

Actual characters also gave Lardner an opportunity for comic misspellings. George Washington Baumgardner could be corrupted into "A righthander named Bumgardner," and Chauncey Dubuc would become "Dubuque, or whatever his name is." The most effective such use of an actual name was Lardner's corruption of the name of the ship on which the White Sox crossed the Pacific in 1913, *Empress of Japan*, into *Umpires of Japan*, to delineate the parochial limitations of Keefe's view of the world.

On the whole, Lardner's dropping of actual teammates and real surroundings from his fiction in 1915 must be considered a mistake. In the process, he muted the vividness of the settings of the stories, forewent some opportunities for humor, and reduced the historical interest of his fiction. It is not surprising that he returned to the practice toward the end of his life.

* * *

---

50. Letter to George W. Hilton, May 24, 1972.

51. Alcock (1890–1944) was sent to New York as the first sports editor of the New York *Daily News* when the *Tribune* established the tabloid in 1919. In 1936 he returned to Chicago, where he became a sports writer for the *Herald-Examiner*.

Ring Lardner's baseball stories indisputably have flaws. As Patrick pointed out, the form of the sequence set produces neither the individuality of short stories nor the continuity of novels.[52] It was best suited to initial publication at short-story length, the stories separated usually by a month or more. The technique of vast sentences that Lardner developed as the Keefe stories progressed becomes tedious with long exposure, so that attempting to read all five of the sequence sets of Keefe stories seriatim, as one might the Sherlock Holmes stories or the D'Artagnan novels, would tax endurance. Finally, Lardner is criticized fairly universally for the total absence of sexual urges in his characters. Because of his own puritanism his characters lack a major dimension; surely an actual busher would have attempted more than the tepid letters and handholding he allowed Jack Keefe.

Withal, however, the stories are the masterpieces of post-*Huckleberry Finn* American letters that they have usually been considered to be. In Jack Keefe and Frank X. Farrell, Lardner gave us two of American literature's most individual figures. In the background he constructed, he delineated a world that surely must have seemed as permanent to him as Victorian society had looked to Trollope and Thackeray. It was a world of baseball, Western Union, the Pullman car, the detachable collar, the saloon, the streetcar, and the manual typewriter. Of it all, baseball has survived better than the rest, even though the major leagues have expanded, the surfaces are now frequently artificial, and the modern designated-hitter rule would have denied us any knowledge of Keefe's batting ability. Still, intrinsically, baseball remains the game of Lardner's time. The White Sox played in Keefe's Comiskey Park for 81 seasons, and to its last game on September 30, 1990, those of us who loved it agreed with Keefe's judgment: "and believe me its some park. . . ."

Baseball, seemingly in decline in 1970, is currently flourishing. Its popularity moves cyclically, inversely with social stress. The Central League is long gone, and the minor leagues in which Fromholtz and Fittery built careers are now principally short-term training grounds for the majors. Attendance at major-league games is several-fold what Lardner knew, but baseball no longer dominates the sports pages as it

52. Patrick, *Ring Lardner*, p. 63. The unsuccessful effort of Maxwell Perkins, Scribner's editor, to induce Lardner to write a novel for the firm is well known. Their correspondence on the subject is published in Clifford M. Caruthers, *Ring around Max: The Correspondence of Ring Lardner and Max Perkins* (DeKalb, Ill.: Northern Illinois University Press, 1973).

did when he wrote for them. Though it is not in the nature of economic institutions to last forever, we might hope that, if any of them does so, it might be baseball. If so, these stories will retain their interest, both for their intrinsic merit and for the insight into the baseball of their period that they provide. If not, let them stand as the literary monuments to the institution we loved, and to help future generations understand the source of our enthusiasm.

The Jack Keefe Stories, 1914-1919

A Busher's Letters Home

TERRE HAUTE, INDIANA, SEPTEMBER 6. ◆

Friend Al: Well, Al old pal I suppose you seen in the paper where I been sold to the White Sox. Believe me Al it comes as a supprise to ◆

You Know Me Al was published in book form in New York by the George H. Doran Company in 1916. The earliest of its stories, "A Busher's Letters Home," first appeared in *The Saturday Evening Post*, CLXXXVI (March 7, 1914), 6–8, 57–58.

◆ *Busher*—A player in the bush leagues, the lower minor leagues; or a player freshly recruited by a major league team but deemed no better than that by his teammates or opponents, in talent or character.

◆ *September 6*—As will be apparent, the chronology of the Jack Keefe stories is not entirely consistent, but in this case the sequence of events places the date in 1912.

◆ *sold*—Baseball was at the time, as it remained until 1976, a *collusive monopsony*, that is, a cartel of buyers in which the ballplayers were denied freedom of choice of employers, by the collusion of the owners. Most but not all players of the time were, like the hero, men of limited education with relatively unattractive employments alternative to baseball. If successful, the collusion would have reduced players' salaries to what they could have earned outside of baseball, plus some compensation for practicing a profession in which, in that era, most participants were finished by the age of 35. The monopsony had its origin in a clandestine meeting of club owners of the National League of Professional Baseball Clubs on September 30, 1879, in Buffalo, N.Y. For its history and economic rationale, see *Organized Baseball*: Report of the Subcommittee on the Study of Monopoly Power of the Committee on the Judiciary (Washington: Government Printing Office, 1952); Lee Lowenfish and Tony Lupien, *The Imperfect Diamond* (Briarcliff Manor,

me and I bet it did to all you good old pals down home. You could of knocked me over with a feather when the old man come up to me and ◆ says Jack I've sold you to the Chicago Americans.

I didn't have no idea that anything like that was coming off. For five minutes I was just dum and couldn't say a word.

He says We aren't getting what you are worth but I want you to go up to that big league and show those birds that there is a Central ◆ League on the map. He says Go and pitch the ball you been pitching

---

(*continued from page 33*)
N.Y.: Stein and Day, 1980); Simon Rottenberg, "The Baseball Players' Labor Market," *Journal of Political Economy*, LXIV (1956), 242–58.

White Sox—The Chicago White Sox, a charter member of the American League of Professional Baseball Clubs from its initial operation as a major league in 1901. The team had its origins as the Sioux City club of the Western League in 1894. After that season Charles A. Comiskey bought the team and moved it to St. Paul. He then moved it to Chicago for the 1900 season in anticipation of the newly named American League's escalation to major league status in the following year. Comiskey believed strongly that Chicago was the best baseball market in the country and that a team there would dominate the new major league. The club had won the American League's pennants of 1900, 1901 and 1906. In 1912 the team finished fourth and, viewed retrospectively, was in the early stages of a rebuilding that culminated in the world championship of 1917. It would have been entirely reasonable for Keefe to have viewed his acquisition by the White Sox as favorably as he did. On the team's history, see Warren Brown, *The Chicago White Sox* (New York: G. P. Putnam's Sons, 1952); Richard Whittingham, *The White Sox: A Pictorial History* (Chicago: Contemporary Books, 1982); Richard Lindberg, *Who's on 3rd? The Chicago White Sox Story* (South Bend, Ind.: The Icarus Press, 1983).

◆ *the old man*—The owner of the Central League's Terre Haute club in 1912 was A. W. Wagner, an officer of the Terre Haute Malleable Iron Works. A later passage, however, indicates that Lardner was referring to Louis D. Smith, owner of the team during Lardner's tenure on the South Bend *Times*. Smith was a conservative operator whose personality was consistent with the quotation attributed to him immediately below. The story antedates the development of farm systems. Minor league clubs, typically, were locally owned, and operated at a loss. They endeavored to go into the black at the end of each season by sales of players' contracts to teams of higher classification, as occurs in this instance.

◆ *Central League*—A large and relatively successful minor league established in 1903. In the classification of the minor leagues, based initially on population, the Central was Class B. In 1912 it consisted of 12 clubs: Fort Wayne, Youngstown, Erie, Springfield (Ohio), Dayton, Wheeling, Canton, Akron, Grand Rapids, Terre Haute, Zanesville, and South Bend. The franchises in Akron, Youngstown, Canton, and Erie had been absorbed from the Ohio & Pennsylvania League, which was suffering financial difficulties. For 1913 the Central League contracted to six teams: Grand Rapids, Fort Wayne, Springfield (Ohio), Dayton, Terre Haute, and Evansville, which had been the core of its traditional franchises. With several hiatuses (1918–19, 1923–27, 1933–47), the league survived through the 1951 season.

down here and there won't be nothing to it. He says All you need is the nerve and Walsh or no one else won't have nothing on you. ◆

So I says I would do the best I could and I thanked him for the treatment I got in Terre Haute. They always was good to me here and though I did more than my share I always felt that my work was apresiated. We are finishing second and I done most of it. I can't ◆ help but be proud of my first year's record in professional baseball and you know I am not boasting when I say that Al.

Well Al it will seem funny to be up there in the big show when I never was really in a big city before. But I guess I seen enough of life not to be scared of the high buildings eh Al?

I will just give them what I got and if they don't like it they can send me back to the old Central and I will be perfectly satisfied.

I didn't know anybody was looking me over, but one of the boys told me that Jack Doyle the White Sox scout was down here looking ◆ at me when Grand Rapids was here. I beat them twice in that serious. You know Grand Rapids never had a chance with me when I was right. I shut them out in the first game and they got one run in the second on account of Flynn misjuging that fly ball. Anyway Doyle ◆ liked my work and he wired Comiskey to buy me. Comiskey come ◆

◆ *Walsh*—Edward Augustine "Big Ed" Walsh (1881–1959), customarily considered the greatest White Sox pitcher. Walsh had been a member of the team since 1904, and in 1908 had won 40 games, the second-largest seasonal total in modern (i.e., twentieth-century) baseball. In 1911 he had a record of 27–18, and in 1912, 27–17. Thereafter a weak arm ended his effectiveness, although he remained with the team through 1916. His lifetime record, 195–126, was logged entirely with the White Sox, except for a single loss with the Boston Braves in 1917. His lifetime earned run average of 1.82 remains the lowest ever recorded. Walsh was elected to the Baseball Hall of Fame in 1946. See George W. Hilton, "Edward Augustine Walsh," in David L. Porter, ed., *Biographical Dictionary of American Sports: Baseball* (Westport, Conn.: Greenwood Press, 1987), pp. 586–88.

◆ *finishing second*—At no time in the period of the story did Terre Haute finish second. In 1912 the team finished tenth in the 12-team league.

◆ *Jack Doyle*—John Joseph Doyle (1869–1958), the White Sox chief scout. Doyle had had a successful career as an infielder, hitting .301 in 1,564 games, mainly in the National League. Scouting the Central League for the White Sox, as he does in the story, Doyle became acquainted with Lardner during the writer's tenure on the South Bend *Times*, in 1906–7. See Al Arthurs, "Jack Doyle," in Mike Shatzkin, ed., *The Ballplayers: Baseball's Ultimate Biographical Reference* (New York: William Morrow & Co., 1990), p. 290.

◆ *Flynn*—Apparently a fictional character.

◆ *Comiskey*—Charles Albert Comiskey (1859–1931). A first baseman notable for his fielding while putting up a lifetime batting average of .264 in 1,390 games, playing chiefly for St. Louis of the American Association and Cincinnati of the National League, from 1882 to 1894. Comiskey achieved his early fame as manager

A BUSHER'S LETTERS HOME

Incidents Following a Call to the Big Show as Told in Some Letters From Jack Keefe, Pitcher, to His Pal, Al Blanchard, in Bedford, Indiana

By Ring W. Lardner

ILLUSTRATED BY MARTIN JUSTICE

TERRE HAUTE, Indiana, September 6.

FRIEND AL: Well, Al old pal I suppose you seen in the paper where I been sold to the White Sox. Believe me Al it comes as a supprise to me and I bet it did to all you good old pals down home. You could of knocked me over with a feather when the old man come up to me and says Jack I've sold you to the Chicago Americans.

I didn't have no idea that anything like that was coming off. For five minutes I was just dum and couldn't say a word.

He says We aren't getting what you are worth but I want you to go up to that big league and show those birds that there is a Central League on the map. He says Go and pitch the ball you been pitching down here and there won't be nothing to it. He says All you need is the nerve and Walsh or no one else won't have nothing on you.

So I says I would do the best I could and I thanked him for the treatment I got in Terre Haute. They always was good to me here and though I did more than my share I always felt that my work was appresiated. We are finishing second and I done most of it. I can't help but be proud of my first year's record in professional baseball and you know I am not boasting when I say that Al.

Well Al it will seem funny to be up there in the big show when I never was really in a big city before. But I guess I seen enough of life not to be scared of the high buildings eh Al?

I will just give them what I got and if they don't like it they can send me back to the old Central and I will be perfectly satisfied.

I didn't know anybody was looking me over, but one of the boys told me that Jack Doyle the White Sox scout was down here looking at me when Grand Rapids was here. I beat them twice in that serious. You know Grand Rapids never had a chance with me when I was right. I shut them out in the first game and they got one run in the second on account of Flynn misjuging that fly ball. Anyway Doyle liked my work and he wired Comiskey to buy me. Comiskey come back with an offer and they excepted it. I don't know how much they got but anyway I am sold to the big league and believe me Al I will make good.

Well Al I will be home in a few days and we will have some of the good old times. Regards to all the boys and tell them I am still their pal and not all swelled up over this big-league business. Your pal, JACK.

CHICAGO, Illinois, December 14.

OLD PAL: Well Al I have not got much to tell you. As you know Comiskey wrote me that if I was up in Chi this month to drop in and see him. So I got here Thursday morning and went to his office in the afternoon. His office is out to the ball park and believe me its some park and some office.

I went in and asked for Comiskey and a young fellow says He is not here now but can I do anything for you? I told him who I am and says I had an engagment to see Comiskey. He says The boss is out of town hunting and did I have to see him personally?

I says I wanted to see about signing a contract. He told me I could sign as well with him as Comiskey and he took me into another office. He says What salary did you think you ought to get? and I says I wouldn't think of playing ball in the big league for less than three thousand dollars per annum. He laughed and says You don't want much. You better stick round town till the boss comes back. So here I am and it is costing me a dollar a day to stay at the hotel on Cottage Grove Avenue and that don't include my meals.

I generally eat at some of the cafes round the hotel but I had supper downtown last night and it cost me fifty-five cents. If Comiskey don't come back soon I won't have no more money left.

Speaking of money I won't sign no contract unless I get the salary you and I talked of, three thousand dollars. You know what I was getting in Terre Haute, a hundred and fifty a month, and I know it's going to cost me a lot more to live here. I made inquiries round here and find I can get board and room for eight dollars a week but I will be out of town half the time and will have to pay for my room when I am away or look up a new one when I come back. Then I will have to buy cloths to wear on the road in places like New York. When Comiskey comes back I will name him three thousand dollars as my lowest figure and I guess he will come through when he sees I am in ernest. I heard that Walsh was getting twice as much as that.

The papers says Comiskey will be back here sometime tomorrow. He has been hunting with the president of the league so he ought to feel pretty good. But I don't care how he feels. I am going to get a contract for three thousand and if he don't want to give it to me he can do the other thing. You know me Al. Yours truly, JACK.

CHICAGO, Illinois, December 16.

DEAR FRIEND AL: Well I will be home in a couple of days now but I wanted to write you and let you know how I come out with Comiskey. I signed my contract yesterday afternoon. He is a great old fellow Al and no wonder everybody likes him. He says Young man will you have a drink? But I was to smart and wouldn't take nothing. He says You was with Terre Haute? I says Yes I was. He says Doyle tells me you were pretty wild. I says Oh no I got good control. He says Well do you want to sign? I says Yes if I get my figure. He asks What is my figure and I says three thousand dollars per annum. He says Don't you want the office furniture too? Then he says I thought you was a young ballplayer and I didn't know you wanted to buy my park.

We kidded each other back and forth like that a while and then he says You better go out and get the air and come back when you feel better. I says I feel O. K. now and I want to sign a contract because I have got to get back to Bedford. Then he calls the secretary and tells him to make out my contract. He give it to me and it calls for two hundred and fifty a month. He says You know we always have a city serious here in the fall where a fellow picks up a good bunch of money. I hadn't thought of that so I signed up. My yearly salary will be fifteen hundred dollars besides what the city serious brings me. And that is only for the first year. I will demand three thousand or four thousand dollars next year.

I would of started home on the evening train but I ordered a suit of cloths from a tailor over on Cottage Grove and it won't be done till tomorrow. It's going to cost me twenty bucks but it ought to last a long time. Regards to Frank and the bunch. Your Pal, JACK.

He Bawled Me Awful

PASO ROBLES, California, March 2.

OLD PAL AL: Well Al we been in this little berg now a couple of days and its bright and warm all the time just like June. Seems funny to have it so warm this early in March but I guess this California climate is all they said about it and then some.

It would take me a week to tell you about our trip out here. We came on a Special Train De Lukes and it was some train. Every place we stopped there was crowds down to the station to see us go through and all the people looked me over like I was a actor or something. I guess my hight and shoulders attracted their attention. Well Al we finally got to Oakland which is across part of the ocean from Frisco. We will be back here later on for practice games.

We stayed in Oakland a few hours and then took a train for here. It was another night in a sleeper and believe me I was tired of sleepers before we got here. I have road one night at a time but this was four straight nights. You know Al I am not built right for a sleeping car birth.

The hotel here is a great big place and got good eats. We got in at breakfasttime and I made a B line for the dining room. Kid Gleason who is a kind of asst. manager to Callahan come in and sat down with me. He says Leave something for the rest of the boys because they will be just as hungry as you. He says Ain't you afraid you will cut your throat with that knife. He says There ain't no extra charge for using the forks. He says You shouldn't ought to eat so much because you're overweight now. I says You may think I am fat, but it's all solid bone and muscle. He says Yes I suppose it's all solid bone from the neck up. I guess he thought I would get sore but I will let them kid me now because they will take off their hats to me when they see me work.

Manager Callahan called us all to his room after breakfast and give us a lecture. He says there would be no work for us the first day but that we must all take a long walk over the hills. He also says we must not take the training trip as a joke. Then the colored trainer give us our suits and I went to my room and tried mine on. I ain't a bad looking guy in the White Sox uniform Al. I will have my picture taken and send you boys some.

My roommate is Allen a lefthander from the Coast League. He don't look nothing like a pitcher but you can't never tell about them dam left handers. Well I didn't go on the long walk because I was tired out. Walsh stayed at the hotel too and when he seen me he says Why didn't you go with the bunch? I says I was too tired. He says Well when Callahan comes back you better keep out of sight or tell him you are sick. I says I don't care nothing for Callahan. He says No but Callahan is crazy about you. He says You better obey orders and you will git along better. I guess Walsh thinks I am some rube.

When the bunch come back Callahan never said a word to me but Gleason come up and says Where was you? I told him I was too tired to go walking. He says Well I will borrow a wheelbarrow some place and push you round. He says Do you sit down when you pitch? I let him kid me because he has not saw my stuff yet.

Next morning half the bunch mostly vetrans went to the ball park which isn't no better than the one we got at home. Most of them was vetrans as I say but I was in the bunch. That makes things look pretty good for me don't it Al? We tossed the ball round and hit fungos and run round and then Callahan asks Scott and Russell and I to warm up easy and pitch a few to the batters. It was warm and I felt pretty good so I warmed up pretty good. Scott pitched to them first and kept laying them right over with nothing on them. I don't believe a man gets any batting practice that way. So I went in and after I lobbed a few over I cut loose my fast one. Lord was to bat and he ducked out of the way and then throwed his bat to the bench. Callahan says What's the matter Harry? Lord says I forgot to pay up my life insurance. He says I ain't ready for Walter Johnson's July stuff.

Well Al I will make them think I am Walter Johnson before I get through with them. But Callahan come out to me and says What are you trying to do kill somebody? He says Save your smoke because you're going to need it later on. He says Go easy with the boys at first or I won't have no batters. But he was laughing and I guess he was pleased to see the stuff I had.

There is a dance in the hotel tonight and I am up in my room writing this in my underwear while I get my

back with an offer and they excepted it. I don't know how much they got but anyway I am sold to the big league and believe me Al I will make good.

Well Al I will be home in a few days and we will have some of the good old times. Regards to all the boys and tell them I am still their pal and not all swelled up over this big league business.

Your pal, Jack. ◇

Facing page:
◇ *Your pal, Jack*—Jack Keefe's first appearance, *The Saturday Evening Post*, March 7, 1914.

CHICAGO, ILLINOIS, DECEMBER 14.

Old Pal: Well Al I have not got much to tell you. As you know Comiskey wrote me that if I was up in Chi this month to drop in and see him. So I got here Thursday morning and went to his office in the afternoon. His office is out to the ball park and believe me its some park ◆◇ and some office.

I went in and asked for Comiskey and a young fellow says He is not here now but can I do anything for you? I told him who I am and says I had an engagment to see Comiskey. He says The boss is out of town hunting and did I have to see him personally? ◆

I says I wanted to see about signing a contract. He told me I could

---

(*continued from page 35*)
of the St. Louis Browns of the American Association in 1883 and 1885–89. He then became manager of the Chicago club of the Players League in 1890 for that league's one season of operation, and returned to the Browns in 1891 for the Association's last year of existence. Comiskey became manager of the Cincinnati Reds for the 1892–94 seasons, and it was in Cincinnati that he met Ban Johnson, with whom he conceived the founding of the American League. Comiskey was elected to the Hall of Fame in 1939. His descendants remained in control of the White Sox until 1959, when the club passed into the hands of Bill Veeck and his associates. The White Sox were the last major league club to remain in the hands of the founding family. See G. W. Axelson, *Commy* (Chicago: Reilly & Lee Co., 1919); Steven A. Riess, "Charles Albert Comiskey," *Biographical Dictionary of American Sports: Baseball*, pp. 107–8.

◆ *the ball park*—Comiskey Park, at 35th Street and Shields Avenue. Originally known as White Sox Park, the stadium had been built by Comiskey, mainly with the proceeds of the successful seasons of 1906–08. The building was designed by the Chicago architect Zachary Taylor Davis (1872–1946) to replace a thoroughly inadequate wooden structure at 39th Street and Princeton Avenue. The park opened on July 1, 1910, with the White Sox losing 2–0 to the St. Louis Browns. Comiskey Park initially seated 28,500, but was expanded to 32,000 in 1917 and, via a major revision in 1926–27, to 52,000. The White Sox played in Comiskey Park through the 1990 season. See George W. Hilton, "Comiskey Park," in L. Robert Davids, ed., *Insider's Baseball* (New York: Charles Scribner's Sons, 1983), pp. 23–30.

◆ *hunting*—Comiskey, an avid outdoorsman, maintained a hunting lodge at Rhinelander, Wis., and in December he would very likely have been there.

◇ *and believe me its some park*—Comiskey Park in its original configuration of 1910. Following the 1926 season the pavilions in the right- and left-field foul areas were double-decked and the bleachers were replaced with double-decked stands. (Barnes-Crosby photograph, Chicago Historical Society)

sign as well with him as Comiskey and he took me into another office. He says What salary did you think you ought to get? and I says I wouldn't think of playing ball in the big league for less than three thousand dollars per annum. He laughed and says You don't want much. You better stick round town till the boss comes back. So here I am and it is costing me a dollar a day to stay at the hotel on Cottage ◆ Grove Avenue and that don't include my meals.

I generally eat at some of the cafes round the hotel but I had supper downtown last night and it cost me fifty-five cents. If Comiskey don't come back soon I won't have no more money left.

◆ *Cottage Grove Avenue*—A major business street of the South Side, about a mile east of Comiskey Park. The area had been one of high-income residences in the nineteenth century, but by 1912 had become a middle-class neighborhood. It was later to descend into one of the city's worst slums.

Speaking of money I won't sign no contract unless I get the salary you and I talked of, three thousand dollars. You know what I was getting in Terre Haute, a hundred and fifty a month, and I know it's going to cost me a lot more to live here. I made inquiries round here and find I can get board and room for eight dollars a week but I will be out of town half the time and will have to pay for my room when I am away or look up a new one when I come back. Then I will have to buy cloths to wear on the road in places like New York. When Comiskey comes back I will name him three thousand dollars as my lowest figure and I guess he will come through when he sees I am in ernest. I heard that Walsh was getting twice as much as that.

The papers says Comiskey will be back here sometime tomorrow. He has been hunting with the president of the league so he ought to ◆ feel pretty good. But I don't care how he feels. I am going to get a contract for three thousand and if he don't want to give it to me he can do the other thing. You know me Al. *Yours truly, Jack.*

CHICAGO, ILLINOIS, DECEMBER 16.

Dear Friend Al: Well I will be home in a couple of days now but I wanted to write you and let you know how I come out with Comiskey. I signed my contract yesterday afternoon. He is a great old fellow Al and no wonder everybody likes him. He says Young man will you have a drink? But I was to smart and wouldn't take nothing. He says You was with Terre Haute? I says Yes I was. He says Doyle tells me you were pretty wild. I says Oh no I got good control. He says Well do you want to sign? I says Yes if I get my figure. He asks What is my figure

---

◆ *president of the league*—Byron Bancroft "Ban" Johnson (1865–1931). Johnson, born in Norwalk, Ohio, entered Marietta College in 1883, but left in the following year. He enrolled at the University of Cincinnati Law School, but there, as well, left without taking a degree. In 1886 he joined the sports staff of the Cincinnati *Commercial-Gazette*, rising to sports editor in 1887. In that post he became acquainted with Comiskey, who was managing the Reds at the time. Later, the two were associated in the formation of the Western League, in 1894, and in its reformation into the American League, in 1900–01. The two men were firm friends during that period, but after 1905 their relation began alternating between friendship and acrimony. In the years following the 1918 season, when Johnson awarded the contract of Jack Quinn to the New York Yankees instead of the White Sox, the two were permanently estranged. The present reference dates from their period of ambivalence, and thus their hunting together was anything but an assurance of Comiskey's good humor. Johnson remained president of the American League until 1927, but his authority eroded steadily after 1919. See Eugene C. Murdock, *Ban Johnson: Czar of Baseball* (Westport, Conn.: Greenwood Press, 1982).

and I says three thousand dollars per annum. He says Don't you want the office furniture too? Then he says I thought you was a young ballplayer and I didn't know you wanted to buy my park.

We kidded each other back and forth like that a while and then he says You better go out and get the air and come back when you feel better. I says I feel O. K. now and I want to sign a contract because I have got to get back to Bedford. Then he calls the secretary and tells ◆ him to make out my contract. He give it to me and it calls for two hundred and fifty a month. He says You know we always have a city ◆ serious here in the fall where a fellow picks up a good bunch of money. I hadn't thought of that so I signed up. My yearly salary will be fifteen hundred dollars besides what the city serious brings me. And that is only for the first year. I will demand three thousand or four thousand dollars next year.

I would of started home on the evening train but I ordered a suit of cloths from a tailor over on Cottage Grove and it won't be done till

---

◆ *Bedford*—Bedford, Ind., a town of 10,349 (in 1910) on the Monon Route 246 miles south of Chicago, was the center of the Indiana limestone industry.

the secretary—The secretary of the White Sox, as he had been since the team's founding, was Charles Augustus Fredericks (1877–1916). Fredericks, however, had lost his eyesight in 1911, and thereafter served only as the corporate officer. The functions of the secretary, who in the baseball of the time combined the role of traveling secretary with whatever duties of a general manager the owner did not himself execute, were already being seen to by Harry Grabiner (1891–1948), to whom the passage almost certainly refers. Grabiner had gone onto the White Sox payroll in 1904 at the age of 13, when he wandered into the 39th Street ballpark and helped Comiskey clean up the field after a rainstorm. He began by selling scorecards, but had risen to assistant secretary by 1912, and succeeded Fredericks upon the latter's death early in 1916. Grabiner was to rise to vice-president and general manager in a tenure that lasted through the 1945 season. He was an able and conservative operator, but because of Comiskey's practice of making favorable announcements himself and leaving the unfavorable ones to Grabiner, he was not as popular a figure as his ability and his loyalty to Comiskey warranted. He became vice-president of the Cleveland Indians when Bill Veeck bought the club in 1946 and died on October 24, 1948, almost immediately after the Indians won the World Series of that year.

◆ *city serious*—Beginning in 1903 the White Sox and Cubs met in a city series in most years when neither won the pennant. By 1913 they had met four times, the Cubs winning in 1905 and 1909, and the White Sox in 1911 and 1912; the 1903 series ended in a tie at seven games each. The 1906 World Series, in which the White Sox defeated the Cubs, is usually included in the city-series tally. The series continued through 1942, when the Cubs decided that the players should not be rewarded for failing to win a pennant. By that time, the White Sox had won 18 series and the Cubs six. "Serious" was apparently Lardner's favorite comic misspelling, for he attributed it to almost all his ballplayers—an inconsistency in what was otherwise a careful effort to give each of them individuality.

◇ *Paso Robles, California*—The California farming town of Paso Robles, where the White Sox took their spring training for the 1913 season, had the attraction of relative isolation and a pleasant, warm climate. The photograph shows the town about 20 years later, in the deep Depression years. The Paso Robles Hot Springs Hotel, where the White Sox stayed, is at upper left. (C. E. Smith collection)

tomorrow. It's going to cost me twenty bucks but it ought to last a long time. Regards to Frank and the bunch, *Your pal, Jack.*

PASO ROBLES, CALIFORNIA, MARCH 2.◆◇

Old Pal Al: Well Al we been in this little berg now a couple of days and its bright and warm all the time just like June. Seems funny to have it so warm this early in March but I guess this California climate is all they said about it and then some.

It would take me a week to tell you about our trip out here. We came on a Special Train De Lukes and it was some train. Every place◆◇ we stopped there was crowds down to the station to see us go through and all the people looked me over like I was a actor or something. I

◆ *Paso Robles, California, March 2*—Paso Robles was a town of 1,441 (in 1910) at the head of the Salinas Valley, 212 miles south of San Francisco and 258 miles north of Los Angeles, on the Coast Line of the Southern Pacific. Comiskey shifted his training base from Mineral Wells, Tex., to Paso Robles for the spring of 1913, when he arranged the series of exhibition games with the San Francisco, Oakland, and Los Angeles clubs of the Pacific Coast League treated in the text. The White Sox made an estimated $10,000 from these games. Training in Paso Robles had the incidental advantage of allowing the managements of the White Sox and the San Francisco club to evaluate young talent jointly; San Francisco was Comiskey's preferred club in the higher minors for optioning players for development.

◆ *Special Train De Lukes*—The White Sox traveled west on an eight-car special that followed the Overland Route, the Chicago & North Western, the Union

◇ *Special Train De Lukes*—Comiskey's practice was to take the team to spring training on a special train. There is no known photograph of the 1913 train, but the train of 1910 is well depicted. Here Comiskey is at the center in the high soft-gray hat that was his trademark. The train is on the Denver & Rio Grande at the hanging bridge in the Royal Gorge of the Arkansas River, west of Pueblo, Colorado. The party was en route to its training base in San Francisco. (George L. Beame photograph, Denver & Rio Grande Western Railroad Collection, courtesy Jackson C. Thode)

guess my hight and shoulders attracted their attention. Well Al we finally got to Oakland which is across part of the ocean from Frisco. We will be back here later on for practice games.

We stayed in Oakland a few hours and then took a train for here. It was another night in a sleeper and believe me I was tired of sleepers before we got here. I have road one night at a time but this was four straight nights. You know Al I am not built right for a sleeping car birth.

The hotel here is a great big place and got good eats. We got in at ◆ breakfasttime and I made a B line for the dining room. Kid Gleason ◆◇

(*continued from page 41*)
Pacific, and the Southern Pacific. The special left Chicago on February 20 and arrived in Oakland on Sunday, February 23. After a night's layover, the train proceeded to Paso Robles on the following day. The party of 94 people, made up of executives, players, support personnel and correspondents, included Lardner, who made the trip as a writer for the Chicago *Examiner*.

◆ *The hotel*—The Paso Robles Hot Springs Hotel, a resort of wide reputation.

◆ *Kid Gleason*—William J. Gleason (1866–1933), a career baseball man who had played for 22 seasons (1888–1908 and 1912) with six National and American League teams. Although mainly a second baseman, he played every position except catcher, batting .261 in 1,966 games and amassing a pitching record of 138–131. Although he played only one game for the White Sox, he became one of Comiskey's most valued employees. His role as coach is accurately delineated

◇ *Kid Gleason*—Kid Gleason, center, with Ed Walsh at left and Nixey Callahan at right. The photograph was probably taken in spring training of 1912 in Callahan's first year as manager of the White Sox. Walsh wears the home uniform of 1911, and Gleason, then a coach, wears the team's road blues. (See also photos on pp. 228 and 310.) (National Baseball Library, Cooperstown, New York)

who is a kind of asst. manager to Callahan come in and sat down with ◆ me. He says Leave something for the rest of the boys because they will be just as hungry as you. He says Ain't you afraid you will cut your throat with that knife. He says There ain't no extra charge for using the forks. He says You shouldn't ought to eat so much because you're

---

(*continued from page 42*)
in the stories. At the time, customary practice was not to have coaches of Gleason's character, but rather, as in the minor leagues at present, to delegate coaching duties to senior part-time players. In 1919 Gleason succeeded Pants Rowland as manager of the White Sox, which ensured that he would be in charge during the Black Sox scandal of that year. He held the position through 1923 and was subsequently a coach for the Athletics. See Garrett J. Kelleher, "More Than A Kid: The Story of Kid Gleason," *Baseball Research Journal*, XVII (1988), 79–81.

◆ *Callahan*—James Joseph "Nixey" Callahan (1874–1934). After playing for Philadelphia and Chicago in the National League in the 1890's, Callahan joined the White Sox upon the team's achieving major league status in 1901, playing for the Sox through 1905 and again in 1911–13. He, too, played every position but catcher, batting .273 in 923 games and ringing up a 99–73 pitching record. He managed the White Sox in 1903 and for 41 games in 1904, and later returned to the post, managing the team to fourth-, fifth-, and sixth-place finishes in 1912, 1913, and 1914. In 1916 and for 61 games of the 1917 season, he managed the Pittsburgh Pirates. See John J. Ward, "Callahan, the Cast Off Manager," *Baseball Magazine*, XVII, No. 4 (August 1916), 53–58.

overweight now. I says You may think I am fat, but it's all solid bone and muscle. He says Yes I suppose it's all solid bone from the neck up. I guess he thought I would get sore but I will let them kid me now because they will take off their hats to me when they see me work.

Manager Callahan called us all to his room after breakfast and give us a lecture. He says there would be no work for us the first day but that we must all take a long walk over the hills. He also says we must not take the training trip as a joke. Then the colored trainer give us our suits and I went to my room and tried mine on. I ain't a bad looking guy in the White Sox uniform Al. I will have my picture taken and send you boys some.

My roommate is Allen a lefthander from the Coast League. He ◆ don't look nothing like a pitcher but you can't never tell about them dam left handers. Well I didn't go on the long walk because I was tired out. Walsh stayed at the hotel too and when he seen me he says Why didn't you go with the bunch? I says I was too tired. He says Well when Callahan comes back you better keep out of sight or tell him you are sick. I says I don't care nothing for Callahan. He says No but Callahan is crazy about you. He says You better obey orders and you will git along better. I guess Walsh thinks I am some rube.

When the bunch come back Callahan never said a word to me but Gleason come up and says Where was you? I told him I was too tired to go walking. He says Well I will borrow a wheelbarrow some place and push you round. He says Do you sit down when you pitch? I let him kid me because he has not saw my stuff yet.

Next morning half the bunch mostly vetrans went to the ball park which isn't no better than the one we got at home. Most of them was vetrans as I say but I was in the bunch. That makes things look pretty good for me don't it Al? We tossed the ball round and hit fungos and run round and then Callahan asks Scott and Russell and I to warm ◆◇

◆ *Allen*—A fictional character. Actually, 19 players from the Pacific Coast League accompanied the White Sox to Paso Robles. Because the league was classified AA, two levels higher than was the Central League, there is a presumption that Allen was more nearly ready for major league ball than Keefe was.

◆ *Scott*—James "Death Valley Jimmy" Scott (1888–1957), a pitcher who spent his entire career, 1909–17, with the White Sox, achieving a lifetime record of 111–113. He was at his peak in the years of the stories, 20–21 in 1913, 16–18 in 1914, and 24–11 in 1915. From Lander, Wyo., he attended Nebraska Wesleyan College. See John J. Ward, "'Death Valley' Jim Scott," *Baseball Magazine*, XVI, No. 6 (April 1916), 43–46.

Russell—Ewell Albert "Reb" Russell (1889–1973), a Mississippian who pitched for the White Sox from 1913 to 1919, going 74–60 overall. His best season was

◇ *Russell*—Reb Russell in batting practice during his second career as an outfielder for the Pirates, ca. 1922. For most of his career he had been a pitcher. (George E. Brace collection)

up easy and pitch a few to the batters. It was warm and I felt pretty good so I warmed up pretty good. Scott pitched to them first and kept laying them right over with nothing on them. I don't believe a man gets any batting practice that way. So I went in and after I lobbed a few over I cut loose my fast one. Lord was to bat and he ducked out of the way and then throwed his bat to the bench. Callahan says What's

(*continued from page 44*)
that of the story, 1913, when his record was 21–17 in a league-leading 51 games, with a 1.91 earned run average. In that year he pitched seven shutouts, a record for a rookie not broken until Fernando Valenzuela pitched eight for the Los Angeles Dodgers in 1981. After encountering arm trouble he returned to the minor leagues, playing in the outfield for the Minneapolis Millers of the American Association, and came back to the majors for two seasons in the outfield for the Pittsburgh Pirates, hitting .368 in 1922 and .289 in 1923. See Richard C. Lindberg, "Reb Russell," *The Ballplayers*, pp. 948–49.

the matter Harry? Lord says I forgot to pay up my life insurance. He ◆ says I ain't ready for Walter Johnson's July stuff. ◆

Well Al I will make them think I am Walter Johnson before I get through with them. But Callahan come out to me and says What are you trying to do kill somebody? He says Save your smoke because you're going to need it later on. He says Go easy with the boys at first or I won't have no batters. But he was laughing and I guess he was pleased to see the stuff I had.

There is a dance in the hotel tonight and I am up in my room writing this in my underwear while I get my suit pressed. I got it all mussed up coming out here. I don't know what shoes to wear. I asked Gleason and he says Wear your baseball shoes and if any of the girls gets fresh with you spike them. I guess he was kidding me.

Write and tell me all the news about home. *Yours truly, Jack.*

PASO ROBLES, CALIFORNIA, MARCH 7.

Friend Al: I showed them something out there today Al. We had a game between two teams. One team was made up of most of the regulars and the other was made up of recruts. I pitched three innings for the recruts and shut the old birds out. I held them to one hit and that was a ground ball that the recrut shortstop Johnson ought to of ◆ ate up. I struck Collins out and he is one of the best batters in the ◆

◆ *Lord*—Harry Donald Lord (1882–1948), the White Sox field captain and their regular third baseman since 1911. Lord broke in with the Boston Red Sox in 1907 and came to the White Sox in mid-season of 1910. In his best season, 1911, he hit .321. During the Federal League war, Lord jumped the White Sox to become the playing manager of the Buffalo Electrics for 1915. Including his Federal League service, he hit .278 in 972 games. See Richard E. Beverage, "Harry Lord," *The Ballplayers*, p. 636.

◆ *Walter Johnson*—Walter Perry Johnson (1887–1946), righthander for the Washington Senators, and generally considered the greatest of all pitchers. Between 1907 and 1927, "The Big Train" won 416 games and lost 279, struck out 3,508 batters, and pitched a staggering 110 complete shutouts. In 1913, at the peak of his powers, Johnson went 36–7 with a 1.09 earned run average and 12 shutouts. His fastball, thrown sidearm with no whip of the wrist, was probably the fastest of any effective pitcher in history. Batters complained that after 4:00 P.M. they could barely see it. The veneration with which Lardner's characters, both real and fictional, speak of Johnson is wholly consistent with the retrospective views of him of the actual ballplayers interviewed by Lawrence F. Ritter for his *The Glory Of Their Times* (New York: The Macmillan Co., 1966). Johnson was a charter member of the Baseball Hall of Fame in 1936. See John L. Evers, "Walter Perry Johnson," *Biographical Dictionary of American Sports: Baseball*, pp. 288–89.

◆ *Johnson*—Apparently a fictional character.

◆ *Collins*—John Francis "Shano" Collins (1885–1955), regular rightfielder for the White Sox. Collins played for the White Sox from 1910 through 1920, ending

bunch. I used my fast ball most of the while but showed them a few spitters and they missed them a foot. I guess I must of got Walsh's goat with my spitter because him and I walked back to the hotel together and he talked like he was kind of jealous. He says You will have to learn to cover up your spitter. He says I could stand a mile away and tell when you was going to throw it. He says Some of these days I will learn you how to cover it up. I guess Al I know how to cover it up all right without Walsh learning me.

I always sit at the same table in the dining room along with Gleason and Collins and Bodie and Fournier and Allen the young lefthander I told you about. I feel sorry for him because he never says a word. Tonight at supper Bodie says How did I look today Kid? Gleason says Just like you always do in the spring. You looked like a cow. Gleason seems to have the whole bunch scared of him and they let him say anything he wants to. I let him kid me to but I ain't scared of him. Collins then says to me You got some fast ball there boy. I says I was not as fast today as I am when I am right. He says Well then I don't want to hit against you when you are right. Then Gleason says to

---

(*continued from page 46*)
his career with the Boston Red Sox from 1921 to 1925. In 16 years he hit .264 in 1,798 games. Collins managed the Red Sox in 1931 and for part of the 1932 season. Judging from the fact that he had hit .292 in the 1912 season, second on the team only to Ping Bodie's .294, Keefe's characterization of Collins' hitting has to be seen as atypically lacking in hyperbole. See Richard A. Lindberg, "Shano Collins," *The Ballplayers*, pp. 212–13.

◆ *spitters*—The spitter, or spitball, is a ball thrown with wet fingers, which was entirely legal at the time. The ball usually took the trajectory of a hard sinker, breaking down sharply as it approached the plate. The pitch was outlawed in 1920, but its working practitioners were allowed to continue using it for the remainder of their careers. Because Walsh was the most successful spitball pitcher, his admonition to Keefe came from the highest authority.

◆ *Bodie*—Frank Stephan "Ping" Bodie, playing name of Francesco Stephano Pezzolo (1887–1961), the White Sox regular centerfielder. He played for the team from 1911 to 1914, for the Philadelphia Athletics in 1917, and for the New York Yankees from 1918 to 1921, hitting .275 in 1,049 games. Bodie, who was 5′8″ and 195 pounds, was slow afoot because of the weight problem noted in this passage. See A. D. Suehsdorf, "Ping Bodie," *The Ballplayers*, p. 87.

Fournier—John Frank "Jacques" Fournier (1892–1973), one of the best fielding first basemen of his day, but not yet the accomplished hitter he was to become. Fournier had come to the White Sox in 1912 and hit just .192 in 35 games. In 1913 he hit .233 in 68 games as second-string first baseman behind Hal Chase. He played for the White Sox into the 1917 season, then for the Yankees, Cardinals, Dodgers, and Braves through 1927. In 1,530 games over the course of 15 seasons, he hit .313 and had no record in a single pitching appearance for the Cardinals. He was subsequently a minor league manager, a scout, and, from 1934 to 1938, baseball coach at the University of California, Los Angeles. See Steven P. Savage, "John Frank Fournier," *Biographical Dictionary of American Sports: Baseball*, p. 193.

Collins Cut that stuff out. Then he says to me Don't believe what he tells you boy. If the pitchers in this league weren't no faster than you I would still be playing ball and I would be the best hitter in the country.

After supper Gleason went out on the porch with me. He says Boy you have got a little stuff but you have got a lot to learn. He says You field your position like a washwoman and you don't hold the runners up. He says When Chase was on second base today he got such a lead ◆ on you that the little catcher couldn't of shot him out at third with a rifle. I says They all thought I fielded my position all right in the Central League. He says Well if you think you do it all right you better go back to the Central League where you are appresiated. I says You can't send me back there because you could not get waivers. He says ◆ Who would claim you? I says St. Louis and Boston and New York. ◆

◆ *Chase*—Harold Harris "Hal" Chase (1883–1947), the team's regular first baseman and one of the most adept fielders in the history of his position. The reference to Chase in spring training is an error, for he did not come to the White Sox from the New York Yankees until June 1, 1913, in trade for Rollie Zeider and Babe Borton. He remained with the team only until early in the 1914 season, when after 58 games he served the team with ten days' notice of his intention to leave it for Buffalo of the Federal League. The standard baseball contract provided that the *club* might release *him* on ten days' notice, but offered the player no such option. Chase shrewdly used this imbalance to show lack of mutuality in the baseball contract, and in the landmark case of *American League Baseball Club of Chicago v. Chase* (86 N.Y. Misc. 441 [1914]) defeated the White Sox in their effort to enjoin him from leaving. Subsequently, he played for Cincinnati and New York of the National League. While playing for the Giants in 1919 he learned of the impending Black Sox scandal, tried to profit from it, and was one of those indicted in the criminal action of 1920. He did not attempt to play major league baseball after 1919, but would probably have been banned had he done so. His guilty knowledge of the plot plus numerous earlier allegations of complicity in game-throwing have presumably denied him entry into the Baseball Hall of Fame. He batted .291 in 15 seasons, with 2,158 hits in 1,917 games. He was one of the few lefthanded players capable of playing other infield positions, and recorded 39 games at second base, shortstop, and third base. See Joseph E. King, "Harold Harris Chase," *Biographical Dictionary of American Sports: Baseball*, pp. 89–90; Robert C. Hoie, "The Hal Chase Case," *Baseball Research Journal*, III (1974), 26–34.

◆ *waivers*—In baseball's organization of the monopsony it was necessary under certain circumstances—as it remains today—to secure waivers from other clubs before sending a player to the minor leagues. The purpose of the arrangement, like several other rules in the monopsony, was to allow a veteran player to play at the highest level open to him, even if he would be more valuable to another club at a lower level. Keefe, who was on his first trip to the major leagues, would not have had to clear waivers to be sent to a minor league club.

◆ *St. Louis and Boston and New York*—An odd set of clubs: in 1912 Boston had won the American League pennant, St. Louis finished seventh, and New York finished last.

You know Al what Smith told me this winter. Gleason says Well if ◆ you're not willing to learn St. Louis and Boston and New York can have you and the first time you pitch against us we will steal fifty bases. Then he quit kidding and asked me to go to the field with him early tomorrow morning and he would learn me some things. I don't think he can learn me nothing but I promised I would go with him.

There is a little blonde kid in the hotel here who took a shine to me at the dance the other night but I am going to leave the skirts alone. She is real society and a swell dresser and she wants my picture. Regards to all the boys. *Your friend, Jack.*

P.S. The boys thought they would be smart tonight and put something over on me. A boy brought me a telegram and I opened it and it said You are sold to Jackson in the Cotton States League. For just a ◆ minute they had me going but then I happened to think that Jackson is in Michigan and there's no Cotton States League round there.

PASO ROBLES, CALIFORNIA, MARCH 9.

Dear Friend Al: You have no doubt read the goods news in the papers before this reaches you. I have been picked to go to Frisco with the first team. We play practice games up there about two weeks while the ◆ second club plays in Los Angeles. Poor Allen had to go with the second ◆◇ club. There's two other recrut pitchers with our part of the team but my name was first on the list so it looks like I had made good. I knowed they would like my stuff when they seen it. We leave here tonight. You got the first team's address so you will know where to send my mail. Callahan goes with us and Gleason goes with the second club. Him

---

◆ *Smith*—Louis D. Smith (1861–1925), a local businessman who owned the Terre Haute Hottentots from 1901 to July 21, 1911. Smith was the city's leading bookseller, but also sold sporting goods and dealt in railroad tickets. For biographical information on Smith I am indebted to the late Paul C. Frisz. See "Louis D. Smith Called by Death," Terre Haute *Tribune*, March 21, 1925.

◆ *Cotton States League*—In 1913 the Class D Cotton States League consisted of Jackson, Columbus, Clarksdale, and Meridian (all in Mississippi), Pensacola (Fla.), and Selma (Ala.).

◆ *first team*—Callahan announced the personnel of the two teams on March 3. He followed normal practice in assigning the younger or weaker pitchers to the first team and the veteran pitchers to the second. The first team was initially assigned only two veteran pitchers, Walsh and Frank Lange. Apart from tending to equalize talent between the two teams, this arrangement allowed the managements of the White Sox and the San Francisco Seals to decide upon pitchers to be optioned to San Francisco.

◆ *second club*—This assignment implies that the management had at least tentatively decided to retain Allen.

◇ *the second club*—The portion of the White Sox split squad sent to the San Francisco Bay Area stayed at the Hotel Oakland. Ray Schalk is at the wheel of the hotel's station van. (National Baseball Library, Cooperstown, New York)

and I have got to be pretty good pals and I wish he was going with us even if he don't let me eat like I want to. He told me this morning to remember all he had learned me and to keep working hard. He didn't learn me nothing I didn't know before but I let him think so.

The little blonde don't like to see me leave here. She lives in Detroit and I may see her when I go there. She wants me to write but I guess I better not give her no encouragement.

Well Al I will write you a long letter from Frisco,

Yours truly, Jack.

OAKLAND, CALIFORNIA, MARCH 19. ◆

Dear Old Pal: They have gave me plenty of work here all right. I have pitched four times but have not went over five innings yet. I worked

◆ *March 19*—By this date the White Sox' first team had won seven and lost three against the San Francisco, Oakland, and Sacramento clubs. The first team then headed south, and the second team left Los Angeles for the Bay Area.

against Oakland two times and against Frisco two times and only three runs have been scored off me. They should only ought to of had one but Bodie misjuged a easy fly ball in Frisco and Weaver made a wild ◆ peg in Oakland that let in a run. I am not using much but my fast ball but I have got a world of speed and they can't foul me when I am right. I whiffed eight men in five innings in Frisco yesterday and could of did better than that if I had of cut loose.

Manager Callahan is a funny guy and I don't understand him sometimes. I can't figure out if he is kidding or in ernest. We road back to Oakland on the ferry together after yesterday's game and he ◆ says Don't you never throw a slow ball? I says I don't need no slow ball with my spitter and my fast one. He says No of course you don't need it but if I was you I would get one of the boys to learn it to me. He says And you better watch the way the boys fields their positions and holds up the runners. He says To see you work one might think they had a rule in the Central League forbidding a pitcher from leaving the box or looking toward first base.

I told him the Central didn't have no rule like that. He says And I noticed you taking your wind up when What's His Name was on second base there today. I says Yes I got more stuff when I wind up.

◆ *Weaver*—George Davis "Buck" Weaver (1890–1956), the team's regular shortstop. The reference to Weaver's wild throw is apt; his main handicap in his early years was an erratic arm. Comiskey had acquired Weaver from York of the Tri-State League in 1911, and in 1912 optioned him to San Francisco to work out his throwing problem.

At the White Sox training camp in Texas in 1912, Weaver, as a rookie, encountered Lardner, whom he had met while playing for Saginaw in the Southern Michigan League in 1909. Lardner particularly liked Weaver for his agreeable personality, his enthusiasm for the game, and his talent as an infielder. Weaver spent his entire career with the White Sox, making 1,254 hits in nine seasons between 1912 and 1920, while establishing a .272 lifetime batting average. Weaver, regular third baseman on the 1919 champions, participated in the planning of the Black Sox scandal, but withdrew from the conspiracy before the World Series. Although he neither engaged in the effort to throw games nor shared in the spoils, he was declared ineligible for having guilty knowledge of the plot. Lardner, along with most other observers of the scandal, felt strongly that Weaver's penalty was excessive. Weaver tried throughout his lifetime to have the ban lifted, but died without succeeding. A biography highly sympathetic to Weaver is Irving M. Stein, *The Ginger Kid: The Buck Weaver Story* (Dubuque: The Elysian Fields Press [Brown & Benchmark], 1992) See also Eliot Asinof, *Eight Men Out: The Black Sox and the 1919 World Series* (New York: Holt, Rinehart and Winston, 1963).

◆ *yesterday's game*—Actually, on March 18, the White Sox played Portland of the Pacific Coast League at Visalia, winning 5–4.

◇ *Cobb*—Ty Cobb in batting practice, 1918 or 1919. (National Baseball Library, Cooperstown, New York)

He says Of course you have but if you wind up like that with Cobb on ◆◇ base he will steal your watch and chain. I says Maybe Cobb can't get on base when I work against him. He says That's right and maybe San Francisco Bay is made of grapejuice. Then he walks away from me.

He give one of the youngsters a awful bawling out for something

---

◆ *Cobb*—Tyrus Raymond "Ty" Cobb (1886–1961), outfielder of the Detroit Tigers. In 22 seasons for the Tigers plus two final years with the Athletics, Cobb appeared in 3,033 games, went to bat 11,429 times, made 4,191 hits, scored 2,244 runs, stole 892 bases, and hit .367 overall—a figure that remains the highest lifetime average ever recorded. His speed, audacity, and competitiveness are legendary. He managed the Tigers with moderate success from 1921 to 1926, and was a charter member of the Baseball Hall of Fame in 1936. See Ty Cobb with Al Stump, *My Life in Baseball: The True Record* (Garden City: Doubleday, 1961); John D. McCallum, *The Tiger Wore Spikes* (New York: A. S. Barnes & Co., 1956); Charles C. Alexander, *Ty Cobb* (New York: Oxford University Press, 1984); Ring W. Lardner, "Tyrus: The Greatest of 'Em All," *The American Magazine*, LXXIX (June 1915), 19–23, 78.

he done in the game at supper last night. If he ever talks to me like he done to him I will take a punch at him. You know me Al.

I come over to Frisco last night with some of the boys and we took in the sights. Frisco is some live town Al. We went all through China Town and the Barbers' Coast. Seen lots of swell dames but they was ◆ all painted up. They have beer out here that they call steam beer. I ◆ had a few glasses of it and it made me logey. A glass of that Terre ◆ Haute beer would go pretty good right now.

We leave here for Los Angeles in a few days and I will write you from there. This is some country Al and I would love to play ball round here. *Your Pal, Jack.*

P.S.—I got a letter from the little blonde and I suppose I got to answer it.

LOS ANGELES, CALIFORNIA, MARCH 26. ◆

Friend Al: Only four more days of sunny California and then we start back East. We got exhibition games in Yuma and El Paso, Texas, and ◆ Oklahoma City and then we stop over in St. Joe, Missouri, for three

---

◆ *Barbers' Coast*—The Barbary Coast, San Francisco's traditional section of bars and brothels, on Pacific Avenue east of Kearny Street.

◆ *steam beer*—The traditional beer of San Francisco's blue-collar workers since the gold rush of 1849. To compensate for the high cost of refrigeration, local brewers developed a process of double fermentation at room temperature—essentially a krausening without refrigeration—wherein the brew produced from the malt and hops was initially allowed to go flat. Then an injection of newly fermenting wort and yeast was injected into the beer in closed tanks, causing the beer to build up a pressure of 65 to 70 pounds per square inch, and creating the steam of the name. The product is a heavy, highly carbonated beer of the character of some English ales. Its full body and heavy hopping could, as Keefe observed, make one logy. The process—which is, remarkably, the only brewing method invented in America—lent itself to small-scale brewing. There were once 27 breweries producing steam beer in San Francisco and over 100 more in the mining region. It continues to be produced with great recent success by the Anchor Brewing Co. of San Francisco.

◆ *Terre Haute beer*—Champagne Velvet, a traditional American light lager, produced by the Terre Haute Brewing Co. from around the turn of the century to 1958. The brewer, which once rose to eighth largest in the United States, distributed widely beyond the Terre Haute area.

◆ *March 26*—On this date the White Sox played the Venice team of the Pacific Coast League, opening its new ballpark.

◆ *Yuma and El Paso*—The schedule to which Keefe refers was:

March 31	Yuma	April 3–4	Omaha at Oklahoma City
April 1	El Paso	April 5–8	St. Joseph, Mo.
April 2	Amarillo		

days before we go home. You know Al we open the season in Cleveland and we won't be in Chi no more than just passing through. We don't play there till April eighteenth and I guess I will work in that serious all right against Detroit. Then I will be glad to have you and the boys come up and watch me as you suggested in your last letter.

I got another letter from the little blonde. She has went back to Detroit but she give me her address and telephone number and believe me Al I am going to look her up when we get there the twenty-ninth of April.

She is a stenographer and was out here with her uncle and aunt.

I had a run in with Kelly last night and it looked like I would have to take a wallop at him but the other boys seperated us. He is a bush outfielder from the New England League. We was playing poker. You know the boys plays poker a good deal but this was the first time I got in. I was having pretty good luck and was about four bucks to the good and I was thinking of quitting because I was tired and sleepy. Then Kelly opened the pot for fifty cents and I stayed. I had three sevens. No one else stayed. Kelley stood pat and I drawed two cards. And I catched my fourth seven. He bet fifty cents but I felt pretty safe even if he did have a pat hand. So I called him. I took the money and told them I was through.

Lord and some of the boys laughed but Kelly got nasty and begun to pan me for quitting and for the way I played. I says Well I won the pot didn't I? He says Yes and he called me something. I says I got a notion to take a punch at you.

He says Oh you have have you? And I come back at him. I says Yes I have have I? I would of busted his jaw if they hadn't stopped me. You know me Al.

I worked here two times once against Los Angeles and once against Venice. I went the full nine innings both times and Venice beat me

---

◆ *we open the season in Cleveland*—The White Sox were indeed scheduled to do so, on April 10.

◆ *that serious . . . against Detroit*—The White Sox were scheduled to open at home against Cleveland on April 17. Detroit followed Cleveland into Comiskey Park on April 21.

◆ *Kelly*—Apparently a fictional character.

◆ *New England League*—A minor league established in 1892. In 1912 it was classified B, as was the Central League. The New England League, after four hiatuses, disbanded permanently after the 1949 season.

◆ *Venice*—A Los Angeles suburb, a real estate promotion along the coast, later to become a bohemian area. Venice was a member of the Pacific Coast League for

four to two. I could of beat them easy with any kind of support. I walked a couple of guys in the forth and Chase drops a throw and Collins lets a fly ball get away from him. At that I would of shut them out if I had wanted to cut loose. After the game Callahan says You didn't look so good in there today. I says I didn't cut loose. He says Well you been working pretty near three weeks now and you ought to be in shape to cut loose. I says Oh I am in shape all right. He says Well don't work no harder than you have to or you might get hurt and then the league would blow up. I don't know if he was kidding me or not but I guess he thinks pretty well of me because he works me lots oftener than Walsh or Scott or Benz. ◆◇

I will try to write you from Yuma, Texas, but we don't stay there only a day and I may not have time for a long letter. *Yours truly, Jack.*

◇ *Benz*—Joe "Blitzen" Benz at an old-timer's event in a White Sox uniform of the late 1930's or 1940's. (George E. Brace collection)

YUMA, ARIZONA, APRIL 1.

Dear Old Al: Just a line to let you know we are on our way back East. This place is in Arizona and it sure is sandy. They haven't got no regular ball club here and we play a pick-up team this afternoon. ◆ Callahan told me I would have to work. He says I am using you because we want to get through early and I know you can beat them quick. That is the first time he has said anything like that and I guess he is wiseing up that I got the goods.

We was talking about the Athaletics this morning and Callahan says None of you fellows pitch right to Baker. I was talking to Lord and ◆◇

(*continued from page 54*)
1913 and 1914. In 1915 the franchise reverted to Vernon, a south-central suburb of Los Angeles, where it had played in 1912.

◆ *Benz*—Joseph Louis "Blitzen" Benz (1886–1957), another pitcher who spent his entire career with the White Sox, winning 73 and losing 76 between 1911 and 1919. In 1913 Benz had a poor year, 6–10. His best record was 15–11 in 1915. (In 1911, not by coincidence, a racing model of the Benz automobile known as the Blitzen Benz broke the world's land speed record.) See Richard A. Lindberg, "Joe Benz," *The Ballplayers*, p. 70.

◆ *a pick-up team*—The White Sox played a team from the U.S. Reclamation Service in Yuma, winning 9–0. The Sox lent pitcher Doc White and catcher Red Kuhn to the local team to help equalize the talent.

◆ *Baker*—John Franklin Baker (1886–1963), third baseman of the Philadelphia Athletics. By the standards of the day, Baker was a hitter of great power, having led the American League in home runs from 1911 through 1914 with 9, 10, 12, and 8, respectively. Hitting two home runs in the 1911 World Series earned him the nickname of "Home Run" Baker, by which he is still customarily known. He played for the Athletics from 1908 to 1914, held out for all of 1915, and then played for the New York Yankees between 1916 and 1922. Baker hit .307 in 1,575

◇ *Baker*—The John Franklin Baker plaque at the National Baseball Hall of Fame and Museum, Cooperstown, New York.

Scott afterward and I say to Scott How do you pitch to Baker? He says I use my fadeaway. I says How do you throw it? He says Just like you ◆ throw a fast ball to anybody else. I says Why do you call it a fadeaway then? He says Because when I throw it to Baker it fades away over the fence.

This place is full of Indians and I wish you could see them Al. They don't look nothing like the Indians we seen in that show last summer.

Your old pal, Jack.

OKLAHOMA CITY, APRIL 4.

Friend Al: Coming out of Amarillo last night I and Lord and Weaver ◆ was sitting at a table in the dining car with a old lady. None of us were talking to her but she looked me over pretty careful and seemed to kind of like my looks. Finally she says Are you boys with some football club? Lord nor Weaver didn't say nothing so I thought it was up to me and I says No ma'am this is the Chicago White Sox Ball Club. She says I knew you were athaletes. I says Yes I guess you could spot us for athaletes. She says Yes indeed and specially you. You certainly look healthy. I says You ought to see me stripped. I didn't see nothing funny about that but I thought Lord and Weaver would die laughing. Lord had to get up and leave the table and he told everybody what I said.

All the boys wanted me to play poker on the way here but I told them I didn't feel good. I know enough to quit when I am ahead Al. Callahan and I sat down to breakfast all alone this morning. He says Boy why don't you get to work? I says What do you mean? Ain't I working? He says You ain't improving none. You have got the stuff to make a good pitcher but you don't go after bunts and you don't cover first base and you don't watch the baserunners. He made me kind of sore talking that way and I says Oh I guess I can get along all right.

(*continued from page 55*)
games and hit 93 home runs. He was elected to the Baseball Hall of Fame in 1955. See Stephen D. Bodayla, "John Franklin Baker," *Biographical Dictionary of American Sports: Baseball*, pp. 19–20.

◆ *fadeaway*—A pitch particularly identified with Christy Mathewson, who described it as essentially the modern screwball, a reverse curveball thrown by revolving the hand inward (rather than outward) just before the instant of delivery. It has long been thought to be hard on a pitcher's arm.

◆ *Amarillo*—On April 2 the White Sox defeated the Amarillo Panhandlers, who do not appear to have been in Organized Baseball, 12–2. On April 3 the White Sox defeated Omaha of the Western League at Oklahoma City, 18–5. Omaha won on April 4, 3–1.

He says Well I am going to put it up to you. I am going to start you over in St. Joe day after tomorrow and I want you to show me something. I want you to cut loose with all you've got and I want you to get round the infield a little and show them you aren't tied in that box. I says Oh I can field my position if I want to. He says Well you better want to or I will have to ship you back to the sticks. Then he got up and left. He didn't scare me none Al. They won't ship me to no sticks after the way I showed on this trip and even if they did they couldn't get no waivers on me.

Some of the boys have begun to call me Four Sevens but it don't bother me none. *Yours truly, Jack.*

ST. JOE, MISSOURI, APRIL 7. ◆

Friend Al: It rained yesterday so I worked today instead and St. Joe done well to get three hits. They couldn't of scored if we had played all week. I give a couple of passes but I catched a guy flatfooted off of first base and I come up with a couple of bunts and throwed guys out. When the game was over Callahan says That's the way I like to see you work. You looked better today than you looked on the whole trip. Just once you wound up with a man on but otherwise you was all O. K. So I guess my job is cinched Al and I won't have to go to New York or St. Louis. I would rather be in Chi anyway because it is near home. I wouldn't care though if they traded me to Detroit. I hear from Violet right along and she says she can't hardly wait till I come to Detroit. She says she is strong for the Tigers but she will pull for me when I work against them. She is nuts over me and I guess she has saw lots of guys to.

I sent her a stickpin from Oklahoma City but I can't spend no more dough on her till after our first payday the fifteenth of the month. I had thirty bucks on me when I left home and I only got about ten left including the five spot I won in the poker game. I have to tip the waiters about thirty cents a day and I seen about twenty picture shows on the coast besides getting my cloths pressed a couple of times.

◆ *St. Joe, Missouri*—St. Joseph, the pioneer city on the Missouri River, was considered a hotbed of enthusiasm for the White Sox; Comiskey frequently scheduled exhibitions there. The local team was the St. Joseph Drummers of the Class A Western League, which in 1912 had finished sixth in an eight-team circuit. In the exhibitions there, Benz beat the Drummers 2–0 on April 5, but the local team beat Walsh 3–1 on April 6. The game of April 7 was called because of cold weather, and the teams were rained out on April 8.

The contraction to St. Joe was locally considered offensive, but less so than Keefe's habitual use of "Frisco."

We leave here tomorrow night and arrive in Chi the next morning. The second club joins us there and then that night we go to Cleveland ◆ to open up. I asked one of the reporters if he knowed who was going to pitch the opening game and he says it would be Scott or Walsh but I guess he don't know much about it.

These reporters travel all round the country with the team all season and send in telegrams about the game every night. I ain't seen no Chi papers so I don't know what they been saying about me. But I should worry eh Al? Some of them are pretty nice fellows and some of them got the swell head. They hang round with the old fellows and play poker most of the time.

Will write you from Cleveland. You will see in the paper if I pitch the opening game. *Your old pal, Jack.*

CLEVELAND, OHIO, APRIL 10.

Old Friend Al: Well Al we are all set to open the season this afternoon. ◇ I have just ate breakfast and I am sitting in the lobby of the hotel. I eat at a little lunch counter about a block from here and I saved seventy cents on breakfast. You see Al they give us a dollar a meal and ◆ if we don't want to spend that much all right. Our rooms at the hotel are paid for.

The Cleveland papers says Walsh or Scott will work for us this afternoon. I asked Callahan if there was any chance of me getting

---

◆ *The second club*—The second team had returned via the central route, playing exhibitions in Ogden, Salt Lake City, Grand Junction, Des Moines, Ottumwa, and Davenport.

◆ *a dollar a meal*—Comiskey issued a meal allowance of $3 per day, whereas other major league teams provided $4. This was a standing irritant to White Sox players, other than the hero.

◆ (*Page 59*) *Lajoie*—Napoleon Lajoie (1875–1959), a second baseman so distinguished that his team, the Cleveland Naps, was named for him. Lajoie had broken into the major leagues with the Philadelphia Phillies in 1896, but shifted to the Athletics in 1901 upon their formation. The Phillies sought and secured an injunction to prevent his playing for the Athletics, but were granted the injunction only because Lajoie's contract with the Phillies had a series of options rather than a reserve clause, i.e., it was not a restraint of trade. This action resulted in Lajoie's being traded to Cleveland, where Ohio courts were unwilling to restrain his appearance. He managed the team from 1905 to 1909. Upon his return to the Athletics in 1915, the Cleveland team was renamed "Indians" following a popular contest. Lajoie played in 2,481 games in 21 seasons, made 3,251 hits, and batted .339. He was elected to the Baseball Hall of Fame in its second year, in 1937. See J. M. Murphy, "Napoleon Lajoie: Modern Baseball's First Superstar," *The National Pastime*, VII, No. 1 (Spring 1988), entire issue; Alan R. Asnen, "Napoleon Lajoie," *Biographical Dictionary of American Sports: Baseball*, pp. 321–22.

into the first game and he says I hope not. I don't know what he meant but he may surprise these reporters and let me pitch. I will beat them Al. Lajoie and Jackson is supposed to be great batters but the bigger ◆ they are the harder they fall.

◇ *we are all set to open the season*—Keefe's team, the Chicago White Sox of 1913, in its road blues. (George E. Brace collection)

Jackson—Joseph Jefferson "Shoeless Joe" Jackson (1887–1951), outfielder of the Cleveland Naps. An illiterate millhand from South Carolina, Jackson was a hitter of enormous talent but ultimately a tragic figure. After playing briefly for the Athletics in 1908 and 1909, Jackson became a member of the Naps in 1910. In 1911 he hit .408, becoming the only man ever to hit .400 without winning the batting championship (Cobb hit .420). Comiskey acquired Jackson during the 1915 season as one of the major moves in his assembly of the championship teams of 1917 and 1919. Jackson played an ambiguous role in the Black Sox scandal. He reportedly participated in planning the game-throwing, but then wished to dissociate himself from the plot, to the extent of asking Comiskey not to play him in the Series. He hit .375 in the Series and fielded perfectly, and was not accused of foul play. In his confession before Judge Charles MacDonald and the Grand Jury, the transcript of which was lost before the criminal trial, he is alleged to have admitted some intentional misplays, but he always denied this and without the transcript the question cannot be reexamined. He accepted $5,000 from his close friend Claude Williams as his share of the payoff, but when he tried to turn the money in to Comiskey, he was rebuffed. Jackson also reportedly complained to ringleader Chick Gandil that he should have received the $20,000 on which they had agreed. This degree of complicity caused him to be banned from baseball after the 1920 season, and prevented his election to the Baseball Hall of Fame. Jackson's lifetime batting average of .356 over the course of 1,330 games in 13

The second team joined us yesterday in Chi and we practiced a little. Poor Allen was left in Chi last night with four others of the recrut pitchers. Looks pretty good for me eh Al? I only seen Gleason for a few minutes on the train last night. He says, Well you ain't took off much weight. You're hog fat. I says Oh I ain't fat. I didn't need to take off no weight. He says One good thing about it the club don't have to engage no birth for you because you spend all your time in the dining car. We kidded along like that a while and then the trainer rubbed my arm and I went to bed. Well Al I just got time to have my suit pressed before noon. *Yours truly, Jack.*

CLEVELAND, OHIO, APRIL 11. ◆

Friend Al: Well Al I suppose you know by this time that I did not pitch and that we got licked. Scott was in there and he didn't have nothing. ◇ When they had us beat four to one in the eight inning Callahan told me to go out and warm up and he put a batter in for Scott in our ninth. But Cleveland didn't have to play their ninth so I got no chance to work. But it looks like he means to start me in one of the games here. We got three more to play. Maybe I will pitch this afternoon. I got a postcard from Violet. She says Beat them Naps. I will give them a battle Al if I get a chance.

Glad to hear you boys have fixed it up to come to Chi during the Detroit serious. I will ask Callahan when he is going to pitch me and let you know. Thanks Al for the papers. *Your friend, Jack.*

ST. LOUIS, MISSOURI, APRIL 15. ◆

Friend Al: Well Al I guess I showed them. I only worked one inning

---

(*continued from page 59*)
seasons remains the third-highest ever achieved, behind only Cobb and Hornsby. For evaluations favorable to Jackson, see Donald Gropman. *Say It Ain't So, Joe! The Story of Shoeless Joe Jackson* (Boston: Little, Brown & Co., 1979), and Harvey Frommer, *Shoeless Joe and Ragtime Baseball* (Dallas: Taylor Publishing Co., 1992).

◆ *Cleveland, Ohio, April 11*—The scheduled opener in Cleveland on April 10 was rained out. In the actual opener of April 11, Scott started and showed little, giving up six hits in six innings before being removed for a pinch hitter and losing 3–1. This is apparently the only regular-season game that Lardner both wrote up as a working sportswriter and treated fictionally before giving up game-by-game reporting for the role of columnist. His account of the game for the *Examiner* is reproduced on the facing page.

◆ *April 15*—On this date the White Sox were, in fact, playing in St. Louis. Walsh defeated the Browns, 5–3.

WHITE SOX LOSE OPENER TO JACKSON, GREGG AND LAJOIE

Cleveland's Great Trio Defeats Hose, 3 to 1, in Icy Battle Before 15,000 Fans; Cicotte Replaces Scott on Slab.

BY R. W. LARDNER.

CLEVELAND, Ohio, April 11.—Cleveland's three great assets, Vean Gregg, Joe Jackson and Nap Lajoie, proved more valuable than fifteen Chicago ballplayers to-day and the opening game of the year in this town was a 3 to 1 defeat for Jimmy Callahan's brave Sox. The score could have been 3 to 2, for Mattick had a chance to walk home in the ninth with a second run, but he couldn't even risk the walk, for the tally wouldn't have benefited anybody but Mattick himself.

Jim Scott's smoke and Callahan's generalship went for naught against the combined efforts of the three stars named above. Nothing but shutout pitching could have won for Chicago, and Lajoie and Jackson, particularly the latter, were there to prevent anything like that. While they were employed in gathering runs for Charley Somers, Gregg was successfully foiling the attempts of the Sox to get some for themselves. Some one told us the other day that Gregg wasn't in condition to pitch. Perhaps that was true, but the lank left-hander gave a pretty fair imitation of a person in the pink for the first seven innings of play. After that, in the eighth and ninth, he showed a few signs of weakness, but it was too late to do our side any good.

RIGHT-HAND BATTERS PUT IN.

When Vean had demonstrated to the Sox leader that he had a great deal too much for our left-handed batters, Cal began substituting and by the time the ninth was with us Jack Fournier was the only one in the Sox lineup who swings from the first base side of the plate. To make his attack as strong as possible Cal started Mattick in left field in place of the left-handed Davy Jones, and late in the day Berger and Zeider went in for Rath and Lord. Callahan himself took a hand in the pastime, batting for Borton in the eighth and making good with the single that scored the only Chicago run.

Until the eighth opened it looked as if the Sox would be pretty lucky to leave the park with two hits, less than Jackson alone had made. The substitutions and the weakening of Gregg occurred simultaneously, however, and the five swats collected in the eighth and ninth gave the Hose the doubtful honor of outbatting their rivals.

Scotty didn't have a bit of trouble except during the three separate and distinct innings in which Jackson and Lajoie had turns at bat. If these two demons could have been enjoined from meddling in the game the Sox to-night would be up there in front instead of associating with Frank Chance and Garland Stahl at the foot of the class.

RATH AND WEAVER OFF STRIDE.

Morris Rath and Buck Weaver committed errors which ably assisted the Naps in scoring, but Joseph and Larry were strong enough to whip us without violations of the fielding rules on the part of those two young infielders.

Jackson faced Scott three times and broke into the American League averages for the year with a percentage of 1.000. He started with a double, came back with a triple and finished with another double. His first two-bagger and his triple collided with the right field wall. His second double went on a line to Mattick's right in left field. Lajoie contributed a single which put Joe in position to score the initial run in the second inning, and a sacrifice fly, or line drive, rather, that brought the Carolinan in from third in the fourth.

Two were out in the sixth when Jackson appeared for the third time and doubled. On this occasion the large Frenchman fell down on the job and rolled out to Weaver, but he probably knew that Cleveland had already made enough runs to win.

It was not an ideal day for the opening, for the clouds hung over the city all day and it was cold. A crowd of close to 15,000 witnessed the daring operations of Gregg, Jackson and Larry. Only for a moment or two, late in the day, did the sun give any signs of existence, and its quick withdrawal behind the clouds once more seemed to throw an extra chill into the atmosphere.

OPENING CELEBRATIONS MISSING.

There were no opening scenes of any kind, and, strange to say, the bugs and the athletes seemed to go along just as well without them. The moving picture men were busy on the field before play began, and the two managers spent a little more than the usual time in apparently needless discussion of ground rules and in pointing exercises with the umpires. We have always been curious to know what four people can find so interesting to talk about when 15,000 are waiting for them to get through. If it's a good story why not let everybody in on it?

Joe Benz and Jim Scott had warmed up for the Sox, and Willie Mitchell had worked out with Gregg, so it was not until the megaphone boys got busy that the fans were informed on the subject of the rival pitchers. Scott's experience won him the position over Benz and Gregg was picked over Mitchell after he had frankly told his boss that he felt like working.

Scotty was successful except against the supermen in the Cleveland outfield. He was extracted in the seventh, so that Lange could strike out for him. The last two Nap innings were pitched by Ed Cicotte, and, believe us, the French Canadian had something on the ball. Only six men faced him and four of them struck out, three whiffing in succession in the eighth. Perhaps if Eddie had started, etc., but how was Callahan to know that in advance?

Jack Collins and Morris Rath divided the sensational fielding for the day with a brilliant catch apiece. Shano's grab was of the Lajoie drive that went down as the books as a sacrifice fly. Morris took a single away from Birmingham in the second, but immediately repaired that damage to Cleveland's chances by cutting loose a costly wild throw.

The Sox hit in hard luck several times. A line hit by Rath went straight at Chapman, and Weaver's hardest wallop was aimed at Graney's paws. Schalk met the ball squarely in the ninth, with two men on bases and nobody out, but instead of doing any good the drive was turned into a double play that saved Turner's skin.

With Weaver safe on a muffed fly ball, Morris Rath nearly drew one of his famous passes the first time up. But Gregg suddenly acquired the control, which Morris thought he had left behind him, and the Sox second baseman was declared out on a strike that cut the corner. Then Chapman missed Lord's grounder. Collins flied out to short center and our champion stole second, getting the decision by virtue of a dandy first slide. Bodie wasted a second strike and Gregg retired the side by whiffing the fence buster.

Jackson Smashes Double.

Jackson's catch on Scott was a pretty one and Joe received a double measure of applause when he took his place at bat. He paid for it by pounding out a double past Collins. Lajoie's single through Lord sent him to third and he scored when Rath went out into center field and grabbed Birmy's floater. Lajoie thought the ball would drop safe and he was far off first when Rath caught it. Rath tried to peg to Borton for a double play, but the throw went to the bleachers and the ground rules permitted Lary to go to third. Graney walked and was nailed stealing. Land grounded to Weaver and Buck was guilty of a low heave to first that saved the runner and scored Lajoie. Gregg struck out.

The reserves were called forth in the Chicago eighth. Berger, batting for Rath, died on a grounder to Larry. Zeider came up for Lord and shot a wicked single past Olson's ear. Collins flied to Birmingham, but Bodie sent Rollie to third with a safe one just out of Graney's reach in left, and Callahan, hitting for Borton, drove the run across with a warm shot between Olson's Swedish feet. Ping stopped at second, but was too deeply interested for his own good in watching Mattick's efforts to connect. Suddenly Land pegged to Chapman and Bodie was tagged out.

Jackson's Day's Work

CHICAGO.

	AB.	R.	H.	SH.	SB.	BB.	PO.	A.	E.
Rath, 2b...	3	0	0	0	0	0	4	0	1
Berger, 2b..	1	0	0	0	0	0	0	0	0
Lord, 3b....	3	0	0	0	1	0	0	1	0
Zeider, 3b..	1	1	1	0	0	0	0	0	0
Collins, rf..	4	0	1	0	0	0	2	0	0
Bodie, cf...	4	0	1	0	0	0	1	0	0
Borton, 1b..	3	0	1	0	0	1	8	0	0
†Callahan ..	1	0	1	0	0	0	0	0	0
Fournier, 1b	0	0	0	0	0	0	1	0	0
Mattick, lf..	4	0	1	0	0	0	1	0	0
Weaver, ss..	4	0	1	0	0	0	1	2	1
Schalk, c...	4	0	0	0	0	0	6	6	0
Scott, p....	2	0	0	0	0	0	0	2	0
*Lang	1	0	0	0	0	0	0	0	0
Cicotte, p..	1	0	0	0	0	0	0	0	0
Totals...34		1	7	0	1	1	24	11	2

*Lange batted for Scott in seventh.
†Callahan batted for Borton in eighth.

CLEVELAND.

	AB.	R.	H.	SH.	SB.	BB.	PO.	A.	E.
Johnston, 1b	4	0	0	0	0	0	5	0	0
Chapman, ss	3	0	1	0	0	1	3	1	1
Olson, 3b...	3	0	0	0	0	0	0	3	0
Jackson, rf..	3	2	3	0	0	0	5	0	0
Lajoie, 2b..	2	1	1	1	0	0	3	2	0
Bir'ham, cf.	2	0	0	1	0	0	5	0	0
Graney, lf..	2	0	1	0	0	1	1	0	1
Land, c....	3	0	0	0	0	0	5	1	0
Gregg, p....	3	0	0	0	0	0	0	1	0
Totals...25		3	6	2	0	2	27	8	2

Chicago	0	0	0	0	0	0	0	1	0	—1
Hits	0	0	0	1	0	1	0	3	2	—7
Cleveland	0	2	0	1	0	0	0	0	*	—3
Hits	0	2	0	2	0	2	0	0	*	—6

Hits made—Off Scott, 6 in 6 innings. Two-base hits—Jackson (2), Collins, Mattick. Three-base hit—Jackson. Double play—Chapman to Lajoie to Johnston. Bases on balls—Off Gregg, 1; off Scott, 2. Struck out—By Gregg, 5 (Rath, Bodie, Mattick, Scott, Lange); by Scott, 4 (Johnston (2), Gregg, Birmingham); by Cicotte, 4 (Birmingham, Gregg, Johnston, Chapman). Hit by pitched ball—Lord. Umpires—O'Loughlin and Ferguson. Time—1:45.

STANDING OF CLUBS

AMERICAN LEAGUE.

	St. Louis	Philadelphia	Washington	Cleveland	Chicago	Boston	New York	Detroit	Won	Percentage
St. Louis	—	0	0	0	0	0	0	2	2	1.000
Philadelphia ..	0	—	0	0	0	1	0	0	1	1.000
Washington ...	0	0	—	0	0	0	1	0	1	1.000
Cleveland	0	0	0	—	1	0	0	0	1	1.000
Chicago	0	0	0	0	—	0	0	0	0	.000
Boston	0	0	0	0	0	—	0	0	0	.000
New York	0	0	0	0	0	0	—	0	0	.000
Detroit	0	0	0	0	0	0	0	—	0	.000
Lost	0	0	0	0	1	1	1	2		

NATIONAL LEAGUE.

	Boston	Brooklyn	Philadelphia	Chicago	St. Louis	Pittsburgh	Cincinnati	New York	Won	Percentage
Boston	—	0	0	0	0	0	0	1	1	1.000
Brooklyn	0	—	1	0	0	0	0	0	1	.500
Philadelphia ..	0	1	—	0	0	0	0	0	1	.500
Chicago	0	0	0	—	0	0	0	0	0	.000
St. Louis	0	0	0	0	—	0	0	0	0	.000
Pittsburgh	0	0	0	0	0	—	0	0	0	.000
Cincinnati	0	0	0	0	0	0	—	0	0	.000
New York	0	0	0	0	0	0	0	—	0	.000
Lost	0	1	1	0	0	0	0	1		

YESTERDAY'S RESULTS.

AMERICAN LEAGUE.

Cleveland, 3; Chicago, 1.
St. Louis, 8; Detroit, 6.
Philadelphia-Boston, postponed; rain.
New York-Washington, postponed; rain.

NATIONAL LEAGUE.

All National League games postponed; rain.

GAMES TO-DAY.

AMERICAN LEAGUE.

Detroit at St. Louis.
Chicago at Cleveland.
Philadelphia at Boston.
New York at Washington.

NATIONAL LEAGUE.

St. Louis at Chicago.
Boston at New York.
Brooklyn at Philadelphia.
Pittsburgh at Cincinnati.

◇ *Scott was in there and he didn't have nothing*—Lardner's account of the opening game of the 1913 season, from the Chicago *Examiner* of April 12, 1913. (Chicago Historical Society)

Lardner's Sox Notes

CLEVELAND, Ohio, April 11.—Schalk's throwing was great stuff. Three Naps tried to steal and all three of them were so far out that they didn't even stop to kick.

Ban Johnson's new time saving device which provides for the substitution of a new ball every time a ball was hit was forgotten several times by athletes and umpires, but on one or two occasions it worked. Everybody will like it as soon as the players and umps get used to it.

The Chicago players had on their new blue suits and with them blue caps. Some of the players looked so strange in these new top pieces that we had difficulty in placing them.

Directly after to-morrow's game the Sox will leave for St. Louis, taking their train at a station near the new ball park.

Joe Benz will pitch to-morrow's game and Birmingham is likely to use his other left-hander, Mitchell, or his prize youngster, Stee.

◇ *A righthander named Bumgardner* —A Cracker Jack baseball card of St. Louis Browns righthanded pitcher George Washington Baumgardner. (Captain William T. Loughman collection)

but I guess them Browns is glad I wasn't in there no longer than that. They had us beat seven to one in the sixth and Callahan pulls Benz out. I honestly felt sorry for him but he didn't have nothing, not a thing. They was hitting him so hard I thought they would score a hundred runs. A righthander named Bumgardner was pitching for ◆◇ them and he didn't look to have nothing either but we ain't got much ◆ of a batting team Al. I could hit better than some of them regulars. Anyway Callahan called Benz to the bench and sent for me. I was

---

◆ *A righthander named Bumgardner*—George Washington Baumgardner (1891–1970), a second-year pitcher who was in the process of turning in a creditable 10–20 season for the last-place Browns. Baumgardner actually pitched the game of April 16, losing to Cicotte 3–2 in the ninth inning. In five seasons, all with the inept Browns, Baumgardner won 36 and lost 49. He was a relatively early player to gain a reputation as a relief pitcher; he won six games in relief in 1914. See William A. Borst, "George Baumgardner," *The Ballplayers*, p. 56.

◆ *we ain't got much of a batting team*—Quite so. The White Sox team batting average in 1913 was .236, worst in the American League. Because of the club's large ballpark, which tended to discourage power hitters, most White Sox teams have been light-hitting, stressing speed, defense, and pitching.

down in the corner warming up with Kuhn. I wasn't warmed up good but you know I got the nerve Al and I run right out there like I meant business. There was a man on second and nobody out when I come in. I didn't know who was up there but I found out afterward it was Shotten. He's the centerfielder. I was cold and I walked him. Then I got warmed up good and I made Johnston look like a boob. I give him three fast balls and he let two of them go by and missed the other one. I would of handed him a spitter but Schalk kept signing for fast ones and he knowns more about them batters than me. Anyway I whiffed Johnston. Then up come Williams and I tried to make him hit at a couple of bad ones. I was in the hole with two balls and nothing and come right across the heart with my fast one. I wish you could of saw the hop on it. Williams hit it right straight up and Lord was camped under it. Then up come Pratt the best hitter on their club. You know what I done to him don't you Al? I give him one spitter and

---

◆ *Kuhn*—Walter Charles "Red" Kuhn (1884–1935), the White Sox reserve catcher. Between 1912 and 1914 Kuhn appeared in 118 games, batting only .205.

◆ *Shotten*—Burton Edward Shotton (1884–1962), an outfielder for the Browns since 1909. In 1913 he hit .297, highest on a weak team. In 14 seasons with the Browns, Senators, and Cardinals, Shotton hit .270 in 1,388 games. Subsequently, and for many years, he was a major league coach and manager. He managed the Phillies from 1928 through 1933 and the Dodgers from 1947 through 1950, including the National League championship teams of 1947 and 1949. See Jack Kavanagh, "Burt Shotton," *The Ballplayers*, p. 998.

◆ *Johnston*—John Thomas Johnston (1890–1940), an outfielder whose entire major league career consisted of the 1913 season with the Browns. He hit .224 in 109 games, playing mainly in left field.

◆ *Schalk*—Raymond William Schalk (1892–1970), the White Sox first-string catcher. Schalk played 1,755 games for the team from 1912 to 1928, and managed it in 1927 and 1928. A fine receiver and a fiery competitor, he hit only .253 over the course of 18 seasons, including five games with the New York Giants in 1929. Nonetheless, Schalk was made a member of the Baseball Hall of Fame in 1955. See John L. Evers, "Raymond William Schalk," *Biographical Dictionary of American Sports: Baseball*, p. 501.

◆ *Williams*—August "Gloomy Gus" Williams (1888–1964), regular rightfielder for the Browns in 1913 and 1914. In five years with the Browns (1911–15) he hit .263 in 408 games. On April 24, 1913, Williams hit three triples in a nine-inning game. His only other notable achievement was negative: he led the American League in strikeouts in 1914, with 120. See Sheldon Fairchild Stewart, "Gus Williams," *The Ballplayers*, p. 1176.

◆ *Pratt*—Derrill Burnham "Del" Pratt (1888–1977), second baseman of the Browns, and previously an outstanding back on the University of Alabama football team. Pratt had been the Browns' leading batter with a .302 average in 1912, and was on his way to a .296 average in 1913. In a 13-year career with the Browns, Yankees, Red Sox, and Tigers (1912–24), Pratt achieved very respectable totals: 1,996 hits in 1,835 games, and a .292 lifetime batting average. See A. D. Suehsdorf, "Del Pratt," *The Ballplayers*, pp. 881–82.

◇ *Schalk*—Ray Schalk, catcher for the White Sox. (National Baseball Library, Cooperstown, New York)

another he didn't strike at that was a ball. Then I come back with two fast ones and Mister Pratt was a dead baby. And you notice they didn't steal no bases neither.

In our half of the seventh inning Weaver and Schalk got on and I was going up there with a stick when Callahan calls me back and sends Easterly up. I don't know what kind of managing you call that. I hit ◆ good on the training trip and he must of knew they had no chance to score off me in the innings they had left while they were liable to

◆ *Easterly*—Theodore Harrison Easterly (1886–1951), the White Sox leading pinch hitter. He had led the league with 13 pinch hits in 1912 and made eight in

murder his other pitchers. I come back to the bench pretty hot and I says You're making a mistake. He says If Comiskey had wanted you to manage this team he would of hired you.

Then Easterly pops out and I says Now I guess you're sorry you didn't let me hit. That sent him right up in the air and he bawled me awful. Honest Al I would of cracked him right in the jaw if we hadn't been right out where everybody could of saw us. Well he sent Cicotte ◆ in to finish and they didn't score no more and we didn't neither.

I road down in the car with Gleason. He says Boy you shouldn't ought to talk like that to Cal. Some day he will lose his temper and bust you one. I says He won't never bust me. I says He didn't have no right to talk like that to me. Gleason says I suppose you think he's going to laugh and smile when we lost four out of the first five games. He says Wait till tonight and then go up to him and let him know you are sorry you sassed him. I says I didn't sass him and ain't sorry.

So after supper I seen Callahan sitting in the lobby and I went over and sit down by him. I says When are you going to let me work? He says I wouldn't never let you work only my pitchers are all shot to pieces. Then I told him about you boys coming up from Bedford to watch me during the Detroit serious and he says Well I will start you in the second game against Detroit. He says But I wouldn't if I had any pitchers. He says A girl could get out there and pitch better than some of them have been doing.

(*continued from page 64*)
1913. Easterly, who had been acquired from Cleveland in mid-1912, spent the entire season of 1913 with the White Sox, catching 19 games and pinch-hitting 37 times. In five years in the American League (1909–13) and two in the Federal, Easterly hit an even .300 in 704 games. See Morris A. Eckhouse, "Ted Easterly," *The Ballplayers*, p. 304.

◆ *Cicotte*—Edward Victor Cicotte (1884–1969), the White Sox leading pitcher of the decade. After appearing in three games for the Tigers in 1905, Cicotte returned to the major leagues in 1908 with the Boston Red Sox, from whom the White Sox acquired him on July 22, 1912. Almost immediately he became one of the stars of the team, going 18–12 in 1913. He specialized in a non-revolving pitch, the shine ball, which his opponents claimed he adulterated with parafin, incidentally changing the ball from white to light brown. Cicotte had his finest seasons in the Sox' two championship years, recording totals of 28–12 in 1917 and 29–7 in 1919. Because Cicotte felt particularly victimized by Comiskey's penurious administration of the team, Chick Gandil was able to enlist him in the Black Sox plot of 1919. Cicotte was particularly culpable in the game-throwing, and especially eager to confess in 1920. Up to the time of his banishment from baseball, he had amassed a 210–148 record. Second only to Joe Jackson, Cicotte was the player most probably deprived of membership in the Baseball Hall of Fame by the scandal. See Lowell L. Blaisdell, "Edward Victor Cicotte," *Biographical Dictionary of American Sports: Baseball*, pp. 93–94.

So you see Al I am going to pitch on the nineteenth. I hope you guys can be up there and I will show you something. I know I can beat them Tigers and I will have to do it even if they are Violet's team.

I notice that New York and Boston got trimmed today so I suppose ◆ they wish Comiskey would ask for waivers on me. No chance Al.

Your old pal, Jack.

P.S.—We play eleven games in Chi and then go to Detroit. So I will ◆ see the little girl on the twenty-ninth.

Oh you Violet!

CHICAGO, ILLINOIS, APRIL 19. ◆

Dear Old Pal: Well Al it's just as well you couldn't come. They beat me and I am writing you this so as you will know the truth about the game and not get a bum steer from what you read in the papers.

I had a sore arm when I was warming up and Callahan should never ought to of sent me in there. And Schalk kept signing for my fast ball and I kept giving it to him because I thought he ought to know something about the batters. Weaver and Lord and all of them kept kicking them round the infield and Collins and Bodie couldn't catch nothing.

Callahan ought never to of left me in there when he seen how sore my arm was. Why, I couldn't of threw hard enough to break a pain of glass my arm was so sore.

They sure did run wild on the bases. Cobb stole four and Bush and ◆

◆ *New York and Boston*—Actually, these teams played each other on April 15, with New York winning, 3–2.

◆ *eleven games in Chi*—As stated, the White Sox were scheduled for 11 games at home before opening on the road in Detroit on April 29.

◆ *April 19*—Necessarily, the game is entirely fictional. On this date the White Sox played Cleveland behind pitcher Frank Lange, who did no better than Keefe, losing 9–2.

◆ *Cobb*—Cobb on this date was still holding out for a higher salary.

Bush—Owen Joseph "Donie" Bush (1887–1972), shortstop of the Tigers. Lardner had attempted without success to interest the White Sox in Bush while the young infielder was playing in the Central League in 1906 and 1907. Active with the Tigers from 1908 to 1921 and then with Washington until 1923, Bush hit .250, making 1,804 hits in 1,946 games. He managed the Senators in 1923, the Pittsburgh Pirates in 1927–29, the White Sox in 1930–31, and the Reds in 1933. For many years he owned the Indianapolis Indians of the American Association. The ballpark in Indianapolis, his home city, bears his name. See Jack Kavanagh, "Donie Bush," *The Ballplayers*, p. 140.

Crawford and Veach about two apiece. Schalk didn't even make a peg◆◇ half the time. I guess he was trying to throw me down.

The score was sixteen to two when Callahan finally took me out in the eighth and I don't know how many more they got. I kept telling him to take me out when I seen how bad I was but he wouldn't do it. They started bunting in the fifth and Lord and Chase just stood there and didn't give me no help at all.

I was all O. K. till I had the first two men out in the first inning. Then Crawford come up. I wanted to give him a spitter but Schalk signs me for the fast one and I give it to him. The ball didn't hop much and Crawford happened to catch it just right. At that Collins ought to of catched the ball. Crawford made three bases and up come Cobb. It was the first time I ever seen him. He hollered at me right off the reel. He says You better walk me you busher. I says I will walk you back to the bench. Schalk signs for a spitter and I gives it to him and Cobb misses it.

Then instead of signing for another one Schalk asks for a fast one and I shook my head no but he signed for it again and yells Put something on it. So I throwed a fast one and Cobb hits it right over second base. I don't know what Weaver was doing but he never made a move for the ball. Crawford scored and Cobb was on first base. First thing I knowed he had stole second while I held the ball. Callahan yells Wake up out there and I says Why don't your catcher tell me when they are going to steal. Schalk says Get in there and pitch and shut your mouth. Then I got mad and walked Veach and Moriarty

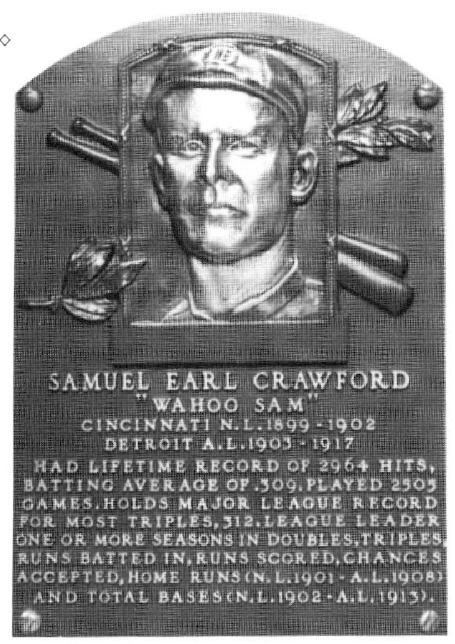

◇ *Crawford*—The Samuel Earl Crawford plaque at the National Baseball Hall of Fame and Museum, Cooperstown, New York.

◆ *Crawford*—Samuel Earl "Wahoo Sam" Crawford (1880–1968), the Tigers rightfielder, a player of great ability whose reputation was eclipsed by his long association with Ty Cobb—whom he disliked. Crawford played for 19 years, from 1899 to 1902 with the Cincinnati Reds and from 1903 to 1917 with the Tigers. An early power hitter who ran well, he scattered 50 inside-the-park home runs across his career. Crawford made 2,964 hits in 2,517 games, hitting .309. He later played with Los Angeles of the Pacific Coast League and umpired in the league. In 1957 he was belatedly made a member of the Baseball Hall of Fame. See Charles C. Alexander, "Samuel Earl Crawford," *Biographical Dictionary of American Sports: Baseball*, pp. 121–22.

Veach—Robert Hayes "Bobby" Veach (1888–1945), third member of the Tigers' distinguished outfield. Veach came up to the Tigers late in 1912 and was in his first full season as the team's regular leftfielder. In 14 seasons, 12 with the Tigers, Veach made 2,064 hits and batted .310. He is the only member of the Cobb-Crawford-Veach outfield not a member of the Baseball Hall of Fame. See David S. Matz and Luther W. Spoehr, "Robert Hayes Veach," *Biographical Dictionary of American Sports: Baseball*, pp. 572–73.

◇ *Veach*—Bobby Veach out at home. (National Baseball Library, Cooperstown, New York)

but before I walked Moriarty Cobb and Veach pulled a double steal ◆ on Schalk. Gainor lifts a fly and Lord drops it and two more come in. ◆ Then Stanage walks and I whiffs their pitcher. ◆

I come in to the bench and Callahan says Are your friends from Bedford up here? I was pretty sore and I says Why don't you get a catcher? He says We don't need no catcher when you're pitching because you can't get nothing past their bats. Then he says You better leave your uniform in here when you go out next inning or Cobb will steal it off your back. I says My arm is sore. He says Use your other one and you'll do just as good.

Gleason says Who do you want to warm up? Callahan says Nobody. He says Cobb is going to lead the league in batting and basestealing ◆

◆ *Moriarty*—George Moriarty (1884–1964), third baseman of the Tigers. In 13 years with the Cubs, New York Yankees, Tigers, and, for his final seven major league games, the White Sox, Moriarty hit .251 in 1,071 games. He is mainly known for his service as an American League umpire, from 1917 to 1926 and from 1929 to 1940. See Rich Marazzi and Jack Kavanagh, "George Moriarty," *The Ballplayers*, pp. 762–63.

◆ *Gainor*—Delos Charles "Del" Gainor (1886–1947), the Tigers regular first baseman. An excellent fielder, he batted .272 in 546 games over ten seasons for the Tigers, Red Sox, and Cardinals. See Joseph Lawler, "Del Gainor," *The Ballplayers*, p. 370.

◆ *Stanage*—Oscar Harland Stanage (1883–1964), catcher for the Tigers from 1909 through 1925, a weak hitter who batted .234 in 1,094 games. See Jack Kavanagh, "Oscar Stanage," *The Ballplayers*, p. 1035.

◆ *Cobb is going to lead the league in batting and basestealing*—This was an eminently

anyway so we might as well give him a good start. I was mad enough to punch his jaw but the boys winked at me not to do nothing.

Well I got some support in the next inning and nobody got on. Between innings I says Well I guess I look better now don't I? Callahan says Yes but you wouldn't look so good if Collins hadn't jumped up on the fence and catched that one off Crawford. That's all the encouragement I got Al.

Cobb come up again to start the third and when Schalk signs me for a fast one I shakes my head. Then Schalk says All right pitch anything you want to. I pitched a spitter and Cobb bunts it right at me. I would of threw him out a block but I stubbed my toe in a rough place and fell down. This is the roughest ground I ever seen Al. Veach bunts and for a wonder Lord throws him out. Cobb goes to second and honest Al I forgot all about him being there and first thing I knowed he had stole third. Then Moriarty hits a fly ball to Bodie and Cobb scores though Bodie ought to of threw him out twenty feet.

They batted all round in the forth inning and scored four or five more. Crawford got the luckiest three-base hit I ever see. He popped ◆ one way up in the air and the wind blowed it against the fence. The wind is something fierce here Al. At that Collins ought to of got under it.

I was looking at the bench all the time expecting Callahan to call me in but he kept hollering Go on and pitch. Your friends wants to see you pitch.

Well Al I don't know how they got the rest of their runs but they had more luck than any team I ever seen. And all the time Jennings ◆◇ was on the coaching line yelling like a Indian. Some day Al I'm going to punch his jaw.

After Veach had hit one in the eight Callahan calls me to the bench

---

(*continued from page 68*)
reasonable presumption. Cobb did lead the American League in batting with .390, but Clyde Milan led in stolen bases, with 75 to Cobb's 52.

◆ *the luckiest three-base hit I ever see*—Crawford was the most proficient hitter of triples in the history of baseball. His 312 triples still constitute the major league record—one of the records least menaced by the recent generations of players. Among batters who played most of their careers after World War II, the best lifetime total is Stan Musial's 177.

◆ *Jennings*—Hugh Ambrose Jennings (1869–1928), manager of the Tigers from 1907 to 1920. Jennings had managed the Tigers to the pennants of 1907–09, but was on his way to a sixth-place finish in 1913. He had a moderately distinguished playing career spanning 17 seasons between 1891 and 1918, in which he hit .311 in 1,285 games. Jennings was famous for flamboyant behavior in the third-base coaching box, especially for endeavoring to distract pitchers with his Indian yell,

◇ *Jennings*—Hughie Jennings, manager of the Tigers, in action in the third base coaching box, ca. 1909. (National Baseball Library, Cooperstown, New York)

and says You're through for the day. I says It's about time you found out my arm was sore. He says I ain't worrying about your arm but I'm afraid some of our outfielders will run their legs off and some of them poor infielders will get killed. He says The reporters just sent me a message saying they had run out of paper. Then he says I wish some of the other clubs had pitchers like you so we could hit once in a while. He says Go in the clubhouse and get your arm rubbed off. That's the only way I can get Jennings sore he says.

Well Al that's about all there was to it. It will take two or three stamps to send this but I want you to know the truth about it. The way my arm was I ought never to of went in there. *Yours truly, Jack.*

(*continued from page 69*)
"Ee-Yah." He was one of the few major league managers to have been lawyers. See Charles C. Alexander, "Hugh Ambrose Jennings," *Biographical Dictionary of American Sports: Baseball*, pp. 281–82.

CHICAGO, ILLINOIS, APRIL 25.

Friend Al: Just a line to let you know I am still on earth. My arm feels pretty good again and I guess maybe I will work at Detroit. Violet writes that she can't hardly wait to see me. Looks like I got a regular girl now Al. We go up there the twenty-ninth and maybe I won't be glad to see her. I hope she will be out to the game the day I pitch. I will pitch the way I want to next time and them Tigers won't have such a picnic.

I suppose you seen what the Chicago reporters said about that game. I will punch a couple of their jaws when I see them.

Your pal, Jack.

CHICAGO, ILLINOIS, APRIL 29. ◆

Dear Old Al: Well Al it's all over. The club went to Detroit last night and I didn't go along. Callahan told me to report to Comiskey this morning and I went up to the office at ten o'clock. He give me my pay to date and broke the news. I am sold to Frisco.

I asked him how they got waivers on me and he says Oh there was no trouble about that because they all heard how you tamed the Tigers. Then he patted me on the back and says Go out there and work hard boy and maybe you'll get another chance some day. I was kind of choked up so I walked out of the office.

I ain't had no fair deal Al and I ain't going to no Frisco. I will quit ◆ the game first and take that job Charley offered me at the billiard hall.

I expect to be in Bedford in a couple of days. I have got to pack up first and settle with my landlady about my room here which I engaged for all season thinking I would be treated square. I am going to rest and lay round home a while and try to forget this rotten game. Tell the boys about it Al and tell them I never would of got let out if I hadn't worked with a sore arm.

I feel sorry for that little girl up in Detroit Al. She expected me there today. *Your old pal, Jack.*

P.S. I suppose you seen where that lucky lefthander Allen shut out Cleveland with two hits yesterday. The lucky stiff.

◆ *April 29*—The White Sox closed their home stand against the Browns on April 27, and, as stated, opened against the Tigers in Detroit on April 29.

◆ *Frisco*—Keefe's option to San Francisco indicates that he was making normal advancement, with the same progression that Buck Weaver had made a year earlier.

The Busher Comes Back

SAN FRANCISCO, CALIFORNIA, MAY 13.

Friend Al: I suppose you and the rest of the boys in Bedford will be supprised to learn that I am out here, because I remember telling you when I was sold to San Francisco by the White Sox that not under no circumstances would I report here. I was pretty mad when Comiskey give me my release, because I didn't think I had been given a fair show by Callahan. I don't think so yet Al and I never will but Bill ◆ Sullivan the old White Sox catcher talked to me and told me not to pull no boner by refuseing to go where they sent me. He says You're only hurting yourself. He says You must remember that this was your first time up in the big show and very few men no matter how much stuff they got can expect to make good right off the reel. He says All

---

"The Busher Comes Back," the second of the stories later collected as *You Know Me Al*, was published in *The Saturday Evening Post*, CLXXXVI (May 23, 1914), 18–20, 61–62.

◆ *Bill Sullivan*—William Joseph Sullivan, Sr. (1875–1965), a superb defensive catcher for the White Sox since 1901. As befits his lifetime average of .212, Sullivan had been a star of the Hitless Wonders, the world champions of 1906. He had been active to 1912, and had managed the team to a fourth-place finish in 1909. Including earlier service with the Braves and one game with the Tigers in 1916, Sullivan played in 1,146 games and made 777 hits. See Richard E. Beverage, "Billy Sullivan," *The Ballplayers*, pp. 1058–59.

you need is experience and pitching out in the Coast League will be just the thing for you.

So I went in and asked Comiskey for my transportation and he says That's right Boy go out there and work hard and maybe I will want you back. I told him I hoped so but I don't hope nothing of the kind Al. I am going to see if I can't get Detroit to buy me, because I would rather live in Detroit than anywheres else. The little girl who got stuck on me this spring lives there. I guess I told you about her Al. Her name is Violet and she is some queen. And then if I got with the Tigers I wouldn't never have to pitch against Cobb and Crawford, though I believe I could show both of them up if I was right. They ain't got much of a ball club here and hardly any good pitchers outside ◆ of me. But I don't care.

I will win some games if they give me any support and I will get back in the big league and show them birds something. You know me, Al. *Your pal, Jack.*

LOS ANGELES, CALIFORNIA, MAY 20. ◆

Al: Well old pal I don't suppose you can find much news of this league in the papers at home so you may not know that I have been standing this league on their heads. I pitched against Oakland up home and shut them out with two hits. I made them look like suckers Al. They hadn't never saw no speed like mine and they was scared to death the minute I cut loose. I could of pitched the last six innings with my foot and trimmed them they was so scared.

Well we come down here for a serious and I worked the second game. They got four hits and one run, and I just give them the one run. Their shortstop Johnson was on the training trip with the White ◆ Sox and of course I knowed him pretty well. So I eased up in the last inning and let him hit one. If I had of wanted to let myself out he

◆ *hardly any good pitchers*—A correct judgment. The San Francisco Seals finished fourth in the Pacific Coast League with barely over a .500 record, 104–103. The team had only one outstanding pitcher, Charles "Skeeter" Fanning, who went 28–15. (Because of the mild climate in its cities, the league habitually played a longer season than the major leagues do.)

◆ *May 20*—Actually, the Seals played in Sacramento on this date.

◆ *Their shortstop Johnson*—Presumably the fictional shortstop referred to previously. The actual shortstop for Oakland was Albert "Pete" Cook. Neither Fanning nor Cook ever played in the major leagues.

couldn't of hit me with a board. So I am going along good and Howard ◆ our manager says he is going to use me regular. He's a pretty nice manager and not a bit sarkastic like some of them big leaguers. I am fielding my position good and watching the baserunners to. Thank goodness Al they ain't no Cobbs in this league and a man ain't scared of haveing his uniform stole off his back.

But listen Al I don't want to be bought by Detroit no more. It is all off between Violet and I. She wasn't the sort of girl I suspected. She is just like them all Al. No heart. I wrote her a letter from Chicago telling her I was sold to San Francisco and she wrote back a postcard saying something about not haveing no time to waste on bushers. What do you know about that Al? Calling me a busher. I will show them. She wasn't no good Al and I figure I am well rid of her. Good riddance is rubbish as they say.

I will let you know how I get along and if I hear anything about being sold or drafted. *Yours truly, Jack.*

SAN FRANCISCO, CALIFORNIA, JULY 20.

Friend Al: You will forgive me for not writeing to you oftener when you hear the news I got for you. Old pal I am engaged to be married. Her name is Hazel Carney and she is some queen, Al—a great big strapping girl that must weigh one hundred and sixty lbs. She is out to every game and she got stuck on me from watching me work.

Then she writes a note to me and makes a date and I meet her down on Market Street one night. We go to a nickel show together and have some time. Since then we been together pretty near every evening except when I was away on the road.

Night before last she asked me if I was married and I tells her No and she says a big handsome man like I ought not to have no trouble finding a wife. I tells her I ain't never looked for one and she says Well you wouldn't have to look very far. I asked her if she was married and she said No but she wouldn't mind it. She likes her beer pretty well

◆ *Howard*—George Elmer "Del" Howard (1877–1956), manager of the Seals. Howard had an undistinguished major league career between 1905 and 1909, batting .263 in 536 games, about evenly divided between the infield and the outfield. After playing regularly for the Pirates and Braves, he became a reserve on the Cubs' championship teams of 1907 and 1908. Howard managed the Seals in 1913 and 1914, but became associated mainly with the Oakland team of the Coast League. He managed it from 1916 to 1922 and, as business manager, vice-president, and part owner, remained affiliated with the team until 1929. See Bob Carroll, "Del Howard," *The Ballplayers*, p. 491.

and her and I had several and I guess I was feeling pretty good. Anyway I guess I asked her if she wouldn't marry me and she says it was O. K. I ain't a bit sorry Al because she is some doll and will make them all sit up back home. She wanted to get married right away but I said No wait till the season is over and maybe I will have more dough. She asked me what I was getting and I told her two hundred dollars a month. She says she didn't think I was getting enough and I don't neither but I will get the money when I get up in the big show again.

Anyway we are going to get married this fall and then I will bring her home and show her to you. She wants to live in Chi or New York but I guess she will like Bedford O. K. when she gets acquainted.

I have made good here all right Al. Up to a week ago Sunday I had won eleven straight. I have lost a couple since then, but one day I wasn't feeling good and the other time they kicked it away behind me.

I had a run in with Howard after Portland had beat me. He says Keep on running round with that skirt and you won't never win another game.

He says Go to bed nights and keep in shape or I will take your money. I told him to mind his own business and then he walked away from me. I guess he was scared I was going to smash him. No manager ain't going to bluff me Al. So I went to bed early last night and didn't keep my date with the kid. She was pretty sore about it but business before pleasure Al. Don't tell the boys nothing about me being engaged. I want to supprise them. *Your pal, Jack.*

SACRAMENTO, CALIFORNIA, AUGUST 16. ◆

Friend Al: Well Al I got the supprise of my life last night. Howard called me up after I got to my room and tells me I am going back to the White Sox. Come to find out, when they sold me out here they ◆ kept a option on me and yesterday they exercised it. He told me I would have to report at once. So I packed up as quick as I could and then went down to say good-by to the kid. She was all broke up and

---

◆ *Sacramento, California, August 16*—The Seals were actually at home playing Venice on this date.

◆ *they kept a option*—The arrangements by which a player could be sent to the minor leagues for development were as Keefe describes them, a sale of the player's contract by the major league club to the minor league club, with an option to repurchase it. To retrieve a player, the major league club had to notify his minor league team by August 15 for a recall on August 20. Otherwise, the player's contract became the property of the minor league club unless the major league club gave it some compensation in order to retain rights to him. On the role of

wanted to go along with me but I told her I didn't have enough dough to get married. She said she would come anyway and we could get married in Chi but I told her she better wait. She cried all over my sleeve. She sure is gone on me Al and I couldn't help feeling sorry for her but I promised to send for her in October and then everything will be all O. K. She asked me how much I was going to get in the big league and I told her I would get a lot more money than out here because I wouldn't play if I didn't. You know me Al.

I come over here to Sacramento with the club this morning and I am leaveing tonight for Chi. I will get there next Tuesday and I guess Callahan will work me right away because he must of seen his mistake in letting me go by now. I will show them Al.

I looked up the skedule and I seen where we play in Detroit the ◆ fifth and sixth of September. I hope they will let me pitch there Al. Violet goes to the games and I will make her sorry she give me that kind of treatment. And I will make them Tigers sorry they kidded me last spring. I ain't afraid of Cobb or none of them now, Al.

Your pal, Jack.

CHICAGO, ILLINOIS, AUGUST 27.

Al: Well old pal I guess I busted in right. Did you notice what I done to them Athaletics, the best ball club in the country? I bet Violet wishes ◆ she hadn't called me no busher.

I got here last Tuesday and set up in the stand and watched the game that afternoon. Washington was playing here and Johnson pitched. I was anxious to watch him because I had heard so much about him. Honest Al he ain't as fast as me. He shut them out, but they never was much of a hitting club. I went to the clubhouse after the game and shook hands with the bunch. Kid Gleason the assistant

---

(*continued from page 75*)
the option process in the organization of the monopsony, see Gerald W. Scully, *The Business of Major League Baseball* (Chicago: University of Chicago Press, 1989), pp. 4, 26, and *passim*. The number of players who could be optioned is limited; by an agreement of 1912, the major league clubs limited themselves to 25 players in the regular season, with eight additional players reserved on option. A given player might be optioned in three seasons.

◆ *the fifth and sixth of September*—The White Sox played in St. Louis on these dates.

◆ *them Athaletics*—The Philadelphia Athletics of 1913 won the American League pennant with a 96–57 record, and defeated the New York Giants in the World Series, four games to one. The Athletics played in Chicago August 21–23, winning two of the three games. Cicotte beat them 7–4 on August 23.

manager seemed pretty glad to see me and he says Well have you learned something? I says Yes I guess I have. He says Did you see the game this afternoon? I says I had and he asked me what I thought of Johnson. I says I don't think so much of him. He says Well I guess you ain't learned nothing then. He says What was the matter with Johnson's work? I says He ain't got nothing but a fast ball. Then he says Yes and ◆ Rockefeller ain't got nothing but a hundred million bucks. ◆

Well I asked Callahan if he was going to give me a chance to work and he says he was. But I sat on the bench a couple of days and he didn't ask me to do nothing. Finally I asked him why not and he says I am saving you to work against a good club, the Athaletics. Well the Athaletics come and I guess you know by this time what I done to them. And I had to work against Bender at that but I ain't afraid of ◆ none of them now Al.

Baker didn't hit one hard all afternoon and I didn't have no trouble with Collins neither. I let them down witih five blows all though the ◆

◆ *nothing but a fast ball*—More precisely, Johnson had a perfectly adequate curveball, but he was unable to throw it with the sidearm motion he used for his fastball. He was forced to throw the curve overhand, thereby telegraphing his pitches in a fashion usually thought fatal to effectiveness. Customarily, Johnson did not attempt a curveball until he had two strikes on a batter, and in close games he threw few curves. Batters as able as Eddie Collins took the fastballs and waited hopefully for the curve.

◆ *Rockefeller*—John Davison Rockefeller (1839–1937), head of the Standard Oil Company, founder of the University of Chicago, and usually thought the richest American of the day. The estimate of his wealth at $100 million is conservative.

◆ *Bender*—Charles Albert Bender (1883–1954), star righthander of the Athletics. Known as "Chief" because of his part Chippewa ancestry, Bender was Connie Mack's preferred pitcher for crucial games. In 1913 he had his second-best season, 21–10, plus two victories in the World Series. With the Athletics from 1903 to 1914 and in relatively unsuccessful later seasons with the Baltimore club of the Federal League, the Phillies, and the White Sox, Bender won 210 games and lost 128 in 16 years. Bender entered the Baseball Hall of Fame in 1953. He did not pitch in the series of August 21–23, 1913. See Frank V. Phelps, "Charles Albert Bender," *Biographical Dictionary of American Sports: Baseball*, pp. 33–34.

◆ *Collins*—Edward Trowbridge Collins (1887–1951), second baseman of the Athletics' "Hundred Thousand Dollar Infield." A graduate of Columbia University, Collins was a highly intelligent and well-educated man in a game in which, as Lardner was demonstrating perhaps too well, such figures were not the norm. Active from 1906 to 1930, Collins made 3,311 hits, batted .333 in 2,826 games, and stole 743 bases. In 1913 he hit .345.

Comiskey acquired Collins from the Athletics in the course of Connie Mack's dissolution of his championship team of 1914. Comiskey incidentally acquired Collins' salary of $14,500, negotiated with the Athletics while the Federal League provided a rival to Organized Baseball. This salary was more than double what the White Sox stars of the period earned, and hostility to Collins for his high

papers give them seven. Them reporters here don't no more about scoreing than some old woman. They give Barry a hit on a fly ball that ◆ Bodie ought to of eat up, only he stumbled or something and they handed Oldring a two base hit on a ball that Weaver had to duck to ◆ get out of the way from. But I don't care nothing about reporters. I beat them Athaletics and beat them good, five to one. Gleason slapped me on the back after the game and says Well you learned something after all. Rub some arnicky on your head to keep the swelling down and you may be a real pitcher yet. I says I ain't got no swell head. He says No. If I hated myself like you do I would be a moveing-picture actor.

Well I asked Callahan would he let me pitch up to Detroit and he says Sure! He says Do you want to get revenge on them? I says, Yes I did. He says Well you have certainly got some comeing. He says I never seen no man get worse treatment than them Tigers give you last spring. I says Well they won't do it this time because I will know how to pitch to them. He says How are you going to pitch to Cobb? I says I am going to feed him on my slow one. He says Well Cobb had ought to make a good meal off of that. Then we quit jokeing and he says You have improved a hole lot and I am going to work you right along regular and if you can stand the gaff I may be able to use you in the city serious. You know Al the White Sox plays a city serious every fall with the Cubs and the players makes quite a lot of money. The winners

---

(*continued from page 77*)
income and superior education was in large part responsible for Chick Gandil's conceiving the Black Sox plot. Collins was a member of the White Sox from 1915 to 1926, playing more than half his games in a White Sox uniform. He managed the team in 1925 and 1926, before returning to the Athletics to finish his playing career. He was subsequently general manager of the Boston Red Sox. Collins was elected to the Baseball Hall of Fame in 1939. See John L. Evers, "Edward Trowbridge Collins, Sr." *Biographical Dictionary of American Sports: Baseball*, pp. 103–4.

◆ *Barry*—John Joseph "Jack" Barry (1887–1961), shortstop of the Athletics. A weak hitter but a reliable infielder, Barry was active for the Athletics from 1908 to 1915, when he went to the Red Sox in Mack's liquidation of his team. In eleven seasons from 1908 to 1919, Barry hit .243. In 1917 he managed the Red Sox to a second-place finish. Barry was for many years baseball coach at the College of the Holy Cross in Worcester, Mass., his alma mater. See Sheldon Fairchild Stewart, "Jack Barry," *The Ballplayers*, p. 53.

◆ *Oldring*—Reuben Henry Oldring (1884–1961), outfielder for the Athletics from 1906 through 1916. In 1,237 games for the Athletics and Yankees between 1905 and 1918 Oldring hit .270. See Jack Kavanagh, "Rube Oldring," *The Ballplayers*, p. 822.

gets about eight hundred dollars a peace and the losers about five hundred. We will be the winners if I have anything to say about it.

I am tickled to death at the chance of working in Detroit and I can't hardly wait till we get there. Watch my smoke Al. *Your pal, Jack.*

P.S. I am going over to Allen's flat to play cards a while tonight. Allen is the left-hander that was on the training trip with us. He ain't got a thing, Al, and I don't see how he gets by. He is married and his wife's sister is visiting them. She wants to meet me but it won't do her much good. I seen her out to the game today and she ain't much for looks.

DETROIT, MICH., SEPTEMBER 6.

Friend Al: I got a hole lot to write but I ain't got much time because we are going over to Cleveland on the boat at ten P. M. I made them ◆ Tigers like it Al just like I said I would. And what do you think Al, Violet called me up after the game and wanted to see me but I will tell you about the game first.

They got one hit off of me and Cobb made it a scratch single that he beat out. If he hadn't of been so dam fast I would of had a 0 hit game. At that Weaver could of threw him out if he had of started after the ball in time. Crawford didn't get nothing like a hit and I whiffed him once. I give two walks both of them to Bush but he is such a little guy that you can't pitch to him.

When I was warming up before the game Callahan was standing beside me and pretty soon Jennings come over. Jennings says You ain't going to pitch that bird are you? And Callahan said Yes he was. Then Jennings says I wish you wouldn't because my boys is all tired out and can't run the bases. Callahan says They won't get no chance today. No, says Jennings I suppose not. I suppose he will walk them all and they won't have to run. Callahan says He won't give no bases on balls, he says. But you better tell your gang that he is liable to bean them and they better stay away from the plate. Jennings says He won't never hurt my boys by beaning them. Then I cut in. Nor you neither, I says. Callahan laughs at that so I guess I must of pulled a pretty good one. Jennings didn't have no comeback so he walks away.

◆ *the boat at ten P. M.*—The elegant sidewheelers of the Detroit & Cleveland Navigation Company provided overnight service between the two cities until 1950. In 1913 the scheduled departure time was 10:45 P.M. The White Sox management considered the water trip a pleasant relief from train travel and used the steamers as late as the post-World War II period.

Then Cobb come over and asked if I was going to work. Callahan told him Yes. Cobb says How many innings? Callahan says All the way. Then Cobb says Be a good fellow Cal and take him out early. I am lame and can't run. I butts in then and said Don't worry, Cobb. You won't have to run because we have got a catcher who can hold them third strikes. Callahan laughed again and says to me You sure did learn something out on that Coast.

Well I walked Bush right off the real and they all begun to holler on the Detroit bench There he goes again. Vitt come up and Jennings ◆ yells Leave your bat in the bag Osker. He can't get them over. But I got them over for that bird all O. K. and he pops out trying to bunt. And then I whiffed Crawford. He starts off with a foul that had me scared for a minute because it was pretty close to the foul line and it went clear out of the park. But he missed a spitter a foot and then I supprised them Al. I give him a slow ball and I honestly had to laugh to see him lunge for it. I bet he must of strained himself. He throwed his bat away like he was mad and I guess he was. Cobb came pranceing up like he always does and yells Give me that slow one Boy. So I says All right. But I fooled him. Instead of giveing him a slow one like I said I was going to I handed him a spitter. He hit it all right but it was a line drive right in Chase's hands. He says Pretty lucky Boy but I will get you next time. I come right back at him. I says Yes you will.

Well Al I had them going like that all through. About the sixth inning Callahan yells from the bench to Jennings What do you think of him now? And Jennings didn't say nothing. What could he of said?

Cobb makes their one hit in the eighth. He never would of made it if Schalk had of let me throw him spitters instead of fast ones. At that Weaver ought to of threw him out. Anyway they didn't score and we made a monkey out of Dubuque, or whatever his name is. ◆

◆ *Vitt*—Oscar Joseph Vitt (1890–1963), a third baseman and outfielder in his second major league season. Active with the Tigers from 1912 to 1918 and the Boston Red Sox from 1919 to 1921, Vitt hit .238 in 1,062 games. As manager of the Cleveland Indians from 1938 to 1940, Vitt suffered a well-publicized player revolt in the course of barely missing the 1940 pennant. See Jack Kavanagh, "Ossie Vitt," *The Ballplayers*, p. 1124.

◆ *Dubuque, or whatever his name is*—Jean Arthur "Chauncey" Dubuc (1888–1958), a pitcher of French-Canadian extraction. With a record of 16–14 in 1913, he led Tiger pitchers in victories. In nine seasons with the Reds, Tigers, Red Sox, and Giants between 1908 and 1919, Dubuc won 85 and lost 75.

Dubuc received a telegram from the gambler Sleepy Bill Burns giving him advance knowledge of the Black Sox plot. He remains on baseball's permanently ineligible list. See Tom Jozwik, "Jean Dubuc," *The Ballplayers*, p. 295.

Well Al I got back to the hotel and snuck down the street a ways and had a couple of beers before supper. So I come to the supper table late and Walsh tells me they had been several phone calls for me. I go down to the desk and they tell me to call up a certain number. So I called up and they charged me a nickel for it. A girl's voice answers the phone and I says Was they some one there that wanted to talk to Jack Keefe? She says You bet they is. She says Don't you know me, Jack? This is Violet. Well, you could of knocked me down with a peace of thread. I says What do you want? She says Why I want to see you. I says Well you can't see me. She says Why what's the matter, Jack? What have I did that you should be sore at me? I says I guess you know all right. You called me a busher. She says Why I didn't do nothing of the kind. I says Yes you did on that postcard. She says I didn't write you no postcard.

Then we argued along for a while and she swore up and down that she didn't write me no postcard or call me no busher. I says Well then why didn't you write me a letter when I was in Frisco? She says she had lost my address. Well Al I don't know if she was telling me the truth or not but maybe she didn't write that postcard after all. She was crying over the telephone so I says Well it is too late for I and you to get together because I am engaged to be married. Then she screamed and I hang up the receiver. She must of called back two or three times because they was calling my name round the hotel but I wouldn't go near the phone. You know me Al.

Well when I hang up and went back to finish my supper the dining room was locked. So I had to go out and buy myself a sandwich. They soaked me fifteen cents for a sandwich and a cup of coffee so with the nickel for the phone I am out twenty cents altogether for nothing. But then I would of had to tip the waiter in the hotel a dime.

Well Al I must close and catch the boat. I expect a letter from Hazel in Cleveland and maybe Violet will write to me too. She is stuck on me all right Al. I can see that. And I don't believe she could of wrote that postcard after all. *Yours truly, Jack.*

BOSTON, MASSACHUSETTS, SEPTEMBER 12. ◆

Old Pal: Well I got a letter from Hazel in Cleveland and she is comeing

---

◆ *Boston, Massachusetts, September 12*—The chronology here does not correspond to the actual schedule. On this date the White Sox were in Philadelphia. They had not come from Cleveland, as stated below.

to Chi in October for the city serious. She asked me to send her a hundred dollars for her fare and to buy some cloths with. I sent her thirty dollars for her fare and told her she could wait till she got to Chi to buy her cloths. She said she would give me the money back as soon as she seen me but she is a little short now because one of her girl friends borrowed fifty off of her. I guess she must be pretty soft-hearted Al. I hope you and Bertha can come up for the wedding because I would like to have you stand up with me.

I all so got a letter from Violet and they was blots all over it like she had been crying. She swore she did not write that postcard and said she would die if I didn't believe her. She wants to know who the lucky girl is who I am engaged to be married to. I believe her Al when she says she did not write that postcard but it is too late now. I will let you know the date of my wedding as soon as I find out.

I guess you seen what I done in Cleveland and here. Allen was going awful bad in Cleveland and I relieved him in the eighth when we had a lead of two runs. I put them out in one-two-three order in the eighth but had hard work in the ninth due to rotten support. I walked Johnston and Chapman and Turner sacrificed them ahead. Jackson come up then and I had two strikes on him. I could of whiffed him but Schalk makes me give him a fast one when I wanted to give him a slow one. He hit it to Berger and Johnston ought to of been

---

◆ *thirty dollars for her fare*—Coach fare from San Francisco to Chicago, effective April 1, 1913, was $65.00.

◆ *Johnston*—Wheeler Roger "Doc" Johnston (1887–1961), a first baseman in his second year with the Naps, in which he hit .255 in 133 games. In 11 seasons with the Reds, Naps, Pirates, and Athletics, Johnson batted .263 in 1,055 games. He was the regular first baseman on the Indians' championship team of 1920. See Joseph Lawler, "Doc Johnston," *The Ballplayers*, p. 538.

Chapman—Raymond John Chapman (1891–1920), shortstop of the Naps. In 1913 Chapman hit .258 in 140 games. In 1,050 games in nine seasons, all with Cleveland, he hit .278 and stole 233 bases. Chapman's principal distinction is a very melancholy one; on August 16, 1920, in New York, he was hit in the head by a pitch from the submarine-ball pitcher Carl Mays. He died on the following day, to date the only man to be killed in a major league game. See Morris A. Eckhouse, "Ray Chapman," *The Ballplayers*, pp. 178–79.

Turner—Terrence Lamont Turner (1881–1960), third baseman of the Naps. Turner played in 1,617 games for Cleveland from 1904 to 1918, the club record. Including a portion of the 1901 season with the Pirates and the 1919 season with the Athletics, Turner made 1,497 hits in 1,685 games for a .253 lifetime average. See Morris A. Eckhouse, "Terry Turner," *The Ballplayers*, p. 1105.

◆ *Berger*—Joseph August Berger (1886–1956), a utility infielder for the White Sox in 1913 and 1914. Berger hit just .191 in 124 games in his two seasons in the major leagues.

threw out at the plate but Berger fumbles and then has to make the play at first base. He got Jackson all O. K. but they was only one run behind then and Chapman was on third base. Lajoie was up next and Callahan sends out word for me to walk him. I thought that was rotten manageing because Lajoie or no one else can hit me when I want to cut loose. So after I give him two bad balls I tried to slip over a strike on him but the lucky stiff hit it on a line to Weaver. Anyway the game was over and I felt pretty good. But Callahan don't appresiate good work Al. He give me a call in the clubhouse and said if I ever disobeyed his orders again he would suspend me without no pay and lick me too. Honest Al it was all I could do to keep from wrapping his jaw but Gleason winks at me not to do nothing.

I worked the second game here and give them three hits two of which was bunts that Lord ought to of eat up. I got better support in Frisco than I been getting here Al. But I don't care. The Boston bunch couldn't of hit me with a shovvel and we beat them two to nothing. I worked against Wood at that. They call him Smoky Joe and they say ◆ he has got a lot of speed.

Boston is some town, Al, and I wish you and Bertha could come here sometime. I went down to the wharf this morning and seen them unload the fish. They must of been a million of them but I didn't have time to count them. Every one of them was five or six times as big as a blue gill.

Violet asked me what would be my address in New York City so I am dropping her a post card to let her know all though I don't know what good it will do her. I certainly won't start no correspondents with her now that I am engaged to be married. *Yours truly, Jack.*

◆ *Wood*—Howard Ellsworth "Smokey Joe" Wood (1889–1985), right-handed pitcher for the Red Sox. After a lackluster beginning, Wood became one of the leading pitchers in the American League, with a 23–17 record in 1911, including a no-hit game against the Browns on July 29. In 1912 he achieved one of the most impressive seasons a pitcher has ever recorded, 34–5 with 35 complete games, ten shutouts, and a 1.91 earned run average. Thereafter, arm trouble limited his effectiveness; in 1913 he was 11–5 with only 12 complete games. He joined the Cleveland Indians in 1917, developing a creditable career as an outfielder, winding it up by hitting .297 in 1922. His lifetime pitching record was 116–57, and his lifetime batting average .283. He was baseball coach at Yale University from 1923 to 1942, and in 1984 Yale granted him the honorary degree of Doctor of Humane Letters. See Ellery H. Clark, Jr., "Joe Wood," *Biographical Dictionary of American Sports: Baseball*, pp. 624–25.

Friend Al: I opened the serious here and beat them easy but I know you must of saw about it in the Chi papers. At that they don't give me no fair show in the Chi papers. One of the boys bought one here and I seen in it where I was lucky to win that game in Cleveland. If I knowed which one of them reporters wrote that I would punch his jaw.

Al I told you Boston was some town but this is the real one. I never seen nothing like it and I been going some since we got here. I walked down Broadway the Main Street last night and I run into a couple of the ballplayers and they took me to what they call the Garden but it ◆ ain't like the gardens at home because this one is indoors. We sat down to a table and had several drinks. Pretty soon one of the boys asked me if I was broke and I says No, why? He says You better get some lubricateing oil and loosen up. I don't know what he meant but pretty soon when we had had a lot of drinks the waiter brings a check and hands it to me. It was for one dollar. I says Oh I ain't paying for all of them. The waiter say This is just for that last drink.

I thought the other boys would make a holler but they didn't say nothing. So I give him a dollar bill and even then he didn't act satisfied so I asked him what he was waiting for and he said Oh nothing, kind of sassy. I was going to bust him but the boys give me the sign to shut up and not to say nothing. I excused myself pretty soon because I wanted to get some air. I give my check for my hat to a boy and he brought my hat and I started going and he says Haven't you forgot something? I guess he must of thought I was wearing a overcoat.

Then I went down the Main Street again and some man stopped me and asked me did I want to go to the show. He said he had a ticket. I asked him what show and he said the Follies. I never heard of it but I told him I would go if he had a ticket to spare. He says I will spare you this one for three dollars. I says You must take me for some boob. He says No I wouldn't insult no boob. So I walks on but if he had of insulted me I would of busted him.

I went back to the hotel then and run into Kid Gleason. He asked

---

◆ *September 16*—On this date the White Sox were in Washington.

◆ *the Garden*—The second Madison Square Garden, built in 1890 at Madison and Fourth avenues, between 26th and 27th streets. The arena was used for horse shows, flower shows, and the like, but the complex included a theater, concert hall and ballroom, restaurant, and roof garden. It was superseded by the sports arena on Eighth Avenue built by Tex Rickard in 1925.

me to take a walk with him so out I go again. We went to the corner and he bought me a beer. He don't drink nothing but pop himself. ◆ The two drinks was only ten cents so I says This is the place for me. He says Where have you been? and I told him about paying one dollar for three drinks. He says I see I will have to take charge of you. Don't go round with them ballplayers no more. When you want to go out and see the sights come to me and I will stear you. So tonight he is going to stear me. I will write to you from Philadelphia.

Your pal, Jack.

PHILADELPHIA, PA., SEPTEMBER 19. ◆

Friend Al: They won't be no game here today because it is raining. We all been loafing round the hotel all day and I am glad of it because I got all tired out over in New York City. I and Kid Gleason went round together the last couple of nights over there and he wouldn't let me spend no money. I seen a lot of girls that I would of like to of got acquainted with but he wouldn't even let me answer them when they spoke to me. We run in to a couple of peaches last night and they had us spotted too. One of them says I'll bet you're a couple of ballplayers. But Kid says You lose your bet. I am a bellhop and the big rube with me is nothing but a pitcher.

One of them says What are you trying to do kid somebody? He says Go home and get some soap and remove your disguise from your face. I didn't think he ought to talk like that to them and I called him about it and said maybe they was lonesome and it wouldn't hurt none if we treated them to a soda or something. But he says Lonesome! If I don't get you away from here they will steal everything you got. They won't even leave you your fast ball. So we left them and he took me to a picture show. It was some California pictures and they made me think of Hazel so when I got back to the hotel I sent her three postcards.

◆ *He don't drink nothing but pop himself.*—Surviving biographical information does not establish whether Gleason was a teetotaler, but given the prominence Lardner accords Gleason in the stories, the role assigned to him to shepherd Keefe about, and Lardner's preoccupation with his own alcohol problem, there is a strong presumption the statement is correct.

◆ *Philadelphia, Pa., September 19*—Lardner, in response to a suggestion from a copy editor of *The Saturday Evening Post* that Keefe would unfailingly have misspelled Philadelphia, replied that, no, Keefe would get it right, either because it was on the hotel stationery in front of him, or because he would look it up, or ask someone to spell it for him. See Donald Elder, *Ring Lardner* (Garden City, N.Y.: Doubleday & Co., 1956), p. 123.

On this date the White Sox were in New York.

Gleason made me go to my room at ten o'clock both nights but I was pretty tired anyway because he had walked me all over town. I guess we must of saw twenty shows. He says I would take you to the grand opera only it would be throwing money away because we can hear Ed Walsh for nothing. Walsh has got some voice Al a loud high tenor.

Tomorrow is Sunday and we have a double header Monday on account of the rain today. I thought sure I would get another chance to beat the Athaletics and I asked Callahan if he was going to pitch me here but he said he thought he would save me to work against Johnson in Washington. So you see Al he must figure I am about the best he has got. I'll beat him Al if they get a couple of runs behind me.

Yours truly, Jack.

P.S. They was a letter here from Violet and it pretty near made me feel like crying. I wish they was two of me so both them girls could be happy.

WASHINGTON, D.C., SEPTEMBER 22.

Dear Old Al: Well Al here I am in the capital of the old United States. We got in last night and I been walking round town all morning. But I didn't tire myself out because I am going to pitch against Johnson this afternoon.

This is the prettiest town I ever seen but I believe they is more colored people here than they is in Evansville or Chi. I seen the White House and the Monumunt. They say that Bill Sullivan and Gabby St. ◆ once catched a baseball that was threw off of the top of the Monumunt but I bet they couldn't catch it if I throwed it.

I was in to breakfast this morning with Gleason and Bodie and Weaver and Fournier. Gleason says I'm supprised that you ain't sick in bed today. I says Why?

He says Most of our pitchers gets sick when Cal tells them they are

◆ *the Monumunt*—The Washington Monument, the largest obelisk in the world, 555 feet high, completed in 1884. The earlier of the two events referred to was Gabby Street (1882–1951), a catcher for the Senators, catching a ball thrown from the monument on August 21, 1908. On the thirteenth try, Street caught a ball dropped by Preston Gibson, a local sportsman. In its account of the event the Washington *Evening Star* estimated the speed of the ball at 135 feet per second, or about 92 miles per hour, the speed of a major league fastball. Thus the problem for Street was estimating the ball's trajectory rather than absorbing its impact. The White Sox catcher Billy Sullivan duplicated the feat on August 24, 1910, catching three balls dropped by Ed Walsh and Doc White.

going to work against Johnson. He says Here's these other fellows all feeling pretty sick this morning and they ain't even pitchers. All they have to do is hit against him but it looks like as if Cal would have to send substitutes in for them. Bodie is complaining of a sore arm which he must of strained drawing to two-card flushes. Fournier and Weaver have strained their legs doing the tango dance. Nothing could cure them except to hear that big Walter had got throwed out of his machine and wouldn't be able to pitch against us this serious.

I says I feel O. K. and I ain't afraid to pitch against Johnson and I ain't afraid to hit against him neither. Then Weaver says Have you ever saw him work? Yes, I says, I seen him in Chi. Then Weaver says Well if you have saw him work and ain't afraid to hit against him I'll bet you would go down to Wall Street and holler Hurrah for Roosevelt. ◆ I says No I wouldn't do that but I ain't afraid of no pitcher and what is more if you get me a couple of runs I'll beat him. Then Fournier says Oh we will get you a couple of runs all right. He says That's just as easy as catching whales with a angleworm.

Well Al I must close and go in and get some lunch. My arm feels great and they will have to go some to beat me Johnson or no Johnson. *Your pal, Jack.*

WASHINGTON, D.C., SEPTEMBER 22.

Friend Al: Well I guess you know by this time that they didn't get no two runs for me, only one, but I beat him just the same. I beat him ◆ one to nothing and Callahan was so pleased that he give me a ticket to the theater. I just got back from there and it is pretty late and I already have wrote you one letter today but I am going to sit up and tell you about it.

It was cloudy before the game started and when I was warming up I made the remark to Callahan that the dark day ought to make my speed good. He says Yes and of course it will handicap Johnson.

While Washington was takeing their practice their two coaches Schaefer and Altrock got out on the infield and cut up and I pretty ◆

◆ *Hurrah for Roosevelt*—Presumably, the cry would evoke the financial community's hostility to Theodore Roosevelt for splitting the Republican Party with his Bull Moose campaign of 1912, which allowed Woodrow Wilson, a Democrat, to assume the presidency.

◆ *I beat him one to nothing*—Losing 1–0 was rather a specialty of Walter Johnson's. He did it 26 times, still a major league record.

◆ *Schaefer*—Herman A. "Germany" Schaefer (1878–1919), a player of limited talent, but famous for his sense of humor. In a career extending from 1901 to

near busted laughing at them. They certainly is funny Al. Callahan asked me what was I laughing at and I told him and he says That's the first time I ever seen a pitcher laugh when he was going to work against Johnson. He says Griffith is a pretty good fellow to give us ◆ something to laugh at before he shoots that guy at us.

I warmed up good and told Schalk not to ask me for my spitter much because my fast one looked faster than I ever seen it. He says it won't make much difference what you pitch today. I says Oh, yes, it will because Callahan thinks enough of me to work me against Johnson and I want to show him he didn't make no mistake. Then Gleason says No he didn't make no mistake. Wasteing Cicotte or Scotty would of been a mistake in this game.

Well, Johnson whiffs Weaver and Chase and makes Lord pop out in the first inning. I walked their first guy but I didn't give Milan ◆

(*continued from page 87*)
1918, he hit .257 in 1,143 games with the Cubs, four American League clubs, and Newark of the Federal League. By 1913 he was a utility player for the Senators, appearing in only 52 games. Schaefer, who was an obvious candidate for dabbling in vaudeville, earlier had an off-season act with his Tiger teammate Charley O'Leary. See Warner Oliver Rockford, "Germany Schaefer," *The Ballplayers*, p. 966.

Altrock—Nicholas Altrock (1876–1965), a left-handed pitcher who had won 20, 22, and 21 games for the White Sox in 1904, 1905, and 1906, respectively. The rest of his career was unimpressive; from 1898 to 1918 his record was 87–75. It was as a clown-coach for the Washington Senators, especially when he teamed with Al Schacht in the 1920's, that he found his greatest fame. In that vein, he made token appearances as a pitcher or batter as late as 1933. See Jack Kavanagh, "Nick Altrock," *The Ballplayers*, p. 18.

◆ *Griffith*—Clark Calvin Griffith (1869–1953), manager and part owner of the Washington Senators. As a player, Griffith was an outstanding pitcher, winning 20 or more games annually for Chicago in the National League from 1894 to 1899. He became the White Sox first manager in 1901, incidentally leading the league in won-lost average with a 24–7 record. After one additional year with the White Sox, Griffith served as manager of the New York Highlanders from 1903 to mid-1908. The experience in New York was an unhappy one, which left him with a dislike of the Yankees that he retained for life. After managing Cincinnati in 1909–11, he became manager of the Senators in 1912, taking a 10-percent interest in the club and serving as director. He bought a majority interest in the club in 1919 and gave up the managership in 1920, remaining in control of the team until his death. Partly for his 242–131 pitching record and his 1,491–1,367 managerial record, and partly for his long service as an owner, Griffith was elected to the Baseball Hall of Fame in 1946. See Alan R. Asnen, "Clark Calvin Griffith," *Biographical Dictionary of American Sports: Baseball*, pp. 225–28.

◆ *Milan*—Jesse Clyde Milan (1887–1953), the Senators centerfielder and, along with Tris Speaker, Cobb's leading rival in defensive play and speed on the basepaths. In 16 years, entirely with the Senators (1907–1922) and entirely in the outfield, Milan made 2,100 hits in 1,981 games, hit .285, and stole 495 bases. Milan

nothing to bunt and finally he flied out. And then I whiffed the next two. On the bench Callahan says That's the way, boy. Keep that up and we got a chance.

Johnson had fanned four of us when I come up with two out in the third inning and he whiffed me to. I fouled one though that if I had ever of got a good hold of I would of knocked out of the park. In the first seven innings we didn't have a hit off of him. They had got five or six lucky ones off of me and I had walked two or three, but I cut loose with all I had when they was men on and they couldn't do nothing with me. The only reason I walked so many was because my fast one was jumping so. Honest Al it was so fast that Evans the umpire ◆◇ couldn't see it half the time and he called a lot of balls that was right over the heart.

Well I come up in the eighth with two out and the score still nothing and nothing. I had whiffed the second time as well as the first but it was account of Evans missing one on me. The eighth started with Shanks muffing a fly ball off of Bodie. It was way out by the fence so ◆ he got two bases on it and he went to third while they was throwing Berger out. Then Schalk whiffed.

Callahan says Go up and try to meet one Jack. It might as well be you as anybody else. But your old pal didn't whiff this time Al. He

◇ *Evans the umpire*—The William George Evans plaque at the National Baseball Hall of Fame and Museum, Cooperstown, New York.

(*continued from page 88*)
managed the Senators in 1922 and subsequently was a coach and scout for the team for many years. He died, in fact, in uniform, while hitting fungoes in spring training in 1953. His reputation did not survive his playing career well, and he is not yet a member of the Baseball Hall of Fame. See Anthony J. Papalas, "Jesse Clyde Milan," *Biographical Dictionary of American Sports: Baseball*, p. 400.

◆ *Evans*—William George "Billy" Evans (1884–1956), an American League umpire from 1906 to 1927. Evans had been a sportswriter for the Youngstown *Vindicator* but turned quickly to umpiring in the Ohio & Pennsylvania League, and then to umpiring in the American League—all by the age of 22. After retiring as an umpire, he served as general manager of the Cleveland Indians, farm director of the Boston Red Sox, general manager of the Cleveland Rams of the National Football League, president of the Southern Association, and general manager of the Detroit Tigers. He retired in 1951 and was elected to the Baseball Hall of Fame in 1973. See Dan E. Krueckeberg, "William George Evans," *Biographical Dictionary of American Sports: Baseball*, p. 169.

◆ *Shanks*—Howard Samuel "Hank" Shanks (1890–1941), leftfielder of the Senators. In 1913, in his second season, Shanks hit .254 in 109 games. He played for the Senators through 1922, for the Red Sox in 1923 and 1924, and finally for the Yankees, in 1925. In his one outstanding season, 1921, as the Senators' third baseman, he hit .302 and led the American League with 19 triples. Overall, in 1,663 games he hit .253. See Jack Kavanagh, "Howard Shanks," *The Ballplayers*, pp. 988–89.

gets two strikes on me with fast ones and then I passed up two bad ones. I took my healthy at the next one and slapped it over first base. I guess I could of made two bases on it but I didn't want to tire myself out. Anyway Bodie scored and I had them beat. And my hit was the only one we got off of him so I guess he is a pretty good pitcher after all Al.

They filled up the bases on me with one out in the ninth but it was pretty dark then and I made McBride and their catcher look like ◆ suckers with my speed.

I felt so good after the game that I drunk one of them pink cocktails. I don't know what their name is. And then I sent a postcard to poor little Violet. I don't care nothing about her but it don't hurt me none to try and cheer her up once in a while. We leave here Thursday night for home and they had ought to be two or three letters there for me from Hazel because I haven't heard from her lately. She must of lost my road addresses. *Your pal, Jack.*

P.S. I forgot to tell you what Callahan said after the game. He said I was a real pitcher now and he is going to use me in the city serious. If he does Al we will beat them Cubs sure.

CHICAGO, ILLINOIS, SEPTEMBER 27.

Friend Al: They wasn't no letter here at all from Hazel and I guess she must of been sick. Or maybe she didn't think it was worth while writeing as long as she is comeing next week.

I want to ask you to do me a favor Al and that is to see if you can find me a house down there. I will want to move in with Mrs. Keefe, don't that sound funny Al? sometime in the week of October twelfth. Old man Cutting's house or that yellow house across from you would be O. K. I would rather have the yellow one so as to be near you. Find out how much rent they want Al and if it is not no more than twelve dollars a month get it for me. We will buy our furniture here in Chi when Hazel comes.

◆ *McBride*—George Florian McBride (1880–1973), the Senators shortstop from 1908 through 1920. His lifetime average for 1,658 games was .218, and in 1913 he hit .214 in 150 games. He managed the Senators to a fourth-place finish in 1921. A lifelong resident of Milwaukee, he was active in baseball in the city throughout his life, and gained local fame as the last living member of the Brewers of 1901, Milwaukee's short-lived charter member of the American League. See George W. Hilton, "Milwaukee's Charter Membership in the American League," *The Historical Messenger*, XXX, No. 1 (1974), 2–17.

We have a couple of days off now Al and then we play St. Louis two games here. Then Detroit comes to finish the season the third and ◆ fourth of October. *Your pal, Jack.*

CHICAGO, ILLINOIS, OCTOBER 3.

Dear Old Al: Thanks Al for getting the house. The one-year lease is O. K. You and Bertha and me and Hazel can have all sorts of good times together. I guess the walk needs repairs but I can fix that up when I come. We can stay at the hotel when we first get there.

I wish you could of came up for the city serious Al but anyway I want you and Bertha to be sure and come up for our wedding. I will let you know the date as soon as Hazel gets here.

The serious starts Tuesday and this town is wild over it. The Cubs ◆ finished second in their league and we was fifth in ours but that don't scare me none. We would of finished right on top if I had of been here all season.

Callahan pitched one of the bushers against Detroit this afternoon and they beat him bad. Callahan is saveing up Scott and Allen and Russell and Cicotte and I for the big show. Walsh isn't in no shape and ◆ neither is Benz. It looks like I would have a good deal to do because most of them others can't work no more than once in four days and Allen ain't no good at all.

We have a day to rest after tomorrow's game with the Tigers and then we go at them Cubs. *Your pal, Jack.*

P.S. I have got it figured that Hazel is fixing to surprise me by dropping in on me because I haven't heard nothing yet.

◆ *Detroit comes to finish the season*—Actually, the Browns played at Chicago on September 26 and 27, and the White Sox moved on to Detroit to finish the season. The game of October 3 was rained out, and the teams split a doubleheader on October 4. The White Sox closed the season by losing to the Tigers 9–8 on October 5.

◆ *The Cubs finished second in their league*—The Cubs actually finished third in 1913, 88–65, a game behind the Phillies. The White Sox, as stated, finished fifth, 78–74, two games behind the Red Sox.

◆ *Walsh isn't in no shape and neither is Benz*—In the 1912 City Series, Walsh had had one of his most glittering performances, appearing in six games as the White Sox won four games to three. He won the clincher 16–0 on five hits. Walsh had ruined his arm by straining a ligament while throwing a medicine ball in the 1913 spring-training camp at Paso Robles, and his absence was expected to weigh heavily against the White Sox in the 1913 series. Benz, according to the anticipations of reporters (and contrary to Keefe's view), was in shape and expected to pitch as may have been required.

CHICAGO, ILLINOIS, OCTOBER 7.

Friend Al: Well Al you know by this time that they beat me today and ◆ tied up the serious. But I have still got plenty of time Al and I will get them before it is over. My arm wasn't feeling good Al and my fast ball didn't hop like it had ought to. But it was the rotten support I got that beat me. That lucky stiff Zimmerman was the only guy that got a real ◆ hit off of me and he must of shut his eyes and throwed his bat because the ball he hit was a foot over his head. And if they hadn't been makeing all them errors behind me they wouldn't of been nobody on bases when Zimmerman got that lucky scratch. The serious now stands one and one Al and it is a cinch we will beat them even if they are a bunch of lucky stiffs. They has been great big crowds at both games and it looks like as if we should ought to get over eight hundred dollars a peace if we win and we will win sure because I will beat them three straight if nessary.

But Al I have got bigger news than that for you and I am the happyest man in the world. I told you I had not heard from Hazel for a long time. Tonight when I got back to my room they was a letter waiting for me from her.

Al she is married. Maybe you don't know why that makes me happy but I will tell you. She is married to Kid Levy the middle weight. I ◆ guess my thirty dollars is gone because in her letter she called me a cheap skate and she inclosed one one-cent stamp and two twos and said she was paying me for the glass of beer I once bought her. I bought her more than that Al but I won't make no holler. She all so said not for me to never come near her or her husband would bust my jaw. I ain't afraid of him or no one else Al but they ain't no danger of me ever bothering them. She was no good and I was sorry the minute I agreed to marry her.

But I was going to tell you why I am happy or maybe you can guess. Now I can make Violet my wife and she's got Hazel beat forty ways.

◆ *they . . . tied up the serious*—The actual City Series opened on October 8, with Russell and Scott combining to win 6–4. Jim "Hippo" Vaughn of the Cubs beat the White Sox in 13 innings, 6–5, in the second game on October 9.

◆ *Zimmerman*—Henry "Heinie" Zimmerman (1887–1969), the Cubs third baseman. In 1912 he had had an outstanding year, winning the batting championship with a .372 average, and in 1913 he had hit .313. Zimmerman hit .295 in 1,456 games in the National League, between 1907 and 1916 with the Cubs and finally, for three more years, with the Giants. He was declared permanently ineligible for allegedly attempting to bribe teammates on the 1919 Giants to lose a game to the Cubs. See Jack Kavanagh, "Heinie Zimmerman," *The Ballplayers*, pp. 1223–24.

◆ *Kid Levy*—Apparently a fictional character.

She ain't nowheres near as big as Hazel but she's classier Al and she will make me a good wife. She ain't never asked me for no money.

I wrote her a letter the minute I got the good news and told her to come on over here at once at my expense. We will be married right after the serious is over and I want you and Bertha to be sure and stand up with us. I will wire you at my own expence the exact date.

It all seems like a dream now about Violet and I haveing our misunderstanding Al and I don't see how I ever could of accused her of sending me that postcard. You and Bertha will be just as crazy about her as I am when you see her Al. Just think Al I will be married inside of a week and to the only girl I ever could of been happy with instead of the woman I never really cared for except as a passing fancy. My happyness would be complete Al if I had not of let that woman steal thirty dollars off of me. *Your happy pal, Jack.*

P.S. Hazel probibly would of insisted on us takeing a trip to Niagara falls or somewheres but I know Violet will be perfectly satisfied if I take her right down to Bedford. Oh you little yellow house.

CHICAGO, ILLINOIS, OCTOBER 9.

Friend Al: Well Al we have got them beat three games to one now and will wind up the serious tomorrow sure. Callahan sent me in to save poor Allen yesterday and I stopped them dead. But I don't care now Al. I have lost all interest in the game and I don't care if Callahan pitches me tomorrow or not. My heart is just about broke Al and I wouldn't be able to do myself justice feeling the way I do.

I have lost Violet Al and just when I was figureing on being the happyest man in the world. We will get the big money but it won't do me no good. They can keep my share because I won't have no little girl to spend it on.

Her answer to my letter was waiting for me at home tonight. She is engaged to be married to Joe Hill the big lefthander Jennings got ◆ from Providence. Honest Al I don't see how he gets by. He ain't got no more curve ball than a rabbit and his fast one floats up there like a big balloon. He beat us the last game of the regular season here but it was because Callahan had a lot of bushers in the game.

I wish I had knew then that he was stealing my girl and I would of made Callahan pitch me against him. And when he come up to bat I would of beaned him. But I don't suppose you could hurt him by

◆ *Joe Hill*—Apparently a fictional character.

hitting him in the head. The big stiff. Their wedding ain't going to come off till next summer and by that time he will be pitching in the Southwestern Texas League for about fifty dollars a month. ◆

Violet wrote that she wished me all the luck and happyness in the world but it is too late for me to be happy Al and I don't care what kind of luck I have now.

Al you will have to get rid of that lease for me. Fix it up the best way you can. Tell the old man I have changed my plans. I don't know just yet what I will do but maybe I will go to Australia with Mike ◆ Donlin's team. If I do I won't care if the boat goes down or not. I don't believe I will even come back to Bedford this winter. It would drive me wild to go past that little house every day and think how happy I might of been.

Maybe I will pitch tomorrow Al and if I do the serious will be over tomorrow night. I can beat them Cubs if I get any kind of decent support. But I don't care now Al. *Yours truly, Jack.*

CHICAGO, ILLINOIS, OCTOBER 12.

Al: Your letter received. If the old man won't call it off I guess I will have to try and rent the house to some one else. Do you know of any couple that wants one Al? It looks like I would have to come down there myself and fix things up someway. He is just mean enough to stick me with the house on my hands when I won't have no use for it.

They beat us the day before yesterday as you probably know and it rained yesterday and today. The papers says it will be all O. K. to-morrow and Callahan tells me I am going to work. The Cub pitchers ◇ was all shot to peaces and the bad weather is just nuts for them because

---

◆ *Southwestern Texas League*—There had actually been a Southwest Texas League in the lower Rio Grande Valley in 1910 and 1911, but it had subsequently disbanded. A Southern Texas League had attempted to operate in 1912, but failed to finish the season.

◆ *Mike Donlin*—Michael Joseph "Turkey Mike" Donlin (1878–1933), an outfielder who hit .333 in 1,050 games in a tempestuous career with six major league clubs between 1893 and 1914. In 1913 he played 36 games for Jersey City of the International League, but mainly devoted himself to his secondary career in vaudeville. The reference to the tour to Australia is apparently to the White Sox–Giants world tour, which would be treated anachronistically at the end of *You Know Me Al.* Donlin was a member of that tour. See A. D. Suehsdorf, "Michael Joseph Donlin," *Biographical Dictionary of American Sports: Baseball*, pp. 153–54.

◊ *Callahan*—Nixey Callahan caught off first base by George Stovall of the St. Louis Browns at Comiskey Park on April 12, 1912 (see footnote, p. 43). (Chicago Historical Society)

it will give Cheney a good rest. But I will beat him Al if they don't kick ◆ it away behind me.

I must close because I promised Allen the little lefthander that I would come over to his flat and play cards a while tonight and I must wash up and change my collar. Allen's wife's sister is visiting them again and I would give anything not to have to go over there. I am through with girls and don't want nothing to do with them.

I guess it is maybe a good thing it rained today because I dreamt about Violet last night and went out and got a couple of high balls before breakfast this morning. I hadn't never drank nothing before breakfast before and it made me kind of sick. But I am all O. K. now.

Your pal, Jack.

◆ *Cheney*—Laurance Russell "Larry" Cheney (1886–1969), the Cubs ace pitcher. A righthander and a practitioner of the spitball and knuckleball, Cheney won 26 and lost 10 in 1912 to lead the National League with a .722 percentage. He won 20 in 1913 and again in 1914. In nine seasons with the Cubs, Dodgers, Braves, and Phillies, concluding in 1919, Cheney won 114 and lost 100. On September 14, 1913, he set a major league record by allowing 14 hits while shutting out the Giants. See Jack Kavanagh, "Larry Cheney," *The Ballplayers*, p. 182.

CHICAGO, ILLINOIS, OCTOBER 13.

Dear Old Al: The serious is all over Al. We are the champions and I ◆ done it. I may be home the day after tomorrow or I may not come for a couple of days. I want to see Comiskey before I leave and fix up about my contract for next year. I won't sign for no less than five thousand and if he hands be a contract for less than that I will leave the White Sox flat on their back. I have got over fourteen hundred dollars now Al with the city serious money which was $814.30 and I don't have to worry.

Them reporters will have to give me a square deal this time Al. I had everything and the Cubs done well to score a run. I whiffed Zimmerman three times. Some of the boys say he ain't no hitter but he is a hitter and a good one Al only he could not touch the stuff I got. The umps give them their run because in the fourth inning I had Leach flatfooted off of second base and Weaver tagged him O. K. but ◆ the umps wouldn't call it. Then Schulte the lucky stiff happened to ◆◇ get a hold of one and pulled it past first base. I guess Chase must of been asleep. Anyway they scored but I don't care because we piled up six runs on Cheney and I drove in one of them myself with one of the prettiest singles you ever see. It was a spitter and I hit it like a shot. If I had hit it square it would of went out of the park.

Comiskey ought to feel pretty good about me winning and I guess

---

◆ *We are the champions and I done it.*—The White Sox did, in fact, win the 1913 City Series, four games to two. Scott won the final game on October 13, 5–2.

◆ *Leach*—Thomas William "Tommy" Leach (1877–1969), a diminutive outfielder who was nearing the end of a long career in the National League. He had played with the Pirates from 1900 to late in the 1912 season, and was in the first of two full seasons with the Cubs. As the passage implies, Leach was notable chiefly as a runner, stealing 361 bases over the course of his career and scoring 1,355 runs. He made 2,144 hits in 2,155 games, hitting just .269. See Luther W. Spoehr, "Thomas William Leach," *Biographical Dictionary of American Sports: Baseball*, pp. 326–27.

◆ *Schulte*—Frank "Wildfire" Schulte (1882–1949), the Cubs rightfielder, a veteran of the team since 1904. Schulte, a player whom Lardner particularly liked personally, was an excellent outfielder, and by the standards of the day a hitter of considerable power. In 1911 he had hit .300 and led the National League with 21 home runs and 107 runs batted in, incidentally winning the Chalmers Award as the league's most valuable player. Schulte remained with the Cubs until mid-season of 1916, before playing with the Pirates and Phillies and finishing his career with the Senators in 1918. Schulte hit .270 in 1,806 games over 15 seasons. See Art Ahrens, "Wildfire Schulte," *The Ballplayers*, p. 975.

For Lardner's delineation of Schulte's personality, see the story "Sick 'Em," below.

◇ *Schulte*—Frank "Wildfire" Schulte in the Cubs road uniform of 1906. (George E. Brace collection)

he will give me a contract for anything I want. He will have to or I will go to the Federal League. ◆

We are all invited to a show tonight and I am going with Allen and his wife and her sister Florence. She is O. K. Al and I guess she thinks the same about me. She must because she was out to the game today and seen me hand it to them. She maybe ain't as pretty as Violet and Hazel but as they say beauty isn't only so deep.

Well Al tell the boys I will be with them soon. I have gave up the

◆ *the Federal League*—The Federal League, promoted by James Gilmore and his associates, was an unsuccessful effort at a third major league. In 1913 the league operated as an independent, with teams in Cleveland, Chicago, St. Louis, Indianapolis, Pittsburgh, and Kansas City. On November 13, 1913, Gilmore announced, simultaneously with adding Baltimore and Buffalo, the elevation of the league to

idea of going to Australia because I would have to buy a evening full-dress suit and they tell me they cost pretty near fifty dollars.

Yours truly, Jack.

CHICAGO, ILLINOIS, OCTOBER 14.

Friend Al: Never mind about that lease. I want the house after all Al and I have got the supprise of your life for you.

When I come home to Bedford I will bring my wife with me. I and ◆ Florence fixed things all up after the show last night and we are going to be married tomorrow morning. I am a busy man today Al because I have got to get the license and look round for furniture. And I have also got to buy some new cloths but they are haveing a sale on Cottage Grove Avenue at Clark's store and I know one of the clerks there. ◆

I am the happyest man in the world Al. You and Bertha and I and Florence will have all kinds of good times together this winter because I know Bertha and Florence will like each other. Florence looks something like Bertha at that. I am glad I didn't get tied up with Violet or Hazel even if they was a little bit prettier than Florence.

Florence knows a lot about baseball for a girl and you would be supprised to hear her talk. She says I am the best pitcher in the league

---

(*continued from page 97*)
major status, and applied to Organized Baseball for recognition. Ban Johnson responded early in 1914 that baseball could not accommodate a third major league. Gilmore, however, correctly interpreting the reserve clause of baseball contracts as unenforceable, announced that the Federal League would begin hiring major league players. This the league did, with mixed success. Although the promoters did attract Hal Chase, Ted Easterly, George Mullin, Jack Quinn, Cy Falkenberg, Joe Tinker, Eddie Plank (in 1915), and several other established major leaguers, the average standard of play was below the level of the two older leagues. By late 1915 the Federal League was clearly failing, but it threatened to place a team in New York for the 1916 season. Because Organized Baseball imposed a three-year boycott on players who jumped to "outlaw" leagues—i.e. leagues that were not parties to the monopsony—the Federal League had to offer its players three-year contracts. Accordingly, any settlement liquidating the Federal League necessarily entailed some disposal of the players, who had a third and final year on their contracts. Because the major league club owners were eager to replace their colleagues in Chicago and St. Louis, the settlement also entailed the owners of the Federal League clubs in those cities taking over the franchises of the Cubs and Browns. See Marc Okkonen, *The Federal League of 1914–15: Baseball's Third Major League* (Garrett Park, Md.: Society for American Baseball Research, 1989).

◆ *I will bring my wife with me*—At the end of the 1913 season Reb Russell married Charlotte Benz, a cousin of his roommate, Joe Benz. This match may have given Lardner the prototype for the upcoming romance.

◆ *Clark's store*—Apparently a fictional enterprise.

and she has saw them all. She all so says I am the best-looking ballplayer she ever seen but you know how girls will kid a guy Al. You will like her O. K. I fell for her the first time I seen her. *Your old pal, Jack.*

P.S. I signed up for next year. Comiskey slapped me on the back when I went in to see him and told me I would be a star next year if I took good care of myself. I guess I am a star without waiting for next year Al. My contract calls for twenty-eight hundred a year which is a thousand more than I was getting. And it is pretty near a cinch that I will be in on the World Serious money next season.

P.S. I certainly am relieved about that lease. It would of been fierce to of had that place on my hands all winter and not getting any use out of it. Everything is all O. K. now. Oh you little yellow house.

The Busher's Honeymoon

CHICAGO, ILLINOIS, OCTOBER 17.

Friend Al: Well Al it looks like as if I would not be writeing so much to you now that I am a married man. Yes Al I and Florrie was married the day before yesterday just like I told you we was going to be and Al I am the happyest man in the world though I have spent $30 in the last 3 days incluseive. You was wise Al to get married in Bedford where not nothing is nearly half so dear. My expenses was as follows:

License	$2.00
Preist	3.50
Haircut and shave	.35
Shine	.05
Carfair	.45
New suit	14.50
Show tickets	3.00
Flowers	.50
Candy	.30
Hotel	4.50
Tobacco both kinds	.25

"The Busher's Honeymoon," the third of the stories later collected as *You Know Me Al*, was published in *The Saturday Evening Post*, CLXXXVII (July 11, 1914), 12–14, 33–34.

You see Al it costs a hole lot of money to get married here. The sum of what I have wrote down is $29.40 but as I told you I have spent $30 and I do not know what I have did with that other $0.60. My new brother-in-law Allen told me I should ought to give the preist $5 and I thought it should be about $2 the same as the license so I split the difference and give him $3.50. I never seen him before and probily won't never see him again so why should I give him anything at all when it is his business to marry couples? But I like to do the right thing. You know me Al.

I thought we would be in Bedford by this time but Florrie wants to stay here a few more days because she says she wants to be with her sister. Allen and his wife is thinking about takeing a flat for the winter instead of going down to Waco Texas where they live. I don't see no sense in that when it costs so much to live here but it is none of my business if they want to throw their money away. But I am glad I got a wife with some sense though she kicked because I did not get no room with a bath which would cost me $2 a day instead of $1.50. I says I guess the clubhouse is still open yet and if I want a bath I can go over there and take the shower. She says Yes and I suppose I can go and jump in the lake. But she would not do that Al because the lake here is cold at this time of the year.

When I told you about my expenses I did not include in it the meals because we would be eating them if I was getting married or not getting married only I have to pay for six meals a day now instead of three and I didn't used to eat no lunch in the playing season except once in a while when I knowed I was not going to work that afternoon. I had a meal ticket which had not quite ran out over to a resturunt on Indiana Ave and we eat there for the first day except at night when I ◆ took Allen and his wife to the show with us and then he took us to a chop-suye resturunt. I guess you have not never had no chop-suye Al and I am here to tell you you have not missed nothing but when Allen was going to buy the supper what could I say? I could not say nothing.

Well yesterday and to-day we been eating at a resturunt on Cottage Grove Ave near the hotel and at the resturunt on Indiana that I had the meal ticket at only I do not like to buy no new meal ticket when I am not going to be round here no more than a few days. Well Al I guess the meals has cost me all together about $1.50 and I have eat

---

◆ *Indiana Ave*—Another major north-south business street east of Comiskey Park.

very little myself. Florrie always wants desert ice cream or something and that runs up into money faster than regular stuff like stake and ham and eggs.

Well Al Florrie says it is time for me to keep my promise and take her to the moveing pictures which is $0.20 more because the one she likes round here costs a dime apeace. So I must close for this time and will see you soon. *Your pal, Jack.*

CHICAGO, ILLINOIS, OCTOBER 12.

Al: Just a note Al to tell you why I have not yet came to Bedford yet where I expected I would be long before this time. Allen and his wife have took a furnished flat for the winter and Allen's wife wants Florrie to stay here untill they get settled. Meentime it is costing me a hole lot of money at the hotel and for meals besides I am paying $10 a month rent for the house you got for me and what good am I getting out of it? But Florrie wants to help her sister and what can I say? Though I did make her promise she would not stay no longer than next Saturday at least. So I guess Al we will be home on the evening train Saturday and then may be I can save some money.

I know Al that you and Bertha will like Florrie when you get acquainted with her spesially Bertha though Florrie dresses pretty swell and spends a hole lot of time fusing with her face and her hair.

She says to me to-night Who are you writeing to and I told her Al Blanchard who I have told you about a good many times. She says I bet you are writeing to some girl and acted like as though she was kind of jealous. So I thought I would tease her a little and I says I don't know no girls except you and Violet and Hazel. Who is Violet and Hazel? she says. I kind of laughed and says Oh I guess I better not tell you and then she says I guess you will tell me. That made me kind of mad because no girl can't tell me what to do. She says Are you going to tell me? and I says No.

Then she says If you don't tell me I will go over to Marie's that is her sister Allen's wife and stay all night. I says Go on and she went downstairs but I guess she probily went to get a soda because she has some money of her own that I give her. This was about two hours ago and she is probily down in the hotel lobby now trying to scare me by makeing me believe she has went to her sister's. But she can't fool me Al and I am now going out to mail this letter and get a beer. I won't never tell her about Violet and Hazel if she is going to act like that.

Yours truly, Jack.

CHICAGO, ILLINOIS, OCTOBER 24.

Friend Al: I guess I told you Al that we would be home Saturday evening. I have changed my mind. Allen and his wife has a spair bedroom and wants us to come there and stay a week or two. It won't cost nothing except they will probily want to go out to the moveing pictures nights and we will probily have to go along with them and I am a man Al that wants to pay his share and not be cheap.

I and Florrie had our first quarrle the other night. I guess I told you the start of it but I don't remember. I made some crack about Violet and Hazel just to tease Florrie and she wanted to know who they was and I would not tell her. So she gets sore and goes over to Marie's to stay all night. I was just kidding Al and was willing to tell her about them two poor girls whatever she wanted to know except that I don't like to brag about girls being stuck on me. So I goes over to Marie's after her and tells her all about them except that I turned them down cold at the last mintue to marry her because I did not want her to get all swelled up. She made me sware that I did not never care nothing about them and that was easy because it was the truth. So she come back to the hotel with me just like I knowed she would when I ordered her to.

They must not be no mistake about who is the boss in my house. Some men lets their wife run all over them but I am not that kind. You know me Al.

I must get busy and pack my suitcase if I am going to move over to Allen's. I sent three collars and a shirt to the laundrey this morning so even if we go over there to-night I will have to take another trip back this way in a day or two. I won't mind Al because they sell my kind of beer down to the corner and I never seen it sold nowheres else in Chi. You know the kind it is, eh Al? I wish I was lifting a few with you to-night. *Your pal, Jack.*

CHICAGO, ILLINOIS, OCTOBER 28.

Dear Old Al: Florrie and Marie has went downtown shopping because Florrie thinks she has got to have a new dress though she has got two changes of cloths now and I don't know what she can do with another one. I hope she don't find none to suit her though it would not hurt none if she got something for next spring at a reduckshon. I guess she must think I am Charles A. Comiskey or somebody. Allen has went to a colledge football game. One of the reporters give him a pass. I don't see nothing in football except a lot of scrapping between little slobs that I could lick the whole bunch of them so I did not care to go. The reporter is one of the guys that travled round with our club all summer. He called up and said he hadn't only the one pass but he was not hurting my feelings none because I would not go to no rotten football game if they payed me.

The flat across the hall from this here one is for rent furnished. They want $40 a month for it and I guess they think they must be lots of suckers running round loose. Marie was talking about it and says Why don't you and Florrie take it and then we can be right together all winter long and have some big times? Florrie says It would be all right with me. What about it Al? I says What do you think I am? I don't have to live in no high-price flat when I got a home in Bedford where they ain't no people trying to hold everybody up all the time. So they did not say no more about it when they seen I was in ernest. Nobody cannot tell me where I am going to live sister-in-law or no sister-in-law. If I was to rent the rotten old flat I would be paying $50 a month rent includeing the house down in Bedford. Fine chance Al.

Well Al I am lonesome and thirsty so more later.

Your pal, Jack.

CHICAGO, ILLINOIS, NOVEMBER 2.

Friend Al: Well Al I got some big news for you. I am not comeing to Bedford this winter after all except to make a visit which I guess will be round Xmas. I changed my mind about that flat across the hall from the Allens and decided to take it after all. The people who was in it and owns the furniture says they would let us have it till the 1 of May if we would pay $42.50 a month which is only $2.50 a month more than they would of let us have it for for a short time. So you see we got a bargain because it is all furnished and everything and we won't have to blow no money on furniture besides the club goes to California the middle of Febuery so Florrie would not have no place to stay while I am away.

The Allens only subleased their flat from some other people till the 2 of Febuery and when I and Allen goes West Marie can come over and stay with Florrie so you see it is best all round. If we should of boughten furniture it would cost us in the neighborhood of $100 even without no piano and they is a piano in this here flat which makes it nice because Florrie plays pretty good with one hand and we can have lots of good times at home without it costing us nothing except just the bear liveing expenses. I consider myself lucky to of found out about this before it was too late and somebody else had of gotten the tip.

Now Al old pal I want to ask a great favor of you Al. I all ready have payed one month rent $10 on the house in Bedford and I want you to see the old man and see if he won't call off that lease. Why should I be paying $10 a month rent down there and $42.50 up here when the house down there is not no good to me because I am liveing up here all winter? See Al? Tell him I will gladly give him another month rent to call off the lease but don't tell him that if you don't have to. I want to be fare with him.

If you will do this favor for me, Al, I won't never forget it. Give my kindest to Bertha and tell her I am sorry I and Florrie won't see her right away but you see how it is Al. *Yours, Jack.*

CHICAGO, ILLINOIS, NOVEMBER 30.

Friend Al: I have not wrote for a long time have I Al but I have been very busy. They was not enough furniture in the flat and we have been buying some more. They was enough for some people maybe but I and Florrie is the kind that won't have nothing but the best. The furniture them people had in the liveing room was oak but they had a bookcase bilt in in the flat that was mohoggeny and Florrie would not stand for no joke combination like that so she moved the oak chairs and table in to the spair bedroom and we went downtown to buy some mohoggeny. But it costs too much Al and we was feeling pretty bad about it when we seen some Sir Cashion walnut that was prettier even than the mohoggeny and not near so expensive. It is not no real Sir Cashion walnut but it is just as good and we got it reasonable. Then we got some mission chairs for the dining room because the old ones was just straw and was no good and we got a big lether couch for $9 that somebody can sleep on if we get to much company.

I hope you and Bertha can come up for the holidays and see how comfertible we are fixed. That is all the new furniture we have boughten but Florrie set her heart on some old Rose drapes and a red table lamp that is the biggest you ever seen Al and I did not have the heart to say no. The hole thing cost me in the neighborhood of $110 which is very little for what we got and then it will always be ourn even when we move away from this flat though we will have to leave the furniture that belongs to the other people but their part of it is not no good anyway.

I guess I told you Al how much money I had when the season ended. It was $1400 all told includeing the city serious money. Well Al I got in the neighborhood of $800 left because I give $200 to Florrie to send down to Texas to her other sister who had a bad egg for a husband that managed a club in the Texas Oklahoma League and this ◆ was the money she had to pay to get the divorce. I am glad Al that I was lucky enough to marry happy and get a good girl for my wife that has got some sense and besides if I have got $800 left I should not worry as they say. *Your pal, Jack.*

CHICAGO, ILLINOIS, DECEMBER 7.

Dear Old Al: No I was in ernest Al when I says that I wanted you and Bertha to come up here for the holidays. I know I told you that I might come to Bedford for the holidays but that is all off. I have gave up the idea of comeing to Bedford for the holidays and I want you to be sure and come up here for the holidays and I will show you a good time. I would love to have Bertha come to and she can come if she wants to only Florrie don't know if she would have a good time or not and thinks maybe she would rather stay in Bedford and you come alone. But be sure and have Bertha come if she wants to come but maybe she would not injoy it. You know best Al.

I don't think the old man give me no square deal on that lease but if he wants to stick me all right. I am greatful to you Al for trying to fix it up but maybe you could of did better if you had of went at it in a different way. I am not finding no fault with my old pal though. Don't think that. When I have a pal I am the man to stick to him threw thick and thin. If the old man is going to hold me to that lease I guess I will have to stand it and I guess I won't starv to death for no $10 a month because I am going to get $2800 next year besides the city serious money and maybe we will get into the World Serious too. I know we will if Callahan will pitch me every 3d day like I wanted him to last season. But if you had of approached the old man in a different way maybe you could of fixed it up. I wish you would try it again Al if it is not no trouble.

We had Allen and his wife here for thanksgiveing dinner and the dinner cost me better than $5. I thought we had enough to eat to last a weak but about six oclock at night Florrie and Marie said they was hungry and we went downtown and had dinner all over again and I payed for it and it cost me $5 more. Allen was all ready to pay for it when Florrie said No this day's treat is on us so I had to pay for it but

◆ *Texas Oklahoma League*—A Class D minor league in the area immediately north of Dallas. In 1913 the league consisted of Denison, Paris, Texarkana, Sherman, and Bonham, Tex., and Hugo, Ardmore, and Durant, Okla.

I don't see why she did not wait and let me do the talking. I was going to pay for it any way.

Be sure and come and visit us for the holidays Al and of coarse if Bertha wants to come bring her along. We will be glad to see you both. I won't never go back on a friend and pal. You know me Al.

Your old pal, Jack.

CHICAGO, ILLINOIS, DECEMBER 20.

Friend Al: I don't see what can be the matter with Bertha because you know Al we would not care how she dressed and would not make no kick if she come up here in a night gown. She did not have no license to say we was to swell for her because we did not never think of nothing like that. I wish you would talk to her again Al and tell her she need not get sore on me and that both her and you is welcome at my house any time I ask you to come. See if you can't make her change her mind Al because I feel like as if she must of took offense at something I may of wrote you. I am sorry you and her are not comeing but I suppose you know best. Only we was getting all ready for you and Florrie said only the other day that she wished the holidays was over but that was before she knowed you was not comeing. I hope you can come Al.

Well Al I guess there is not no use talking to the old man no more. You have did the best you could but I wish I could of came down there and talked to him. I will pay him his rotten old $10 a month and the next time I come to Bedford and meet him on the street I will bust his jaw. I know he is a old man Al but I don't like to see nobody get the best of me and I am sorry I ever asked him to let me off. Some of them old skinflints has no heart Al but why should I fight with a old man over chicken feed like $10? Florrie says a star pitcher like I should not ought never to scrap about little things and I guess she is right Al so I will pay the old man his $10 a month if I have to.

Florrie says she is jealous of me writeing to you so much and she says she would like to meet this great old pal of mine. I would like to have her meet you to Al and I would like to have you change your mind and come and visit us and I am sorry you can't come Al.

Yours truly, Jack.

CHICAGO, ILLINOIS, DECEMBER 27.

Old Pal: I guess all these lefthanders is alike though I thought this Allen had some sense. I thought he was different from the most and was not no rummy but they are all alike Al and they are all lucky that somebody don't hit them over the head with a ax and kill them but I ◆ guess at that you could not hurt no lefthanders by hitting them over the head. We was all down on State St. the day before Xmas and the girls was all tired out and ready to go home but Allen says No I guess we better stick down a while because now the crowds is out and it will be fun to watch them. So we walked up and down State St. about a hour longer and finally we come in front of a big jewlry store window and in it was a swell dimond ring that was marked $100. It was a ladies' ring so Marie says to Allen Why don't you buy that for me? and Allen says Do you really want it? And she says she did.

So we tells the girls to wait and we goes over to a salloon where Allen has got a friend and gets a check cashed and we come back and he bought the ring. Then Florrie looks like as though she was getting all ready to cry and I asked her what was the matter and she says I had not boughten her no ring not even when we was engaged. So I and Allen goes back to the salloon and I gets a check cashed and we come back and bought another ring but I did not think the ring Allen had boughten was worth no $100 so I gets one for $75. Now Al you know I am not makeing no kick on spending a little money for a present for my own wife but I had allready boughten her a rist watch for $15 and a rist watch was just what she had wanted. I was willing to give her the ring if she had not of wanted the rist watch more than the ring but when I give her the ring I kept the rist watch and did not tell her nothing about it.

Well I come downtown alone the day after Xmas and they would not take the rist watch back in the store where I got it. So I am going to give it to her for a New Year's present and I guess that will make Allen feel like a dirty doose. But I guess you cannot hurt no lefthander's feelings at that. They are all alike. But Allen has not got nothing but a dinky curve ball and a fast ball that looks like my slow one. If Comiskey was not good-hearted he would of sold him long ago.

I sent you and Bertha a cut-glass dish Al which was the best I could get for the money and it was pretty high pricet at that. We was glad to get the pretty pincushions from you and Bertha and Florrie says to

---

◆ *I guess at that you could not hurt no lefthanders by hitting them over the head.*—Keefe's bigoted view of lefthanded pitchers embodies a stereotype of lefthanders as eccentric and given to alcoholism, dating from the personality problems of George "Rube" Waddell, a lefthander of great ability but of monumental self-destructive properties. Even his manager, the mild-mannered Connie Mack, thought Waddell somewhat unbalanced.

tell you that we are well supplied with pincushions now because the ones you sent makes a even half dozen. Thanks Al for remembering us and thank Bertha too though I guess you paid for them.

Your pal, Jack.

CHICAGO, ILLINOIS, JANUERY 3.

Old Pal: Al I been pretty sick ever since New Year's eve. We had a table at 1 of the swell resturunts downtown and I never seen so much wine drank in my life. I would rather of had beer but they would not sell us none so I found out that they was a certain kind that you can get for $1 a bottle and it is just as good as the kind that has got all them fancy names but this lefthander starts ordering some other kind about 11 oclock and it was $5 a bottle and the girls both says they liked it better. I could not see a hole lot of difference myself and I would of gave $0.20 for a big stine of my kind of beer. You know me Al. Well Al you know they is not nobody that can drink more than your old pal and I was all O. K. at one oclock but I seen the girls was getting kind of sleepy so I says we better go home.

Then Marie says Oh, shut up and don't be no quiter. I says You better shut up yourself and not be telling me to shut up, and she says What will you do if I don't shut up? And I says I would bust her in the jaw. But you know Al I would not think of busting no girl. Then Florrie says You better not start nothing because you had to much to drink or you would not be talking about busting girls in the jaw. Then I says I don't care if it is a girl I bust or a lefthander. I did not mean nothing at all Al but Marie says I had insulted Allen and he gets up and slaps my face. Well Al I am not going to stand that from nobody not even if he is my brother-in-law and a lefthander that has not got enough speed to brake a pain of glass.

So I give him a good beating and the waiters butts in and puts us all out for fighting and I and Florrie comes home in a taxi and Allen and his wife don't get in till about 5 oclock so I guess she must of had to of took him to a doctor to get fixed up. I been in bed ever since till just this morning kind of sick to my stumach. I guess I must of eat something that did not agree with me. Allen come over after breakfast this morning and asked me was I all right so I guess he is not sore over the beating I give him or else he wants to make friends because he has saw that I am a bad guy to monkey with.

Florrie tells me a little while ago that she paid the hole bill at the resturunt with my money because Allen was broke so you see what kind of a cheap skate he is Al and some day I am going to bust his jaw. She won't tell me how much the bill was and I won't ask her to no more because we had a good time outside of the fight and what do I care if we spent a little money? *Yours truly, Jack.*

CHICAGO, ILLINOIS, JANUERY 20.

Friend Al: Allen and his wife have gave up the flat across the hall from us and come over to live with us because we got a spair bedroom and why should they not have the bennifit of it? But it is pretty hard for the girls to have to cook and do the work when they is four of us so I have a hired girl who does it all for $7 a week. It is great stuff Al because now we can go round as we please and don't have to wait for no dishes to be washed or nothing. We generally almost always has dinner downtown in the evening so it is pretty soft for the girl too. She don't generally have no more than one meal to get because we generally run round downtown till late and don't get up till about noon.

That sounds funny don't it Al, when I used to get up at 5 every morning down home. Well Al I can tell you something else that may sound funny and that is that I lost my taste for beer. I don't seem to care for it no more and I found I can stand allmost as many drinks of other stuff as I could of beer. I guess Al they is not nobody ever lived can drink more and stand up better under it than me. I make the girls and Allen quit every night.

I only got just time to write you this short note because Florrie and Marie is giving a big party to-night and I and Allen have got to beat it out of the house and stay out of the way till they get things ready. It is Marie's berthday and she says she is 22 but say Al if she is 22 Kid Gleason is 30. Well Al the girls says we must blow so I will run out and mail this letter. *Yours truly, Jack.*

CHICAGO, ILLINOIS, JANUERY 31.

Al: Allen is going to take Marie with him on the training trip to California and of course Florrie has been at me to take her along. I told her postivly that she can't go. I can't afford no stunt like that but still I am up against it to know what to do with her while we are on the trip because Marie won't be here to stay with her. I don't like to leave her here all alone but they is nothing to it Al I can't afford to take her along. She says I don't see why you can't take me if Allen takes Marie. And I says That stuff is all O. K. for Allen because him and Marie has been grafting off of us all winter. And then she gets mad and tells me I should not ought to say her sister was no grafter.

I did not mean nothing like that Al but you don't never know when a woman is going to take offense.

If our furniture was down in Bedford everything would be all O. K. because then I could leave her there and I would feel all O. K. because I would know that you and Bertha would see that she was getting along O. K. But they would not be no sense in sending her down to a house that has not no furniture in it. I wish I knowed somewheres where she could visit Al. I would be willing to pay her bord even.

Well Al enough for this time. *Your old pal, Jack.*

CHICAGO, ILLINOIS, FEBUERY 4.

Friend Al: You are a real old pal Al and I certainly am greatful to you for the invatation. I have not told Florrie about it yet but I am sure she will be tickled to death and it is certainly kind of you old pal. I did not never dream of nothing like that. I note what you say Al about not axcepting no bord but I think it would be better and I would feel better if you would take something say about $2 a week.

I know Bertha will like Florrie and that they will get along O. K. together because Florrie can learn her how to make her cloths look good and fix her hair and fix up her face. I feel like as if you had took a big load off of me Al and I won't never forget it.

If you don't think I should pay no bord for Florrie all right. Suit yourself about that old pal.

We are leaveing here the 20 of Febuery and if you don't mind I will bring Florrie down to you about the 18. I would like to see all the old bunch again and spesially you and Bertha. *Yours, Jack.*

P.S. We will only be away till April 14 and that is just a nice visit. I wish we did not have no flat on our hands.

CHICAGO, ILLINOIS, FEBUERY 9.

Old Pal: I want to thank you for asking Florrie to come down there and visit you Al but I find she can't get away. I did not know she had no engagements but she says she may go down to her folks in Texas and she don't want to say that she will come to visit you when it is so indefanate. So thank you just the same Al and thank Bertha too.

Florrie is still at me to take her along to California but honest Al I can't do it. I am right down to my last $50 and I have not payed no rent for this month. I owe the hired girl 2 weeks' salery and both I and Florrie needs some new cloths.

Florrie has just came in since I started writeing this letter and we have been talking some more about California and she says maybe if

I would ask Comiskey he would take her along as the club's guest. I had not never thought of that Al and maybe he would because he is a pretty good scout and I guess I will go and see him about it. The league has its skedule meeting here to-morrow and maybe I can see ◆ him down to the hotel where they meet at. I am so worried Al that I can't write no more but I will tell you how I come out with Comiskey.

Your pal, Jack.

CHICAGO, ILLINOIS, FEBUERY 11.

Friend Al: I am up against it right Al and I don't know where I am going to head in at. I went down to the hotel where the league was holding its skedule meeting at and I seen Comiskey and got some money off of the club but I owe all the money I got off of them and I am still wondering what to do about Florrie.

Comiskey was busy in the meeting when I went down there and they was not no chance to see him for a while so I and Allen and some of the boys hung round and had a few drinks and fanned. This here Joe Hill the busher that Detroit has got that Violet is hooked up to was round the hotel. I don't know what for but I felt like busting his jaw only the boys told me I had better not do nothing because I might kill him and any way he probily won't be in the league much longer. Well finally Comiskey got threw the meeting and I seen him and he says Hello young man what can I do for you? And I says I would like to get $100 advance money. He says Have you been takeing care of yourself down in Bedford? And I told him I had been liveing here all winter and it did not seem to make no hit with him though I don't see what business it is of hisn where I live.

So I says I had been takeing good care of myself. And I have Al. You know that. So he says I should come to the ball park the next day which is to-day and he would have the secretary take care of me but I says I could not wait and so he give me $100 out of his pocket and says he would have it charged against my salery. I was just going to brace him about the California trip when he got away and went back to the meeting.

Well Al I hung round with the bunch waiting for him to get threw again and we had some more drinks and finally Comiskey was threw

◆ *skedule meeting*—The American League held its annual meeting at the Congress Hotel in Chicago on November 6, 1913, and its spring meeting, to which the reference is presumably made, at the Biltmore Hotel in New York on February 12, 1914.

again and I braced him in the lobby and asked him if it was all right to take my wife along to California. He says Sure they would be glad to have her along. And than I says Would the club pay her fair? He says I guess you must of spent that $100 buying some nerve. He says Have you not got no sisters that would like to go along to? He says Does your wife insist on the drawing room or will she take a lower birth? He says Is my special train good enough for her?

Then he turns away from me and I guess some of the boys must of heard the stuff he pulled because they was laughing when he went away but I did not see nothing to laugh at. But I guess he ment that I would have to pay her fair if she goes along and that is out of the question Al. I am up against it and I don't know where I am going to head in at. *Your pal, Jack.*

CHICAGO, ILLINOIS, FEBUERY 12.

Dear Old Al: I guess everything will be all O. K. now at least I am hopeing it will. When I told Florrie about how I come out with Comiskey she bawled her head off and I thought for a while I was going to have to call a doctor or something but pretty soon she cut it out and we sat there a while without saying nothing. Then she says If you could get your salery razed a couple of hundred dollars a year would you borrow the money ahead somewheres and take me along to California? I says Yes I would if I could get a couple hundred dollars more salery but how could I do that when I had signed a contract for $2800 last fall allready? She says Don't you think you are worth more than $2800? And I says Yes of coarse I was worth more than $2800. She says Well if you will go and talk the right way to Comiskey I believe he will give you $3000 but you must be sure you go at it the right way and don't go and ball it all up.

Well we argude about it a while because I don't want to hold nobody up Al but finally I says I would. It would not be holding nobody up anyway because I am worth $3000 to the club if I am worth a nichol. The papers is all saying that the club has got a good chance to win the pennant this year and talking about the pitching staff and I guess they would not be no pitching staff much if it was not for I and one or two others—about one other I guess.

So it looks like as if everything will be all O. K. now Al. I am going to the office over to the park to see him the first thing in the morning and I am pretty sure that I will get what I am after because if I do not he will see that I am going to quit and then he will see what he is up against and not let me get away.

I will let you know how I come out. *Your pal, Jack.*

CHICAGO, ILLINOIS, FEBUERY 14.

Friend Al: Al old pal I have got a big supprise for you. I am going to the Federal League. I had a run in with Comiskey yesterday and I guess I told him a thing or 2. I guess he would of been glad to sign me at my own figure before I got threw but I was so mad I would not give him no chance to offer me another contract.

I got out to the park at 9 oclock yesterday morning and it was a hour before he showed up and then he keep me waiting another hour so I was pretty sore when I finally went in to see him. He says Well young man what can I do for you? I says I come to see about my contract. He says Do you want to sign up for next year all ready? I says No I am talking about this year. He says I thought I and you talked business last fall. And I says Yes but now I think I am worth more money and I want to sign a contract for $3000. He says If you behave yourself and work good this year I will see that you are took care of. But I says That won't do because I have got to be sure I am going to get $3000.

Then he says I am not sure you are going to get anything. I says What do you mean? And he says I have gave you a very fare contract and if you don't want to live up to it that is your own business. So I give him a awful call Al and told him I would jump to the Federal League. He says Oh, I would not do that if I was you. They are haveing a hard enough time as it is. So I says something back to him and he did not say nothing to me and I beat it out of the office.

I have not told Florrie about the Federal League business yet as I am going to give her a big supprise. I bet they will take her along with me on the training trip and pay her fair but even if they don't I should not worry because I will make them give me a contract for $4000 a year and then I can afford to take her with me on all the trips.

I will go down and see Tinker to-morrow morning and I will write ◆◇

JOSEPH B. TINKER
FAMOUS AS A MEMBER OF ONE OF BASEBALL'S GREATEST DOUBLE PLAY COMBINATIONS-FROM TINKER TO EVERS TO CHANCE. A BIG LEAGUER FROM 1902 THROUGH 1916 WITH THE CHICAGO CUBS AND CINCINNATI REDS AND THE CHICAGO FEDS. MANAGER CINCINNATI 1913 AND CHICAGO N.L. 1916. SHORTSTOP ON CUBS' TEAM THAT WON PENNANTS IN 1906,'07'08 AND 1910.

◇ *Tinker*—The Joseph B. Tinker plaque at National Baseball Hall of Fame and Museum, Cooperstown, New York.

◆ *Tinker*—Joseph Bert Tinker (1880–1948), manager of the Chicago Whales of the Federal League in 1914 and 1915. Tinker had won more fame than his playing record appears to warrant. He hit .263 in 1,804 games in 15 seasons, mainly as shortstop for the Cubs between 1902 and 1912. In 1913 he managed the Cincinnati Reds. In the dissolution of the Federal League the Whales and Cubs were essentially merged as a playing entity, but Tinker remained as manager for the 1916 season. He was elected to the Hall of Fame in 1946. See Allen R. Asnen and John E. Findling, "Joseph Bert Tinker," *Biographical Dictionary of American Sports: Baseball*, pp. 556–57.

you to-morrow night Al how much salery they are going to give me. But I won't sign for no less than $4000. You know me Al.

Yours, Jack.

CHICAGO, ILLINOIS, FEBUERY 15.

Old Pal: It is pretty near midnight Al but I been to bed a couple of times and I can't get no sleep. I am worried to death Al and I don't know where I am going to head in at. Maybe I will go out and buy a gun Al and end it all and I guess it would be better for everybody. But I cannot do that Al because I have not got the money to buy a gun with.

I went down to see Tinker about signing up with the Federal League and he was busy in the office when I come in. Pretty soon Buck Perry ◆ the pitcher that was with Boston last year come out and seen me and as Tinker was still busy we went out and had a drink together. Buck shows me a contract for $5000 a year and Tinker had allso gave him a $500 bonus. So pretty soon I went up to the office and pretty soon Tinker seen me and called me into his private office and asked what did I want. I says I was ready to jump for $4000 and a bonus. He says I thought you was signed up with the White Sox. I says Yes I was but I was not satisfied. He says That does not make no difference to me if you are satisfied or not. You ought to of came to me before you signed a contract. I says I did not know enough but I know better now. He says Well it is to late now. We cannot have nothing to do with you because you have went and signed a contract with the White Sox. I ◆ argude with him a while and asked him to come out and have a drink so we could talk it over but he said he was busy so they was nothing for me to do but blow.

So I am not going to the Federal League Al and I will not go with the White Sox because I have got a raw deal. Comiskey will be sorry for what he done when his team starts the season and is up against it for good pitchers and then he will probily be willing to give me anything I ask for but that don't do me no good now Al. I am way in debt and no chance to get no money from nobody. I wish I had of stayed with Terre Haute Al and never saw this league.

Your pal, Jack.

◆ *Buck Perry*—Apparently a fictional character.

◆ *you have went and signed a contract with the White Sox*—The Federal League behaved in this fashion at the outset, honoring the current contract but treating the reserve clause as unenforceable.

CHICAGO, ILLINOIS, FEBRUARY 17.

Friend Al: Al don't never let nobody tell you that these here lefthanders is right. This Allen my own brother-in-law who married sisters has been grafting and spongeing on me all winter Al. Look what he done to me now Al. You know how hard I been up against it for money and I know he has got plenty of it because I seen it on him. Well Al I was scared to tell Florrie I was cleaned out and so I went to Allen yesterday and says I had to have $100 right away because I owed the rent and owed the hired girl's salery and could not even pay no grocery bill. And he says No he could not let me have none because he has got to save all his money to take his wife on the trip to California. And here he has been liveing on me all winter and maybe I could of took my wife to California if I had not of spent all my money takeing care of this no good lefthander and his wife. And Al honest he has not got a thing and ought not to be in the league. He gets by with a dinky curve ball and has not got no more smoke than a rabbit or something.

Well Al I felt like busting him in the jaw but then I thought No I might kill him and then I would have Marie and Florrie both to take care of and God knows one of them is enough besides paying his funeral expenses. So I walked away from him without takeing a crack at him and went into the other room where Florrie and Marie was at. I says to Marie I says Marie I wish you would go in the other room a minute because I want to talk to Florrie. So Marie beats it into the other room and then I tells Florrie all about what Comiskey and the Federal League done to me. She bawled something awful and then she says I was no good and she wished she had not never married me. I says I wisht it too and then she says Do you mean that and starts to cry.

I told her I was sorry I says that because they is not no use fusing with girls Al specially when they is your wife. She says No California trip for me and then she says What are you going to do? And I says I did not know. She says Well if I was a man I would do something. So then I got mad and I says I will do something. So I went down to the corner salloon and started in to get good and drunk but I could not do it Al because I did not have the money.

Well old pal I am going to ask you a big favor and it is this I want you to send me $100 Al for just a few days till I can get on my feet. I do not know when I can pay it back Al but I guess you know the money is good and I know you have got it. Who would not have it when they live in Bedford? And besides I let you take $20 in June 4 years ago Al and you give it back but I would not have said nothing to you if you had of kept it. Let me hear from you right away old pal.

Yours truly, Jack.

CHICAGO, ILLINOIS, FEBUERY 19.

Al: I am certainly greatful to you Al for the $100 which come just a little while ago. I will pay the rent with it and part of the grocery bill and I guess the hired girl will have to wait a while for hern but she is sure to get it because I don't never forget my debts. I have changed my mind about the White Sox and I am going to go on the trip and take Florrie along because I don't think it would not be right to leave her here alone in Chi when her sister and all of us is going.

I am going over to the ball park and up in the office pretty soon to see about it. I will tell Comiskey I changed my mind and he will be glad to get me back because the club has not got no chance to finish nowheres without me. But I won't go on no trip or give the club my services without them giveing me some more advance money so as I can take Florrie along with me because Al I would not go without her.

Maybe Comiskey will make my salery $3000 like I wanted him to when he sees I am willing to be a good fellow and go along with him and when he knows that the Federal League would of gladly gave me $4000 if I had not of signed no contract with the White Sox.

I think I will ask him for $200 advance money Al and if I get it may be I can send part of your $100 back to you but I know you cannot be in no hurry Al though you says you wanted it back as soon as possible. You could not be very hard up Al because it don't cost near so much to live in Bedford as it does up here.

Anyway I will let you know how I come out with Comiskey and I will write you as soon as I get out to Paso Robles if I don't get no time to write you before I leave. *Your pal, Jack.*

P.S. I have took good care of myself all winter Al and I guess I ought to have a great season.

P.S. Florrie is tickled to death about going along and her and I will have some time together out there on the Coast if I can get some money somewheres.

CHICAGO, ILLINOIS, FEBUERY 21.

Friend Al: I have not got the heart to write this letter to you Al. I am up here in my $42.50 a month flat and the club has went to California and Florrie has went too. I am flat broke Al and all I am asking you is to send me enough money to pay my fair to Bedford and they and all their leagues can go to hell Al.

I was out to the ball park early yesterday morning and some of the boys was there allready fanning and kidding each other. They tried to kid me to when I come in but I guess I give them as good as they give me. I was not in no mind for kidding Al because I was there on business and I wanted to see Comiskey and get it done with.

Well the secretary come in finally and I went up to him and says I wanted to see Comiskey right away. He says The boss was busy and what did I want to see him about and I says I wanted to get some advance money because I was going to take my wife on the trip. He says This would be a fine time to be telling us about it even if you was going on the trip.

And I says What do you mean? And he says You are not going on no trip with us because we have got wavers on you and you are sold to Milwaukee. ◆

Honest Al I thought he was kidding at first and I was waiting for him to laugh but he did not laugh and finally I says What do you mean? And he says Cannot you understand no English? You are sold to Milwaukee. Then I says I want to see the boss. He says It won't do you no good to see the boss and he is to busy to see you. I says I want to get some money. And he says You cannot get no money from this club and all you get is your fair to Milwaukee. I says I am not going to no Milwaukee anyway and he says I should not worry about that. Suit yourself.

Well Al I told some of the boys about it and they was pretty sore and says I ought to bust the secretary in the jaw and I was going to do it when I thought No I better not because he is a little guy and I might kill him.

I looked all over for Kid Gleason but he was not nowheres round and they told me he would not get into town till late in the afternoon. If I could of saw him Al he would of fixed me all up. I asked 3 or 4 of the boys for some money but they says they was all broke.

But I have not told you the worst of it yet Al. When I come back to the flat Allen and Marie and Florrie was busy packing up and they asked me how I come out. I told them and Allen just stood there

---

◆ *Milwaukee*—The city had a strong franchise in the American Association. Because of its proximity to Chicago, 89 miles away, it was an attractive place for the White Sox to option players.

stareing like a big rummy but Marie and Florrie both begin to cry and I almost felt like as if I would like to cry to only I am not no baby Al.

Well Al I told Florrie she might just is well quit packing and make up her mind that she was not going nowheres till I got money enough to go to Bedford where I belong. She kept right on crying and it got so I could not stand it no more so I went out to get a drink because I still had just about a dollar left yet.

It was about 2 oclock when I left the flat and pretty near 5 when I come back because I had ran in to some fans that knowed who I was and would not let me get away and besides I did not want to see no more of Allen and Marie till they was out of the house and on their way.

But when I come in Al they was nobody there. They was not nothing there except the furniture and a few of my things scattered round. I sit down for a few minutes because I guess I must of had to much to drink but finally I seen a note on the table addressed to me and I seen it was Florrie's writeing.

I do not remember just what was there in the note Al because I tore it up the minute I read it but it was something about I could not support no wife and Allen had gave her enough money to go back to Texas and she was going on the 6 oclock train and it would not do me no good to try and stop her.

Well Al they was not no danger of me trying to stop her. She was not no good Al and I wisht I had not of never saw either she or her sister or my brother-in-law.

For a minute I thought I would follow Allen and his wife down to the deepo where the special train was to pull out of and wait till I see him and punch his jaw but I seen that would not get me nothing.

So here I am all alone Al and I will have to stay here till you send me the money to come home. You better send me $25 because I have got a few little debts I should ought to pay before I leave town. I am not going to Milwaukee Al because I did not get no decent deal and nobody cannot make no sucker out of me.

Please hurry up with the $25 Al old friend because I am sick and tired of Chi and want to get back there with my old pal.

Yours, Jack.

P.S. Al I wish I had of took poor little Violet when she was so stuck on me.

A New Busher Breaks In

CHICAGO, ILLINOIS, MARCH 2.

Friend Al: Al that peace in the paper was all O. K. and the right dope just like you said. I seen president Johnson the president of the league to-day and he told me the peace in the papers was the right dope and Comiskey did not have no right to sell me to Milwaukee because the Detroit Club had never gave no wavers on me. He says the Detroit Club was late in fileing their claim and Comiskey must of tooken it for granted that they was going to wave but president Johnson was pretty sore about it at that and says Comiskey did not have no right to sell me till he was positive that they was not no team that wanted me.

It will probily cost Comiskey some money for acting like he done and not paying no attention to the rules and I would not be supprised if president Johnson had him throwed out of the league.

Well I asked president Johnson should I report at once to the Detroit Club down south and he says No you better wait till you hear from Comiskey and I says What has Comiskey got to do with it now? And he says Comiskey will own you till he sells you to Detroit or

"A New Busher Breaks In," the fourth of the stories later collected as *You Know Me Al*, was published in *The Saturday Evening Post*, CLXXXVII (September 12, 1914), 15–17, 53–54.

somewheres else. So I will have to go out to the ball park to-morrow and see is they any mail for me there because I probily will get a letter from Comiskey telling me I am sold to Detroit.

If I had of thought at the time I would of knew that Detroit never would give no wavers on me after the way I showed Cobb and Crawford up last fall and I might of knew too that Detroit is in the market for good pitchers because they got a rotten pitching staff but they won't ◆ have no rotten staff when I get with them.

If necessary I will pitch every other day for Jennings and if I do we will win the pennant sure because Detroit has got a club that can get 2 or 3 runs every day and all as I need to win most of my games is 1 run. I can't hardly wait till Jennings works me against the White Sox and what I will do to them will be a plenty. It don't take no pitching to beat them anyway and when they get up against a pitcher like I they might as well leave their bats in the bag for all the good their bats will do them.

I guess Cobb and Crawford will be glad to have me on the Detroit Club because then they won't never have to hit against me eccept in practice and I won't pitch my best in practice because they will be teammates of mine and I don't never like to show none of my teammates up. At that though I don't suppose Jennings will let me do much pitching in practice because when he gets a hold of a good pitcher he won't want me to take no chances of throwing my arm away in practice.

Al just think how funny it will be to have me pitching for the Tigers in the same town where Violet lives and pitching on the same club with her husband. It will not be so funny for Violet and her husband though because when she has a chance to see me work regular she will find out what a mistake she made takeing that left-hander instead of a man that has got some future and soon will be makeing 5 or $6000 a year because I won't sign with Detroit for no less than $5000 at most. Of coarse I could of had her if I had of wanted to but still and all it will make her feel pretty sick to see me winning games for Detroit while her husband is batting fungos and getting splinters in ◆ his unie from slideing up and down the bench.

◆ *they got a rotten pitching staff*—Quite right. Tiger pitchers had given up 720 runs in 1913, highest in the American League by a margin of 51 runs. Their collective earned run average of 3.41 was also the worst in the league.

◆ *batting fungos*—Hitting fungoes—throwing the ball a few feet up and hitting it to the outfielders with a light bat as it descends into the strike zone—is a

As for her husband the first time he opens his clam to me I will haul off and bust him one in the jaw but I guess he will know more than to start trouble with a man of my size and who is going to be one of their stars while he is just holding down a job because they feel sorry for him. I wish he could of got the girl I married instead of the one he got and I bet she would of drove him crazy. But I guess you can't drive a left-hander crazyer than he is to begin with.

I have not heard nothing from Florrie Al and I don't want to hear nothing. I and her is better apart and I wish she would sew me for a bill of divorce so she could not go round claiming she is my wife and disgraceing my name. If she would consent to sew me for a bill of divorce I would gladly pay all the expenses and settle with her for any sum of money she wants say about $75.00 or $100.00 and they is no reason I should give her a nichol after the way her and her sister Marie and her brother-in-law Allen grafted off of me. Probily I could sew her for a bill of divorce but they tell me it costs money to sew and if you just lay low and let the other side do the sewing it don't cost you a nichol.

It is pretty late Al and I have got to get up early to-morrow and go to the ball park and see is they any mail for me. I will let you know what I hear old pal. *Your old pal, Jack.*

CHICAGO, ILLINOIS, MARCH 4.

Al: I am up against it again. I went out to the ball park office yesterday and they was nobody there eccept John somebody who is asst secretary ◆ and all the rest of them is out on the Coast with the team. Maybe this here John was trying to kid me but this is what he told me. First I says Is they a letter here for me? And he says No. And I says I was expecting word from Comiskey that I should join the Detroit Club and he says What makes you think you are going to Detroit? I says Comiskey asked wavers on me and Detroit did not give no wavers. He says Well

---

(*continued from page 121*)
characteristic task of coaches and reserve pitchers during fielding practice. On the etymology of the term, see Paul Dickson, *The Dickson Baseball Dictionary* (New York: Facts on File, 1989), pp. 172–74.

◆ *John somebody*—Whoever the officer named John might have been, he was definitely not the assistant secretary. The assistant or acting secretary of the White Sox, owing to Fredericks' disability, was Harry Grabiner, and his assistant was Joe O'Neill. The passage may refer to John Hand, a White Sox front-office official who had acted as traveling secretary for the second team in spring training of 1913, but he, like Grabiner and O'Neill, was west with the team in spring training of 1914.

that is not no sign that you are going to Detroit. If Comiskey can't get you out of the league he will probily keep you himself and it is a cinch he is not going to give no pitcher to Detroit no matter how rotten he is.

I says What do you mean? And he says You just stick round town till you hear from Comiskey and I guess you will hear pretty soon because he is comeing back from the Coast next Saturday. I says Well the only thing he can tell me is to report to Detroit because I won't never pitch again for the White Sox. Then John gets fresh and says I suppose you will quit the game and live on your saveings and then I blowed out of the office because I was scared I would loose my temper and break something.

So you see Al what I am up against. I won't never pitch for the White Sox again and I want to get with the Detroit Club but how can I if Comiskey won't let me go? All I can do is stick round till next Saturday and then I will see Comiskey and I guess when I tell him what I think of him he will be glad to let me go to Detroit or anywheres else. I will have something on him this time because I know that he did not pay no attention to the rules when he told me I was sold to Milwaukee and if he tries to slip something over on me I will tell president Johnson of the league all about it and then you will see where Comiskey heads in at.

Al old pal that $25.00 you give me at the station the other day is all shot to peaces and I musk ask you to let me have $25.00 more which will make $75.00 all together includeing the $25.00 you sent me before I come home. I hate to ask you this favor old pal but I know you have got the money. If I am sold to Detroit I will get some advance money and pay up all my dedts incluseive.

If he don't let me go to Detroit I will make him come across with part of my salery for this year even if I don't pitch for him because I signed a contract and was ready to do my end of it and would of if he had not of been nasty and tried to slip something over on me. If he refuses to come across I will hire a attorney at law and he will get it all. So Al you see you have got a cinch on getting back what you lone me but I guess you know that Al without all this talk because you have been my old pal for a good many years and I have allways treated you square and tried to make you feel that I and you was equals and that my success was not going to make me forget my old friends.

Wherever I pitch this year I will insist on a salery of 5 or $6000 a year. So you see on my first pay day I will have enough to pay you up and settle the rest of my dedts but I am not going to pay no more rent for this rotten flat because they tell me if a man don't pay no rent for a while they will put him out. Let them put me out. I should not worry but will go and rent my old room that I had before I met Florrie and got into all this trouble.

The sooner you can send me that $35.00 the better and then I will owe you $85.00 incluseive and I will write and let you know how I come out with Comiskey. *Your pal, Jack.*

CHICAGO, ILLINOIS, MARCH 12.

Friend Al: I got another big supprise for you and this is it I am going to pitch for the White Sox after all. If Comiskey was not a old man I guess I would of lost my temper and beat him up but I am glad now that I kept my temper and did not loose it because I forced him to make a lot of consessions and now it looks like as though I would have a big year both pitching and money.

He got back to town yesterday morning and showed up to his office in the afternoon and I was there waiting for him. He would not see me for a while but finally I acted like as though I was getting tired of waiting and I guess the secretary got scared that I would beat it out of the office and leave them all in the lerch. Anyway he went in and spoke to Comiskey and then come out and says the boss was ready to see me. When I went into the office where he was at he says Well young man what can I do for you? And I says I want you to give me my release so as I can join the Detroit Club down South and get in shape. Then he says What makes you think you are going to join the Detroit Club? Because we need you here. I says Then why did you try to sell me to Milwaukee? But you could not because you could not get no wavers.

Then he says I thought I was doing you a favor by sending you to Milwaukee because they make a lot of beer up there. I says What do you mean? He says You been keeping in shape all this winter by trying to drink this town dry and besides that you tried to hold me up for more money when you allready had signed a contract allready and so I was going to send you to Milwaukee and learn you something and besides you tried to go with the Federal League but they would not take you because they was scared to.

I don't know where he found out all that stuff at Al and besides he was wrong when he says I was drinking too much because they is not nobody that can drink more than me and not be effected. But I did not say nothing because I was scared I would forget myself and call him some name and he is a old man. Yes I did say something. I says

Well I guess you found out that you could not get me out of the league and then he says Don't never think I could not get you out of the league. If you think I can't send you to Milwaukee I will prove it to you that I can. I says You can't because Detroit won't give no wavers on me. He says Detroit will give wavers on you quick enough if I ask them.

Then he says Now you can take your choice you can stay here and pitch for me at the salery you signed up for and you can cut out the monkey business and drink water when you are thirsty or else you can go up to Milwaukee and drownd yourself in one of them brewrys. Which shall it be? I says How can you keep me or send me to Milwaukee when Detroit has allready claimed my services? He says Detroit has claimed a lot of things and they have even claimed the pennant but that is not no sign they will win it. He says And besides you would not want to pitch for Detroit because then you would not never have no chance to pitch against Cobb and show him up.

Well Al when he says that I knowed he appresiated what a pitcher I am even if he did try to sell me to Milwaukee or he would not of made that remark about the way I can show Cobb and Crawford up. So I says Well if you need me that bad I will pitch for you but I must have a new contract. He says Oh I guess we can fix that up O. K. and he steps out in the next room a while and then he comes back with a new contract. And what do you think it was Al? It was a contract for 3 years so you can see I am sure of my job here for 3 years and ◆ everything is all O. K.

The contract calls for the same salery a year for 3 years that I was going to get before for only 1 year which is $2800.00 a year and then I will get in on the city serious money too and the Detroit Club don't have no city serious and have no chance to get into the World's Serious with the rotten pitching staff they got. So you see Al he fixed me up good and that shows that he must think a hole lot of me or he would of sent me to Detroit or maybe to Milwaukee but I don't see how he could of did that without no wavers.

Well Al I allmost forgot to tell you that he has gave me a ticket to

---

◆ *I am sure of my job here for 3 years*—This course of action assured Comiskey of the services of an improving player for three years at his existing salary, incidentally preventing any further Federal League incursions for the three-year period of Federal League contracts. Because the contract provided for the player's release on ten days' notice, it gave Keefe no additional security.

Los Angeles where the 2d team are practicing at now but where the ◆ 1st team will be at in about a week. I am leaveing to-night and I guess before I go I will go down to president Johnson and tell him that I am fixed up all O. K. and have not got no kick comeing so that president Johnson will not fine Comiskey for not paying no attention to the rules or get him fired out of the league because I guess Comiskey must be all O. K. and good-hearted after all.

I won't pay no attention to what he says about me drinking this town dry because he is all wrong in regards to that. He must of been jokeing I guess because nobody but some boob would think he could drink this town dry but at that I guess I can hold more than anybody and not be effected. But I guess I will cut it out for a while at that because I don't want to get them sore at me after the contract they give me.

I will write to you from Los Angeles Al and let you know what the boys says when they see me and I will bet that they will be tickled to death. The rent man was round to-day but I seen him comeing and he did not find me. I am going to leave the furniture that belongs in the flat in the flat and allso the furniture I bought which don't amount to much because it was not no real Sir Cashion walnut and besides I don't want nothing round me to remind me of Florrie because the sooner her and I forget each other the better.

Tell the boys about my good luck Al but it is not no luck neither because it was comeing to me. *Yours truly, Jack.*

LOS ANGELES, CALIFORNIA, MARCH 16.

Al: Here I am back with the White Sox again and it seems to good to be true because just like I told you they are all tickled to death to see me. Kid Gleason is here in charge of the 2d team and when he seen me come into the hotel he jumped up and hit me in the stumach but he acts like that whenever he feels good so I could not get sore at him though he had no right to hit me in the stumach. If he had of did it in ernest I would of walloped him in the jaw.

He says Well if here ain't the old lady-killer. He ment Al that I am

---

◆ *Los Angeles*—The White Sox again trained in Paso Robles in 1914, so as to continue the exhibitions with Pacific Coast League clubs.

the 2d team—The White Sox second team, called the "Goofs," wound up two weeks in Southern California on March 15. As stated, Gleason managed the team, which won only three games against Coast League and other opposition. Keefe's assignment to the second team probably represented an advancement over 1913.

◇ *Bodie*—Ping Bodie in his road uniform, probably in 1912 (see footnote, p. 47). (National Baseball Library, Cooperstown, New York)

strong with the girls but I am all threw with them now but he don't know nothing about the troubles I had. He says Are you in shape? And I told him Yes I am. He says Yes you look in shape like a barrel. I says They is not no fat on me and if I am a little bit bigger than last year it is because my mussels is bigger. He says Yes your stumach mussels is emense and you must of gave them plenty of exercise. Wait till Bodie sees you and he will want to stick round you all the time ◇ because you make him look like a broom straw or something. I let him kid me along because what is the use of getting mad at him? And besides he is all O.K. even if he is a little rough.

I says to him A little work will fix me up all O. K. and he says You bet you are going to get some work because I am going to see to it myself. I says You will have to hurry because you will be going up to Frisco in a few days and I am going to stay here and join the 1st club. Then he says You are not going to do no such a thing. You are going right along with me. I knowed he was kidding me then because Callahan would not never leave me with the 2d team no more after what I done for him last year and besides most of the stars generally allways goes with the 1st team on the training trip.

Well I seen all the rest of the boys that is here with the 2d team and they all acted like as if they was glad to see me and why should not they be when they know that me being here with the White Sox and not with Detroit means that Callahan won't have to do no worrying about his pitching staff? But they is four or 5 young recrut pitchers with the team here and I bet they is not so glad to see me because what chance have they got?

If I was Comiskey and Callahan I would not spend no money on new pitchers because with me and 1 or 2 of the other boys we got the best pitching staff in the league. And instead of spending the money ◆ for new pitching recruts I would put it all in a lump and buy Ty Cobb or Sam Crawford off of Detroit or somebody else who can hit and Cobb and Crawford is both real hitters Al even if I did make them look like suckers. Who wouldn't?

Well Al tomorrow A. M. I am going out and work a little and in the P. M. I will watch the game between we and the Venice Club but I won't pitch none because Gleason would not dare take no chances of me hurting my arm. I will write to you in a few days from here because no matter what Gleason says I am going to stick here with the 1st team because I know Callahan will want me along with him for a attraction. *Your pal, Jack.*

SAN FRANCISCO, CALIFORNIA, MARCH 20.

Friend Al: Well Al here I am back in old Frisco with the 2d team but ◆ I will tell you how it happened Al. Yesterday Gleason told me to pack up and get ready to leave Los Angeles with him and I says No I am going to stick here and wait for the 1st team and then he says I guess

---

◆ *best pitching staff in the league*—In 1914 the White Sox pitchers gave up 568 runs, fifth best in the American League, but had the second-best earned run average, 2.48.

◆ *the 2d team*—The second team, somewhat strengthened, went to San Francisco on March 14.

I must of overlooked something in the papers because I did not see nothing about you being appointed manager of the club. I says No I am not manager but Callahan is manager and he will want to keep me with him. He says I got a wire from Callahan telling me to keep you with my club but of coarse if you know what Callahan wants better than he knows it himself why then go ahead and stay here or go jump in the Pacific Ocean.

Then he says I know why you don't want to go with me and I says Why? And he says Because you know I will make you work and won't let you eat everything on the bill of fair includeing the name of the hotel at which we are stopping at. That made me sore and I was just going to call him when he says Did not you marry Mrs. Allen's sister? And I says Yes but that is not none of your business. Then he says Well I don't want to butt into your business but I heard you and your wife had some kind of a argument and she beat it. I says Yes she give me a rotten deal. He says Well then I don't see where it is going to be very pleasant for you traveling round with the 1st club because Allen and his wife is both with that club and what do you want to be mixed up with them for? I says I am not scared of Allen or his wife or no other old hen.

So here I am Al with the 2d team but it is only for a while till Callahan gets sick of some of them pitchers he has got and sends for me so as he can see some real pitching. And besides I am glad to be here in Frisco where I made so many friends when I was pitching here for a short time till Callahan heard about my work and called me back to the big show where I belong at and nowheres else.

Yours truly, Jack.

SAN FRANCISCO, CALIFORNIA, MARCH 25.

Old Pal: Al I got a supprise for you. Who do you think I seen last night? Nobody but Hazel. Her name now is Hazel Levy because you know Al she married Kid Levy the middleweight and I wish he was champion of the world Al because then it would not take me more than about a minute to be champion of the world myself. I have not got nothing against him though because he married her and if he had not of I probily would of married her myself but at that she could not of treated me no worse than Florrie. Well they was setting at a table in the café where her and I use to go pretty near every night. She spotted me when I first come in and sends a waiter over to ask me to come and have a drink with them. I went over because they was no use being nasty and let bygones be bygones.

She interduced me to her husband and he asked me what was I drinking. Then she butts in and says Oh you must let Mr. Keefe buy the drinks because it hurts his feelings to have somebody else buy the drinks. Then Levy says Oh he is one of these here spendrifts is he? and she says Yes he don't care no more about a nichol than his right eye does. I says I guess you have got no holler comeing on the way I spend my money. I don't steal no money anyway. She says What do you mean? and I says I guess you know what I mean. How about that $30.00 that you borrowed off of me and never give it back? Then her husband cuts in and says You cut that line of talk out or I will bust you. I says Yes you will. And he says Yes I will.

Well Al what was the use of me starting trouble with him when he has got enough trouble right to home and besides as I say I have not got nothing against him. So I got up and blowed away from the table and I bet he was relieved when he seen I was not going to start nothing. I beat it out of there a while afterward because I was not drinking nothing and I don't have no fun setting round a place and lapping up ginger ail or something. And besides the music was rotten.

Al I am certainly glad I throwed Hazel over because she has grew to be as big as a horse and is all painted up. I don't care nothing about them big dolls no more or about no other kind neither. I am off of them all. They can all of them die and I should not worry.

Well Al I done my first pitching of the year this P. M. and I guess I showed them that I was in just as good a shape as some of them birds that has been working a month. I worked 4 innings against my old team the San Francisco Club and I give them nothing but fast ones but they sure was fast ones and you could hear them zip. Charlie ◆ O'Leary was trying to get out of the way of one of them and it hit his bat and went over first base for a base hit but at that Fournier would of eat it up if it had of been Chase playing first base instead of Fournier.

That was the only hit they got off of me and they ought to of been

◆ *Charlie O'Leary*—Charles Timothy O'Leary (1881–1941), regular third baseman of the San Francisco Seals in 1914. O'Leary had been a light-hitting infielder for the Tigers from 1904 to 1912, and for the Cardinals in 1913. A pleasant and witty man, he was active in vaudeville. After his playing career, O'Leary was a manager at Indianapolis and elsewhere in the minor leagues and coached for the Yankees and Cubs. While working for the Browns at the age of 52 in 1934, he requested an opportunity to go to bat, in hopes of raising his lifetime batting average of .226. He singled in one pinch-hit appearance. See Jack Kavanagh, "Charley O'Leary," *The Ballplayers*, p. 822.

ashamed to of tooken that one. But Gleason don't appresiate my work and him and I allmost come to blows at supper. I was pretty hungry and I ordered some stake and some eggs and some pie and some ice cream and some coffee and a glass of milk but Gleason would not let me have the pie or the milk and would not let me eat more than 1/2 the stake. And it is a wonder I did not bust him and tell him to mind his own business. I says What right have you got to tell me what to eat? And he says You don't need nobody to tell you what to eat you need somebody to keep you from floundering yourself. I says Why can't I eat what I want to when I have worked good?

He says Who told you you worked good and I says I did not need nobody to tell me. I know I worked good because they could not do nothing with me. He says Well it is a good thing for you that they did not start bunting because if you had of went to stoop over and pick up the ball you would of busted wide open. I says Why? and he says Because you are hog fat and if you don't let up on the stable and fancy groceries we will have to pay 2 fairs to get you back to Chi. I don't remember now what I says to him but I says something you can bet on that. You know me Al.

I wish Al that Callahan would hurry up and order me to join the 1st team. If he don't Al I believe Gleason will starve me to death. A little slob like him don't realize that a big man like I needs good food and plenty of it. *Your pal, Jack.*

SALT LAKE CITY, UTAH, APRIL 1.

Al: Well Al we are on our way East and I am still with the 2d team and I don't understand why Callahan don't order me to join the 1st team but maybe it is because he knows that I am allright and have got the stuff and he wants to keep them other guys round where he can see if they have got anything.

The recrut pitchers that is along with our club have not got nothing and the scout that reckommended them must of been full of hops or something. It is not no common thing for a club to pick up a man that has got the stuff to make him a star up here and the White Sox was pretty lucky to land me but I don't understand why they throw their money away on new pitchers when none of them is no good and besides who would want a better pitching staff than we got right now without no raw recruts and bushers.

I worked in Oakland the day before yesterday but he only let me go the 1st 4 innings. I bet them Oakland birds was glad when he took me out. When I was in that league I use to just throw my glove in the box and them Oakland birds was licked and honest Al some of them turned white when they seen I was going to pitch the other day.

I felt kind of sorry for them and I did not give them all I had so they got 5 or 6 hits and scored a couple of runs. I was not feeling very good at that and besides we got some awful excuses for a ball player on this club and the support they give me was the rottenest I ever seen gave anybody. But some of them won't be in this league more than about 10 minutes more so I should not fret as they say.

We play here this afternoon and I don't believe I will work because the team they got here is not worth wasteing nobody on. They must be a lot of boobs in this town Al because they tell me that some of them has got ½ a dozen wives or so. And what a man wants with 1 wife is a misery to me let alone a ½ dozen.

I will probily work against Denver because they got a good club and was champions of the Western League last year. I will make them ◆ think they are champions of the Epworth League or something. ◆

Yours truly, Jack.

DES MOINES, IOWA, APRIL 10.

Friend Al: We got here this A. M. and this is our last stop and we will be in old Chi to-morrow to open the season. The 1st team gets home to-day and I would be there with them if Callahan was a real manager who knowed something about manageing because if I am going to open the season I should ought to have 1 day of rest at home so I would have all my strenth to open the season. The Cleveland Club will be there to open against us and Callahan must know that I have got them licked any time I start against them.

As soon as my name is announced to pitch the Cleveland Club is licked or any other club when I am right and they don't kick the game away behind me.

Gleason told me on the train last night that I was going to pitch here to-day but I bet by this time he has got orders from Callahan to let me rest and to not give me no more work because suppose even if I did not start the game to-morrow I probily will have to finish it.

Gleason has been sticking round me like as if I had a million bucks

◆ *champions of the Western League last year.*—Denver led the Western League for virtually all of the 1913 season and won the pennant by a ten-game margin. In 1914, however, the team was to finish second to Sioux City.

◆ *the Epworth League*—The temperance organization of the Methodist Church.

or something. I can't even sit down and smoke a cigar but what he is there to knock the ashes off of it. He is O. K. and good-hearted if he is a little rough and keeps hitting me in the stumach but I wish he would leave me alone sometimes espesially at meals. He was in to breakfast with me this A. M. and after I got threw I snuck off down the street and got something to eat. That is not right because it costs me money when I have to go away from the hotel and eat and what right has he got to try and help me order my meals? Because he don't know what I want and what my stumach wants.

My stumach don't want to have him punching it all the time but he keeps on doing it. So that shows he don't know what is good for me. But he is a old man Al otherwise I would not stand for the stuff he pulls. The 1st thing I am going to do when we get to Chi is I am going to a resturunt somewheres and get a good meal where Gleason or no one else can't get at me. I know allready what I am going to eat and that is a big stake and a apple pie and that is not all.

Well Al watch the papers and you will see what I done to that Cleveland Club and I hope Lajoie and Jackson is both in good shape because I don't want to pick on no cripples. *Your pal, Jack.*

CHICAGO, ILLINOIS, APRIL 16.

Old Pal: Yesterday was the 1st pay day old pal and I know I promised to pay you what I owe you and it is $75.00 because when I asked you for $35.00 before I went West you only sent me $25.00 which makes the hole sum $75.00. Well Al I can't pay you now because the pay we drawed was only for 4 days and did not amount to nothing and I had to buy a meal ticket and fix up about my room rent.

And then they is another thing Al which I will tell you about. I come into the clubhouse the day the season opened and the 1st guy I seen was Allen. I was going up to bust him but he come up and held his hand out and what was they for me to do but shake hands with him if he is going to be yellow like that? He says Well Jack I am glad they did not send you to Milwaukee and I bet you will have a big year. I says Yes I will have a big year O. K. if you don't sick another 1 of your sister-in-laws on to me. He says Oh don't let they be no hard feelings about that. You know it was not no fault of mine and I bet if you was to write to Florrie everything could be fixed up O. K.

I says I don't want to write to no Florrie but I will get a attorney at law to write to her. He says You don't even know where she is at and I says I don't care where she is at. Where is she? He says She is down to her home in Waco, Texas, and if I was you I would write to her myself and not let no attorney at law write to her because that would get her mad and besides what do you want a attorney at law to write to her about? I says I am going to sew her for a bill of divorce.

Then he says On what grounds? and I says Dessertion. He says You better not do no such thing or she will sew you for a bill of divorce for none support and then you will look like a cheap guy. I says I don't care what I look like. So you see Al I had to send Florrie $10.00 or maybe she would be mean enough to sew me for a bill of divorce on the ground of none support and that would make me look bad.

Well Al, Allen told me his wife wanted to talk to me and try and fix things up between I and Florrie but I give him to understand that I would not stand for no meeting with his wife and he says Well suit yourself about that but they is no reason you and I should quarrel.

You see Al he don't want no mix-up with me because he knows he could not get nothing but the worst of it. I will be friends with him but I won't have nothing to do with Marie because if it had not of been for she and Florrie I would have money in the bank besides not being in no danger of getting sewed for none support.

I guess you must have read about Joe Benz getting married and I ◆ guess he must of got a good wife and 1 that don't bother him all the time because he pitched the opening game and shut Cleveland out with 2 hits. He was pretty good Al, better than I ever seen him and they was a couple of times when his fast ball was pretty near as fast as mine.

I have not worked yet Al and I asked Callahan to-day what was the matter and he says I was waiting for you to get in shape. I says I am in shape now and I notice that when I was pitching in practice this A. M. they did not hit nothing out of the infield. He says That was because you are so spread out that they could not get nothing past you. He says The way you are now you cover more ground than the grand stand. I says Is that so? And he walked away.

We go out on a trip to Cleveland and Detroit and St. Louis in a few days and maybe I will take my regular turn then because the other pitchers has been getting away lucky because most of the hitters has

---

◆ *Joe Benz getting married*—Benz married Alice Leddy of Chicago at Our Lady of Mercy Chapel on West Jackson Boulevard, Chicago, on March 10, 1914. He did not, as stated, pitch the opener. Rather, Scott opened the season by beating Cleveland, 5–2, on April 14. Benz made his first start of the season on April 16, defeating Cleveland, 4–0, on four hits.

not got their batting eye as yet but wait till they begin hitting and then it will take a man like I to stop them.

The 1st of May is our next pay day Al and then I will have enough money so as I can send you the $75.00. *Your pal, Jack.*

DETROIT, MICHIGAN, APRIL 28. ◆

Friend Al: What do you think of a rotten manager that bawls me out and fines me $50.00 for loosing a 1 to 0 game in 10 innings when it was my 1st start this season? And no wonder I was a little wild in the 10th when I had not had no chance to work and get control. I got a good notion to quit this rotten club and jump to the Federals where a man gets some kind of treatment. Callahan says I throwed the game away on purpose but I did not do no such a thing Al because when I throwed that ball at Joe Hill's head I forgot that the bases was full and besides if Gleason had not of starved me to death the ball that hit him in the head would of killed him.

And how could a man go to 1st base and the winning run be forced in if he was dead which he should ought to of been the lucky left-handed stiff if I had of had my full strenth to put on my fast one instead of being ½ starved to death and weak. But I guess I better tell you how it come off. The papers will get it all wrong like they generally allways does.

Callahan asked me this A. M. if I thought I was hard enough to work and I was tickled to death, because I seen he was going to give me a chance. I told him Sure I was in good shape and if them Tigers scored a run off of me he could keep me setting on the bench the rest of the summer. So he says All right I am going to start you and if you go good maybe Gleason will let you eat some supper.

Well Al when I begin warming up I happened to look up in the grand stand and who do you think I seen? Nobody but Violet. She smiled when she seen me but I bet she felt more like crying. Well I smiled back at her because she probily would of broke down and made a seen or something if I had not of. They was not nobody warming up for Detroit when I begin warming up but pretty soon I looked over to their bench and Joe Hill Violet's husband was warming up. I says to myself Well here is where I show that bird up if they got nerve enough to start him against me but probily Jennings don't want to waste no real pitcher on this game which he knows we got cinched and

◆ *April 28*—On this date the Tigers beat the White Sox at Detroit, 4–1.

we would of had it cinched Al if they had of got a couple runs or even 1 run for me.

Well, Jennings come passed our bench just like he allways does and tried to pull some of his funny stuff. He says Hello are you still in the league? I says Yes but I come pretty near not being. I came pretty near being with Detroit. I wish you could of heard Gleason and Callahan laugh when I pulled that one on him. He says something back but it was not no hot comeback like mine.

Well Al if I had of had any work and my regular control I guess I would of pitched a 0 hit game because the only time they could touch me was when I had to ease up to get them over. Cobb was out of the game and they told me he was sick but I guess the truth is that he knowed I was going to pitch. Crawford got a couple of lucky scratch hits off of me because I got in the hole to him and had to let up. But the way that lucky left-handed Hill got by was something awful and if I was as lucky as him I would quit pitching and shoot craps or something.

Our club can't hit nothing anyway. But batting against this bird was ◆ just like hitting fungos. His curve ball broke about ½ a inch and you could of wrote your name and address on his fast one while it was comeing up there. He had good control but who would not when they put nothing on the ball?

Well Al we could not get started against the lucky stiff and they could not do nothing with me even if my suport was rotten and I give a couple or 3 or 4 bases on balls but when they was men waiting to score I zipped them threw there so as they could not see them let alone hit them. Every time I come to the bench between innings I looked up to where Violet was setting and give her a smile and she smiled back and once I seen her clapping her hands at me after I had made Moriarty pop up in the pinch.

Well we come along to the 10th inning, 0 and 0, and all of a sudden we got after him. Bodie hits one and Schalk gets 2 strikes and 2 balls and then singles. Callahan tells Alcock to bunt and he does it but Hill ◆ sprawls all over himself like the big boob he is and the bases is full

---

◆ *Our club can't hit nothing anyway.*—In 1914 the White Sox hit .239, second-worst in the American League.

◆ *Alcock*—John Forbes "Scotty" Alcock (1885–1973), an infielder who played in 54 games for the White Sox in 1914. He hit .173 in this, his only major league season.

with nobody down. Well Gleason and Callahan argude about should they send somebody up for me or let me go up there and I says Let me go up there because I can murder this bird and Callahan says Well they is nobody out so go up and take a wallop.

Honest Al if this guy had of had anything at all I would of hit 1 out of the park, but he did not have even a glove. And how can a man hit pitching which is not no pitching at all but just slopping them up? When I went up there I hollered to him and says Stick 1 over here now you yellow stiff. And he says Yes I can stick them over allright and that is where I got something on you.

Well Al I hit a foul off of him that would of been a fare ball and broke up the game if the wind had not of been against it. Then I swung and missed a curve that I don't see how I missed it. The next 1 was a yard outside and this Evans calls it a strike. He has had it in for me ever since last year when he tried to get funny with me and I says something back to him that stung him. So he calls this 3d strike on me and I felt like murdering him. But what is the use?

I throwed down my bat and come back to the bench and I was glad Callahan and Gleason was out on the coaching line or they probily would of said something to me and I would of cut loose and beat them up. Well Al Weaver and Blackburne looked like a couple of rums up ◆ there and we don't score where we ought to of had 3 or 4 runs with any kind of hitting.

I would of been all O. K. in spite of that peace of rotten luck if this big Hill had of walked to the bench and not said nothing like a real pitcher. But what does he do but wait out there till I start for the box and I says Get on to the bench you lucky stiff or do you want me to hand you something? He says I don't want nothing more of yourn. I allready got your girl and your goat.

Well Al what do you think of a man that would say a thing like that? And nobody but a left-hander could of. If I had of had a gun I would of killed him deader than a doornail or something. He starts for the bench and I hollered at him Wait till you get up to that plate and then I am going to bean you.

◆ *Blackburne*—Russell Aubrey "Lena" Blackburne (1886–1968), a light-hitting infielder who had replaced Harry Lord as the White Sox second baseman when Lord jumped to the Federal League. Playing in 144 games, Blackburne batted only .222 in 1914. His lifetime average was even worse, .214 in 548 games over the course of eight seasons. He was later a coach for many years, and managed the White Sox in 1928 and 1929. See Jack Kavanagh, "Lena Blackburne," *The Ballplayers*, p. 81.

Honest Al I was so mad I could not see the plate or nothing. I don't even know who it was come up to bat 1st but whoever it was I hit him in the arm and he walks to first base. The next guy bunts and Chase tries to pull off 1 of them plays of hisn instead of playing safe and he don't get nobody. Well I kept getting madder and madder and I walks Stanage who if I had of been myself could not foul me.

Callahan has Scotty warming up and Gleason runs out from the bench and tells me I am threw but Callahan says Wait a minute he is going to let Hill hit and this big stiff ought to be able to get him out of the way and that will give Scotty a chance to get warm. Gleason says You better not take a chance because the big busher is hogwild, and they kept argueing till I got sick of listening to them and I went back to the box and got ready to pitch. But when I seen this Hill up there I forgot all about the ball game and I cut loose at his bean.

Well Al my control was all O. K. this time and I catched him square on the fourhead and he dropped like as if he had been shot. But pretty soon he gets up and gives me the laugh and runs to first base. I did not know the game was over till Weaver come up and pulled me off the field. But if I had not of been ½ starved to death and weak so as I could not put all my stuff on the ball you can bet that Hill never would of ran to first base and Violet would of been a widow and probily a lot better off than she is now. At that I never should ought to of tried to kill a left-hander by hitting him in the head.

Well Al they jumped all over me in the clubhouse and I had to hold myself back or I would of gave somebody the beating of their life. Callahan tells me I am fined $50.00 and suspended without no pay. I asked him What for and he says They would not be no use in telling you because you have not got no brains. I says Yes I have to got some brains and he says Yes but they is in your stumach. And then he says I wish we had of sent you to Milwaukee and I come back at him. I says I wish you had of.

Well Al I guess they is no chance of getting square treatment on this club and you won't be supprised if you hear of me jumping to the Federals where a man is treated like a man and not like no white slave.

Yours truly, Jack.

CHICAGO, ILLINOIS, MAY 2.

Al: I have got to disappoint you again Al. When I got up to get my pay yesterday they held out $150.00 on me. $50.00 of it is what I was fined for loosing 1 to 0 10-inning game in Detroit when I was so weak that I should ought never to of been sent in there and the $100.00 is the advance money that I drawed last winter and which I had forgot all about and the club would of forgot about it to if they was not so tight-fisted.

So you see all I get for 2 weeks' pay is about $80.00 and I sent $25.00 to Florrie so she can't come no none-support business on me.

I am still suspended Al and not drawing no pay now and I got a notion to hire a attorney at law and force them to pay my salery or else jump to the Federals where a man gets good treatment.

Allen is still after me to come over to his flat some night and see his wife and let her talk to me about Florrie but what do I want to talk about Florrie for or talk about nothing to a nut left-hander's wife?

The Detroit Club is here and Cobb is playing because he knows I am suspended but I wish Callahan would call it off and let me work against them and I would certainly love to work against this Joe Hill again and I bet they would be a different story this time because I been getting something to eat since we been home and I got back most of my strenth. *Your old pal, Jack.*

CHICAGO, ILLINOIS, MAY 5.

Friend Al: Well Al if you been reading the papers you will know before this letter is received what I done. Before the Detroit Club come here Joe Hill had win 4 strate but he has not win no 5 strate or won't neither Al because I put a crimp in his winning streek just like I knowed I would do if I got a chance when I was feeling good and had all my strenth. Callahan asked me yesterday A. M. if I thought I had enough rest and I says Sure because I did not need no rest in the 1st place. Well, he says, I thought maybe if I layed you off a few days you would do some thinking and if you done some thinking once in a while you would be a better pitcher.

Well anyway I worked and I wish you could of saw them Tigers trying to hit me Cobb and Crawford incluseive. The 1st time Cobb come up Weaver catched a lucky line drive off of him and the next time I eased up a little and Collins run back and took a fly ball off of the fence. But the other times he come up he looked like a sucker eccept when he come up in the 8th and then he beat out a bunt but allmost anybody is liable to do that once in a while.

Crawford got a scratch hit between Chase and Blackburne in the 2d inning and in the 4th he was gave a three-base hit by this Evans who should ought to be writeing for the papers instead of trying to umpire. The ball was 2 feet foul and I bet Crawford will tell you the same thing if you ask him. But what I done to this Hill was awful. I give him my curve twice when he was up there in the 3d and he missed it a foot. Then I come with my fast ball right past his nose and I bet if he had not of ducked it would of drove that big horn of hisn clear up in the press box where them rotten reporters sits and smokes their hops. Then when he was looking for another fast one I slopped up my slow one and he is still swinging at it yet.

But the best of it was that I practally won my own game. Bodie and Schalk was on when I come up in the 5th and Hill hollers to me and says I guess this is where I shoot one of them bean balls. I says Go ahead and shoot and if you hit me in the head and I ever find it out I will write and tell your wife what happened to you. You see what I was getting at Al. I was insinuateing that if he beaned me with his fast one I would not never know nothing about it if somebody did not tell me because his fast one is not fast enough to hurt nobody even if it should hit them in the head. So I says to him Go ahead and shoot and if you hit me in the head and I ever find it out I will write and tell your wife what happened to you. See, Al?

Of coarse you could not hire me to write to Violet but I did not mean that part of it in ernest. Well sure enough he shot at my bean and I ducked out of the way though if it had of hit me it could not of did no more than tickle. He takes 2 more shots and misses me and then Jennings hollers from the bench What are you doing pitching or trying to win a cigar? So then Hill sees what a monkey he is makeing out of himself and tries to get one over, but I have him 3 balls and nothing and what I done to that groover was a plenty. She went over Bush's head like a bullet and got between Cobb and Veach and goes clear to the fence. Bodie and Schalk scores and I would of scored to if anybody else besides Cobb had of been chaseing the ball. I got 2 bases and Weaver scores me with another wallop.

Say, I wish I could of heard what they said to that baby on the bench. Callahan was tickled to death and he says Maybe I will give you back that $50.00 if you keep that stuff up. I guess I will get that $50.00 back next pay day and if I do Al I will pay you the hole $75.00.

Well Al I beat them 5 to 4 and with good support I would of held them to 1 run but what do I care as long as I beat them? I wish though that Violet could of been there and saw it. *Yours truly, Jack.*

CHICAGO, ILLINOIS, MAY 29.

Old Pal: Well Al I have not wrote to you for a long while but it is not because I have forgot you and to show I have not forgot you I am incloseing the $75.00 which I owe you. It is a money order Al and you can get it cashed by takeing it to Joe Higgins at the P. O.

Since I wrote to you Al I been East with the club and I guess you know what I done in the East. The Athaletics did not have no right to win that 1 game off of me and I will get them when they come here the week after next. I beat Boston and just as good as beat New York twice because I beat them 1 game all alone and then saved the other for Eddie Cicotte in the 9th inning and shut out the Washington Club and would of did the same thing if Johnson had of been working against me instead of this left-handed stiff Boehling. ◆

Speaking of left-handers Allen has been going rotten and I would not be supprised if they sent him to Milwaukee or Frisco or somewheres.

But I got bigger news than that for you Al. Florrie is back and we are liveing together in the spair room at Allen's flat so I hope they don't send him to Milwaukee or nowheres else because it is not costing us nothing for room rent and this is no more than right after the way the Allens grafted off of us all last winter.

I bet you will be supprised to know that I and Florrie has made it up and they is a secret about it Al which I can't tell you now but maybe next month I will tell you and then you will be more supprised than ever. It is about I and Florrie and somebody else. But that is all I can tell you now.

We got in this A. M. Al and when I got to my room they was a slip of paper there telling me to call up a phone number so I called it up and it was Allen's flat and Marie answered the phone. And when I reckonized her voice I was going to hang up the phone but she says Wait a minute somebody wants to talk to you. And then Florrie come to the phone and I was going to hang up the phone again when she pulled this secret on me that I was telling you about.

So it is all fixed up between us Al and I wish I could tell you the secret but that will come later. I have tooken my baggage over to

---

◆ *Boehling*—John Joseph Boehling (1891–1941), the Senators leading lefthander of the period. At 12–8 he was the Senators fourth-best pitcher in 1914. With the team from 1912 to 1916, and with Cleveland from 1916 to 1920, Boehling won 53 and lost 49. See Jack Kavanagh, "Joe Boehling," *The Ballplayers*, p. 87.

Keefe is ungenerous not to mention the two major events of this period. On May 14, 1914, in Washington, Jim Scott held the Senators hitless for nine innings, but lost on two hits in the tenth, 1–0, and on May 30 Joe Benz was to pitch a no-hitter against Cleveland in Chicago, winning 6–1.

Allen's and I am there now writeing to you while Florrie is asleep. And after a while I am going out and mail this letter and get a glass of beer because I think I have got 1 comeing now on account of this secret. Florrie says she is sorry for the way she treated me and she cried when she seen me. So what is the use of me being nasty Al? And let bygones be bygones. *Your pal, Jack.*

CHICAGO, ILLINOIS, JUNE 16. ◆

Friend Al: Al I beat the Athaletics 2 to 1 to-day but I am writeing to you to give you the supprise of your life. Old pal I got a baby and he is a boy and we are going to name him Allen which Florrie thinks is after his uncle and aunt Allen but which is after you old pal. And she can call him Allen but I will call him Al because I don't never go back on my old pals. The baby was born over to the hospital and it is going to cost me a bunch of money but I should not worry. This is the secret I was going to tell you Al and I am the happyest man in the world and I bet you are most as tickled to death to hear about it as I am.

The baby was born just about the time I was makeing McInnis look ◆ like a sucker in the pinch but they did not tell me nothing about it till after the game and then they give me a phone messige in the clubhouse. I went right over there and everything was all O. K. Little Al is a homely little skate but I guess all babys is homely and don't have no looks till they get older and maybe he will look like Florrie or I and then I won't have no kick comeing.

Be sure and tell Bertha the good news and tell her everything has came out all right eccept that the rent man is still after me about that flat I had last winter. And I am still paying the old man $10.00 a month for that house you got for me and which has not never done me no good. But I should not worry about money when I got a real family. Do you get that Al, a real family?

◆ *June 16*—On this date the Athletics defeated the White Sox, 10–7.

◆ *McInnis*—John Phalen "Stuffy" McInnis (1890–1960), first baseman of the Athletics from 1909 to 1917. Keefe may reasonably have taken pride in retiring McInnis in a pinch situation, for the star infielder was in the process of hitting .314 and driving in 95 runs for the 1914 season. In 19 years with the Athletics, Cleveland, both Boston clubs, Pittsburgh, and the Phillies, McInnis hit .308 in 2,128 games, making 2,406 hits. He managed the Phillies to a last-place finish in 1927. He was later baseball coach at Norwich and Harvard universities. Remarkably, McInnis is not a member of the Baseball Hall of Fame. See Joseph Lawler, "John Phalen McInnis," *Biographical Dictionary of American Sports: Baseball*, pp. 357–58.

Well Al I am to happy to do no more writeing to-night but I wanted you to be the 1st to get the news and I would of sent you a telegram only I did not want to scare you. *Your pal, Jack.*

CHICAGO, ILLINOIS, JULY 2.

Old Pal: Well old pal I just come back from St. Louis this A. M. and found things in pretty fare shape. Florrie and the baby is out to Allen's and we will stay there till I can find another place. The Dr. was out to look at the baby this A. M. and the baby was waveing his arm round in the air. And Florrie asked was they something the matter with him that he kept waveing his arm. And the Dr. says No he was just getting his exercise.

Well Al I noticed that he never waved his right arm but kept waveing his left arm and I asked the Dr. why was that. Then the Dr. says I guess he must be left-handed. That made me sore and I says I guess you doctors don't know it all. And then I turned round and beat it out of the room.

Well Al it would be just my luck to have him left-handed and Florrie should ought to of knew better than to name him after Allen. I am going to hire another Dr. and see what he has to say because they must be some way of fixing babys so as they won't be left-handed. And if nessary I will cut his left arm off of him. Of coarse I would not do that Al. But how would I feel if a boy of mine turned out like Allen and Joe Hill and some of them other nuts?

We have a game with St. Louis to-morrow and a double header on the 4th of July. I guess probily Callahan will work me in one of the ◆ 4th of July games on account of the holiday crowd. *Your pal, Jack.*

P.S. Maybe I should ought to leave my kid left-handed so as he can have some of their luck. The lucky stiffs.

◆ *the 4th of July*—The White Sox were, in fact, scheduled to play the Browns in Chicago on July 3 and in a doubleheader on July 4. On July 3 the White Sox won, 3–2, and on July 4 won both games, 4–3 and 9–0.

The Busher's Kid

CHICAGO, ILLINOIS, JULY 31.

Friend Al: Well Al what do you think of little Al now? But I guess I better tell you first what he done. Maybe you won't believe what I am telling you but did you ever catch me telling you a lie? I guess you know you did not Al. Well we got back from the East this A. M. and I ◆ don't have to tell you we had a rotten trip and if it had not of been for me beating Boston once and the Athaletics two times we would of been ashamed to come home.

I guess these here other pitchers thought we was haveing a vacation and when they go up in the office to-morrow to get there checks they should ought to be arrested if they take them. I would not go nowheres near Comiskey if I had not of did better than them others but I can go and get my pay and feel all O. K. about it because I done something to ern it.

Me loseing that game in Washington was a crime and Callahan says so himself. This here Weaver throwed it away for me and I would not

---

"The Busher's Kid," the fifth of the stories later collected as *You Know Me Al*, was published in *The Saturday Evening Post*, CLXXXVII (October 3, 1914), 20–22, 53–54.

◆ *we got back from the East this* A. M.—Rather, the team had been in a home stand against eastern clubs since July 25.

◇ *Scott*—Death Valley Jim Scott warming up at the Polo Grounds, ca. 1912. (George E. Brace collection)

be surprised if he done it from spitework because him and Scott is pals and probily he did not want to see me winning all them games when Scott was getting knocked out of the box. And no wonder when ◆◇ he has not got no stuff. I wish I knowed for sure that Weaver was throwing me down and if I knowed for sure I would put him in a hospittal or somewheres.

But I was going to tell you what the kid done Al. So here goes. We are still liveing at Allen's and his wife. So I and him come home together from the train. Well Florrie and Marie was both up and the baby was up too—that is he was not up but he was woke up. I beat it right into the room where he was at and Florrie come in with me. I says Hello Al and what do you suppose he done. Well Al he did not

◆ *Scott was getting knocked out of the box.*—Scott was, indeed, having trouble finishing games. In 1914 he pitched only 12 complete games in 33 starts, a poor performance by the standards of the time.

say Hello pa or nothing like that because he is not only one month old. But he smiled at me just like as if he was glad to see me and I guess maybe he was at that.

I was tickled to death and I says to Florrie Did you see that. And she says See what. I says The baby smiled at me. Then she says They is something the matter with his stumach. I says I suppose because a baby smiles that is a sign they is something the matter with his stumach and if he had the toothacke he would laugh. She says You think your smart but I am telling you that he was not smileing at all but he was makeing a face because they is something the matter with his stumach. I says I guess I know the difference if somebody is smileing or makeing a face. And she says I guess you don't know nothing about babys because you never had none before. I says How many have you had. And then she got sore and beat it out of the room.

I did not care because I wanted to be in there alone with him and see would he smile at me again. And sure enough Al he did. Then I called Allen in and when the baby seen him he begin to cry. So you see I was right and Florrie was wrong. It don't take a man no time at all to get wise to these babys and it don't take them long to know if a man is there father or there uncle.

When he begin to cry I chased Allen out of the room and called Florrie because she should ought to know by this time how to make him stop crying. But she was still sore and she says Let him cry or if you know so much about babys make him stop yourself. I says Maybe he is sick. And she says I was just telling you that he had a pane in his stumach or he would not of made that face and that you said was smileing at you.

I says Do you think we should ought to call the doctor but she says No if you call the doctor every time he has the stumach acke you might just as well tell him he should bring his trunk along and stay here. She says All babys have collect and they is not no use fussing about it but come and get your breakfast.

Well Al I did not injoy my breakfast because the baby was crying all the time and I knowed he probily wanted I should come in and visit with him. So I just eat the prunes and drunk a little coffee and did not wait for the rest of it and sure enough when I went back in our room and started talking to him he started smileing again and pretty soon he went to sleep so you see Al he was smileing and not makeing no face and that was a hole lot of bunk about him haveing the collect. But I don't suppose I should ought to find fault with Florrie for not knowing no better because she has not never had no babys before but still and all I should think she should ought to of learned something about them by this time or ask somebody.

Well Al little Al is woke up again and is crying and I just about got time to fix him up and get him asleep again and then I will have to go to the ball park because we got a poseponed game to play with ◆ Detroit and Callahan will probily want me to work though I pitched the next to the last game in New York and would of gave them a good beating eccept for Schalk dropping that ball at the plate but I got it on these Detroit babys and when my name is announced to pitch they feel like forfiting the game. I won't try for no strike-out record because I want them to hit the first ball and get the game over with quick so as I can get back here and take care of little Al. *Your pal, Jack.*

P. S. Babys is great stuff Al and if I was you I would not wait no longer but would hurry up and adopt 1 somewheres.

CHICAGO, ILLINOIS, AUGUST 15.

Old Pal: What do you think Al. Kid Gleason is comeing over to the flat and look at the baby the day after to-morrow when we don't have no game skeduled but we have to practice in the A. M. because we been going so rotten. I had a hard time makeing him promise to come but he is comeing and I bet he will be glad he come when he has came. I says to him in the clubhouse Do you want to see a real baby? And he says You're real enough for me Boy.

I says No I am talking about babys. He says Oh I thought you was talking about ice-cream soda or something. I says No I want you to come over to the flat to-morrow and take a look at my kid and tell me what you think of him. He says I can tell you what I think of him without takeing no look at him. I think he is out of luck. I says What do you mean out of luck. But he just laughed and would not say no more.

I asked him again would he come over to the flat and look at the baby and he says he had troubles enough without that and kidded along for a while but finally he seen I was in ernest and then he says he would come if I would keep the missus out of the room while he was there because he says if she seen him she would probily be sorry she married me.

He was just jokeing and I did not take no eccepshun to his remarks

◆ *we got a poseponed game to play with Detroit*—Rather, on July 31, 1914, the White Sox played Boston in Chicago.

because Florrie could not never fall for him after seeing me because he is not no big strapping man like I am but a little runt and look at ◆ how old he is. But I am glad he is comeing because he will think more of me when he sees what a fine baby I got though he thinks a hole lot of me now because look what I done for the club and where would they be at if I had jumped to the Federal like I once thought I would. I will tell you what he says about little Al and I bet he will say he never seen no prettyer baby but even if he don't say nothing at all I will know he is kidding.

The Boston Club comes here to-morrow and plays 4 days includeing ◆ the day after to-morrow when they is not no game. So on account of the off day maybe I will work twice against them and if I do they will wish the grounds had of burned down. *Yours truly, Jack.*

CHICAGO, ILLINOIS, AUGUST 17.

Al: Well old pal what did I tell you about what I would do to that Boston Club? And now Al I have beat every club in the league this year because yesterday was the first time I beat the Boston Club this year but now I have beat all of them and most of them severel times.

This should ought to of gave me a record of 16 wins and 0 defeats because the only game I lost was throwed away behind me but instead of that my record is 10 games win and 6 defeats and that don't include the games I finished up and helped the other boys win which is about 6 more alltogether but what do I care about my record Al? because I am not the kind of man that is allways thinking about there record and playing for there record while I am satisfied if I give the club the best I got and if I win all O. K. And if I lose who's fault is it. Not mine Al.

I asked Callahan would he let me work against the Boston Club again before they go away and he says I guess I will have to because you are going better than anybody else on the club. So you see Al he ◆

◆ *a little runt and look at how old he is*—Gleason was 5′7″, 158 pounds, and at the time, 47 years old.

◆ *The Boston Club comes here to-morrow and plays 4 days includeing the day after to-morrow when they is not no game.*—This sentence is presumably its own justification. The White Sox were actually in St. Louis on August 15, and were to proceed to Boston to play on August 18.

◆ *you are going better than anybody else on the club.*—The White Sox were, in fact, going badly. After playing over .500 ball for the first half of the season, the team had sunk to fifth place and .495 on this date.

is beginning to appresiate my work and from now on I will pitch in my regular turn and a hole lot offtener then that and probily Comiskey will see the stuff I am made from and will raise my salery next year even if he has got me signed for 3 years for the same salery I am getting now.

But all that is not what I was going to tell you Al and what I was going to tell you was about Gleason comeing to see the baby and what he thought about him. I sent Florrie and Marie downtown and says I would take care of little Al and they was glad to go because Florrie says she should ought to buy some new shoes though I don't see what she wants of no new shoes when she is going to be tied up in the flat for a long time yet on account of the baby and nobody cares if she wears shoes in the flat or goes round in her bear feet. But I was glad to get rid of the both of them for a while because little Al acts better when they is not no women round and you can't blame him.

The baby was woke up when Gleason come in and I and him went right in the room where he was laying. Gleason takes a look at him and says Well that is a mighty fine baby and you must of boughten him. I says What do you mean? And he says I don't believe he is your own baby because he looks humaner than most babys. And I says Why should not he look human. And he says Why should he.

Then he goes to work and picks the baby right up and I was a-scared he would drop him because even I have not never picked him up though I am his father and would be a-scared of hurting him. I says Here, don't pick him up and he says Why not? He says Are you going to leave him on that there bed the rest of his life? I says No but you don't know how to handle him. He says I have handled a hole lot bigger babys than him or else Callahan would not keep me.

Then he starts patting the baby's head and I says Here, don't do that because he has got a soft spot in his head and you might hit it. He says I thought he was your baby and I says Well he is my baby and he says Well then they can't be no soft spot in his head. Then he lays little Al down because he seen I was in ernest and as soon as he lays him down the baby begins to cry. Then Gleason says See he don't want me to lay him down and I says Maybe he has got a pane in his stumach and he says I would not be supprised because he just took a good look at his father.

But little Al did not act like as if he had a pane in his stumach and he kept sticking his finger in his mouth and crying. And Gleason says He acts like as if he had a toothacke. I says How could he have a toothacke when he has not got no teeth? He says That is easy. I have saw a lot of pitchers complane that there arm was sore when they did not have no arm.

Then he asked me what was the baby's name and I told him Allen but that he was not named after my brother-in-law Allen. And Gleason says I should hope not. I should hope you would have better sense than to name him after a left-hander. So you see Al he don't like them no better then I do even if he does jolly Allen and Russell along and make them think they can pitch.

Pretty soon he says What are you going to make out of him, a ball player? I says Yes I am going to make a hitter out of him so as he can join the White Sox and then maybe they will get a couple of runs once in a while. He says If I was you I would let him pitch and then you won't have to give him no educasion. Besides, he says, he looks now like he would divellop into a grate spitter.

Well I happened to look out of the window and seen Florrie and Marie comeing acrost Indiana Avenue and I told Gleason about it. And you ought to of seen him run. I asked him what was his hurry and he says it was in his contract that he was not to talk to no women but I knowed he was kidding because I allready seen him talking to severel of the players' wifes when they was on trips with us and they acted like as if they thought he was a regular comeedion though they really is not nothing funny about what he says only it is easy to make women laugh when they have not got no grouch on about something.

Well Al I am glad Gleason has saw the baby and maybe he will fix it with Callahan so as I won't have to go to morning practice every A. M. because I should ought to be home takeing care of little Al when Florrie is washing the dishs or helping Marie round the house. And besides why should I wear myself all out in practice because I don't need to practice pitching and I could hit as well as the rest of the men on our club if I never seen no practice.

After we get threw with Boston, Washington comes here and then we go to St. Louis and Cleveland and then come home and then go East again. And after that we are pretty near threw eccept the city serious. Callahan is not going to work me no more after I beat Boston again till it is this here Johnson's turn to pitch for Washington. And I hope it is not his turn to work the 1st game of the serious because then I would not have no rest between the last game against Boston and the 1st game against Washington.

But rest or no rest I will work against this here Johnson and show him up for giveing me that trimming in Washington, the lucky stiff. I wish I had a team like the Athaletics behind me and I would loose about 1 game every 6 years and then they would have to get all the best of it from these rotten umpires. *Your pal, Jack.*

NEW YORK, NEW YORK, SEPTEMBER 16.

Friend Al: Al it is not no fun running round the country no more and I wish this dam trip was over so as I could go home and see how little Al is getting along because Florrie has not wrote since we was in Philly which was the first stop on this trip. I am a-scared they is something the matter with the little fellow or else she would of wrote but then if they was something the matter with him she would of sent me a telegram or something and let me know.

So I guess they can't be nothing the matter with him. Still and all I don't see why she has not wrote when she knows or should ought to know that I would be worrying about the baby. If I don't get no letter to-morrow I am going to send her a telegram and ask her what is the matter with him because I am positive she would of wrote if they was not something the matter with him.

The boys has been trying to get me to go out nights and see a show or something but I have not got no heart to go to shows. And besides Callahan has not gave us no pass to no show on this trip. I guess probily he is sore on account of the rotten way the club has been going but still he should ought not to be sore on me because I have win 3 out of my last 4 games and would of win the other if he had not of started me against them with only 1 day's rest and the Athaletics at that, who a man should ought not to pitch against if he don't feel good.

I asked Allen if he had heard from Marie and he says Yes he did but she did not say nothing about little Al eccept that he was keeping her awake nights balling. So maybe Al if little Al is balling they is something wrong with him. I am going to send Florrie a telegram to-morrow—that is if I don't get no letter.

If they is something the matter with him I will ask Callahan to send me home and he won't want to do it neither because who else has he got that is a regular winner. But if little Al is sick and Callahan won't let me go home I will go home anyway. You know me Al.

Yours truly, Jack.

BOSTON, MASSACHUSETTS, SEPTEMBER 24.

Al: I bet if Florrie was a man she would be a left-hander. What do you think she done now Al? I sent her a telegram from New York when I did not get no letter from her and she did not pay no atension to the telegram. Then when we got up here I sent her another telegram and it was not more than five minutes after I sent the 2d telegram till I got a letter from her. And it said the baby was all O. K. but she had been so busy takeing care of him that she had not had no time to write.

Well when I got the letter I chased out to see if I could catch the boy who had took my telegram but he had went allready so I was spending $.60 for nothing. Then what does Florrie do but send me a telegram after she got my second telegram and tell me that little Al is all O. K., which I knowed all about then because I had just got her letter. And she sent her telegram c. o. d. and I had to pay for it at this end because she had not paid for it and that was $.60 more but I bet if I had of knew what was in the telegram before I read it I would of told the boy to keep it and would not of gave him no $.60 but how did I know if little Al might not of tooken sick after Florrie had wrote the letter?

I am going to write and ask her if she is trying to send us both to the Poor House or somewheres with her telegrams. I don't care nothing about the $.60 but I like to see a woman use a little judgement though I guess that is impossable.

It is my turn to work to-day and to-night we start West but we have got to stop off at Cleveland on the way. I have got a nosion to ask Callahan to let me go right on threw to Chi if I win to-day and not stop off at no Cleveland but I guess they would not be no use because I have got that Cleveland Club licked the minute I put on my glove. So probily Callahan will want me with him though it don't make no difference if we win or lose now because we have not got no chance ◆ for the pennant. One man can't win no pennant Al I don't care who he is.

Your pal, Jack.

CHICAGO, ILLINOIS, OCTOBER 2.

Friend Al: Well old pal I am all threw till the city serious and it is all fixed up that I am going to open the serious and pitch 3 of the games if nessary. The club has went to Detroit to wind up the season and ◆ Callahan did not take me along but left me here with a couple other pitchers and Billy Sullivan and told me all as I would have to do was

---

◆ *we have not got no chance for the pennant.*—The White Sox had not been a contender at any time in the season.

◆ *The club has went to Detroit to wind up the season*—Actually, the season ended in Chicago with a series against the Browns on October 2–4.

◇ *Yes I suppose I should ought to give him weeny worst or something*—Drawing by Martin Justice for *The Saturday Evening Post*, October 3, 1914.

go over to the park the next 3 days and warm up a little so as to keep in shape. But I don't need to be in no shape to beat them Cubs Al. But it is a good thing Al that Allen was tooken on the trip to Detroit or I guess I would of killed him. He has not been going good and he has been acting and talking nasty to everybody because he can't win no games.

Well the 1st night we was home after the trip little Al was haveing a bad night and was balling pretty hard and they could not nobody in the flat get no sleep. Florrie says he was haveing the collect and I says Why should he have the collect all the time when he did not drink nothing but milk? She says she guessed the milk did not agree with him and upsetted his stumach. I says Well he must take after his mother if his stumach gets upsetted every time he takes a drink because if he took after his father he could drink a hole lot and not never be effected. She says You should ought to remember he has only got a little stumach and not a great big resservoire. I says Well if the milk don't agree with him why don't you give him something else? She says Yes I suppose I should ought to give him weeny worst or something. ◇

Allen must of heard us talking because he hollered something and I did not hear what it was so I told him to say it over and he says Give the little X-eyed brat poison and we would all be better off. I says You better take poison yourself because maybe a rotten pitcher like you could get by in the league where you're going when you die. Then I says Besides I would rather my baby was X-eyed then to have him left-handed. He says It is better for him that he is X-eyed or else he might get a good look at you and then he would shoot himself. I says Is that so? and he shut up. Little Al is not no more X-eyed than you or I are Al and that was what made me sore because what right did Allen have to talk like that when he knowed he was lying?

Well the next morning Allen nor I did not speak to each other and I seen he was sorry for the way he had talked and I was willing to fix things up because what is the use of staying sore at a man that don't know no better.

But all of a sudden he says When are you going to pay me what you owe me? I says What do you mean? And he says You been liveing here all summer and I been paying all the bills. I says Did not you and Marie ask us to come here and stay with you and it would not cost us nothing. He says Yes but we did not mean it was a life sentence. You are getting more money than me and you don't never spend a nichol. All I have to do is pay the rent and buy your food and it would take a millionare or something to feed you.

Then he says I would not make no holler about your grafting off of me if that brat would shut up nights and give somebody a chance to sleep. I says You should ought to get all the sleep you need on the bench. Besides, I says, who done the grafting all last winter and without no invatation? If he had of said another word I was going to bust him but just then Marie come in and he shut up.

The more I thought about what he said and him a rotten left-hander that should ought to be hussling freiht the more madder I got and if he had of opened his head to me the last day or 2 before he went to Detroit I guess I would of finished him. But Marie stuck pretty close to the both of us when we was together and I guess she knowed they was something in the air and did not want to see her husband get the worst of it though if he was my husband and I was a woman I would push him under a st. car.

But Al I won't even stand for him saying that I am grafting off of him and I and Florrie will get away from here and get a flat of our own as soon as the city serious is over. I would like to bring her and the kid down to Bedford for the winter but she wont listen to that.

I allmost forgot Al to tell you to be sure and thank Bertha for the little dress she made for little Al. I don't know if it will fit him or not because Florrie has not yet tried it on him yet and she says she is going to use it for a dishrag but I guess she is just kidding.

I suppose you seen where Callahan took me out of that game down to Cleveland but it was not because I was not going good Al but it was because Callahan seen he was makeing a mistake wasteing me on that ◆ bunch who allmost any pitcher could beat. They beat us that game at that but only by one run and it was not no fault of mine because I was tooken out before they got the run that give them the game.

Your old pal, Jack.

CHICAGO, ILLINOIS, OCTOBER 4.

Friend Al: Well Al the club winds up the season at Detroit to-morrow and the serious starts the day after to-morrow and I will be in there giveing them a battle. I wish I did not have nobody but the Cubs to pitch against all season and you bet I would have a record that would make Johnson and Mathewson and some of them other swell heads ◆ look like a dirty doose.

I and Florrie and Marie has been haveing a argument about how could Florrie go and see the city serious games when they is not nobody here that can take care of the baby because Marie wants to go and see the games to even though they is not no more chance of Callahan starting Allen than a rabbit or something.

Florrie and Marie says I should ought to hire a nurse to take care of little Al and Florrie got pretty sore when I told her nothing doing because in the first place I can't afford to pay no nurse a salery and in

---

◆ *that bunch who allmost any pitcher could beat.*—The 1914 Cleveland club was, indeed, dismal. It won 51, lost 102, and finished last, 18½ games out of seventh place. The White Sox played at Cleveland September 29–30, losing 10–4 on the 29th and 6–5 in 12 innings on the 30th.

◆ *Mathewson*—Christopher "Christy" Mathewson (1880–1925), leading pitcher of the New York Giants, and along with Walter Johnson one of the two most highly esteemed pitchers of the early twentieth century. Mathewson pitched for the Giants from 1900 until 1916, when he became manager of the Cincinnati Reds. Including one game he pitched and won against his old adversary, Mordecai Brown, while managing the Reds, Mathewson won 373 games and lost 188. Jointly with Grover Cleveland Alexander he holds the National League record for victories. He won 20 or more games 13 times, a record for post-1900 baseball that he holds jointly with Warren Spahn. Mathewson was particularly effective in World Series play. His ten complete games and four shutouts in World Series play remain records. The 1914 season was Mathewson's last as an effective pitcher. That year he posted a 24–13 record, winning 20 or more games for the twelfth consecutive year. In 1915 he was 8–14, and in 1916, 4–4. A poison-gas victim in World War I, he died prematurely of tuberculosis. Mathewson was a charter member of the Baseball Hall of Fame in 1936. See Ring W. Lardner, "Matty," *The American Magazine*, LXXX (August 1915), 26–29; Steven A. Riess, "Christopher Mathewson," *Biographical Dictionary of American Sports: Baseball*, pp. 390–91.

the second place I would not trust no nurse to take care of the baby because how do I know the nurse is not nothing but a grafter or a dope fiend maybe and should ought not to be left with the baby?

Of coarse Florrie wants to see me pitch and a man can't blame her for that but I won't leave my baby with no nurse Al and Florrie will have to stay home and I will tell her what I done when I get there. I might of gave my consent to haveing a nurse at that if it had not of been for the baby getting so sick last night when I was takeing care of him while Florrie and Marie and Allen was out to a show and if I had not of been home they is no telling what would of happened. It is a cinch that none of them bonehead nurses would of knew what to do.

Allen must of been out of his head because right after supper he says he would take the 2 girls to a show. I says All right go on and I will take care of the baby. Then Florrie says Do you think you can take care of him all O. K.? And I says Have not I tooken care of him before allready? Well, she says, I will leave him with you only don't run in to him every time he cries. I says Why not? And she says Because it is good for him to cry. I says You have not got no heart or you would not talk that way.

They all give me the laugh but I let them get away with it because I am not picking no fights with girls and why should I bust this Allen when he don't know no better and has not got no baby himself. And I did not want to do nothing that would stop him takeing the girls to a show because it is time he spent a peace of money on somebody.

Well they all went out and I went in on the bed and played with the baby. I wish you could of saw him Al because he is old enough now to do stunts and he smiled up at me and waved his arms and legs round and made a noise like as if he was trying to say Pa. I did not think Florrie had gave me enough covers so I rapped him up in some more and took a blanket off of the big bed and stuck it round him so as he could not kick his feet out and catch cold.

I thought once or twice he was going off to sleep but all of a sudden he begin to cry and I seen they was something wrong with him. I gave him some hot water but that made him cry again and I thought maybe he was to cold yet so I took another blanket off of Allen's bed and wrapped that round him but he kept on crying and trying to kick inside the blankets. And I seen then that he must have collect or something.

So pretty soon I went to the phone and called up our regular Dr. and it took him pretty near a hour to get there and the baby balling all the time. And when he come he says they was nothing the matter eccept that the baby was to hot and told me to take all them blankets off of him and then soaked me 2 dollars. I had a nosion to bust his jaw. Well pretty soon he beat it and then little Al begin crying again and kept getting worse and worse so finally I got a-scared and run down to the corner where another Dr. is at and I brung him up to see what was the matter but he said he could not see nothing the matter but he did not charge me a cent so I thought he was not no robber like our regular doctor even if he was just as much of a boob.

The baby did not cry none while he was there but the minute he had went he started crying and balling again and I seen they was not no use of fooling no longer so I looked around the house and found the medicine the doctor left for Allen when he had a stumach acke once and I give the baby a little of it in a spoon but I guess he did not like the taste because he hollered like a Indian and finally I could not stand it no longer so I called that second Dr. back again and this time he seen that the baby was sick and asked me what I had gave it and I told him some stumach medicine and he says I was a fool and should ought not to of gave the baby nothing. But while he was talking the baby stopped crying and went off to sleep so you see what I done for him was the right thing to do and them doctors was both off of there nut.

This second Dr. soaked me 2 dollars the 2d time though he had not did no more than when he was there the 1st time and charged me nothing but they is all a bunch of robbers Al and I would just as leave trust a policeman.

Right after the baby went to sleep Florrie and Marie and Allen come home and I told Florrie what had came off but instead of giveing me credit she says If you want to kill him why don't you take a ax? Then Allen butts in and says Why don't you take a ball and throw it at him? Then I got sore and I says Well if I did hit him with a ball I would kill him while if you was to throw that fast ball of yours at him and hit him in the head he would think the musketoes was biteing him and brush them off. But at that, I says, you could not hit him with a ball eccept you was aiming at something else.

I guess they was no comeback to that so him and Marie went to there room. Allen should ought to know better then to try and get the best of me by this time and I would shut up anyway if I was him after getting sent home from Detroit with some of the rest of them when he only worked 3 innings up there and they had to take him out or play the rest of the game by electrick lights.

I wish you could be here for the serious Al but you would have to stay at a hotel because we have not got no spair room and it would cost you a hole lot of money. But you can watch the papers and you will see what I done. *Yours truly, Jack.*

CHICAGO, ILLINOIS, OCTOBER 6.

Dear Old Pal: Probily before you get this letter you will of saw by the paper that we was licked in the first game and that I was tooken out but the papers don't know what really come off so I am going to tell you and you can see for yourself if it was my fault.

I did not never have no more stuff in my life then when I was warming up and I seen the Cubs looking over to our bench and shakeing there heads like they knowed they did not have no chance. O'Day was going to start Cheney who is there best bet and had him ◆ warming up but when he seen the smoke I had when I and Schalk was warming up he changed his mind because what was the use of useing his best pitcher when I had all that stuff and it was a cinch that no club in the world could score a run off of me when I had all that stuff?

So he told a couple others to warm up to and when my name was announced to pitch Cheney went and set on the bench and this here left-hander Pierce was announced for them. ◆

Well Al you will see by the paper where I sent there 1st 3 batters back to the bench to get a drink of water and all 3 of them good

---

◆ *O'Day*—Henry F. "Hank" O'Day (1863–1935), manager of the Cubs in 1914. As a pitcher and occasional utility player, O'Day played with five clubs in seven seasons between 1884 and 1890 in the American Association, National League, and Players League. His pitching record was 71–112. He had managed the Cincinnati Reds in 1912. O'Day is mainly known as an umpire, however, serving in the National League at various times from 1888 to 1926 and in the Players League in 1890. He made the famous call on Fred Merkle of the Giants, declaring him out at second base on September 23, 1908, thus precipitating the playoff by which the Chicago Cubs won the 1908 pennant. See Rich Marazzi, "Hank O'Day," *The Ballplayers*, pp. 817–18.

◆ *Pierce*—George Thomas Pearce (1888–1935), a lefthander who pitched for the Cubs from 1912 to 1916 and for the Cardinals in 1917, amassing a record of 33–27 in 103 games. Considering Pearce's 6–12 record in 1914, he would have been an eccentric choice to open the City Series. In the actual first game of the series on October 8, Scott opposed Larry Cheney. Keefe's spelling of "Pierce" conformed to the typical newspaper practice of the day. See Dennis Bingham, "George Pearce," *The Ballplayers*, p. 850.

hitters Leach and Good and this here Saier that hits a hole lot of home ◆ runs but would not never hit one off of me if I was O. K. Well we scored a couple in our half and the boys on the bench all says Now you got enough to win easy because they won't never score none off of you.

And they was right to because what chance did they have if this thing that I am going to tell you about had not of happened? We goes along seven innings and only 2 of there men had got to 1st base one of them on a bad peg of Weaver's and the other one I walked because this blind Evans don't know a ball from a strike. We had not did no more scoreing off of Pierce not because he had no stuff but because our club could not take a ball in there hands and hit it out of the infield.

Well Al I did not tell you that before I come out to the park I kissed little Al and Florrie good-by and Marie says she was going to stay home to and keep Florrie Co. and they was not no reason for Marie to come to the game anyway because they was not a chance in the world for Allen to do nothing but hit fungoes. Well while I was doing all this here swell pitching and makeing them Cubs look like a lot of rummys I was thinking about little Al and Florrie and how glad they would be when I come home and told them what I done though of coarse little Al is not only a little over 3 months of age and how could he appresiate what I done? But Florrie would.

Well Al when I come in to the bench after there ½ of the 7th I happened to look up to the press box to see if the reporters had gave Schulte a hit on that one Weaver throwed away and who do you think I seen in a box right alongside of the press box? It was Florrie and Marie and both of them claping there hands and hollering with the rest of the bugs.

◆ *Good*—Wilbur David Good (1885–1963), a journeyman outfielder who played a full 154 games for the Cubs in 1914 after a lackluster history with the Yankees, Naps, and Braves since 1905. He was to remain with the Cubs through 1915 and would then play with the Phillies, in 1916, and the White Sox, in 1918. In 1914 Good hit .272, well above his lifetime average of .258 in 750 games. See Art Ahrens, "Wilbur Good," *The Ballplayers*, p. 399.

Saier—Victor Sylvester Saier (1891–1967), the Cubs first baseman from 1911 to 1917. Saier had the thankless task of replacing Frank Chance. After his wartime service he played 58 games for the Pirates in 1919, and in his eight seasons in the National League he hit .263 in 864 games. In 1914 Saier hit .240, and his 18 home runs that year were only one less than the league leader, Gavvy Cravath of the Phillies, had hit. See Art Ahrens, "Vic Saier," *The Ballplayers*, p. 956.

Well old pal I was never so supprised in my life and it just took all the heart out of me. What was they doing there and what had they did with the baby? How did I know that little Al was not sick or maybe dead and balling his head off and nobody round to hear him?

I tried to catch Florrie's eyes but she would not look at me. I hollered her name and the bugs looked at me like as if I was crazy and I was to Al. Well I seen they was not no use of standing out there in front of the stand so I come into the bench and Allen was setting there and I says Did you know your wife and Florrie was up there in the stand? He says No and I says What are they doing here? And he says What would they be doing here—mending there stockings? I felt like busting him and I guess he seen I was mad because he got up off of the bench and beat it down to the corner of the field where some of the others was getting warmed up though why should they have anybody warming up when I was going so good?

Well Al I made up my mind that ball game or no ball game I was not going to have little Al left alone no longer and I seen they was not no use of sending word to Florrie to go home because they was a big crowd and it would take maybe 15 or 20 minutes for somebody to get up to where she was at. So I says to Callahan You have got to take me out. He says What is the matter? Is your arm gone? I says No my arm is not gone but my baby is sick and home all alone. He says Where is your wife? And I says She is setting up there in the stand.

Then he says How do you know your baby is sick? And I says I don't know if he is sick or not but he is left home all alone. He says Why don't you send your wife home? And I says I could not get word to her in time. He says Well you have only got two innings to go and the way your going the game will be over in 10 minutes. I says Yes and before 10 minutes is up my baby might die and are you going to take me out or not? He says Get in there and pitch you yellow dog and if you don't I will take your share of the serious money away from you.

By this time our part of the inning was over and I had to go out there and pitch some more because he would not take me out and he has not got no heart Al. Well Al how could I pitch when I kept thinking maybe the baby was dying right now and maybe if I was home I could do something? And instead of paying attension to what I was doing I was thinking about little Al and looking up there to where Florrie and Marie was setting and before I knowed what come off they had the bases full and Callahan took me out.

Well Al I run to the clubhouse and changed my cloths and beat it for home and I did not even hear what Callahan and Gleason says to me when I went by them but I found out after the game that Scott went in and finished up and they batted him pretty hard and we was licked 3 and 2.

When I got home the baby was crying but he was not all alone after all Al because they was a little girl about 14 years of age there watching him and Florrie had hired her to take care of him so as her and Marie could go and see the game. But just think Al of leaveing little Al with a girl 14 years of age that did not never have no babys of her own! And what did she know about takeing care of him? Nothing Al.

You should ought to of heard me ball Florrie out when she got ◇ home and I bet she cried pretty near enough to flood the basemunt. We had it hot and heavy and the Allens butted in but I soon showed them where they was at and made them shut there mouth.

◇ *You should ought to of heard me ball Florrie out*—Drawing by Martin Justice for *The Saturday Evening Post*, October 3, 1914.

I had a good nosion to go out and get a hole lot of drinks and was just going to put on my hat when the doorbell rung and there was Kid Gleason. I thought he would be sore and probily try to ball me out and I was not going to stand for nothing but instead of balling me out he come and shook hands with me and interduced himself to Florrie and asked how was little Al.

Well we all set down and Gleason says the club was depending on me to win the serious because I was in the best shape of all the pitchers. And besides the Cubs could not never hit me when I was right and he was telling the truth to.

So he asked me if I would stand for the club hireing a train nurse to stay with the baby the rest of the serious so as Florrie could go and see her husband win the serious but I says No I would not stand for that and Florrie's place was with the baby.

So Gleason and Florrie goes out in the other room and talks a while and I guess he was persuadeing her to stay home because pretty soon they come back in the room and says it was all fixed up and I would not have to worry about little Al the rest of the serious but could give the club the best I got. Gleason just left here a little while ago and I won't work to-morrow Al but I will work the day after and you will see what I can do when I don't have nothing to worry me.

Your pal, Jack.

CHICAGO, ILLINOIS, OCTOBER 8.

Old Pal: Well old pal we got them 2 games to one now and the serious is sure to be over in three more days because I can pitch 2 games in that time if nessary. I shut them out to-day and they should ought not to of had four hits but should ought to of had only 2 but Bodie don't cover no ground and 2 fly balls that he should ought to of eat up fell safe.

But I beat them anyway and Benz beat them yesterday but why should he not beat them when the club made 6 runs for him? All they made for me was three but all I needed was one because they could not hit me with a shuvvel. When I come to the bench after the 5th inning they was a note there for me from the boy that answers the phone at the ball park and it says that somebody just called up from the flat and says the baby was asleep and getting along fine. So I felt good Al and I was better then ever in the 6th.

When I got home Florrie and Marie was both there and asked me how did the game come out because I beat Allen home and I told them all about what I done and I bet Florrie was proud of me but I supose Marie is a little jellus because how could she help it when Callahan is depending on me to win the serious and her husband is wearing out the wood on the bench? But why should she be sore when it is me that is winning the serious for them? And if it was not for me Allen and all the rest of them would get about $500.00 apeace instead of the winner's share which is about $750.00 apeace.

Cicotte is going to work to-morrow and if he is lucky maybe he can get away with the game and that will leave me to finish up the day after to-morrow but if nessary I can go in to-morrow when they get to hitting Cicotte and stop them and then come back the following day and beat them again. Where would this club be at Al if I had of jumped to the Federal? *Yours truly, Jack.*

CHICAGO, ILLINOIS, OCTOBER 11.

Friend Al: We done it again Al and I guess the Cubs won't never want to play us again not so long as I am with the club. Before you get this letter you will know what we done and who done it but probily you could of guessed that Al without seeing no paper.

I got 2 more of them phone messiges about the baby dureing the game and I guess that was what made me so good because I knowed then that Florrie was takeing care of him but I could not help feeling sorry for Florrie because she is a bug herself and it must of been pretty hard for her to stay away from the game espesially when she knowed I was going to pitch and she has been pretty good to sacrifice her own plesure for little Al.

Cicotte was knocked out of the box the day before yesterday and then they give this here Faber a good beating but I wish you could of saw what they done to Allen when Callahan sent him in after the game

◇ *this here Faber*—Red Faber in 1932, toward the end of a long career spent entirely with the White Sox. (George E. Brace collection)

was gone allready. Honest Al if he had not of been my brother in law I would of felt like laughing at him because it looked like as if they would have to call the fire department to put the side out. They had Bodie and Collins hollering for help and with there tongue hanging out from running back to the fence.

Anyway the serious is all over and I won't have nothing to do but ◆ stay home and play with little Al but I don't know yet where my home

◆ (*Page 162*) *Faber*—Urban Clarence "Red" Faber (1888–1976), a rookie right-hander who was to become one of the White Sox' most distinguished pitchers. Coming up from Des Moines of the Western League, Faber recorded 10–9 in 1914. In 1915 he would win 24 games to tie Scott for the club leadership, the first of Faber's four 20-game seasons, and in 1917 he would defeat the Giants three times in the World Series. In 1919, however, he was relatively ineffective, exacerbating the team's excessive dependence on Eddie Cicotte and Claude Williams, which in turn helped cause Chick Gandil to conceive the Black Sox plot. On his retirement in 1933 Faber was the last member of the 1917 and 1919 champions still active with the White Sox. In 20 seasons, he won 254 and lost 212, second only to Ted Lyons's 260 victories among White Sox pitchers. Faber was elected to the Baseball Hall of Fame in 1964. See Thomas L. Karnes, "Urban Clarence Faber," *Biographical Dictionary of American Sports: Baseball*, pp. 173–74.

◆ *the serious is all over*—In the actual City Series of 1914, the White Sox defeated the Cubs four games to three. The events do not correspond to this account, however. On October 9 the Cubs defeated Benz, not Cicotte, 2–1. Faber appeared only in relief in the game of October 12, preserving a victory for Scott, 3–1. In the final game on October 15, Cicotte, in relief of Scott, beat the Cubs, 3–2.

is going to be at because it is a cinch I won't stay with Allen no longer. He has not came home since the game and I suppose he is out somewheres lapping up some beer and spending some of the winner's share of the money which he would not of had no chance to get in on if it had not of been for me.

I will write and let you know my plans for the winter and I wish Florrie would agree to come to Bedford but nothing doing Al and after her staying home and takeing care of the baby instead of watching me pitch I can't be too hard on her but must leave her have her own way about something. *Your pal, Jack.*

CHICAGO, ILLINOIS, OCTOBER 13.

Al: I am all threw with Florrie Al and I bet when you hear about it you won't say it was not no fault of mine but no man liveing who is any kind of a man would act different from how I am acting if he had of been decieved like I been.

Al Florrie and Marie was out to all them games and was not home takeing care of the baby at all and it is not her fault that little Al is not dead and that he was not killed by the nurse they hired to take care of him while they went to the games when I thought they was home takeing care of the baby. And all them phone messiges was just fakes and maybe the baby was sick all the time I was winning them games and balling his head off instead of being asleep like they said he was.

Allen did not never come home at all the night before last and when he come in yesterday he was a sight and I says to him Where have you been? And he says I have been down to the Y. M. C. A. but that is not none of your business. I says Yes you look like as if you had been to the Y. M. C. A. and I know where you have been and you have been out lushing beer. And he says Suppose I have and what are you going to do about it? And I says Nothing but you should ought to be ashamed of yourself and leaveing Marie here while you was out lapping up beer.

Then he says Did you not leave Florrie home while you was getting away with them games, you lucky stiff? And I says Yes but Florrie had to stay home and take care of the baby but Marie don't never have to stay home because where is your baby? You have not got no baby. He says I would not want no X-eyed baby like yourn. Then he says So you think Florrie stayed to home and took care of the baby do you? And I says What do you mean? And he says You better ask her.

So when Florrie come in and heard us talking she busted out crying and then I found out what they put over on me. It is a wonder Al that

I did not take some of that cheap furniture them Allens got and bust it over there heads, Allen and Florrie. This is what they done Al. The club give Florrie $50.00 to stay home and take care of the baby and she said she would and she was to call up every so offten and tell me the baby was all O. K. But this here Marie told her she was a sucker so she hired a nurse for part of the $50.00 and then her and Marie went to the games and beat it out quick after the games was over and come home in a taxicab and chased the nurse out before I got home.

Well Al when I found out what they done I grabbed my hat and goes out and got some drinks and I was so mad I did not know where I was at or what come off and I did not get home till this A. M. And they was all asleep and I been asleep all day and when I woke up Marie and Allen was out but Florrie and I have not spoke to each other and I won't never speak to her again.

But I know now what I am going to do Al and I am going to take little Al and beat it out of here and she can sew me for a bill of divorce and I should not worry because I will have little Al and I will see that he is tooken care of because I guess I can hire a nurse as well as they can and I will pick out a train nurse that knows something. Maybe I and him and the nurse will come to Bedford Al but I don't know yet and I will write and tell you as soon as I make up my mind. Did you ever hear of a man getting a rottener deal Al? And after what I done in the serious too. *Your pal, Jack.*

CHICAGO, ILLINOIS, OCTOBER 17.

Old Pal: I and Florrie has made it up Al but we are threw with Marie and Allen and I and Florrie and the baby is staying at a hotel here on Cottage Grove Avenue the same hotel we was at when we got married only of coarse they was only the 2 of us then.

And now Al I want to ask you a favor and that is for you to go and see old man Cutting and tell him I want to ree-new the lease on that house for another year because I and Florrie has decided to spend the winter in Bedford and she will want to stay there and take care of little Al while I am away on trips next summer and not stay in no high-price flat up here. And may be you and Bertha can help her round the house when I am not there.

I will tell you how we come to fix things up Al and you will see that I made her apollojize to me and after this she will do what I tell her to and won't never try to put nothing over. We was eating breakfast—I and Florrie and Marie. Allen was still asleep yet because I guess he must of had a bad night and he was snoreing so as you could hear him in the next st. I was not saying nothing to nobody but pretty soon Florrie says to Marie I don't think you and Allen should ought to kick on the baby crying when Allen's snoreing makes more noise than a hole wagonlode of babys. And Marie got sore and says I guess a man has got a right to snore in his own house and you and Jack has been grafting off of us long enough.

Then Florrie says What did Allen do to help win the serious and get that $750.00? Nothing but set on the bench eccept when they was makeing him look like a sucker the 1 inning he pitched. The trouble with you and Allen is you are jellous of what Jack has did and you know he will be a star up here in the big league when Allen is tending bar which is what he should ought to be doing because then he could get stewed for nothing.

Maries says Take your brat and get out of the house. And Florrie says Don't you worry because we would not stay here no longer if you hired us. So Florrie went in her room and I followed her in and she says Let's pack up and get out.

Then I says Yes but we won't go nowheres together after what you done to me but you can go where you dam please and I and little Al will go to Bedford. Then she says You can't take the baby because he is mine and if you was to take him I would have you arrested for kidnaping. Besides, she says, what would you feed him and who would take care of him?

I says I would find somebody to take care of him and I would get him food from a resturunt. She says He can't eat nothing but milk and I says Well he has the collect all the time when he is eating milk and he would not be no worse off if he was eating watermelon. Well, she says, if you take him I will have you arrested and sew you for a bill of divorce for dessertion.

Then she says Jack you should not ought to find no fault with me for going to them games because when a woman has a husband that can pitch like you can do you think she wants to stay home and not see her husband pitch when a lot of other women is cheering him and makeing her feel proud because she is his wife?

Well Al as I said right along it was pretty hard on Florrie to have to stay home and I could not hardly blame her for wanting to be out there where she could see what I done so what was the use of argueing?

So I told her I would think it over and then I went out and I went and seen a attorney at law and asked him could I take little Al away and he says No I did not have no right to take him away from his mother and besides it would probily kill him to be tooken away from her and then he soaked me $10.00 the robber.

Then I went back and told Florrie I would give her another chance and then her and I packed up and took little Al in a taxicab over to this hotel. We are threw with the Allens Al and let me know right away if I can get that lease for another year because Florrie has gave up and will go to Bedford or anywheres else with me now.

Yours truly, Jack.

CHICAGO, ILLINOIS, OCTOBER 20.

Friend Al: Old pal I won't never forget your kindnus and this is to tell you that I and Florrie axcept your kind invatation to come and stay with you till we can find a house and I guess you won't regret it none because Florrie will livun things up for Bertha and Bertha will be crazy about the baby because you should ought to see how cute he is now Al and not yet four months old. But I bet he will be talking before we know it.

We are comeing on the train that leaves here at noon Saturday Al and the train leaves here about 12 o'clock and I don't know what time ◆ it gets to Bedford but it leaves here at noon so we shall be there probily in time for supper.

I wish you would ask Ben Smith will he have a hack down to the deepo to meet us but I won't pay no more than $.25 and I should think he should ought to be glad to take us from the deepo to your house for nothing.

Your pal, Jack.

P. S. The train we are comeing on leaves here at noon Al and will probily get us there in time for a late supper and I wonder if Bertha would have spair ribs and crout for supper. You know me Al.

◆ *the train leaves here about 12 o'clock*—So it did. The Monon in 1914 scheduled an Indianapolis express, No. 33, from Dearborn Station, Chicago, at noon. At the town of Monon the train connected at 2:29 P.M. with a local for French Lick Springs, which arrived at Bedford at 8:08 P.M. Thus, Keefe's prospective arrival would have required what was by the standards of Bedford a very late supper, and the dish he requested for dinner would have required at least two hours' preparation. On the railroad, see George W. Hilton, *Monon Route* (Berkeley: Howell-North Books, 1978).

The Busher Beats It Hence

CHICAGO, ILL., OCT. 20.

Friend Al: I guess may be you will begin to think I dont never do what I am going to do and that I change my mind a hole lot because I wrote and told you that I and Florrie and little Al would be in Bedford today and here we are in Chi yet on the day when I told you we would get to Bedford and I bet Bertha and you and the rest of the boys will be dissapointed but Al I dont feel like as if I should ought to leave the White Sox in a hole and that is why I am here yet and I will tell you how it come off but in the 1st place I want to tell you that it wont make a diffrence of more than 5 or 6 or may be 7 days at least and we will be down there and see you and Bertha and the rest of the boys just as soon as the N. Y. giants and the White Sox leaves here and starts a ◆ round the world. All so I remember I told you to fix it up so as a hack

"The Busher Beats It Hence," the sixth and last of the stories later collected as *You Know Me Al,* was published in *The Saturday Evening Post,* CLXXXVII (November 7, 1914), 21–23, 38–40.

◆ *a round the world*—Here Lardner introduces a major anachronism. The Giants and White Sox world tour occurred after the 1913 season. Obviously, the outbreak of World War I would have made the trip impossible after the 1914 season. Lardner does adhere closely to the chronology of the 1913 trip, however. Although he had not made the trip himself, his first book was an account of the tour, *March*

would be down to the deepo to meet us tonight and you wont get this letter in time to tell them not to send no hack so I supose the hack will be there but may be they will be some body else that gets off of the train that will want the hack and then every thing will be all O. K. but if they is not nobody else that wants the hack I will pay them ½ of what they was going to charge me if I had of came and road in the hack though I dont have to pay them nothing because I am not going to ride in the hack but I want to do the right thing and besides I will want a hack at the deepo when I do come so they will get a peace of money out of me any way so I dont see where they got no kick comeing even if I dont give them a nichol now.

I will tell you why I am still here and you will see where I am trying to do the right thing. You knowed of coarse that the White Sox and the N. Y. giants was going to make a trip a round the world and they been after me for a long time to go a long with them but I says No I would not leave Florrie and the kid because that would not be fare and besides I would be paying rent and grocerys for them some wheres and me not getting nothing out of it and besides I would probily be spending a hole lot of money on the trip because though the club pays all of our regular expences they would be a hole lot of times when I felt like blowing my self and buying some thing to send home to the Mrs and to good old friends of mine like you and Bertha so I turned them down and Callahan acted like he was sore at me but I dont care nothing for that because I got other people to think a bout and not Callahan and besides if I was to go a long the fans in the towns where we play at would want to see me work and I would have to do a hole lot of pitching which I would not be getting nothing for

---

(*continued from page 168*)
6th: The Home Coming of Charles A. Comiskey, John J. McGraw and James J. Callahan (Chicago: The Blakeley Printing Co., 1914), in collaboration with Edward C. Heeman.

Isaac E. Clark notes that, as in the passage at hand, Keefe in this story divides almost every word that could remotely be considered divisible and drops apostrophes. Clark argues that Keefe is consistently delineated as a man who was exposed in school to correct English, but very imperfectly apprehended it. Keefe continually experiments with locutions that he thinks may be correct, occasionally succeeding but more often failing. Clark also notes that Keefe's punctuation, spelling, syntax, and choice of parts of speech are all at their worst in this story. This may have reflected a conscious attempt on Lardner's part to show the strain on Keefe of the decision whether or not to join the world tour. Isaac Edgar Clark, "An Analysis of Ring Lardner's American Language, or Who Learnt You Grammar Bud?" unpublished M.A. thesis, University of Texas, 1944, pp. 59–62, 65, and *passim*.

it and it would not count in no standing because the games is to be just for fun and what good would it do me and besides Florrie says I was not under no circumstance to go and of coarse I would go if I wanted to go no matter what ever she says but all and all I turned them down and says I would stay here all winter or rather I would not stay here but in Bedford. Then Callahan says All right but you know before we start on the trip the giants and us is going to play a game right here in Chi next Sunday and after what you done in the city serious the fans would be sore if they did not get no more chance to look at you so will you stay and pitch part of the game here and I says I would think it over and I come home to the hotel where we are staying at and asked Florrie did she care if we did not go to Bedford for an other week and she says No she did not care if we dont go for 6 years so I called Callahan up and says I would stay and he says Thats the boy and now the fans will have an other treat so you see Al he appresiates what I done and wants to give the fans fare treatment because this town is nuts over me after what I done to them Cubs but I could do it just the same to the Athaletics or any body else if it would of been them in stead of the Cubs. May be we will leave here the A. M. after the game that is Monday and I will let you know so as you can order an other hack and tell Bertha I hope she did not go to no extra trouble a bout getting ready for us and did not order no spair ribs and crout but you can eat them up if she all ready got them and may be she can order some more for us when we come but tell her it dont make no diffrence and not to go to no trouble because most anything she has is O. K. for I and Florrie accept of coarse we would not want to make no meal off of sardeens or something.

Well Al I bet them N. Y. giants will wish I would of went home before they come for this here exibishun game because my arm feels grate and I will show them where they would be at if they had to play ball in our league all the time though I supose they is some pitchers in our league that they would hit good against them if they can hit at all but not me. You will see in the papers how I come out and I will write and tell you a bout it. *Your pal, Jack.*

CHICAGO, ILL., OCT. 25.

Old Pal: I have not only got a little time but I have got some news for you and I knowed you would want to hear all a bout it so I am writeing this letter and then I am going to catch the train. I would be saying good by to little Al instead of writeing this letter only Florrie wont let me wake him up and he is a sleep but may be by the time I get this letter wrote he will be a wake again and I can say good by to him. I am going with the White Sox and giants as far as San Francisco or may be Van Coover where they take the boat at but I am not going a round the world with them but only just out to the coast to help them out because they is a couple of men going to join them out there and untill them men join them they will be short of men and they got a hole lot of exibishun games to play before they get out there so I am going to help them out. It all come off in the club house after the game today and I will tell you how it come off but 1st I want to tell you a bout the game and honest Al them giants is the luckyest team in the world and it is not no wonder they keep wining the penant in that ◆ league because a club that has got there luck could win ball games with out sending no team on the field at all but staying down to the hotel.

They was a big crowd out to the park so Callahan says to me I did not know if I was going to pitch you or not but the crowd is out here to see you so I will have to let you work so I warmed up but I knowed the minute I throwed the 1st ball warming up that I was not right and I says to Callahan I did not feel good but he says You wont need to feel good to beat this bunch because they heard a hole lot a bout you and you would have them beat if you just throwed your glove out there in the box. So I went in and tried to pitch but my arm was so lame it pretty near killed me every ball I throwed and I bet if I was some other pitchers they would not never of tried to work with my arm so sore but I am not like some of them yellow dogs and quit because I would not dissapoint the crowd or throw Callahan down when he wanted me to pitch and was depending on me. You know me Al. So I went in there but I did not have nothing and if them giants could of hit at all in stead of like a lot of girls they would of knock down the fence because I was not my self. At that they should not ought to of had only the 1 run off of me if Weaver and them had not of begin kicking the ball a round like it was a foot ball or something. Well Al what with dropping fly balls and booting them a round and this in that the giants was gave 5 runs in the 1st 3 innings and they should ought to of had just the 1 run or may be not that and that ball Merkle hit in to the seats I was trying to waist it and a man that is a ◆

◆ *They keep wining the penant in that league*—The Giants had won the 1911, 1912, and 1913 pennants, before finishing second to the Braves by a margin of 10½ games in 1914.

◆ *Merkle*—Frederick Charles Merkle (1888–1956), first baseman of the Giants. Unfortunately remembered for his failure to touch second base in a crucial game,

◇ *Mcgraw*—Drawing of John McGraw by Lawrence Semon. (National Baseball Library, Cooperstown, New York)

good hitter would not never of hit at it and if I was right this here Merkle could not foul me in 9 years. When I was comeing into the bench after the 3th inning this here smart alex Mcgraw come passed ◆◇ me from the 3 base coaching line and he says Are you going on the trip and I says No I am not going on no trip and he says That is to bad because if you was going we would win a hole lot of games and I give him a hot come back and he did not say nothing so I went in to the bench and Callahan says Them giants is not such rotten hitters is they and I says No they hit pretty good when a man has got a sore arm against them and he says Why did not you tell me your arm was sore and I says I did not want to dissapoint no crowd that come out here to see me and he says Well I guess you need not pitch no more because if I left you in there the crowd might begin to get tired of watching you a bout 10 oclock tonight and I says What do you mean and he did not say nothing more so I set there a while and then went ◆ to the club house. Well Al after the game Callahan come in to the club house and I was still in there yet talking to the trainer and getting my arm rubbed and Callahan says Are you getting your arm in shape for next year and I says No but it give me so much pane I could not stand it and he says I bet if you was feeling good you could make them giants look like a sucker and I says You know I could make them look like a sucker and he says Well why dont you come a long with us and

---

(*continued from page 171*)
thus costing the Giants the 1908 pennant, Merkle was a good though not outstanding first baseman for 16 seasons ranging from 1907 to 1926. He played regularly for the Giants until 1916, thereafter with the Dodgers, Cubs, and Yankees. In 1,637 games he made 1,579 hits for a .273 average. In 1914 he hit .258 and led the National League in strikeouts with 80. After his playing career he managed in the minor leagues. See Norman L. Macht, "Fred Merkle," *The Ballplayers*, pp. 731–32.

◆ *Mcgraw*—John Joseph McGraw (1873–1934), manager of the Giants. Known mainly as a fiery third baseman with the Baltimore Orioles in the 1890's, McGraw hit .334 in 1,099 games spread over 16 seasons. He became manager of the Orioles of the National League in 1899, and returned to Baltimore as manager in the American League in 1901. His leaving the team in 1902 was partly responsible for the team's failure and its transfer to New York, where it became the Highlanders and later the Yankees. McGraw became manager of the Giants in midseason in 1902 and remained until discharged in 1932. In the interim he won ten pennants, a number equaled only by Casey Stengel. McGraw entered the Baseball Hall of Fame in 1937. See Frank Graham, *McGraw of the Giants* (New York: G. P. Putnam's Sons, 1944; Charles C. Alexander, *John McGraw* (New York: Viking Penguin Inc., 1988).

◆ *and then went to the club house.*—In the actual White Sox–Giants exhibition in Chicago, the Giants defeated Russell, 3–1, on October 19, 1913.

you will get an other chance at them when you feel good and I says I would like to get an other crack at them but I could not go a way on no trip and leave the Mrs and the baby and then he says he would not ask me to make the hole trip a round the world but he wisht I would go out to the coast with them because they was hard up for pitchers and he says Mathewson of the giants was not only going as far as the ◆ coast so if the giants had there star pitcher that far the White Sox should ought to have theren and then some of the other boys coaxed me would I go so finely I says I would think it over and I went home and seen Florrie and she says How long would it be for and I says a bout 3 or 4 weeks and she says If you dont go will we start for Bedford right a way and I says Yes and then she says All right go a head and go but if they was any thing should happen to the baby while I was gone what would they do if I was not a round to tell them what to do and I says Call a Dr. in but dont call no Dr. if you dont have to and besides you should ought to know by this time what to do for the baby when he got sick and she says Of coarse I know a little but not as much as you do because you know it all. Then I says No I dont know it all but I will tell you some things before I go and you should not ought to have no trouble so we fixed it up and her and little Al is to stay here in the hotel untill I come back which will be a bout the 20 of Nov. and then we will come down home and tell Bertha not to get to in patient and we will get there some time. It is going to cost me $6.00 a week at the hotel for a room for she and the baby besides there meals but the babys meals dont cost nothing yet and Florrie should not ought to be very hungry because we been liveing good and besides she will get all she can eat when we come to Bedford and it wont cost me nothing for meals on the trip out to the coast because Comiskey and Mcgraw pays for that.

I have not even had no time to look up where we play at but we stop off at a hole lot of places on the way and I will get a chance to make them giants look like a sucker before I get threw and Mcgraw wont be so sorry I am not going to make the hole trip. You will see by the papers what I done to them before we get threw and I will write as soon as we stops some wheres long enough so as I can write and now I am going to say good by to little Al if he is a wake or not a wake and wake him up and say good by to him because even if he is not

◆ *Mathewson of the giants was not only going as far as the coast*—Mathewson did go only as far as the Coast.

only 5 months old he is old enough to think a hole lot of me and why not. I all so got to say good by to Florrie and fix it up with the hotel clerk a bout she and the baby staying here a while and catch the train. You will hear from me soon old pal. *Your pal, Jack.*

ST. JOE, MISS., OCT. 29. ◆

Friend Al: Well Al we are on our way to the coast and they is quite a party of us though it is not no real White Sox and giants at all but some players from off of both clubs and then some others that is from other clubs a round the 2 leagues to fill up. We got Speaker from the Boston club and Crawford from the Detroit club and if we had them with us all the time Al I would not never loose a game because one or the other of them 2 is good for a couple runs every game and that is all I need to win my games is a couple of runs or only 1 run and I would win all my games and would not never loose a game.

I did not pitch today and I guess the giants was glad of it because no matter what Mcgraw says he must of saw from watching me Sunday that I was a real pitcher though my arm was so sore I could not hardly raze it over my sholder so no wonder I did not have no stuff but at that I could of beat his gang with out no stuff if I had of had some kind of decent suport. I will pitch against them may be tomorrow or may be some day soon and my arm is all O. K. again now so I will show them up and make them wish Callahan had of left me to home. Some of the men has brung there wife a long and besides that there is some other men and there wife that is not no ball players but are going a long for the trip and some more will join the party out the coast before they get a bord the boat but of coarse I and Mathewson ◇ will drop out of the party then because why should I or him go a round the world and throw our arms out pitching games that dont count in no standing and that we dont get no money for pitching them out side of just our bare expences. The people in the towns we played at so far has all wanted to shake hands with Mathewson and I so I guess they know who is the real pitchers on these here 2 clubs no matter what them reporters says and the stars is all ways the men that the people wants to shake there hands with and make friends with them but Al this here Mathewson pitched today and honest Al I dont see how he gets by and either the batters in the National league dont

---

◆ *St. Joe, Miss.*—As before, St. Joseph, Missouri. On this date the White Sox defeated the Giants, 7–1, in Muskogee, Okla.

◇ *Mathewson*—Christy Mathewson warming up for the Giants, 1913 or 1914 (see footnote, p. 155). (National Baseball Library, Cooperstown, New York)

know nothing a bout hitting or else he is such a old man that they feel ◆ sorry for him and may be when he was a bout 10 years younger then he is may be then he had some thing and was a pretty fare pitcher but all as he does now is stick the 1st ball right over with 0 on it and pray that they dont hit it out of the park. If a pitcher like he can get by in the National league and fool them batters they is not nothing I would like better then to pitch in the National league and I bet I would not get scored on in 2 to 3 years. I heard a hole lot a bout this here fade a way that he is supposed to pitch and it is a ball that is throwed out between 2 fingers and falls in at a right hand batter and they is not no body cant hit it but if he throwed 1 of them things today he done it while I was a sleep and they was not no time when I was not wide a

◆ *he is such a old man*—Mathewson was 34 years old. The reference is apparently to the game of October 25, when the White Sox defeated Mathewson in St. Joseph, 4–3.

wake and looking right at him and after the game was over I says to him Where is that there fade a way I heard so much a bout and he says O I did not have to use none of my regular stuff against your club and I says Well you would have to use all you got if I was working against you and he says Yes if you worked like you done Sunday I would have to do some pitching or they would not never finish the game. Then I says a bout me haveing a sore arm Sunday and he says I wisht I had a sore arm like yourn and a little sence with it and was your age and I would not never loose a game so you see Al he has heard a bout me and is jellus bcause he has not got my stuff but they cant every body expect to have the stuff that I got or ½ as much stuff. This smart alex Mcgraw was trying to kid me today and says Why did not I make friends with Mathewson and let him learn me some thing a bout pitching and I says Mathewson could not learn me nothing and he says I guess thats right and I guess they is not nobody could learn you nothing a bout nothing and if you was to stay in the league 20 years probily you would not be no better then you are now so you see he had to add mit that I am good Al even if he has not saw me work when my arm was O. K.

Mcgraw says to me tonight he says I wisht you was going all the way and I says Yes you do. I says Your club would look like a sucker after I had worked against them a few times and he says May be thats right to because they would not know how to hit against a regular pitcher after that. Then he says But I dont care nothing a bout that but I wisht you was going to make the hole trip so as we could have a good time. He says We got Steve Evans and Dutch Schaefer going a long ◆ and they is both of them funny but I like to be a round with boys that is funny and dont know nothing a bout it. I says Well I would go a long only for my wife and baby and he says Yes it would be pretty tough on your wife to have you a way that long but still and all think how glad she would be to see you when you come back again and besides them dolls acrost the ocean will be pretty sore at I and Callahan if we tell them we left you to home. I says Do you supose the people

---

◆ *Steve Evans*—Louis Richard Evans (1885–1943), an outfielder who had played for the Giants briefly in 1908, but in 1909–13 played for the Cardinals. He jumped to the Federal League in 1914, ending his career there in 1915. In 987 games Evans hit .287. On the 1913–14 world tour, Evans played left field for the White Sox. As stated, he was one of baseball's best-known comics; his antics caused McGraw to trade him to the Cardinals after just two games, at the outset of his career. See William A. Borst, "Steve Evans," *The Ballplayers*, p. 318.

over there has heard a bout me and he says Sure because they have wrote a lot of letters asking me to be sure and bring you and Mathewson a long. Then he says I guess Mathewson is not going so if you was to go and him left here to home they would not be nothing to it. You could have things all your own way and probily could marry the Queen of europe if you was not all ready married. He was giveing me the strate dope this time Al because he did not crack a smile and I wisht I could go a long but it would not be fare to Florrie but still and all did not she leave me and beat it for Texas last winter and why should not I do the same thing to her only I am not that kind of a man. You know me Al.

We play in Kansas city tomorrow and may be I will work there ◆ because it is a big town and I have got to close now and write to Florrie. *Your old pal, Jack.*

ABILENE, TEXAS, NOV. 4.

Al: Well Al I guess you know by this time that I have worked against them 2 times since I wrote to you last time and I beat them both times and Mcgraw knows now what kind of a pitcher I am and I will tell you how I know because after the game yesterday he road down to the place we dressed at a long with me and all the way in the automobile he was after me to say I would go all the way a round the world and finely it come out that he wants I should go a long and pitch for his club and not pitch for the White Sox. He says his club is up against it for pitchers because Mathewson is not going and all they got left is a man named Hern that is a young man and not got no experiense and ◆ Wiltse that is a left hander. So he says I have talked it over with ◆

◆ *We play in Kansas city tomorrow*—The two teams had played in Kansas City on October 26, the Giants winning, 6–2.

◆ *Hern*—Bunn "Bunny" Hearn (1891–1959), an obscure lefthander who was, indeed, short of experience. Hearn had started five games for the Cardinals in 1910, recording a 1–3 season. He failed to get a decision in two relief appearances for the Cardinals in 1911. With the Giants in 1913, Hearn started twice, pitched one complete game, and posted a 1–1 record. He had his best season, 5–6, with the Braves, in 1918. Including the 1915 season in the Federal League, he had a 13–24 record over six seasons. He pitched in the minor leagues from 1910 to 1931, compiling a record of 247–146. Hearn was baseball coach at the University of North Carolina for 27 years. See Morris A. Eckhouse, "Bunny Hearn," *The Ballplayers*, p. 455; "Bunn Hearn," *Minor League Baseball Stars* (Society for American Baseball Research), III (1992), 159.

◆ *Wiltse*—George LeRoy "Hooks" Wiltse (1880–1959), a lefthander of great talent a half dozen years earlier, but now nearing the end of his career. He had

Callahan and he says if I could get you to go a long it was all O. K. with him and you could pitch for us only I must not work you to hard because he is depending on you to win the penant for him next year. I says Did not none of the other White Sox made no holler because may be they might have to bat against me and he says Yes Crawford and Speaker says they would not make the trip if you was a long and pitching against them but Callahan showed them where it would be good for them next year because if they hit against you all winter the pitchers they hit against next year will look easy to them. He was crazy to have me go a long on the hole trip but of coarse Al they is not no chance of me going on acct. of Florrie and little Al but you see Mcgraw has cut out his trying to kid me and is treating me now like a man should ought to be treated that has did what I done.

They was not no game here today on acct. of it raining and the ◆ people here was sore because they did not see no game but they all come a round to look at us and says they must have some speechs from the most prommerent men in the party so I and Comiskey and Mcgraw and Callahan and Mathewson and Ted Sullivan that I guess ◆ is puting up the money for the trip made speechs and they clapped there hands harder when I was makeing my speech then when any 1

(*continued from page 177*)
peaked at 23–14 in 1908, but was 0–0 in 17 appearances in 1913 and 1–1 in 1914. Except for the 1915 season in the Federal League, Wiltse spent his entire career with the Giants, winning 138 and losing 85 in a Giant uniform. One of the best fielding pitchers, Wiltse occasionally played at first base and in the outfield. See Jack Kavanagh, "Hooks Wiltse," *The Ballplayers*, p. 1189.

Hearn and Wiltse were the only pitchers McGraw had available for the trip. The White Sox lent Red Faber to the Giants for the tour, presumably providing Lardner's prototype for the proposed lending of Keefe. Faber, an articulate and intelligent man, was not in other respects a prototype for Keefe.

◆ *on acct. of it raining*—The White Sox and Giants were rained out in Abilene, Tex., on November 4, 1913.

◆ *Ted Sullivan*—Timothy Paul Sullivan (1852–1929), managing director of the world tour, and a long-time associate of Comiskey. He had signed Comiskey to his first minor league contract at Dubuque of the Northwestern League in 1879. Sullivan had been among the founders of the Northwestern League, and was also active in founding the Western and Texas leagues and the Southern Association. In 1884 he managed Kansas City of the Union Association to an eleventh-place finish, and inserted himself in three games, making three hits in nine at bats—the limit of his major league experience. He also managed St. Louis of the American Association for part of the 1883 season and Washington of the National League for part of the 1888 season. Sullivan wrote a pamphlet, *History of World's Tour, Chicago White Sox and New York Giants* (Chicago: M. A. Donohue & Co., 1914). He remained active as a White Sox scout into the 1920's.

of the others was makeing there speech. You did not know I was a speech maker did you Al and I did not know it neither untill today but I guess they is not nothing I cant do if I make up my mind and 1 of the boys says that I done just as well as Dummy Taylor could of. ◆

I have not heard nothing from Florrie but I guess may be she is to busy takeing care of little Al to write no letters and I am not worring none because she give me her word she would let me know was they some thing the matter. *Yours truly, Jack.*

SAN DAGO, CAL., NOV. 9. ◆

Friend Al: Al some times I wisht I was not married at all and if it was not for Florrie and little Al I would go a round the world on this here trip and I guess the boys in Bedford would not be jellus if I was to go a round the world and see every thing they is to be saw and some of the boys down home has not never been no futher a way then Terre Haute and I dont mean you Al but some of the other boys. But of coarse Al when a man has got a wife and a baby they is not no chance for him to go a way on 1 of these here trips and leave them a lone so they is not no use I should even think a bout it but I cant help thinking a bout it because the boys keeps after me all the time to go. Callahan was talking a bout it to me today and he says he knowed that if I was to pitch for the giants on the trip his club would not have no chance of wining the most of the games on the trip but still and all he wisht I would go a long because he was a scared the people over in Rome and Paris and Africa and them other countrys would be awful sore if the 2 clubs come over there with out bringing none of there star pitchers along. He says We got Speaker and Crawford and Doyle and Thorp◆◇

◇ *Doyle*—Drawing of Larry Doyle by Lawrence Semon. (National Baseball Library, Cooperstown, New York)

◆ *Dummy Taylor*—Luther Hayden Taylor (1875–1958), a deaf-mute who pitched for the Giants from 1900 to 1908, except for four games for the Cleveland Naps in 1902. His lifetime record was 117–116 in 274 games. Taylor later became a staff member of the Illinois School for the Deaf. See Jack Kavanagh, "Dummy Taylor," *The Ballplayers*, p. 1071.

◆ *Nov. 9*—The Giants and White Sox played to a 7–7 tie in Los Angeles on November 9, 1913, and the Giants won 4–3 at San Diego on November 10.

◆ *Doyle*—Lawrence Joseph "Laughing Larry" Doyle (1886–1974), a second baseman who played with the Giants from 1907 through 1920, with the exception of the last nine games of the 1916 season and all of 1917, which he spent with the Cubs. Doyle hit .290 in 1,765 games; his principal achievement was leading the National League with a .320 average in 1915. See Alan R. Asnen, "Lawrence Joseph Doyle," *Biographical Dictionary of American Sports: Baseball*, pp. 156–57.

Thorp—James Francis Thorpe (1886–1953), America's finest all-around athlete of the period, star of the 1912 Olympics, and one of football's leading running

and some of them other real stars in all the positions accept pitcher and it will make us look bad if you and Mathewson don't neither 1 of you come a long. I says What is the matter with Scott and Benz and ◆ this here left hander Wiltse and he says They is not nothing the matter with none of them accept they is not no real stars like you and Mathewson and if we cant show them forreners 1 of you 2 we will feel like as if we was cheating them. I says You would not want me to pitch my best against your club would you and he says O no I would not want you to pitch your best or get your self all wore out for next year but I would want you to let up enough so as we could make a run oncet in a while so the games would not be to 1 sided. I says Well they is not no use talking a bout it because I could not leave my wife and baby and he says Why dont you write and ask your wife and tell her how it is and can you go. I says No because she would make a big holler and besides of coarse I would go any way if I wanted to go with out no I yes or no from her only I am not the kind of a man that runs off and leaves his family and besides they is not no body to leave her with because her and her sister Allens wife has had a quarrle. Then Callahan says Where is Allen at now is he still in Chi. I says I dont know where is he at and I dont care where he is at because I am threw with him. Then Callahan says I asked him would he go on the trip before the season was over but he says he could not and if I knowed where was he I would wire a telegram to him and ask him again. I says What would you want him a long for and he says Because Mcgraw is shy of pitchers and I says I would try and help him find 1. I says Well you should ought not to have no trouble finding a man like Allen to go along because his wife probily would be glad to get rid of him. Then Callahan says Well I wisht you would get a hold of where Allen is at and let me know so as I can wire him a telegram. Well Al I know where Allen is at all O. K. but I am not going to give his adress to

---

(*continued from page 179*)
backs. To call him a "real star" in baseball is an overstatement; Thorpe was a fine outfielder, but an unimpressive hitter. In 298 games with the Giants, Reds, and Braves between 1913 and 1919, he hit only .252. In 1913 he had hit only .143 for the Giants. His performance in the 1912 Olympics at Stockholm had brought him international prominence, and he was thus one of the tour's principal drawing cards. Thorpe played right field for the Giants on the tour. See Robert W. Wheeler, *Jim Thorpe: The World's Greatest Athlete* (Norman: University of Oklahoma Press, 1979).

◆ *Scott*—Scott, in general, made the best impression on foreign sports writers of any of the pitchers on the tour.

Callahan because Mcgraw has treated me all O. K. and why should I wish a man like Allen on to him and besides I am not going to give Allen no chancet to go a round the world or no wheres else after the way he acted a bout I and Florrie haveing a room in his flat and asking me to pay for it when he give me a invatation to come there and stay. Well Al it is to late now to cry in the sour milk but I wisht I had not never saw Florrie untill next year and then I and her could get married just like we done last year only I dont know would I do it again or not but I guess I would on acct. of little Al. *Your pal, Jack.*

SAN FRANCISCO, CAL., NOV. 14.

Old Pal: Well old pal what do you know a bout me being back here in San Francisco where I give the fans such a treat 2 years ago and then I was not nothing but a busher and now I am with a team that is going a round the world and are crazy to have me go a long only I cant because of my wife and baby. Callahan wired a telegram to the reporters here from Los Angeles telling them I would pitch here and I guess they is going to be 20 or 25000 out to the park and I will give them the best I got.

But what do you think Florrie has did Al. Her and the Allens has made it up there quarrle and is friends again and Marie told Florrie to write and tell me she was sorry we had that there argument and let by gones be by gones. Well Al it is all O. K. with me because I cant help not feeling sorry for Allen because I dont beleive he will be in the league next year and I feel sorry for Marie to because it must be pretty tough on her to see how well her sister done and what a misstake she made when she went and fell for a left hander that could not fool a blind man with his curve ball and if he was to hit a man in the head with his fast ball they would think there nose iched. In Florries letter she says she thinks us and the Allens could find an other flat like the 1 we had last winter and all live in it to gether in stead of going to Bedford but I have wrote to her before I started writeing this letter all ready and told her that her and I is going to Bedford and the Allens can go where they feel like and they can go and stay on a boat on Michigan lake all winter if they want to but I and Florrie is comeing to Bedford. Down to the bottom of her letter she says Allen wants to know if Callahan or Mcgraw is shy of pitchers and may be he would change his mind and go a long on the trip. Well Al I did not ask either Callahan nor Mcgraw nothing a bout it because I knowed they was looking for a star and not for no left hander that could not brake a pane of glass with his fast 1 so I wrote and told Florrie to tell Allen they was all filled up and would not have no room for no more men.

It is pretty near time to go out to the ball park and I wisht you could be here Al and hear them San Francisco fans go crazy when they hear my name anounced to pitch. I bet they wish they had of had me here this last year. *Yours truly, Jack.*

MEDFORD, ORGAN, NOV. 16.

Friend Al: Well Al you know by this time that I did not pitch the hole ◆ game in San Francisco but I was not tooken out because they was hitting me Al but because my arm went back on me all of a sudden and it was the change in the clime it that done it to me and they could not hire me to try and pitch another game in San Francisco. They was the biggest crowd there that I ever seen in San Francisco and I guess they must of been 40000 people there and I wisht you could of heard them yell when my name was anounced to pitch. But Al I would not never of went in there but for the crowd. My arm felt like a wet rag or some thing and I knowed I would not have nothing and besides the people was packed in a round the field and they had to have ground rules so when a man hit a pop fly it went in to the crowd some wheres and was a 2 bagger and all them giants could do against me was pop my fast ball up in the air and then the wind took a hold of it and dropped it in to the crowd the lucky stiffs. Doyle hit 3 of them pop ups in to the crowd so when you see them 3 2 base hits oposit his name in the score you will know they was not no real 2 base hits and the infielders would of catched them had it not of been for the wind. This here Doyle takes a awful wallop at a ball but if I was right and he swang at a ball the way he done in San Francisco the catcher would all ready be throwing me back the ball a bout the time this here Doyle was swinging at it. I can make him look like a sucker and I done it both in Kansas city and Bonham and if he will get up there and bat ◆ against me when I feel good and when they is not no wind blowing I will bet him a $25.00 suit of cloths that he cant foul 1 off of me. Well when Callahan seen how bad my arm was he says I guess I should ought to take you out and not run no chance of getting killed in there and so I quit and Faber went in to finnish it up because it dont make no diffrence if he hurts his arm or dont. But I guess Mcgraw knowed

---

◆ *the hole game in San Francisco*—The game, played on November 14, 1913, was won by the Giants, 4–3. On November 16 the teams were playing in Oakland.

◆ *Bonham*—The two teams played at Bonham, Tex., on October 30, 1913. The Giants won, 4–1.

my arm was sore to because he did not try and kid me like he done that day in Chi because he has saw enough of me since then to know I can make his club look rotten when I am O. K. and my arm is good. On the train that night he come up and says to me Well Jack we catched you off your strid today or you would of gave us a beating and then he says What your arm needs is more work and you should ought to make the hole trip with us and then you would be in fine shape for next year but I says You cant get me to make no trip so you might is well not do no more talking a bout it and then he says Well I am sorry and the girls over to Paris will be sorry to but I guess he was just jokeing a bout the last part of it.

Well Al we go to 1 more town in Organ and then to Washington but of coarse it is not the same Washington we play at in the summer but this is the state Washington and have not got no big league club and the boys gets there boat in 4 more days and I will quit them and then I will come strate back to Chi and from there to Bedford.

Your pal, Jack.

PORTLAND, ORGAN, NOV. 17. ◆

Friend Al: I have just wrote a long letter to Florrie but I feel like as if I should ought to write to you because I wont have no more chance for a long while that is I wont have no more chance to male a letter because I will be on the pacific Ocean and un less we should run passed a boat that was comeing the other way they would not be no chance of getting no letter maled. Old pal I am going to make the hole trip clear a round the world and back and so I wont see you this winter after all but when I do see you Al I will have a lot to tell you a bout my trip and besides I will write you a letter a bout it from every place we head in at.

I guess you will be supprised a bout me changeing my mind and makeing the hole trip but they was not no way for me to get out of it and I will tell you how it all come off. While we was still in that there Medford yesterday Mcgraw and Callahan come up to me and says was they not no chance of me changeing my mind a bout makeing the hole trip. I says No they was not. Then Callahan says Well I dont know what are we going to do then and I says Why and he says Comiskey just got a letter from president Wilson the President of the united

◆ *Nov. 17*—The White Sox defeated the Giants at Portland, 2–0, on November 18.

states and in the letter president Wilson says he had got an other letter from the king of Japan who says that they would not stand for the White Sox and giants comeing to Japan un less they brought all there stars a long and president Wilson says they would have to take there stars a long because he was a scared if they did not take there stars a long Japan would get mad at the united states and start a war and then where would we be at. So Comiskey wired a telegram to president Wilson and says Mathewson could not make the trip because he was so old but would everything be all O.K. if I was to go a long and president Wilson wired a telegram back and says Yes he had been talking to the priest from Japan and he says Yes it would be all O.K. I asked them would they show me the letter from president Wilson because I thought may be they might be kiding me and they says they could not show me no letter because when Comiskey got the letter he got so mad that he tore it up. Well Al I finely says I did not want to brake up there trip but I knowed Florrie would not stand for letting me go so Callahan says All right I will wire a telegram to a friend of mine in Chi and have him get a hold of Allen and send him out here and we will take him a long and I says It is to late for Allen to get here in time and Mcgraw says No they was a train that only took 2 days ◆ from Chi to where ever it was the boat is going to sale from because the train come a round threw canada and it was down hill all the way. Then I says Well if you will wire a telegram to my wife and fix things up with her I will go a long with you but if she is going to make a holler it is all off. So we all 3 went to the telegram office to gether and we wired Florrie a telegram that must of cost $2.00 but Callahan and Mcgraw payed for it out of there own pocket and then we waited a round a long time and the anser come back and the anser was longer then the telegram we wired and it says it would not make no diffrence to her but she did not know if the baby would make a holler but he was hollering most of the time any way so that would not make no diffrence but if she let me go it was on condishon that her and the Allens could get a flat to gether and stay in Chi all winter and not go to no Bedford and hire a nurse to take care of the baby and if I would send her a check for the money I had in the bank so as she could put it in her name and draw it out when she need it. Well I says at 1st I

◆ *No they was a train that only took 2 days from Chi*—The fastest service from Chicago to Vancouver via the Soo Line and Canadian Pacific Railway required four nights.

would not stand for nothing like that but Callahan and Mcgraw showed me where I was makeing a mistake not going when I could see all them diffrent countrys and tell Florrie all a bout the trip when I come back and then in a year or 2 when the baby was a little older I could make an other trip and take little Al and Florrie a long so I finely says O. K. I would go and we wires still an other telegram to Florrie and told her O. K. and then I set down and wrote her a check for ½ the money I got in the bank and I got $500.00 all together there so I wrote the check for ½ of that or $250.00 and maled it to her and if she cant get a long on that she would be a awfull spendrift because I am not only going to be a way untill March. You should ought to of heard the boys cheer when Callahan tells them I am going to make the hole trip but when he tells them I am going to pitch for the giants and not for the White Sox I bet Crawford and Speaker and them wisht I was going to stay to home but it is just like Callahan says if they bat against me all winter the pitchers they bat against next season will look easy to them and you wont be supprised Al if Crawford and Speaker hits a bout 500 next year and if they hit good you will know why it is. Steve Evans asked me was I all fixed up with cloths and I says No but I was going out and buy some cloths includeing a full dress suit of evening cloths and he says You dont need no full dress suit of evening cloths because you look funny enough with out them. This Evans is a great kidder Al and no body never gets sore at the stuff he pulls some thing like Kid Gleason. I wisht Kid Gleason was going on the trip Al but I will tell him all a bout it when I come back.

Well Al old pal I wisht you was going a long to and I bet we could have the time of our life but I will write to you right a long Al and I will send Bertha some post cards from the diffrent places we head in at. I will try and write you a letter on the boat and male it as soon as we get to the 1st station which is either Japan or Yokohama I forgot which. Good by Al and say good by to Bertha for me and tell her how sorry I and Florrie is that we cant come to Bedford this winter but we will spend all the rest of the winters there and her and Florrie will have a plenty of time to get acquainted. Good by old pal.

Your pal, Jack.

SEATTLE, WASH., NOV. 18.

Al: Well Al it is all off and I am not going on no trip a round the world and back and I been looking for Callahan or Mcgraw for the last ½ hour to tell them I have changed my mind and am not going to make no trip because it not be fare to Florrie and besides that I think I should ought to stay home and take care of little Al and not leave him to be tooken care of by no train nurse because how do I know what would she do to him and I am not going to tell Florrie nothing a bout it but I am going to take the train tomorrow night right back to Chi and supprise her when I get there and I bet both her and little Al will be tickled to death to see me. I supose Mcgraw and Callahan will be sore at me for a while but when I tell them I want to do the right thing and not give my famly no raw deal I guess they will see where I am right.

We was to play 2 games here and was to play 1 of them in Tacoma and the other here but it rained and so we did not play neither 1 and the people was pretty mad a bout it because I was announced to pitch and they figured probily this would be there only chance to see me in axion and they made a awful holler but Comiskey says No they would not be no game because the field neither here or in Tacoma was in no ◆ shape for a game and he would not take no chance of me pitching and may be slipping in the mud and straneing my self and then where would the White Sox be at next season. So we been laying a round all the P. M. and I and Dutch Schaefer had a long talk to gether while some of the rest of the boys was out buying some cloths to take on the trip and Al I bought a full dress suit of evening cloths at Portland yesterday and now I owe Callahan the money for them and am not going on no trip so probily I wont never get to ware them and it is just $45.00 throwed a way but I would rather throw $45.00 a way then go on a trip a round the world and leave my family all winter.

Well Al I and Schaefer was talking to gether and he says Well may be this is the last time we will ever see the good old US and I says What do you mean and he says People that gos acrost the pacific Ocean most generally all ways has there ship recked and then they is not no more never heard from them. Then he asked me was I a good swimer and I says Yes I had swam a good deal in the river and he says Yes you have swam in the river but that is not nothing like swiming in the pacific Ocean because when you swim in the pacific Ocean you cant move your feet because if you move your feet the sharks comes up to the top of the water and bites at them and even if they did not bite your feet clean off there bite is poison and gives you the hiderofobeya and when you get that you start barking like a dog and the

◆ *the field neither here or in Tacoma was in no shape for a game*—As stated, both these games were rained out.

water runs in to your mouth and chokes you to death. Then he says Of coarse if you can swim with out useing your feet you are all O.K. but they is very few can do that and especially in the pacific Ocean because they got to keep useing there hands all the time to scare the sord fish a way so when you dont dare use your feet and your hands is busy you got nothing left to swim with but your stumach mussles. Then he says You should ought to get a long all O. K. because your stumach mussles should ought to be strong from the exercise they get so I guess they is not no danger from a man like you but men like Wiltse and Mike Donlin that is not hog fat like you has not got no chance. Then he says Of coarse they have been times when the boats got acrost all O. K. and only a few lifes lost but it dont offten happen and the time the old Minneapolis club made the trip the boat went ◆ down and the only thing that was saved was the catchers protector that was full of air and could not do nothing else but flote. Then he says May be you would flote to if you did not say nothing for a few days.

I asked him how far would a man got to swim if some thing went wrong with the boat and he says O not far because they is a hole lot of ilands a long the way that a man could swim to but it would not do a man no good to swim to these here ilands because they dont have nothing to eat on them and a man would probily starve to death un less he happened to swim to the sandwich ilands. Then he says But by the time you been out on the pacific Ocean a few months you wont care if you get any thing to eat or not. I says Why not and he says the pacific Ocean is so ruff that not nothing can set still not even the stuff you eat. I asked him how long did it take to make the trip acrost if they was not no ship reck and he says they should ought to get acrost a long in febuery if the weather was good. I says Well if we dont get there until febuery we wont have no time to train for next season and he says You wont need to do no training because this trip will take all the weight off of you and every thing else you got. Then he says But you should not ought to be a scared of getting sea sick because they is 1 way you can get a way from it and that is to not eat nothing at all while you are on the boat and they tell me you dont eat hardly nothing any way so you wont miss it. Then he says Of coarse if we should have

◆ *the old Minneapolis club made the trip*—The event, it need hardly be said, is fictional. As far as is known, the Minneapolis Millers never barnstormed west of Denver.

good luck and not get in to no ship reck and not get shot by 1 of them war ships we will have a grate time when we get acrost because all the girls in europe and them places is nuts over ball players and especially stars. I asked what did he mean saying we might get shot by 1 of them war ships and he say we would have to pass by Swittserland and the Swittserland war ships was all the time shooting all over the ocean and of coarse they was not trying to hit no body but they was as wild as most of them left handers and how could you tell what was they going to do next.

Well Al after I got threw talking to Schaefer I run in to Jack Sheridan the umpire and I says I did not think I would go on no trip and I told him some of the things Schaefer was telling me and Sheridan says Schaefer was kiding me and they was not no danger at all and of coarse Al I did not believe ½ of what Schaefer was telling me and that has not got nothing to do with me changeing my mind but I dont think it is not hardly fare for me to go a way on a trip like that and leave Florrie and the baby and supose some of them things really did happen like Schaefer said though of coarse he was kiding me but if 1 of them was to happen they would not be no body left to take care of Florrie and little Al and I got a $1000.00 insurence policy but how do I know after I am dead if the insurence co. comes acrost and gives my famly the money.

Well Al I will male this letter and then try again and find Mcgraw and Callahan and then I will look up a time table and see what train can I get to Chi. I dont know yet when I will be in Bedford and maybe Florrie has hired a flat all ready but the Allens can live in it by them self and if Allen says any thing a bout I paying for ½ of the rent I will bust his jaw. *Your pal, Jack.*

VICTORIA, CAN., NOV. 19.

Dear Old Al: Well old pal the boat gos tonight I am going a long and I would not be takeing no time to write this letter only I wrote to you yesterday and says I was not going and you probily would be expecting

---

◆ *Jack Sheridan*—John F. Sheridan (c. 1852–1914), an American League umpire from 1901 to 1914. After a short playing career in the minor leagues, he began umpiring in the California League in 1886, and later served in the Pacific Coast, Southern, and Western leagues. Sheridan umpired in the Players League of 1890 and reached the National League in 1892. He was a charter member of the American League staff, and served on the world tour of 1913.

◆ *Victoria, Can., Nov. 19*—The White Sox–Giants party sailed from Victoria, British Columbia, on November 19, 1913.

to see me blow in to Bedford in a few days and besides Al I got a hole lot of things to ask you to do for me if any thing happens and I want to tell you how it come a bout that I changed my mind and am going on the trip. I am glad now that I did not write Florrie no letter yesterday and tell her I was not going because now I would have to write her an other letter and tell her I was going and she would be expecting to see me the day after she got the 1st letter and in stead of seeing me she would get this 2nd. letter and not me at all. I have all ready wrote her a good by letter today though and while I was writeing it Al I all most broke down and cried and espesially when I thought a bout leaveing little Al so long and may be when I see him again he wont be no baby no more or may be some thing will of happened to him or that train nurse did some thing to him or may be I wont never see him again no more because it is pretty near a cinch that some thing will either happen to I or him. I would give all most any thing I got Al to be back in Chi with little Al and Florrie and I wisht she had not of never wired that telegram telling me I could make the trip and if some thing happens to me think how she will feel when ever she thinks a bout wireing me that telegram and she will feel all most like as if she was a murderer.

Well Al after I had wrote you that letter yesterday I found Callahan and Mcgraw and I tell them I have changed my mind and am not going on no trip. Callahan says Whats the matter and I says I dont think it would be fare to my wife and baby and Callahan says Your wife says it would be all O.K. because I seen the telegram my self. I says Yes but she dont know how dangerus the trip is and he says Whos been kiding you and I says They has not no body been kiding me. I says Dutch Schaefer told me a hole lot of stuff but I did not beleive none of it and that has not got nothing to do with it. I says I am not a scared of nothing but supose some thing should happen and then where would my wife and my baby be at. Then Callahan says Schaefer has been giveing you a lot of hot air and they is not no more danger on this trip then they is in bed. You been in a hole lot more danger when you was pitching some of them days when you had a sore arm and you would be takeing more chances of getting killed in Chi by 1 of them taxi cabs or the dog catcher then on the Ocean. This here boat we are going on is the Umpires of Japan and it has went acrost◆◇

◆ *the Umpires of Japan*—The *Empress of Japan*, a steamer of the Canadian Pacific Railway, on which the party crossed the Pacific. The ship, which had handsome

◇ *the Umpires of Japan*—The Canadian Pacific Railway's transpacific liner *Empress of Japan*. (Maritime Museum of British Columbia)

the Ocean a million times with out nothing happening and they could not nothing happen to a boat that the N. Y. giants was rideing on because they is to lucky. Then I says Well I have made up my mind to not go on no trip and he says All right then I guess we might is well call the trip off and I says Why and he says You know what president Wilson says a bout Japan and they wont stand for us comeing over there with out you a long and then Mcgraw says Yes it looks like as if the trip was off because we dont want to take no chance of starting no war between Japan and the united states. Then Callahan says You will be in fine with Comiskey if he has to call the trip off because you are a scared of getting bit by a fish. Well Al we talked and argude for a hour or a hour and ½ and some of the rest of the boys come a round and took Callahan and Mcgraws side and finely Callahan says it looked like as if they would have to posepone the trip a few days untill he could get a hold of Allen or some body and get them to take my place

---

(*continued from page 189*)
yacht-like lines, was built in 1891 by the Naval Construction & Armaments Co. of Barrow, England. A sister of the *Empress of India* and *Empress of China*, she was the only one of the three ships to survive World War I. Because of restrictions on Asian immigration she was laid up at Vancouver in 1922 and sold for scrap in 1925. Her figurehead is mounted in Stanley Park, overlooking the entrance to Vancouver Harbour.

so finely I says I would go because I would not want to brake up no trip after they had made all there plans and some of the players wifes ◆ was all ready to go and would be dissapointed if they was not no trip. So Mcgraw and Callahan says Thats the way to talk and so I am going Al and we are leaveing tonight and may be this is the last letter you will ever get from me but if they does not nothing happen Al I will write to you a lot of letters and tell you all a bout the trip but you must not be looking for no more letters for a while untill we get to Japan where I can male a letter and may be its likely as not we wont never get to Japan.

Here is the things I want to ask you to try and do Al and I am not asking you to do nothing if we get threw the trip all right but if some thing happens and I should be drownded here is what I am asking you to do for me and that is to see that the insurence co. dont skin Florrie out of that $1000.00 policy and see that she all so gets that other $250.00 out of the bank and find her some place down in Bedford to live if she is willing to live down there because she can live there a hole lot cheaper then she can live in Chi and besides I know Bertha would treat her right and help her out all she could. All so Al I want you and Bertha to help take care of little Al untill he grows up big enough to take care of him self and if he looks like as if he was going to be left handed dont let him Al but make him use his right hand for every thing. Well Al they is 1 good thing and that is if I get drownded Florrie wont have to buy no lot in no cemetary and hire no herse.

Well Al old pal you all ways been a good friend of mine and I all ways tried to be a good friend of yourn and if they was ever any thing I done to you that was not O.K. remember by gones is by gones. I want you to all ways think of me as your best old pal. Good by old pal.

Your old pal, Jack.

P.S. Al if they should not nothing happen and if we was to get acrost the Ocean all O.K. I am going to ask Mcgraw to let me work the 1st game against the White Sox in Japan because I should certainly ought to be right after giveing my arm a rest and not doing nothing at all on the trip acrost and I bet if Mcgraw lets me work Crawford and Speaker will wisht the boat had of sank. You know me Al.

◆ *some of the players wifes was all ready to go and would be dissapointed if they was not no trip*—Present on the trip were the wives of players Larry Doyle, Hooks Wiltse, Hans Lobert (of the Phillies), and Jim Thorpe, plus the wives of several of the management.

Call for Mr. Keefe!

ST. LOUIS, APRIL 10. ◆

Friend Al: Well Al the training trips over and we open up the season here tomorrow and I suppose the boys back home is all anxious to know about our chances and what shape the boys is in. Well old pal you can tell them we are out after that old flag this year and the club that beats us will know they have been in a battle. I'll say they will.

Speaking for myself personly I never felt better in my life and you know what that means Al. It means I will make a monkey out of this league and not only that but the boys will all have more confidence in themself and play better baseball when they know my arms right and that I can give them the best I got and if Rowland handles the club ◆◇ right and don't play no favorites like last season we will be so far out

"Call for Mr. Keefe!" was published in *The Saturday Evening Post*, CXC (March 9, 1918), 3–4, 78, 80, 82, and has been reprinted in Matthew J. Bruccoli and Richard Layman, eds., *Some Champions: Sketches and Fiction by Ring Lardner* (New York: Charles Scribner's Sons, 1976), pp. 99–116.

◆ *April 10*—As stated, the White Sox were in St. Louis, and would open the season on April 11, 1917. Jim Scott won in relief of Claude Williams, 7–2.

◆ *Rowland*—Clarence Henry "Pants" Rowland (1879–1969), who had succeeded Callahan as manager of the White Sox in 1915. He proved a great success, leading the team to third place in 1915, to second in 1916, and to the pennant in 1917. The team, fully up to Keefe's expectations, proved to be the only White Sox team

◇ *Rowland*—Pants Rowland, at right, with Eddie Cicotte before the 1917 World Series (see footnote, p. 65). (National Baseball Library, Cooperstown, New York)

in front by the middle of July that Boston and the rest of them will ◆ think we have jumped to some other league.

Well I suppose the old towns all excited about Uncle Sam declairing ◆ war on Germany. Personly I am glad we are in it but between you and I Al I figure we ought to of been in it a long time ago right after the Louisiana was sank. I often say alls fair in love and war but that don't ◆ mean the Germans or no one else has got a right to murder American citizens but thats about all you can expect from a German and anybody that expects a square deal from them is a sucker. You don't see none

(*continued from page 192*)
to win 100 games. It won a notable World Series from the Giants. Rowland's last year as manager was 1918, when the team, much of whose personnel went to work in shipyards or war factories, finished sixth. Rowland, who never played major league baseball, later served as president of the Pacific Coast League and as a front-office official of the Chicago Cubs. See Norman L. Macht, "Pants Rowland," *The Ballplayers*, p. 942.

◆ *Boston*—The Red Sox, who had won the pennants of 1915 and 1916, were widely expected to win the 1917 pennant. They were to finish second, ten games behind the White Sox.

◆ *Uncle Sam declairing war on Germany.*—President Woodrow Wilson requested a declaration of war in a message to Congress on April 2, 1917. The Senate complied on April 4 and the House of Representatives on April 6.

◆ *Louisiana*—Obviously, the *Lusitania*, one of the great passenger liners of the day, torpedoed off the coast of Ireland on May 7, 1915.

of them umpireing in our league but at that they couldn't be no worse than the ones we got. Some of ours is so crooked they can't lay in a birth only when the trains making a curve.

But speaking about the war Al you couldn't keep me out of it only for Florrie and little Al depending on me for sport and of course theys the ball club to and I would feel like a trader if I quit them now when it looks like this is our year. So I might just as well make up my mind to whats got to be and not mop over it but I like to kid the rest of the boys and make them think I'm going to enlist to see their face fall and tonight at supper I told Gleason I thought I would quit the club and join the army. He tried to laugh it off with some of his funny stuff. He says "They wouldn't take you." "No," I said. "I suppose Uncle Sam is turning down men with a perfect physic." So he says "They don't want a man that if a shell would hit him in the head it would explode all over the trench and raise havioc." I forget what I said back to him.

Well Al I don't know if I will pitch in this serious or not but if I do I will give them a touch of high life but maybe Rowland will save me to open up at Detroit where a mans got to have something besides ◆ their glove. It takes more than camel flags to beat that bunch. I'll say it does. *Your pal, Jack.*

CHICAGO, APRIL 15. ◆

Friend Al: Well Al here I am home again and Rowland sent some of us home from St. Louis instead of takeing us along to Detroit and I suppose he is figureing on saveing me to open up the home season ◆ next Thursday against St. Louis because they always want a big crowd on opening day and St. Louis don't draw very good unless theys some extra attraction to bring the crowd out. But anyway I was glad to get home and see Florrie and little Al and honest Al he is cuter than ever and when he seen me he says "Who are you?" Hows that for a 3 year old?

Well things has been going along pretty good at home while I was away only it will take me all summer to pay the bills Florrie has ran

---

◆ *to open up at Detroit*—The White Sox opened at Detroit on April 15, winning 6–2 behind Jim Scott.

◆ *April 15*—Unaccountably, Keefe neglects to mention that Eddie Cicotte pitched the only no-hit game of his career on April 14, shutting out the Browns, 11–0.

◆ *to open up the home season next Thursday against St. Louis*—The White Sox opened the home season against St. Louis on Thursday, April 19, losing to Eddie Plank, 6–2. Scott started, but was knocked out in the third inning.

up on me and you ought to be thankfull that Bertha aint 1 of these Apollos thats got to keep everybody looking at them or they can't eat. Honest Al to look at the clothes Florrie has boughten you would think we was planning to spend the summer at Newport News or somewhere. ◆ And she went and got herself a hired girl that sticks us for $8.00 per week and all as she does is cook up the meals and take care of little Al and run wild with a carpet sweeper and dust rag every time you set down to read the paper. I says to Florrie "What is the idea? The 3 of us use to get along O. K. without no help from Norway." So she says "I got sick in tired of staying home all the time or dragging the baby along with me when I went out." So I said I remembered when she wouldn't leave no one else take care of the kid only herself and she says "Yes but that was when I didn't know nothing about babys and every time he cried I thought he had lumbago or something but now I know he has got no intentions of dying so I quit worring about him."

So I said "Yes but I can't afford no high price servants to say nothing about dressing you like an actor and if you think I am going to spend all my salary on silks and satans and etc. you will get a big supprise." So she says "You might as well spend your money on me as leave the ball players take it away from you in the poker game and show their own wives a good time with it. But if you don't want me to spend your money I will go out and get some of my own to spend." Then I said "What will you do teach school?" And she says "No and I won't teach school either." So I said "No I guess you won't. But if you think you want to try standing up behind a cigar counter or something all day why go ahead and try it and we'll see how long you will last." So she says "I don't have to stand behind no counter but I can go in business for myself and make more then you do." So I said "Yes you can" and she didn't have no come back.

Imagine Al a girl saying she could make more money then a big league pitcher. Probably theys a few of them that does but they are movie actors or something and I would like to see Florrie try to be a movie actor because they got to look pleasant all the time and Florrie would strain herself.

Well Al the ski jumper has got dinner pretty near ready and after

---

◆ *Newport News*—Presumably, Keefe meant the patrician seaside resort of Newport, Rhode Island, rather than the shipbuilding center and coal port of Newport News, Virginia.

dinner I am going over North and see what the Cubs look like and I ◆ wish I pitched in that league Al and the only trouble is that I would feel ashamed when I went after my pay check. *Your old pal, Jack.*

CHICAGO, MAY 19.

Dear Friend Al: Well old pal if we wasn't married we would all have to go to war now and I mean all of us thats between 21 and 30. I suppose you seen about the Govt. passing the draft law and a whole lot of the baseball players will have to go but our club won't loose nobody except 1 or 2 bushers that don't count because all as they do any way is take up room on the bench and laugh when Rowland springs a joke.

When I first seen it in the paper this morning I thought it meant everybody that wasn't crippled up or something but Gleason explained it to me that if you got somebody to sport they leave you home and thats fair enough but he also says they won't take no left handers on acct. of the guns all being made for right handed men and thats just like the lucky stiffs to set in a rocking chair and take it easy while the regular fellows has got to go over there and get shot up but anyway the yellow stiffs would make a fine lot of soldiers because the first time a German looked X eyed at them they would wave a flag of truants.

But I can't help from wishing this thing had of come off before I seen Florrie or little Al and if I had money enough saved up so as they wouldn't have to worry I would go any way but I wouldn't wait for no draft. Gleason says I will have to register family or no family when the time comes but as soon as I tell them about Florrie they will give me an excuse. I asked him what they would do with the boys that wasn't excused and if they would send them right over to France and he says No they would keep them here till they had learned to talk German. He says "You can't fight nobody without a quarrel and you can't quarrel with a man unless they can understand what you are calling them." So I asked him how about the aviators because their

---

◆ *see what the Cubs look like*—The Cubs of 1917 were to finish fifth with a 74–80 record. The team was in the second year of its tenancy of Weeghman Park, former home of the Chicago Whales of the Federal League, now Wrigley Field, at Clark and Addison streets. Keefe's statement that he would be ashamed to pick up his paycheck there is, off the evidence of a later passage attributed to Gleason, a gesture of contempt for National League hitting. Although in Cobb, Jackson, Speaker, Eddie Collins, and others, the American League had the outstanding individual hitters of the time, the overall averages of the two leagues were not significantly different. In 1917 the American League hit .248 and the National .249. Nor could it be argued that the quality of the pitching differed significantly, one league from the other.

machines would be makeing so much noise that they couldn't tell if the other one was talking German or rag time and he said "Well if you are in an areoplane and you see a German areoplane coming tords you you can pretty near guess that he don't want to spoon with you."

Thats what I would like to be Al is an aviator and I think Gleasons afraid I'm going to bust into that end of the game though he pretends like he don't take me in ernest. "Why don't you?" he said "You could make good there all right because the less sense they got the better. But I wish you would quit practiceing till you get away from here." I asked him what he meant quit practiceing. "Well" he said "you was up in the air all last Tuesday afternoon." ◆

He was refering to that game I worked against the Phila. club but honest Al my old souper was so sore I couldn't cut loose. Well Al a ◆ mans got a fine chance to save money when they are married to a girl like Florrie. When I got paid Tuesday the first thing when I come home she wanted to borrow $200.00 and that was all I had comeing so I said "What am I going to do the next 2 weeks walk back and forth to the ball park and back?" I said "What and the hell do you want with $200.00?" So then she begin to cry so I split it with her and give her a $100.00 and she wouldn't tell me what she wanted it for but she says she was going to supprise me. Well Al I will be supprised if she don't land us all out to the county farm but you can't do nothing with them when they cry. *Your pal, Jack.*

CHICAGO, MAY 24.

Friend Al: What do you think Florrie has pulled off now? I told you she was fixing to land us in the poor house and I had the right dope. With the money I give her and some she got somewheres else she has opened up a beauty parlor on 43th St. right off of Michigan. Her and ◆ a girl that worked in a place like it down town.

◆ *last Tuesday afternoon*—Actually, on Tuesday, May 15, Joe Benz beat the Athletics, 11–0.

◆ *souper*—Here Keefe uses a common contraction for "soupbone," a term for a pitcher's throwing arm that dates from about 1910. Paul Dickson, in his *Baseball Dictionary*, states that the word had its origin in a pitcher's evaluation of his arm being as important to his performance as a soupbone is to soup. See *The Dickson Baseball Dictionary*, p. 365. Alternatively, it may be a term of self-derogation for a well-used piece of bone and muscle.

◆ *43th St. right off of Michigan*—A location a mile south of the ballpark and about a half-mile to the east. The shop would have drawn on a densely populated neighborhood of apartment buildings in the immediate vicinity, and on the affluent Kenwood development of single-family homes to the southeast.

Well Al when she sprung it on me you couldn't of knocked me down with a feather. I always figured girls was kind of crazy but I never seen one loose her mind as quick as that and I don't know if I ought to have them take her to some home or leave her learn her lesson and get over it.

I know you ain't got no beauty parlor in Bedford so I might as well tell you what they are. They are for women only and the women goes to them when they need something done to their hair or their face or their nails before a wedding or a eucher party or something. For inst. you and Bertha was up here and you wanted to take her to a show and she would have to get fixed up so she would go to this place and tell them to give her the whole treatment and first they would wash the grime out of her hair and then comb it up fluffy and then they would clean up her complexion with buttermilk and either get rid of the moles or else paint them white and then they would put some eyebrows on her with a pencil and red up her lips and polish her teeth and pair her finger nails and etc. till she looked as good as she could and it would cost her $5.00 or $10.00 according to what they do to her and if they would give her a bath and a massage I suppose its extra.

Well theys plenty of high class beauty parlors down town where women can go and know they will get good service but Florrie thinks she can make it pay out here with women that maybe haven't time to go clear down town because their husband or their friend might loose his mind in the middle of the afternoon and phone home that he had tickets for the Majestic or something and then of course they would ◆ have to rush over to some place in the neighborhood for repairs.

I didn't know Florrie was wise to the game but it seems she has been takeing some lessons down town without telling me nothing about it and this Miss Nevins thats in partners with her says Florrie is a darb. Well I wouldn't have no objections if I thought they was a chance for them to make good because she acts like she liked the work and its right close to where we live but it looks to me like their expenses would eat them up. I was in the joint this morning and the different smells alone must of cost them $100.00 to say nothing about all the bottles and cans and tools and brushs and the rent and furniture besides. I

◆ *the Majestic*—The city's leading vaudeville theater of the day, located on Monroe Street, just west of State Street. After standing idle for most of the interwar period, the theater was reopened after World War II as the Schubert and remains in operation today.

told Florrie I said "You got everything here but patients." She says "Don't worry about them. They will come when they find out about us." She says they have sent their cards to all the South Side 400.

"Well" I said "if they don't none of them show up in a couple of months I suppose you will call on the old meal ticket." So she says "You should worry." So I come away and went over to the ball park.

When I seen Kid Gleason I told him about it and he asked me where Florrie got the money to start up so I told him I give it to her. "You" he says "Where did you get it?" So just jokeing I said "Where do you suppose I got it? I stole it." So he says "You did if you got it from this ball club." But he was kidding Al because of course he knows I'm no thief. But I got the laugh on him this afternoon when Silk ◆ O'Loughlin chased him out of the ball park. Johnson was working against us and they was two out and Collins on second base and Silk called a third strike on Gandil that was down by his corns. So Gleason ◆◇ hollered "All right Silk you won't have to go to war. You couldn't pass the eye test." So Silk told him to get off of the field. So then I hollered something at Silk and he hollered back at me "That will be all from you you big busher." So I said "You are a busher yourself you busher." So he said:

◆ *this afternoon*—In the actual game of May 24, Reb Russell beat George Dumont of the Senators, 1–0 in 12 innings.

Silk O'Loughlin—Francis H. O'Loughlin (c. 1870–1918), a highly regarded umpire in the American League from 1902 until his death in the influenza epidemic of 1918. He holds the record for working the most no-hit games, seven. He did not work the game of May 24. See Rich Marazzi, "Silk O'Loughlin," *The Ballplayers*, p. 825.

◆ *Gandil*—Charles Arnold "Chick" Gandil (1888–1970), the White Sox first baseman, notorious as the organizer of the infamous "Black Sox" plot. A rough-and-ready character more typical of western mining towns or lumber camps than of his staid birthplace of St. Paul, Minn., Gandil had been a semipro baseball player, boxer, and boilermaker in his youth. He had played 77 games for the White Sox in 1910, then played for Washington from 1912 to 1915, and for Cleveland in 1916. Returning to the White Sox in 1917, Gandil proved a steady hitter in the .270–.290 range, and a fine fielder. A righthanded first baseman, he rarely made a one-handed catch. In his nine seasons in the American League, ending in 1919, he hit .277 in 1,147 games. Gandil held out for $10,000 in 1920, and, failing to get it, played and managed in an "outlaw" league in Idaho. He was, of course, declared permanently ineligible for Organized Baseball following the revelation of the scandal late in the 1920 season. He spent most of the rest of his life as a plumber in Oakland, Calif. For Gandil's version of the scandal, which differs radically from orthodox interpretations, see Arnold "Chick" Gandil, as told to Melvin Durslag, "This Is My Story of the Black Sox Series," *Sports Illustrated*, V, No. 12 (September 17, 1956), 62–68. Briefly, Gandil states that the players first agreed with the gamblers to throw the Series, but then reneged, so that no games were thrown. This argument has had little or no acceptance.

◇ *Gandil*—Chick Gandil in the uniform of the 1917 White Sox, illustrating his two-handed style of fielding first base. (National Baseball Library, Cooperstown, New York)

"Get off of the bench and let one of the ball players set down."

So I and Gleason stalled a while and finely come into the club house and I said "Well Kid I guess we told him something that time." "Yes" says Gleason "you certainly burned him up but the trouble with me is I can't never think of nothing to say till it's to late." So I said "When a man gets past sixty you can't expect their brain to act quick." And he didn't say nothing back.

Well we win the ball game any way because Cicotte shut them out. The way some of the ball players was patting him on the back afterwards you would have thought it was the 1st. time anybody had ever pitched a shut out against the Washington club but I don't see no reason to swell a man up over it. If you shut out Detroit or Cleveland you are doing something but this here Washington club gets a bonus ◆ every time they score a run.

But it does look like we was going to cop that old flag and play the Giants for the big dough and it will sure be the Giants we will have to play against though some of the boys seem to think the Cubs have got

◆ *this here Washington club gets a bonus every time they score a run*—The Senators' poor hitting is a recurring theme in Lardner's baseball fiction, but the 1917 club was not outstandingly weak in this respect. The team finished in fifth place, and also fifth in runs scored, with 543.

a chance on acct. of them just winning 10 straight on their eastren ◆ trip but as Gleason says how can a club help from winning 10 straight in that league? *Your pal, Jack.*

CHICAGO, JUNE 6.

Friend Al: Well Al the clubs east and Rowland left me home because ◆ my old souper is sore again and besides I had to register yesterday for the draft. They was a big crowd down to the place we registered and you ought to seen them when I come in. They was all trying to get up close to me and I was afraid some of them would get hurt in the jam. All of them says "Hello Jack" and I give them a smile and shook hands with about a dozen of them. A man hates to have everybody stareing at you but you got to be pleasant or they will think you are swelled up and besides a man can afford to put themself out a little if its going to give the boys any pleasure.

I don't know how they done with you Al but up here they give us a card to fill out and then they give us another one to carry around with us to show that we been registered and what our number is. I had to put down my name on the first card and my age and where I live and the day I was born and what month and etc. Some of the questions was crazy like "Was I a natural born citizen?" I wonder what they think I am. Maybe they think I fell out of a tree or something. Then I had to tell them I was born in Bedford, Ind. and it asked what I done for a liveing and I put down that I was a pitcher but the man made me change it to ball player and then I had to give Comiskey's name and address and then name the people that was dependent on me so I put down a wife and one child.

And the next question was if I was married or single. I supposed they would know enough to know that a man with a wife dependent on him was probably married. Then it says what race and I had a notion to put down "pennant" for a joke but the man says to put down white. Then it asked what military service had I had and of course I says none and then come the last question Did I claim exemption and what grounds so the man told me to write down married with dependents.

◆ *them just winning 10 straight*—The Cubs did win ten straight, beginning with victories over Pittsburgh at home on May 6 and 7, and ending with a win at Boston on May 17.

◆ *the clubs east*—The White Sox opened their first eastern trip on June 1 at Philadelphia. Red Faber did not make the trip, but was expected to rejoin the team in a week to ten days.

Then the man turned over to the back of the card and wrote down about my looks. Just that I was tall and medium build and brown eyes and brown hair. And the last question was if I had lost an arm or leg or hand or foot or both eyes or was I other wise disabled so I told him about my arm being sore and thats why I wasn't east with the club but he didn't put it down. So thats all they was to it except the card he give me with my number which is 3403.

It looks to me like it was waisting a mans time to make you go down there and wait for your turn when they know you are married and got a kid or if they don't know it they could call up your home or the ball park and find it out but of course if they called up my flat when I or Florrie wasn't there they wouldn't get nothing but a bunch of Swede talk that they couldn't nobody understand and I don't believe the girl knows herself what she is talking about over the phone. She can talk english pretty good when shes just talking to you but she must think all the phone calls is long distance from Norway because the minute she gets that receiver up to her ear you can't hardly tell the difference between she and Hughey Jennings on the coaching line.

I told Florrie I said "This girl could make more then $8.00 per week if she would get a job out to some ball park as announcer and announce the batterys and etc. She has got the voice for it and she would be right in a class with the rest of them because nobody could make heads or tales out of what she was trying to get at."

Speaking about Florrie what do you think Al? They have had enough suckers to pay expenses and also pay up some of the money they borrowed and Florrie says if their business gets much bigger they will have to hire more help. How would you like a job Al white washing some dames nose or levelling off their face with a steam roller? Of course I am just jokeing Al because they won't allow no men around the joint but wouldn't it be some job Al? I'll say so. *Your old pal, Jack.*

CHICAGO, JUNE 21.

Dear Al: Well Al I suppose you read in the paper the kind of luck I ◆ had yesterday but of course you can't tell nothing from what them dam reporters write and if they know how to play ball why aint they playing it instead of trying to write funny stuff about the ball game

◆ *the kind of luck I had yesterday*—On June 20, the White Sox played Cleveland in Chicago, winning 3–2 as Claude Williams held the Indians to four hits.

but at that some of it is funny Al because its so rotten its good. For inst. one of them had it in the paper this morning that I flied out to Speaker in that seventh inning. Well listen Al I hit that ball right on ◆ the pick and it went past that shortstop so fast that he didn't even have time to wave at it and if Speaker had of been playing where he belongs that ball would of went between he and Graney and bumped against ◆◇ the wall. But no. Speakers laying about ten feet back of second base and over to the left and of course the ball rides right to him and there was the whole ball game because that would of drove in 2 runs and made them play different then they did in the eigth. If a man is supposed to be playing center field why don't he play center field and of course I thought he was where he ought to been or I would of swung different.

Well the eigth opened up with the score 1 and 1 and I get 2 of them out but I got so much stuff I can't stick it just where I want to and I give Chapman a base on balls. At that the last one cut the heart of the plate but Evans called it a ball. Evans lives in Cleveland. Well I said ◆ "All right Bill you won't have to go to war. You couldn't pass the eye test."

◆ *Speaker*—Tristam E. "Tris" Speaker (1888–1958), the Indians centerfielder and Ty Cobb's only serious rival as the greatest outfielder of the dead-ball era. Speaker broke in with the Red Sox in 1907 and went to the Indians in 1916, the year in which his .386 broke Cobb's otherwise continuous series of batting championships from 1907 to 1919. Speaker became manager of the Indians during the 1919 season and held the post through 1926. He played for Washington in 1927 and finally joined Cobb with the Athletics in 1928. In 22 seasons Speaker played 2,789 games, made 3,515 hits, including 793 doubles (a lifetime record that still stands), and hit .344 (sixth all-time). He was considered the best defensive centerfielder of his day, and today is still considered one of the best ever. The passage accurately describes Speaker's style of playing center field: he played a shallow position, so as to be able to participate in double plays, and made use of his great speed to go back on fly balls. He was elected to the Baseball Hall of Fame in 1937. See Ellery H. Clark, Jr., "Tristam E. Speaker," *Biographical Dictionary of American Sports: Baseball*, pp. 528–30.

◆ *Graney*—John Gladstone Graney (1886–1978), the Indians' veteran leftfielder. A Canadian, Graney failed in a brief trial as a pitcher with Cleveland in 1908, then returned as an outfielder in 1910. He played with Cleveland through the 1922 season, hitting .250 in 1,402 games. Graney is notable as the first baseball player to become a full-time broadcaster. As the regular radio voice of the Indians from 1932 to 1953, Graney was crisp, authoritative, and extremely effective. His familiarity with American League ballparks made him unequaled in the recreation of games from telegraphic accounts, and his fiery loyalty to the Indians, evident in a passage below, came through his broadcasts clearly. See Ted Patterson, "Jack Graney: The First Player-Broadcaster," *Baseball Research Journal*, II (1973), 80–86.

◆ *Evans lives in Cleveland*—As stated, Evans lived in Cleveland, although he neither was born there nor died there.

◇ *Graney*—Cleveland Indians leftfielder Jack Graney in fielding practice. (National Baseball Library, Cooperstown, New York)

So he says "You must of read that one in a book." "No" I said "I didn't read it in no book either."

So up comes this Speaker and I says "What do you think you are going to do you lucky stiff?" So he says "I'm going to hit one where theys nobody standing in the way of it." I said "Yes you are." But I had to hold Chapman up at first base and Schalk made me waist 2 thinking Chapman was going and then of course I had to ease up and Speaker cracked one down the first base line but Gandil got his glove on it and if he hadn't of messed it all up he could of beat Speaker to the bag himself but instead of that they all started to ball me out for not covering. I told them to shut their mouth. Then Roth come up and I ◆ took a half wind up because of course I didn't think Chapman would

◆ *Roth*—Robert Frank "Braggo" Roth (1892–1936), an outfielder who played 34 games for the White Sox in 1914 and 70 in 1915 before moving on to the Indians, for whom he played regularly from 1915 to 1918. Between 1919 and 1921 he played successively for the Red Sox, Athletics, Senators, and Yankees. A

be enough of a bone head to steal third with 2 out but him and Speaker pulled a double steal and then Rowland and all of them begin to yell at me and they got my mind off of what I was doing and then Schalk asked for a fast one though he said afterwards he didn't but I would of made him let me curve the ball if they hadn't got me all nervous yelling at me. So Roth hit one to left field that Jackson could of caught in his hip pocket if he had been playing right. So 2 runs come in and then Rowland takes me out and I would of busted him only for makeing a seen on the field.

I said to him "How can you expect a man to be at his best when I have not worked for a month?" So he said "Well it will be more than a month before you will work for me again." "Yes" I said "because I am going to work for Uncle Sam and join the army." "Well," he says "you won't need no steel helmet." "No" I said "and you wouldn't either." Then he says "I'm afraid you won't last long over there because the first time they give you a hand grenade to throw you will take your wind up and loose a hand." So I said "If Chapman is a smart ball player why and the hell did he steal third base with 2 out?" He couldn't answer that but he says "What was you doing all alone out in No Mans Land on that ball of Speakers to Gandil?" So I told him to shut up and I went in the club house and when he come in I didn't speak to him or to none of the rest of them either.

Well Al I would quit right now and go up to Fort Sheridan and try ◆ for a captain only for Florrie and little Al and of course if it come to a show down Comiskey would ask me to stick on acct. of the club being in the race and it wouldn't be the square thing for me to walk out on him when he has got his heart set on the pennant. *Your pal, Jack.*

CHICAGO, JULY 5.

Friend Al: Just a few lines Al to tell you how Florrie is getting along and I bet you will be surprised to hear about it. Well Al she paid me back my $100.00 day before yesterday and she showed me their figures for the month of June and I don't know if you will beleive it or not but

---

(*continued from page 204*)
remarkably consistent player, Roth hit .284 in 811 games, never going above .294 or below .268. His seven home runs in 1915 tied Sam Crawford's record of 1908 for the lowest number ever to lead the American League. See Jack Kavanagh, "Braggo Roth," *The Ballplayers*, p. 940.

◆ *Fort Sheridan*—A military installation at Highwood, Illinois, in the Chicago north suburbs, the principal facility of the U.S. Army in the Chicago area.

she and Miss Nevins cleared $400.00 for the month or $200.00 a peace over and above all expenses and she says the business will be even better in the fall and winter time on acct. of more people going to partys and theaters then. How is that for the kind of a wife to have Al and the best part of it is that she is stuck on the work and a whole lot happier then when she wasn't doing nothing. They got 2 girls working besides themself and they are talking about moveing into a bigger store somewheres and she says we will have to find a bigger flat so as we can have a nurse and a hired girl instead of just the one.

Tell Bertha about it Al and tell her that when she comes up to Chi she can get all prettied up and I will see they don't charge her nothing for it.

The clubs over in Detroit but it was only a 5 day trip so Rowland ◆ left me home to rest up my arm for the eastren clubs and Phila. is due ◆ here the day after tomorrow and all as I ask is a chance at them. My arm don't feel just exactly right but I could roll the ball up to the plate and beat that club.

Its a cinch now that the Giants is comeing through in the other ◆ league and if we can keep going it will be some worlds serious between ◇ the 2 biggest towns in the country and the club that wins ought to grab off about $4500.00 a peace per man. Is that worth going after Al? I'll say so. *Your old pal, Jack.*

CHICAGO, JULY 20.

Friend Al: Well Al I don't suppose you remember my draft number and I don't remember if I told it to you or not. It was 3403 Al. And it ◆ was the 5th number drawed at Washington.

◆ *it was only a 5 day trip*—It was in fact a seven-day trip, June 30–July 2 in Cleveland and July 3–6 in Detroit.

◆ *Phila. is due here the day after tomorrow*—The Athletics were due on the 22nd—a prospect to bring joy to any opposing pitcher. Connie Mack, feeling that his championship club of 1914 was past its peak, and fearing depredations by the Federal League or the draft board (should the United States become a participant in World War I), broke up the team, beginning in 1915. He then endeavored to rebuild, largely with college players, but it was a slow process, producing seven consecutive last-place teams—still the major league record. The team had hit bottom in 1916 with its 36–117 performance; the 1917 club was a considerable improvement, finishing 55–98, only a game and a half behind the Browns.

◆ *the Giants is comeing through in the other league*—On July 5 the Giants led the National League by a four-game margin over Philadelphia.

◆ *3403*—This was actually the fourth number drawn at the draft lottery on July 20. The order was 258, 2522, 458, and 3403.

◇ *some worlds serious between the 2 biggest towns in the country*—As Keefe predicted, the World Series would indeed match the White Sox against the Giants. The White Sox adopted a new uniform for the series, with a patriotic motif of thirteen stars on the "S" in the team logo and an American flag on each sleeve. Here the uniform is worn by Joe Jackson, left, and Happy Felsch. (National Baseball Library, Cooperstown, New York)

Well old pal they can wipe the town of Washington off of the map and you won't hear no holler from me. The day before yesterday ◆ Rowland sends me in against the Washington club and of course it had to be Johnson for them. And I get beat 3 and 2 and I guess its the only time this season that Washington scored 3 runs in 1 day. And the next thing they announce the way the draft come out and I'm No. 5 and its a misery to me why my number wasn't the 1st. they drawed out instead of the 5th.

◆ *The day before yesterday Rowland sends me in against the Washington club*—On July 18 the White Sox beat Washington 4–0 and 7–4 at Chicago behind Benz and Dave Danforth. Johnson did not pitch. Rather, he did so on the 17th, losing to Faber in the second game of a doubleheader.

Well Al of course it don't mean I got to go if I don't want to. I can get out of it easy enough by telling them about Florrie and little Al and besides Gleason says they have promised Ban Johnson that they won't take no baseball stars till the seasons over and maybe not then and besides theys probably some White Sox fans that will go to the front for me and get me off on acct. of the club being in the fight for the pennant and they can't nobody say I'm trying to get excused because I said all season that I would go in a minute if it wasn't for my family and the club being in the race and I give $50.00 last week for a liberty bond that will only bring me in $1.75 per annum which is nothing you might say. You couldn't sport a flee on $1.75 per annum.

Florrie wanted I should go right down to the City Hall or where ever it is you go and get myself excused but Gleason says the only thing to do is just wait till they call me and then claim exemptions. I read somewheres a while ago that President Wilson wanted baseball kept up because the people would need amusement and I asked Gleason if he had read about that and he says "Yes but that won't get you nothing because the rest of the soldiers will need amusement even more then the people."

Well Al I don't know what your number was or how you come out but I hope you had better luck but if you did get drawed you will probably have a hard time getting out of it because you don't make no big salary and you got no children and Bertha could live with your mother and pick up a few dollars sowing. Enough to pay for her board and clothes. Of course they might excuse you for flat feet which they say you can't get in if you have them. But if I was you Al I would be tickled to death to get in because it would give you a chance to see something outside of Bedford and if your feet gets by you ought to be O. K.

I guess they won't find fault with my feet or anything about me as far physical goes. Hey Al?

I will write as soon as I learn anything. *Your pal, Jack.*

CHICAGO, AUG. 6.

Friend Al: Well Al I got notice last Friday that I was to show up right away over to Wendell Phillips high school where No. 5 board of ◆

◆ *Wendell Phillips high school*—The principal public high school of the White Sox neighborhood, on 39th Street near Michigan Boulevard. It bears the name of Wendell Phillips (1811–1884), the abolitionist orator of the mid-nineteenth-century. The draft was administered locally through the Chicago public-school system.

exemptions was setting but when I got over there it was jamed so I went back there today and I have just come home from there now.

The 1st. man I seen was the doctor and he took my name and number and then he asked me if my health was O. K. and I told him it was only I don't feel good after meals. Then he asked me if I was all sound and well right now so I told him my pitching arm was awful lame and that was the reason I hadn't went east with the club. Then he says "Do you understand that if a man don't tell the truth about themself here they are libel to prison?" So I said he didn't have to worry about that.

So then he made me strip bear and I wish you had seen his eyes pop out when he got a look at my shoulders and chest. I stepped on the scales and tipped the bean at 194 and he measured me at 6 ft. 1 and a half. Then he went all over me and poked me with his finger and counted my teeth and finely he made me tell him what different letters was that he held up like I didn't know the alphabet or something. So when he was through he says "Well I guess you ain't going to die right away." He signed the paper and sent me to the room where the rest of the board was setting.

Well 1 of them looked up my number and then asked me did I claim exemptions. I told him yes and he asked me what grounds so I said "I sport a wife and baby and besides I don't feel like it would be a square deal to Comiskey for me to walk out on him now." So he says "Have you got an affidavit from your wife that you sport her?" So I told him no and he says "Go and get one and bring it back here tomorrow but you don't need to bring none from Comiskey." So you see Comiskey must stand pretty good with them.

So he give me a blank for Florrie to fill out and when she gets home we will go to a notary and tend to it and tomorrow they will fix up my excuse and then I won't have nothing to think about only to get the old souper in shape for the big finish. *Your pal, Jack.*

CHICAGO, AUG. 8.

Dear Old Pal: Well old pal it would seem like the best way to get along in this world is to not try and get nowheres because the minute a man gets somewheres they's people that can't hardly wait to bite your back.

The 1st thing yesterday I went over to No. 5 board and was going to show them Florrie's affidavit but while I was pulling it out of my pocket the man I seen the day before called me over to 1 side and says "Listen Keefe I am a White Sox fan and don't want to see you get none the worst of it and if I was you I would keep a hold of that paper." So I asked him what for and he says "Do you know what the law is about telling the truth and not telling the truth and if you turn in an affidavit thats false and we find it out you and who ever made the affidavit is both libel to prison?" So I said what was he trying to get at and he says "We got information that your wife is in business for herself and makeing as high as $250.00 per month which is plenty for she and your boy to get along on." "Yes" I said "but who pays for the rent of our flat and the hired girl and what we eat?" So he says "That don't make no difference. Your wife could pay for them and that settles it."

Well Al I didn't know what to say for a minute but finely I asked him where the informations come from and he says he was tipped off in a letter that who ever wrote it didn't sign their name the sneaks and I asked him how he knowed that they was telling the truth. So he says "Its our business to look them things up. If I was you I wouldn't make no claim for exemptions but just lay quiet and take a chance."

Then all of a sudden I had an idea Al and I will tell you about it but 1st. as soon as it come to me I asked the man if this here board was all the board they was and he says no that if they would not excuse me I could appeal to the Dist. board but if he was me he wouldn't do it because it wouldn't do no good and might get me in trouble. So I said "I won't get in no trouble" and he says "All right suit yourself." So I said I would take the affadavit and go to the Dist. board but he says no that I would have to get passed on 1st. by his board and then I could appeal if I wanted to.

So I left the affidavit and he says they would notify me how I come out so then I beat it home and called up Florrie and told her they was something important and for her to come up to the flat.

Well Al here was the idea. I had been thinking for a long time that while it was all O. K. for Florrie to earn a little money in the summer when I was tied up with the club it would be a whole lot better if we was both free after the season so as we could take little Al and go on a trip somewheres or maybe spend the winter in the south but of course if she kept a hold of her share in the business she couldn't get away so the best thing would be to sell out to Miss Nevins for a good peace of money and we could maybe buy us a winter home somewheres with what she got and whats comeing to me in the worlds serious.

So when Florrie got home I put it up to her. I said "Florrie I'm sick in tired of haveing you tied up in business because it don't seem right for a married woman to be in business when their husbands in the big league and besides a womans place is home especially when they got a baby so I want you to sell out and when I get my split of the worlds serious we will go south somewheres and buy a home."

Well she asked me how did I come out with the affidavit. So I said "The affidavit is either here nor there. I am talking about something else" and she says "Yes you are." And she says "I been worring all day about that affidavit because if they find out about it what will they do to us." So I said "You should worry because if this board won't excuse me I will go to the Dist. board and mean while you won't be earning nothing because you will be out of business." Well Al she had a better idea then that. She says "No I will hold on to the business till you go to the Dist. board and then if they act like they wouldn't excuse you you can tell them I am going to sell out. And if they say all right I will sell out. But if they say its to late why then I will still have something to live on if you have to go."

So when she said that about me haveing to go we both choked up a little but pretty soon I was O. K. and now Al it looks like a cinch I would get my exemptions from the Dist. board because if Florrie says she wants to sell out they can't stop her. *Your pal, Jack.*

CHICAGO, AUG. 22.

Friend Al: Well Al its all over. The Dist. board won't let me off and between you and I Al I am glad of it and I only hope I won't have to go before I have had a chance at the worlds serious.

My case come up about noon. One of the men asked me my name and then looked over what they had wrote down about me. Then he says "Theys an affidavit here that says your wife and child depends on you. Is that true?" So I said yes it was and he asked me if my wife was in business and I said yes but she was thinking about selling out. So he asked me how much money she made in her business. I said "You can't never tell. Some times its so much and other times different." So he asked me what the average was and I said it was about $250.00 per month. Then he says "Why is she going to sell out?" I said "Because we don't want to live in Chi all winter" and he said "You needn't to worry." Then he said "If she makes $250.00 per month how do you figure she is dependent on you?" So I said "Because she is because I pay for the rent and everything." And he asked me what she done with the $250.00 and I told him she spent it on clothes.

So he says "$250.00 per month on clothes. How does she keep warm this weather?" I said "I guess they don't nobody have no trouble keeping warm in August." Then he says "Look here Keefe this affidavit mitigates against you. We will have to turn down your appeal and I guess your wife can take care of herself and the boy." I said "She can't when she sells out." "Well" he said "you tell her not to sell out. It may be hard for her at first to sport herself and the boy on $250.00 but if the worst comes to the worst she can wear the same shoes twice and she will find them a whole lot more comfortable the second time." So I said "She don't never have no trouble with her feet and if she did I guess she knows how to fix them."

Florrie was waiting for me when I got home. "Well" I said "now you see what your dam beauty parlor has done for us." And then she seen what had happened and begin to cry and of course I couldn't find no more fault with her and I called up the ball park and told them I was sick and wouldn't show up this P. M. and I and Florrie and little Al stayed home together and talked. That is little Al done all the talking. I and Florrie didn't seem to have nothing to say.

Tomorrow I am going to tell them about it over to the ball park. If they can get me off till after the worlds serious all right. And if they can't all right to. *Your old pal, Jack.*

P. S. Washington comes tomorrow and I am going to ask Rowland to leave me pitch. The worst I can get is a tie. They scored a run in St. ◆ Louis yesterday and that means they are through for the week.

CHICAGO, AUG. 23.

Dear Al: Well Al the one that laughs last gets all the best of it. Wait till you hear what come off today.

When I come in the club house Rowland and Gleason was there all alone. I told them hello and was going to spring the news on them but when Rowland seen me he says "Jack I got some bad news for you." So I said what was it. So he says "The boss sold you to Washington this morning."

Well Al at first I couldn't say nothing and I forgot all about that I wanted to tell them. But then I remembered it again and here is what I pulled. I said "Listen Manager I beat the boss to it." "What do you mean?" he said so I said "I'm signed up with Washington all ready only I ain't signed with Griffith but with Uncle Sam." Thats what I ◇ pulled on them Al and they both got it right away. Gleason jumped

---

◆ *They scored a run in St. Louis yesterday and that means they are through for the week*— They were in fact rained out in St. Louis on August 21. Washington was scheduled to play at Chicago on the 23rd.

up and shook hands with me and so did Rowland and then Rowland said he would have to hurry up in the office and tell the Old Man."But wait a minute" I said. "I am going to quit you after this game because I don't know when I will be called and theys lots of things I got to fix up." So I stopped and Rowland asked me what I wanted and I said "Let me pitch this game and I will give them the beating of their life."

So him and Gleason looked at each other and then Rowland says "You know we can't afford to loose no ball games now. But if you think you can beat them I will start you."

So then he blowed and I and Gleason was alone.

"Well kid" he says "you make the rest of us look like a monkey. This game ain't nothing compared to what you are going to do. And when you come back they won't be nothing to good for you and your kid will be proud of you because you went while a whole lot of other kids dads stayed home."

So he patted me on the back and I kind of choked up and then the trainer come in and I had him do a little work on my arm.

Well Al you will see in the paper what I done to them. Before the ◆ game the boss had told Griffith about me and called the deal off. So while I was warming up Griffith come over and shook hands. He says "I would of like to had you but I am a good looser." So I says "You ought to be." So he couldn't help from laughing but he says "When you come back I will go after you again." I said "Well if you don't get somebody on the club between now and then that can hit something besides fouls I won't come back." So he kind of laughed again and walked away and then it was time for the game.

Well Al the official scorer give them 3 hits but he must be McMullins ◆

CLARK C. GRIFFITH
ASSOCIATED WITH MAJOR LEAGUE BASEBALL FOR MORE THAN 50 YEARS AS A PITCHER, MANAGER AND EXECUTIVE. SERVED AS A MEMBER OF THE CHICAGO AND CINCINNATI TEAMS IN THE N.L. AND THE CHICAGO, NEW YORK AND WASHINGTON CLUBS IN THE A.L. COMPILED MORE THAN 200 VICTORIES AS A PITCHER. MANAGER OF THE CINCINNATI N.L. AND CHICAGO, NEW YORK AND WASHINGTON A.L. TEAMS FOR 20 YEARS.

◇ *Griffith*—The Clark C. Griffith plaque at the National Baseball Hall of Fame and Museum, Cooperstown, New York (see footnote, p. 88).

◆ *Well Al you will see in the paper what I done to them*—In the actual game of August 23 Cicotte beat Washington at Chicago, 6–0, on Military Day.

◆ *McMullin*—Frederick William McMullin (1891–1952), utility infielder for the White Sox from 1916 to 1920. He had played in a single game at shortstop for Detroit in 1914. For the White Sox he played most frequently at third base, beside his close friend, shortstop Swede Risberg. McMullin was a member of the Black Sox plot, but the one who played the most minor role and the one who could most easily have avoided participation. Overhearing Gandil and Risberg discuss the plot in the locker room, McMullin asked to be included. When banned permanently in 1920, McMullin had hit .256 in 304 games. See A. D. Suehsdorf, "Fred McMullin," *The Ballplayers*, p. 722.

As the text implies, McMullin played third base in the game of August 23. Clyde Milan, who had food poisoning, did not play. His brother Horace Milan (1894–1955) did so, and hit one triple, but made no such infield hit as Keefe describes.

◇ *Milan*—Clyde Milan in the Senators uniform of the early 1920's (see footnote, pp. 88–89). (National Baseball Library, Cooperstown, New York)

brother in law or something because McMullin ought to of throwed Milan out from here to Berlin on that bunt. But any way 3 hits and ◇ no runs is pretty good for a finish and between you and I Al I feel like I got the last laugh on Washington and Rowland to.

Your pal, Jack.

CHICAGO, SEPT. 18.

Friend Al: Just time for a few lines while Florrie finishs packing up my stuff. I leave with the bunch tomorrow A. M. for Camp Grant at Rockford. I don't know how long we will stay there but I suppose long enough to learn to talk German and shoot and etc.

We just put little Al to bed and tonight was the first time we told him I was going to war. He says "Can I go to daddy?" Hows that for a 3 year old Al?

Well he will be proud of me when I come back and he will be proud of me if I don't come back and when he gets older he can go up to the kids that belong to some of these left handers and say "Where and the hell was your father when the war come off?"

Good by Al and say good by to Bertha for me. *Your pal, Jack.*

P. S. I won't be in the serious against New York but how about the real worlds serious Al? Won't I be in that? I'll say so.

The Busher Reenlists

CHI, DEC. 2. ◆

Friend Al: Well Al I was down to see the Dr. for the last time today as he said they wasn't no use in me comeing down there again as my arm is just as good is new though of course its weak yet on acct. of being in a sling all this wile and I haven't used it and I suppose if it was my right arm it would take me a long wile to get it strenthened up again to where I could zip the old ball through there the way like I use to but thank god its the left arm that the Dutchmens shot full of holes. ◆ But at that it wouldn't make no differents if it was the left arm or the old souper either one as I have gave up the idear of going back in to the old game.

"The Busher Reenlists" was published in *The Saturday Evening Post*, CXCI (April 19, 1919), 3–4, 147, 151, 155.

◆ *The Busher Reenlists*—Keefe, notwithstanding his continual protestations that he had enlisted to serve his country, had actually been drafted in the story "Call for Mr. Keefe!" above. Thus, the title implies that his return to the White Sox was also not voluntary. On his being drafted and on his military experience, see the Introduction to this volume.

◆ *Chi, Dec. 2*—The year is 1918; the subsequent events are unambiguously of the 1919 season.

◆ *the left arm that the Dutchmens shot full of holes*—In accord with his claim that he enlisted, Keefe misrepresents his wound: actually, he was shot by a soldier from his own outfit during an unauthorized crawl in No-Man's Land.

I bet you will be surprised to hear that Al as I am still a young man just a kid you might say compared to some of the other birds that is still pitching yet and getting by with it and I figure that if I would stick in the game my best yrs. is yet to come. But that isn't the point Al but the point is that after a man has took part in the war game all the other games seems like they was baby games and after what I went through acrost the old pond how could a man take any interest in baseball and it would be like as if a man set up all night in a poker game with the sky for the limit and when they come home their wife asked them to play a hand of jack straws to see which one of them had to stick the ice card in the window. No man can do themself justice Al if you don't take your work in ernest whether its pitching baseball or takeing a bath.

Besides that Al I figure that even a man like I am that's put up like a motor Laura you might say can't last forever in baseball and why ◆ not quit wile you are young and have still got the old ambition to start out in some other line of business that a man can last in it all their life and probably by the time I got to be the age where I would half to give up pitching if I stuck at it, why by that time I can work myself up to the head of some business where I would be drawing $15000.00 per annum or something and no danger of getting kicked out of it when the old souper finely lays down on me.

And besides that when a man has got a wife and 2 kiddies that the whole 3 of them has got the world beat why should I go out and pitch baseball and be away from home ½ the yr. around where if I hooked up good in some business here in Chi I wouldn't never half to leave except maybe a run down to N. Y. city once or twice a yr. So in justice to them and myself I don't see nothing to it only give up the game for good in all and get in to something permerant.

Well Al I suppose you will be saying to yourself that I haven't never had no experience in business and what kind of business could I get in to that would pay me the right kind of money. Well old pal if you will stop and think I haven't never tackled no job yet where I didn't make good and in the 1st. place it was pitching baseball and I hadn't only been pitching a little over 2 yrs. when I was in the big league and then come the war game and I was made a corporal a few wks. after I

◆ *motor Laura*—Motor lorry. Keefe's absorption of British English during his overseas experience was as imperfect as his command of American English. He had used this locution throughout *The Real Dope*.

enlisted and might of stayed a corporal or went higher yet only I would rather pal around with the boys and not try and lord it over them and you can bet it won't be no different in whatever business I decide to take up because they isn't nothing that can't be learned Al if a man gos at it the right way and has got something under their hat besides scalp trouble.

As for getting in to the right kind of a place I guess I can just about pick out what kind of a place I want to start in at as everybody that reads the papers knows who I am and how I went in the war wile most of the other baseball boys kept the home fires burning though I had a wife and a kid to look out for besides the baby that came since I went in and for all as I knew might of been here a long wile before that. So it looks like when I make it up in my mind what business I want to tackle I can just go to whoever is at the head of the business and they will say "You bet your life we will find a place for you after what you done both in baseball and for the stars and strips." Because they won't no real man turn a soldier down Al a specially 1 that earned his wound strips acrost the old pond.

So they won't be no trouble about me landing when I decide what I want to go in to and the baseball men can offer me whatever kind of a contract they feel like and I will give them 1 of my smiles and tell them they are barking the wrong tree.

Regards to Bertha. *Your pal, Jack.*

CHI, DEC. 8.

Friend Al: Well Al this is a fine burg where a lot of the business men don't know they's been a war or read the papers or nothing only set in front of the cash register and watch how the money rolls in or else they must of bet 20 cents on the Kaiser and have got a gruge against the boys that stopped him.

The other night I was with a couple of friends of mine that's White Sox fans and we was histing a few and 1 of them is asst. mgr. down to 1 of the big dept. stores so I told him I was going to quit the game and try and bust in to some business where I could work up to something worth wile and he says they was shy of a floor man down to their store and he would speak to the mgr. about me and if I come down maybe I could land the job, as the floor man has to be a man that can wear clothes and carry themself as most of the customers is ladys and you half to give them a smile and make them feel at home and the job pays pretty good jack.

Well I didn't think much of the job only this bird is a kind of an

◇ *I said "I have had the kind of experience that I guess a whole lot of men would give their right eye if they could brag about it, playing in the big league in baseball and the big league in war"*—Drawing by P. Preston for *The Saturday Evening Post*, April 19, 1919.

admire of mine on acct. of baseball so I didn't want to be nasty to him so I went down there yesterday and he introduced me to the mgr. and his name is suppose to be Kelly but I guess Heinz would be closer to what his name is. Well he asked me had I had any experience in dept. stores and I said yes I had had all the experience I wanted the times I had been in there with Florrie shoping and my feet was still sore yet where all the women in Chi had used them for a parade grounds. So he said he meant did I ever have any experience working in a store so I said do I look like a counter jumper or something? I said "I have ◇ had the kind of experience that I guess a whole lot of men would give their right eye if they could brag about it, playing in the big league in baseball and the big league in war and I guess that's enough of experience for a man of my age." So he said "Well our floor men is not suppose to hit the customers with a bat or tickle them with a bayonet either one so I don't see how we can use you right now." So I said "I have got a charge acct. here and here is where my wife does pretty near all her shoping." So he said "Well if we was to give jobs to all our customers why as soon as they had all reported for work in the A. M. we could close the doors and get along without a floor man." Well Al all as I could do was walk away from him as I couldn't very well take a wallop at his jaw on acct. of his asst. being my pal.

Well as long as I was down town I thought I might as well look up some of my other friends so I happened to remember a pal of mine that use to work in the Gas Co. so I dropped in there and asked for him but he wasn't there no more so I asked for whoever was in charge and they showed me to an old bird that must of began to work for them the day they struck gas and I told him my name and who I was and he said about the only thing open was meter readers so I said "Read them yourself" and come away.

That's the kind of birds we have got here Al but they can't all be that way and the next time I will wait for them to come to me before I go around and lay myself libel to insults from a bunch of pro German spys or whatever you have a mind to call them.

Well they's a saloon on Adams St. that it use to be a big hang out ◆ for the fans so I dropped in there before I started home but they wasn't nobody in there that I knew them or they knew me and the bunch that was in there didn't even know their own name but they was all trying to sing tenor and that's about the way it is in all the saloons you drop in to these days and they all seem to think that every day is June 30. Well I couldn't stand for the noise and everybody with ◆ their arm around each other tearing off Smiles so I come home and ◆ Florrie asked me how I had came out and I told her and she says it looked like I better go back in to baseball. So I said if I do go back it will be because they give me a $5000.00 contract in the stead of the $2500.00 I was getting when I quit and enlisted and between you and I Al that's the lowest figure I would sign up for and of course I wouldn't have no trouble getting that if I give Comiskey the word that I was thinking about pitching baseball again. But nothing doing in baseball for me Al when I know I can get in to some big business with a future in it and won't never half to worry about my arm or catching cold in it or nothing and be home every night with the kiddies. But if I did sign up to a $5000.00 contract in baseball it would mean our income would be around $8000.00 per annum as Florrie is kicking out pretty close to $250.00 per mo. clear profit in her beauty parlor.

Well Florrie said if I couldn't get no $5000.00 from the White Sox or find no job that suited me she would give me a job herself so I said "What doing pairing finger nails over in your studio?" So she said "No indeed I would hire you as nurse for little Al and the baby in place of

---

◆ *a saloon on Adams St.*—There were, of course, alternatives, but an attractive possibility is the Berghoff Restaurant on Adams just west of State Street. Owned by the Berghoff brewery of Fort Wayne, Ind., it had a huge, predominantly male clientele. It is still in operation.

◆ *June 30.*—The last day of legal drinking before the Volstead Act took effect in 1920.

◆ *Smiles*—A popular song of World War I.

the one we have got." So I said I wouldn't mind being a nurse for little Al as I and him can have a fine time playing together and I would make a man out of him but I wouldn't sign no contract to take care of little Florrie for no amt. of money as it would mean I would half to stay awake 24 hrs. per day as this little bird don't never close her eyes and I only wished they was a few umpires like her in the American League and maybe a man could get something like a square deal. I have often heard people that had babys brag about how good they was and slept all the wile except when they was getting their chow but little Florrie ain't no relation to them or neither is little Al as he was just as bad when he was a baby and when I hear these storys about these here perfect babys I begin to think that the husbands and wifes that owns them is the same kind that never had a cross word since they been married.

But jokeing to 1 side Al I don't see how the Swede stands it being up all day and then up again all night and sometimes I wished I could help her out by walking the floor with the kid nights but the Dr. said I wasn't to do nothing that might strain my bad arm till I was sure it was O. K. *Your pal, Jack.*

CHI, DEC. 12.

Friend Al: Well Al yesterday was the American League meeting and I ◆ happened to be down town so I dropped in to the hotel where the meeting was at just to see some of the boys as they's always a bunch of them hangs around in the hopes that 1 of the club owners will smile at them or something and any way I dropped in the lobby and the 1st. bird I seen was Bobby Roth that was with us a few yrs. ago and played the outfield for Cleveland last yr. So I says "Hello Bobby." So he said "Hello Jack." Well it was the 1st. time I seen him since I quit baseball for the army but I guess he hadn't never heard that I was in the war or something and any way he didn't say nothing about it but finely he said he supposed I would be back with the White Sox next yr. so then I told him I had made it up in my mind to quit the game and go in to business and he said he was sorry to hear it. So I said "Yes you are because when you was with the Cleveland club I always made you look like a monkey." So he said "I never had a chance to hit against you as they had me batting 4th. at Cleveland and by the time it come my turn

---

◆ *the American League meeting*—The meeting was held at the Congress Hotel, Chicago, on December 12, 1918.

to hit you was took out of the game." So I said "Yes I was" and he didn't have nothing more to say.

Well I walked around a wile and run in to some of the other boys Artie Hofman and Charley O'Leary and Jim Archer and Joe Benz ◆◇ but not a 1 of them mentioned about the war or me being over there and I finely figured it out that it was kind of a sore subject with them so I walked away from them and all of a sudden I seen Rowland the mgr. and I thought sure he would ask me about signing up but I guess Bobby or somebody must of tipped him off about me going in to business so he didn't want to take a chance of me turning him down or maybe he thought he would have a better chance of landing me if he didn't say nothing at this time but just sent me a big fat contract when the time comes. Any way we didn't talk contract but he had heard about me getting shot in the left arm and he mentioned about it and smiled and said it was lucky I wasn't a left hander so you see he has got me on his mind and I suppose the contract will come along in a few days and then I will half to send it back to them and tell them I am through even if the contract meets my figure which is $5000.00 because I wouldn't go back and pitch baseball even for that amt. when I can go in to business and maybe not do that well right at the start but work myself up in to something worth wile.

Well after I left Rowland I bumped in to Hy Pond that I was with ◆ him down in the Central League and he asked me to come in and

---

◆ *Artie Hofman*—Arthur Frederick "Circus Solly" Hofman (1882–1956), outfielder and utility infielder of the Cubs from 1904 to 1912. As centerfielder, he was one of the stalwarts of the Cubs' championship teams of 1906–08 and 1910. Subsequently, he played for the Pittsburgh Pirates, the Brooklyn and Buffalo teams of the Federal League, the Yankees, and again the Cubs. In 14 seasons he hit .269 in 1,193 games. Hofman's most notable moment was when he retrieved Al Bridwell's single and threw to Johnny Evers to force Fred Merkle at second in the game that precipitated the National League playoff game of 1908. See Bob Carroll, "Solly Hofman," *The Ballplayers*, p. 479.

Charley O'Leary—O'Leary was at the meetings for good reason; he was seeking a job. He had closed out his playing career as manager at San Antonio of the Texas League in 1917. The job he found for 1919, managing the Gunthers, a semiprofessional team on Chicago's West Side, was outside of Organized Baseball.

Jim Archer—James Peter Archer (1883–1958), catcher for the Cubs from 1909 to 1917. In 1918 he had played briefly with the Dodgers, Reds, and Pirates to end his playing days. In 12 seasons, including brief performances with Pittsburgh in 1904 and Detroit in 1907, Archer hit .250 in 846 games. He was considered one of the best-throwing catchers. Though he was an obvious figure to be at the meetings looking for a job, he did not find one, and became a hog buyer for Armour & Co. See Jack Kavanagh, "Jimmy Archer," *The Ballplayers*, p. 29.

◆ *Hy Pond that I was with him down in the Central League*—Apparently a fictional character, although he appears in a context in which Lardner would be expected

◇ *Jim Archer*—Jimmy Archer in a Cubs uniform of about 1938. (George E. Brace collection)

have a drink so I went with him and histed a couple beers but it was a mad house and besides wile we was over there takeing the fight out of the Germans the people that stayed home done the same thing to the beer and the way they have got it fixed now you could drink all they have got left without feeling like shock troops so finely I told Hy to make my excuses to the boys and I come along home.

Well I have had 2 or 3 pretty good chances so far to break in to some line of business and 1 of them was an ad I seen in the paper today where they wanted a young man of good appearances to

---

(*continued from page 222*)
to use an actual figure. No player of this name is recorded in Central League records up to its suspension for World War I in 1917, but the passage does not state that Pond was a player. The late Paul C. Frisz, in his research on the Central League, found no evidence of Pond, and the name does not appear in Lardner's accounts of Central League games in the South Bend *Times*. See the discussion of this passage in the Introduction.

represent them in Detroit with $5000.00 per annum to start out but they didn't say what line of business it was and besides I don't feel like moveing to Detroit so I decided to not answer the ad but wait till something showed up where I could stay here in Chi as they's no use of a man rushing in to something blind folded you might say when all as I half to do is play the waiting game and let them come to me with all their offers and then pick out the one that suits me best. Get them bidding against each other for you is the system Al.

Your pal, Jack.

CHI, DEC. 23.

Friend Al: Well Al I just come back from down town where I and Florrie has been all P. M. buying xmas presents and she has been saying ever since I come back from France how lonesome she was all the wile I was away but from the number of xmas presents she had to buy for people I never seen or heard of they couldn't of been more than a couple hours of the time I was over there when she wasn't busy saying please to meet you. But whenever I would raise a holler about the jack she was spending she would swell up and tell me she would pay for it out of her own money so of course I couldn't say nothing though when the bills comes in they will be addressed to me and her check book will of probably got halled away with the garbage.

Well when we got through buying for the city directory she said she was through except for the baby as she had fixed up for little Al last time she was down so she asked me what could I suggest for little Florrie so I said why get her a new rattle as what else is they for a 6 mos. old baby so she said the baby wasn't going to be 6 mos. old all her life. How is that for a bright remark Al but of course a woman can't expect to have the looks and everything else with it, but any way she said she had a idear that she heard about a friend of hers doing it that had a little baby girl and that was to start a pearl necklace for her and 1st. buy the chain and a few pearls and then add a couple pearls every yr. so as when she got old enough to wear it she would have something.

Well I said why not wait till some xmas when we have got a little more jack say in 7 or 8 yrs. and then get enough pearls to make up for the yrs. we passed up and then give them to the little girl and tell her we started buying them before she was a yr. old and she wouldn't know the differents and in the mean wile we could get her something that if she busted it we wouldn't be out no real jack. So Florrie said "You don't suppose I am going to leave her get a hold of the necklace now do you or even show it to her?" So I said "That is a fine way to give a person a xmas present is to buy something and hide it and if that is the system why don't you buy her a couple new undershirts my size and I can wear them and when I have wore them out you can put them away somewheres till she gets old enough to have some sence and then you can hall them out and show them to her and tell her that was what we give her for xmas in 1918."

Well you know how much good it done to argue and finely she picked out a little gold chain and 4 little pearls to go with it and it cost $47.50 but what and the he—ll is $47.50 as long as the baby has a merry xmas.

Well we was shoping all the P. M. but you can bet we didn't go in that smart Alex store where that smart Alex mgr. got so fresh when they offered me that cheap job and we use to spend a lot of jack in there at that but never again and if they want to know why they haven't got no big bill against us like they usually have around xmas time I will tell them and then maybe Mr. Smart will wished he hadn't of been so smart but at that when I seen them floor men on the job today I was tickled to death I turned that job down because the way them women jousled them around I couldn't of never stood for it and I would of felt like busting them in the eye if it had of been me and of course I don't mean that Al as I wouldn't think of hitting a woman but I would of certainly gave them the elbow or accidently parked my heel on a few of their best toes.

Well of course I couldn't buy Florrie no present wile she was along and I half to go back down again tomorrow and try and find something and I haven't the lease idear what will it be and all as I know is that it won't be no pearl necklace for adults. She says she has all ready boughten my present and wait till I see it. Well I suppose it will be a corset or maybe she will give me a set of false teeth and hide them away somewheres till I come of age to put them on.

Well Al we are sending xmas cards to you and Bertha and I only wished it could be something more but we kind of feel this yr. like we shouldn't ought to spend a whole lot of money what with some of the boys still over in France yet and another liberty loan comeing along some time soon and all and all it don't seem hardly right to be blowing jack for xmas presents but maybe next yr. everything will be different and in the mean wile merry xmas to you and Bertha from the both of us.

Your pal, Jack.

◇ *Harry*—Harry Grabiner, secretary of the White Sox. (George E. Brace collection)

CHI, DEC. 31.

Friend Al: Well Al they's not much news to write as everything has been going along about like usual and I haven't made it up in my mind yet what line of business to take up though I have got several good offers hanging in the fire you might say and am just playing the waiting game till I decide which 1 looks best as I would be sorry to get in to 1 thing and then find out they was something else opened up that I would like a whole lot better.

One of the things I have got in mind is takeing up newspaper work and writeing articles about baseball or maybe army life and when the baseball season opens maybe I would go out and see the games and write up the reports and you can bet my articles would be different then some of these birds that's reporting the games as I would at lease know what I was writeing about wile you take the most of these here reporters and all the baseball they know you could carry it around in a eye dropper.

But I don't know whether the papers would pay me the kind of money I would want and if not why I am in a position to laugh at them.

Well I got tired of setting around the house today as Florrie was over to her looks garage and the Swede had both the kiddies out to get the air so I walked around a wile and then I hopped on to a 35th. St. car and rode over west and I happened to look out of the window and we was just passing the ball pk. so I didn't have nothing else to do so I give the conductor the highball and jumped off and went up in ◆ the office to see if they wasn't maybe some mail for me that some of the boys wrote from France not knowing my home address.

Well they wasn't no mail so I set down and fanned a wile with Harry ◇ the secty. of the club and he asked me all about what I seen over acrost the pond and we had quite a talk and finely I thought maybe Comiskey would be sore if he heard I had been up there and hadn't paid my respects but Harry said he wasn't in so then I thought maybe he might of left some word about me and wanted to know if I was going to come back and pitch baseball for him or not but Harry said he hadn't mentioned nothing about it so I guess when the time comes he will just send me my contract and then I will send it back and tell him I have decided to quit baseball and go in to some line of business where they's a future in it.

◆ *highball*—In railroad jargon, the highball is the signal to go, not to stop.

Because they's no use of a man killing himself pitching baseball and then when your arm gives out you haven't got no business to go in to because business men won't hire a man that's 33 or 34 yrs. old and no experience and besides if a man has got a family like mine why not stay home and enjoy them in the stead of traveling on the road ½ the yr. around you might say. So even if Comiskey should send me a contract calling for $4000.00 per annum I would send it back though that is the lease I would sign up for if I was going to sign at all.

Well Al xmas is over and I only wished you could of been here to see how little Al eat it up. Besides all the junk we give him all of Florrie's friends sent something and all together he must of got about 25 presents in the 1st. place and now he has got about 100 as everything he got is broke in to 4 peaces and they also sent the baby a load of play things that means as much to her as the hit and run but Florrie says never mind they will be put away till some xmas when she is old enough to enjoy them and then we won't half to buy her nothing new. Well the idear is O. K. Al but it reminds me like when Sept. comes along and a man has got a straw Kelly that looks pretty good and you give it to your wife to take care of till next June and when it comes June you go and buy yourself a new hat.

Well Florrie's present to me was a phonograph and of course that's a mighty fine present and will cost her or whoever pays for it a bunch of jack but between you and I Al I wouldn't be surprised if she was thinking to herself when she bought it that maybe she might turn it on some times when I am not in the house. What I give her is 1 of these here patent shower bath attachments that you can have it put up on a regular bath tub and you can have a regular tub bath or a shower just as you feel like. They cost real money to Al but what's the differents when its your wife? *Your pal, Jack.*

CHI, JAN. 16. ◆

Friend Al: Well Al I don't know if you have been reading the papers but if you have you probably seen the big news where Kid Gleason ◆◇ has been appointed mgr. of the White Sox. Well old pal that peace of news makes all the differents in the world to your old pal. As you know I had entirely gave up the idear of going back in to baseball and

---

◆ *Chi, Jan. 16*—1919.

◆ *Kid Gleason has been appointed mgr. of the White Sox*—Gleason was appointed manager, replacing Pants Rowland, on January 1, 1919. Rowland had resigned to

◇ *Kid Gleason*—Gleason, at right, with Eddie Collins in the 1919 home uniform of the White Sox (see footnote, pp. 42–43, and photos on pp. 43 and 310). (National Baseball Library, Cooperstown, New York)

figured where I would take up some other line of business and work myself up to something big and I was just about makeing it up in my mind to accept 1 of the offers I got when this news come out.

Well old pal I haven't no idear how things will come out now as I guess you know what friends I and Gleason are. You know he was asst.

(*continued from page* 227)
become part owner of the Milwaukee club of the American Association. The choice was surprising because Gleason, after a salary dispute, did not take his usual coaching post for the White Sox in 1918, but rather sat out the season at his home in Camden, N.J. For a view of Gleason as he rose to the managership, see John J. Ward, "The New Leader of the White Sox," *Baseball Magazine*, XXII, No. 5 (March 1919), 273–74, 309.

mgr. when Callahan had the club and then again the yr. Rowland win the pennant and he seemed to take a fancy to me some way and I guess I may as well come out and say that I was his favorite of any man on the club and I always figured that it was because when he tried his kidding on me I always give him back as good as he sent wile the rest of the boys was a scared of him but he use to kid me just to hear what I would say back to him. Like 1 time we was playing a double header with the St. Louis club and Jim Scott lose the 1st. game and Callahan said I was to work the 2d. game so I was warming up and Gleason come out and stood behind me and I had eat something that didn't set very good so Gleason asked me how I felt and I said "Not very good. I'm not myself today." So he said "Well then it looks like we would break even on the afternoon." So I said "I will break your jaw in a minute."

But a side from all that he was the 1 man that ever give me the credit for the work I done and if he had of been mgr. of the club he would of pitched me in my regular turn in the stead of playing favorites like them other 2 birds and all as I needed was regular work and I would of made them forget Walsh and all the rest of them big 4 flushers.

Well Al Gleason lives in Philly in the winter so I expect he will either wire me a telegram and ask for my terms or else he will run out here and see me if they give me $4000.00 per annum I am afraid they won't be nothing for me to do only sign up though I have got several chances to go in to some business at better money than that and with a future to it. But this here is a matter of friendships Al and after all Gleason done for me why if he says the word I can't hardly do nothing only say yes though of course I am not going to sacrifice myself or sign for a nickel less then $4000.00.

You see Al this will be Gleason's 1st. yr. as a mgr. and he will want to finish up in the race and I don't care how good a mgr. is he can't win unless he has got the men and beleive me he will need all the pitching strenth he can get a hold of as Cleveland and N.Y. has both strenthened up and the Boston club with all their men back from the service has got enough good ball players to finish 1st. and 2d. both if they was room for all of them to play at once. So that is where friendships comes in Al and I figure that it is up to your old pal to pass up my business chances and show the Kid I am true blue and beleive me I will show him something and I will come pretty near winning that old flag single handed.

So all and all it looks like your old pal wouldn't go in to no business adventure this yr. but I will be out there on the old ball field giveing them the best I have got and I guess the fans won't holler their heads off when I walk out there the 1st. time after what I done in France.

Your pal, Jack.

CHI, FEB. 13.

Friend Al: Well Al it says in the paper this A. M. that Gleason is comeing to Chi for a few days to see Comiskey and talk over the plans for the training trip and etc. but they's another reason why he is comeing to Chi and maybe you can guess what it is. Well Al that's the way to work it is to wait and let them come to you in the stead of you going to them as when you make them come to you you can pretty near demand whatever you want and they half to come acrost with it.

That's a fine story Al about him comeing to talk over plans for the training trip as I know Comiskey and you could talk to him for 3 wks. about the plans for the training trip and when you got all through talking he would tell you what the plans was for the training trip so you can bet that Gleason isn't comeing all the way out here from Philly to hear himself talk but what he is comeing for is to get some of the boys in line that lives here and when I say some of the boys I don't half to go no further eh Al?

And all the more because I dropped him a letter a couple wks. ago and said I had made all arrangements to go in to business but if he wanted me I would give up my plans and pitch for him provided he give me my figure which is $3600.00 per annum and I never got no answer to the letter and now I know why I didn't get no answer as he is 1 of the kind that would rather set down and do their talking face to face then set down and take the trouble of writeing a letter when he could just as well hop on the old rattler and come out here and see me personly.

Well Al he will be here next wk. and I have left my phone No. over to the ball pk. so as he will know how to get a hold of me and all they will be to it is he will ask me how much I want and I will tell him $3600.00 and he will say sign here.

Well Al Florrie says she don't know if she is glad or sorry that I am going to be back in the old game as she says she don't like to have me away from home so much but still and all she knows I wouldn't be happy unless I was pitching baseball but she also says that if I do get back in to harness and ern a liveing and they's another war breaks out she will probably half to go as she couldn't claim no exemptions on the grounds of a dependant husband. So I said "I guess they won't ask no women to go to war because the minute they heard 1 of them trench rats give their college yell they would all retreat to the equator or somewheres." So she said "They had women in the Russia army and they didn't retreat." So I said "Yes they did only the men retreated so much faster that the women looked like they was standing still."

Jokeing to 1 side Al I will let you know how I come out with Gleason but they's only 1 way I can come out and that is he will be tickled to death to sign me at my own figure because if he trys any monkey business with me I will laugh in his face and Comiskey to, and give up the game for good and take the best offer I have got in some other line. *Your pal, Jack.*

CHI, FEB. 20.

Friend Al: Well Al I have just came back from the ball pk. and had a long talk with Gleason and the most of it was kidding back and 4th. like usual when the 2 of us gets together but it didn't take no Wm. A. ◆ Pinkerton to see that he is anxious to have me back on the ball club and in a few days they will probably send me a contract at my own figures and then they won't be nothing to do only wait for the rattler to start for the sunny south land.

Well Gleason got in yesterday P. M. and I was expecting him to call up either last night or this A. M. but they didn't no call come and I figured they must of either lost my phone No. over to the office or else the phone was out of order or something and the way the phones has been acting all winter why he might of asked central to give him my No. and the next thing he knew he would be connected with the morgue so any way when they hadn't no call came at noon I jumped on a 35th St. car and went over the pk. and up in the office and the secty. said Gleason was in talking to Comiskey but he would be through in a little while.

Well after about a hr. Gleason come out and seen me setting there and of course he had to start kidding right off of the real so he said "Well here is the big Busher and I hoped you was killed over in France but I suppose even them long distance guns fell short of where you was at." So I said "They reached me all right and they got me in the left arm and wasn't it lucky it wasn't my right arm?" So he said "Its to bad they didn't shoot your head off and made a pitcher out of you."

◆ *Wm. A. Pinkerton*—William Allan Pinkerton (1846–1923), founder of America's most prominent private-detective agency.

So then he asked me all about the war and if I got in to Germany and I told him no that I got my wounds in June and was invalid home. So he said "You fight just like you pitch and they half to take you out in the 5th. inning." So I asked him if he got my letter and he said he got a letter that looked like it might of came from me so he didn't open it. So I said "Well I don't know if you opened it or not but I just as soon tell you right here what I said in the letter. I told you I was going in to some business but I would stay in baseball another yr. to help you out if you met my figure." So he asked what was my figure, so I told him $3000.00 per annum. So he said how much was I getting in the army and I told him I was getting $30.00 per mo. most of the time. So he said "Yes you was getting $30.00 per mo. to get up at 5 G. M. and work like a dog all day and eat beans and stew and sleep in a barn nights with a cow and a pig for your roomies and now you want $3000.00 a yr. to live in the best hotels and eat off the fat of the land and about once in every 10 days when we feel like we can afford to loose a ball game why you half to go out there and stand on your feet pretty near ½ the P. M. and if it happens to be July or Aug. you come pretty close to prespireing."

So I said "You are the same old Gleason always trying to kid somebody but jokeing a side I will sign up for $3000.00 or else I will go in to business." So he asked me what business I was going in to and I told him I had an offer from the Stock Yards. So he said "How much do they offer for you on the hoof?"

Well we kidded along back and 4th. like that for a wile and finely he said he was going out somewheres with Comiskey so I asked him if he wasn't going to talk business to me 1st. So he said "I will tell you how it is boy. They have cut down the limit so as each club can't only ◆ carry 21 men and that means we won't have no room for bench lizards. But the boss says that on acct. of you haveing went to France and wasn't killed why we will take you south if you want to go and you will get a chance to show if you are a pitcher yet or not and if you are like you use to be why maybe the Stock Yards will keep open long enough to take you when we are through with you and you can tell Armour and Swift and them that I will leave them know whether I want you

---

◆ *each club can't only carry 21 men*—Baseball had had a very bad year in 1918, and mistakenly expected another poor one in 1919. The American League club owners, therefore, at their meeting of December 12, 1918, mentioned earlier, decided upon a cut from 25 to 21 active players for the 1919 season.

or not about 3 days after we get to Texas." So I asked him how about salery and he said "The boss will send you a contract in a few days and if I was you I would be satisfied with it."

So it looks now like I was all set for the season Al and Gleason said I would be satisfied with the salery which is just as good as saying it will be $3000.00 as I wouldn't be satisfied with no less, so all I half to do now is wait for the contract and put my name on it and I will be back in the game I love and when a man's heart is in their work how are you going to stop him a specially with the stuff I've got.

Your pal, Jack.

CHI, MARCH 8.

Friend Al: Well Al I am through with baseball for good and am going in to business and I don't know just yet which proposition I will take that's been offered to me but they's no hurry and I will take the one that looks best when the proper time comes.

I suppose you will be surprised to hear that I have gave up the old game but maybe you won't be so surprised when I tell you what come off today.

Well in the 1st. place when the mail man come this A. M. he brought me a contract from Comiskey and the figures amounted to $2400.00 per annum. How is that Al when I was getting $2500.00 per annum before I went to the war. Well at 1st. I couldn't hardly beleive my eyes but that was the figure all right and finely I thought they must be some mistake so I was going to call up Comiskey and demand an explanation but afterwards I thought maybe I better run over and see him.

Well Al I went over there and Harry said the boss was busy but he would find out would he see me. Well after a wile Harry come out and said I was to go in the inside office so I went in and Comiskey was setting at his desk and for a wile he didn't look up but finely he turned around and seen me and shook hands and said "Well young man what can I do for you?" So I said "I come to see you about this here contract." So he asked me if I had signed it and I said no I hadn't so he said "Well they's nothing to see me about then." So I said "Yes because I figure they must of been some mistake in the salery you offered me." So he said "Don't you think you are worth it?" So I said "This here contract calls for $2400.00 per annum and I was getting $2500.00 when I quit and enlisted in the war so it looks like you was fineing me $100.00 per annum for fighting for my country." I said "Gleason said he wanted me and would send me a contract that I would be satisfied with." Well Comiskey said "If Gleason said he wanted you he must of been kidding me when I talked to him but if he wants you bad enough to pay the differents between what that contract calls for and what you want why he is welcome but that is up to him."

Well Al it was all as I could do to hold myself in and if he was a younger man it would of been good night Comiskey but I kept a hold of myself and asked him why didn't he trade me to some club where I could get real jack. So he said "Well I will tell you young man I have got just 1 chance to trade you and that is to Washington and if you think Griffith will pay you more money than I will why I will make the trade." Well I told him to not trouble himself as I was through with baseball any way and had decided to go in to some business so he said good luck and I started out but he said "Here you have left your contract and you better take it along with you because some times when you leave a contract lay around the house a few days the figures gets so big that you wouldn't hardly know them."

Well I seen he was trying to kid me so I said "All right I will take the contract home and tear it up" and I walked out on him.

Well Al that's all they is to it and I am tickled to death that it has came out the way it has and now I can take the best offer that comes along in some good business line and can stay right here in Chi and be home all the yr. around with Florrie and the kiddies.

As for the White Sox I wished them good luck and beleive me they will need it the way Gleason and Comiskey are trying to run things and they will do well to finish in the same league with Boston and Cleveland and N. Y. but at that I don't believe its Gleason that's doing it and the way I figure is that this is his 1st. yr. as mgr and he is a scared to open his clam and if he had his say he would give me the $2800.00 I am holding out for. But its Comiskey himself that's trying to make a monkey out of me. Well god help his ball club is all I can say.

As for leaveing them trade me to Washington that would be a sweet club to pitch for Al where the only time they get a run is when the ◆ president comes out to see them and he's libel to be in France all summer. *Your pal, Jack.*

CHI, MARCH 20.

Friend Al: Well Al this is the last letter you will get from me from Chi

◆ *the only time they get a run is when the president comes out to see them*—The Senators proved to be about as bad as Keefe anticipated, finishing seventh with a team batting average of .260. Only the last-place Athletics were worse, at .244.

for a wile as I am leaveing for Texas with the White Sox tomorrow ◆ night. The scheme worked Al and by setting pretty in the boat and keeping my mouth shut I made them come to me.

I suppose you will be surprised to hear that I am going to get back in to harness but wait till I tell you what come off today and you will where they wasn't no other way out.

Well I went over to the stores this A. M. and when I come back the Swede said some man had called me up on the phone. So of course I knew it must of been the ball pk. so I called them up and the secty. answered the phone and I asked him if anybody wanted to talk to me. So he said no but Gleason was there if I wanted to talk to him.

So I said put him on the wire and pretty soon I heard Gleason's voice and he said "Well Jack are you going along with us?" So I said "What about salery?" So he said "You have got your contract haven't you?" So I said "Yes but it don't call for enough jack." So he said "Well if you earn more jack than your contract calls for you will get it." So I said "If that's a bet I'm on."

So he told me to bring my contract along and come over there and I went over and there was a whole bunch of the boys getting ready for the get away and I wished you could of heard them when they seen me stride in to the office. Well Al they was hand shakes all around and you would of thought it was a family union or something.

Well the business was all tended to in a minute and I signed up and I am going to get $2400.00 which is the same money I was getting when I quit and that's going some Al when you think of the way they have been cutting salerys in baseball. ◆

Well Al I am going to show them that they haven't made no mistake and I am going to work my head off for Gleason and Comiskey and the rest of the boys and wile I hate to be away from Florrie and the kiddies, still and all they's nobody on this ball club that lays awake all night crying for their bottle and if Texas don't do nothing else for me it will at lease give me a chance to get a little sleep. *Your pal, Jack.*

◆ *I am leaveing for Texas with the White Sox tomorrow night*—As stated, the White Sox left for Texas on the Rock Island on March 21, 1919.

◆ *cutting salerys in baseball*—As a further manifestation of their mistaken anticipation of a decline in interest in baseball in 1919, the club owners cut the season to 140 games and collusively reduced salaries.

The Battle of Texas

ON THE RATTLER, MARCH 22.

Friend Al: Well Al I am writeing this on the old rattler bound for sunny Texas and a man has got to write letters or something or you would gap yourself to death. They don't have no more poker game Al but just some baby game like rummy that may be O. K. for birds that has spent all their life at some X roads but take a man like I that was over in France and played in the big game and it kind of sets up a man's stomach to watch a bunch of growed up men popping their eyes out for the fear that they might maybe have a picture card left in their hand when some other bird lays down their cards. So about all they's left for a real man to do is write letters or read the paper or look out at the scenery and I all ready read the papers and as for the scenery we been going through Kas. most of the day and you could pull down the shade most any minute and feel pretty sure you wasn't going to miss nothing.

Well Al we left Chi last night and the 1st. thing Kid Gleason come through the car and asked everybody if they had any bottle goods hid in their grips as he says they are getting strick and if they catch a bird

"The Battle of Texas" was published in *The Saturday Evening Post*, CXCI (May 24, 1919), 12–13, 120, 123.

carring anything in to dry territory they send you to Siberia or somewheres. So when he come along to me he said "Well you big busher I don't half to ask you if you are bringing anything along with you as my nose knows but is any of it in bottles?" So I said "No all I have got with me they would half to operate to find it."

So he said "Well you want to be sure as they are libel to go through everybody's baggage." So I said "I would like to see some fresh Alex make a move to serch my baggage and I would knock him for a gool." ◆

Well they's 2 or 3 of the other boys besides myself that was in the service or that is they call it being in the service though I was the only 1 that got acrost the old pond outside of Joe Jenkins 1 of the catchers ◆ that's still over there yet, but Red Faber was in the navy up to Great Lakes and Ed Collins was in the marines and 1 of the young fellows is wearing a aviation uniform and I suppose he seen the war from Texas and maybe got up so high that the 1st. baseman had to jump for him. But for a wile last night they was all asking me questions about what I seen over there and this in that but every time I would tell them something Collins or 1 of the other smart Alex would say he read about it in the papers and it was different so I said "All right if you seen it in the papers that way it must be so only I kind of figured that me being right up to the front I might be in a position to know something about the war where you take the most of these here

---

◆ *I would knock him for a gool*—This is the first of Keefe's 14 uses of this obscure expression. Harold Wentworth and Stuart Berg Flexner, in their *Dictionary of American Slang*, second supplemented edition (New York: Thomas Y. Crowell, 1975), p. 233, state that "gool" is a corruption of "goal," in use since about 1840. They define "gool" as a transitive verb meaning "To elicit great applause from an audience by one's entertainment," paralleling the phraseology of the passage. The context of Keefe's use of the term is never that, but rather the delivery of a blow. It would have been consistent with Keefe's imperfect apprehension of English to have heard the phrase, misinterpreted it, and adopted it for intensive use for a short period. On the other hand, my only acquaintance with the term is in the context in which Keefe used it. In high school in Chicago in the early 1940's my fellow students occasionally used it, invariably as a transitive verb, as in "I gooled him!" I interpreted it as making a verb out of "ghoul," meaning "I treated him as one would a ghoul." Retrospectively, however, it seems more likely that those who used it, unmindful of its real origins, meant, "I treated him as a ghoul would, devouring his carcass."

◆ *Joe Jenkins*—Joseph Daniel Jenkins (1890–1974), the White Sox third-string catcher. He played 19 games with the Browns in 1914, 10 with the White Sox in 1917, and 11 in 1919 after coming out of the army. In his 40 games in the major leagues, Jenkins hit only .133. Keefe was correct in saying that Jenkins was still in Europe. A lieutenant, he did not receive his discharge until well after the majority of players, who had typically been enlisted men, had been released from service.

reporters and for all they seen of it they might as well of been on Pikes Peek with a pair of opera glasses looking west." So that shut them up.

Well Al we are supposed to get to Mineral Wells tomorrow noon ◆ and they can't get us there to soon to suit me as I am wild to get out there in the old ball yard and show Gleason that I have got something left and he was telling me this A. M. that he had picked up a lot of good looking young right handers and I would half to step along to hold a job or the next thing I knowed I would be up to Minneapolis ◆ wearing a white beard and pitching for Joe Cantillon. But the new recruits that I have met on the train so far that thinks they are pitchers couldn't pass the physical examination for the Portugal army so it looks like I wouldn't have much trouble if I get a square deal and if I don't I will knock somebody for a gool. *Your pal, Jack.*

MINERAL WELLS, MARCH 24.

Friend Al: Well Al we landed here yesterday noon and it was raining ◆ when we got here and still raining and don't look like it would ever stop and a man might almost think we had came to France by a mistake. And the only differents is that the harder it rained in France why they would see that we was all out in it wile here they's nothing to do only lay around the hotel. Well Al I don't know how many people they have got in Texas but they are all stopping at this hotel and on a rainy day it would take Houdini to get through the lobby. They call ◆

◆ *Mineral Wells*—A resort town about 40 miles due west of Fort Worth. Its population in 1910 was 3,950.

◆ *up to Minneapolis wearing a white beard and pitching for Joe Cantillon.*—Joseph D. "Pongo Joe" Cantillon (1861–1930), was manager and part owner of the Minneapolis Millers of the American Association from 1910 to 1923. The reference to the white beard is to Cantillon's practice of hiring former major leaguers for their final years of play. Cantillon, who never played major league baseball, is mainly known as Walter Johnson's first manager with the Senators in 1907. Cantillon managed the Senators for three years, finishing eighth in 1907, seventh in 1908, and eighth in 1909. He had been an umpire in the American League from 1901 to 1903 and umpired in the American Association in 1929. In the mid-1920's he was a scout for the White Sox. On Cantillon and the Millers generally, see Stew Thornley, *On to Nicollet: The Glory and Fame of the Minneapolis Millers* (Minneapolis: Nodin Press, 1988).

◆ *it was raining when we got here and still raining*—It rained continually through March 25. The aridity of the climate, ironically, was one of Comiskey's criteria in choosing Mineral Wells as a training base.

◆ *Houdini*—Harry Houdini (1874–1926), the best-known stage magician of the day, and a notable escape artist.

this hotel the Crazy Wells on acct. of 1 of the wells that they say it ◆ cures crazy people but it would half to be some well to cure some of the birds on our club a specially after they been jammed up together in this hotel a couple of rainy days with nothing to do only gap at each other.

Well we got in to Ft. Worth yesterday A. M. they switched us on to the R. R. that runs over here at lease they call it a R. R. and its the Weatherford Mineral Wells and North Western but Buck Weaver says ◆ the letters stands for Whoa Mule Whoa now Whoa. So I said if you think this R. R. balks you should ought to ride around France in some of them horse cars so Buck said "I wished I was a extra catcher so as I could set down in the bull pen with you all summer and learn all about France." He said "You boys that went to France thinks you had a tough time of it but what about we birds that has to listen to it all the rest of our life." So I said shut your mouth. But any way Al this R.R. isn't only 28 miles long from 1 end to the other so even if the trains do run like old Cy Young was paceing them you get to where ◆ you was going some time, where the roads we was on in France never seemed to know where to leave off.

Well we couldn't of done no work yesterday any way on acct. of just getting in and unpacking and getting our uniforms and everything but Gleason was certainly sore when we woke up this A. M. and it was still poring rain and I set with him at the breakfast table and the waiter said this rain was makeing a big hit with the people in Texas as they

---

◆ *Crazy Wells*—The hotel was a notable spa, the waters of which were advertised for their medicinal properties, even if they did not have the psychotherapeutic effect Keefe attributed to them. The minerals from the water were marketed under the trade name "Crazy Water Crystals."

◆ *the Weatherford Mineral Wells and North Western*—Mineral Wells was on a short line, the Weatherford, Mineral Wells & North-Western Railway, 22 miles west of the junction with the Texas & Pacific Railway at Weatherford. The T&P and the WMW&NW ran through coaches and Pullman cars from Fort Worth to the resort.

◆ *Cy Young*—Denton True Young (1867–1955), a pitcher of almost legendary fame. Pitching for Cleveland of the National League from 1890 to 1898, for St. Louis of the National in 1899 and 1900, for Boston of the American League from 1901 to 1908, for the Cleveland Naps from 1909 to 1911, and finally for the Boston Braves in 1911, Young won 511 games and lost 313, neither figure ever closely approached by later players. He also leads all pitchers in games started, 816; complete games, 753; innings pitched, 7,356; and hits allowed, 7,092. He threw 77 shutouts. Young was elected to the Baseball Hall of Fame in 1937. The modern award for outstanding pitcher of the year was named in Young's honor in 1956.

The reference is to Young's sluggish speed afoot. He became quite stout in his final years, and claimed to have retired because of his inability to field bunts. See Ellery H. Clark, Jr., "Denton True Young," *Biographical Dictionary of American Sports: Baseball*, pp. 635–37.

hadn't had no rain for so long that pretty near everything was drying up so Gleason said "Well you better make it unanimous." He meant for the waiter to dry up to and shut his mouth.

Well Gleason said we would half to go out and work tomorrow rain or shine and he said after this everybody would half to be down for breakfast at 8 bells or they wouldn't get no breakfast and if they didn't get down for breakfast he would go up to their rooms and use his razor strap on them. That's the way he generally always does Al on the new recruits is go after them with his razor strap to show them he is in ernest but of course he wouldn't dast do that on 1 of we old timers and if he ever tried it on me I would knock him for a gool.

I told him that this A. M. and he said "Well they's no danger of you ever comeing late to a meal and the only thing I am a scared of is that you will get here before they open up the dinning rm. and bust down the door and get us put out of the hotel."

Well Al I am glad of 1 thing and that is most of the people stopping at the hotel is men and very few gals not that the gals would make any differents in my young life only in most of these southern hotels they's generally always a flock of gals that wants to make a fuss over the ball players and usually 1 of them takes a kind of a shine to me but this time I have made it up in my mind to tend to business and show Gleason that he didn't make no mistake in meeting my terms so I am glad I won't have nothing to take my mind off of my work though they's 1 little gal stopping here that the boys says she is a swell heiress from St. Louis that's here with her mother that's got rheumatism and I noticed she give me a long look when I come in the dinning rm. this noon but I looked straight ahead and pretended like I didn't notice it. Her name is Miss Krug and she is some looker but she is certainly wasteing them goggly eyes on me as I am down here to get my arm in shape to pitch and not hold hands or something.

The clerk tells me that she has got a big car that she drives around in it all the wile her mother is takeing the treatments but as far as I am conserned if she gets lonesome driveing she will half to talk to the spare tire. *Your pal, Jack.*

MINERAL WELLS, MARCH 26.

Friend Al: Well Al if nerve was all that a bird needed to make good in the big league they's 1 bird down here trying to be a pitcher on our club that has all ready made good. But it takes something besides nerve Al but listen to what come off today and you will say this bird is chesty enough if he only had something to go with it.

Well this bird's name is Belden and he was a semi pro up in Chi but ◆ he got catched in the draft and went to France and he just got back from over there last month and somebody recomended him to Comiskey and so he is down here on the trip. Well he is a right hander so he is a rival of mine you might say but to look at him I guess they's no hurry about me packing up my grip and go home.

Well the rain had stopped this A. M. and Gleason said everybody must be out to the pk. at 10 bells so we started out about 9:30 and I was walking with Buck Weaver and Eddie Cicotte and this here Belden. They was about a ft. of mud on the road and Cicotte made some remark about the mud and Belden said "This isn't nothing to what it was in France and over there we would think this was a drout." Well they's a cemetery on the way out to the pk. and wile we was going past it Buck Weaver made the remark that that was where we left most of the young pitchers every spring so Belden said "You can't scare me with no stuff about cemeterys as I seen to many of them in France." So then Buck says "Is they any subject we can talk about that won't remind you of something you seen in France?" So that shut him up for a wile but after a wile Cicotte asked him what battles he was in over there and he said he was in the Marne and the Oregon forest and Bellow Woods. So Cicotte says "Its no wonder the Germans took such a licking in them places as the whole American army was there." So Belden said oh no they wasn't and what made him think that. So Cicotte said "Because every soldier I have seen that's came back from France was in the Oregon forest and Bellow Woods."

Well we finely got out to the pk. and they wasn't no chance for a real practice on acct. of the mud but Gleason found a dry spot over in 1 corner and marked off the pitching distants and had us all throw a few and honest Al my old super never felt better in my life and I cut loose a couple that pretty near knocked Schalk for a gool but Gleason finely come up and stopped me and told me to not go to strong the 1st. day. Well I watched this Belden wile he throwed a few and I was standing along side of Cicotte and he was watching him to so I asked him what he thought of him. So Cicotte said "He looks like he will make a mighty valuable man for us as when he is in there pitching Schalk can set on the bench and rest as he won't never get nothing past the batter."

◆ *Belden*—A fictional character. In the Central League was a career outfielder named Billy Belden, from whom Lardner presumably adapted the name.

Well we finely come out of the pk. and started back towards the hotel and the 1st. thing you know they was a machine come hunking up behind us and it was Miss Krug the St. Louis heiress that's stopping at the hotel and she slowed up and asked if anybody wanted a ride. Well Al she was looking right at me but I pretended like I didn't understand but I just give her a kind of a smile and the next thing you know Belden had ran out and jumped in the drivers seat with her and away they went.

How is that for nerve Al when it was me she was looking at and this other bird that's been in the league about 5 minutes you might say jumps in and rides with her and I bet the little gal felt pretty sick when she seen what she had got wished on to and she didn't come in for supper tonight as I suppose she thought some of the boys would make fun of her though she needn't have no fears on that score as if any of them tried it I would knock them for a gool. *Your pal, Jack.*

MINERAL WELLS, MARCH 29.

Friend Al: Well old pal I guess they's no more question about me makeing good and sticking with the club and you will say the same thing when I tell you what Gleason said yesterday. We played a game out to the pk. between the 1st. and 2d. clubs and the game was to go 7 innings and Gleason told me I could pitch a part of it for the 2d. club so my arm was feeling so good that I asked him to let me work 4 of the 7 innings. Well Al when I got through the 1st. club had 1 hit and never found out where 2d. base was located. So when it was over Gleason come up to me and said "Well Jack I don't know what the war done to you but I never seen you look better then that in the spring and right now you look like the best man I have got down here pitching." He said "Now don't go and swell up but keep working hard and do like I tell you and you may turn out to be the bird I need to round out my pitching staff." Well the club was going over to play Ft. Worth and Dallas Saturday and Sunday and I thought of course we would all go along but after my showing yesterday Gleason figured he wouldn't take no chances so he left me here to work out with Faber and Wolfgang wile the rest of the boys is gone. He said "I wouldn't ◆ pitch you in either of them games after working you yesterday and I

◆ *Wolfgang*—Melford John "Mellie" Wolfgang (1890–1947), a short, righthanded spitballer who had pursued a lackluster career with the White Sox since 1914. His best season, at 7–5, was his first, in the course of which he beat Walter Johnson twice in three days. Four additional seasons brought his career record to 14–14.

want you to do a little work here with these other 2 boys and behave just like I was here watching you." So I said "What and the he—ll could a man do only behave himself in this town?" Well he said "I mean for you to not try and eat for the whole club just because they are not here to eat for themself."

So you see Al it looks like I had made good right from the start this time and that means they will half to come acrost with more jack before long as Gleason promised before I come south that he would give me more then my contract calls for if I show him the right kind of stuff.

Well the bunch went away early this A. M. and was gone before I got up and I had breakfast with Faber and Wolfgang and we decided to go out and work about 11 o'clock so I and the other 2 went out to the pk. and throwed the ball around a wile and done some running but I got tired pretty quick on acct. of pitching yesterday so pretty soon I said I thought I would call it a day so I started back to the hotel and I hadn't no sooner then got outside of the pk. and all of a sudden along come Miss Krug in her machine.

Well they wasn't no getting away from her this time without turning her down cold so I kind of waved to her and she stopped the machine and I got in and we drove back to the hotel.

Well Al she is some gal and it is a pleasure to talk to a gal like she as you take most gals and they can't kid along with a man but about all as they can do is giggle and act silly but this baby can give you as good as you send.

Well I said "You must be pretty lonesome today with Belden gone." So she said "Oh I don't know." So then I said "He is sure some lady killer." So she said "I'll say so. But you notice I am still alive." So after a wile she said "Belden tells me you was in France too." So I said "You and Belden seems to of talked together a whole lot." "Well" she said "I haven't had no one else to talk to." So I said "Well you have got some one else to talk to now." "Yes" she says "but you always run away from me. I suppose you real stars gets tired of haveing girls run after you." So I said "Oh I don't know."

Well we kidded back and 4th. like that till we come to the hotel and

---

(*continued from page 242*)
He served mainly as the White Sox' batting-practice pitcher in 1917 and 1918. Wolfgang failed to make the team in 1919 and was released to Milwaukee on April 12. See Bob Carroll, "Mellie Wolfgang," *The Ballplayers*, p. 1194.

then I asked her was she doing anything this P. M. and she said she had a date with her mother but I took her to the picture show tonight and tomorrow she is going to take me for another ride. Well Al it does a man good to be around with a gal like that that keeps a man on edge what to say next as she always gives you as good as you send and from what she said she must be kind of tired of hearing Belden tell how he win the battle of Bellow Woods and etc. and any way I feel like a little rest would be the best thing for me after pitching them 4 innings yesterday. So I will play around with her tomorrow and then forget her when the bunch gets back Monday A. M. and go to work in ernest but if a man works to hard right at the start you are libel to go stale.

Well Al I had a letter from Florrie today and little Florrie has got 1 tooth and another 1 showing and she says little Al misses me pretty bad and asks every day why daddy don't hurry up and come home. Well they will all be proud of daddy before this season is over eh Al.

Your pal, Jack

MINERAL WELLS, MARCH 31.

Friend Al: Well Al the boys is back from Ft. Worth and Dallas and I guess they didn't show up any to good over there and any way Gleason ◆ don't look like he enjoyed the trip and he told the boys out to the pk. this P. M. they would half to show a whole lot more pep or he would leave some of them in Texas all summer to graze.

Well he give us a long work out and he stood behind me wile I throwed a few to Schalkie and he said I didn't look as fast as when I pitched them 4 innings last Friday but he wasn't throwing no boquets at any of the boys today so I didn't pay no tension. But I couldn't help from laughing at 1 of the young catchers name Cosgrove that was ◆ standing up there catching in the batting pracice and Joe Jackson hit a foul ball straight up and Cosgrove throwed off his mask and begin running a mile around a 4 ft. track and finely the ball came down and hit him in the cheek bone and knocked him for a gool. Well he layed there and the trainer come running out to tend to him but Gleason says "Get away from him as he is just as good laying there as standing up and maybe after this he will know enough to keep his mask on after a high foul ball."

◆ *they didn't show up any to good over there*—The White Sox beat Fort Worth, 3–0, on March 29 and were rained out at Dallas on March 30.

◆ *Cosgrove*—Apparently a fictional character.

Well it was pretty near supper time when he let us off and I tried to be 1 of the 1st. out of the pk. but they was a whole bunch out ahead of me and when Miss Krug come along with her car they all seen me jump in and you ought to of seen Belden when he seen us drive away together and all the boys yelled their head off.

Well I come back here to the hotel and got dressed and come down for supper and after a wile Gleason come in and I was setting with 3 of the other boys but he made 1 of them get up and give him his seat so as he could set down and kid me.

"Well Jack" he says "I hear you worked pretty hard wile we was gone and I suppose you can pretty near run the car by this time."

Well I knew he wasn't sore at me but just sore on acct. of how rotten the young fellows was showing up so I just give him a smile.

"After this" he says "you and all the whole rest of the club will ride back and 4th. between the ball pk. and back on your own dogs. They's to much rideing on this club but after this I will do all of it and everybody on this club will get rode to death if they don't quit loafing on me. So remember every one of you will stay out of machines going to the ball pk. and comeing back and besides that when you go up to your rms. you can use the stairs and take a load off the elevator."

Well Al he may be my mgr. out on the old ball field but he can't tell me how to get upstairs or from 1 place to another but I left him get away with it rather then start trouble in the dinning rm. of the hotel in front of the other boys to say nothing of the guests.

But I wonder what he would say if he knew how I spent Sunday. Well old pal I had some time. Miss Krug knows all the roads and we drove pretty near all day and she is some gal Al and smart as a whip. Everything you say to her she has got a come back and for inst. wile we was driveing yesterday she happened to ask me where I come from and I told her Indiana and she said "That's a good place to come from." She meant it was a good place to get away from. So I said "I guess it hasn't got nothing on St. Louis at that." "Oh I don't know" she said.

Well it looks like I had Belden's time beat and I suppose I ought to of left him a clear field on acct. of him being single but the gal says herself that she can't stand him on acct. of him talking about himself all the wile and besides his looks is against him and besides a man has got to amuse themself some way in a burg like this or it would take more then the crazy wells to stop you from turning in to squirrel meat.

Your pal, Jack.

Friend Al: Well Al tomorrow is the last day here as we leave for Houston and play there Saturday and Sunday and then Austin and Georgetown and after that we go to Dallas for a few days and play a couple games there before we start north. Gleason was kidding me again tonight and said he wanted to apologize for the schedule that takes us away from here so soon and if he had of known how I was going to enjoy Mineral Wells he would of arranged to stay here longer. But he said I was to be sure and start in saying good by soon enough so as I would be through by train time. Well Al I wonder what he would say if I told him Miss Krug is going to be in Dallas wile we are there as she is going to drive over there with her mother. It kind of looks like she hates me eh Al?

Well we played another ball game today between the 1st. and 2d. club and I pitched 5 innings for the 1st. club and they got 5 runs off of me but most of them was on acct. of the way Weaver and Collins was kicking the ball around the infield and then when they had filled up the bases on me Shano Collins caught a hold of 1 that was a mile over his head and the wind blowed it down in the right field corner and the right field fence in this pk. is as far as from here to France and the ground was hard and of course the dam ball rolled and Shano could of ran around the bases twice so when the inning was over Gleason said to me "When you are pitching to a man like Collins you want to say to yourself I am pitching to Collins and not be thinking about some garbage contractor's daughter from St. Louis." So I said "He hit a ball that was over his head." So Gleason said "Yes and over Liebold's head to." He says "The next time I pick out a spot to train a ◆ ball club it will be in a man's convent where they's no gals." So I walked away from him.

But wait till you hear what this Belden pulled today Al. Dureing the game some of the boys was trying their hit and run signs and etc.

◆ *Liebold*—Harry Loran "Nemo" Leibold (1892–1977), the White Sox regular rightfielder. After breaking in with Cleveland in 1913, Leibold came to the White Sox at the waiver price during the 1915 season. Only 5′6½″ and 157 pounds, Leibold had little power, and in spite of a .302 batting average was considered the weakest starter on the team. He typically played only against righthanded pitching, and was replaced by Shano Collins against lefthanders. Leibold played for the White Sox through 1920, and then for the Red Sox and Senators. He wound up a 13-year career in 1925 with a lifetime average of .266 in 1,258 games. Later, Leibold was a successful, if notoriously belligerent, minor league manager. See Jack Kavanagh, "Nemo Leibold," *The Ballplayers*, p. 614.

and they got them all balled up so Gleason made us stay out there after the game was over and practice up on our signs and wile he was talking to some of the boys this Belden cut in and said he thought it would be a good idear if instead of slideing their hand up and down the bat or pulling their cap or something if they would learn a few French words and give their signs in French out loud and they couldn't none of the other clubs understand them and for inst. if a man was up there hitting and wanted the man on 1st. base to go down on the next ball he would holler allay at him on acct. of that being the French for go. So Cicotte said it was a great idear only about the 9th. or 10th. time we worked it on some club and they seen the man go every time they might maybe suspect what it meant and then we would half to find out the Russian word for go and use that and he thought the only Russian word for go meant go back and the base runner would get mixed up and think the batter meant he was going to hit a foul ball.

Well Miss Krug had some engagement with her mother tonight so I went with some of the boys to a picture show and Belden went along with us an 1 of the pictures was old last yr. stuff that showed a lot of different places in France and etc. and every time they would show a picture Cicotte would ask Belden if he was there and he said yes every time and finely Cicotte asked him how long he was in France all together and he said 4 mos, so Cicotte said "Well if you was only in France 4 mos. and seen all them places its no wonder you wasn't shot as you never stood still a minute."

Well Al this is the last letter you will get from me here as I will be busy packing up tomorrow and saying good by to my friends but I will try and drop you a line from Houston or somewheres along the line and let you know how things is comeing on. *Your pal, Jack.*

GEORGETOWN, APRIL 8.

Friend Al: Well I guess Gleason won't half to worry no more about at least 1 member of his pitching staff after what I done over in Houston ◆ Saturday and here again today. I worked 5 innings against the Houston club Saturday and believe me Al they have got some club but I made them look like they ought to of paid their way in. They was only 1 ball got out of the infield and Weaver could of nailed that only he didn't

◆ *what I done over in Houston Saturday*—Actually, Cicotte beat Houston, 5–1, on Saturday, April 5. Houston had finished fifth in a Texas League reduced to six teams in 1918, and was to finish fourth and second in the normal eight-team league in a split season in 1919.

◇ *Williams*—Claude "Lefty" Williams in the White Sox 1917 home uniform. (George E. Brace collection)

start in time and the rest of the wile they was popping them up in the air or missing them all together. Well Williams the left hander followed ◆◇ me and he was pretty good to though he didn't have anywheres near the stuff I showed but we trimmed them 6 to 0 and Gleason was all smiles.

◆ *Williams*—Claude Preston ("Lefty") Williams (1893–1959), the White Sox' leading lefthander and, after Cicotte, the team's second-best pitcher. Williams pitched six games for Detroit in 1913 and 1914, with a record of 1–4. He came to the White Sox in 1916 and turned in a 13–7 record. On the 1917 championship team Williams had a 17–8 record and made one relief appearance in the World Series. In a partial season in 1918 he had only a 6–4 record, but he reached stardom in 1919 with 23–11. Williams, who was making less than $3,000 per year, was the fourth player lined up by Chick Gandil to throw the 1919 World Series. Williams was to lose three games in the Series, including the final game. He had a 22–14 record in 1920 before being declared ineligible. An inarticulate, moody man, he did not lend himself even to an attempt at personality delineation by Lardner. See Norman L. Macht, "Lefty Williams," *The Ballplayers*, p. 1177.

Well of course I didn't work there again Sunday or yesterday at ◆ Austin and the boys didn't look so good behind the pitching they got but today we was up against a bunch of collegers and Gleason sent ◆ me the whole distants to see how I could stand it and I guess I showed him. Well Al I honestly felt sorry for some of these scollege boys and they couldn't of got a base hit off me with a shovel only their teachers and friends was watching them so I eased up in the last 2 innings and they got a couple of base hits and they felt so good about them that I wished I had of let them get some more.

Well Gleason come to me afterwards and he said "Now Jack you look like that 1st. day at the Wells and if you can just keep going like that I have got the 4 pitchers I want to work regular and you are 1 of them. You showed me in Houston and here what you can do when you haven't got your mind on some millionaire janitor's daughter from St. Louis with rheumatism on the mother's side. You had a fast ball in there to-day that looked like Johnson at his best and you have pretty near got where you can slow ball them without everybody in the pk. calling it on you. You just keep pitching that way and I will get you some dough that is some dough."

So it looks like I was all set Al and the only thing now is to keep him from finding out about Miss Krug and her mother comeing to Dallas and I don't care if I see her or not only it wouldn't seem hardly fair to have she and her mother come all the way over there and then me not even take her to a picture show. But what Gleason don't know won't hurt him and that stuff about girls bothering me is all in his eye as I can pitch when my arm feels good and I can't pitch when it don't feel good girls or no girls. *Your pal, Jack.*

FORT WORTH, APRIL 13.

Friend Al: Well Al I don't know whether to quit baseball or not and maybe I won't quit if I can get away to some other club but I can't work no more under Gleason and do myself justice.

Wait till you hear what come off in Dallas yesterday and I bet you will say I would be a sucker to stand for the kind of stuff he is trying to put over.

◆ *yesterday at Austin*—The White Sox varsity defeated the University of Texas, 9–1, on April 7.

◆ *collegers*—The White Sox first team beat Southwestern College in Georgetown, Tex., on April 8, 11–3, behind Dave Danforth.

Well Al the second day we was there I got a phone call and it was Miss Krug and her and her mother was stopping at a certain hotel so I asked her would she like to go to a picture show or somewheres and she said she would so I said I would meet her that night and we would go somewheres and see a show. Well I was in the lobby of our hotel when the phone call come and of course they had to page me and Gleason heard them so after I got through phoneing he come up to me and asked if the bell of St. Louis was folling me around. So I said no I supposed she was in Mineral Wells. So he said where was I going that evening and I said nowheres and he said all right he wanted me to go to a picture show with him. So then I said I had forgot I had a date to go with 1 of the other boys on the club so he said all right he would go along with us. Well Al they wasn't no shakeing lose from him so finely I had to own up that I was going to take Miss Krug to a show so he said he would go along and pay for it. Well he went along all right and it was the worst picture I ever seen and when it was over Gleason asked Miss Krug and I if we wouldn't have a soda or something.

Well they wasn't nothing to do only go with him and we hadn't no sooner then give our order when he said to her "What do you think of big Jack here?" Well she said she thought I was all right. So Gleason said "Well I never thought so myself but I guess he must be or he couldn't of never got such a sweet wife like he's got up in Chi." Well I couldn't say nothing or neither could the gal. So then Gleason asked me did I have the Mrs. picture with me or either 1 of the 2 kids. Well Al they's no use telling you any more about it only we had our soda and took the gal back to her hotel and then I and Gleason come back to our hotel together and he never said a word all the way home or neither did I only just before he left me to go up to his rm. he said "You pitch tomorrow Jack" and that's all he said.

Well of course they won't be no more picture shows for Miss Krug and I and of course it don't make no differents to me as I was just going to tell her about me being married and everything and her and I was just good friends and liked to talk to each other but its haveing him cut in on my private affairs and try to run them that makes me sore and he must think this is the army the way he acts.

Well Al I pitched the game in Dallas yesterday and they couldn't do nothing with me but I wouldn't of never pitched it at all only they had me advertised and I have got a whole lot of good friends there that I wouldn't disapoint them. But as for sticking with the club after that kind of business I couldn't do myself justice and as soon as we get home I will put it up to Comiskey and ask him to trade me to some other club or else I will quit and go in to some business where a man does his work and gets through and when he is through the mgr. of the store don't go noseing around in to your private affairs.

Your pal, Jack.

LOUISVILLE, APRIL 18.

Friend Al: Well Al I have only got time for a few lines as we are leaveing in a little wile for Cincy for games tomorow and Sunday and I am going to pitch 5 innings Sunday and then rest till Wednesday when we open up the season in St. Louis. Gleason hasn't gave it out to the papers yet Al but between you and I it looks like a cinch I would pitch the opening game in St. Louis. Gleason and all the rest of the boys admits that I have been going better then any other pitcher on the club and you know how crazy every club is to win the opening game and that is why it looks like I would be the man that is chose.

Well Al I will give them everything I have got and if I only feel as good as I felt yesterday in Nashville why the St. Louis boys might just ◆ as well leave their bats in the bag.

Well I guess the last time I wrote you I was kind of on the outs with Gleason and I didn't speak to him for pretty near a wk. but a man can't stay sore at him very long on acct. of the stuff he pulls and 1st. thing you know you half to bust right out laughing and then of course its good night.

I guess I told you about Belden the young pitcher from Chi that was in France and tried to get us to give our signs in French. Well he was with the 2d. club that left us before we come away from Texas and they went up north the other way and yesterday I was setting in the ◆ hotel at Nashville talking to Felsch and Gleason come along and Felsch ◆ asked him if he had heard how Belden was comeing along with the

---

◆ *Nashville*—The White Sox beat Nashville of the Southern Association, 5–3, on April 17.

◆ *they went up north the other way*—The second team returned via Des Moines and other midwestern points.

◆ *Felsch*—Oscar Emil "Happy" Felsch (1891–1964), centerfielder for the White Sox since 1915. An above-average hitter, Felsch had hit .300 in 1916 and .308 for the 1917 champions. A sixth-grade dropout from Milwaukee, he was easy prey for Gandil, and readily joined the Black Sox conspiracy. In 1920, before being declared ineligible, Felsch had his finest year, batting .338. His career encompassed six seasons, over the course of which he hit .293 in 749 games. See Richard E. Beverage, "Happy Felsch," *The Ballplayers*, p. 328.

2d. club. So Gleason said "He got along a whole lot faster then the club he was with as he is all ready back in Chi." He said "I wired to Shano Collins and asked him if they was anybody on his 2d. club that looked like he could get along without them so he wired back that he could rap Belden up and send him home because though they wasn't no doubt that he had beat Germany it didn't look like he would ever last 2 innings vs. Boston and Cleveland." So when Gleason pulled that I couldn't help from laughing and then he kicked me in the shins like old times and now we are pals again.

Well I haven't no more time to write from here but will try and drop you a line from Cincy but in the mean wile you can tell the boys that it looks like a cinch I will open the season in St. Louis and if any of them has a chance to get a bet down on your old pal they can't go wrong. I wasn't never as good as I am this spring Al and I will knock them for a gool. *Your pal, Jack.*

CINCY, APRIL 20. ◆

Friend Al: Well Al just a few words before we go out to the pk. and this will be my last game before the opening and Gleason says I and Lefty Williams will pitch 5 and 4 innings today for a final work out so it looks like a cinch I will open up Wednesday in St. Louis.

Speaking about St. Louis Al I guess I told you about that Miss Krug that was down to the Wells wile we was there and kind of lost her head over me and finely I had to get Gleason to tell her I was a married man. Well I had forgot all about her but this A. M. when I come down for breakfast they was a letter in my box and it was from this same gal and she is back in St. Louis and wanted to know if maybe I couldn't call her up when I get there just for old time sake and any way she said she would be out to the opening game Wednesday and pulling for us even if she is a St. Louis gal.

Well I was reading the letter at breakfast and Gleason come in and asked me what was the news from home and I said I hadn't heard nothing from home since we was in Memphis so he said who was the letter from then. So I said "You may be the mgr. of this ball club but you are not my mother." So he said "No and if I was I would give you a spanking." He says "You don't half to tell me who the letter is from because I can tell by your rosy cheeks who it is from and I can just

◆ *Cincy, April 20*—On this date Dickie Kerr beat the Reds in 10 innings, 3–1.

about tell what's in it." So then I said "All right if you are such a smart Alex they's no use in me telling you anything." So then he asked me what was my home address in Chi as he said he wanted all the boys addresses and phone numbers. So I give him mine and he walked away.

Well Al I have got to get ready to go out to the pk. and give these National Leaguers a treat and I bet by the time I get through with them they will be thanking god that they don't half to look at this kind of pitching all summer or they would hit about 6 and 7-8.

Your pal, Jack.

ST. LOUIS, APRIL 24.

Friend Al: Well old pal I suppose by this time you have got a hold of the Chi papers and seen what I done yesterday and all as I have seen so far is the St. Louis papers and every 1 of them says it was 1 of the best pitched games they ever seen for an opening game. ◆

Well Al they couldn't of nobody beat me yesterday and either 1 of the 2 hits I give them could of been scored either way and a specially Sisler's but I guess he ain't bragging much this A. M. at that as I sent ◆ him back twice for a drink of water.

Well old pal I have had lots of big days in my career both in baseball and in Uncle Sam's service but I don't believe I was ever so happy in my life as when Schalkie caught that foul ball off of Gedeon and made ◆ the last out and the way Gleason and the rest of the boys slapped me on the back.

◆ *opening game*—Actually, it was Williams who defeated the Browns in the opener, 13–4.

◆ *Sisler*—George Harold Sisler (1893–1973), the leading player of the St. Louis Browns in their undistinguished history and, along with Lou Gehrig, one of the two usual choices as the game's premier first basemen. Sisler, a fine fielder as well as a great hitter, played for the Browns from 1915 to 1927, then with the Washington Senators and Boston Braves, ending his career in 1930. In 15 seasons he made 2,811 hits for a .340 batting average in 2,054 games. Sisler hit over .400 twice, .407 in 1920 and .420 in 1922. His 257 hits in 1920 remain the major league record. He also had a 5–6 pitching record with the Browns in 1915–16, and made occasional pitching appearances as late as 1928. An intelligent man with a degree in mechanical engineering from the University of Michigan, Sisler managed the Browns from 1924 to 1926, and later served as a scout and batting instructor. He was elected to the Baseball Hall of Fame in 1939. See Lowell L. Blaisdell, "George Harold Sisler," *Biographical Dictionary of American Sports: Baseball*, pp. 515–17.

◆ *Gedeon*—Elmer Joseph Gedeon (1894–1941), the Browns second baseman. A journeyman infielder, Gedeon broke in with Washington in 1913, returned to the minor leagues in 1914, came up to the Yankees in 1916, and went to the Browns

◇ *her setting there in the stand—* Two sides of a pass for the 1919 season at Comiskey Park. (Collection of the Editor)

WHITE SOX AT COMISKEY PARK, 1919

St. Louis	May 1, 2, 3, 4
Detroit	May 5, 6, 7
Boston	May 14, 15, 16
Philadelphia	May 17, 18, 19, 20
New York	May 21, 22, 23, 24
Washington	May 25, 26, 27
Cleveland	May 30, 30, 31, June 1
Cleveland	June 23, 24, 25
Detroit	July 4, 4, 5, 6
Philadelphia	July 9, 10, 11
Boston	July 12, 13, 14, 15
Washington	July 16, 17, 18, 19
New York	July 20, 21, 22
St. Louis	July 24, 25, 26, 27
Boston	Aug. 14, 15, 16
Philadelphia	Aug. 17, 18, 19
Washington	Aug. 20, 21, 22
New York	Aug. 23, 24, 25
Cleveland	Sept. 5, 6, 7
St. Louis	Sept. 24, 25
Detroit	Sept. 26, 27, 28

(continued from page 253)
in 1918, where he played regularly through 1920, hitting .244 in 581 games in his seven-year career. Gedeon was a close friend of Swede Risberg, the White Sox shortstop, who was a party to Gandil's plot. Risberg wired Gedeon to bet on the Reds, making him one of several people to have advance knowledge of the fix. Gedeon came forth to tell what he knew to Comiskey shortly after the Series, but Comiskey took no action, ostensibly considering Gedeon's information inconclusive. Gedeon was banned for having guilty knowledge, however. See Jack Kavanagh, "Joe Gedeon," *The Ballplayers*, p. 381.

But wait till I tell you the funny part of it Al. Gleason sent us all to bed early Tuesday night and before I went to the hay he told me to get plenty of rest as he was going to pitch me if I looked good out there before the game.

So I didn't get up till pretty near 9 o'clock and it was a quarter to 10 when I come down for breakfast and when I got in the lobby who do you think was there waiting for me? Well Al it was Florrie, all dolled up like the state fair.

Well to make a short story out of it it seems like Gleason had wrote her a letter from Cincy and asked her to come down here at the club's expense and watch me open up the season but to not say nothing to me about she was comeing and believe me Al it was some surprise and pleasant surprise to see her and I never seen her look prettier in her life.

Well Al I guess with the stuff I had I could of beat them without her setting there in the stand but just the same I worked a whole lot harder for knowing she was up there watching me and I guess the club won't grudge the jack they spent getting her down here.

Well when we come back to the hotel for dinner last night Gleason come in the dinning rm. with us and insisted on buying us a bottle of wine and I never seen nobody in my life so tickled over winning 1 ball game as him. Well of course he has got a good reason to be tickled as he will need all the pitching he can get and me makeing this showing means about half his worrys is gone.

Well you will read about the game in the papers and they isn't much more to write about only I can't help from kind of wondering if Miss Krug was out there and seen it but after all what and the he—ll do I care if she was or wasn't? *Your pal, Jack.*

Along Came Ruth

ST. LOUIS, APRIL 26.

Friend Al: Well Al this is our last day here and we win the 1st. 2 games ◆ and lose yesterday and have got 1 more game to play and tonight we leave for Detroit. Well if we lose today we will have a even break on the serious and a club that can't do no better then break even with this St. Louis club better take up some other line of business but ◆ Gleason instead of useing a little judgement sent a left hander in against them yesterday and they certainly give him a welcome and the more I see of left handers I am certainly glad I pitch with my right arm the way God intended for a man.

Well the boys on our club was feeling pretty cocky the 1st. 2 days ◇ about how they could hit but yesterday they could of played in a 16 ft. ring without no ground rules as the most of the time they was missing the ball all together and when they did hit it it acted like a geyser and it was Bert Gallia pitching against us and they all kept ◆◇

"Along Came Ruth" was published in *The Saturday Evening Post*, CXCII (July 26, 1919), 12–13, 120, 123.

◆ *we win the 1st. 2 games and lose yesterday*—Correct. Cicotte won the second game of the season, 5–2, on April 24. In the third, the Browns easily beat Dave Danforth, 7–2. In the final game of the series on April 26, Faber won, 9–4.

◆ *this St. Louis club*—The Browns finished fifth at 67–72, in 1919.

saying he didn't have nothing but when he got through with us we didn't have nothing either and that's the way it always goes when a pitcher makes a sucker out of a club he didn't have nothing but when they knock him out of the park he's pretty good.

Well any way I told Gleason last night that it looked like we wouldn't get no better then a even break here unless he stuck me in there to pitch the last game today. So he says "No I was figureing on you to open up in Detroit Sunday but of course if you are afraid of Detroit I can make different plans." So I said "I am not afraid of Detroit or nobody else and you know yourself that they can't no club beat me the way I am going whether its Detroit or no matter who it is." So he said "All right then keep your mouth shut about who is going to pitch

◆ (*Page 256*) *Bert Gallia*—Melvin Allys Gallia (1891–1976), a righthander who started 24 games for the Browns in 1919. Gallia pitched for the Senators from 1912 to 1917, reaching his peak with 16–10 in 1915 and 17–13 in 1916. He came to the Browns in 1917, and in 1919 was in the process of recording an 11–14 season. After two games of the 1920 season he went to the Phillies, where he closed his career. Gallia won 63 and lost 68 in nine years in the major leagues. See Norman L. Macht, "Bert Gallia," *The Ballplayers*, p. 371.

◇ *the boys on our club*—The Chicago White Sox of 1919. *Bottom row*: Eddie Collins, Nemo Leibold, Eddie Cicotte, Erskine Mayer, Claude Williams, Byrd Lynn. *Middle row*: Ray Schalk, Shano Collins, Harvey McClellan, Dickie Kerr, Happy Felsch, Chick Gandil, Buck Weaver. *Top row*: Kid Gleason, John Sullivan, Roy Wilkinson, Grover Lowdermilk, Swede Risberg, Fred McMullin, Big Bill James, Eddie Murphy, Joe Jackson, Joe Jenkins.

The photograph shows the personnel of the team in the first two weeks of September 1919, after the release of Dave Danforth on August 31 and before the return of Red Faber to the team on September 15 and the acquisition of Wyn Noyes

(*continued*)

(*continued from page 257*)
from the Athletics on September 19. The photograph, which shows the team in its home uniforms, was probably taken at Comiskey Park during the series with Cleveland on September 5, 6, and 7.

By this time Chick Gandil had conceived the plot to throw the World Series but had not yet lined up the participants. As is well known, the plot stemmed in part from factionalism on the team. The better-educated faction, which was loyal to the management, centered around Ray Schalk and Eddie Collins, who are at the extreme left of the photograph. Dickie Kerr, at the center of the middle row, and Red Faber, who is not in the photograph, were part of this group. The contrary clique of players, who participated in the plot—Chick Gandil, Happy Felsch, Buck Weaver, Claude Williams, Joe Jackson, Swede Risberg, and Fred McMullin—range from the upper center to the right. Eddie Cicotte, who took no sides in the feud and had not yet committed himself to the plot, sits at front row center. Kid Gleason, instead of taking the manager's usual position at the center, stands at the extreme left, distancing himself from Gandil's clique as far as possible. Gandil's expression is unambiguous. See George W. Hilton, "The 1919 White Sox Depicted," *Baseball Research Journal* 4 (1975): 42–44. (National Baseball Library, Cooperstown, New York)

because if you are going to manage the club I won't have no job left." Well let him try and run the ball club the way he wants to but if I was running the ball club and had a pitcher that is going the way I am going I would work him every other day and get a start on the other clubs as the games we win now counts just as much as the games we win in Sept.

Well Al Florrie went back to Chi last night though I wanted her to stick with the club and go on to Detroit with us but she said she had to get back, and tend to business at the beauty parlor so I told Gleason that and he said he was sorry she was going to leave us as it was a releif for him to look at something pretty once in a wile when most of the time he had to watch ball players but he admired her for tending to business and he wished it run in the family. He says "You should ought to be thankfull that your Mrs. is what she is as most wifes is a drug on their husband but your Mrs. makes more jack then you and if she give up her business it would keep you hustleing to make both ends meet the other, where if you missed a meal some time and died from it your family would be that much ahead." So I said "Yes and that is because your cheap skate ball club is only paying me a salary of $2400.00 per annum instead of somewheres near what I am worth." So he said "I have all ready told you that if you keep working hard and show me something I will tear up your contract and give you a good one but before I do it I will half to find out if you are going to win ball games for me or just use up 1 lower birth like in old times." So I told him to shut his mouth.

Well Al I thought the war with Germany was all over but Joe Jenkins ◆ joined the club here and now the whole war is being played over again. He is 1 of the catchers on the club and he was in France and if they was any battles he wasn't in its because he can't pronounce them but anybody that thinks the U. S. troop movements was slow over there ought to listen to some of these birds that's came back and some of them was at Verdun 1 evening and Flanders the next A. M. then down to Nice the next day for a couple hours rest and up in the Oregon forest the folling afternoon and etc. till its no wonder the Germans was dazzled. If some of these birds that was in the war could get around the bases like they did around the western front all as the catchers would dast do when they started to steal second base would be walk up the base line towards third with the ball in their hand and try to scare them from comeing all the way home.

Well its Detroit tomorrow and 3 more days after that and then home and I haven't been there since the middle of March and I guess they's 2 kids that won't be tickled to death to see sombeody eh Al?

Your pal, Jack.

DETROIT, APRIL 28. ◆

Friend Al: Well old pal I suppose you read in the papers what come off here yesterday and I guess Gleason won't have no more to say after this about me being afraid of Detroit. The shoe points the other way now and Detroit is the one that's afraid of me and no wonder.

I didn't have the stuff that I had down to St. Louis for the opening but I had enough to make a monkey out of Cobb and Veach and I

Facing page:
◇ *Bert Gallia*—Melvin Gallia in the road uniform of the St. Louis Browns. The White Sox habitually found him tough to hit. (National Baseball Library, Cooperstown, New York)

◆ *Joe Jenkins joined the club here*—As stated, Jenkins joined the White Sox in St. Louis upon his release from the army.

◆ *Detroit, April 28*—The White Sox won the opener in Detroit, 6–4, behind Williams.

couldn't help from feeling sorry for this new outfielder they have got name Flagstaff or something and I guess he was about half mast ◆ before I got through with him.

Well its a cinch now that I will open in Chi Thursday and I will give St. Louis another spanking and then I will make Gleason come acrost with the contract he has been promiseing me and if he trys to stall I will tell him he must either give me the jack or trade me to some other club and he has got good sence even if he don't act like it sometimes and they's a fine chance of him tradeing me though they's 7 other clubs in this league that would jump at it and Detroit is 1 of them though the Detroit club would be takeing a big chance if they got a hold of somebody that would realy pitch as the fans up here would die from surprise.

Well I had a letter from Florrie today and it was just like the most of her letters when you got through reading it you wondered what she had in mind and about all as she said was that she had a surprise to tell me when I got home and I use to get all excited when she wrote about them surprises but now I can guess what it is. She probably seen a roach in the apartment or something and any way I guess I can wait till I get home and not burn up the wires trying to find out before hand.

Your pal, Jack.

DETROIT, APRIL 30. ◆

Friend Al: Well Al we leave for home tonight and open up the season in Chi tomorrow but I won't be out there pitching unless Gleason apologizes for what he pulled on me last night. It was more rotten ◆ weather yesterday just like we been haveing ever since the 1st. day in St. Louis and I near froze to death setting out there on the bench so when we come back to the hotel they was a friend of mine here in Detroit waiting for me here in the lobby and he come up in the room

---

◆ *name Flagstaff or something*—Ira James Flagstead (1893–1940), who had inherited the right-field position so long occupied by Sam Crawford and Harry Heilmann. Flagstead, who had played in four games in 1917, was in his first season as a regular for the Tigers, hitting .331 in 97 games. He played for the Tigers into the 1923 season, then for the Red Sox, Senators, and Pirates through 1930. An excellent defensive outfielder and a good hitter with little power, Flagstead hit .290 in 1,217 games in 13 seasons. See Ed Walton, "Ira Flagstead," *The Ballplayers*, p. 341.

◆ *April 30*—On this date Dickie Kerr defeated the Tigers, 9–7, and the White Sox did head for home.

◆ *rotten weather*—The series in Detroit had been played in cold, rainy weather.

with me and I was still shivering yet with the cold and he said how would I like something to warm me up. So I said "That's a fine line of talk to hand out in a dry town." So he said I could easy get a hold of some refreshments if I realy wanted some and all as I would half to do would be call a bell hop and tell him what I wanted.

Well I felt like a good shot would just about save my life so I called a boy and told him to go fetch me some bourbon and he said O. K. and he went out and come back in about a half hr. and he had a qt. with him and I asked him how much did we owe him and he said $15.00. How is that for reasonable Al and I guess it was the liquor men themselfs that voted Michigan dry and you can't blame them. ◆ Well my friend seemed to of had a stroke in his arm so as he couldn't even begin to reach in his pocket so I dug down and got 15 berrys and handed it to the kid and he still stood there yet like he expected a tip so I told him to beat it or I would tip him 1 in the jaw.

Well I asked my friend would he have a shot and his arm was O. K. again and he took the bottle and went to it without waiting for no glass or nothing but he got the neck of the bottle caught in his teeth and before he could pry it loose they was about a quarter of the bourbon gone.

Well I was just going to pore some of it out for myself and all of a sudden they come a rap at the door and I said come in and who walked in but Gleason. So I asked him what did he want.

So he said "Well you wasn't the 1st. one in the dinning rm. so I thought you must be pretty sick so I come up to see what was the matter." Well it was to late to hide the bottle and he come over to the table where I was setting and picked it up and looked at it and then he pored out a couple drops in the glass and tasted it and said it tastes like pretty good stuff. So I said it ought to be pretty good stuff as it cost enough jack so he asked me how much and I told him $15.00.

So he said "Well they's some of the newspaper boys has been asking me to try and get a hold of some stuff for them so I will just take this along."

So I said I guest the newspaper boys could write crazy enough without no help from the Michigan boot legs and besides the bottle belongs to me as I payed good money for it. So Gleason said "Oh I wouldn't think of stealing it off of you but I will take it and pay you

---

◆ *voted Michigan dry*—Michigan anticipated national Prohibition, going dry on May 1, 1918.

for it. You say it cost $15.00 but they's only about $11.00 and a half worth of it left so I will settle with you for $11.00 and a half." Well I didn't want to quarrel with him in the front of a outsider so I didn't say nothing and he took the bottle and started out of the rm. and I said hold on a minute where is my $11.00 and a half? So he said "Oh I am going to fine you $11.00 and a half for haveing liquor in your rm. but instead of takeing the fine out of your check I will take what's left in the bottle and that makes us even." So he walked out.

Well Al only for my friend being here in the rm. I would of took the bottle away from Gleason and cracked his head open with it but I didn't want to make no seen before a outsider as he might tell it around and people would say the White Sox players was fighting with their mgr. So I left Gleason get away with $11.00 and a half worth of bourbon that I payed $15.00 for it and never tasted it and don't know now if it was bourbon or cat nip.

Well my friend said "What kind of a bird are you to let a little scrimp like that make a monkey out of you?" So I said I didn't want to make no seen in the hotel. So he said "Well if it had of been me I would of made a seen even if it was in church." So I says "Well they's no danger of you ever haveing a chance to make a seen in church and a specialy with Gleason but if you did make a seen with Gleason you would be in church 3 days later and have a box right up close to the front."

Well Al I have told Gleason before this all ready that I would stand for him manageing me out on the old ball field but I wouldn't stand for him trying to run my private affairs and this time I mean it and if he don't apologize this P. M. or tonight on the train he will be shy of a pitcher tomorrow and will half to open up the home season with 1 of them other 4 flushers that claims they are pitchers but if Jackson and Collins didn't hit in 7 or 8 runs every day they would be beating rugs in the stead of ball clubs.

Well any way we go home tonight and tomorrow I will be where it don't cost no $15.00 per qt. and if Gleason walks in on me he can't only rob me of $.20 worth at a time unless he operates.

Your pal, Jack.

CHI., MAY 3.

Friend Al: Well Al I have just now came back from the ball pk. and will set down and write you a few lines before supper. I give the St. Louis club another good trimming today Al and that is 3 games I have pitched and win them all and only 1 run scored off of me in all 3 games together and that was the 1 the St. Louis club got today and they wouldn't of never had that if Felsch had of been playing right for Tobin. But 1 run off of me in 3 games is going some and I should ◆ worry how many runs they scratch in as long as I win the ball game.

Well you know we was to open up here Thursday and it rained and ◆ we opened yesterday and I was waiting for Gleason to tell me I was going to pitch and then I was going to tell him I would pitch if he would apologize to me for what he done in Detroit but instead of picking me to pitch he picked Lefty Williams and the crowd was sore at him for not picking me and before the 1st inning was over he was sore at himself and Lefty was enjoying the shower bath. Gallia give us ◆ another beating and after it was over Gleason come up to me in the club house and said he was going to start me today. So I said "How about what you pulled on me in Detroit?" So he says "Do you mean about grabbing that bottle off of you?" So I said yes and he says "Look at here Jack you have got a great chance to get somewheres this yr. and if you keep on pitching like the way you started you will make a name for yourself and I will see that you get the jack. But you can't do it and be stewed all the wile so that is the reason I took that bottle off of you." So I said "They's no danger of me being stewed all the wile or any part of the wile when bourbon is $15.00 per qt. and me getting a bat boy's salery." So he said "Well you lay off of the old burb and pitch baseball and you won't be getting no bat boy's salery. And besides I have told the newspaper boys that you are going to pitch and it will be in the morning papers and if you don't pitch the bugs will jump out of the stand and knock me for a gool." So as long as he put it up to me that way I couldn't do nothing only say all right.

So sure enough it come out in the papers this A. M. that I was going

---

◆ *Tobin*—John Thomas "Jack" Tobin (1892–1969), the Browns leftfielder. One of the few outstanding players to come to the established major leagues from the Federal League, Tobin played for two years for the St. Louis Feds and stayed on when owner Phil Ball assumed control of the Browns. In 1919 Tobin had an excellent year, hitting .327. He was active for the Browns until 1925, then with the Senators and Red Sox until 1927. He hit .308 in 1,618 games in 13 seasons, and was later a coach and scout for the Browns. See Jack Kavanagh, "Jack Tobin," *The Ballplayers*, p. 1092.

◆ *it rained*—As stated, the opener against the Browns on Thursday, May 1, was rained out.

◆ *Gallia give us another beating*—Bert Gallia did beat the White Sox, 11–4, in the home opener on May 2, but Williams was knocked out in the second inning, rather than the first. As the phrasing indicates, Gallia was habitually extremely effective against the White Sox.

to pitch and you ought to seen the crowd out there today Al and you ought to heard them when my name was gave out to pitch and when ◆ I walked out there on the field. Well I got away to a bad start you might say as Felsch wasn't laying right for Tobin and he got a two base hit on a ball that Felsch ought to of caught in his eye and then after I got rid of Gedeon this Sisler hit at a ball he couldn't hardly reach and it dropped over third base and Tobin scored and after that I made a monkey out of them and the 1st. time I come up to bat the fans give me a traveling bag and I suppose they think I have been running around the country all these yrs. with my night gown in a peach basket but I suppose we can give it to 1 of Florrie's friends next xmas and besides it shows the fans of old Chi have got a warm spot for old Jack.

Speaking about Florrie Al when we was in Detroit she wrote and said she had a surprise for me and I thought little Al had picked up a couple hives or something but no it seems like wile I was on the road she met some partys that runs a beauty parlor down town and they wanted she should sell her interest in the one out south and go in pardners with them and they would give her a third interest for $3000.00 and pay her a salery of $300.00 per mo. and a share of the receits and she could pay for her interest on payments. So she asked me what I thought about it and I said if I was her I would stick to what she had where she was makeing so good but no matter what I thought she would do like she felt like so what was the use of asking me so she said she didn't like to make a move without consulting me. That's a good one Al as the only move she ever made and did consult me about it was when we got married and then it wouldn't of made no differents to her what I said.

Well she will do as she pleases and if she goes into this here down town parlor and gets stung we should worry as I will soon be getting real jack and it looks like a cinch we would be in the world serious besides, and besides that the kids would be better off if she was out of business and could be home with them more as the way it is now they don't hardly ever see anybody only the Swede nurse and 1st. thing as we know they will be saying I ban this and I ban that and staying away from the bldg. all the wile like the janitor. *Your pal, Jack.*

◆ *when I walked out there on the field*—On May 3 the White Sox were scheduled to play the Browns but were rained out.

CHI, MAY 6.

Friend Al: 4 straight now Al. How is that for a way to start out the season? It was Detroit again today and that is twice I have beat them and twice I have beat St. Louis and it don't look like I was never going to stop. They got 2 runs off of me today but it was after we had 7 and had them licked and I kind of eased up to save the old souper for the Cleveland serious. But I wished you could of heard the 1 I pulled on Cobb. You know I have always kind of had him on the run ever since I come in the league and he would as leaf have falling archs as see me walk out there to pitch.

Well the 1st. time he come up they was 2 out and no one on and I had him 2 strikes and nothing and in place of monking with him I stuck a fast one right through the groove and he took it for a third strike. Well he come up again in the 4th. inning and little Bush was on third base and 1 out and Cobb hit the 1st. ball and hit it pretty good towards left field but Weaver jumped up and stabbed it with his glove hand and then stepped on third base and the side was out. Well Cobb hollered at me and said "You didn't put that strike acrost on me." So I said "No why should I put strikes acrost on you when I can hit your bat and get 2 out at a time? You ought to of heard the boys give him the laugh.

Well he hit one for 3 bases in the 7th. inning with Bush and Ellison both on and that's how they got their 2 runs but he wouldn't of never hit the ball only I eased up on acct. of the lead we had and besides I felt sorry for him on acct. of the way the crowd was rideing him. So wile he was standing over there on third base I said "You wouldn't of hit that one Ty only I eased up." So he said "Yes I knew you was easeing up and I wouldn't take advantage of you so that's why I bunted."

Well 1 more game with Detroit and then we go down to Cleveland and visit Mr. Speaker and the rest of the boys and Speaker hasn't been going any to good against them barbers that's supposed to pitch for Detroit and St. Louis so God help him when he runs up against Williams and Cicotte and I. *Your pal, Jack.*

◆ *4 straight now Al*—The White Sox had opened extremely well, had a 6–2 record, and were in first place, ahead of the Red Sox by a game.

◆ *It was Detroit again today*—On May 6 Williams beat Detroit, 3–1.

◆ *Ellison*—Herbert Spencer "Babe" Ellison (1896–1955), a utility player in 135 games for the Tigers between 1916 and 1920. In 1919 he appeared in 56 games, batting .216, which by coincidence was his lifetime batting average.

CLEVELAND, MAY 9.

Friend Al: Well Gleason told me today he wasn't going to pitch me here till the Sunday game to get the crowd. We have broke even on ◆ the 2 games so far and ought to of win them both only for bad pitching but we can't expect to win them all and you really can't blame the boys for not pitching baseball when we run into weather like we have got down here and it seems like every place we go its colder then where we just come from and I have heard about people going crazy with the heat but we will all be crazy with the cold if it keeps up like this way and Speaker was down to our hotel last night and said the Cleveland club had a couple of bushers from the Southren league that's all ready lost their mind and he told us what they pulled off wile the St. Louis club was here.

Well it seems like Cleveland was beat to death 1 day and they thought they would give some of the regulars a rest and they put in a young catcher name Drew and the 1st. time he come up to bat they ◆ was men on first and second and 1 out and Sothoron was pitching for ◆ St. Louis and 1 of the St. Louis infielders yelled at him "Don't worry about this bird as he will hit into a double play." Well Drew stood up there and took 3 strikes without never takeing the bat off his shoulder so then he come back to the bench and said "Well I crossed them on their double play."

Well in another game Bagby was pitching and he had them licked ◆ 8 to 1 in the 7th inning and he had a bad finger so they took him out and sent in a busher name Francis to finish the game. Well he got ◆

◆ *We have broke even on the 2 games so far*—Actually, the White Sox won the first game at Cleveland on May 8, and were rained out there on May 9.

◆ *Drew*—Apparently a fictional character.

◆ *Sothoron*—Allen Sutton Sothoron (1893–1939), the Browns ace, on his way to a 20–13 season. Sothoron, a righthander, had brief trials with the Browns in 1914 and 1915, and was a regular starter for the team from 1917 through 1920. Subsequently, he pitched for the Red Sox, Indians, and Cardinals until 1926, ending an 11-year career with a 92–100 record. See Jack Kavanagh, "Allen Sothoron," *The Ballplayers*, p. 1021.

◆ *Bagby*—James Charles Jacob Bagby, Sr. (1887–1954), one of the Indians' two leading pitchers. Bagby was turning in a 17–11 record in 1919, but in the Indians' pennant year of 1920 he led the league in victories with a 31–12 record. After a brief trial with Cincinnati in 1912, Bagby became a regular starter for the Indians in 1916, and pitched for the team until 1922. Including a final season for the Pirates in 1923, Bagby won 128 and lost just 88 in nine seasons. His son, Jim, Jr., pitched for the Indians in the 1940's, with somewhat less success. See Morris A. Eckhouse, "Jim Bagby, Sr.," *The Ballplayers*, p. 38.

◆ *Francis*—Apparently a fictional character.

through 1 inning and when he come up to hit they was a man on 3d. base and 2 out and Davenport was pitching for St. Louis and he was ◆ kind of wild and he throwed 3 balls to Francis. So then he throwed a strike and Francis took it and then he throwed one that was over the kid's head but he took a cut at it and hit it over Tobin's head and made 3 bases on it. So when the inning was over Larry Gardner heard him ◆ calling himself names and balling himself out and Larry asked him what was the matter and he said he was just thinking that if he had of left that ball go by he would of had a base on balls.

Well I had a letter from Florrie today and she has closed up that deal and sold out her interest in the place out near home and went in pardners in that place down town and she said she thought it was a wise move and she would clean up a big bunch of jack and it won't only take her a little wile to pay for her interest in the new parlor as with what she had saved up and what she got out of the other joint she had over $2000.00 cash to start in with.

Well I don't know who her new pardners is but between you and I it looks to me like she was pulling a boner to leave a place where she knew her pardners was friends and go into pardners with a couple women that's probably old hands at the game and maybe wanted some new capital or something and are libel to get her role and then can her out of the firm but as I say they's no use me trying to tell her what to do and I might just is well tell Gleason to take Collins off of second base and send for Jakey Atz. ◆◇

◆ *Davenport*—David W. Davenport (1890–1954), a righthander who broke in with the Reds in 1914, then pitched for St. Louis in the Federal League in 1914 and 1915. He remained in St. Louis with the Browns, for whom 1919 was his last season. His record that year was 3–11, and in his six seasons, 74–83. See Norman L. Macht, "Dave Davenport," *The Ballplayers*, p. 254.

◆ *Larry Gardner*—William Lawrence Gardner (1886–1976), a veteran third baseman who played for the Red Sox from 1908 to 1917, the Athletics in 1918, and the Indians from 1919 to 1924. In 17 years Gardner hit .289 in 1,922 games. Gardner was baseball coach at the University of Vermont, his alma mater, for 25 years, and its athletic director for eight. See Anthony J. Papalas, "William Lawrence Gardner," *Biographical Dictionary of American Sports: Baseball*, p. 208.

◆ *Jakey Atz*—Jacob Henry "Jake" Atz (1879–1945), playing name of John Jacob Zimmerman, who had tired of being last in alphabetical order. He had been the White Sox' part-time second baseman from 1907 to 1909. In four seasons, including three games for Washington in 1902, Atz hit .219 in 208 games. He had been distinguished about equally for lack of talent and for sense of humor, a combination that could only have endeared him to Lardner. Atz became a notable minor league manager, particularly with Fort Worth in the Texas League. See Vern Luse, "The 1920–1925 Fort Worth Panthers," *Baseball Research Journal*, VI (1977), 16–19.

◇ *Jakey Atz*—Jake Atz in his most familiar role, as manager of the Fort Worth Cats of the Texas League. (National Baseball Library, Cooperstown, New York)

Well Al nothing to do till Sunday and if I beat them it will make me 5 straight and you can bet I will beat them Al as I am going like a crazy man and they can't no club stop me. *Your pal, Jack.*

CHI, MAY 12.

Friend Al: Well old pal its kind of late to be setting up writeing a letter but I had a little run in with Florrie tonight and I don't feel like I could go to sleep and besides I don't half to work tomorrow as I win yesterday's game in Cleveland and Gleason is saveing me for the Boston serious.

Well we got in from Cleveland early this A. M. and of course I hurried right home and I was here before 8 o'clock but the Swede said Florrie had left home before 7 as she didn't want to be late on the new job and she would call me up dureing the forenoon. Well it got pretty near time to start over to the ball pk. before the phone rung and it was Florrie and I asked her if she wasn't going to congratulate me and she says what for and I said for what I done in Cleveland yesterday and she said she hadn't had time to look at the paper. So I told her I had win my 5th straight game and she acted about as interested as if I said we had a new mail man so I got kind of sore and told her I would half to hang up and go over to the ball pk. So she said she would see me at supper and we hung up.

Well we had a long game this P. M. and it seemed longer on acct. of ◆ how anxious I was to get back home and when I finely got here it was half past 6 and no Florrie. Well the Swede said she had called up and said she had to stay down town and have supper with some business friends and she would try and be home early this evening.

Well the kids was put in bed and I tried to set down and eat supper alone and they didn't nothing taste right and finaly I give it up and put on my hat and went out and went in a picture show but it was as old as Pat and Mike so I blew it and went in Kramer's to get a couple ◆ drinks but I had kind of promised Gleason to lay off of the hard stuff and you take the beer you get now days and its cheaper to stay home and draw it out of the sink so I come back here and it was 8 bells and still no Florrie.

Well I set down and picked up the evening paper and all of a sudden the phone rung and it was a man's voice and he wanted to know if Mrs. Keefe had got home. So I done some quick thinking and I said "Yes she is here who wants her?" So he said "That's all right. I just wanted to know if she got home O. K." So I said who is it but he had hung up. Well I rung central right back and asked her where that party had called from and she said she didn't know and I asked her what and the he—ll she did know and she begun to play some jazz on my ear drum so I hung up.

Well in about 10 minutes more Florrie come in and come running over to give me a smack like usual when I get back off a trip. But she didn't get by with it. So she asked what was the matter. So I said "They's nothing the matter only they was a bird called up here a wile

---

◆ *Well we had a long game this P. M.*—The White Sox defeated the Browns, 4–3, on this date. Bert Gallia was wild, working long counts on many batters and, as stated, producing a long game.

◆ *Kramer's*—George Kramer's Saloon, 3549 Cottage Grove Avenue, one of the principal haunts of White Sox fans. George Kramer (1868–1957) was a friend of Comiskey, a frequent hunting companion, and a member of Comiskey's support group, the Woodland Bards. For identification of this saloon I am indebted to the late Lucius W. Hilton, and for George Kramer's dates of birth and death, to the Donnellan Funeral Home, Chicago.

ago and wanted to know if you was home." So she says "Well what of it?" So I said "I suppose he was 1 of them business friends that you had to stay down town to supper with them." So she said "Maybe he was." So I said "Well you ought to know if he was or not." So she says "Do you think I can tell you who all the people are that calls me up when I haven't even heard their voice? I don't even know a one of the girls that keeps calling up and asking for you." So I said "They don't no gals call up here and ask for me because they have got better sence but even if they did I couldn't help it as they see me out there on the ball field and want to get aquainted."

Then she swelled up and says "It may be hard for you to believe but there is actualy men that want to get aquainted with me even if they never did see me out there on the ball field." So I said "You tell me who this bird is that called up on the phone." So she said "I thought they was only the 2 babys in this apartment but it seems like there is 3." So then she went in her rm. and shut the door.

Well Al that's the way it stands and if it wasn't for the kiddies I would pack up and move somewheres else but kiddies or no kiddies she has got to explain herself tomorrow morning and meanwile Al you should ought to thank God that you married a woman that isn't flighty and what if a wife ain't the best looker in the world if she has got something under her hat besides marcel wavers? *Your pal, Jack.*

CHI, MAY 14.

Friend Al: Well old pal it looks like your old pal was through working for nothing you might say and by tomorrow night I will be signed up to a new contract calling for a $600.00 raise or $3000.00 per annum. I guess I have all ready told you that Gleason promised to see that I got real jack provide it I showed I wasn't no flash out of the pan and this noon we come to a definite understanding.

We was to open against the Boston club and I called him to 1 side in the club house and asked him if I was to pitch the game. So he says you can suit yourself. So I asked him what he meant and he said "I am going to give you a chance to get real money. If you win your game against the Boston club I will tear up your old contract and give you a contract for $3000.00. And you can pick your own spot. You can work against them today or you can work against them tomorrow just as you feel like. They will probably pitch Mays against us today and Ruth tomorrow and you can take your choice." Well Al Mays has always been good against our club and besides my old souper is better this kind of weather the longer I give it a rest so after I thought it over I said I would wait and pitch against Ruth tomorrow. So tomorrow is my big day and you know what I will do to them old pal and if the boys only gets 1 run behind me that is all as I ask.

That's all we got today Al was 1 run but Eddie Cicotte was in there with everything and the 1 run was a plenty. They was only 1 time ◆ when they had a chance and it looked that time like they couldn't hardly help from scoreing but Eddie hates to beat this Boston club on acct. they canned him once and he certainly give a exhibition in there that I would of been proud of myself. This inning I am speaking of Scott got on and Schang layed down a bunt and Eddie tried to force ◆ Scott at second base but he throwed bad and the ball went to center field and Scott got around to third and Schang to second and they wasn't nobody out. Well Mays hit a fly ball to Jackson but it was so ◆◇

◆ *the 1 run was a plenty.*—As stated, the White Sox defeated Boston, 1–0, on May 14, as Cicotte won a pitching duel from Carl Mays. The inning described below was the sixth. The Chicago *Tribune*'s account of the game differs somewhat from the description in this paragraph, reporting that Weaver, not Cicotte, threw the ball into center field, and that Hooper popped up to Risberg, not to Collins. As stated below, Cicotte struck out Ruth twice. This passage is solid testament to Lardner's respect for Cicotte as a pitcher.

◆ *Scott*—Lewis Everett Scott (1892–1960), shortstop for the Red Sox since 1914. A notable iron man, Scott held the major league record for consecutive games played, 1,307, before being displaced by Lou Gehrig. In 1922 Scott became one of the many members of the Red Sox to pass to the Yankees in the so-called Rape of the Red Sox. Scott played for 13 years and hit .249 in 1,654 games. In 1919 he was to hit .278 for the Red Sox. See A. D. Suehsdorf, "Everett Scott," *The Ballplayers*, pp. 977–78.

Schang—Walter Henry "Wally" Schang (1889–1965), a durable catcher who spent 19 years in the American League. After breaking in with Philadelphia in 1913, Schang managed to participate in both of the mass liquidations of the era: Connie Mack sold him to the Red Sox after the 1917 season, and Harry Frazee sold him to the Yankees for the 1921 season. Later, he moved to the Browns in 1926, back to the Athletics in 1930, and finally to the Tigers in 1931. In 1,839 games, he hit .284. In 1919, one of his best seasons, he hit .306. An excellent receiver, he handled many of the best pitchers of all time in the course of playing on world-championship teams for three clubs—a distinction only he holds. He is not a member of the Baseball Hall of Fame. See Jack Kavanagh, "Wally Schang," *The Ballplayers*, pp. 967–68.

◆ *Mays*—Carl William Mays (1891–1971), a righthanded submarine-ball pitcher of great distinction. After a 5–5 season with the Red Sox in 1915, Mays recorded 19–13, 22–9, and 21–13 in the following three seasons, all with the Red Sox. Mays's switch to the Yankees in the 1919 season bulks large in the plot of this set of stories. Mays pitched for the Yankees through 1923, leading the league with 27 victories in 1921. After the 1923 season he went to the Reds, where he won 20 games in 1924 and 19 in 1926. Mays finished his career with the Giants in 1929, with a lifetime record of 208–126. See Eugene C. Murdock, "Carl William Mays," *Biographical Dictionary of American Sports: Baseball*, pp. 392–93.

◇ *Jackson*—Joe Jackson in the uniform of the 1919 White Sox, probably at the home dugout in Comiskey Park (see footnote, pp. 59–60). (National Baseball Library, Cooperstown, New York)

short that Scott didn't dast go in. Then Hooper popped up to Collins◆◇
and Barry hit the 1st. ball and fouled out to Schalkie. Some pitching ◆
eh Al and that is the kind I will show them tomorrow. And another
thing Eddie done was make a monkey out of Ruth and struck him out◆◇

HARRY BARTHOLOMEW HOOPER
BOSTON A.L. 1909-1920
CHICAGO A.L. 1921-1925
LEADOFF HITTER AND RIGHT FIELDER OF 1912-15-16-18 WORLD CHAMPION RED SOX. NOTED FOR SPEED AND STRONG ARM. COLLECTED 2,466 HITS FOR .281 CAREER AVERAGE. HAD 3,981 PUTOUTS AND 344 ASSISTS. LIFETIME FIELDING AVERAGE .966.

◇ *Hooper*—The Harry Bartholomew Hooper plaque at the National Baseball Hall of Fame and Museum, Cooperstown, New York.

◆ *Hooper*—Harry Bartholomew Hooper (1887–1974), the Red Sox' veteran rightfielder. Hooper had broken in with the team in 1909 and rarely missed a game after 1910. During Harry Frazee's liquidation of the Red Sox, his unusual fate was to be dealt off to the White Sox rather than to the Yankees. With the White Sox from 1921 to 1925, Hooper had his best years, hitting over .300 three out of the five seasons. In 17 years in the American League Hooper made 2,466 hits in 2,308 games, hitting .281. A well-educated man with a degree in civil engineering from St. Mary's College, he was baseball coach at Princeton University in 1931 and 1932. Hooper was elected to the Baseball Hall of Fame in 1971. See Ellery H. Clark, Jr., "Harry Bartholomew Hooper," *Biographical Dictionary of American Sports: Baseball*, pp. 259–60; Lawrence S. Ritter, *The Glory of Their Times*, pp. 131–45.

◆ *Barry*—Jack Barry again, in his last season in the major leagues, played 31 games for the Red Sox in 1919.

◆ *Ruth*—George Herman "Babe" Ruth (1895–1948), baseball's premier slugger, its most famous player, and probably the most important athlete in social impact

◇ *Ruth*—Babe Ruth in a Red Sox uniform. (National Baseball Library, Cooperstown, New York)

(*continued from page* 272)
in American history. Ruth came to the Red Sox in 1914 from Baltimore of the International League as a lefthanded pitcher, but he quickly demonstrated his batting ability as well. His pitching was instrumental in the Red Sox' championships of 1915, 1916, and 1918, and he was particularly proud of pitching 25 consecutive scoreless innings in the Series of 1916 and 1918, a record broken only in 1961, by Whitey Ford, long after Ruth's death. By 1918 Ruth had begun to play also in the outfield and at first base. In 1919 he pitched only 17 games, while playing 111 in

twice and they claim he is a great hitter Al but all you half to do is pitch right to him and pitch the ball anywheres but where he can get a good cut at it.

Well they never had another look in against Eddie and we got a run when Barry booted one on Collins and Jackson plastered one out between Ruth and Strunk for 2 bases. ◆

Well Al I am feeling pretty good again as I and Florrie kind of made up our quarrel last night. She come home to supper and I was still acting kind of cross and she asked me if I was still mopping over that bird that called her up and I didn't say nothing so she said "Well that was a man that was the husband of 1 of the girls I had supper with and he was there to and him and his wife wanted to bring me home but I told them I didn't want nobody to bring me home so his wife probably told him to call up and see if I got home all right as they was worried." So she asked me if I was satisfied and I said I guessed I was but why couldn't she of told me that in the 1st. place and she said because she liked to see me jealous. Well I left her think I was jealous but between you and I it was just a kind of a kid on my part as of course I knew all the wile that she was O. K. only I wanted to make her give in and I knew she would if I just held out and

---

(*continued from page 273*)
the outfield and four at first base. Even as a part-time batter, he hit .322 and led the league in home runs with 29, runs with 103, and runs batted in with 112.

In the following season Frazee dealt Ruth to the Yankees for $125,000 and a loan of $300,000. In New York, of course, he went on to fame in the seven Yankee championship teams of the 1920's and early 1930's. Ruth pitched only five games for the Yankees, mainly as promotions, but he won all five. In 22 years, including a final season with the Braves in 1935, Ruth made 2,873 hits, including 714 home runs, batted in 2,204 runs, and hit .342. As a pitcher, he won 94 and lost 46, with a career earned run average of 2.28. His fame rests mainly on his home run totals, which were not exceeded until Roger Maris hit 61 homers in 1961 and Henry Aaron hit his 715th homer on April 8, 1974, but Ruth's greatest merit was his versatility: no other player has been one of the great hitters *and* one of the great pitchers. He was a charter member of the Baseball Hall of Fame in 1936. The literature on Ruth is extensive, but see in particular Robert Creamer, *Babe: The Legend Comes to Life* (New York: Simon and Schuster, 1974), and Marshall Smelser, *The Life That Ruth Built: A Biography* (New York: Quadrangle Books, 1975).

◆ *Strunk*—Amos Aaron Strunk (1889–1979), a strong defensive outfielder who came to the Red Sox in 1918 after playing for the Athletics since 1908. As centerfielder, he was a mainstay of the Red Sox' 1918 championship club. Strunk would return to the Athletics on June 27, 1919. He came to the White Sox in mid-1920, and finally returned to the Athletics in 1924. In 17 seasons, he hit .283 in 1,507 games. See Ellery H. Clark, Jr., "Amos Strunk," *The Ballplayers*, p. 1056.

As stated, the White Sox won the game on a triple by Jackson.

pretended like I was sore. Make them come to you Al is the way to get along with them.

I haven't told Florrie what this game tomorrow means to us as I want to surprise her and if I win I will take her out somewheres on a party tomorrow night. And now old pal I must get to bed as I want to get a good rest before I tackle those birds. Oh you $600.00 baseball game. *Your pal, Jack.*

CHI, MAY 16. ◆

Friend Al: Well Al I don't care if school keeps or not and all as I wish is that I could get the flu or something and make a end out of it. I have quit the ball club Al and I have quit home and if I ever go back again to baseball it depends on whether I will have my kiddies to work for or whether they will be warded to her.

It all happened yesterday Al and I better start at the start and tell you what come off. Florrie had eat her breakfast and went down town before I got up but she left word with the ski jumper that she was going to try and get out to the ball game and maybe bring the rest of her pardners with her and show me off to them.

Well to make it a short story I was out to the pk. early and Gleason asked me how I felt and I told him fine and I certainly did Al and Danforth was working against us in batting practice to get us use to a ◆ left hander and I was certainly slapping the ball on the pick and Gleason said it looked like I was figureing on winning my own game. Well we got through our batting practice and I looked up to where Florrie usualy sets right in back of our bench but she wasn't there but after a wile it come time for me to warm up and I looked over and Ruth was warming up for them so then I looked up in the stand again

---

◆ *Chi, May 16*—Keefe's emotional turmoil prevents his describing a game of exceptional interest on this date. Babe Ruth, starting for the Red Sox in left field, came in to pitch, relieving Joe Bush in the second inning and surviving to win a hard-fought game from the White Sox, 6–5.

◆ *Danforth*—David Charles Danforth (1890–1970), a tall, thin lefthander whose chronically sore pitching arm gave him a highly inconsistent record. After partial seasons with the Athletics in 1911 and 1912, Danforth came up to the White Sox in 1916. In the championship year of 1917 he was the team's leading relief pitcher, making 41 relief appearances in addition to nine starts. His record of 15–6 led the American League in average, at .714. In 1919 he had a 1–2 record in 15 games before being released at the end of August. He returned to the majors in 1922 with the Browns and was quite effective, winning 16 in 1923 and 15 in 1924. In 1925 Danforth closed a ten-year major league career in which he won 74 and lost 66. See Jack Kavanagh, "Dave Danforth," *The Ballplayers*, p. 250.

and there was Florrie. She was just setting down Al and she wasn't alone.

Well Al I had to look up there twice to make sure I wasn't looking cock eyed. But no I was seeing just what was there and what I seen was she and a man with her if that's what you want to call him.

Well I guess I couldn't of throwed more than 4 or 5 balls when I couldn't stand it no more so I told Lynn to wait a minute and Gleason ◆ was busy hitting to the infield so I snuck out under the bench and under the stand and I seen 1 of the ushers and sent word up to Florrie to come down a minute as I wanted to see her. Well I waited and finely she come down and we come to the pt. without waisting no time. I asked her to explain herself and do it quick. So she said "You needn't act so crazy as they's nothing to explain. I said I was going to bring my pardner out here and the gentleman with me is him." "Your pardner" I said "What does a man do in a beauty parlor?" "Well" she said "This man happens to do a whole lot.

"Besides owning two thirds of the business he is 1 of the best artists in the world on quaffs." Well I asked her what and the he—ll was quaffs and she said it meant fixing lady's hair.

Well by this time Gleason had found out I wasn't warming up and sent out to find me. So all as I had time to say was to tell her she better get that bird out of the stand before I come up there and quaffed him in the jaw. Then I had to leave her and go back on the field.

Well I throwed about a dozen more balls to Lynn and then I couldn't throw no more and Gleason come over and asked me what was the matter and I told him nothing so he said "Are you warmed up enough?" and I said "I should say I am."

Well Al to make it a short story pretty soon our names was announced to pitch and I walked out there on the field.

Well when I was throwing them practice balls to Schalk I didn't know if he was behind the plate or up in Comiskey's office and when Hooper stepped in the batters box I seen a dozen of him. Well I don't know what was signed for but I throwed something up there and

◆ *Lynn*—Byrd Lynn (1889–1940), the White Sox second-string catcher. Ray Schalk so dominated the team's catching that Lynn saw little action. With the White Sox from 1916 to 1920, Lynn came to bat only 211 times in 116 games, hitting .237. Though he was Claude Williams' roommate, Lynn was not implicated in the Black Sox scandal, seemed unaware of it—or, alternatively, denied to himself that it was happening—and was particularly devastated by the revelation in 1920.

Hooper hit it to right field for 2 bases. Then I throwed something else to Barry and he cracked it out to Jackson on the 1st. hop so fast that Hooper couldn't only get to third base. Well wile Strunk was up there I guess I must of looked up in the stand again and any way the ball I pitched come closer to the barber then it did to Strunk and before they got it back in the game Hooper had scored and Barry was on third base.

Then Schalkie come running out and asked me what was the matter so I said I didn't know but I thought they was getting our signs. "Well" he said "you certainly crossed them on that one as I didn't sign you for no bench ball." Then he looked over at Gleason to have me took out but Gleason hollered "Let him stay in there and see what kind of a money pitcher he is."

Well Al I didn't get one anywheres near close for Strunk and walked him and it was Ruth's turn. The next thing I seen of the ball it was sailing into the right field bleachers where the black birds sets. And ◆ that's all I seen of the ball game.

Well old pal I didn't stop to look up in the stand on the way out and I don't remember changing clothes or nothing but I know I must of rode straight down town and when I woke up this A. M. I was still down town and I haven't called up home or the ball pk. or nowheres else and as far is I am concerned I am through with the both of them as a man can't pitch baseball and have any home life and a man can't have the kind of home life I have got and pitch baseball.

All that worrys me is the kiddies and what will become of them if they don't ward them to me. And another thing I would like to know is who put me to bed in this hotel last night as who ever undressed me forgot to take off my clothes. *Your pal, Jack.*

CHI, MAY 20.

Friend Al: Well Al I am writeing this from home and that means that everything is O. K. again as I decided to give in and let bygones be bygones for the kiddies sake and besides I found out that this bird

---

◆ *the right field bleachers where the black birds sets*—Prior to its extension and enclosure after the 1926 season, Comiskey Park had bleachers in both left and right fields. The right-field bleacher was never literally a Jim Crow section, but many of the team's black fans sat there. Although Comiskey Park was close to Chicago's highest concentration of black population, the team has never had much success in engendering interest within the black community—a problem with which Bill Veeck and some other owners later wrestled.

that Florrie is pardners with him is O. K. and got a Mrs. of his own and she works down there with him and Florrie is cleaning up more jack then she could of ever made in the old parlor out south so as long as she is makeing good and everything is O. K. why they would be no sence in me makeing things unpleasant.

Well I told you about me staying down town 1 night and I stayed down till late the next P. M. and finely I called up the Swede and told her to pack up my things as I was comeing out there the next day and get them. Well the Swede said that Gleason had been there the night before looking for me and he left word that I was to call him up at the ball pk. So I thought maybe he might have a letter out there for me or something or maybe I could persuade him to trade me to some other club so I called him up and just got him before he left the pk. and he asked me where I was at and said he wanted to see me so I give him the name of the hotel where I was stopping and he come down and met me there at 6 o'clock that night.

"Well" he says "I was over to see your little wife last night and I have got a notion to bust you in the jaw." So I asked him what he meant and he said "She sported your kids wile you was in the war and she is doing more than you to sport them now and she goes in pardners with a man that's O. K. and has got a wife of his own that works with him and you act like a big sap and make her cry and pretty near force her out of a good business and all for nothing except that you was born a busher and can't get over it."

So I said to him "You mind your own business and keep out of my business and trade me to some ball club where I can get a square deal and we will all get along a hole lot better." So he said where did I want to be traded and I said Boston. "Oh no" he said. "I would trade you to Boston in a minute only Babe Ruth wouldn't stand for it as he likes to have you on our club." But he said "The 1st. thing is what are you going to do about your family?" So I said I would go back to my family if Florrie would get out of that down town barber shop. So Gleason said "Now listen you are going back home right now tonight and your Mrs. isn't going to sacrifice her business neither." So I said "You can't make me do nothing I don't want to do." So he says "No I can't make you but I can tell your Mrs. about that St. Louis janitor's daughter that was down in Texas and then if she wants to get rid of you she can do it and be better off."

Well Al I thought as long as Florrie was all rapped up in this new business it wasn't right to make her drop it and pull out and besides there was the kiddies to be considered so I decided to not make no trouble. So I promised Gleason to go home that night.

So then I asked him about the ball club. "Well," he said "you still belong to us." "Yes" I said "but I can't work for no $2400.00."

"Well" he said "we are scheduled against a club now that hasn't no Ruths on it and its a club that even you should ought to beat and if you want to try it again why I will leave you pick your day to work against the Philadelphia club and the same bet goes." ◆

So yesterday was the day I picked Al and Roth got a base hit and ◆ Burns got a base hit and that's all the base hits they got and the only ◆ 2 runs we got I drove in myself. But they was worth $600.00 to me Al and I guess Gleason knows now what kind of a money pitcher I am.

Your pal, Jack.

◆ *the Philadelphia club*—The 1919 Athletics were the fifth of Connie Mack's seven consecutive last-place clubs, and not the best. The team was to play 36–104 baseball in the 140-game season. It finished 52 games out of first place and 20 games out of seventh.

◆ *So yesterday was the day I picked*—On that date, Monday, May 19, there was no game, although the Athletics played in Chicago on May 17, 18, and 20.

◆ *Burns*—George Henry Burns (1893–1978), a much-traveled firstbaseman. Burns played for Detroit from 1914 to 1917, and for the Athletics from 1918 until mid-1920. Subsequently, he played for Cleveland, the Red Sox, the Yankees, and again for the Athletics. Burns was the most valuable player in the American League in 1926, batting .358 with 216 hits, 64 doubles, and 114 runs-batted-in. He ended a 16-year career in 1929 with a .307 lifetime average. See Jack Kavanagh, "George Burns," *The Ballplayers*, p. 137.

The Courtship of T. Dorgan

CHI, MAY 22.

Friend Al: Well Al I suppose you seen what I done to the N. Y. bunch ◆ yesterday and when it was over Gleason called me to 1 side in the club house and says he thought it was about time I was getting the real jack so if I would bring my old contract over to the pk. today he would give me a new 1 calling for $3000.00 per annum. So today I took my old contract over to the pk. and Gleason told me to take it up in the office and I took it up there and the old man give me my new 1 and says now go ahead and show me you are worth it. Well I will show him Al and when a man gets fair treatment from a club why you work all the harder for them.

Well Gleason told me to not say nothing to none of the other ball players about the matter as they might maybe take it in their head to hold up the club for more jack so I didn't tell nobody only Tom Dorgan ◆

"The Courtship of T. Dorgan" was published in *The Saturday Evening Post*, CXCII (September 6, 1919), 8–9, 173–74, 177.

◆ *you seen what I done to the N. Y. bunch yesterday*—There was no game on May 21, although the Yankees opened a series in Chicago on the following day.

◆ *Tom Dorgan*—The catcher is a fictional character, but the name is that of Lardner's close friend and neighbor at Great Neck, Long Island, the sports cartoonist Thomas Aloysius "Tad" Dorgan (1877–1929).

that rooms with me when we are out on the road and the best pal a man ever had and they's no danger of him asking for more jack as he is just a 3th string catcher and all the closer he ever gets to the ball game is down in the bull pen warming up somebody but he is a regular guy and I only wished he could get in there and show them something.

Well when I told him about my new contract he said I was a lucky stiff to be getting all that jack and besides that have a beautiful wife and a couple kiddies and a nice home where all as he has got is 1 dinky little rm. over on Grand Blvd. that he can't squeeze in or out of ◆ it without barking his ears. So I told him I said "I can't get you no more jack old pal but the next gal that looks X eyed at me I will turn her over to you and welcome as 1 wife is about all as I can handle and then some."

At that I would like to find him some nice gal Al as a man don't know they are liveing till you get married and I can't help from feeling sorry for a bird that has to go home nights after the ball game and open up the close closet and talk to his other suit.

Well when I told Florrie about me getting the $600.00 raise she asked me what would we do with it and I said I didn't know yet and she says why not buy a car as we could have some time rideing around old Chi in a car evenings and take in the different pks. and etc. and take our friends along and show them a time. So I said "You have got a fine idear of what cars costs these days and for $600.00 you can't even buy a tire rench." So she begin telling me about the 2d hand car the Dumonts which is her new pardners in the beauty parlor down town and they got it for $700.00 and its a 1917 5 passenger Peel and ◆ runs and looks like new and they must be a whole lot more bargains if a person would just get out and look for them so just to stall her I said I would keep my eyes open and if I seen a real bargain I would grab it off but what and the he—ll is the use of us blowing our jack on a car when the Dumonts has all ready got 1 and all as we half to do is call them up and ask for the correct time and they would probably invite us out for a spin.

Personly Al I don't see no use in anybody buying a car now as they

◆ *Grand Blvd.*—A major north-south boulevard on the South Side east of Comiskey Park, later known as South Parkway and, currently, as Martin Luther King, Jr., Drive.

◆ *Peel*—Apparently a fictional make of automobile.

won't be nowheres to go after the 1 of July and besides when I am out on the road with the club Florrie would want to drive it herself and we would half to hire a steeple jack to get she and the car down off in the top of the Boston store.

Well Al I won't half to work no more vs. the N. Y. club this serious but will probably work vs. the Washington club which comes next and he will save me for the game Walter pitchs as Walter is going pretty good now and a man has just about got to shut them out to beat him.

Your pal, Jack.

CHI, MAY 27.

Friend Al: Well Al the way some people runs a ball club its a wonder we can stay in the U. S. let alone 1st place. Well yesterday Griffith started Jim Shaw against us and Gleason thought it was a good spot to try out big Lowdermilk so the 2 of them went to it but pretty soon they was both out of there and it come along the 8th inning with the Washington club a couple runs ahead and he stuck me in there to stop them and next thing you know Johnson was in there for them to try and hold the lead but we knocked his can off and beat them out.

Well of course I hadn't no idear that Gleason would send me back

---

◆ *the 1 of July*—The date in 1920 when Prohibition was to become effective.

◆ *the Boston store*—The Boston Store was one of Chicago's principal department stores, located on the west side of State Street immediately north of Madison Street in the Loop—one of the most prominent locations in the city.

◆ *Walter is going pretty good now*—Quite so. Johnson was running up a 20–14 record in 1919 and would lead the league with a 1.49 earned run average, 147 strikeouts, and seven shutouts.

◆ *Jim Shaw*—James Aloysius "Grunting Jim" Shaw (1893–1962), a righthander who won 83 and lost 98 for the Senators from 1913 through 1921. In 1919 his record was 16–17, but he led the league in innings pitched, with 306. A hip injury was to end his career two years later. See Jack Kavanagh, "Jim Shaw," *The Ballplayers*, p. 991.

◆ *Lowdermilk*—Grover Cleveland Lowdermilk (1885–1968), a journeyman righthander whom the White Sox acquired from the Browns for cash on May 17, 1919. His acquisition tacitly recognized the team's desperation for pitching beyond Cicotte and Williams. Lowdermilk, who was 6′4″, had worked for the Cardinals, Cubs, Tigers, and Indians since 1909. He was considered very fast, but lacking in control. He turned in a 5–5 record for the White Sox in 20 games in 1919, and closed out his major league career with the team in 1920, without earning another decision. His lifetime record was 23–39 in 122 games. See William A. Borst, "Grover Lowdermilk," *The Ballplayers*, p. 637.

◆ *we knocked his can off and beat them out*—This report is close to the actual events of the game of Sunday, May 25. Lowdermilk started against Shaw. Walter Johnson was sent in to protect a two-run lead in the eighth, but failed. Danforth finished the game for the White Sox, in the manner attributed to Keefe.

at them today after the work I done so the Dumonts was out to the game with Florrie and after the game I come out and the Dumonts had a mighty sweet looking doll with them named Miss Mulvihill or something so Dumont made the remark that it was pretty dry in Chi on a Sunday so why didn't we all hop in his car and go out to Lyons ◆ where they was plenty to eat and drink.

Well then Florrie said it didn't seem right for Miss Mulvihill to not have no man along when her and Mrs. Dumont both had their husband so Dumont asked me if they wasn't 1 of the ball players that was single that would like to go along. So I happened to think about Tom Dorgan so I went back in the club house and got him and you ought to seen his eyes pop out when he got a look at the Mulvihill trick. Well we went out to the car and it was the 1st time I seen it and Florrie had told me it looked like new but if it does why Jack Lapp has got a ◆◇ pompador. And when they said it was a 5 passenger car they meant 4 people and a weather strip.

Well the next thing was how was we going to set and Mrs. Dumont said she always set in the front seat to keep her husband from driveing to fast so that left I and Florrie and Miss Mulvihill and Tom for the soap box in back so Florrie said it looked like Miss Mulvihill would half to set on Tom's lap. Well both partys had a hemorage to the cheek when they heard that and Miss Mulvihill said she guessed not and why didn't Florrie set on my lap and Florrie said she had tried that to many times so any way the way we went was with Florrie and Miss Mulvihill squeezed along the side of me and Tom on my lap and I don't know how far it is to Lyons but by the time we got there I thought we must be all of us in the Coast League.

Well we set out on the porch of the joint out there and ordered up a few drinks and everybody acted like they had came to the morgue to identify a body till finely I begin pulling some of my stuff and I wished you could of heard Miss Mulvihill split her sides only I kind of felt sorry for poor Dorgan as he acted like the cat had his tongue or something and the gal must of thought she had been pared off with Dummy Taylor. Well we had some more drinks and a chicken dinner

---

◆ *Lyons*—A suburban town southwest of Chicago. Lyons still has a concentration of bars and restaurants on Ogden Avenue, U.S. route 34.

◆ *Jack Lapp*—John Wallace Lapp (1884–1920), a reserve catcher who hit .263 with the Athletics from 1908 to 1915 and with the White Sox in 1916. Lapp was notoriously bald. He died of pneumonia only a year after the events depicted by the story. See Norman L. Macht, "Jack Lapp," *The Ballplayers*, p. 602.

◇ *Jack Lapp*—Catcher Jack Lapp in an Athletics uniform, 1913. (George E. Brace collection)

and when the check come around Dorgan was still speechless and Dumont was danceing with Florrie so I was elected on the 1st ballad and Miss Mulvihill made the remark that I shouldn't ought to pay for everything and just jokeing I said I was tickled to death to pay for being in her company and she blushed up like a school girl and give me a smile and I couldn't help from feeling sorry for Dorgan but I can't help it if that's the way the gals feels Al and I only wished I could be just friends with them and nothing more.

Well when it come time to go home I made the remark that I wasn't crazy about holding Tom on my lap again along with the extra load he had picked up in the mean wile so what does Miss Mulvihill do but say that if Florrie did not mind she would just as leaf set on my lap and Florrie said go ahead so that's the way we come home and even with Dumont zig zaging all over the road and hitting her up about 12 miles per hr. all the way it didn't seem more then 5 minutes when we come to where Miss Mulvihill lived and dropped her off and I seen her to the door and I said to her how did she like my friend Mr. Dorgan and she said "Why don't you speak for yourself John?" How is that Al she calling me John the 1st time she ever seen me and I didn't know they was anybody realy knew my name was John as they all been calling me Jack ever since I was a knee high grass hopper you might say.

Well when I and Florrie got home I got the silent treatmunt but she will get over it Al like they all do and anybody would think it was my fault that I wasn't born with a hair lip or something.

But wait till I tell you what come off today. It wasn't till pretty near 5 this A. M. when we rolled in this A. M. and I got up about 11 this A. M. and finely got over to the ball pk. and I felt like the supper dishs and finely it come time for batting practice and Gleason said you work today and I said what was he talking about as I worked yesterday and he said yes but it wasn't only 2 innings just long enough to warm up so I had to get in there and try and pitch and of course it had to be the day when Weaver and Collins and all of them went to he—ll behind me and the Washington club went mad and got 4 runs which is more then they usually get all through May and Harper shut us out ◆ with 3 hits though he didn't even have a nightgown on the ball and after the game Gleason asked me where I was last night and I told him I was out and he said yes and you are out today again to the amt. of $50.00. Well Al if he makes that fine stick I will quit baseball and go in some business where a man can get fair treatmunt and sometimes I think I better get out of baseball any way as a man that is a star in the game if he has got any looks at all why the gals all loose their nut about him and bother you to death even if you turn your back every time they look at you and a man hasn't no business being before the public in a position where the gals can look you over and make a fool out of themself when you have got a wife and 2 kiddies.

Your pal, Jack.

◆ *Harper*—Harry Clayton Harper (1895–1963), a lefthander on his way to a 6–21 season in 1919, a performance sufficiently futile to lead the American League in losses. Harper pitched for Washington from 1913 to 1919, and later for the Red Sox, Yankees, and Dodgers, amassing a 56–77 record in ten seasons. Against the White Sox, however, Harper was usually effective. In the 1919 season Washington batted .260 and scored only 533 runs, both figures the second-worst in the league. The team finished seventh. Harper was to become a successful industrialist in New Jersey. See Jack Kavanagh, "Harry Harper," *The Ballplayers*, p. 444.

In the actual game of May 27, Cicotte defeated Walter Johnson, 4–3.

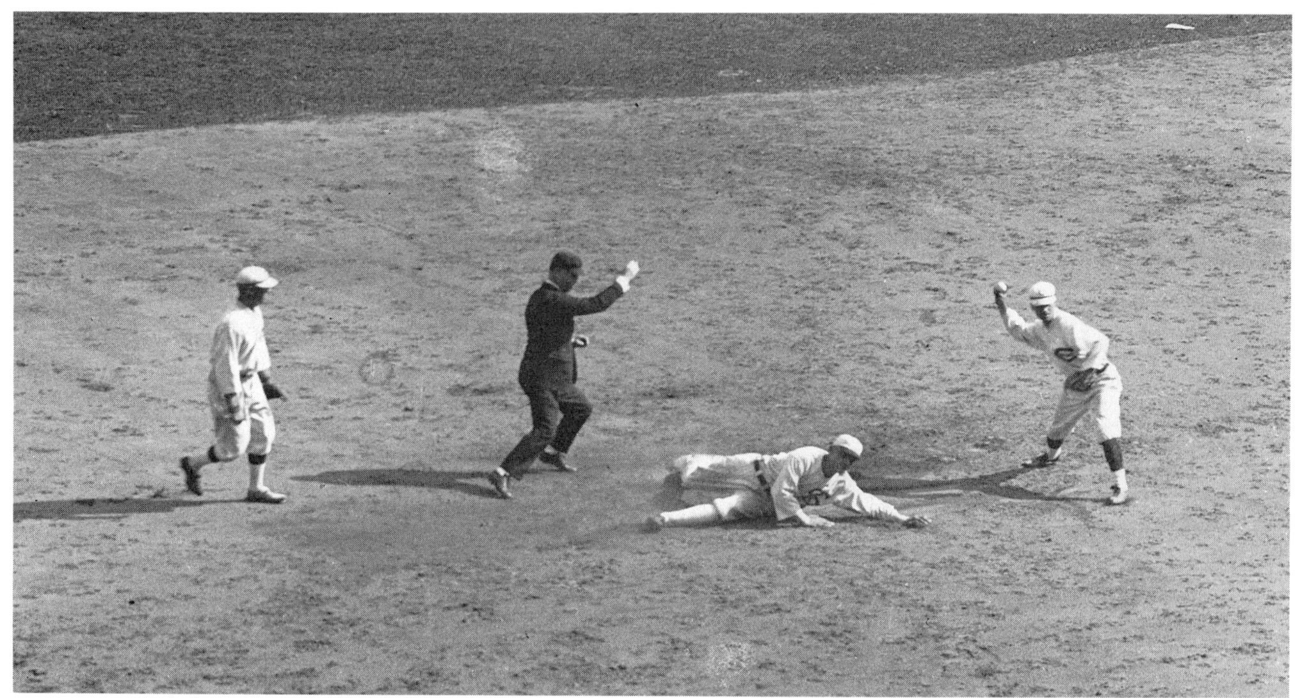

◇ *Gandil*—Chick Gandil out attempting to steal second base in the 1919 World Series. The Cincinnati second baseman is Maurice Rath; the shortstop, Larry Kopf. (See footnotes, pp. 199 and 287, and photo, p. 200.) (Chicago Historical Society)

CHI, JUNE 1.

Friend Al: Well Al I just come back from the pk. and Cleveland give us a trimming but it was about time as we win the 1st 3 we played with ◆ them. We leave for Detroit tonight and go east from there and won't be back in old Chi till the last of the mo.

Well Al they was some excitement out in the old ball yard yesterday but beleive me it wouldn't of never came off if I had of been in there pitching or even down there on the bench. The way that it come off was that I pitched the P. M. game Decoration Day and give them a ◆ good licking and Gleason called off the $50.00 fine he plastered on me last wk. and said I didn't need to dress yesterday but could set up in the stand with Florrie. Well the Dumonts and Miss Mulvihill was also out to the game and we all set together and I kind of explained the game to Miss Mulvihill and I kept talking fast for the fear she would bring up something personal. Well the game wasn't much of a game as we had them licked to death but along in the 8th inning the Cleveland bunch was sore on acct. of the way we was makeing them

◆ *we win the 1st 3*—As stated, the White Sox won 4–1 and 3–2 on May 30 and 5–2 on May 31, after which Cleveland won, 5–3, on June 1.
◆ *the P. M. game Decoration Day*—In the actual second game on Memorial Day, Claude Williams defeated the Indians, 3–2.

like it and Speaker hit a ball down towards Gandil and Chick made ◇ quite a stop of the ball and run over and stepped on the bag long before Spoke got there but Spoke was kind of sore so he slid in to the bag and that made Gandil sore and they begin barking at each other and next thing you know they was at each other and the rest of the boys was all scared and left them go to it and finely Gandil had his shirt tore off and the umps put them both off of the field. Well Al it ◆ wouldn't of never of happened if I had of been in there as the minute Speaker had of started anything I would knocked him for a gool and it would of been good night Mr. Speaker. Just like I told Jack Graney out there on the field today I said "Speaker better not never try no monkey business like that on me or Fohl will be scarring the bushs for ◆ a new center fielder."

Well Miss Mulvihill was setting next to me when the fight come off and I could feel her kind of tremble so I guess I must of kind of squeezed her hand and I told her to not worry because if I seen that either 1 of them was realy going to get hurt I would run down there and knock them both for a gool. So she give me a smile and made some remarks about how nice it must be to be so big and I kind of laughed it off and then I seen Florrie kind of looking at us so I cut it out.

Well the fight must of kind of went to Dumont's bean and any way he asked us all down to the Dearborn for supper and Mrs. Dumont ◆ said we better get Tom Dorgan along so as Miss Mulvihill would have somebody to play with and she kind of made a face but didn't say nothing so I got a hold of him and we went down there. Well Tom is a pretty fair dancer and he kept asking Miss Mulvihill to dance and of

---

◆ *the umps put them both off of the field.*—The fight between Speaker and Gandil described here actually occurred on May 31, 1919. The fact that the White Sox did not go to Gandil's aid was interpreted at the time (and subsequently) as demonstrating his unpopularity with his teammates. Keefe's response to the episode in the rest of the paragraph in part reflects the character's typical braggadocio, but at minimum it shows no hostility to Gandil and possibly demonstrates outright identification with him. This is consistent with the interpretation set forth in the Introduction to this volume that Gandil should easily have been able to line up Keefe for the Black Sox plot.

◆ *Fohl*—Leo Alexander "Lee" Fohl (1870–1965), manager of the Indians from 1915 until his replacement by Tris Speaker on July 19, 1919. Subsequently, Fohl managed the Browns from 1921 to 1923, and the Red Sox from 1924 to 1926. His major league playing career, as a catcher, was limited to a game with Pittsburgh in 1902 and four with Cincinnati in 1903. As a manager, he won 713 and lost 792 in 11 seasons. See Norman L. Macht, "Lee Fohl," *The Ballplayers*, p. 345.

◆ *the Dearborn*—The Dearborn Hotel, 666 South State Street, Chicago.

course she couldn't say no though I guess she would of rather set at the table and talk things over but I was glad he kept her danceing at that as I was afraid things might get to personal if her and I was left at the table alone. Well finely we started home and on the way she managed to ask me where we was going to stop in Detroit and I told her so I suppose she will be sending me a post card or a night letter or something and if she does why all as I can do is just pretend like I didn't get it. But any way we are on our way tonight Al and if we can come back from this trip in 1st place why the race is as good as win you might say as the way I and Cicotte and Williams is going they's no club in the league can catch us in the stretch. Personly Al wile I don't never like to leave home I am kind of glad we are going this time for Miss Muvihill's sakes if nothing else as the less she sees of me for a wile she will be better off.

I will write to you from Detroit or somewheres in the east.

Your pal, Jack.

N. Y., JUNE 5.

Friend Al: Well Al we just got in from Detroit and we played against Jennings club like we was the Red X 2d team and if we finish up the trip like we started we will be lucky to come home in a passenger train. ◆ I suppose you read about how they beat me Al and it looks like they was enough bad breaks against me to last a whole season and the only peace of luck I had all the while we was there didn't have nothing to do with baseball but I did happen to run acrost a bird that wants to sell a car and its a 1918 Blaine that hasn't only been drove 4000 miles ◆ and it looks like it was just out of the shop. I took Cracker Schalk out to see it and he said I would be a sucker to not grab it off but the bird wants $1200.00 which is about twice as much is I figured on paying for a car so I didn't do nothing but I kind of think he took a fancy to me and if I hold off a wile he will come down to somewheres near my price. Any way I have got his name and address and if I decide I want to pay somewheres near his price why all as I half to do is wire him.

Well Al I didn't get no word from that little gal Miss Mulvihill wile we was in Detroit and I hope she finely got some sence in her head

◆ *we will be lucky to come home in a passenger train.*—The White Sox had lost to the Tigers 5–3 and 2–1 on June 2 and 7–3 on June 3. Gandil was under suspension for his fight with Speaker, greatly weakening the team at first base. Gandil was not restored to eligibility until June 7.

◆ *Blaine*—Apparently a fictional make of automobile.

but speaking about Miss Mulvihill I have kind of got a idear that this here Tom Dorgan is stuck on her as whenever we get up in the rm. together that is about all as he can talk about and the day we left Detroit he asked me if I thought it would do any harm him writeing her and of course I said why no it wouldn't and I felt like telling him it wouldn't do no good neither one but I guess he will find that out for himself soon enough without me telling him. Only I can't help from kind of feeling sorry for the both of them and I feel sorry for him because he has fell for a gal that has left her heart run away from her to a place where it won't get her nothing and I feel sorry for her for looseing her nut over a man that has all ready got a wife and troubles of my own.

But Dorgan of course don't know nothing about what has past between her and I and wile we was setting together on the train comeing east he asked me if I thought they was anything I could do to help him get in right with her. Well I told him I would do the best I could as I would like to see them both happy but between you and I Al about the only thing I could do to help his case along would be to put myself out of the way and maybe in time she would forget me but I have got Florrie and the kiddies to think of and after all a man's family comes before your friends.

Well old pal I expect to pitch 1 of the games here and the N. Y. ◆ club is going like wild men wile we act like we was trying to see who could hit the highest foul but after the luck I had in Detroit I should ought to get some kind of luck here and all as I ask is a even break and I will make Pipp and some of the rest of them think they have ◆ got the pip eh Al? *Your pal, Jack.* ◆

BOSTON, JUNE 11.

Friend Al: Well old pal it looks like your old pal should ought to start a matrimony burro and charge a commission for fixing it up between couples that wants to get married though this time I guess the want

---

◆ *the N. Y. club is going like wild men*—New York had won 19 and lost 11.

◆ *Pipp*—Walter Clement Pipp (1893–1965), first baseman of the Yankees. After a trial with Detroit in 1913 Pipp came up to the Yankees in 1915 and played regularly until the arrival of Lou Gehrig in 1925. He then played for the Cincinnati Reds from 1926 to 1928. In 15 seasons Pipp played 1,872 games, made 1,941 hits, and batted .281. See Jack Kavanagh, "Wally Pipp," *The Ballplayers*, pp. 871–72.

◆ *the pip*—A disease of fowl in which mucus forms in the throat and scale forms on the tongue.

to is all on 1 side and I am afraid my efforts is going to be waisted. I suppose you will wonder what am I talking about. Well I guess I told you about Josie Mulvihill that little queen out in Chi that Tom Dorgan went nuts over her well instead of them hitting it off why she kind of lost her noodle over me without me never looking X eyed at her and of course she is waisting her time over me as I have all ready got a wife and beleive me 1 of them is enough.

Well any way Dorgan can't think of nothing else only she and this A. M. up in the rm. he asked me did I think they was any chance for him in that direction and of course I couldn't come out and tell him what I realy thought so I said "Well you can't never tell till you try." So he says "Yes but I am a busher in the lady league and I don't know how to go about it and if I was to ask her and she node me I wouldn't never dast face 1 of them again." He said "How would it be if you was to just drop her a friendily letter and kind of mention my name in it and ask her what she thinks about me and kind of give me a boost and feel her out and if she answers you back why we can come pretty close to telling if I have got a chance or have not got a chance."

Well Al I couldn't do nothing only say O. K. so I have wrote her a letter giveing Tom a boost and I am going to mail it to her special and here is what it says in it.

Dear Miss Mulvihill: Well Miss Mulvihill I suppose you will be surprised recieveing a letter from 1 who you have hardily had time to get acquainted and a specially a married man but I am writeing this in behalf of a pal of mine who I won't half to tell you his name as you can guess who it is when I say that you have been out a couple times on partys with him which I was along at the same time with the wife and the Dumonts.

This man Miss Mulvihill has not yet win his spurrs in the big league yet and might do better if traded to another club as a young catcher breaking in has not got much of a chance on our club with a man like Ray Schalk a specially when you have got a couple of faults that a youngster has got to over come before they will make a big league catcher. I know you don't know a whole lot about baseball and if you seen this boy stand up there behind the plate and catch you might think he was O. K. and as good as anybody where a man that knew baseball could tell you what was the matter with him. 1 thing wile he has got a fair arm he has got to get in a certain position to peg and looses time before he can cut the ball loose and another thing he is what we call spike shy that is when a man is comeing in to the plate it seems like he has not got the nerve to block them off but trys to stand to 1 side and tag them as they are slideing past. But this boy may overcome these faults or he might make a grand catcher for some minor league club.

Well Miss Mulvihill I and this boy has been rooming together on the road ever since the season opened and wile he don't draw no star salery I wouldn't ask for a better roomy and when we have a little beer or something up in the rm. I am always glad to pay for it and I feel towards him like he was a young brother that hasn't got started yet in a money way you might say but if he keeps his eyes open and works hard he has got a chance to make good in the big league or at lease in Class A.

Now I don't want you to feel like as if I am butting in and trying to run your fairs but this boy asked me would I put in a word for him and try and find out how he stands with you and I can say to you Miss Mulvihill that you could do a whole lot worse then give this boy a chance and wile you may not like him just at the 1st he is 1 of these birds that the more you see of him he is just the same all the wile so if he gives you a ring on the phone when we get home why it won't hurt nothing if you make a date with him.

As for you and I personly girlie you know how matters stands with me and some times its to late to mend like in this case but a person can forget anybody if they try and we can be just good friends like I am with other girlies that is friends of my wife and all go out and have a good time together and no harm done. So if you will give this boy a chance and let by gones be by gones why it looks to me like it would be a good move both ways and remember that looks is not everything or money neither one.

With my personal regards and of course I don't half to tell you to not let this go no father and if you can't see your way clear why no harm done but I wished you would try and find time to write and tell me: how you feel in regards to this matter and beleive me your sinsere friend.

So that is what I wrote her Al and I signed my name and I feel like I had killed 2 birds with the same stone as she won't make no more fuss over me and she will either give this boy a chance when he gets home or else she will tell him right off in the real where to head in at and the sooner he gets the bad news he will get over it that much sooner.

Well I suppose you seen in the paper what I done to Babe Ruth yesterday and its no wonder they call him Babe Al as I had him swinging like a baby in a cradle and the only 2 times he even fouled the ball was when Liebold run back and catched the fly ball and another time when Gandil speered that line drive off in him but he would of struck out on that ball only it was a bran new ball and I tried to curve it and it didn't break like I intend it.

Well we leave here for Philly Friday night and after we get through with them we go to Washington and then Detroit for 1 game and then home. In the mean wile kindest regards to Bertha and don't take no bad money. *Your pal, Jack.*

DETROIT, JUNE 22.

Friend Al: Well Al we leave in a couple hrs. for old Chi and play the Cleveland club there tomorrow and I thought I was going to work here today but I guess Gleason wanted to save me up for the Cleveland club. Well I will make them like it and maybe they won't feel so cocky after I get done with them.

Well Al it looks like I would soon be a Barney Oldfield or something. ◆ I guess I told you that they was a bird here in Detroit that wants to sell me a 1918 Blaine car for $1200.00 and all the boys that seen it said I was a sucker if I didn't grab it off. Well when we got here today the 1st bird I seen was the bird that owns this car and he wanted to know if I had made up my mind or not. So I told him no I had not and he would half to give me a little more time or else cut down on the price. So he said he couldn't do neither as he had a offer from a man here in Detroit to take it off in his hands at $1200.00 and the man wants it right away and will pay cash and the only reason why he hadn't sold it to him was on acct. of takeing a kind of a fancy to me and he would rather see me get it then anybody else as he felt like we was old friends on acct. of him seeing me on the ball field so often. So I said well I only had about $800.00 in the bank and I would half to talk it over with the wife 1st any way so finely he said that if I would give him a $100.00 for a option on it he would hold on to it for a wk. before he sold it to somebody else and then I could wire him if I want it or not and that will give me plenty of time to talk it over with Florrie.

Well Al it looks like such a bargain that I would be a fool to not take it and Florrie will feel the same way when I tell her about it and I have gave the bird my check for a $100.00 and if Florrie will go in with me 50 50 why I will wire the bird and tell him the deal is closed

---

◆ *Barney Oldfield*—Barna Eli Oldfield (1878–1946), the leading American automobile race driver from 1902 until his retirement in 1918.

and then I will ask Gleason to leave me run over here from Chi some night and drive it back the next day and that way I won't only loose 1 day all together and when I get that old car back in old Chi beleive me I will burn up old Michigan Ave. only they will be 1 understanding and that is that Florrie can't drive the car neither wile I am in Chi or out on the road as I don't trust no woman to drive a car and a specially 1 that is always looking all over the st. to see if they's some dame that has got sporter close then her.

The bird took me out to the ball pk. this P. M. in the machine and it run like a watch charm and he asked me if I didn't want to try and run it a wile to see how easy it run but I don't want to take no chance of running a machine that don't belong to me and besides it won't take me no time to learn how to run it by myself as they's nothing I ever tried yet that I couldn't pick it up like childs play.

Well its pretty near train time Al and besides they isn't much news to write. I guess I told you about me writeing to Josie Mulvihill in Chi that Tom Dorgan is nuts over her and I wrote to try and give him a boost and see how he stood with her. Well the last day we was in Washington I had a night letter from her and all as it said was "Tell Mr. Dorgan the same thing I told you once why don't he speak for himself." So I showed him the message and his face kind of fell and I couldn't help from feeling sorry for him as it looks like he is barking on the wrong tree but I guess he will get over it and I hope the poor little gal will have sence enough to get over something herself as she must know they can't be nothing only friendship between her and I and the sooner she forgets all about me so everybody will be better off. *Your pal, Jack.*

CHI, JUNE 24.

Friend Al: Well Al from all I ever seen of Bertha I wouldn't never accuse her from being a spend drift but beleive me she has not got nothing on Florrie. When I got back from Detroit yesterday A. M. and told her about this here car that I had took a option on it and could get it for $1200.00 and everybody said it was a bargain and I would be sucker to not grab it off so she said well why don't you buy it. So I said that is all right to talk about buying it but I am about $600.00 shy and I figured that as long as I and you is both going to get the benefits out of the car you would go in with me 50 50 and pay for half of the car. So she said "All right I will pay for half of the car if you will agree that it belongs to the both of us and not just you and I can take it out and drive it when ever I feel like it." So I said nothing

◇ *a 60 passenger 35th st. limousine* —A car of the 35th Street crosstown line stopped at Wallace Street, about a quarter mile west of Comiskey Park, in 1948. The car is one of an order of 1914, and except for the light towers on the ballpark, which were installed in 1939, the scene is little different from what Keefe knew. (Tom Desnoyers)

doing as I wouldn't trust her to drive a lawn more let alone a car and a specially in town like Chi where its a dull day when a 100 people don't get bumped off in a automobile wreck.

So she said all right then nothing doing and you can either pay for the car yourself or go without it so I thought if she was going to be stubborn why I would be stubborn to as 2 could play in that game so it looks like we wouldn't have no car as I am not going to buy no cheap 1 for no $600.00 after seen that Blaine that is worth $2000.00 or better and the bird trying to give it to me for $1200.00 you might say. So it looks like I would do my motoring in a 60 passenger 35th st.◆◇ limousine eh Al?

◆ *a 60 passenger 35th st. limousine*—I.e., the 35th Street crosstown streetcar of the ubiquitous Chicago Surface Lines.

Well Gleason started me vs. the Cleveland club yesterday and as usual the boys wasn't hitting behind me and it come up to the 7th inning with the score 3 and 2 against us and we had a couple men on and 2 out and Gleason takes me out and sends Jack Collins up to hit ◆ and Coumbe made a monkey out of him and that's the way it always ◆ goes and some day Gleason will get wise to himself and find out that I can hit as good as anybody on the club against left handers. Any way Danforth went in to finish and they got a couple more off in him and finely beat us 5 and 3. ◆

But beleive me Al they come near being more excitement out there then just the baseball game. I was warming up before the game and Speaker come over towards our bench and I thought he was going in the club house or somewheres but he stopped along side of me and he said "Jack Graney said you wanted to see me." So I said I hadn't told Graney nothing of the kind so he said "Well what he said was that if I ever started anything with you Fohl would half to start scarring the bushs for a new center fielder." So I said "I never said nothing like that Spoke and if Graney told you that he was just kidding." So then Speaker hollered to Graney to come over and he come over and Speaker says "This big goof says he never said what you said." So Graney says "Well he did and if he says he didn't he is a liar." So I said "You better not call me a liar or I will liar you all over the ball pk." So Graney said it looked like I and him would half to settle it but Speaker said "No I will take it off in your hands."

Well Al it was all as I could do to keep from socking the both of them and I was just going to sock Speaker when I happened to think that it would probably mean I would get put off in the field and Gleason was depending on me to work the game so I pretended like I thought they was jokeing and I said "I don't want no trouble with neither of you 2 boys out here on the field but if you are looking for trouble I will come down to your hotel tonight and we can settle it there." So Spoke said all right and don't forget where we are stopping at and the clerk will give you the rm. No.

◆ *Jack Collins*—I.e., Shano Collins.

◆ *Coumbe*—Frederick Nicholas "Fritz" Coumbe (1889–1978), a lefthander with the Indians who pitched in only eight games in 1919, finishing with a 1–1 record. In eight seasons (1914–21) for the Red Sox, Indians, and Reds, Coumbe finished at 38–38. His only strong season was 1918, when he turned in a 13–7 record for the Indians. See A. D. Suehsdorf, "Fritz Coumbe," *The Ballplayers*, p. 227.

◆ *finely beat us 5 and 3.*—In the actual game of June 24 the Indians, behind Jim Bagby, beat Cicotte, 3–2.

Well what they was trying to do Al was start a fight with me and get me put off the field and Gleason is up against it for pitchers and besides he didn't have nobody else warmed up but I was to smart for them and didn't fall for it. But beleive me if it hadn't of been for us being up in the race and every game counts I would of socked the both of them.

Well finely the game started and the 1st ball I throwed come pretty close to Graney's bean and he said I better not try none of that business or he would hit me with a bat so I just laughed at him and I tried to throw the next 1 at his head but the ball kind of slipped and went right in his groove and he happened to catch it just right and hit it to left field and made 2 bases. Well I got the next bird but Speaker come up and said to throw 1 at his head and see what would happen. Well I wasn't going to leave him bluff me so I tried to get 1 close enough to scare him but I wasn't warmed up good yet and kind of wild and I got the ball outside and he hit it down the left foul line for 2 bases and at that Jackson should ought to of held him to a single but any way Graney scored and then Liebold let a fly ball get away from him and Speaker scored and that is how they got 2 of their runs. Well Graney and Speaker tried to ride me all the P. M. but I give them back what they sent and what they was trying to do was start a scrap so as I would get suspend it but I was to foxy for them. Well Al I was going down to their hotel last night and call their bluff and knock the both of them for a gool but when I got home the baby was acting kind of croopy and I was afraid to leave the house.

Well we play Cleveland here once more tomorrow and then we go to St. Louis and I will work 1 of the games there and I will make a monkey out of them.

Tom Dorgan told me tonight that he had called up Josie Mulvihill and was going to take her out somewheres tonight to a picture or somewheres and dance and I suppose she made the date so as she could tell him once in for all that they wasn't no chance for him and I only hope she lets him down easy as he is 1 of these silent birds that takes it mighty hard when the gals treats you rough.

Your pal, Jack.

ST. LOUIS, JUNE 28.

Friend Al: Well Al it looks like I am going to be a demon motorist after all Florrie or no Florrie. I just wired a telegram to the bird in Detroit saying I would buy the Blaine for $1200.00 if he would hold on to it for me till the 7 of July. We have got a off day in the schedule that day and I can easy get leaf from Gleason to run over to Detroit and get the old boat and drive her back to Chi and won't even loose a day.

Well I suppose you will wonder what has happened to change my mind and if somebody has gave me a birthday present of $600.00 or something. Well nothing like that old pal but still and all its going to be just the same like a birthday present and instead of the whole amt. comeing out of our family I am going to spend the $600.00 like I planned and 3 poor suckers is comeing through with the rest of it.

Well I suppose you will wonder have I went crazy or what am I talking about. Well Al I have went crazy like a fox and you will say so to when I tell you what I am going to pull off. Well they's a bird here in St. Louis name Jack Casey that I have ran around with him ever since I been comeing here and maybe you have heard of him but any way he has got a stable of fighters and he has put on some bouts himself here in St. Louis and he knows the game from A to Z. Well he has gave me a steer on a whole lot of fights how to bet on them and I never loose a nickle yet on his dope. Well I was out with him last night and we was all over St. Louis lapping them up and we run in to a bunch of boxers and boys that is interested in the fight game and as soon is they heard who I was they popped their eyes out and said they had been a admirer of mine for a long wile and always wanted to meet me and if Jimmy Burke had a few pitchers like myself maybe the St. Louis club could get somewheres.

Well finely the talk got around to the Willard Dempsey fight in

---

◆ *the 7 of July*—The White Sox played Detroit at home July 4–6 and Philadelphia at home July 9–11. Thus Keefe would have had time to make the trip to Detroit for the car, as stated.

◆ *Jack Casey*—Apparently a fictional character.

◆ *Jimmy Burke*—James Timothy "Sunset Jimmy" Burke (1874–1942), manager of the Cardinals for 49 games in 1905 and of the Browns from mid-season of 1918 through 1920. As a player, Burke had participated in 548 games, mainly at third base, between 1898 and 1905, with Cleveland of the National League, Chicago and Milwaukee of the American, and Pittsburgh and St. Louis of the National, hitting .244. His major league managerial record was 189–213. Burke also managed several minor league clubs (see below, in the footnotes to the story "Sick 'Em") and coached for the Cubs and Yankees in the 1920's and 1930's. See Jack Kavanagh, "Jimmy Burke," *The Ballplayers*, p. 135.

◆ *Willard*—Jess Willard (1883–1968), heavyweight champion of the world. Willard had won the championship by defeating Jack Johnson in Havana on April 15, 1915, in a fight that Johnson later claimed to have thrown.

Dempsey—William Harrison "Jack" Dempsey (1895–1983), challenger in the fight at Toledo, Ohio, on July 4.

Toledo the 4 of July and I asked some of the boys how they thought it was comeing out and they all kind of stalled and said it looked pretty even and it looked like a even money bet and etc. but I could see they was stalling and finely Casey come out with it. Well Al these birds is all in a position to know and they couldn't have nothing only the right dope and here is what they give me.

It seems like Tex Ricketts that is running the fight has spent a whole ◆ lot of jack building the arena in Toledo and he can't expect to break better than even on the 1 fight and if Dempsey was to win why they wouldn't be nobody left for him to fight so they are going to leave the arena up and Willard is going to get the decision in this fight and then they are going to match them up again for Labor Day and get the crowd back there a 2d time and clean up a bunch of jack and the 2d time they fight it will be on the level but this time the cards is all stacked for the big fellow to win and any way he is to big for this other guy to reach him. So Casey said if he was I and wanted to clean up a peace of jack why to go ahead and bet my head off on the big fellow to win this bout and they wasn't no way I could loose unless Willard drops dead from cramps or something when they get in the ring.

Well I said I would think it over and 1 of the boys said I better not think to long as it might be to late as it is only 5 more days now before the fight and he said if I wanted to put up my jack he knew a friend of his that wasn't on the inside and he couldn't see nothing only Dempsey and this friend would take any bet I would make and this bird said he would see that I got the jack when I win. Well I said I didn't want to rob no friend of his and besides I didn't have the jack along with me to put it up and he said he would take me check but I said I would rather wait till I get to Cleveland and maybe the odds ◆ would be different and I could get some odds on the big fellow instead of even money.

Well that's the dope Al and these birds know what they are talking about and if I was you and had a few dollars to bet why I would put

◆ *Tex Ricketts*—George Lewis "Tex" Rickard (1871–1929), promoter of the Willard-Dempsey fight and all of Dempsey's other major fights through 1927. Rickard is usually given the major share of credit for boxing's rise to respectability. He was the builder of the Madison Square Garden of 1925.

◆ *maybe . . . I could get some odds on the big fellow*—Odds on the fight favored Willard 7–5 on the morning of July 4. Lardner, in the *Tribune*, predicted that Willard would win. Dempsey won by a technical knockout in the third round. Retrospectively, Willard was widely thought to be overweight and out of condition, as Keefe mentions in his next letter home.

it up on big Jess and not say nothing about what I have told you as the more people that knows about it why it will effect the betting.

Personly when I was through with Casey and his friends I come back to the hotel and some of the boys was still setting around the lobby in the hotel and I set down with them and told them what I had found out and Buck Weaver is 1 of these smart Alex that always knows more then anybody else so he says "Well I will tell you what I think of your dope I will take all the jack you want to bet on the big fellow." So 1 word lead to another and I said I didn't want to rob no pals that was on the same club with me but they kept acting smarty and finely I kind of loose my temper and I said I would bet $600.00 even money if I didn't half to put it up and Weaver said he would take $200.00 of it and a couple more of the boys took $200.00 a peace and they covered the whole $600.00 and God help them but it will learn them not to be so smarty in the future.

So you see Al that I am going to have the big car after all and I am glad I can get it without Florrie putting in her jack as now I will own the car all myself and she won't half nothing to say only ask me to take her rideing and when I am out on the road with the club I will have the old buggy locked up in some garage where she can't get a hold of it and try to clime trees.

Well I made a monkey out of this club today and won't half to work no more till we get to Cleveland where I can get another whack at Speaker and Graney and if they try any more of their smart business on me I will give them the Jess Willard only they won't want to come back for no 2d dose on Labor Day or no other day and speaking about Cleveland reminds me that they are going to make us go there Sunday night and play a postpone game Monday and I can't see no sence to it only that is the last day before the country goes dry and I suppose they want us to spend it in a dry town for the fear we might enjoy ourself.

That is 1 place where poor Tom Dorgan has got it on us as Gleason has left him home this trip and he will be in old Chi the night of the 30 of June where he can get all as he wants to drink so he isn't so unlucky after all even if the ladys don't go nuts over him.

Well Al its time to go to bed and don't forget what I said about betting your jack on the big fellow if you have got any to spare and in the mean wile come on you big Jessica.

Your pal, Jack.

CHI, JULY 5.

Friend Al: Well Al its good night car and good night everything else and the way I feel I don't care if school keeps or not. I am glad I didn't advise you to bet no dough on the big fellow and if you bet some on your own hook why all as I have got to say is that I am sorry and it wasn't my fault or them boys down to St. Louis neither one as I have knew Casey several yrs. and I know he wouldn't give me no bad steer and the way it looks like to me is that Dempsey double crossed the big fellow and everybody else and of course only for what they told me down there I would of bet my jack on Dempsey instead of on the other fellow as in the 1st place Jess wasn't in no shape to fight and besides when a bird 24 yrs. old fights a man pretty near 40 why its 10 to 1 he will knock him for a gool.

Well Al your old pal will do his rideing around on st. cars this summer at lease unless we win the world serious and then of course I will have enough jack to buy the finest car made and not no broke down 2d hand Blaine and they say it costs a million dollars to run a Blaine any way as they are he—ll on tires and the cylinders keeps getting gumed up. Well they's 1 good thing and that is that Florrie don't know nothing about it and if she did why I wouldn't never hear the last of it but I am not the kind to cry over sour milk and whatever is comeing to me why I take it with a smile and go on my way. I suppose that bird in Detroit will try and hold on to the $100.00 I give him for a option but he won't never get away with that Al and I have all ready wired him a telegram to send it back to me at once and if he don't why the next time we hit Detroit I will knock him for a gool.

Speaking about Detroit I suppose you seen what happened in the game yesterday P. M. and when a busher like Flagstead can get to me ◆ for 3 hits why you know I am not myself.

Well Al I am to sick in tired of everything to write you much of a letter and besides they's nothing to write about you might say only except 1 thing and that is that Tom Dorgan called me to 1 side in the club house after the game this P. M. and said to not leave till he was ready to go with me so we come down under the stand together and there was this Mulvihill dame waiting for him and grinning like a

---

◆ *when a busher like Flagstead can get to me for 3 hits why you know I am not myself*— On July 4 the White Sox defeated Detroit twice, 8–1 and 2–1. Flagstead appeared only as a defensive replacement. He was, however, hitting .339 at the time. Note that by this time Keefe could spell Flagstead's name.

monkey and Tom couldn't hardily talk he was so fussed up but finely it come out that they are engaged to be married and they wanted to thank me for kind of helping them fix it up and she is wearing a big diamond solitary stone that he just bought for her this A. M. and he told me on the quite that he bought it with some of the jack he win on the fight down to Toledo.

Well good luck to them Al and they can have each other as far is I am concerned and I am glad she is off in my hands as she was getting to be a kind of a pest writeing me letters and night telegrams and 1 thing another and she might of knew that a married man don't want nothing to do with even a young gal let alone 1 that's way up in the paints. So I say good luck to them both Al and God help them.

Well the boys on the club has began calling me Jess and I guess they think its a joke or something but 1 of these days when I ain't feeling my best they won't think its such a joke when they pull some of their funny stuff on me and I Jess them in the jaw. *Your pal, Jack.*

The Busher Pulls a Mays

N. Y., JULY 29.

Friend Al: Well old pal here we are on the gay white way but they don't nobody on this ball club feel gay and no wonder. In the 1st. place to look at our club you would think we had just came back from the Marne as Gandil was left home in a hospital with appendix and Felsch ◆ is so lame that he can't cover no more ground then where his dogs is parked and Cracker Schalk has to be wheeled up to the plate and back you might say and to cap off the climax I got stomach trouble from something I eat or something and wile I don't pitch with my stomach a man can't do themself justice when the old feed bag acts up.

To make it worse Detroit has got a hold of a couple pitchers that can do something besides make 9 men on the field and Jennings club

"The Busher Pulls a Mays" was published in *The Saturday Evening Post,* CXCII (October 18, 1919), 16–17, 182, 185–86.

◆ *Gandil was left home in a hospital with appendix*—Gandil was out of action with a knee injury after July 17; Swede Risberg replaced him at first base. While out of action, Gandil had an attack of appendicitis, but characteristically refused surgery and returned to the team on August 5 in Philadelphia. Following the World Series he had an appendectomy.

Felsch is so lame—Felsch was reported to be limping at the time.

◇ *Carl Mays the Boston pitcher*— Carl Mays in the Red Sox road uniform of 1915–18, in the follow-through of his submarine-ball delivery (see footnote, p. 271). (National Baseball Library, Cooperstown, New York)

is comeing like a house on fire and all and all it looks like we was a bad bet and will be mighty lucky to get back off of this trip in 1st. place. For inst. Cicotte pitched a nice game today and lose it because ◆ they was a couple fly balls hit to center field that Felsch only had to take 3 or 4 steps to get under them but his sick dog layed down on him and wouldn't buge and zowey they went for 3 base hits. So as I say they can call this the gay white way but they can't hardily call us the gay White Sox eh Al.

Well I suppose you seen in the paper what Carl Mays the Boston ◆◇

◆ *Cicotte pitched a nice game today*—Not very. The Yankees defeated the White Sox 10–1 on this date; Cicotte gave up 12 hits in five innings.

◆ *what Carl Mays the Boston pitcher pulled off*—On July 13, 1919, as stated, Carl Mays left the field at Comiskey Park during a game and announced that he would never again pitch for the Red Sox, citing poor support from his teammates. Actually, some personal emotional problems may have been responsible. Mays returned home and refused the appeals of club president Harry Frazee and

pitcher pulled off and you will half to hand it to him. He walked out on the Boston club wile they was playing us out in Chi and said he wouldn't pitch no more baseball for them and of course they was out of the race for the pennant though when the season opened up and they had all their men back from the service we all of us thought they would be the club we would half to beat as they had 2 stars for every position you might say and they could stick 1 club in the field 1 day and a whole different club the next day and 1 of them as good is the other but any way they blowed up like Willard and it got so as they felt cocky when they only lose 1 game per day so Mays said he was through and instead of the club suspending him why they pretty near kissed him you might say and all the other clubs in the league begun biding for him.

Well we would of had him only I guess the Boston club insisted on Gleason giveing them Cocky Collins or Schalk or myself or somebody so of course Gleason give them the razz and finely Huggins got him for the N. Y. club for 4 or 5 ball players and the liberty loan and now Mr. Mays is with a club that has got a chance to get in the world serious and it shows what a sucker a ball player is to stick with a club where you can't get nothing only the worst of it.

Well Al I guess if I was to have a run in now with Gleason or something I will know what to do as the minute he looks X eyed at me I will Mays him and I guess they wouldn't some clubs jump at the

---

(*continued from page 303*)
general manager Ed Barrow to return to the club. The Red Sox suspended him for insubordination and began to entertain offers for him. Chicago, Cleveland, New York, Detroit, and St. Louis expressed interest in Mays, and on July 29 the Red Sox accepted the offer of the Yankees of $40,000 plus pitchers Allan Russell and Bob McGraw. Ban Johnson sought to prevent the transfer, recognizing it as a serious breach in the monopsony's power over players. The Yankees went to court, securing an injunction against Johnson's interference with Mays' playing for the team. The Red Sox and White Sox allied themselves with the Yankees, while the rest of the clubs remained loyal to Johnson. The dispute nearly tore the American League apart. The three insurrectionist clubs were even reported to be considering shifting to the National League, which they hoped could be expanded to a 12-team circuit. The American League survived the episode intact, but Johnson's power had been irretrievably diminished. As stated in the Introduction, the Mays affair was the principal cause of ending rule of baseball by a National Commission (consisting of the presidents of the two major leagues and Garry Herrmann of the Cincinnati Reds) in favor of unilateral control by a Commissioner, Kenesaw Mountain Landis. The subsequent Black Sox scandal, which demonstrated a problem of integrity in baseball, simply provided a universally acceptable reason for making the change. See Harold Seymour, *Baseball*, II, *The Golden Age* (New York: Oxford University Press, 1971), 264–68.

chance to get a hold of me and specially Detroit as Jennings is makeing a great fight for the old rag without hardily any pitching at all you might say and what would he do with a man like I on the club to go in there every 3d. day and take my own turn besides helping the other birds out when they begin to weaken.

Well old N. Y. is some dry town since the 1 of July and the only way a man can get a drink here is go in a saloon and the only differents between old times is what they soak you for it now which is plenty but when a man has got to have it he has got to have like today after the game for inst. my old stomach was freting pretty bad and I got myself 6 high balls on the way back from the pk. and it set me back $2.40 but as I say what is $2.40 compared to a man's health. *Your pal, Jack.*

BOSTON, AUG. 2.

Friend Al: Well Al we are haveing a fine trip and the way we been going you would think we must of clumb in to 1st. place some night ◆ after dark but we won't be there long if Gleason don't wake up and use his pitchers right. He acts like Cicotte and Williams was Adam ◆ and Eve and they wasn't nobody else in the world and he keeps yelping about what tough shape he is in on acct. of not only haveing 2 pitchers and as far is the rest of us is conserned we might as well be takeing tickets.

Well a man can't hardily blame him for going slow with birds like Kerr and Faber and Lowdermilk that when they do throw a ball ◆ somewheres close to the plate somebody's bat gets in the way but just because I lose them games to the St. Louis and N. Y. clubs in Chi with my stomach why that isn't no reason I should spend August with my feet on the water cooler and as I said to Gleason today he might as well of left me home and he says yes and the rest of the club to.

Well you don't see Jennings trying to cop the old rag with 2 pitchers

---

◆ *we must of clumb in to 1st. place some night after dark*—The White Sox regained first place on July 10, and on August 2 led Detroit by 6½ games.

◆ *He acts like Cicotte and Williams was Adam and Eve*—This sentence demonstrates how intelligently Gandil chose the pitchers for his plot. Cicotte started 35 times in 1919 and led the league with 29 complete games. Williams led the league with 40 starts and completed 27 of them. Gleason started them as often as possible, filled in with other pitchers as available, and made no real effort to develop the usual four-man rotation of the time. It is difficult, then, to see why Gandil spread the plot as far as he did, when all he needed was the cooperation of Cicotte and Williams. The other players he brought in simply divided the spoils further and added to the risk of exposure.

but he works his staff in turn like a mgr. should and some A. M. we will wake up and find ourself a few laps behind Detroit instead of leading them and all because Jennings gives his pitchers a chance but instead of Gleason giveing me a chance he sets around and mones about what tough shape we are in and if he could only get a hold of some pitcher like Page with the Phila. club but it looks to me like if Page was so dam good the Athaletics would get rid of him. We have all ready signed up Pat Ragan that every club in the National League tried him and I don't know what and the he—ll they can expect him to do here where a man has got to have something besides acquaintences in all the big citys and it looks to me like Gleason has went plain cuckoo and it wouldn't surprise me to see him bark like a dog.

Well I suppose you seen where Ban Johnson stepped in and suspend it Mays after it come out that the N. Y. club had boughten him and I don't see what Ban has got to say about it now and I suppose we will be reading pretty soon where he has plastered a $5.00 fine on Hap Felsch for limping.

◇ *Ban Johnson*—The Byron Bancroft Johnson plaque at the National Baseball Hall of Fame and Museum, Cooperstown, New York (see footnote, p. 39).

(*continued from page 305*)

◆ *Kerr*—Richard Henry "Dickie" Kerr (1893–1963), a rookie lefthander who won 13 and lost 7 in 1919. Kerr immediately became part of a clique of the better-educated members of the team, consisting of Eddie Collins, Ray Schalk, and Red Faber. Kerr, who was particularly disliked by Gandil's clique, won two games in the 1919 World Series and lost none. In 1920 Kerr ran up a 21–9 record, one of four White Sox pitchers to win 20 games, but after a 19–17 season in 1921, Comiskey denied Kerr a $500 raise. Kerr held out for the entire season of 1922, and was suspended by the team in 1923 and 1924. Comiskey's handling of Kerr is usually interpreted as his worst example of ingratitude, with the possible exception of his habitually shabby treatment of Ed Walsh. In 1925 Kerr appeared in 12 games with a record of only 0–1. Kerr later managed in the minor leagues, where his most famous accomplishment was converting Stan Musial from pitcher to outfielder. See Jack Kavanagh, "Dickey [sic] Kerr," *The Ballplayers*, p. 566.

◆ *Page*—A fictional character, but one vital to the denouement of the story. The White Sox were endeavoring unsuccessfully to secure a pitcher, Scott Perry, from the Athletics, and Perry was presumably the model for Page.

◆ *Pat Ragan*—Don Carlos Patrick Ragan (1888–1956), a righthander who was as shopworn as Keefe indicates. Since 1909 Ragan had pitched for the Reds, Cubs, Dodgers, Braves, and Giants before being picked up at the waiver price by the White Sox on August 2, 1919. His acquisition was the clearest indication yet of the team's desperate hunger for pitching. Ragan pitched in relief in one game for the White Sox against the Yankees on August 25, neither winning nor losing. He finished his major league career with a single game with the Phillies in 1923. In eleven seasons, his record was 75–104, all recorded in the National League. See Thomas Griesel, "Pat Ragan," *The Ballplayers*, p. 891.

◆ *Ban Johnson stepped in and suspend it Mays*—Johnson suspended Mays on July 31 after the Washington, Detroit, and St. Louis managements vigorously protested Mays' transfer to New York. Lardner correctly recognized that Johnson lacked the power to implement his policy in this case.

Ban said a few yrs. ago that Ty Cobb wouldn't never play another ◆ game in this league but the last time we played the Detroit club they had somebody in center field that looked a whole lot like Cobb and Jennings and the rest of the boys called him Ty.

Well this old burg isn't running as wide open as N. Y. and if a man wants a little refreshmunts they have got to go out and hunt for it like tonight I and 1 of the boys thought we better lay in a qt. to last over the sabath and 1 of the boys on the Boston club told us where to go get it so we got a qt. of it and it cost $7.00 and that means $7.00 a drink as they couldn't nobody in the world take more then 1 swallow and I wouldn't be surprised if that is what ails the Boston club. They are poisoned. Well the qt. all but 2 drinks is standing on my burro and that is where it is going to spend the sabath and when we leave here I will give it to the chamber horse for a tip and tell her what it cost and she will know she died a high price death. In the old days when we was here on a Sunday they closed up the bars but you could walk in the hotel cafe and order up a drink as long is you ordered sandwichs with it and if they knowed you they would bring you the same sandwichs every trip.

Well 1 more game here Monday and then we go to Philly and maybe we will win 1 there as we have got 4 to play and if Mack ever win 4 in ◆◇ a row he would put on a auction sale. *Your pal, Jack.*

◇ *Mack*—Connie Mack, co-owner and manager of the Philadelphia Athletics, probably about 1930. (George E. Brace collection)

◆ *Ban said a few yrs. ago that Ty Cobb wouldn't never play another game in this league*—The reference is to an episode in New York on May 15, 1912, in which Cobb went into the stands to attack a heckling fan, Claude Lueker. Johnson suspended Cobb indefinitely, precipitating a brief strike of Detroit players in support of Cobb. Cobb returned to the Tiger lineup on May 26 in Chicago.

◆ *Mack*—Connie Mack, playing name of Cornelius Alexander MacGillicuddy (1862–1956), manager of the Philadelphia Athletics for the entire first half of the twentieth century, from 1901 to 1950. From 1886 to 1896, Mack had been a light-hitting catcher; a season with Buffalo of the Players League in 1890 separated his years in Washington and Pittsburgh of the National League. He began managing at Pittsburgh in 1894, and became manager of the Milwaukee club of the Western League in 1897. The Milwaukee post brought him into a long and favorable relation with Ban Johnson. When Johnson and Comiskey raised the American League to major status, Johnson arranged that the Philadelphia franchise be given to Mack and Ben Shibe, an executive of the Reach sporting-goods firm. Mack's equity in the club allowed him to set a record of 7,878 games managed in the major leagues, probably the most unattainable of all baseball records. He won 3,776 and lost 4,025, winning nine pennants but finishing last 17 times. He became a member of the Baseball Hall of Fame in 1937. See Frederick G. Lieb, *Connie Mack* (New York: G. Putnam's Sons, 1945); Connie Mack, *My Sixty-six Years in the Big Leagues* (New York: John C. Winston Co., 1950).

Friend Al: Well Al just a line to let you know I am here in Philly and the club still up in Boston yet and don't get here till tomorrow. Well that means that I am going to take my regular turn from now on and will start against this club either tomorrow or the next day and Gleason ◆ sent me on ahead to rest up along with Cicotte. You see in the old days the ball clubs use to get a party rate on the R. R. and it saved them money to all travel together from town to town but now everybody ◆ has got to pay full fare so if a mgr. wants to send a couple of his star pitchers a day or 2 ahead to the next town to rest them up why it don't cost nothing so that is how it come that I and Cicotte is here in Phila.

I didn't have no idear I was comeing on ahead till yesterday A. M. when I run in to Gleason in the hotel dinning rm. up in Boston and he motioned me to come and set down with him. Well he said how is your heart so I asked him what did he mean. "Well" he says "in them last 2 games you pitched vs. St. Louis and N. Y. out in Chi it looked to me like you was missing." So I said I guest my heart was O. K. but my stomach has been freting me on acct. of something I eat. I said "I would of made them 2 clubs look like a bum only a man can't work when your stomach aint right." "No" he says "and your stomach won't never get right on that liquid diet." So I asked him what he meant and he says you know what I mean and I should think you would get wise to yourself. So I says I guest I was wise enough so he says "Well if your wise you will cut out the rough stuff and get to work." So I asked him how could I get to work when he wouldn't give me no chance and he said "I will tell you what I will do with you. Cicotte is going over to Phila. tonight to rest up and you can go along with him and rest up includeing your stomach and if you aint in shape to pitch when I call on you it won't be nobody's fault only your own. And remember they won't be nobody over there watching you and you can behave yourself or not just as you feel like but when I get there I will know if you been behaveing."

◆ *Gleason sent me on ahead to rest up along with Cicotte*—Newspaper accounts do not indicate that Cicotte was sent ahead of the team.

◆ *now everybody has got to pay full fare*—The United States Railroad Administration, the federal body that operated the railroads from late 1917 until 1920 as a wartime expedient, eliminated group fares for the 1919 season. The USRA's motive was to end the competition between railroads for the traffic of large groups to conventions, which had previously been one of the limited number of competitive practices in the noncompetitively organized industry. See *The Railway Age*, LXVI (March 28, 1919), 857–58.

So he had Joe O'Neill buy me a ticket and birth and I and Cicotte ◆ got here this A. M. and have the whole day to ourself and maybe we will go out this P. M. and see the game as the St. Louis club is playing ◆ here and besides we will have a chance to study Mack's batters. They are some study Al but maybe we can set where we can watch foxy Connie waggle his score card and maybe get his signs though it looks to me like he would do a whole lot better if he give up his score card long enough to have a few good ball players names printed on it.

Well 1 of the waiters here in the hotel tells me a man can get all they want to drink here in Phila. if they go at it right but nothing doing Al as I am going to be in shape to give Gleason the best I got though 3 or 4 wouldn't hurt me and what Gleason don't know won't hurt him. *Your pal, Jack.*

PHILA., AUG. 6.

Friend Al: Well Al I guess they's no use of a man trying to go along with a mgr. that has went cuckoo and if it wasn't for the rest of the boys on the club I would pull a Mays and walk out on the club and go to some club where a man can get a square deal but if I done that it might maybe cost this club the pennant and it wouldn't be the right thing towards the rest of the boys.

Well I guess I told you that I and Cicotte was sent on here ahead of the rest of the club to rest up so as we would be in good shape for the serious here and we layed around the hotel here all Monday A. M. and after lunch Eddie said he was going out to the ball pk. and did I want to go along. Well I said I guest I seen enough of baseball without spending a P. M. looking at a couple clubs like Burke and Mack has got a hold of and the more a man seen of Mack's club why the lest he would know about how to pitch to them and besides the best thing for me would be to get my mind off of baseball. So Eddie went out to the game and pretty soon I got kind of lonesome so I called up a friend of mine that is quite a fan and we found a place where you can still get it and we histed a few and then he said how about running down to Atlantic City.

◆ *Joe O'Neill*—Joseph O'Neill (c. 1885–1920), traveling secretary for the White Sox. He was in his last season in this office; he died of tuberculosis on March 9 of the following year.

◆ *the St. Louis club is playing here*—As stated, the Browns were scheduled to play the Athletics in Philadelphia on Monday, August 4.

◇ *Gleason*—Kid Gleason, at left, with Ed Walsh at Comiskey Park in 1923 (see also footnotes on pp. 42–43 and 227–28, and photos on pp. 43 and 228). (National Baseball Library, Cooperstown, New York)

Well Al we went down there and seen the sights and took a dip and my friend says he wondered why all the queens was giveing us the double O as they didn't never pay no tension to him when he was alone so I just laughed and didn't say nothing and didn't even look X eyed at 1 of them as I leave the flirting game to birds that hasn't no wife or no respect for the ones they have got so we got a dinj to dig us up a qt. and we was comeing back here at 11 P. M. but they must of been sleeping powders or something in that stuff we got and any way we layed down on the beach to rest for a few minutes after supper and the both of us overslept ourselfs and missed the train. Well Al we finely got back here at 9 o'clock yesterday A. M. and the club was all ready here and Gleason was setting in the lobby when I come in. Well ◇ he said where have you been. So I told him I had been out for a walk and he didn't say nothing so I come up to my rm. and layed down.

Well when we got out to the ball pk. he had both Cicotte and I take our turn in batting practice and when it come time to warm up he said it would be me. Well I didn't feel any to good but I warmed up pretty good and finely the game started and I hadn't pitched for pretty near 2 wks. and no wonder I couldn't start right out as good as ever but instead of giveing me a chance to get started he halls me out of there after I walked the 1st. 2 men. Well Cicotte went in and I come in to the bench and Gleason begin to rave and I said how can a man pitch when you don't even leave him get started. "Well" he says "you was out for 1 walk this morning and you was out for 2 walks this afternoon and I thought 3 walks a day would be enough for you." "Where was you last night?" he says and I told him nowheres. So he said "Yes you was. You was out for a board walk down to Atlantic City and I have got a notion to board walk you 1 in the jaw."

Well Al I don't know how he could of knew where I had been but I am not the kind that trys to lie out of something so I says yes I went down to Atlantic City and took a dip. So he says you mean you took a dipper. Well they's no use argueing with a crazy man Al so all as I could do was walk away from him before my temper got the best of me so I went in the club house and dressed and went up in the stand and watched the rest of the game. Well they didn't score off of Cicotte and we got 1 run in the 11th. off of Page and beat them 1 to 0 but I ◆ might of shut them out just the way Cicotte done if he had of left me in there but he has went cuckoo Al and to show you how bad he is he has signed up Mayer that has been in the National League 20 or 30 ◆ yrs. and the next thing you know he will be sending for Geo. Van ◆ Haltren or somebody. Well I only wished I was off this club and I

◆ *we . . . beat them 1 to 0*—The game attributed to August 6 is entirely fictional. The White Sox and Athletics did not play on that date. After several rain-outs the teams played a doubleheader on August 7. Cicotte beat Perry, 2–1, in the opener, but Williams lost to Rollie Naylor, 3–2, in the second game.

◆ *Mayer*—James Erskine Mayer (1891–1957), a righthanded pitcher who had starred for the Phillies in 1914 and 1915, winning 21 games each year. His only other effective season was 1918, when he went 16–7 in a season split between the Phillies and Pirates. The White Sox acquired his contract from Pittsburgh on August 6, 1919, in yet another of the management's efforts to beef up the woeful pitching staff. Erskine Mayer appeared in just six games for the White Sox, winning one and losing three. This ended his major league career, leaving him with a record of 91 wins and 70 losses. See A. D. Suehsdorf, "Erskine Mayer," *The Ballplayers*, p. 690.

◆ *Geo. Van Haltren*—George Edward Martin Van Haltren (1866–1945), a player who doubled as pitcher and outfielder. As a pitcher he was of no great merit, winning 40 games and losing 31 in nine seasons with Chicago, Baltimore, and

would walk out on them in a minute only for the rest of the boys that has got their heart set on winning. *Your pal, Jack.*

WASHINGTON, AUG. 9. ◆

Friend Al: Well old pal don't be surprised if you pick up a paper some A. M. and see where I have walked out on this bunch of cuckoos and pulled a Mays on them only it won't be no 2 or 3 wks. before I land somewheres else as they's a certain club in this league that would give their eye to get a hold of me as it would mean the pennant. Don't think I am bosting Al as I am just giveing you the facts and when I tell you what come off yesterday you will know who I refer. Even if the deal don't come off I can give Gleason a good scare and maybe come to some kind of a understanding with him.

Well yesterday was our last day in Philly and the Detroit club had finished up their serious in Washington the day before and their whole bunch was over in Philly yesterday and out to see our game. Well afterwards we seen the whole bunch of them and Jennings kind of smiled at me like he wanted to see me alone so I give him the chance and he says what was on my mind. So I seen he was trying to give me a opening so I said I was tired of pitching for Gleason. So he says "Well I been watching the box scores where you pitched lately and it didn't look to me like you was pitching for Gleason." He is a great kidder Al but that is just his way.

Well he humed and haud and finely he says they was no use him talking to me as Gleason wouldn't trade no pitcher to a club that was fighting him for the pennant. So I said maybe he wouldn't trade me but suppose I walked out on him like Mays done on Boston why then maybe he would give me to the club that made the best offer.

So Jennings said "Yes but we tried to get Mays but all as we could offer for him was jack and we couldn't offer nothing else for you and

---

(continued from page 311)
New York of the National League, Brooklyn of the Players League, and Baltimore of the American Association, between 1887 and 1901. As an outfielder, however, he was thoroughly respectable. He played 1,827 games in the outfield, mainly for the Giants, between 1894 and 1903. Van Haltren's overall batting average was .316 in 1,984 games. Partly because of his mediocre pitching talents, partly because his career was so far in the past, he was an excellent choice for this passage. See Jack Kavanagh, "George Van Haltren," *The Ballplayers*, p. 1113.

◆ *Washington, Aug. 9*—The White Sox finished in Philadelphia on August 8 and opened in Washington on August 9, as stated.

when a club offers money to Comiskey why it is like takeing coal to a castle."

So I said "Well it looks to me like it would be to your int. to offer something besides jack as Gleason could use a couple of your ball players." Yes said Jennings but when you begin talking trade to Gleason he can't only talk in words of 1 sylable Cobb and Bush. Well I said if I make up my mind to walk out on him Cleveland or N. Y. will get me either 1 and you know what that means. So he says "I guess you won't go to neither 1 of them clubs." That is what he said Al and they's only 1 way to take it but at that it wasn't so much what he said as how he looked when he said it. He kind of half smiled and give me a kind of a wink and walked away from me and besides he was scared to make it to strong as a mgr. of a club is not supposed to temper with a player on another club. But last night just before we left for here I seen Bush of the Detroit club and I told him what had came off and he says why didn't I go ahead and pull a Mays and see what happened. He says "We are going to win the pennant any way so you better take a chance of getting on a live 1."

Well old pal I am not going to do nothing I will be sorry for and if our club wakes up and begins to show something I won't leave them in the lerch but Gleason better get help to himself or he will wake up some A. M. and I won't be around for him to snarl at me.

Well comeing over on the train I set with 1 of the reporters that travels with the club and he told me that Gleason had been trying to get this here Page that pitched the 11 inning game vs. Cicotte and Gleason wanted to pay cash for him but Mack must of been unconsious or something and any way he turned it down so it looks like Gleason would half to struggle along without Mr. Page and I guess we will get along just as good without him as from what I seen of him you could write up the game on his fast ball wile its comeing up there but maybe he would bring us luck as a bird that can make us go 11 innings for 1 run must have god with him.

Well I asked this reporter if Gleason had said anything about me lately and he said nothing that could be printed so I said well maybe I will have a story for you 1 of these mornings so he asked me what I meant and I said well if Gleason didn't give me a square deal I would maybe pull a Mays on him and go to some club where I can get fair treatmunt. "Well" he says "if I was you I would cut out that line of talk as it may get back to Gleason and he will beat you to it." Well Al I should worry if it gets back to Gleason or not as it might give him a scare but I don't want him to know nothing about it yet a wile till I see how things comes along so I haven't told nobody about my plans only a couple of the boys on the club that knows enough to keep their mouth shut and in the mean wile mum is the word till we see how matters comes along. *Your pal, Jack.*

ON TRAIN, AUG. 12.

Friend Al: Well old pal we are on our way back to old Chi and everybody is happy even the Washington club though we took 2 out of 3 from them but they made more jack out of our serious then they ever seen before and what is 2 or 3 ball games to them you might say. Well Gleason didn't start me but you notice he stuck me in there yesterday in the 8th inning when Lefty Williams begin to wilt and put ◆ the brakes on them and that ball Judge hit would have been nuts for ◆ Gandil only for him being weak on acct. of his appendix.

Well when Gleason 1st. told me to go in there I had a notion to go in there and dink the ball up there and let the Washington boys get their name in the averages for once in their life and show Gleason I didn't give a dam but then I thought of the rest of the boys and it wasn't square to them to not give them the best I got so I cut loose and you see what happened. ◆

Well Gleason patted me on the back when it was over and tried to give me the old oil but I just kind of smiled and pertended like I fell

---

◆ *Lefty Williams begin to wilt*—Williams did, in fact, defeat the Senators, 7–4, on August 11, and the White Sox took the series, two games to one. Williams pitched a complete game; he needed no relief.

◆ *Judge*—Joseph Ignatius Judge (1894–1963), long-time first baseman of the Senators and one of their most popular players. Judge played for the Senators from 1915 to 1932, starring on the championship teams of 1924 and 1925. Including two final years with the Brooklyn Dodgers and Boston Red Sox, Judge made 2,350 hits in 2,166 games, for a career batting average of .297. Only 5′8½″, he compensated for his size with exceptional agility at first base. See James K. Skipper, Jr., "Joseph Ignatius Judge," *Biographical Dictionary of American Sports: Baseball*, pp. 293–94.

◆ *you see what happened*—As this paragraph clearly demonstrates, Lardner recognized, however implicitly, that the stresses on the team were so severe that the players would want to lose. Gandil had conceived the plot in July, and by this time, mid-August, was endeavoring to interest Cicotte in it. Cicotte agreed in a Pullman car on the team's last trip to Boston, on September 18, and by September 21, when an organizational meeting was held in Gandil's room in the Ansonia Hotel in New York, he had lined up the rest of the conspirators. As stated in the Introduction, Gandil would have had no incentive to enroll Keefe in the plot, and Keefe had in any case been let go before the organizational meeting, but this remarkable passage indicates unambiguously that Keefe would have been predisposed to participation.

for it but that is the way he is Al when you win you are aces but when you have a bad day your as welcome is a gangrene.

Well it looks now like we would go right through and win the old rag as everybody has got so as they can waggle their legs without groaning and Gandil will soon have his strength back and then look out as about all as we half to do is break even and Detroit will have 1 he—ll of a time catching up with us so it looks like your old pal will get in once on the world serious dough and about time after all I have did for this club and would of been in on it in 1917 only I give up everything for my country wile the rest of the boys stayed home and made nasty remarks about the Kaiser.

Speaking about the world serious Al it looks now like Cincinnati ◆ would give the Giants some battle in the other league and if Moran ◆ can keep his club going they have got a good chance and I guess that old burg wouldn't go cuckoo if they win a championship. Well I guess the ball pk. down there can't handle the crowd that we would draw in ◆ the Polo Grounds but even if we can't make as much jack out of a serious down there all the boys on our club would about as leaf play them as it would save us time as we can get it over in 4 days if we play them where it would probably take 5 days vs. N. Y. on acct. of 1 day to make the jump. The boys was talking this A. M. about what Cicotte and Williams should ought to do to Moran's club and they would make a bum out of them and etc. but I guess after what I showed in Washington Gleason can't do no lest then start me in 1 game at the outside and then we will see if Roush and Groh is such wales when ◆◇ they get up vs. real pitching after the dead arm Dicks they been looking at all season.

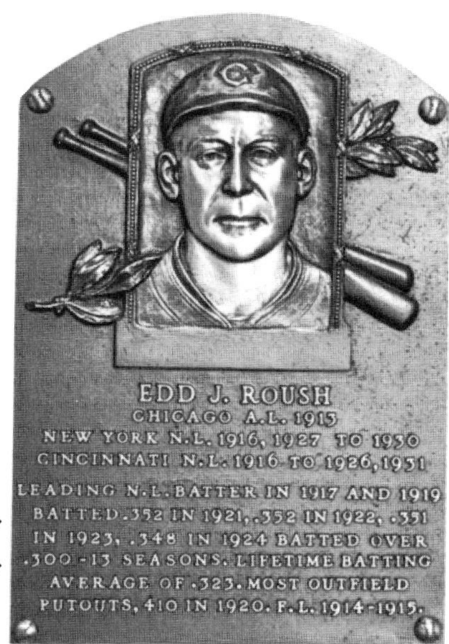

◇ *Roush*—The Edd J. Roush plaque at the National Baseball Hall of Fame and Museum, Cooperstown, New York.

◆ *it looks now like Cincinnati would give the Giants some battle in the other league*—The Reds now led the Giants by four games.

◆ *Moran*—Patrick Joseph Moran (1876–1924), manager of the Cincinnati Reds. From 1901 to 1914, Moran had been an undistinguished catcher with the Braves, Cubs, and Phillies, batting .235 in 817 games, but he had led the Phillies to their first pennant in his first season as manager, in 1915. He remained with the Phillies through 1918, and then managed the Reds from 1919 to 1923. See Art Ahrens, "Pat Moran," *The Ballplayers*, p. 759.

◆ *the ball pk. down there can't handle the crowd*—Redland Field, later Crosley Field, accommodated only 22,000 in 1919, as compared with 52,000 for the Polo Grounds. It was expanded with temporary seating for the World Series.

◆ *Roush*—Edd J Roush (1893–1988), centerfielder of the Reds and, with an average of .321, batting champion of the National League in 1919. Roush broke into the major leagues in nine games with the White Sox in 1913, then played for the Indianapolis-Newark club of the Federal League. After 39 games with the Giants in 1916 he came to the Reds, where he won the 1917 batting championship

Well old pal it is pretty near time to stick the old nose in the old feed bag and we land in old Chi this P. M. and no game tomorrow but Thursday we open up vs. Boston and I suppose it will be Cicotte as Gleason sent him on ahead to get ready. Well if he can't cut her they's others on the old pitching staff that can and 1 of them is

Your pal, Jack.

CHI, AUG. 15.

Friend Al: Well Al I suppose you seen what the Boston club done to ◆ Cicotte yesterday and Gleason had to take him out so as Felsch and Liebold could stand still and rest a minute but when he come in to the bench all as Gleason said to him was better luck next time Ed instead of fuming at the mouth like he done to me in Philly. So I said to Gleason I says "You send this bird on ahead of the club to be ready for this game and they make a bum out of him and all as you say to him is better luck next time Ed and the same thing came off in Philly the day I started and you went cuckoo and barked like a dog." So Gleason says "Yes you big stiff but the reason they got to Eddie was because he didn't have no stuff when he got in there but your trouble was that you had to much stuff before you ever went in." So I just laughed at him.

Well it looks more then ever like Pat Moran was going to cop in the other league the way his club made a bum out of the Giants in the ◆ serious down there and I was just thinking tonight if the big show

---

(*continued from page 315*)
with a .341 average. With the Reds through 1926, the Giants from 1927 to 1929, and the Reds again in 1931, Roush made 2,376 hits in 1,967 games for a .323 career average. He was elected to the Baseball Hall of Fame in 1962. Roush, who had particularly disliked spring training, in fact died at a Reds' spring-training game on March 21, 1988. Of the men mentioned in these stories, he was the last to die. See David L. Porter, "Edd J. Roush," *Biographical Dictionary of American Sports: Baseball*, pp. 488–89.

Groh—Henry Knight "Heinie" Groh (1889–1968), the Reds' third baseman. Groh, who was on his way to a .310 season, had played for the Reds since 1913. In 1922 he went to the Giants, with whom he had broken in in 1912. He ended his career with Pittsburgh in 1927 with a lifetime average of .292 in 1,676 games. Groh was notable for using a bat with a thin handle and an abrupt taper from the handle to the barrel–the bottle bat. He managed the Reds briefly in 1918. See Jack Kavanagh, "Heinie Groh," *The Ballplayers*, p. 420.

◆ *you seen what the Boston club done to Cicotte yesterday*—On August 14, the Red Sox beat Cicotte 15–6.

◆ *his club made a bum out of the Giants in the serious down there*—The Reds played three consecutive doubleheaders at New York, August 13–15. On the 13th the

comes off in Cincinnati why couldn't you hop on a train and breeze down there for the 1st. game that is scheduled down there and maybe that will be the game I pitch or 1 of them and it would tickle me to death to know my old pal was up there in the stand pulling for me and I promise you won't be ashamed of saying your my friend when you see me out there. It wouldn't only cost you about $6.00 or $7.00 R. R. fare and you wouldn't half to bother about no ticket to the game as the boys on our club can get 2 of them a peace to every game at the ◆ regular prices and I would leave you use 1 of mine 1 day and it wouldn't only cost you $2.00 or $3.00 and after the game we could go somewheres and hist a few as its a cinch they have still got some tucked away somewheres in that old burg as even the babys would die down there without their beer.

Maybe you will think you shouldn't ought to make no trip like that and leave Bertha home but between you and I Al the ladys is a nusance when it comes to a trip like that and besides no matter how good a man and their wife gets along when you have lived with them a few yrs. its like a sweet dream to be away from them a day or 2. Think it over Al and leave me know how you feel about it and I would say come up to 1 of the games here only what with the Swede and the 2 kids we wouldn't have no place to park you and besides we could have a better time somewheres where Florrie wasn't folling us around all the wile like a caboose.

Speaking about Florrie we had a long talk last night and it seems like she is about ready to sell out her share in the beauty parlor as she don't get along very good with the Dumonts and besides as I always say a womans place is home so I guess she is about through pairing finger nails and etc. and I am glad of it as with my salery and what I

(*continued from page 316*)
Reds won, 4–3 and 2–1. On the 14th the Giants won, 2–1 and 9–3. On the 15th the Reds won, 4–3 and 4–0. The Reds were not thereafter closely challenged for the pennant.

◆ *at the regular prices*—The Reds established a price scale for individual World Series games ranging from $6 for box seats to $1 for the added right-field bleachers. (See the Cincinnati *Enquirer*, September 12, 1919, p. 6.) Because this was the Reds' first pennant of the twentieth century, the management expected a huge demand for tickets, with as many as half a million applications. Scalping was inevitable. Thus, offering to sell his best friend a ticket at face price was about as close to generosity or reciprocation for emotional support as Keefe could be expected to go. A $2 or $3 ticket would have put Al in the rear of the upper deck or in the permanent bleachers.

◇ *hello handsome*—Nick Altrock. (National Baseball Library, Cooperstown, New York)

pick up in the world serious and etc. I guess they won't be no over the hills to the poor house for Mr. and Mrs. Keefe yet a wile.

Your pal, Jack.

CHI, AUG. 20.

Friend Al: Well Al I and Gleason had some words today and I guess he knows now where I stand and if he don't why it is his own look out. We was playing the Washington club and Nick Altrock was out on the ◆ coaching line and I begin to kid him from the bench and I hollered hello handsome at him. So he turned around and hollered why hello ◆◇ Carl I didn't know you was still with us. So Gleason says why is he calling you Carl and I said I didn't know so Gleason says "Yes you do he is calling you Carl after Carl Mays because you told some of the boys you was going to Mays me and walk out on the club and Nick has heard about it." So I said "Well maybe I did say that in a jokeing way." So Gleason says "What was the joke." So I said "Well maybe they wasn't no joke but I just made the remark to some of the boys that I

◆ *We was playing the Washington club*—As stated, Washington opened a series in Chicago on August 20.

◆ *hello handsome*—See the accompanying photograph of Altrock.

liked to pitch and it looked like they wasn't no chance for me to pitch here so I wished I was somewheres where I could pitch." So Gleason said "Well I will send you somewheres where you can pitch." So I said "I can pitch here if you will give me a chance." "Well" Gleason says "I am not running this club to muse you but I am trying to win a pennant and I can't take no chances with a bird that has only turned out 2 good innings for me in a month." So I said "Well I can't turn out no more good innings till you stick me in there." So Gleason said "Well I will stick you in there when I get good in ready and if you want to walk out on me why walk as far is you like." So I says "I don't half to walk as the Michigan Central will take me as far is I want to go." So ◆ that shut him up Al as he knows now that if I jumped I would have a place to light and he can't afford to strengthen a club that is right on our tail you might say.

You have got to hand it to Jennings for the race they are makeing Al though we been going good to thanks to a whole lot of luck like today for inst. Cicotte was in there against a Swede name Erickson ◆ that the Washington club got from Detroit and the boys went out and got 10 runs for Eddie and a man that can't win with 10 runs better study for a janitor or something and a specially vs. the Washington club that if they ever scored 10 runs in 1 day the other clubs would ask for a recount. Well this Erickson certainly was good and the only boys on our club that could hit him was those that batted against him. Well Al you never see them pile up 10 runs behind me when I am in there pitching and about the only way as we can score at all with me in there is 3 bases on balls and a balk.

Well Al Florrie told the Dumonts today that she was going to quit them and sell out her share of the business and they wasn't no tears shed on neither side. She hasn't only payed in about $250.00 for the stock they was going to sell her so she will have that comeing besides a few dollars salery as she had drew ahead. Any way I am glad she is

---

◆ *the Michigan Central*—The New York Central System's line from Chicago to Detroit.

◆ *a Swede name Erickson*—Eric George Adolph Erickson (1892–1965), a genuine Swede born in Gothenburg. As indicated, Washington had picked him up from Detroit only recently, in a trade for Doc Ayers on July 5, 1919. Erickson had pitched one game for the Giants in 1914, then played for Detroit since 1916. He remained with the Senators until 1922. In 1919 he was 0–2 for Detroit and 6–11 for Washington. The game was as described, with Cicotte defeating Erickson, 10–3. In seven seasons Erickson won 34 and lost 57. See Jack Kavanagh, "Eric Erickson," *The Ballplayers*, p. 313.

out of it and can stay home and pay a little tension to the kiddies and we are going to throw a party Sat. night to celebrate and as long is you can't be here Al why I suppose I will half to hist a couple for you. *Your pal, Jack.*

CHI, AUG. 25.

Friend Al: Well Al I am through. Not through with pitching but through working for a cuckoo that treats a man like a dog. They's only 1 condition that I will go back to him Al and that is a contract calling for more money or a bonus or something and he has got to understand that I work in my regular turn which is the only way a pitcher can do themself justice. But he won't agree to my turns Al as trying to manage a ball club has went to his head and his brains has been A. W. O. L. for the last 2 mos. you might say. So its going to be moveing day pretty soon for your old pal and I guess you know where I am going to move without me telling you. I have all ready wired a telegram to Jennings telling him what come off and things ought to begin to pop by tomorrow at lease.

Well Al I will tell you what come off and you can judge for yourself what kind of a cuckoo this bird is. Well the lst half of last wk. he had me down in the bull pen every day warming up though he didn't have no intentions of sticking me in there and God knows I was warm enough without going out and looking for it but every time I would ease up a little and try and rest he would look down there from the bench and motion to me to get busy and by the time the game was over Sat. P. M. my old souper squeeked like a rat every time I throwed a ball.

Well Sat. night we throwed a party over to the house in honor of Florrie retireing from business and I had 4 qts. of the old hard stuff layed away and I and a couple of Florrie's friends husbands finished 1 of them before supper and after supper we turned on the jazz and triped the life fantastic and I half to be oiled or I can't dance so by 11 o'clock the serch and sieze her birds could of had the run of the house and welcome. Well 1 of the husbands said he knowed a place where they had escaped from the epidemic so we went down there and they served us rat poison in tea cups and I only histed a couple to be polite but I eat something that didn't set right and when I finely got home and put on my night gown I wished it was a sroud.

Well Al I couldn't eat nothing when I got up and whatever it was I had eat the night before had gave me a fever and Florrie wanted I should call up the ball pk. and tell them I was sick but it was Williams's turn to pitch and I thought all as I would half to do would be get down in the bull pen and go through the motions but when I get to the pk. what does this cuckoo do but tell me to take my turn in the batting practice as I am going to work. So I asked him what was the matter with Williams and Gleason said he don't feel good. "Well" I ◆ said "if he felt like I do his family would be out shopping for 1 left handed casket." So Gleason said what and the he—ll is the matter with you now. So I told him my stomach. "Well" said Gleason "get in there and give them your fast one and curve and I will tell Schalk not to sign for your stomach." So that was all as I could get out of him Al and they wasn't nothing to do only grip my teeth and try and make ◆ the best of it.

Well Al to make a short story out of it I went in there so dizzy that Vick of the N. Y. club looked like he was hitting from both sides of ◆◇ the plate and I tried to throw a ball between him. Well I seen him fall ◇ over but he couldn't get out of the way as I catched him right over the ear and if I had of had my regular stuff on the ball they would of been brains splashing clear up in the grand stand. Well I got 1 over for Peck and he past it up and then Schalk thought they was going to ◆ hit and run so he signed me to waist 1 and I waisted 4 and then up come Baker and I had 2 balls and nothing on him and I looked in to the bench but Gleason wasn't looking at me and I looked out to the

---

◆ *Williams . . . don't feel good*—Williams had an alcohol problem, but he had assured Gleason that he would not let it interfere with his pitching assignments. With occasional deviations, he observed the agreement, but this passage implies that a lapse was occurring.

◆ *make the best of it.*—The White Sox were, in fact, playing the Yankees in Chicago on Sunday, August 24, Williams pitched, winning 4–1.

◆ *Vick*—Samuel Bruce Vick (1895–1986), the Yankees' rightfielder. Vick was playing his only season as a regular, appearing in 106 games and hitting .248—which was by coincidence his lifetime average. Vick, an alumnus of Millsaps College, played for the Yankees from 1917 to 1920 and for the Red Sox in 1921. His chief claim to historical notice is being the man whom Babe Ruth replaced upon joining the Yankees. The fictional beaning described here did not interfere with his longevity; on his death in his native Mississippi at 91 he was the last but one of the players mentioned in these stories.

◆ *Peck*—Roger Thorpe Peckinpaugh (1891–1977), the Yankees' shortstop. Peckinpaugh had broken in with Cleveland in 1910, but had played for the Yankees since 1913. In 1919 he was enjoying an excellent season, which included a 29-game hitting streak. In 1922 Peckinpaugh went to Washington, where he was to star on the 1924 and 1925 championship teams. He was chosen the most valuable player in the American League in 1925, but ended his playing career with the White Sox just two years later. In 2,012 games over 17 seasons, Peckinpaugh hit .259. He managed the Indians from 1928 to 1933 and again in 1941, and was general manager of the team from 1942 to 1946. See A. D. Suehsdorf, "Roger Peckinpaugh," *The Ballplayers*, p. 850.

◇ *Vick*—Outfielder Sam Vick, shown in the uniform of his principal minor league club, the Memphis Chickasaws of the Southern Association. (*The Sporting News*)

bull pen and they wasn't nobody warming up so I pitched again and got 1 over the plate. Well I don't know what kind of baseball it is for a man to hit with 2 and 0 with birds on 1st. and 2d. and nobody out and the pitcher hog wild but that is what this bird done Al is take a lunge at the ball and Liebold couldn't of catched it without a pass out check.

Well I looked in to the bench again and Gleason didn't say I yes or no but I wasn't going to stay out there and faint away for him or no other cuckoo. So I walked in to the dug out and said I'm through. "Through with what" Gleason says. "Through with a mgr. like you that makes a man go in there and try to pitch when I am so sick I don't know what I am doing." So Gleason said "That is the way you have always pitched." So I said "Well I am not going to pitch that way or no other way for you no more but I am going to pitch for a mgr. that don't ask a man to work when he is only 2 laps this side of a corps." Who are you going to pitch for? I am going to pitch for Detroit. "Well"

◇ *Well I seen him fall over but he couldn't get out of the way as I catched him right over the ear*—Drawing by M. L. Blumenthal for *The Saturday Evening Post*, October 18, 1919.

says Gleason "that puts them out of the race as Jennings is so crazy ◆ now that he eats grass and when you get there he will start in on his ball club." Well I said something back to him and went in the club house.

That is what come off Al and I will leave it to you if I didn't do right as how can a man work for a cuckoo that makes a bench lizard out of you for a mo. and then pitchs you 64 innings in 3 days in the bull pen and then when your sick and wore out and your souper whines every time you raise it.

Well he as much is said he wished I would go to Detroit so he can't go back on that Al or try and block the deal so as I say I wired a telegram to Jennings that I am through here and for him to hurry up with his offer.

Well Gleason and the club leaves to-night for St. Louis and I have been kind of expecting that he would call up and try and square things with me but not a peep out of him and as I say he is so cuckoo

---

◆ *that puts them out of the race*—The Tigers on August 25 were in second place, six games behind the White Sox.

that he probably won't come down off of his horse. But I should worry Al as I will soon be with a club that can win the pennant with a little help and I am the bird that can give them the kind of help they need.

I will keep you posted Al and let you know the minute I hear news. In the mean wile come on you Tigers. *Your pal, Jack.*

CHI, AUG. 29.

Friend Al: Well Al no news yet and I called up the ball pk. today to see if maybe they wasn't a telegram there for me though I wired Jennings my home address. They wasn't no telegram there and I don't know what to think only it may be that Jennings is wireing back and 4th. to Gleason trying to make the trade and they can't agree on turns. Well Gleason is not a sucker enough to not make some kind of a deal when he knows that I won't never work for him again but or course its natural for him to hold out for the best man he can get and its natural for Jennings to not give more for me than he has to. But if it comes to a show down you can bet that Jennings will give up anybody he has to outside of Cobb or maybe Bush and I wouldn't be surprised if the final deal was me for Bob Veach and no money on the side. The ◆◇ White Sox has got room for another outfielder God knows wile on the other hand Veach's strength is hitting which is wasted in Detroit as they can all hit up there but dam few of them can pitch.

Of course Veach is in the game every day where most pitchers don't only work about every 4th. day but for a man like Jennings I would go in there every day the rest of the season if he asked me and work my head off to bring the old flag home to Detroit.

In the mean wile I should worry as news is sure to come sooner or later and I and Florrie is enjoying ourselfs and getting acquainted with the kiddies and still got enough jack to keep the wolfs from the door a couple of wks. at the outside.

Your pal, Jack.

◆ *Bob Veach*—Bobby Veach had a fine year in 1919, leading the American League in hits with 191, doubles with 45, and triples with 17. He batted .355, second only to Cobb's .384; his slugging average was .519, third to Ruth and Sisler; and he batted in 101 runs, second to Ruth's 114.

The White Sox has got room for another outfielder God knows—Keefe refers to the White Sox' problem in right field, where Nemo Leibold and Shano Collins played.

◇ *Bob Veach*—Bobby Veach at the plate in batting practice during World War I (see footnote, p. 67). (National Baseball Library, Cooperstown, New York)

CHI, AUG. 31. ◆

Friend Al: Well Al I suppose you seen the news in the paper Sat. and I am leaveing for the east tonight to join my new pals. Don't never get it in your head Al that I am not tickled to death to play for Connie Mack as he has always had my respect even if the Athaletics has been tail enders for the last few yrs. He has got the right idear Al and that is to build up a young ball club and learn them the game and by the time they are ready they are still young enough to play their best baseball and when they get good they don't win 1 championship and then crall back in their hole to die but they win 3 or 4 in a row and

◆ *Aug. 31*—At this time the White Sox led the league by seven games. They did release a pitcher on this date, sending Dave Danforth to Columbus of the American Association. Danforth refused to report and joined a semiprofessional team in Baltimore.

get enough jack to live in ease and luxery the rest of their life. Besides Al a man that plays ball for Mack knows that he will be treated like a gentleman and not barked at like a dog when things goes wrong.

Well Al the news come to me in a funny way. I was out late Friday night and overslept myself and when I woke up Florrie was up and dressed and I heard her in the next rm. and it sounded like she was sobing. Well I couldn't figure what and the he—ll she had to whine about so I hollered to her and she come in with the morning paper in 1 hand and her nose in the other. "Oh Jack" she says "its in the paper." So I said what was in the paper and she says "They have traded you to Philadelphia you and $5000.00 for Page."

Well for a minute I felt kind of stuned and then I snatched the paper out of her hand and read it over and over again and finely I got it through my head that it was true and Florrie was still snuffleing and I guess maybe I snuffled a little to.

Well finely I seen they wasn't no use makeing a baby out of ourselfs so I griped my teeth and I says "Well lets cut out the sob stuff as this here story don't mean nothing in our young life. They can trade me to Philadelphia for all the Pages in the book but I won't go." So Florrie spruced up to and she says "That's right you just tell them they can either send you to some decent club or you will quit the game for good."

So for a wile we talked along that line Al but Sat. P. M. I said something about going down town for supper and take in a picture show and Florrie begin to snuffle again. We can't afford no partys now she said. She says "You haven't no job and I haven't and we have got less then $200.00 to our name and what is going to become of us."

Well we stayed home and we talked things over and to make a short story out of it we seen where we was makeing a sucker out of ourselfs as when you come to think of it they's no better town in the league to live in then Phila. and its near Atlantic City so as Florrie and the kids can be down there all summer you might say and I can go down nights when the club is playing at home and Florrie thinks maybe she can get in a beauty parlor there and make enough jack to help out this winter.

So all and all Al I am tickled to death the way things has came along and wile I won't get in the world serious this yr. its the long run that counts after all and when we do get going in Philly it will still be a young ball club yet that can stand the pace and cop the old rag 2 or 3 seasons in a row. And about that time Gleason's club and Jennings's to will be in the old folks home lapping up gruel.

Well I have looked up the schedule and Detroit comes to Philly the ◆ 9 of Sept. and the White Sox the 13 and I am going to ask Connie to let me work twice against the both of them and then I will show Gleason and Jennings what a fool they made out of themself and what kind of a pitcher old Jack Keefe is when I am working for a man that can talk to you without barking like a dog. *Your pal, Jack.*

◆ *I have looked up the schedule*—The schedule information is correct. By September 9 the Athletics were 14 games behind seventh-place Washington. Note that Keefe, since November 1913, had learned to spell "schedule." Even at the end he was still learning.

The Individual Short Stories, 1914-1917

My Roomy

I

No—I ain't signed for next year; but there won't be no trouble about that. The dough part of it is all fixed up. John and me talked it over◆◇ and I'll sign as soon as they send me a contract. All I told him was that he'd have to let me pick my own roommate after this and not sick no wild man on to me.

"My Roomy" was published in *The Saturday Evening Post*, CLXXXVI (May 9, 1914), 17–19, 61–62, 65. The late Professor Eugene C. Murdock of Marietta College, Charles Elston and James L. Stephens of Marietta, Ohio, the library staff of Marietta College, and Arthur Ahrens of Chicago were all extremely helpful in work on this story.

◆ *John*—John Joseph Evers (1881–1947), manager of the third-place Chicago Cubs of 1913, the team on which the action is set. Evers was the second baseman of the famous Chance-Evers-Tinker-Steinfeldt infield of the Cub championship teams of 1906–08. Evers broke in with the Cubs in 1902 and played for the team continuously through 1913. He then was traded to the Braves, whom he assisted to the 1914 pennant. Evers ended his active career with the Phillies in 1917, except for a single game with the White Sox in 1922 and another with the Braves in 1929. Evers made 1,658 hits in 1,762 games over the course of 18 seasons, hitting .270. He also managed the Cubs for 98 games in 1921 and the White Sox for the entire 1924 season, in which the team finished last. Evers was elected to the Baseball Hall of Fame in 1946. See John L. Evers, "John Joseph Evers," *Biographical Dictionary of American Sports: Baseball*, pp. 169–70.

◇ *John*—Johnny Evers in batting practice for the Cubs, 1909. (National Baseball Library, Cooperstown, New York)

You know I didn't hit much the last two months o' the season. Some o' the boys, I notice, wrote some stuff about me gettin' old and losin' my battin' eye. That's all bunk! The reason I didn't hit was because I wasn't gettin' enough sleep. And the reason for that was Mr. Elliott. ◆◇

He wasn't with us after the last part o' May, but I roomed with him long enough to get the insomny. I was the only guy in the club game

◆ *Mr. Elliott*—A fictional character, but the syndrome of psychiatric symptoms attributed to him is so consistent that scholars and psychologists have always presumed Lardner observed it in an actual player. In one of his weekly columns of the 1920's Lardner offered a clue to the prototype. Lardner stated that he, another reporter, an established player, and a young lefthanded player had shared two rooms and a bath in a southern hotel during spring training of the club to which Lardner had been assigned. The lefthander did not sleep the first night, but spent his time talking to himself. On the second night he left the water running into the bathtub to simulate the sound of the dam that was near his home, which he required to sleep. This proves to be one of the principal symptoms attributed to Elliott. The lefthander disappeared from camp after three or four days, but turned up drunk at a card game, intending to beat up the manager, who was not present. Instead, he swung at Lardner, missed, but damaged Lardner's rented typewriter. Lardner was explicit that the man did not make the team. (See Ring W. Lardner, "Sense and Southpaws," San Francisco *Examiner*, April 30, 1922, p. E6. For this reference I am indebted to Professor Howard W. Webb.)

On the basis of Lardner's reference to the dam and the player's physique, ability to sing, weakness in fielding hits, unwillingness to play in the Southern Association, and other evidence cited below, the player is identifiable as Charles

Quartet of Cub Recruits at West Baden.

JOE DONEHUE CURT ELSTON VINCENT CAMPBELL MARTIN WALSH

SOX SWAMP OAKLAND | CALIFORNIA YIELDS TO MIGHT OF SOX SECONDS | TANK STARS TO MEET

◇ *Mr. Elliott*—The Cubs brought only four rookies to spring training in 1908, all of whom are shown in this halftone from the Chicago *Record-Herald* of March 10, 1908. Two of the four appear in "My Roomy." Curt Elston, the apparent model for Elliott, is the shortest of the four, consistent with Lardner's description of his stocky build. Joe Donehue was a pitcher from the Spauldings, a semiprofessional team in Chicago. Vincent Campbell had been a college player, a catcher at Vanderbilt University. Martin Walsh, brother of Ed, was a pitcher from Danville in the Virginia League. He was returned to Danville at the end of spring training. Of the four, only Campbell made the team, and he only for a single game. He did play 545 games as an outfielder for Pittsburgh and Boston of the National League and Indianapolis/Newark of the Federal League, however. (For more on Walsh, see footnote, p. 346.) (Chicago Historical Society)

enough to stand for him; but I was sorry afterward that I done it, because it sure did put a crimp in my little old average.

And do you know where he is now? I got a letter today and I'll read it to you. No—I guess I better tell you somethin' about him first. You fellers never got acquainted with him and you ought to hear the dope to understand the letter. I'll make it as short as I can.

(continued from page 332)
Curtis "Curt" Elston (1879–1950), a lefthanded outfielder from Marietta, Ohio, who was with the Cubs in spring training of 1908, but was released to Fort Wayne of the Central League without appearing in a major league game. Neither the accounts of Elston's career in the minor leagues, which spanned the years 1903–1913, nor biographical information on his personal life give any evidence of psychiatric symptoms of the character of those attributed to Elliott. Either the symptoms attributed to Elliott are entirely fictional, or Lardner observed them in another person and combined them with Elston's superficial physical and mental characteristics. David Eden, a British mental-health professional who was kind enough to comment on this point, wrote, "Unless Lardner is known to have made a study of abnormal psychology I would say he could not have produced this clinically consistent picture except as a result of direct and fairly long-term observation of an individual psychopath" (letter of David Eden to George W. Hilton, May 30, 1991). This implies that Lardner's brief acquaintance with Elston could not have allowed him to observe in Elston the syndrome attributed to Elliott.

He didn't play in no league last year. He was with some semi-pros over in Michigan and somebody writes John about him. So John sends Needham over to look at him. Tom stayed there Saturday and Sunday, ◆ and seen him work twice. He was playin' the outfield, but as luck would have it they wasn't a fly ball hit in his direction in both games. A base hit was made out his way and he booted it, and that's the only report Tom could get on his fieldin'. But he wallops two over the wall in one day and they catch two line drives off him. The next day he gets four blows and two o' them is triples.

So Tom comes back and tells John the guy is a whale of a hitter and ◆ fast as Cobb, but he don't know nothin' about his fieldin'. Then John signs him to a contract—twelve hundred or somethin' like that. We'd been in Tampa a week before he showed up. Then he comes to the ◆ hotel and just sits round all day, without tellin' nobody who he was. Finally the bellhops was going to chase him out and he says he's one o' the ballplayers. Then the clerk gets John to go over and talk to him. He tells John his name and says he hasn't had nothin' to eat for three days, because he was broke. John told me afterward that he'd drew about three hundred in advance—last winter sometime. Well, they took him in the dinin' room and they tell me he inhaled about four meals at once. That night they roomed him with Heine. ◆

Next mornin' Heine and me walks out to the grounds together and Heine tells me about him. He says:

"Don't never call me a bug again. They got me roomin' with the champion o' the world."

◆ *Needham*—Thomas J. Needham (1879–1926), the Cubs bullpen catcher. Needham had made a career of second-string catching with the Braves from 1904 to 1907, the Giants in 1908, and the Cubs from 1909 to 1914. He got into 523 games, but hit only .209. Needham did engage in scouting, as the passage indicates, and after his playing career was a coach and scout for the White Sox. See Norman L. Macht, "Tom Needham," *The Ballplayers*, pp. 787–88.

Elston was actually drafted by the Cubs from Lancaster (Ohio) of the Ohio & Pennsylvania League, where he had hit .303 in 1906 and .318 in 1907, leading the league in the latter season.

◆ *a whale of a hitter*—When Elston reported to the Cubs at West Baden, Ind., W. A. Phelon, the correspondent of the Chicago Daily *Journal*, wrote, on March 6, 1908, "This gentleman is plainly a hitter and nothing else." In 1906, when Elston had reported to the Columbus Senators of the American Association for spring training, the Columbus *Dispatch* for April 7 had stated, "Elston clouted the ball like a fiend. Here is surely a real hitter. The fielding department of his game is the only weakness he shows."

◆ *Tampa*—The Cubs opened training in Tampa, Fla., on February 18, 1913.

◆ *Heine*—Heinie Zimmerman.

"Who is he?" I says.

"I don't know and I don't want to know," says Heine; "but if they stick him in there with me again I'll jump to the Federals. To start with, he ain't got no baggage. I ast him where his trunk was and he says he didn't have none. Then I ast him if he didn't have no suitcase, and he says: 'No. What do you care?' I was goin' to lend him some pajamas, but he put on the shirt o' the uniform John give him last night and slept in that. He was asleep when I got up this mornin'. I seen his collar layin' on the dresser and it looked like he had wore it in Pittsburgh every day for a year. So I throwed it out the window and he comes down to breakfast with no collar. I ast him what size collar he wore and he says he didn't want none, because he wasn't goin' out nowheres. After breakfast he beat it up to the room again and put on his uniform. When I got up there he was lookin' in the glass at himself, and he done it all the time I was dressin'."

When we got out to the park I got my first look at him. Pretty good-lookin' guy, too, in his unie—big shoulders and well put together; ◆ built somethin' like Heine himself. He was talkin' to John when I come up.

"What position do you play?" John was askin' him.

"I play anywheres," says Elliott.

"You're the kind I'm lookin' for," says John. Then he says: "You was an outfielder up there in Michigan, wasn't you?"

"I don't care where I play," says Elliott.

John sends him to the outfield and forgets all about him for a while. Pretty soon Miller comes in and says: ◆

"I ain't goin' to shag for no bush outfielder!"

John ast him what was the matter, and Miller tells him that Elliott ◆

◆ *big shoulders and well put together*—Elston was a stocky player, about 5′8½″ and 183 pounds, with powerful shoulders, as stated. He was considered a fast runner for a man of this build; his physique had earned him the nickname "Groundhog" early in his professional career.

◆ *Miller*—Ward Taylor "Windy" Miller (1884–1958), a part-time outfielder and pinch hitter for the Cubs. Miller pursued this role with the Pirates in 1909, the Reds in 1909–10, and the Cubs in 1912–13. In 1914–15 he played for St. Louis in the Federal League and in 1916–17, for the Browns. Miller batted .278 in 769 games. See A. D. Suehsdorf, "Ward Miller," *The Ballplayers*, p. 743.

◆ *Elliott ain't doin' nothin' but just standin' out there*—Newspaper accounts, which survive for Elston's entire career in Organized Baseball, give no indication of an unwillingness to field or to run the bases. He prided himself on professionalism, and on his ability to play even when injured.

ain't doin' nothin' but just standin' out there; that he ain't makin' no attemp' to catch the fungoes, and that he won't even chase 'em. Then John starts watchin' him, and it was just like Miller said. Larry hit one ◆ pretty near in his lap and he stepped out o' the way. John calls him in and ast him:

"Why don't you go after them fly balls?"

"Because I don't want 'em," says Elliott.

John gets sarcastic and says:

"What do you want? Of course we'll see that you get anythin' you want!"

"Give me a ticket back home," says Elliott.

"Don't you want to stick with the club?" says John, and the busher tells him, No, he certainly did not. Then John tells him he'll have to pay his own fare home and Elliott don't get sore at all. He just says:

"Well, I'll have to stick, then—because I'm broke."

We was havin' battin' practice and John tells him to go up and hit a few. And you ought to of seen him bust 'em!

Lavender was in there workin' and he'd been pitchin' a little all ◆ winter, so he was in pretty good shape. He lobbed one up to Elliott, and he hit it 'way up in some trees outside the fence—about a mile, I guess. Then John tells Jimmy to put somethin' on the ball. Jim comes through with one of his fast ones and the kid slams it agin the right-field wall on a line.

"Give him your spitter!" yells John, and Jim handed him one. He pulled it over first base so fast that Bert, who was standin' down there, ◆ couldn't hardly duck in time. If it'd hit him it'd killed him.

Well, he kep' on hittin' everythin' Jim give him—and Jim had

◆ *Larry*—Pitcher Larry Cheney.

◆ *Lavender*—James Sanford "Jimmy" Lavender (1884–1960), one of the Cubs' starting pitchers. Lavender pitched for the Cubs from 1912 to 1916, and for the Phillies in 1917. His lifetime record was 63–76, and his best record, 15–13, was in his first season, 1912. Lavender gained an odd immortality: Vincent Starrett, a prominent Chicago literary figure, was so enamored of Lavender's name that he used it, with the pitcher's permission, for his fictional detective in several short stories. See Vincent Starrett, *The Case Book of Jimmy Lavender* (New York: Gold Label Books, 1944).

◆ *Bert*—Albert Humphries (1880–1945), a righthander newly acquired by the Cubs from Cincinnati. Humphries was about to lead the National League with an .810 percentage in a 17–4 season. Beginning with the Phillies in 1910 and ending with the Cubs in 1915, Humphries won 53 and lost 43. See Art Ahrens, "Bert Humphries," *The Ballplayers*, p. 503.

somethin' too. Finally John gets Pierce warmed up and sends him out ◆ to pitch, tellin' him to hand Elliott a flock o' curve balls. He wanted to see if lefthanders was goin' to bother him. But he slammed 'em right along, and I don't b'lieve he hit more'n two the whole mornin' that wouldn't of been base hits in a game.

They sent him out to the outfield again in the afternoon, and after a lot o' coaxin' Leach got him to go after fly balls; but that's all he did do—just go after 'em. One hit him on the bean and another on the shoulder. He run back after the short ones and 'way in after the ones that went over his head. He catched just one—a line drive that he couldn't get out o' the way of; and then he acted like it hurt his hands.

I come back to the hotel with John. He ast me what I thought of Elliott.

"Well," I says, "he'd be the greatest ballplayer in the world if he could just play ball. He sure can bust 'em."

John says he was afraid he couldn't never make an outfielder out o' him. He says:

"I'll try him on the infield tomorrow. They must be some place he can play. I never seen a lefthand hitter that looked so good agin lefthand pitchin'—and he's got a great arm; but he acts like he'd never saw a fly ball."

Well, he was just as bad on the infield. They put him at short and he was like a sieve. You could of drove a hearse between him and second base without him gettin' near it. He'd stoop over for a ground ball about the time it was bouncin' up agin the fence; and when he'd try to cover the bag on a peg he'd trip over it.

They tried him at first base and sometimes he'd run 'way over in the coachers' box and sometimes out in right field lookin' for the bag. Once Heine shot one acrost at him on a line and he never touched it with his hands. It went bam! right in the pit of his stomach—and the lunch he'd ate didn't do him no good.

Finally John just give up and says he'd have to keep him on the bench and let him earn his pay by bustin' 'em a couple o' times a week or so. We all agreed with John that this bird would be a whale of a pinch hitter—and we was right too. He was hittin' 'way over five hundred when the blowoff come, along about the last o' May.

◆ *Pierce*—Pitcher George Pearce.

◇ *pretty near everybody in the club.* —The Cubs of 1913. (George E. Brace collection)

II

Before the trainin' trip was over, Elliott had roomed with pretty near ◇ everybody in the club. Heine raised an awful holler after the second night down there and John put the bug in with Needham. Tom stood him for three nights. Then he doubled up with Archer, and Schulte, and Miller, and Leach, and Saier—and the whole bunch in turn, averagin' about two nights with each one before they put up a kick. Then John tried him with some o' the youngsters, but they wouldn't stand for him no more'n the others. They all said he was crazy and they was afraid he'd get violent some night and stick a knife in 'em.

He always insisted on havin' the water run in the bathtub all night, because he said it reminded him of the sound of the dam near his ◆

◆ *the dam near his home*—Dam No. 1 on the Muskingum River, a quarter-mile above the confluence of the Muskingum and the Ohio in Marietta. Elston spent his entire life, with the exception of baseball seasons, within earshot of the dam. His boyhood home was 201 Barber Street (the present 121), about 2,125 feet from the dam. When he married after retiring from baseball, he bought a house at 127 Gilman Street, about 1,250 feet from the dam, and as a widower he lived in an

home. The fellers might get up four or five times a night and shut off the faucet, but he'd get right up after 'em and turn it on again. Carter, ◆ a big bush pitcher from Georgia, started a fight with him about it one ◇ night, and Elliott pretty near killed him. So the rest o' the bunch, when they'd saw Carter's map next mornin', didn't have the nerve to do nothin' when it come their turn.

Another o' his habits was the thing that scared 'em though. He'd brought a razor with him—in his pocket, I guess—and he used to do his shavin' in the middle o' the night. Instead o' doin' it in the bathroom he'd lather his face and then come out and stand in front o' the lookin'-glass on the dresser. Of course he'd have all the lights turned on, and that was bad enough when a feller wanted to sleep; but the worst of it was that he'd stop shavin' every little while and turn round and stare at the guy who was makin' a failure o' tryin' to sleep. Then he'd wave his razor round in the air and laugh, and begin shavin' agin. You can imagine how comf'table his roomies felt!

John had bought him a suitcase and some clothes and things, and charged 'em up to him. He'd drew so much dough in advance that he didn't have nothin' comin' till about June. He never thanked John and he'd wear one shirt and one collar till some one throwed 'em away.

Well, we finally gets to Indianapolis, and we was goin' from there

---

(*continued from page 338*)
apartment at 408 Hamar Street, nearby. All of these addresses are in West Marietta, where the sound of the dam pervaded the neighborhood. The dam was removed in 1969, 19 years after his death.

◆ *Carter, a big bush pitcher from Georgia*—This very strange passage appears to be an unambiguous reference to Paul Warren Carter (1894–1984), a pitcher who won 23 and lost 25 for the Cleveland Indians in 1914–15 and the Cubs from 1916 to 1920. Carter, who was 6′3″ and 175 pounds, was born in Lake Park, Georgia, and died there. In 1913, however, Carter was playing for Maysville, Ky., in the Class D Ohio State League. Newspaper accounts, moreover, give no indication he was in the Cubs training camp in Tampa. The story was published in 1914, two years before the Cubs acquired Carter. See Bob Carroll, "Paul Carter," *The Ballplayers*, p. 163.

Newspaper accounts give only slight evidence of a predisposition to violence in Elston. W. A. Phelon in the Cincinnati *Times-Star* (March 7, 1913) reported that while playing for Providence in the Eastern League Elston attacked a sportswriter who had published a joke about him that Elston found offensive. The writer responded by hitting Elston in the leg with a bat, damaging a ligament. The incident appears not to have been noted in the Providence newspapers. Elston, in 1910, stated with some pride that he had been ejected from a game only once—for defending a deaf-and-dumb second baseman from a bullying umpire. See "Who's Who with the Grays," Providence *Journal*, June 3, 1910.

◇ *a big bush pitcher from Georgia*—Paul Carter at the plate, evidently in the uniform of a minor league team. (George E. Brace collection)

to Cincy to open. The last day in Indianapolis John come and ast me ◆ how I'd like to change roomies. I says I was perfectly satisfied with Larry. Then John says:

"I wisht you'd try Elliott. The other boys all kicks on him, but he seems to hang round you a lot and I b'lieve you could get along all right."

"Why don't you room him alone?" I ast.

"The boss or the hotels won't stand for us roomin' alone," says John. "You go ahead and try it, and see how you make out. If he's too much for you let me know; but he likes you and I think he'll be diff'rent with a guy who can talk to him like you can."

So I says I'd tackle it, because I didn't want to throw John down.

◆ *to Cincy to open*—The Cubs opened the 1913 season against St. Louis in Chicago.

When we got to Cincy they stuck Elliott and me in one room, and we was together till he quit us.

III

I went to the room early that night, because we was goin' to open next day and I wanted to feel like somethin'. First thing I done when I got undressed was turn on both faucets in the bathtub. They was makin' an awful racket when Elliott finally come in about midnight. I was layin' awake and I opened right up on him. I says:

"Don't shut off that water, because I like to hear it run."

Then I turned over and pretended to be asleep. The bug got his clothes off, and then what did he do but go in the bathroom and shut off the water! Then he come back in the room and says:

"I guess no one's goin' to tell me what to do in here."

But I kep' right on pretendin' to sleep and didn't pay no attention. When he'd got into his bed I jumped out o' mine and turned on all the lights and begun stroppin' my razor. He says:

"What's comin' off?"

"Some o' my whiskers," I says. "I always shave along about this time."

"No, you don't!" he says. "I was in your room one mornin' down in Louisville and I seen you shavin' then."

"Well," I says, "the boys tell me you shave in the middle o' the night; and I thought if I done all the things you do mebbe I'd get so's I could hit like you."

"You must be superstitious!" he says. And I told him I was. "I'm a good hitter," he says, "and I'd be a good hitter if I never shaved at all. That don't make no diff'rence."

"Yes, it does," I says. "You prob'ly hit good because you shave at night; but you'd be a better fielder if you shaved in the mornin'."

You see, I was tryin' to be just as crazy as him—though that wasn't hardly possible.

"If that's right," says he, "I'll do my shavin' in the mornin'—because I seen in the papers where the boys says that if I could play the outfield like I can hit I'd be as good as Cobb. They tell me Cobb gets twenty thousand a year."

"No," I says; "he don't get that much—but he gets about ten times as much as you do."

"Well," he says, "I'm goin' to be as good as him, because I need the money."

"What do you want with money?" I says.

He just laughed and didn't say nothin'; but from that time on the water didn't run in the bathtub nights and he done his shavin' after breakfast. I didn't notice, though, that he looked any better in fieldin' practice.

IV

It rained one day in Cincy and they trimmed us two out o' the other three; but it wasn't Elliott's fault.

They had Larry beat four to one in the ninth innin' o' the first game. Archer gets on with two out, and John sends my roomy up to hit—though Benton, a lefthander, is workin' for them. The first thing ◆ Benton serves up there Elliott cracks it a mile over Hobby's head. It ◆ would of been good for three easy—only Archer—playin' safe, o' course—pulls up at third base. Tommy couldn't do nothin' and we ◆ was licked.

The next day he hits one out o' the park off the Indian; but we was ◆ 'way behind and they was nobody on at the time. We copped the last one without usin' no pinch hitters.

I didn't have no trouble with him nights durin' the whole series. He come to bed pretty late while we was there and I told him he'd better not let John catch him at it.

"What would he do?" he says.

◆ *Benton*—John Clebon "Rube" Benton (1887–1937), the Reds' leading lefthander, en route to an 11–7 season with a seventh-place club. Benton pitched for the Reds from 1910 to mid-1915, for the Giants until 1921, and for the Reds again from 1923 to 1925, winning 155 and losing 144.

◆ *Hobby*—Richard Carleton Hoblitzell (1888–1962), the Reds' first baseman since 1908. In mid-1914 Hoblitzell went to the Red Sox, where he finished an 11-year career with a .278 lifetime average in 1,314 games. He retired at 29 to become a dentist, but later returned to baseball as a manager and umpire in the minor leagues. See Jack Kavanagh, "Dick Hoblitzell," *The Ballplayers*, p. 476.

◆ *Tommy*—Outfielder Tommy Leach.

◆ *the Indian*—George Howard "Chief" Johnson (1887–1922), a member of the Winnebago tribe from the reservation in Thurston County, Nebr. Although Johnson was the Reds' leading pitcher in 1913, with a 14–16 record, he pitched only one game for them in 1914, without a decision. He then played for Kansas City in both seasons of the Federal League and thereafter never returned to the major leagues. Including his service in the Federal League, he won 41 and lost 43. Indian players of the time were widely expected to be introversive and defensive about their ancestry, but Johnson was pleasant, voluble, and communicative about his tribal origins. See Normal L. Macht, "Chief Johnson," *The Ballplayers*, p. 530.

"Fine you fifty," I says.

"He can't fine me a dime," he says, "because I ain't got it."

Then I told him he'd be fined all he had comin' if he didn't get in the hotel before midnight; but he just laughed and says he didn't think John had a kick comin' so long as he kep' bustin' the ball.

"Some day you'll go up there and you won't bust it," I says.

"That'll be an accident," he says.

That stopped me and I didn't say nothin'. What could you say to a guy who hated himself like that?

The "accident" happened in St. Louis the first day. We needed two runs in the eighth and Saier and Brid was on, with two out. John tells ◆ Elliott to go up in Pierce's place. The bug goes up and Griner gives ◆ him two bad balls—'way outside. I thought they was goin' to walk him—and it looked like good judgment, because they'd heard what he done in Cincy. But no! Griner comes back with a fast one right over and Elliott pulls it down the right foul line, about two foot foul. He hit it so hard you'd of thought they'd sure walk him then; but Griner gives him another fast one. He slammed it again just as hard, but foul. Then Griner gives him one 'way outside and it's two and three. John says, on the bench:

"If they don't walk him now he'll bust that fence down."

I thought the same and I was sure Griner wouldn't give him nothin' to hit; but he come with a curve and Rigler calls Elliott out. From ◆ where we sat the last one looked low, and I thought Elliott'd make a kick. He come back to the bench smilin'.

John starts for his position, but stopped and ast the bug what was

---

◆ *Brid*—Albert Henry Bridwell (1884–1969), the Cubs shortstop. This was Bridwell's only season for the Cubs. He had played for Cincinnati in 1905, the Braves in 1906–07, the Giants from 1908 to 1911, and the Braves again in 1911–12. He jumped to St. Louis of the Federal League for 1914 and 1915. Including his Federal League service, Bridwell hit .255 in 1,250 games in 11 seasons. See Ritter, *The Glory of Their Times*, pp. 116–29.

◆ *Griner*—Donald Dexter "Dan" Griner (1888–1950), a righthander for the last-place Cardinals, in the process of leading the National League in losses with a 9–22 record. Griner pitched without notable success with the Cardinals from 1912 to 1916 and with the Dodgers in 1918, amassing a lifetime record of 27–55. See Norman L. Macht, "Dan Griner," *The Ballplayers*, pp. 419–20.

◆ *Rigler*—Charles "Cy" Rigler (1882–1935), an umpire in the National League from 1905 to 1935, except for the 1923 season. Because Rigler had umpired in the Central League during Lardner's tenure on the South Bend *Times*, he appears frequently in Lardner's fiction. See Rich Marazzi, "Cy Rigler," *The Ballplayers*, p. 915.

the matter with that one. Any busher I ever knowed would of said, "It was too low," or "It was outside," or "It was inside." Elliott says:

"Nothin' at all. It was right over the middle."

"Why didn't you bust it, then?" says John.

"I was afraid I'd kill somebody," says Elliott, and laughed like a big boob.

John was pretty near chokin'.

"What are you laughin' at?" he says.

"I was thinkin' of a nickel show I seen in Cincinnati," says the bug.

"Well," says John, so mad he couldn't hardly see, "that show and that laugh'll cost you fifty."

We got beat, and I wouldn't of blamed John if he'd fined him his whole season's pay.

Up 'n the room that night I told him he'd better cut out that laughin' stuff when we was gettin' trimmed or he never would have no payday. Then he got confidential.

"Payday wouldn't do me no good," he says. "When I'm all squared up with the club and begin to have a payday I'll only get a hundred bucks at a time, and I'll owe that to some o' you fellers. I wisht we could win the pennant and get in on that World's Series dough. Then I'd get a bunch at once."

"What would you do with a bunch o' dough?" I ast him.

"Don't tell nobody, sport," he says; "but if I ever get five hundred at once I'm goin' to get married."

"Oh!" I says. "And who's the lucky girl?"

"She's a girl up in Muskegon," says Elliott; "and you're right when you call her lucky."

"You don't like yourself much, do you?" I says.

"I got reason to like myself," says he. "You'd like yourself too, if you could hit 'em like me."

"Well," I says, "you didn't show me no hittin' today."

"I couldn't hit because I was laughin' too hard," says Elliott.

"What was it you was laughin' at?" I says.

"I was laughin' at that pitcher," he says. "He thought he had somethin' and he didn't have nothin'."

"He had enough to whiff you with," I says.

"He didn't have nothin'!" says he again. "I was afraid if I busted one off him they'd can him, and then I couldn't never hit agin him no more."

Naturally I didn't have no comeback to that. I just sort o' gasped and got ready to go to sleep; but he wasn't through.

"I wisht you could see this bird!" he says.

"What bird?" I says.

"This dame that's nuts about me," he says.

"Good-looker?" I ast.

"No," he says; "she ain't no bear for looks. They ain't nothin' about her for a guy to rave over till you hear her sing. She sure can holler some."

"What kind o' voice has she got?" I ast.

"A bear," says he.

"No," I says; "I mean is she a barytone or an air?"

"I don't know," he says; "but she's got the loudest voice I ever hear on a woman. She's pretty near got me beat."

"Can you sing?" I says; and I was sorry right afterward that I ast ◆ him that question.

I guess it must of been bad enough to have the water runnin' night after night and to have him wavin' that razor round; but that couldn't of been nothin' to his singin'. Just as soon as I'd pulled that boner he says, "Listen to me!" and starts in on Silver Threads Among the Gold. Mind you, it was after midnight and they was guests all round us tryin' to sleep!

They used to be noise enough in our club when we had Hofman and Sheckard and Richie harmonizin'; but this bug's voice was louder'n ◆

◆ *"Can you sing?—"*—Elston did, in fact, sing. Charles Dryden, in his story from the Cubs' spring-training camp at West Baden, Ind., in the Chicago *Tribune* of March 7, 1908, reported: "Curt Elston, the lefthanded outfielder from Marietta, Ohio, performed for the benefit of the hotel inmates and peasants standing on the balcony."

◆ *Sheckard*—Samuel James Tilden "Jimmy" Sheckard (1878–1947), leftfielder on the Cubs' championship teams of 1906–08 and 1910. Sheckard played for Brooklyn and Baltimore from 1897 to 1905, then for the Cubs from 1906 to 1912. In 1913 he was splitting his last season in the majors between Cincinnati and the Cardinals. In 17 seasons, Sheckard made 2,091 hits, batted .275, and stole 465 bases in 2,121 games. See Lowell L. Blaisdell, "Samuel James Tilden Sheckard," *Biographical Dictionary of American Sports: Baseball*, pp. 510–11.

Richie—Lewis A. "Lurid Lew" Richie (1883–1936), a righthanded pitcher still with the Cubs in 1913, but at the end of his major league tenure. Richie had come into the National League with the Phillies in 1906, gone to the Braves in 1909, and to the Cubs in 1910. He won 15 games for the Cubs in 1911 and 16 in 1912, but was to record only 2–4 in 1913. Overall, he won 75 and lost 64 in eight seasons. Richie teamed with Lardner in pantomimes and pranks on long train trips, and is thought to have been one of the major inspirations for Lardner's first efforts at fiction. See Jack Kavanagh, "Lew Richie," *The Ballplayers*, p. 911.

The reference is to a quartet of players in the Cubs' glory years of 1906–10. On the championship team of 1910 the personnel were Solly Hofman, first tenor, Richie, second tenor and manager, Jimmy Sheckard, baritone, and Orval Overall,

all o' theirn combined. We once had a pitcher named Martin Walsh—◆ brother o' Big Ed's—and I thought he could drownd out the Subway; but this guy made a boiler factory sound like Dummy Taylor. If the whole hotel wasn't awake when he'd howled the first line it's a pipe they was when he cut loose, which he done when he come to "Always young and fair to me." Them words could of been heard easy in East St. Louis.

He didn't get no encore from me, but he goes right through it again—or starts to. I knowed somethin' was goin' to happen before he finished—and somethin' did. The night clerk and the house detective come bangin' at the door. I let 'em in and they had plenty to say. If we made another sound the whole club'd be canned out o' the hotel. I tried to salve 'em, and I says:

"He won't sing no more."

But Elliott swelled up like a poisoned pup.

"Won't I?" he says. "I'll sing all I want to."

"You won't sing in here," says the clerk.

"They ain't room for my voice in here anyways," he says. "I'll go outdoors and sing."

And he puts his clothes on and ducks out. I didn't make no attemp' to stop him. I heard him bellowin' Silver Threads down the corridor and down the stairs, with the clerk and the dick chasin' him all the way and tellin' him to shut up.

Well, the guests make a holler the next mornin'; and the hotel people tells Charlie Williams that he'll either have to let Elliott stay ◆

(*continued from page 345*)
bass. Overall's abrupt retirement from baseball, after losing the opening game of the 1910 World Series, aborted a vaudeville tour projected with the White Sox pitcher Guy Harris "Doc" White, who sang solo with piano accompaniment. See Lardner's account of the end of the quartet in his story, "Cubs Get Losers' Share of Series," Chicago *Tribune*, October 25, 1910.

◆ *Martin Walsh*—Martin Walsh (1889–1954), the youngest of Ed Walsh's 13 siblings, pitched in the minor leagues, mainly the Eastern and Virginia leagues, from 1906 to 1921. The passage refers to Walsh's presence at spring training with the Cubs in 1908. He did not make the team and never appeared in a major league game. Martin Walsh had an excellent tenor voice. He regaled guests at the hotel at West Baden with informal recitals during his spring training with the team, and later recorded several Irish folk songs. His failure to make the team was much regretted, for he was personally very popular, and was expected to become part of the team's quartet.

◆ *Charlie Williams*—Charles G. Williams (c. 1870–1938), secretary of the Chicago Cubs. Williams was in his last season in this position before moving to the Chicago Whales of the Federal League. The merger of 1916 brought him back to the Cubs.

somewheres else or the whole club'll have to move. Charlie tells John, and John was thinkin' o' settlin' the question by releasin' Elliott.

I guess he'd about made up his mind to do it; but that afternoon they had us three to one in the ninth, and we got the bases full, with two down and Larry's turn to hit. Elliott had been sittin' on the bench sayin' nothin'.

"Do you think you can hit one today?" says John.

"I can hit one any day," says Elliott.

"Go up and hit that lefthander, then," says John, "and remember there's nothin' to laugh at."

Sallee was workin'—and workin' good; but that didn't bother the ◆ bug. He cut into one, and it went between Oakes and Whitted like a ◆ shot. He come into third standin' up and we was a run to the good. Sallee was so sore he kind o' forgot himself and took pretty near his full wind-up pitchin' to Tommy. And what did Elliott do but steal home and get away with it clean!

Well, you couldn't can him after that, could you? Charlie gets him a room somewheres and I was relieved of his company that night. The next evenin' we beat it for Chi to play about two weeks at home. He

---

(*continued from page 346*)
Williams was employed by the Cubs or Whales from 1885 to 1917, traveling some 500,000 miles. He was thought to have a remarkable command of the *Official Guide of the Railways*, and was particularly adept at finding obscure trains to which he could have the Cubs' Pullman attached in order to meet scheduled obligations.

◆ *Sallee*—Harry Franklin "Slim" Sallee (1885–1950), a notable lefthander of the period. Sallee, who was 6′3″ but weighed only 180, pitched for the Cardinals from 1908 to mid-1916, for the Giants through 1918, for the Reds until late 1920, and finally for the Giants in 1920–21. His lifetime record was 172–143 in 475 games in 14 seasons. His best single mark was 21–7 in the Reds' pennant year of 1919, when he recorded a remarkably low 20 walks and 24 strikeouts. See A. D. Suehsdorf and Richard J. Thompson, "Slim Sallee's Extraordinary Year," *Baseball Research Journal*, XIX (1990), 10–14.

◆ *Oakes*—Ennis Talmadge "Rebel" Oakes (1886–1948), the Cardinals center-fielder. Oakes, after playing with Cincinnati in 1909, played regularly for St. Louis from 1910 to 1913, before jumping to the Federal League, where he became player-manager of the Pittsburgh club. He did not return to the National League, and wound up his seven years of service with a .279 average in 985 games. See A. D. Suehsdorf, "Rebel Oakes," *The Ballplayers*, p. 815.

Whitted—George Bostic "Possum" Whitted (1890–1962), a utility player who put in eleven seasons in the National League with St. Louis, Boston, Philadelphia, Pittsburgh, and Brooklyn. In 1913 Whitted was in his second season with the Cardinals. Overall, he batted .270 in 1,021 games, divided between the outfield and all four infield positions. His principal distinction is having been traded for Casey Stengel in 1919. See Jack Kavanagh, "Possum Whitted," *The Ballplayers*, pp. 1168.

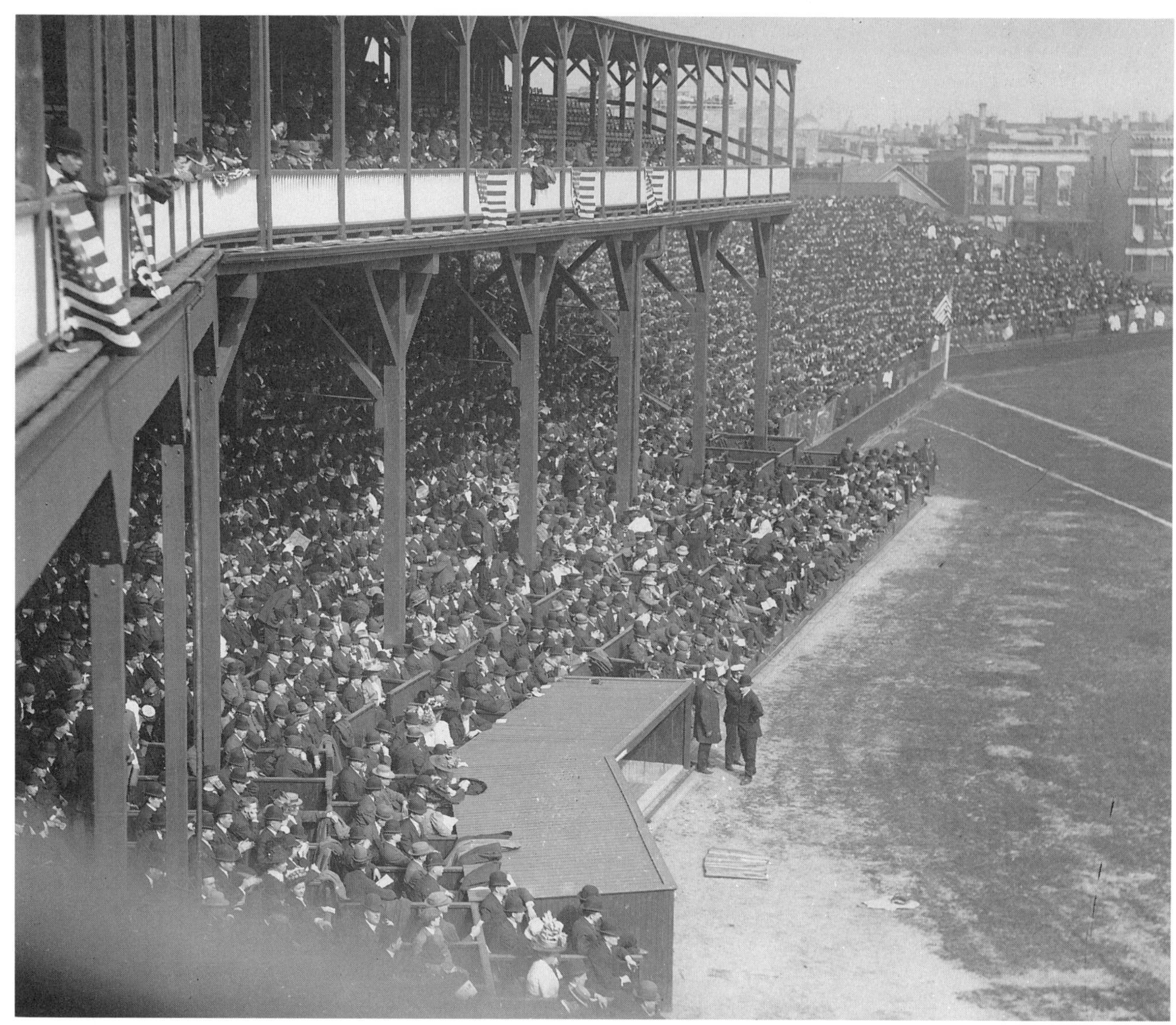

◇ *the park*—The home park of the Cubs at the time of "My Roomy" was a wooden stadium on the West Side of Chicago at Polk, Taylor, Honore, and Wood Streets. This view, probably taken at the 1908 World Series, shows stands erected in that year. (Chicago Historical Society)

didn't tell nobody where he roomed there and I didn't see nothin' of him, 'cep' out to the park. I ast him what he did with himself nights ◇ and he says:

"Same as I do on the road—borrow some dough some place and go to the nickel shows."

"You must be stuck on 'em," I says.

"Yes," he says; "I like the ones where they kill people—because I want to learn how to do it. I may have that job some day."

"Don't pick on me," I says.

"Oh," says the bug, "you never can tell who I'll pick on."

It seemed as if he just couldn't learn nothin' about fieldin', and finally John told him to keep out o' the practice.

"A ball might hit him in the temple and croak him," says John.

But he busted up a couple o' games for us at home, beatin' Pittsburgh once and Cincy once.

V

They give me a great big room at the hotel in Pittsburgh; so the fellers picked it out for the poker game. We was playin' along about ten o'clock one night when in come Elliott—the earliest he'd showed up since we'd been roomin' together. They was only five of us playin' and Tom ast him to sit in.

"I'm busted," he says.

"Can you play poker?" I ast him.

"They's nothin' I can't do!" he says. "Slip me a couple o' bucks and I'll show you."

So I slipped him a couple o' bucks and honestly hoped he'd win, because I knowed he never had no dough. Well, Tom dealt him a hand and he picks it up and says:

"I only got five cards."

"How many do you want?" I says.

"Oh," he says, "if that's all I get I'll try to make 'em do."

The pot was cracked and raised, and he stood the raise. I says to myself: "There goes my two bucks!" But no—he comes out with three queens and won the dough. It was only about seven bucks; but you'd of thought it was a million to see him grab it. He laughed like a kid.

"Guess I can't play this game!" he says; and he had me fooled for a minute—I thought he must of been kiddin' when he complained of only havin' five cards.

He copped another pot right afterward and was sittin' there with about eleven bucks in front of him when Jim opens a roodle pot for ◆ a buck. I stays and so does Elliott. Him and Jim both drawed one card and I took three. I had kings or queens—I forget which. I didn't help 'em none; so when Jim bets a buck I throws my hand away.

"How much can I bet?" says the bug.

◆ *a roodle pot*—A pot in which a token called the roodle, such as the crown from a beer bottle, is placed. The winner of that hand, and thus of the roodle, retains the roodle until the next occasion when he is the dealer. Possession of the roodle gives him the right to determine what type of poker is to be played in the hand he deals. The roodle is then placed in that pot and passes to the winner of the hand. For explication of this point I am indebted to the late Lucius W. Hilton.

"You can raise Jim a buck if you want to," I says.

So he bets two dollars. Jim comes back at him. He comes right back at Jim. Jim raises him again and he tilts Jim right back. Well, when he'd boosted Jim with the last buck he had, Jim says:

"I'm ready to call. I guess you got me beat. What have you got?"

"I know what I've got, all right," says Elliott. "I've got a straight." And he throws his hand down. Sure enough, it was a straight, eight high. Jim pretty near fainted and so did I.

The bug had started pullin' in the dough when Jim stops him.

"Here! Wait a minute!" says Jim. "I thought you had somethin.' I filled up." Then Jim lays down his nine full.

"You beat me, I guess," says Elliott, and he looked like he'd lost his last friend.

"Beat you?" says Jim. "Of course I beat you! What did you think I had?"

"Well," says the bug, "I thought you might have a small flush or somethin'."

When I regained consciousness he was beggin' for two more bucks.

"What for?" I says. "To play poker with? You're barred from the game for life!"

"Well," he says, "if I can't play no more I want to go to sleep, and you fellers will have to get out o' this room."

Did you ever hear o' nerve like that? This was the first night he'd came in before twelve and he orders the bunch out so's he can sleep! We politely suggested to him to go to Brooklyn.

Without sayin' a word he starts in on his Silver Threads; and it wasn't two minutes till the game was busted up and the bunch—all but me—was out o' there. I'd of beat it too, only he stopped yellin' as soon as they'd went.

"You're some buster!" I says. "You bust up ball games in the afternoon and poker games at night."

"Yes," he says; "that's my business—bustin' things."

And before I knowed what he was about he picked up the pitcher of ice-water that was on the floor and throwed it out the window—through the glass and all.

Right then I give him a plain talkin' to. I tells him how near he come to gettin' canned down in St. Louis because he raised so much Cain singin' in the hotel.

"But I had to keep my voice in shape," he says. "If I ever get dough enough to get married the girl and me'll go out singin' together."

"Out where?" I ast.

"Out on the vaudeville circuit," says Elliott.

"Well," I says, "if her voice is like yours you'll be wastin' money if you travel round. Just stay up in Muskegon and we'll hear you, all right!"

I told him he wouldn't never get no dough if he didn't behave himself. That, even if we got in the World's Series, he wouldn't be with us—unless he cut out the foolishness.

"We ain't goin' to get in no World's Series," he says, "and I won't never get a bunch o' money at once; so it looks like I couldn't get married this fall."

Then I told him we played a city series every fall. He'd never thought o' that and it tickled him to death. I told him the losers always got about five hundred apiece and that we were about due to win it and get about eight hundred. "But," I says, "we still got a good chance for the old pennant; and if I was you I wouldn't give up hope o' that yet—not where John can hear you anyway."

"No," he says, "we won't win no pennant, because he won't let me play reg'lar; but I don't care so long as we're sure o' that city-series dough."

"You ain't sure of it if you don't behave," I says.

"Well," says he, very serious, "I guess I'll behave." And he did—till we made our first Eastern trip.

VI

We went to Boston first, and the crazy bunch goes out and piles up a three-run lead on us in seven innin's the first day. It was the pitcher's turn to lead off in the eighth, so up goes Elliott to bat for him. He kisses the first thing they hands him for three bases; and we says, on the bench: "Now we'll get 'em!"—because, you know, a three-run lead wasn't nothin' in Boston.

"Stay right on that bag!" John hollers to Elliott.

Mebbe if John hadn't said nothin' to him everythin' would of been all right; but when Perdue starts to pitch the first ball to Tommy, ◆ Elliott starts to steal home. He's out as far as from here to Seattle.

◆ *Perdue*—Hubbard E. "Hub" Perdue (1882–1968), a Braves righthander in the course of a 16–13 season. Perdue had been with the Cubs in spring training in 1907, but had not made the team. He pitched for the Braves from 1911 through the early part of the 1914 season, then for the Cardinals through 1915, winning 51 and losing 63 in 161 appearances. Perdue's major league record is deceptive;

If I'd been carryin' a gun I'd of shot him right through the heart. As it was, I thought John'd kill him with a bat, because he was standin' there with a couple of 'em, waitin' for his turn; but I guess John was too stunned to move. He didn't even seem to see Elliott when he went to the bench. After I'd cooled off a little I says:

"Beat it and get into your clothes before John comes in. Then go to the hotel and keep out o' sight."

When I got up in the room afterward, there was Elliott, lookin' as innocent and happy as though he'd won fifty bucks with a pair o' treys.

"I thought you might of killed yourself," I says.

"What for?" he says.

"For that swell play you made," says I.

"What was the matter with the play?" ast Elliott, surprised. "It was all right when I done it in St. Louis."

"Yes," I says; "but they was two out in St. Louis and we wasn't no three runs behind."

"Well," he says, "if it was all right in St. Louis I don't see why it was wrong here."

"It's a diff'rent climate here," I says, too disgusted to argue with him.

"I wonder if they'd let me sing in this climate?" says Elliott.

"No," I says. "Don't sing in this hotel, because we don't want to get fired out o' here—the eats is too good."

"All right," he says. "I won't sing." But when I starts down to supper he says: "I'm li'ble to do somethin' worse'n sing."

He didn't show up in the dinin' room and John went to the boxin' show after supper; so it looked like him and Elliott wouldn't run into each other till the murder had left John's heart. I was glad o' that—because a Mass'chusetts jury might not consider it justifiable hommercide if one guy croaked another for givin' the Boston club a game.

I went down to the corner and had a couple o' beers; and then I come straight back, intendin' to hit the hay. The elevator boy had went

---

(*continued from page 351*)
there is reason to believe he was much more able than it indicates. A southerner, he starred in the Southern Association and took pride in several lifetime records he set there. Perdue earned one of the many nicknames bestowed by sportswriter Charles Dryden: the Gallatin Squash—a reference to his hometown of Gallatin, Tenn., and his unathletic build. See Jack Kavanagh, "Hub Perdue," *The Ballplayers*, p. 854.

for a drink or somethin', and they was two old ladies already waitin' in the car when I stepped in. Right along after me comes Elliott.

"Where's the boy that's supposed to run this car?" he says. I told him the boy'd be right back; but he says: "I can't wait. I'm much too sleepy."

And before I could stop him he'd slammed the door and him and I and the poor old ladies was shootin' up.

"Let us off at the third floor, please!" says one o' the ladies, her voice kind o' shakin'.

"Sorry, madam," says the bug; "but this is a express and we don't stop at no third floor."

I grabbed his arm and tried to get him away from the machinery; but he was as strong as a ox and he throwed me agin the side o' the car like I was a baby. We went to the top faster'n I ever rode in an elevator before. And then we shot down to the bottom, hittin' the bumper down there so hard I thought we'd be smashed to splinters.

The ladies was too scared to make a sound durin' the first trip; but while we was goin' up and down the second time—even faster'n the first—they begun to scream. I was hollerin' my head off at him to quit and he was makin' more noise than the three of us—pretendin' he was the locomotive and the whole crew o' the train.

Don't never ask me how many times we went up and down! The women fainted on the third trip and I guess I was about as near it as I'll ever get. The elevator boy and the bellhops and the waiters and the night clerk and everybody was jumpin' round the lobby screamin'; but no one seemed to know how to stop us.

Finally—on about the tenth trip, I guess—he slowed down and stopped at the fifth floor, where we was roomin'. He opened the door and beat it for the room, while I, though I was tremblin' like a leaf, run the car down to the bottom.

The night clerk knowed me pretty well and knowed I wouldn't do nothin' like that; so him and I didn't argue, but just got to work together to bring the old women to. While we was doin' that Elliott must of run down the stairs and slipped out o' the hotel, because when they sent the officers up to the room after him he'd blowed.

They was goin' to fire the club out; but Charlie had a good stand-in with Amos, the proprietor, and he fixed it up to let us stay— ◆

◆ *Amos*—Amos H. Whipple (1856–1916), proprietor of the Copley Square Hotel, at which the Cubs and most other visiting National League teams stayed while in Boston in this period.

providin' Elliott kep' away. The bug didn't show up at the ball park next day and we didn't see no more of him till we got on the rattler for New York. Charlie and John both bawled him, but they give him a berth—an upper—and we pulled into the Grand Central Station without him havin' made no effort to wreck the train.

VII

I'd studied the thing pretty careful, but hadn't come to no conclusion. I was sure he wasn't no stew, because none o' the boys had ever saw ◆ him even take a glass o' beer, and I couldn't never detect the odor o' booze on him. And if he'd been a dope I'd of knew about it—roomin' with him.

There wouldn't of been no mystery about it if he'd been a lefthand pitcher—but he wasn't. He wasn't nothin' but a whale of a hitter and he throwed with his right arm. He hit lefthanded, o' course; but so ◆ did Saier and Brid and Schulte and me, and John himself; and none of us was violent. I guessed he must of been just a plain nut and li'ble to break out any time.

They was a letter waitin' for him at New York, and I took it, intendin' to give it to him at the park, because I didn't think they'd let him room at the hotel; but after breakfast he come up to the room, with his suitcase. It seems he'd promised John and Charlie to be good, and made it so strong they b'lieved him.

I give him his letter, which was addressed in a girl's writin' and come from Muskegon.

"From the girl?" I says.

"Yes," he says; and, without openin' it, he tore it up and throwed it out the window.

"Had a quarrel?" I ast.

"No, no," he says, "but she can't tell me nothin' I don't know already. Girls always writes the same junk. I got one from her in Pittsburgh, but I didn't read it."

◆ *he wasn't no stew*—This is inconsistent with Lardner's account of Elston's searching for Frank Chance while drunk, mentioned at the outset. There is no evidence that Elston had an alcohol problem, and there is some that he did not. While he played for Chattanooga in 1913, the Chattanooga *Times* for July 10 reported that following the release of pitcher Bill Chappelle no one on the team had a drinking problem.

◆ *he throwed with his right arm.*—Elston in fact both batted and threw lefthanded.

"I guess you ain't so stuck on her," I says.

He swells up and says:

"Of course I'm stuck on her! If I wasn't, do you think I'd be goin' round with this bunch and gettin' insulted all the time? I'm stickin' here because o' that series dough, so's I can get hooked."

"Do you think you'd settle down if you was married?" I ast him.

"Settle down?" he says. "Sure, I'd settle down. I'd be so happy that I wouldn't have to look for no excitement."

Nothin' special happened that night 'cep' that he come in the room about one o'clock and woke me up by pickin' up the foot of the bed and droppin' it on the floor, sudden-like.

"Give me a key to the room," he says.

"You must of had a key," I says, "or you couldn't of got in."

"That's right!" he says, and beat it to bed.

One o' the reporters must of told Elliott that John had ast for waivers on him and New York had refused to waive, because next mornin' he come to me with that dope.

"New York's goin' to win this pennant!" he says.

"Well," I says, "they will if some one else don't. But what of it?"

"I'm goin' to play with New York," he says, "so's I can get the World's Series dough."

"How you goin' to get away from this club?" I ast.

"Just watch me!" he says. "I'll be with New York before this series is over."

Well, the way he goes after the job was original, anyway. Rube'd ◆◇ had one of his good days the day before and we'd got a trimmin'; but this second day the score was tied up at two runs apiece in the tenth, and Big Jeff'd been wabblin' for two or three innin's. ◆◇

Well, he walks Saier and me, with one out and Mac sends for Matty,

---

◆ *Rube*—Richard William "Rube" Marquard (1889–1980), the outstanding left-hander of the New York Giants. With the Giants since 1908, Marquard recorded seasons of 24–7 in 1911 and 26–11 in 1912, the latter including a string of 19 consecutive victories, which remains the record for a single season. In 1913 Marquard went 23–10, but he never again won 20. He remained with the Giants into mid-1915, then pitched for Brooklyn, Cincinnati, and the Boston Braves until 1925, winning 205 and losing 177. He was elected to the Baseball Hall of Fame in 1970. See Fred Stein, "Richard William Marquard," *Biographical Dictionary of American Sports: Baseball*, pp. 383–84; Ritter, *The Glory of Their Times*, pp. 1–19.
◆ *Big Jeff*—Charles Monroe "Jeff" Tesreau (1889–1946), the Giants' star right-hander, who was 6′2″ and 218 pounds. Tesreau had a short but spectacular career, 16–7 in his rookie season of 1912, followed by 22–13 in 1913 and 26–10 in 1914.

◇ *Rube*—Rube Marquard in the uniform of the Cincinnati Reds in 1921. (George E. Brace collection)

who was warmed up and ready. John sticks Elliott in in Brid's place and the bug pulls one into the rightfield stand.

It's a cinch McGraw thinks well of him then, and might of went after him if he hadn't went crazy the next afternoon. We're tied up in the ninth and Matty's workin'. John sends Elliott up with the bases choked; but he doesn't go right up to the plate. He walks over to their bench and calls McGraw out. Mac tells us about it afterward.

"I can bust up this game right here!" says Elliott.

"Go ahead," says Mac; "but be careful he don't whiff you."

Then the bug pulls it.

(*continued from page 355*)
Thereafter he was less successful, but in 1918 he wound up his career with a lifetime record of 118–72 in 247 games. In 1919 Tesreau became baseball coach at Dartmouth College, a position he held until his death. See Jack Kavanagh, "Jeff Tesreau," *The Ballplayers*, p. 1077.

◇ *Big Jeff*—Jeff Tesreau warming up for the Giants, 1917. (George E. Brace collection)

"If I whiff," he says, "will you get me on your club?"

"Sure!" says Mac, just as anybody would.

By this time Bill Klem was hollerin' about the delay; so up goes ◆◇ Elliott and gives the worst burlesque on tryin' to hit that you ever see. Matty throws one a mile outside and high, and the bug swings like it was right over the heart. Then Matty throws one at him and he ducks out o' the way—but swings just the same. Matty must of been wise by this time, for he pitches one so far outside that the Chief almost has ◆

◇ *Big Jeff*—Drawing of Jeff Tesreau by Lawrence Semon. (National Baseball Library, Cooperstown, New York)

◆ *Bill Klem*—William J. Klem (1874–1951), most famous of umpires. Klem was active in the National League from 1905 to 1940, and occasionally thereafter while serving as chief of staff of the league's umpires. See Lowell L. Blaisdell, "William Joseph Klem," *Biographical Dictionary of American Sports: Baseball*, pp. 309–10.

◆ *Chief*—John Tortes Meyers (1880–1971), the Giants catcher and one of the outstanding receivers of the period. One of the Mission Indians of Southern California, Meyers attended Dartmouth on funds allocated because of the college's

◇ *Bill Klem*—The William J. Klem plaque at the National Baseball Hall of Fame and Museum, Cooperstown, New York.

to go to the coachers' box after it. Elliott takes his third healthy and runs through the field down to the clubhouse.

We got beat in the eleventh; and when we went in to dress he has his street clothes on. Soon as he seen John comin' he says: "I got to see McGraw!" And he beat it.

John was goin' to the fights that night; but before he leaves the hotel he had waivers on Elliott from everybody and had sold him to Atlanta. ◆

"And," says John, "I don't care if they pay for him or not."

My roomy blows in about nine and got the letter from John out of his box. He was goin' to tear it up, but I told him they was news in it. He opens it and reads where he's sold. I was still sore at him; so I says:

"Thought you was goin' to get on the New York club?"

"No," he says. "I got turned down cold. McGraw says he wouldn't have me in his club. He says he'd had Charlie Faust—and that was ◆ enough for him."

(*continued from page 357*)
origin as a school for Indians. He did not graduate, but rather went into professional baseball. With the Giants from 1909 to 1915 and Brooklyn and Boston in 1916–17, Meyers played 992 games in the National League and hit .291. See Ritter, *The Glory of Their Times*, pp. 162–76.

◆ *Atlanta*—A club of the Class A Southern Association. In 1908 Elston was released to Nashville of the Southern Association, but refused to report, wishing to play closer to his home in Marietta. The Cubs accommodated him by sending him to Fort Wayne. Elston began the 1913 season with Chattanooga of the Southern Association, but disliked playing in the South and wrote to Jack Hendricks, the manager at Denver in the Western League, who had managed Elston at Fort Wayne, requesting a transfer. Hendricks obliged him, and Elston closed out his professional career in Denver at the end of the 1913 season.

At the time of Elston's release by the Cubs, the Chicago *Inter Ocean* for April 5 characterized him as a fair minor league outfielder with a chance to advance. He was said to be "not a dead sure catch," and weak on fielding ground balls or line hits—which is consistent with Lardner's description. He was also said not to have shown much batting ability against minor league pitching, however.

By 1910–12, when he played for Providence of the Eastern (International) League, Elston seems to have overcome his fielding inadequacies, and was considered by the standards of the high minor leagues an adept fielder. Probably because of his age, he never had a second opportunity at the major league level, although most of the writers who covered his teams believed that he deserved one. He had begun his career as a lefthanded pitcher in 1903 after earlier experience as a railroad man in the West. Because of his hitting ability, he shifted to the outfield permanently in 1906. Accordingly, his one major league trial in 1908 was at a relatively late age, 29.

◆ *Charlie Faust*—Charles Victor Faust (1880–1915), a Kansas Farmer who became a human mascot for the Giants. Faust was seemingly just an eccentric, but actually was a psychotic who had been told by a fortune-teller that he could be the greatest

He had a kind o' crazy look in his eyes; so when he starts up to the room I follows him.

"What are you goin' to do now?" I says.

"I'm goin' to sell this ticket to Atlanta," he says, "and go back to Muskegon, where I belong."

"I'll help you pack," I says.

"No," says the bug. "I come into this league with this suit o' clothes and a collar. They can have the rest of it." Then he sits down on the bed and begins to cry like a baby. "No series dough for me," he blubbers, "and no weddin' bells! My girl'll die when she hears about it!"

Of course that made me feel kind o' rotten, and I says:

"Brace up, boy! The best thing you can do is go to Atlanta and try hard. You'll be up here again next year."

"You can't tell me where to go!" he says, and he wasn't cryin' no more. "I'll go where I please—and I'm li'ble to take you with me."

I didn't want no argument, so I kep' still. Pretty soon he goes up to the lookin'-glass and stares at himself for five minutes. Then, all of a sudden, he hauls off and takes a wallop at his reflection in the glass. Naturally he smashed the glass all to pieces and he cut his hand somethin' awful.

Without lookin' at it he come over to me and says: "Well, good-by, sport!"—and holds out his other hand to shake. When I starts to shake with him he smears his bloody hand all over my map. Then he laughed like a wild man and run out o' the room and out o' the hotel.

VIII

Well, boys, my sleep was broke up for the rest o' the season. It might of been because I was used to sleepin' in all kinds o' racket and excitement, and couldn't stand for the quiet after he'd went—or it might of been because I kep' thinkin' about him and feelin' sorry for him.

(*continued from page 358*)
of pitchers if he joined the Giants. He convinced John McGraw—apparently on the basis of his middle name—that he was a source of good luck who could win the 1911 pennant for the Giants. Faust, who was tall and thin, warmed up daily, but was allowed to pitch only twice, both times in relief. He was also with the team in 1912. Faust became a drawing card in baseball and also in vaudeville, but was declared insane in Portland, Oreg., in June 1914, and died a year later. See Ken Turetzky, "Charlie Faust," *The Ballplayers*, p. 326.

I of'en wondered if he'd settle down and be somethin' if he could get married; and finally I got to b'lievin' he would. So when we was dividin' the city-series dough I was thinkin' of him and the girl. Our share o' the money—the losers', as usual— was twelve thousand seven ◆ hundred sixty bucks or somethin' like that. They was twenty-one of us and that meant six hundred seven bucks apiece. We was just goin' to cut it up that way when I says:

"Why not give a divvy to poor old Elliott?"

About fifteen of 'em at once told me that I was crazy. You see, when he got canned he owed everybody in the club. I guess he'd stuck me for the most—about seventy bucks—but I didn't care nothin' about that. I knowed he hadn't never reported to Atlanta, and I thought he was prob'ly busted and a bunch o' money might make things all right for him and the other songbird.

I made quite a speech to the fellers, tellin' 'em how he'd cried when he left us and how his heart'd been set on gettin' married on the series dough. I made it so strong that they finally fell for it. Our shares was cut to five hundred eighty apiece, and John sent him a check for a full share.

For a while I was kind o' worried about what I'd did. I didn't know if I was doin' right by the girl to give him the chance to marry her.

He'd told me she was stuck on him, and that's the only excuse I had for tryin' to fix it up between 'em; but, b'lieve me, if she was my sister or a friend o' mine I'd just as soon of had her manage the Cincinnati Club as marry that bird. I thought to myself:

"If she's all right she'll take acid in a month—and it'll be my fault; but if she's really stuck on him they must be somethin' wrong with her too, so what's the diff'rence?"

Then along comes this letter that I told you about. It's from some friend of hisn up there—and they's a note from him. I'll read 'em to you and then I got to beat it for the station:

"*Dear Sir:* They have got poor Elliott locked up and they are goin' to take him to the asylum at Kalamazoo. He thanks you for the check, and we will use the money to see that he is made comf'table.

"When the poor boy come back here he found that his girl was married to Joe Bishop, who runs a soda fountain. She had wrote to him about it, but he did not read her letters. The news drove him

---

◆ *the losers', as usual*—As noted in *You Know Me Al*, the White Sox won the 1913 City Series, four games to two.

crazy—poor boy—and he went to the place where they was livin' with a baseball bat and very near killed 'em both. Then he marched down the street singin' Silver Threads Among the Gold at the top of his voice. They was goin' to send him to prison for assault with intent to kill, but the jury decided he was crazy.

"He wants to thank you again for the money.

"Yours truly, Jim——"

I can't make out his last name—but it don't make no diff'rence. Now I'll read you his note:

"*Old Roomy:* I was at bat twice and made two hits; but I guess I did not meet 'em square. They tell me they are both alive yet, which I did not mean 'em to be. I hope they got good curve-ball pitchers where I am goin'. I sure can bust them curves—can't I, sport?

"Yours, B. Elliott. ◆

"P. S.—The B stands for Buster."

That's all of it, fellers; and you can see I had some excuse for not hittin'. You can also see why I ain't never goin' to room with no bug again—not for John or nobody else!

◆ *B. Elliott*—Elston's personal history differed diametrically from Elliott's end. Elston married Mrs. Winifred Laurie Little on September 4, 1914, and remained married to her until her death in 1947. He operated the Crescent Cafe, a restaurant in Marietta, until about 1929, and was then stationary engineer at the Peoples Bank & Trust Co. of Marietta until retiring in 1949, a year before his death. *His* history, at least, had a happy ending. See his obituary in the Marietta *Daily Times*, May 17, 1950.

Sick 'Em

This is just between I and you. I don't want it to go no further. In the first place a feller that's had rotten luck as long as Red is entitled to ◆◇ the credit when his club fin'lly comes through and cops. In the second place if I was to tell the newspapers or the public that I was the one that really done it they'd laugh at me. They'd say: "How could you of did it when you was sittin' on the bench all summer?"

But you know I wouldn't lie to you, Jake, and you know I don't care ◆ nothin' about the honor or that bunk.

"Sick 'Em" was published in *The Saturday Evening Post*, CLXXXVII (July 25, 1914), 16–18, 33–35.

◆ *Red*—Charles Sebastian Dooin (1879–1952), manager of the Philadelphia Phillies. A fine defensive catcher, Dooin broke in with the Phillies in 1902 and became manager of the team in 1910. A broken ankle in that year and a broken leg in 1911 reduced his mobility, ending his days as a regular. He remained manager through 1914 and subsequently played for the Reds and Giants in 1915 and 1916. As a player, Dooin hit .240 in 1,289 games. See Norman L. Macht, "Red Dooin," *The Ballplayers*, pp. 286–87.

The chronology of the story is inconsistent between 1913 and 1914, but the preponderance of references are to 1914. On the team, see Rich Westcott and Frank Bilovsky, *The New Phillies Encyclopedia* (Philadelphia: Temple University Press, 1993), p. 46.

◆ *Jake*—Presumably, Jake Atz, who was managing Fort Worth of the Texas League in 1914.

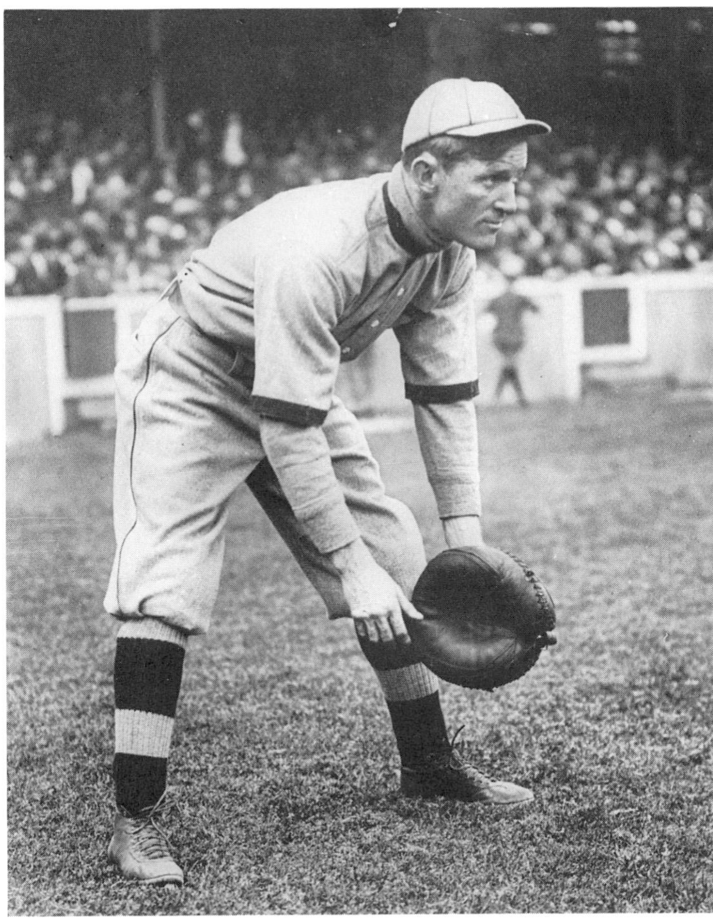

◇ *Red*—Charles Sebastian Dooin, manager of the 1914 Philadelphia Phillies. (National Baseball Library, Cooperstown, New York)

The little old World's Serious check is honor enough for me. So let 'em say that it was Red's managin' and them two guys' pitchin' that won for us, and let it go at that. I'm just tellin' you this to get it offen my chest.

Well, you must of read about Lefty Smith last fall, after we'd grabbed ◆ him. He's a wop and Smith ain't his real name, but it's the one he's went under ever since he started pitchin'. I heard his right name oncet, but I ain't got time to tell it to you to-day. It's longer'n Eppa ◆◇

◆ *Lefty Smith*—A fictional character.

◆ *longer'n Eppa Rixey*—Eppa Rixey, Jr. (1891–1963), the Phillies' budding star lefthander. He had come to the Phillies from the University of Virginia in 1912, and in 1914 was on his way to his worst season, 2–11. He was, however, to be a 20-game winner four times and to amass a lifetime record of 266–251 over the course of 21 seasons. His 266 victories were the National League record for a lefthanded pitcher until broken by Warren Spahn in 1959. After the 1920 season

◇ *longer'n Eppa Rixey*—Eppa Rixey in a Phillies uniform, about 1915. (National Baseball Library, Cooperstown, New York)

Rixey. Anyway, the papers was full o' what him and Fogarty had did ◆ at Fort Wayne; how they'd worked a hundred games between 'em and copped the Central League pennant, and how all the scouts had went ◆ after 'em.

(*continued from page 363*)
Rixey was traded to Cincinnati, where he remained active until 1933. He was elected to the Baseball Hall of Fame in 1963, a month before his death. The reference here is to his height, 6′5″. He was not only the tallest of the great pitchers, but one of the best-educated players: he held a bachelor's degree in chemistry from the University of Virginia, and in the year of the story, 1914, took an M.A. in Latin at the same institution. See Robert G. Weaver, "Eppa Rixey, Jr.," *Biographical Dictionary of American Sports: Baseball*, p. 474; Adam Bell, "Eppa Rixey: A Virginia Gentleman in the Hall of Fame," *University of Virginia Alumni News*, July/August, 1987, pp. 21–24.

◆ *Fogarty*—A fictional character.

◆ *the Central League pennant*—Fort Wayne won the Central League pennant in 1912 and finished second to Grand Rapids in 1913.

Pat had stopped off there when we was goin' West one trip and had ◆ saw 'em both work, and they'd looked so good to him that he'd advised Red to buy the both o' them. Well, Red told the big boss and he bought Smitty; paid five thousand for him, they say. They wanted even more for Fogarty; so we just put in a draft for him. But pretty near all the other clubs done the same and the Cubs got him.

Red thought Smitty'd fit in nice with our bunch. We needed all the pitchers we could get after what the Feds done to us. Most o' these ◆ guys with all the toutin' turns out to be dubs; but Smitty had a whale of a record, full o' no-hit games and shut-outs. He'd whiffed more guys than Rube Waddell or Johnson, and had tooken part in fifty games. Besides, he had some pitchin' sense, which is more'n you can say for most o' them bushers. Fogarty's record was just as good as Smitty's; but, o' course we wasn't so much interested in him. We figured from what Smitty'd did and from what Pat said about him that he'd come right through from the jump and show enough to make Red stick him in there in his reg'lar turn.

Well, we got down South and had a chancet to look him over. You could spot him right off the reel for a wop, but he was a handsome devil, big as a house, and with black eyes and black hair.

He didn't show nothin' for a couple o' weeks, but nobody lost no sleep over that; we thought he was takin' it easy and was one o' them careful birds that comes slow. Along in the third week we had some practice games between ourselves and Red starts Smitty agin the second club in one o' them. Say, he had a fast one like Waddell's and ◆◇

◆ *Pat*—Pat Moran, coach of the Phillies. He was to replace Dooin as manager in 1915 and would go on to win the National League pennant—the Phillies' last until 1950.

◆ *what the Feds done to us*—The Phillies lost two starting pitchers to the Federal League: Tom Seaton, who had led the National League in victories with 27–12 in 1913, and Ad Brennan, who had been 14–12. This passage is consistent only with the story's being laid in 1914.

◆ *Waddell*—George Edward "Rube" Waddell (1876–1914), the brilliant, erratic, and unstable lefthander of the early twentieth century. From 1897 to 1901, Waddell played for Louisville, Pittsburgh, and Chicago of the National League without notable success, then jumped to the American League, where he achieved instant stardom with the Philadelphia Athletics. He led the American League annually in strikeouts through 1907, his last season with the Athletics. He then pitched for the Browns through 1910, finishing with a lifetime major league record of 191–141, an earned run average of 2.16, 50 shutouts, and a remarkable 2,316 strikeouts in only 407 games. Waddell entered the Baseball Hall of Fame in 1946. See Douglas D. Martin, "George Edward Waddell," *Biographical Dictionary of American Sports: Baseball*, pp. 579–80.

◇ *Waddell*—The George Edward Waddell plaque at the National Baseball Hall of Fame and Museum, Cooperstown, New York.

a cross fire like Sallee's! But he seemed to be afraid he'd show too much. He'd begin an innin' by puttin' more stuff on the ball than I ever seen, but after he'd threw two or three he'd ease up and lob 'em over. Them goofs couldn't see 'em when he was tryin'; but, say, they hit 'em acrost the state line when he let up. That didn't bother us none, neither, for we figured that he had the stuff when he wanted to use it, and when he got in shape he'd burn up the league.

We played a few games with them Southern clubs and Smitty kept on the same way. Maybe he'd pitch hard to one guy in a innin', but then he'd quit workin' and just float 'em up there like a balloon. Red told him one day to cut loose and see if he could go the route. He might just as well of told him to shave himself with a dish o' prunes. He went right along the way he'd been doin', pitchin' like a bear cat oncet in a while and sloppin' 'em over the rest o' the time. We was

◇ *Alexander*—Grover Cleveland Alexander in a Phillies uniform, about 1917. (National Baseball Library, Cooperstown, New York)

playin' the Richmond Club and they scored eleven runs, but Red ◆ wouldn't take him out.

After the game Red give him a bawlin' and ast him what was the matter. He said, Nothin'; he was doin' the best he knowed how. Red says: "You ain't doin' no such a thing. You've got the stuff, but you won't let go of it. Are you lazy or what?" Smitty didn't say a word. Then Red ast him if he wasn't in shape, and he said, Yes, he guessed he was. "Well," says Red, "you'll have to cut out the monkey business or I'll put the rollers under you!"

We stopped off in Washin'ton for a couple of exhibition games and ◆ broke even with 'em. Then we went home and tackled the Athaletics in the spring serious. Alexander trimmed 'em and they licked Mayer. ◆◇ Red sent Smitty at 'em in the third game and he was worse'n ever. I ◆ thought he'd be massacreed.

For two innin's they couldn't touch him and then he pulled the old stuff. Cy Young could of run to the plate as fast as the balls this bird throwed. It was just like hittin' fungoes for them Athaletics. A slow ball's all right in its place, but it's got to be mixed up with somethin' else. The way Smitty mixed 'em up was to throw one slow, and then one slower, and then one slower yet. Along in the fourth, before Red took him out, you could of went on one o' them street cars from the hotel to the ball park in St. Louis between the time he let go o' the pill and when one o' them Mackmen kissed it. Pat was crazy. He says:

◇ *Alexander*—The Grover Cleveland Alexander plaque at the National Baseball Hall of Fame and Museum, Cooperstown, New York

◆ *the Richmond club*—A member of the Class C Virginia League.

◆ *We . . . broke even with 'em*—Rather, the Senators won both games, 6–1 on March 26 and 5–2 on March 27.

◆ *Alexander*—Grover Cleveland Alexander (1887–1950), the Phillies' ace and the National League's outstanding pitcher of the period. Alexander had come to the Phillies in 1911 and won 28 games as a rookie. In 1914 he was to win 27, and in 1915 would go 31–10, the first of three consecutive seasons in which he would win 30 games or more. Fearing—correctly—that Alexander would be drafted, the Phillies sold him to the Chicago Cubs before the 1918 season. Alexander pitched for Chicago following the War and until early in the 1926 season, for the Cardinals through 1929, and finally for the Phillies again in 1930. In 20 seasons he won 373, exactly equaling Christy Mathewson's total, lost just 208, pitched 90 shutouts, and walked an almost incredibly low total of 953 batters in 5,189 innings. Because of his well-publicized alcoholism, Alexander's post-major league career was little short of tragic. He was elected to the Hall of Fame in 1938. See A. D. Suehsdorf, "Grover Cleveland Alexander," *Biographical Dictionary of American Sports: Baseball*, pp. 4–6.

◆ *they licked Mayer*—Actually, Joe Oeschger won the first game for the Phillies and Erskine Mayer, as stated, lost the second. The Athletics won the series, four games to three.

"I'd give my glove to know what's the matter with him. He was the best pitcher in the world when I looked him over, and now he couldn't hold a job with a high school. He must of been full o' dope at Fort Wayne."

Meantime I got a hold o' one o' the Chi papers and seen where they was pannin' Fogarty. They said he seemed to be as fast as Johnson and to have a lot o' stuff, but he didn't show no more ambish than a horse car. I read the piece to Smitty.

"Your old sidekick don't seem to be cuttin' up much," I says.

"He ain't no sidekick o' mine," Smitty says.

"You and him was together at Fort Wayne, wasn't you?" says I.

"Yes," says Smitty; "and he's a false alarm."

I thought I'd bruise him.

"He ain't got nothin' on you," I says.

But he took it just as calm as though I'd told him his collar was dirty. Then I says:

"You and Fogarty must of pawned your pepper when you left Fort Wayne. Or maybe you can't get along without your Hoosier hops. Somethin's wrong. You couldn't of won all them games if you worked there like you're doin' here. What's the matter?"

"Matter with who?" he says.

"Both o' you—you and Fogarty," I says.

"They's nothin' the matter with me," says Smitty. "I'm all right; but that slob never had no business tryin' to pitch."

"How did he win them games?" I ast.

"I guess they felt sorry for him," says Smitty.

"They'll be feelin' sorry for you if you don't go and get some ginger," says I.

The season opened and we started off like we always do, playin' 'em off their feet and lookin' like champs. Alexander and Rixey was better'n I'd ever saw 'em, and the boys was all hittin'. It was a rotten day when Cravath or Magee or Luderus, or some o' them, didn't pole ◆◇

◆ *Cravath*—Clifford Carlton "Gavvy" or "Cactus" Cravath (1881–1963), the Phillies' rightfielder since 1912. After trials with the Red Sox, White Sox, and Senators in 1908–09, Cravath blossomed as a power hitter in the cramped confines of Baker Bowl. He led the National League in home runs on six occasions, including the year at hand, 1914. His 24 home runs in the pennant year of 1915 were the highest total in modern baseball until Babe Ruth's 29 in 1919. He remained active with the Phillies through 1920, managing the team to last-place finishes in both 1919 and 1920. In 1,219 games Cravath batted .287 and hit 119 home runs. See Ralph S. Graber, "Clifford Clarence [sic] Cravath," *Biographical Dictionary of American Sports: Baseball*, pp. 120–21.

◇ *Luderus*—Fred Luderus in the road uniform of the 1915 Phillies. (National Baseball Library, Cooperstown, New York)

(*continued from page 368*)

Magee—Sherwood Robert "Sherry" Magee (1884–1929), the Phillies' veteran outfielder and captain, in his last year with the club. In 1914 Magee had a fine year, hitting .314 and leading the league with 171 hits, 39 doubles, and 103 runs batted in. Magee played subsequently for Boston and Cincinnati, finishing a 16-year career in 1919 with 2,168 hits and a .291 lifetime average in 2,084 games. Magee, who had received a lengthy suspension in 1911 for punching umpire Bill Finneran, in 1928 began a second career as an umpire. The new career appeared quite promising, but Magee died before his second season. See Frank V. Phelps, "Sherwood Robert Magee," *Biographical Dictionary of American Sports: Baseball*, pp. 373–74.

Luderus—Frederick William Luderus (1885–1961), the club's first baseman. Luderus broke in with the Cubs in 1909 but went to the Phillies early in 1910 and remained there until 1920. In 1914 he was to hit .248, but his .315 in 1915 would be a major contribution to the Phillies' pennant. In 12 seasons, in which he never played a position other than first base, Luderus hit .277 in 1,346 games. He was a notoriously poor fielder, however. See A. D. Suehsdorf, "Fred Luderus," *The Ballplayers*, p. 640.

◇ *pole a couple out o' the park*— Baker Bowl, home of the Phillies. The park had a reputation for cheap home runs because of its short right-field fence, only 280 feet from home plate, but it would have been more accurate to call the facility a place for cheap doubles and triples. At the time, the wall was 40 feet high to the top of the advertisements, and a ball hit onto any part of it was in play. The photograph dates probably from 1916; the 1915 pennant flies from the flagpole. (Society for American Baseball Research)

a couple out o' the park. We didn't get excited about it, though. We'd been May champions too often. We was wonderin' when the Old Jinx was goin' to hit us in the eye, and whether we'd get smashed up in a railroad wreck or have a epidemic o' lepersy. The papers was sayin' that we was up to our old tricks and that we'd blow higher'n a kite when the annual cyclone struck us.

Red had started Smitty just oncet. That was agin the Boston bunch, and he'd tooken him out in the first innin' so's we could finish the game that day. The first ball he throwed made a noise like a cannon when it hit Bill's glove. The rest o' them never got that far. One was ◆ all he had the strength to pitch. The first seven guys that come up was expresses—they didn't stop at first or second base. Paskert ast Red to ◆

◆ *Bill*—William Lavier Killefer (1887–1960), the Phillies catcher. Kellefer played with the Browns in 1909 and 1910, and from 1911 to 1917 he was the regular catcher for the Phillies. In 1914 he hit .234 in 98 games. Killefer went to the Cubs with Grover Alexander after the 1917 season, and remained active through 1921, having hit .238 in 1,035 games over the course of 13 seasons. He managed the Cubs from 1921 to 1925 and the Browns from 1930 to 1933, in neither case with much success. See Jack Kavanagh, "Bill Killefer," *The Ballplayers*, pp. 568–69.

◆ *Paskert*—George Henry "Dode" Paskert (1881–1959), centerfielder of the Phillies. After four seasons with Cincinnati, from 1907 to 1910, Paskert played

send him a taxi. Smitty fin'lly was invited to the bench and sat there blinkin' while Red sprung a monologue.

"You're layin' down on me," says Red, "and it's goin' to cost you a month's pay. If you're playin' for your release you're wastin' time. I'd get rid o' you if I could, but nobody'll take you. I've ast for waivers and I know what I'm talkin' about. You're wished on to us for the summer, but you ain't goin' to do no more pitchin'. I wouldn't even let you work in battin' practice, 'cause the fellers couldn't see a real pitcher's stuff after lookin' at your'n. You can help the clubhouse boy, and you can hustle out the canvas when it rains, and you can stand and hold the bottle while the real ball players is gettin' rubbed. And you can stick round after the games and hang up the undershirts.

"We'd ought to sue the Fort Wayne club for swindlin' us! I'd like to manage a team in that league if fellers like you can win a pennant there. I'd give the ground keeper a dollar a day extra to do the pitchin' for me, and I'd go in myself when he was too busy. They give you a salary for playin' ball, but they pinch a man for stealin' a loaf o' bread! If you're the best pitcher in the Central League the rest o' them is paralytics. If we'd spent five thousand for the middle of a doughnut we'd have a better chancet o' realizin' on our investment. If pepper ◇ was worth a million dollars a ounce you'd be rated at ten cents!"

◇ *"If pepper was worth a million dollars a ounce you'd be rated at ten cents!"*—Drawing by Arthur William Brown for *The Saturday Evening Post*, July 25, 1914.

"Can I go in and dress?" says Smitty.

"I doubt it," says Red. "You better take somebody along to help you." Well, that might of been the end o' the bird if he was with any club but our'n. Red had the waivers all right, but couldn't make no deal that'd bring us within four thousand bucks of even. Still, we wasn't gettin' no service out of him and was payin' him salary all the time.

So Red was just about to sell him to a old-clo'es man when the old hoodoo hit us. Alexander strained his souper and Rixey got a pair o' ◆

(*continued from page 370*)
regularly for the Phillies until 1917, then with the Cubs through 1920, and finally for the Reds in 1921. A particular favorite of Lardner's because of their days in the Central League, Paskert hit .268 over the course of 15 seasons in the major leagues. He was a centerfielder of exceptional range, one of the mainstays of the 1915 champions. See A. D. Suehsdorf, "Dode Paskert," *The Ballplayers*, p. 847.

◆ *Alexander strained his souper and Rixey got a pair o' busted fingers, all in the same serious.*—On the basis of newspaper accounts, no such events occurred. Actually, the team had a poor start and spent most of May in sixth place. Rixey did not report until early June. In early September Alexander was reported to have arm trouble, but did not miss a start.

busted fingers, all in the same serious. We was left with one fair pitcher ◆ and a gang o' kids that'd never saw no big-league games till last spring. The bust-up didn't surprise nobody. We figured that we'd been lucky to go till the first o' June without none o' the boys gettin' killed. It was the same old gag with us: Right up near the top and happy for a couple o' months. Then, Blooie!—and the club all shot to pieces.

It wouldn't of been sensible to turn even a rotten pitcher loose at that stage. We had to keep a hold of all o' them, so's when some got their bumps they'd be plenty to take their place. That's how Smitty happened to hang on. Red didn't start him, but he let him finish for some o' the others that wasn't much better. And he kept lookin' worse all the while.

Well, it was the second week in June when Red sent me from Cincy to Dayton to look at a big spitter. ◆

"I ain't strong for the Central League after what they handed me," he says; "but maybe this guy's better'n most o' them, and you can see where we're up agin it. We got to get somebody or we'll go to the bottom so fast they'll pinch us for speedin'. If he's got anything at all and looks like as if he was alive we can use him; but if he's a dope, like this other boob, we don't need him. I don't want to run no lodgin' house for vagrants."

So I beat it over there and seen a double-header between the home ◆ club and Evansville. The guy I was sent after worked one game and ◇ had about as much action as a soft drink. I voted No! before he'd went two innin's. Evansville had a lefthander who knowed how to pitch, but ◆◇

◆ *one fair pitcher*—Necessarily, Erskine Mayer. Early in 1914 the team was almost entirely dependent on Alexander and Mayer.

◆ *a big spitter*—Presumably Jacob George Fromholtz (1886–1952), Evansville's leading pitcher, who went 23–10 in 1914. Fromholtz was, as stated, a big man and a spitball pitcher. His chronic weight problem, in fact, was thought by local sports writers to be the only impediment to his reaching the major leagues, and the narrator's view of him appears to have been shared by actual scouts who saw him. Fromholtz was never given a try at the major leagues. He pitched in the Central League through 1917, never again having an outstanding season. After his military service, he pitched for Portsmouth in the Virginia League in 1920 and 1921, closing his career without rising above Class B baseball. I am indebted to the Pierce mortuary of Lawrenceburg, Ind., for allowing me to search its records for Fromholtz's dates of birth and death.

◆ *a double-header between the home club and Evansville*—The doubleheader is apparently fictional. The only doubleheader Evansville played at Dayton was on July 4, 1914, and neither of the presumed objects of the scouting trip pitched.

◆ *a lefthander who knowed how to pitch*—Paul Clarence Fittery (1891–1974), Evansville's second-leading pitcher at 22–7. He was, as stated, a small man, at 5′8½″

1, Graham; 2, Baker; 3, Knoll, Mgr.; 4, Grefe; 5, Hauger; 6, Fromholtz;
7, Matthews; 8, Tepe; 9, H. W. Stahlhefer, Pres.; 10, Hauser; 11, Fittery;
12, Schultz; 13, Mascot; 14 Kibble.
Mason Photo.

◇ *Evansville*—The Evansville team of the Central League in 1913. (William J. Weiss collection)

they told me he'd been in the league six years; and, besides, he was a little feller.

Well, I spotted old Jack Barnett on the Evansville bench, so I waited ◆ to shake hands with him when the game was over. You know him and

---

(*continued from page 372*)
and 156 pounds. He had pitched in the minors for six years, although not entirely in the Central League. As with Fromholtz, the scouting report is perfectly accurate. Fittery had two chances at the major leagues, neither successful. His strong record at Evansville in 1914 earned him a try with the Cincinnati Reds at the end of the season, and he pitched creditably, losing two complete games in eight appearances. He spent the entire 1917 season with the Phillies, going 1–1 in 17 games. His only major league victory came in the second game of a doubleheader on September 23, 1917, when he defeated the Chicago Cubs, 11–4, in spite of continual wildness. Fittery was an outstanding pitcher in the high minor leagues through the mid-1920's, and remained active while managing in the lower minors until 1930. His lifetime minor league record was 294–228 in 663 games. See "Paul Clarence Fittery," *Minor League Baseball Stars* (Society for American Baseball Research), II (1985), 138.

It might be noted that Lardner considered "feller" an inaccurate and amateurish rendition of illiterate English, and rebuked H. L. Mencken for using it. As in this instance, however, he frequently resorted to it. See H. L. Mencken, *The American Language: An Inquiry into the Development of English in the United States*, 4th ed. (New York: A. A. Knopf, 1936), p. 425n.

◆ *Jack Barnett*—Apparently a fictional character, although—as in the instance of Hy Pond in "The Busher Reenlists" the context is one in which Lardner would normally use an actual player. No player of this name is shown in the Central

◇ *a lefthander who knowed how to pitch*—Paul Fittery in the uniform of Salt Lake City of the Pacific Coast League in 1916. (William J. Weiss collection)

me broke in together at Utica. I found out while we rode downtown ◆ that he'd been with the Fort Wayne Club the last year and was traded to Evansville durin' the winter. I'd sort o' lost track of old Jack 'cause he hadn't been playin' enough in recent years to get his name in the book.

"I see your club's still lucky," he says. "We all thought you had a grand chancet till them two fellers got hurt."

"Yes," I says, "but we're gone now. The young guys we got ought to of been dressmakers instead o' pitchers." Then I happened to think

---

(*continued from page 373*)
League from its founding to 1914. A first baseman named John Barnett played with considerable success in the Blue Grass and Virginia leagues in this period, but he never played in the Central League, and there is no reason to believe Lardner was familiar with him. See the more general discussion of Barnett and of this remarkable passage in the Introduction.

◆ *Utica*—A club in the Class B New York State League. Similarly, no player named Jack Barnett appears in the Utica club's records for the period.

o' Smitty. "Maybe you can tell me somethin'," says I. "How did this here Smitty ever win all them games for you?"

Barnett started to laugh.

"What's the matter?" he ast. "Ain't the big wop worth five thousand?"

"He ain't worth a cigar coupon," I says. "He's a big, lazy tramp."

Barnett kept on laughin'.

"I knowed what'd come off," he says. "I told the fellers what'd happen. I bet Punch Knoll fifty bucks that Smitty wouldn't last the ◆ season. You guys can talk about McGraw and Mack, and them other big-league managers, all you want to, but it's us fellers down here in the sticks that knows how to get the work out of a man."

I ast him what he meant.

"Well," he says, "we had Smitty two years ago and he was a bum. He was sloppin' along with us like he's doin' with you now. At that time the Grand Rapids Club had Fogarty, the guy the Cubs got now. Fogarty's a big right-hander, with a spitter and a good hook and just as good a fast ball as Smitty. He's a big, handsome brute, too, and maybe he don't know it! Up to Grand Rapids he was doin' nothin' but look pretty and draw his pay. He was just as valuable to them as Smitty was to us; but we used to have all kinds o' fun with 'em both, kiddin' 'em about their looks. We'd say to Smitty: 'You'd be the handsomest guy in this league if it wasn't for Fogarty.' And we'd pull the same stuff on Fogarty when we was playin' Grand Rapids. And the both o' them would get as sore as a boil. I never seen nothin' like it.

"At the schedule meetin' a year ago last winter, our club and Grand Rapids pulled off a trade, Bill Peck comin' to us for Joe Hammond ◆

◆ *Punch Knoll*—Charles Elmer Knoll (1881–1960), manager of the Evansville club of the Central League from 1913 to 1917. Knoll, a native of Evansville, broke into professional baseball with Evansville's team in the Three-I League in 1901, and proceeded to Memphis and Nashville before playing 85 games for the Washington Senators in 1905. An outfielder and catcher, Knoll hit .213 in his only major league season. In the minor leagues he played 2,522 games and made 2,448 hits. Knoll began a long and successful career as a minor league manager with Evansville in the Three-I League in 1908–09. In addition to his managerships at Evansville, he managed at Dayton, Ludington, Bay City, Danville, Quincy, Fort Wayne, and Wilkes-Barre before retiring in 1930. Knoll won six pennants as a manager, and on the 50th anniversary of Evansville's entry into the Three-I League in 1951, he was declared the city's "Mr. Baseball." See "Charles Elmer 'Punch' Knoll," *Minor League Baseball Stars* (Society for American Baseball Research), III (1992), 94–95.

◆ *Bill Peck . . . Joe Hammond and Bull Harper*—None of these players appears in Central League records, and all are presumed fictional.

and Bull Harper, a couple of infielders. Jack Burke, our manager, ◆ told the owner o' the Grand Rapids Club that it didn't look fair, givin' up two men for one. So he says: 'All right; I'll throw in Fogarty and then you'll have the two handsomest ball players in the business.' Jack thought he was jokin'; but, sure enough, he turned Fogarty over to us.

"We started in on the pair o' them right off the reel, tryin' to make their life miserable. When Smitty was round we'd talk about Fogarty's pretty red hair; and when Fogarty was with us we'd be wishin' we had big black eyes like Smitty's. I done the most of it, but I didn't have no idea what'd happen.

"Well, to make it short, Smitty come up to Jack a week before the season opened and ast if he could pitch the first game. Jack pretty near dropped dead, 'cause it'd been all he could do the year before to get him to put on his uniform. Mind you, we all knowed then that Smitty had the stuff if he'd only use it. Burke told him he'd think it over and was wonderin' whether to turn him down or not, when up come Fogarty and ast the same thing. Burke decided to take a chancet, so he had the two o' them toss a coin, and Smitty won the toss. He opened up for us and shut Terre Haute out with two hits. And the next day Fogarty worked and shut 'em out again, but give 'em one more hit than Smitty. They was nothin' to it after that. We kept up the good work, gettin' 'em madder and madder at each other. And the madder they got the harder they worked. Either one o' them would of pitched every day if Burke had of let 'em. While Fogarty was workin' Smitty'd slide up and down the bench cussin' to himself and pullin' his head off for the other club. And Fogarty'd do the same thing when Smitty was in there.

"Both o' them was strong for the skirts; and o' course, a pair o' fine-lookin' slobs like them could cop one out in every town. We took up that end of it, too, tellin' Smitty that Fogarty's Marie was prettier than his Julia, and that kind o' stuff.

"You know what they done for us. We'd of finished about sixth without 'em. I never seen such pitchin' in my life, and I never seen

◆ *Jack Burke*—Actually, Jimmy Burke, mentioned above (see the footnotes to the story "The Courtship of T. Dorgan"). Burke managed Fort Wayne in 1913, which accords with the majority of the chronological references that place the story in 1914. This appears to be a confusion with John Patrick Burke (1877–1950), who was also active in minor league managing (see below, in the footnotes to the story "Horseshoes").

two fellers hate each other the way them two done. When you guys bought Smitty and didn't get Fogarty I called the turn. Some o' the boys figured they both might of got the habit o' workin' and might keep it up when they was separated; but I knowed different. And that's why I made the bet with Punch Knoll. Looks like I'll win it easy don't it?"

"Looks like it," I says. "Alexander and Rixey'd both ought to be ready again in a month and then Smitty'll lose his home sure. And we'll be absolutely last by that time."

We was goin' to Chi that night and I didn't see no use o' stickin' in Dayton when I hadn't had no orders to look at no one else but that one guy. Besides, Barnett told me they wasn't nobody else on neither club worth lampin'. I'd of liked to of listened to some more o' the stuff about the two jealous cats, but I had to beat it back to Cincy.

Well, on the way I done some thinkin'; but I was afraid to spring anything on Red for fear he'd laugh at me. We've all knew o' cases where jealousy'd helped a ball club, and a lot more cases where it'd hurt 'em; but I hadn't never heard o' no case like this here one.

We got to Chi and the Cubs proceeded to murder us. Red was desp'rate and so was the rest o' the gang. We dropped the first three and didn't have no hopes o' winnin' the fourth unless Hank lost his ◆ mind and pitched the bat boy agin us.

I hadn't never saw Fogarty. He'd been left to home when the Cubs come East in May. But I spotted him the first day out there to the Cubs' park. He sure was a nice-lookin' devil and big enough to pitch every afternoon and twicet on Sundays. He wasn't doin' no pitchin' for them, though. They was lucky enough to have their reg'lars in shape and wasn't obliged to fill up the box score with ornaments.

Well, I went up to Schulte durin' battin' practice and ast him what was the matter with Fogarty.

"Nothin' at all," says Frank, "I don't figure they can be nothin' the matter with a guy that draws his pay for sittin' on the bench and lookin' beautiful. I wisht I could get away with it."

"Don't he work none?" I ast.

"He pitches to the batters about oncet in two weeks," says Frank. "He does it when Hank can get his consent. And on the days he pitches to us I manage to hide somewheres till the practice is over."

◆ *Hank*—Hank O'Day, manager of the Cubs only in 1914.

"Why?" I ast.

"'Cause," says Frank, "I figure that, barrin' accidents, I got many happy years before me. If he was to happen to put all his stuff on the ball oncet and hit me in the head, they wouldn't be nobody to drive the mules on my peach ranch in Georgia."

"He's got a lot o' stuff, then?" I says.

"Yes," says Frank; "and he's savin' it up for somethin'—maybe to give it away for a birthday present. All he does now is sit and wait for everybody to look away from him, so's he can pull out his pocket mirror and enjoy himself."

This dope fit in perfect with what Jack Barnett had been tellin' me. I made up my mind right there that the thing was worth tryin'; but it took all the nerve I had to spring it on Red. My chancet soon come. He was put off the field in the second innin' and I got myself chased right afterward. He was sittin' in the clubhouse with his head in his hands when I come in.

"Red," I says, "we couldn't be worse off'n we are, could we?" He didn't pay no attention. "We'd be better off if we had somebody that could pitch, wouldn't we?" I says.

"What are you drivin' at?" he ast.

"I want you to try a experiment," I says. "It may not do no good, and then again it might. It might pull us through O. K. if you was willin' to take a chancet."

"Shoot," says Red. "I'll try anything oncet."

"Do you think you could get Fogarty offen the Cubs?" I says.

"Could I get him?" says Red. "Sure I could get him! They just give me notice that they'd ast waivers. But what do I want with Fogarty? He's another one just like this Smitty we got. I give him the oncet over to-day on their bench, and if they's anybody in the world that's lazier'n Smitty, he's him. Don't you think we're carryin' enough excess baggage?"

Then I told him what Barnett'd told me, only I made it even stronger. At first he called me a nut, and it took me pretty near till the game was over to coax him into it. He'd just gave up when the gang come in.

"How bad did they trim us?" ast Red.

"I don't know," says Magee; "but I know I chased back to that fence a hundred and sixteen times."

"Better go see Hank," says I to Red.

I had to pretty near drag him to get him out o' the clubhouse. Hank was just goin' in their door.

"Wait a minute, Hank," I says. "Red wants to see you."

"Just heard you was askin' waivers on Fogarty," says Red. "What do you want for him?"

"I guess you can get him for the waiver price," says Hank; "but you'll have to see the boss."

So me and Red went up to the office and sprung it on 'em. They seemed surprised, but said Red could have him. So Red wired home and got the deal O. K.'d. And Fogarty went with us to St. Louis.

Before we got on the train, Red told me I'd have to do the funny work. I said I'd tackle it, and then I went to Pat and explained the thing to him and ast for help. He was willin' and we fixed it up that I was to room with Fogarty and Pat with Smitty.

Smitty was in his berth, gettin' his beauty sleep, when Fogarty clumb aboard that night. So they didn't see each other till next mornin'. Smitty nailed me comin' out o' the Union Station in St. Louis.

"What's that guy doin' with us?" he says.

"Who do you mean?" I says.

"That big, ugly Mick," says he.

"Ugly!" I says. "If I was you I wouldn't call him ugly. He's a big, handsome boy, and he looks handsomer'n ever alongside a homely wop like you."

He never said a word. He turned away from me like as if I'd ast him for a hundred bucks. Red told me afterward that he come and sat with him in the dinin' room at the hotel and ast if Fogarty was goin' to be with us.

"Sure!" says Red. "I thought it was about time we was gettin' a pitcher."

"A pitcher!" says Smitty. "If they sold him to you for a pitcher you got cheated. He's only a swell-headed pup that don't think about nothin' but the part in his hair."

"Well," says Red, "if I had hair as pretty as his'n I'd be proud of it too."

That shut up Smitty and he left the table without finishin' his Java; but he come to Red in the lobby an hour later and ast if he could work that afternoon! It took Red five minutes to come to. He hadn't had no such request as that from nobody for pretty near three weeks, and Smitty was the last guy on earth he expected it from. You can bet he give his consent.

When our grips come I went to my room to take a nap and a shave; but I didn't get no nap. My new roomy, Fogarty, followed me in and begin talkin' right away.

"What kind o' burg is Philly?" he says.

"Swell!" says I. "You can get anything you want there."

"How about the female population?" he says. "Lots of good lookers?"

"Well," I says, "I guess there's plenty o' pretty girls; but I'm a married man and I ain't got no time for 'em. If you're after information on that subject you better ast Smitty."

"Smitty!" he says. "What does he know about girls?"

"He must know how to grab 'em," says I. "All the real dolls in the burg is bugs over him."

"They must be a fine bunch!" says Fogarty. "It must be they never seen nobody."

"Well," I says, "they ain't looked at nobody since they seen him."

"I can't figure it out," he says.

"That's easy," says I. "In the first place he's a fine-lookin' boy, and in the second place he's a swell pitcher."

"Where do you get that stuff?" says Fogarty. "Don't you think I know nothin'? If he's fine-lookin' I'm a snake. And if he's a swell pitcher, why don't they never start him?"

"He's had a sore arm," I says; "but he's all O. K. now and Red's goin' to work him to-day."

He left the room right after that and I didn't see no more of him till we got out to the park; but Red tipped me that he'd came to him and ast if he could work the game. Red told him he was goin' to start Smitty.

"Good night!" says Fogarty. "They'll get a hundred runs."

But, say, I never seen such a change in a man as they was in Smitty that afternoon. He warmed up with Pat first and was so fast that Pat couldn't hardly keep his glove on. Then Red took him a while and was so pleased that he forgot to get sore when he catched one right on the meat hand.

Well, he didn't shut 'em out—he hadn't had no real work for a long time and he was hog wild; but, say, they couldn't hit him with a shovel! Two blows was what they got, an' we licked 'em, five to two. It was the first game we'd win since we left home; and all through it Fogarty was frothin' at the mouth. Every little while he'd say: "He can't keep it up—the lucky bum! He's slippin'. Better let me warm up!" But Red didn't pay no attention to him.

Maybe you think we didn't feel good in that clubhouse—'specially me and Pat and Red! We was the only ones in on the secret. We'd decided not to ask no help from the other boys for fear they'd make it too raw. I felt the best of anybody, 'cause it was my scheme and I'd been scared that it wouldn't work. It made me look good to myself and to Red too. Before we was dressed, Fogarty'd drew Red aside and got him to promise to pitch him next day.

I wasn't sure yet that success was goin' to be permanent. Still, it was up to I and Pat to go through with our end of it, and my job was to stick close to Fogarty all that evenin' and keep goadin' him. I braced him outside o' the hotel after supper and ast him to take a walk.

"Grand game Smitty pitched to-day!" I says.

"What was grand about it?" says he. "Who couldn't beat that bunch? ◆ He'd ought to of been ashamed of himself for lettin' 'em score."

"He only give 'em two hits," says I.

"Sure!" says Fogarty. "And how was they goin' to get hits when he didn't throw nothin' near the plate?"

"Well," I says, "I don't see no harm in a few walks so long's a feller can get 'em over when he has to. It's pretty hard for a guy with all that smoke to control it right along."

"Yes," he says; "but I claim it takes a lucky bird to give eight bases on balls and get away with the ball game. It don't show no pitchin' on his part; all it shows is that the other club'd ought to try some easier game than baseball. All they had to do was go up there without their bats and they'd of trimmed us; but they didn't even make him pitch. It looked to me like as if their manager'd offered a prize to the one that could miss 'em the furthest. They looked like a vaudeville team rehearsin' a club-swingin' act. At that, Smitty's got a big advantage over most pitchers. He's so dam' homely that it scares a feller to look at him."

"If that's a advantage," I says, "nobody'd never even bunt one safe off o' you."

"You're kiddin' me now," he says. "I ain't stuck on my looks, but they wouldn't be no sense in me pretendin' that I didn't have him beat. I and him was together in the Central, y'know; and I was one o' the most pop'lar if not the pop'larest feller that ever played ball in Fort Wayne. It takes the skirts to judge if a man's good-lookin' or not; and I'm here to tell you without no boastin' that I could of married any

---

◆ *Who couldn't beat that bunch?*—This is probably a reference to the Cardinals of 1913, who finished last with a 51–99 record. The Cardinals of 1914, by contrast, were quite respectable, finishing in third place with an 81–72 mark, the team's best performance up to that point in the twentieth century.

dame in that burg. So far's Smitty was concerned, he couldn't get no girl to look at him."

"Fort Wayne girls ain't like the ones in Philly, then," says I.

"Girls is the same everywheres," says Fogarty. "You can't never make me believe that they'd chase him, unless it's out o' curiosity. You'll often see a crowd round a monkey cage, but it ain't 'cause the monkeys is handsome."

"Some girls likes them big, dark fellers," I says.

"Yes," he says, "and some people likes the smell o' garlic."

"I s'pose we'll get a lickin' to-morrow," I says. "Red ain't got nobody left to work, outside of a few bushers."

"This busher right here works to-morrow," says Fogarty; "and you can bet a month's pay that he won't give no eight bases on balls."

"Maybe you won't be in there long enough," I says.

"I'll be in there just nine innin's," says he; "and at the end o' that time the St. Louis Club won't have nothin' to show they been in a ball game."

"All you need to do," says I, " is to work as good as Smitty done to-day; but that's too much to look for from most bushers."

That stung him.

"They ain't no homely wop got nothin' on me!" he says. "If I can't do no better'n he done I'll quit pitchin' and peddle bananas, which is what he'd ought to be doin'."

Well, I kept him goin' till bedtime and all the next forenoon. He was out to the park and dressed before anybody, and he warmed up enough for three games. Red ast him oncet if he wasn't workin' too hard.

"Not me," he says. "I ain't delicate like some o' these here pitchers. Work's my middle name and you'll find it out before I get through."

Say, they wasn't no kick comin' on the way he done his job! One o' the St. Louis guys got as far as second base and was so surprised that Bill caught him off o' there flatfooted. Three little singles he give 'em and not a man did he walk. Bill told me afterward that it was fast one, fast one, fast one, and hardly three hooks or spitters all through the game. Bill said them fast ones stung right through his big mitt like he'd been barehanded.

And Smitty, on the bench, acted just like Fogarty'd did the day before. He called them St. Louis hitters everything he could think of. When the big Turk whiffed the hull side in the seventh Smitty was so sore he kicked a hole in the ball bag and throwed away his chew.

The rest o' the bunch couldn't help noticin' the way he acted, and

I seen where they'd be wise to the whole game before long.

That night Pat took Smitty took a bunch o' nickel shows and entertained him with conversation about Fogarty's grand performance. The result was that the wop got Red out o' bed at seven the next mornin' and ast him whether he could pitch the game. Red stalled him, 'cause he didn't know then how strong the both o' them was—him and Fogarty.

Anyway, it rained, so Smitty'd had two days' rest before we played again, and Red sent him in to wind up the serious. Gavvy saved St. Louis another whitewashin' by droppin' a fly ball with a guy on; but that run was all they got. Fogarty's game wasn't a bit better'n this second one o' Smitty's, and I kept rubbin' that into Fogarty all the way back to Philly.

They ain't no use goin' on and tellin' you about all the rest o' the games they pitched. They was both beat a few times, but it wasn't 'cause they didn't try. Every pitcher with a arm and a glove'd cop more'n two-thirds of his games if he'd work as hard as these babies done. Some o' the papers come out and said that Red was overworkin' 'em, but the reporters that wrote that didn't know what they was talkin' about. It was all Red could do to keep either o' them on the bench. If they'd of had their way about it they'd of both been out there in the middle o' the diamond every day, fightin' for possession o' the ball.

When Red sent Mayer or one o' the other boys in, the pair o' them'd sit on the bench growlin' and makin' remarks about each other. The minute the feller in there workin' showed any signs o' weakenin', Fogarty and Smitty'd both jump up and race down to the bull pen. And when Red got ready to take the guy out and sent for one or the other o' the two handsome birds the one he didn't pick would slam his glove on the ground and start kickin' it. Everybody on the ball club kept at 'em on the bench; but Red, figurin' they might get suspicious, give orders that nobody but I and Pat was to ride 'em in private.

We was right up on the Giants' heels by the first of August. Then Rixey and Alexander joined us, but all they was ast to do was fill in when Red could persuade Fogarty and Smitty to take a rest. We was about the only club that was beatin' New York, or else we'd of had the flag cinched long before we did. We was runnin' through the rest o' the league like soup through a sieve.

One day Smitty held the Brooklyn Club to six hits in a double-header and beat 'em both games. Fogarty ast me a hundred times in the next few days when we was goin' to have another double-header. And a week before it come off he made Red promise to let him tackle it alone. It was agin the Cubs and he beat 'em clean as a whistle; but they got a couple more hits than Brooklyn'd made agin Smitty. So the big Turk was just as discontented as though he hadn't did nothin' at all. You ought to of heard Hank rave, though! He couldn't figure how Red could get so much work out of a guy who'd been on his bench two or three months and hadn't did nothin' but sleep.

But you know what they done. What I set out to tell you was how I and Pat kept 'em goin'. We soon found out that they wasn't only jealous of each other's looks and their pitchin'. Neither one o' them would let the other have anything on him at all. If I'd make a remark about what a classy necktie Smitty was wearin', Fogarty'd go out and buy the loudest one he could find. If Pat mentioned to Smitty that Fogarty always kept his shoes shined up nice, Smitty'd sneak away to a shine parlor and make the boy work his fool head off for a hour. They just naturally hated each other and acted like a pair o' grand opery stars or a couple o' schoolgirls that was both tryin' to be teacher's pet.

I and Pat would get together and figure out different things to rile 'em up with. Pat was singin' The River Shannon in the clubhouse one day. Fogarty was standin' right by me.

"Pat's got a good voice," he says.

"Fair," says I; "but the best singer on the club is Smitty."

Now I hadn't heard Smitty sing—didn't know whether he could or not. Fogarty'd ought to of knew somethin' about it, as they'd been at Fort Wayne together a hull season; but, regardless o' the fact that neither one o' the two had a voice—as we soon learned—the Turk joined right in with Pat, and it wasn't two seconds before Smitty was whinin' too. Pat quit when he seen he had competition. Everybody stopped talkin' and listened.

I wisht you could of heard it! It was like as though all the ferryboats in East River had got into trouble at once. Their idea o' singin' was to see how many sour notes they could hit and how loud they could hit 'em. The bunch give 'em a hand when they got through, and each o' them figured it was on the square and was for him personally. Well, that was a big laugh with us for a while; but it got so's it was no joke when they done it every day and yelled different songs at the same time.

Another thing we done was to write letters to both o' them and sign a girl's name. The letters was just the same, and they said that she was a great fan and was pullin' for our club and just loved to see them two pitch. We wound them up somethin' like this:

"I think you're so handsome and I would love to meet you. I've already met Mr. Smith." We said Mr. Smith in one and Mr. Fogarty in the other. "I think he's the handsomest man I ever seen, but maybe you're just as handsome when a person sees you up close. I sit in the third or fourth row o' the stand, right back o' your bench, every afternoon."

Say, you'd ought to of seen them birds fall for that! They rubbered for that dame every day we played at home for the last two months o' the season. Sometimes, when neither o' them was working, they'd both get up and lean on the roof o' the bench and try to get a smile from every skirt in the place, thinkin' one o' them must be the girl who'd wrote.

On the road we'd get the telephone girls in the hotels to call up Smitty and ask him if he was Mr. Fogarty. When he'd say no she'd ring off; but she'd call him up again in about ten minutes and ask him the same question. We worked this on Fogarty, too, and both o' them pretty near went nuts 'cause the other was gettin' so many calls.

Pat pulled a hot one in Pittsburgh. He told Smitty that Fogarty was the most generous guy he'd ever met.

"Why?" says Smitty.

"He's so good to the waiters and bell hops," says Pat. "He gives the waiters a quarter tip at every meal and slips the boys two bits when they bring him ice water."

That started a battle that was pretty costly to the both o' them, but mighty sweet for the hops and waiters. If I'd of been Pat I'd of made 'em slip me a commission.

We had 'em both ridin' in taxis to and from all the parks on the last trip West. We had 'em gettin' their clo'es pressed every night, and buyin' new shirts and collars in every burg we blowed into, and gettin' shaved twicet a day, till Red made us cut some of it out, sayin' they was touchin' the club for too much dough. And all season I never seen 'em speak to each other, though neither one couldn't talk about nothin' else but the other when they was separated.

The pennant race was settled when we won a double-header in ◆

◆ *when we won a double-header in Cincy on the fifteenth o' September.*—Because the story was published in *The Saturday Evening Post* of July 25, 1914, the late-season action is fictional. On September 15, 1914, the Phillies defeated the Giants at New York, 4–3. On September 15, 1913, the Phillies did play at Cincinnati, but in a ten-inning 2–2 tie with the Reds, rather than in a doubleheader.

Cincy on the fifteenth o' September. When we got back to the hotel Red told us the lid was off for that night—that we could do anything we wanted to and stay out until breakfast. So they can't blame neither Pat nor I for what come off. One o' the other boys—I never found out who—told Fogarty that Smitty could hold more wine than a barrel. Then he pulled the same thing on Smitty about Fogarty.

I and Pat went to a show. When we blowed back, about eleven, they was a noise like New Year's Eve in the café. We went in to see what it was. They was a gang o' fellers at one table with Smitty, and another bunch at another table with Fogarty. They was four or five empty quart bottles in front o' each o' them. They'd had five or six more pints than they could carry comfortable and was hollerin' for more, but was broke. We got 'em both at one table and ast 'em to sing. Before they was halfway through the first verse o' whatever it was, the night clerk horned in and stopped 'em. Then we took 'em out in the street and told 'em to finish it, but they was too many coppers round.

Most of us was roomin' on the tenth floor and one o' the boys talked the pair into racin' upstairs instead of usin' the elevator. They both fell down at the first landin' and when they hit the floor they was all in. They'd of slept there for a week if we hadn't of carried 'em to the elevator and got 'em up the rest o' the way. Then what did we do but steer 'em both into Pat's room and put 'em to bed together. They was no danger o' them gettin' wise till the next day; they was dead to the world. I and Pat slept in my room and we was up bright and early so's not to miss nothin'. We walked in and found 'em both poundin' their ear. It must of tooken us fifteen minutes to get 'em roused.

"Well, boys," says Pat, "I'm glad to see you friendly and lookin' so fresh."

They looked about as fresh as a old dray horse.

"How did you happen to be roomin' together?" I says.

It wasn't till then that they wised up. Smitty jumped out o' bed lke the hotel was afire.

"I'll murder the guy that done this!" he hollered.

"What do you mean?" says Pat. "Don't you know who you went to bed with?"

"You must of been in bad shape," I says. "Fogarty was all right; he knowed what he was doin'."

Fogarty wanted to deny it, but he couldn't, 'cause if he had of he'd be admittin' that the wine was too much for him. So he just had to shut up and take it.

"I was all right too," says Smitty.

"Then what are you crabbin' about?" says Pat.

They wasn't no answer to that.

"I'm goin' to ring for some ice water," says Fogarty.

"Nobody never wants ice water at this time o' the mornin' unless they had a bad night," I says. "You don't hear Smitty askin' for no ice water."

Smitty'd of gave his right eye for a barrel of it, but he didn't have the nerve to say so.

Well, we made Fogarty get up and we stuck in there while they was dressin'. Fogarty had to go to his own room to get a clean shirt and collar, and we could hear him ringin' for water the minute he got in there. Fin'lly we took pity on Smitty and got him some too. He complained o' headache, and I says:

"That's a funny thing about Fogarty—no matter how much wine he laps up he don't never have no headache the next mornin.' "

We didn't hear no more complaints from Smitty. They both went down to breakfast and tried to eat somethin', but it was hard work. And I noticed that neither o' them bothered Red with requests to pitch that day.

They went to bed—separated—right after supper and was as good as ever the followin' mornin'. I don't s'pose neither o' them had never drank no wine before, and, so far as I know, they didn't tackle it again. They both wanted to pitch in Chi, but Red was anxious to try out some kids; so he told both o' them, on the quiet, that they was the ones he was dependin' on for the World's Serious and he didn't want to risk gettin' 'em hurt.

Well, we wound up the season in Boston, and it was the next to the ◆ last day that we got into a awful jam! You remember readin' about Davis, the infielder Red bought from the New England League? Well, ◆ he'd got married the week before he joined us—married a Boston girl. He'd left her with her folks while he went West with us and she stuck to home till we hit Boston on that last trip. She was goin' to Philly with us to take in the serious.

Davis was a fast little cuss, not much bigger'n Maranville. Red had ◆

◆ *Well, we wound up the season in Boston*—In both 1913 and 1914 the Phillies ended play in New York.

◆ *Davis*—Apparently a fictional character.

◆ *Maranville*—Walter James Vincent "Rabbit" Maranville (1891–1954), a 5′5″, 155-pound shortstop of remarkable durability. Maranville had come up to the Boston Braves in 1912 and in 1914 was hitting .246 in the course of assisting the

tried him out at short agin Pittsburgh and he'd looked good; but he was usin' the reg'lars most o' the time to keep 'em in shape for the big show. Davis had more nerve than any little feller I ever seen. He wouldn't break ground for none o' them Pittsburgh guys when they come into second base. In one o' the games there big Honus had told ◆ him to keep out o' the way or he'd get killed.

"It won't be no big slob like you that'll kill me!" says Davis.

Honus had a license to get sore at that, 'cause he was just slippin' the kid a friendly warnin'; but it shows you what a game little devil Davis was.

Well, as I was sayin', it was the next to the last day up in Boston that somethin' come off that pretty near cost us the big money. Mayer was pitchin' the game and we had the reg'lar club in agin 'em.

In one o' the boxes, right down next to the field, they was the prettiest girl I ever looked at. She was all alone and she was dressed up like a million bucks. She was sittin' where we could lamp her from our bench and all the boys had gave her the oncet over before the game ever started. Fogarty and Smitty wiped the dirt offen their faces and smoothed their hair the minute they piped her.

She was a lot more interestin' than the national pastime and I guess we was all gettin' a eyeful when, all of a sudden, she smiled right at us. Our club was in the field and they was only a few of us on the bench—me and Pat and Davis and the pitchers and one or two others.

(*continued from page 387*)
Braves to the pennant. He played for the Braves through 1920, for the Pirates through 1924, for the Cubs in 1925, the Dodgers in 1926, the Cardinals in 1927–28, and again the Braves, from 1929 to 1933. After a year away he returned to the Braves in 1935 at the age of 43. In 2,670 games in 23 seasons Maranville made 2,605 hits, batting .258. Maranville, who coupled a sly sense of humor with an alcohol problem, was an unlikely managerial choice, but managed the Cubs for 53 games in 1925, finishing last. He was elevated to the Baseball Hall of Fame in 1954. See Horace R. Givens, "Walter James Vincent Maranville," *Biographical Dictionary of American Sports: Baseball*, p. 377.

◆ *Honus*—John Peter Wagner (1874–1955), shortstop of the Pirates. After playing for Louisville from 1897 to 1899, Wagner played in his native Pittsburgh from 1900 to 1917. Remarkably versatile, Wagner played every position but catcher in his 21 seasons. In 2,789 games he made 3,430 hits, batted .328, and stole 722 bases. Wagner managed the Pirates for five games in 1917, long enough to convince him he had no managerial ambitions. Generally considered the National League's greatest player until the coming of Stan Musial, Willie Mays, and Henry Aaron, Wagner was a charter member of the Baseball Hall of Fame. See Edward J. Walsh, "John Peter Wagner," *Biographical Dictionary of American Sports: Baseball*, pp. 581–82.

Well, I was one of a number that returned the salute; but after doin' it oncet I remembered I was a old married man and cut it out. But Fogarty and Smitty give a correct imitation of a toothpaste advertisement all the rest o' the time they sat there. Every three or four minutes she'd smile and then they'd smile back. They was wise to each other and it was a battle to see which one could give her the prettiest grin.

Just before the last half o' the eighth Fogarty ast Red whether he could go in and dress. He hadn't no more'n got permission when Smitty wanted to go too. I had 'em guessed right, and I and Pat was wonderin' which one'd cop. They raced to the clubhouse and Smitty beat him in. Now them two birds was usually awful slow about gettin' their clo'es changed, 'cause they was so partic'lar; but they beat the world's record this time. They was in their street clo'es and down in front o' that box just as the game ended.

Smitty was there first, but lots o' good it done him! He tipped his hat to the girl and got a cold stare. Then Fogarty come up and spoke to her. He was gave just as much encouragement as Smitty.

I begin to laugh, but I stopped quick. Before I knowed what was comin' off, little Davis grabbed a bat and started for the stand. Smitty was leanin' agin the box, with his left hand flat on the rail. Without a word o' warnin' Davis swung the bat overhand and it come down on poor Smitty's hand like a ton o' brick. Smitty yelled and fell over on the ground. Fogarty tried to duck, but he was too late. The little busher aimed the bat at his bean and catched him square on the right arm as he throwed it up to protect himself.

That's all they was to the bout. The first punch is a lot—'specially if you use a baseball bat. Neither o' them showed signs o' fightin' back. Besides, we was all on the job by that time and grabbed Davis. Little as he was, it took three of us to hold him. But, say, they was the devil to pay in the clubhouse! Red was goin' to shoot Davis till the truth come out.

"They went too far with it," says Davis. "They ain't no man can go up and talk to my wife without a introduction! I seen 'em tryin' to flirt with her. Them big bugs is so swell-headed that they think no girl could smile at nobody but them."

"You'd ought to of tipped 'em off," says Red.

"I hadn't ought to of did no such a thing," says Davis. "They'd ought to of knew by lookin' that she wasn't the kind o' girl that'd flirt. But I didn't feel in no danger o' havin' my home broke up, so I let 'em go."

Then Red jumped on me.

"That's what you get for eggin' 'em on," he says. "Where's our chancet in the World's Serious now?"

"Have some sense!" I says. "You wouldn't be thinkin' o' no World's Serious if I hadn't of egged 'em on."

We called a doctor for Smitty and Fogarty, and the news he give us didn't cheer us up none. He said he thought Smitty's hand was broke, but he'd have to take a X ray. The mitt was swole up as big as a ham. Fogarty's souper was hangin' limp as a rag, and the doc didn't believe he'd be able to raise it for a month. Afterward he found out that they was no bones busted in Smitty's hand, but it was in such shape that he couldn't hold a han'kerchief, let alone a baseball. There we was, three days before the start o' the serious, and our pitchin' staff shot to hellangone!

Red sent me and Pat and the trainer home that night with the pair o' cripples. We was to report up to the club's offices next mornin' and have all the doctors in Philly called in. Me and Pat was so sore that we couldn't talk to each other, and I don't think they was a word said on the trip. Yes, they was too; just before Smitty went to sleep he ast me a question:

"Who was that girl?"

"You'd ought to know by this time," I says. "That wasn't nobody but Davis' wife."

"Then what was she smilin' at me for?" he says.

Well, the Philly doctors told us they was absolutely no chancet o' havin' either o' them in shape for the serious and we was gettin' ready to count the losers' share. Red'd been figurin' on alternatin' the two, 'cause none o' the rest was in real shape; but now we didn't have nothin' that you could call a air-tight pitcher.

Rixey and Alexander and Mayer would of made 'em step some if they'd been right, but they wasn't.

I says to Pat:

"Looks like as though I and you and the bat boy would have to work."

"Looks that way," he says, "unless we can bring them two fellers round."

"How can we do that?" I says. "You heard what them doctors said."

"Yes," says Pat; "but they're the only hope we got, and I ain't goin' to give up till I have to."

Red and the bunch got in the next mornin', which was a Sunday. Most o' the gang went to church, and if the Lord'd never heard o' Fogarty and Smitty before I bet He knowed who they was when we got through prayin'. We practiced Monday and went over to Washin'ton that night. ◆

Well, you know what come off. Johnson beat us there and Boehling beat us Wednesday in Philly. With Johnson to come back, twicet if necessary, it looked like a short serious.

And then it begin to rain. It's a wonder the District o' Columbia wasn't washed away. Four straight days of it, includin' Sunday; and I never seen it come down so hard. A cleanin' like that might do Pittsburgh or Chi some good, but it looked like wastin' it in Washin'ton. We was anxious to get the serious over with; and the more it rained, the worse we hated it. We never figured that it was the best thing that could of happened to us!

I'm the guy they'd ought to thank for coppin' the league pennant. And the rain and me together was what saved us from a awful lickin' for the big dough. On Sunday night, while we was still layin' round the hotel in Washin'ton, where we'd been stalled since Thursday, I got my hunch. I went to Red with it.

"Maybe one o' them fellers could help us out now," I says.

"What makes you think so?" says Red.

"Well," I says, "they've had time to get back in shape."

"No use," says Red. "I was just talkin' to Smitty in the dinin' room. He couldn't even hold his knife. He says his mitt feels just as bad as it did the first day."

"How about Fogarty?" I ast.

"He ain't no better off," says Red. "The worst of it is that neither one o' them seems to care."

"Maybe I can wake 'em up," I says.

"You got my permission to try," says Red.

Me and Fogarty wasn't roomin' together. The trainer was doubled up with him and they had another guy lookin' out for Smitty. Neither o' them had put on a suit, but they'd saw us get our two beatin's from the stand. I found Smitty first and took him into the bar.

"How does it look to you?" I says.

"We're licked," says he.

"Don't be too sure!" I says.

◆ *We practiced Monday and went over to Washin'ton that night.*—Needless to say, the Phillies–Senators World Series is entirely fictional; the two teams met in the Series neither in 1914 nor in any other year. The Phillies finished sixth in 1914 and the Senators second. In the actual World Series of 1914, the Braves defeated the Athletics four games to none.

"What do you mean?" he ast me. "What chancet have we got with nobody to pitch?"

"We got somebody to pitch now," I says.

"Who?" says Smitty.

"Fogarty," says I. "The doctor says he's all right and Red's goin' to start him to-morrow."

"You're crazy!" says Smitty. "The doctor said he wouldn't be no good till next year."

"That was pretty near a week ago," I says. "Besides, that doctor didn't know nothin'. We had the best doctor in Washin'ton up to see him to-night—the doctor that looks after the President and all the congressmen. He says they's nothin' at all the matter with him."

I left Smitty then and went lookin' for Fogarty.

I found him in his room gettin' his poor souper rubbed. I spoke my piece over again. I told him Smitty'd been pronounced cured by the President's special surgeon and that he was goin' to start the next day's game.

An hour later I run into Red, and he was smilin' like Davis' wife.

"You've did it, old boy!" he says. "They both been after me till I had to duck out in the wet to get away from 'em. They both insist on workin' to-morrow, and I told 'em I wasn't goin' to decide on my pitcher till mornin'."

"I guess I don't know nothin'!" I says. "Which one are you goin' to start?"

"The one that can throw a ball with the least pain," says Red.

You know the rest of it. The sun shined on us next day, and Smitty shut 'em out and beat Johnson on the wettest grounds I ever seen! I don't know yet how he gripped a wet ball with that hand, but he done it. And Fogarty's game Tuesday was even better. If his arm hurt he kept it to himself.

Smitty come back agin Johnson Wednesday and pitched the prettiest game that was ever pitched. Milan and Gandil and them might just as well of used jackstraws as bats, for all the good their swingin' done. He whiffed plain sixteen men and Johnson's two-bagger was their only wallop. Nobody didn't grudge Walter that one, 'cause he pitched a grand game too.

Well, the honor o' coppin' the final pastime and winnin' the title went to Fogarty; and it pleased him about as much as a toothache. Do you know why? 'Cause the papers was full o' Smitty's two victories over Johnson and didn't say much about nothin' else. Fogarty told me afterward that if he'd thought at the time he'd of refused to pitch

Thursday and made Red work him agin the big blond in the seventh game.

"But," I says, "s'pose Red had pitched Smitty right back and he'd of trimmed 'em and they hadn't been no seventh game anyway. Then where'd you of been at?"

"That's right!" he says. "That wop is just lucky enough to of did it, too, even if he can't pitch up an alley."

Well, I made a little speech in the clubhouse and collected a purse of a hundred and fifty bucks. I'm goin' to send it to Jack Barnett as soon as I can get his address. That'll fix him up on that bet he made with Punch Knoll and give him a little spendin' money besides. If he hadn't of told me that stuff in Dayton we'd of been fightin' the ◆ Cardinals for seventh place. And if he'd of told it to some guys they wouldn't of had sense enough to of tooken advantage of it.

One o' the Philly doctors told Red, and Red told me, that we'd prob'ly ruined both o' them guys for the next season by workin' 'em in the shape they was in. But I should worry! Between me and you, I ain't goin' to be with the Phillies next year. I'm goin' to manage the ◆ Mobile Club; and maybe I can play some in that climate. And I guess I don't know nothin' about managin' a ball club. No; I guess not!

◆ *fightin' the Cardinals for seventh place*—This is another apparent reference to the 1913 season.

◆ *I'm goin' to manage the Mobile Club*—The manager of the Mobile club of the Southern Association in 1915 was Charles "Boss" Schmidt, a former catcher for the Detroit Tigers. Because he had also held the post in 1913 and 1914, Schmidt cannot be identified as the narrator.

Horseshoes

The series ended Tuesday, but I had stayed in Philadelphia an extra ◆ day on the chance of there being some follow-up stuff worth sending. Nothing had broken loose; so I filed some stuff about what the Athletics and Giants were going to do with their dough, and then ◇ caught the eight o'clock train for Chicago.

Having passed up supper in order to get my story away and grab the train, I went to the buffet car right after I'd planted my grips. I sat down at one of the tables and ordered a sandwich. Four salesmen were playing rhum at the other table and all the chairs in the car were occupied; so it didn't surprise me when somebody flopped down in the seat opposite me.

I looked up from my paper and with a little thrill recognized my companion. Now I've been experting round the country with ball players so much that it doesn't usually excite me to meet one face to face, even if he's a star. I can talk with Tyrus without getting all fussed up. But this particular player had jumped from obscurity to fame so suddenly and had played such an important though brief part in the

---

"Horseshoes" was published in *The Saturday Evening Post*, CLXXXVII (August 15, 1914), 8–10, 44–46.

◆ *The Series ended Tuesday*—The reference is to the 1913 World Series between the Giants and Athletics. The Series, which the Athletics won, four games to one, actually ended on a Saturday, October 11.

◇ *the Athletics*—The Philadelphia Athletics of 1913. (National Baseball Library, Cooperstown, New York)

recent argument between the Macks and McGraws that I couldn't help being a little awed by his proximity.

It was none other than Grimes, the utility outfielder Connie had been forced to use in the last game because of the injury to Joyce— ◆ Grimes, whose miraculous catch in the eleventh inning had robbed Parker of a home run and the Giants of victory, and whose own homer—a fluky one—had given the Athletics another World's Championship.

I had met Grimes one day during the spring he was with the Cubs, but I knew he wouldn't remember me. A ball player never recalls a reporter's face on less than six introductions or his name on less than twenty. However, I resolved to speak to him, and had just mustered sufficient courage to open a conversation when he saved me the trouble.

"Whose picture have they got there?" he asked, pointing to my paper.

"Speed Parker's," I replied.

"What do they say about him?" asked Grimes.

"I'll read it to you," I said:

◆ *Joyce . . . Grimes . . . Parker*—All fictional characters.

"Speed Parker, McGraw's great third baseman, is ill in a local hospital with nervous prostration, the result of the strain of the World's Series, in which he played such a stellar rôle. Parker is in such a dangerous condition that no one is allowed to see him. Members of the New York team and fans from Gotham called at the hospital to-day, but were unable to gain admittance to his ward. Philadelphians hope he will recover speedily and will suffer no permanent ill effects from his sickness, for he won their admiration by his work in the series, though he was on a rival team. A lucky catch by Grimes, the Athletics' substitute outfielder, was all that prevented Parker from winning the title for New York. According to Manager Mack, of the champions, the series would have been over in four games but for Parker's wonderful exhibition of nerve and—"

"That'll be a plenty," Grimes interrupted. "And that's just what you might expect from one o' them doughheaded reporters. If all the baseball writers was where they belonged they'd have to build an annex to Matteawan." ◆

I kept my temper with very little effort—it takes more than a peevish ball player's remarks to insult one of our fraternity; but I didn't exactly understand his peeve.

"Doesn't Parker deserve the bouquet?" I asked.

"Oh, they can boost him all they want to," said Grimes; "but when they call that catch lucky and don't mention the fact that Parker is the luckiest guy in the world, somethin' must be wrong with 'em. Did you see the serious?"

"No," I lied glibly, hoping to draw from him the cause of his grouch.

"Well," he said, "you sure missed somethin'. They never was a serious like it before and they won't never be one again. It went the full seven games and every game was a bear. They was one big innin' every day and Parker was the big cheese in it. Just as Connie says, the Ath-a-letics would of cleaned 'em in four games but for Parker; but it wasn't because he's a great ball player—it was because he was born with a knife, fork and spoon in his mouth, and a rabbit's foot hung round his neck.

"You may not know it, but I'm Grimes, the guy that made the lucky catch. I'm the guy that won the serious with a hit—a home-run hit; and I'm here to tell you that if I'd had one-tenth o' Parker's luck they'd of heard about me long before yesterday. They say my homer was lucky.

◆ *Matteawan*—Matteawan State Hospital, New York.

Maybe it was; but, believe me, it was time things broke for me. They been breakin' for him all his life."

"Well," I said, "his luck must have gone back on him if he's in a hospital with nervous prostration."

"Nervous prostration nothin'," said Grimes. "He's in a hospital because his face is all out o' shape and he's ashamed to appear on the street. I don't usually do so much talkin' and I'm ravin' a little to-night because I've had a couple o' drinks; but—"

"Have another," said I, ringing for the waiter, "and talk some more."

"I made two hits yesterday," Grimes went on, "but the crowd only seen one. I busted up the game and the serious with the one they seen. The one they didn't see was the one I busted up a guy's map with—and Speed Parker was the guy. That's why he's in a hospital. He may be able to play ball next year; but I'll bet my share o' the dough that McGraw won't reco'nize him when he shows up at Marlin in the spring." ◆

"When did this come off?" I asked. "And why?"

"It come off outside the clubhouse after yesterday's battle," he said; "and I hit him because he called me a name—a name I won't stand for from him."

"What did he call you?" I queried, expecting to hear one of the delicate epithets usually applied by conquered to conqueror on the diamond.

"'Horseshoes!'" was Grimes' amazing reply.

"But, good Lord!" I remonstrated, "I've heard of ballplayers calling each other that, and Lucky Stiff, and Fourleaf Clover, ever since I was a foot high, and I never knew them to start fights about it."

"Well," said Grimes, "I might as well give you all the dope; and then if you don't think I was justified I'll pay your fare from here to wherever you're goin'. I don't want you to think I'm kickin' about trifles—or that I'm kickin' at all, for that matter. I just want to prove to you that he didn't have no license to pull that Horseshoes stuff on me and that I only give him what was comin' to him."

"Go ahead and shoot," said I.

"Give us some more o' the same," said Grimes to the passing waiter. And then he told me about it.

* * *

◆ *Marlin*—Marlin, Tex. (pop. 3,878 in 1910), seat of Falls County, about 113 miles south of Dallas, spring-training base of the Giants since 1908. The town, which saw some development as a spa, had for John McGraw the attraction of isolation, which allowed him to maintain a disciplined environment in spring training.

Maybe you've heard that me and Speed Parker was raised in the same town—Ishpeming, Michigan. We was kids together, and though he done all the devilment I got all the lickin's. When we was about twelve years old Speed throwed a rotten egg at the teacher and I got expelled. That made me sick o' schools and I wouldn't never go to one again, though my ol' man beat me up and the truant officers threatened to have me hung.

Well, while Speed was learnin' what was the principal products o' New Hampshire and Texas I was workin' round the freighthouse and drivin' a dray.

We'd both been playin' ball all our lives; and when the town organized a semi-pro club we got jobs with it. We was to draw two bucks apiece for each game and they played every Sunday. We played four games before we got our first pay. They was a hole in my pants pocket as big as home plate, but I forgot about it and put the dough in there. It wasn't there when I got home. Speed didn't have no hole in his pocket—you can bet on that! Afterward the club hired a good outfielder and I was canned. They was huntin' for another third baseman too; but, o' course, they didn't find none and Speed held his job.

The next year they started the Northern Peninsula League. We landed with the home team. The league opened in May and blowed up the third week in June. They paid off all the outsiders first and then had just money enough left to settle with one of us two Ishpeming guys. The night they done the payin' I was out to my uncle's farm, so they settled wth Speed and told me I'd have to wait for mine. I'm still waitin'!

Gene Higgins, who was manager o' the Battle Creek Club, lived in Houghton, and that winter we goes over and strikes him for a job. He give it to us and we busted in together two years ago last spring.

I had a good year down there. I hit over .300 and stole all the bases

---

◆ *Ishpeming, Michigan*—An iron-mining town (pop. 12,448 in 1910) in the Upper Peninsula, center of the Marquette iron range.

◆ *Northern Peninsula League*—No league of this name ever operated in Organized Baseball, although it would be surprising if such a league had not operated at least on an amateur, semiprofessional, or "outlaw" level.

◆ *the Battle Creek Club*—Battle Creek had a club in the Southern Michigan Association in 1911. The club placed seventh among the eight teams. The manager was John Patrick Burke; Gene Higgins is apparently a fictional character.

◆ *Houghton*—one of the twin cities of Houghton and Hancock on the Keweenaw Waterway crossing the Keweenaw Peninsula, an arm of the Upper Peninsula.

in sight. Speed got along good too, and they was several big-league scouts lookin' us over. The Chicago Cubs bought Speed outright and four clubs put in a draft for me. Three of 'em—Cleveland and the New York Giants and the Boston Nationals—needed outfielders bad, and it would of been a pipe for me to of made good with any of 'em. But who do you think got me? The same Chicago Cubs; and the only outfielders they had at that time was Schulte and Leach and Good and Williams and Stewart, and one or two others. ◆

Well, I didn't figure I was any worse off than Speed. The Cubs had Zimmerman at third base and it didn't look like they was any danger of a busher beatin' him out; but Zimmerman goes and breaks his leg ◆ the second day o' the season—that's a year ago last April—and Speed jumps right in as a regular. Do you think anything like that could happen to Schulte or Leach, or any o' them outfielders? No, sir! I wore out my uniform slidin' up and down the bench and wonderin' whether they'd ship me to Fort Worth or Siberia.

Now I want to tell you about the miserable luck Speed had right off the reel. We was playin' at St. Louis. They had a one-run lead in the eighth, when their pitcher walked Speed with one out. Saier hits a high fly to center and Parker starts with the crack o' the bat. Both coachers was yellin' at him to go back, but he thought they was two out and he was clear round to third base when the ball come down. And Oakes muffs it! O' course he scored and the game was tied up.

Parker come in to the bench like he'd did something wonderful.

"Did you think they was two out?" ast Hank. ◆

◆ *Williams*—Fred "Cy" Williams (1887–1974), a rookie outfielder with the Cubs in 1912 who appeared in only 28 games, hitting .242. Williams was never oustandingly successful for the Cubs, but upon going to the Phillies after the 1917 season, hit over .300 six times, and by the end of his major league service in 1930 had hit .292 in 2,002 games. Williams, who held a degree in architecture from Notre Dame, became a builder in northeastern Wisconsin after his playing days. See Cappy Gagnon, "Fred C. [sic] Williams," *Biographical Dictionary of American Sports: Baseball*, pp. 610–11.

Stewart—Charles Eugene "Tuffy" Stewart (1883–1934). The reference is an anachronism, for the internal logic of the story requires the events discussed to have occurred in 1912. Stewart's major league career was limited to nine games with the Cubs in 1913 and two in 1914, in which he made a total of one hit in 11 times at bat. Stewart in fact seems an odd choice for the hero's demonstration of the difficulty of making the Cubs' outfield.

◆ *Zimmerman goes and breaks his leg the second day o' the season*—This is a fictional occurrence.

◆ *Hank*—As usual, Hank O'Day. This is a further anachronism, for the action is attributed to 1912 and O'Day managed the Cubs only in 1914.

"No," says Speed, blushin'.

"Then what did you run for?" says Hank.

"I had a hunch he was goin' to drop the ball," says Speed; and Hank pretty near falls off the bench.

The next day he come up with one out and the sacks full, and the score tied in the sixth. He smashes one on the ground straight at Hauser and it looked like a cinch double play; but just as Hauser was ◆ goin' to grab it the ball hit a rough spot and hopped a mile over his head. It got between Oakes and Magee and went clear to the fence. ◆ Three guys scored and Speed pulled up at third. The papers come out and said the game was won by a three-bagger from the bat o' Parker, the Cubs' sensational kid third baseman. Gosh!

We go home to Chi and are havin' a hot battle with Pittsburgh. This time Speed's turn come when they was two on and two out, and Pittsburgh a run to the good—I think it was the eighth innin'. Cooper ◆ gives him a fast one and he hits it straight up in the air. O' course the runners started goin', but it looked hopeless because they wasn't no wind or high sky to bother anybody. Mowrey and Gibson both goes ◆

◆ *Hauser*—Arnold George Hauser (1888–1966), regular shortstop for the Cardinals from 1910 to early 1913. Hauser was mentally ill with a religious mania in 1914, but after recovering played in 23 games for the Chicago Whales in 1915. In 433 games in the National and Federal leagues, he batted .238. See Jack Kavanagh, "Arnold Hauser," *The Ballplayers*, p. 453.

◆ *Magee*—Lee Magee, playing name of Leopold Christopher Hoernschemeyer (1889–1966), a utility player whose 1,034 major league games were about evenly divided between the infield and outfield. For the Cardinals from 1911 to 1914, Magee played mainly center and left fields. Subsequently, he played for Brooklyn of the Federal League and for the Yankees, Browns, Reds, Dodgers, and Cubs through 1919, hitting .275. In the description at hand, Oakes was presumably in center and Magee in left. In 1919 Magee was found guilty of betting against the Dodgers while playing for them; he remains on baseball's list of permanently ineligible players. See Jack Kavanagh, "Lee Magee," *The Ballplayers*, p. 653.

◆ *Cooper*—Arley Wilbur Cooper (1892–1973), the Pirates' greatest lefthanded pitcher. In 1912 Cooper went 3–0 as a rookie, but by the early 1920's he was one of the major leagues' premier lefthanders, winning 20 or more games on four occasions. Including two final years with the Cubs and Tigers in 1925 and 1926, Cooper won 216 and lost 178. His 202 victories for Pittsburgh remain the club record. Cooper was also an excellent hitting pitcher, batting .346 in 1924. He is not a member of the Baseball Hall of Fame. See Raymond D. Kush, "Arley Wilbur Cooper," *Biographical Dictionary of American Sports: Baseball*, pp. 113–14.

◆ *Mowrey*—Harry Harlan "Mike" Mowrey (1887–1947), a third baseman who played in 79 games for the Pirates in 1914. From 1910 to 1913 he had been with the Cardinals. Between 1905 and 1917 Mowrey played in 1,275 games for the Reds, Cardinals, Pirates, Pittsburgh of the Federal League, and the Dodgers,

after the ball; and just as Mowrey was set for the catch Gibson bumps into him and they both fall down. Two runs scored and Speed got to second. Then what does he do but try to steal third—with two out too! And Gibson's peg pretty near hits the left field seats on the fly.

When Speed comes to the bench Hank says:

"If I was you I'd quit playin' ball and go to Monte Carlo."

"What for?" says Speed.

"You're so dam' lucky!" says Hank.

"So is Ty Cobb," says Speed. That's how he hated himself!

First trip to Cincy we run into a couple of old Ishpeming boys. They took us out one night, and about twelve o'clock I said we'd have to go back to the hotel or we'd get fined. Speed said I had cold feet and he stuck with the boys. I went back alone and Hank caught me comin' in and put a fifty-dollar plaster on me. Speed stayed out all night long and Hank never knowed it. I says to myself: "Wait till he gets out there and tries to play ball without no sleep!" But the game that day was called off on account o' rain. Can you beat it?

I remember what he got away with the next afternoon the same as though it happened yesterday. In the second innin' they walked him with nobody down, and he took a big lead off first base like he always does. Benton throwed over there three or four times to scare him back, and the last time he throwed, Hobby hid the ball. The coacher seen it and told Speed to hold the bag; but he didn't pay no attention. He started leadin' right off again and Hobby tried to tag him, but the ball slipped out of his hand and rolled about a yard away. Parker had plenty o' time to get back; but, instead o' that, he starts for second. Hobby picked up the ball and shot it down to Groh—and Groh made a square muff.

Parker slides into the bag safe and then gets up and throws out his chest like he'd made the greatest play ever. When the ball's throwed back to Benton, Speed leads off about thirty foot and stands there in

---

(*continued from page 400*)
hitting .256. He had an unorthodox fielding style of slapping hard ground balls to the dirt with his gloved hand, picking them up barehanded, and throwing to first base. See A. D. Suehsdorf, "Mike Mowrey," *The Ballplayers*, p. 767.

Gibson—George "Moon" Gibson (1880–1967), a Canadian who was the Pirates' catcher from 1905 to 1916. In 14 seasons, including 1917 and 1918 with the Giants, Gibson hit .236 in 1,213 games. He managed the Pirates from 1920 to 1922 and again from 1932 to 1934, as well as the Cubs briefly in 1925. See Morris A. Eckhouse, "George Gibson," *The Ballplayers*, p. 388.

a trance. Clarke signs for a pitch-out and pegs down to second to nip him. He was caught flatfooted—that is, he would of been with a decent throw; but Clarke's peg went pretty near to Latonia. Speed scored and strutted over to receive our hearty congratulations. Some o' the boys was laughin' and he thought they was laughin' with him instead of at him.

It was in the ninth, though, that he got by with one o' the worst I ever seen. The Reds was a run behind and Marsans was on third base with two out. Hobby, I think it was, hit one on the ground right at Speed and he picked it up clean. The crowd all got up and started for the exits. Marsans run toward the plate in the faint hope that the peg to first would be wild. All of a sudden the boys on the Cincy bench begun yellin' at him to slide, and he done so. He was way past the plate when Speed's throw got to Archer. The bonehead had shot the ball home instead o' to first base, thinkin' they was only one down. We was all crazy, believin' his nut play had let 'em tie it up; but he comes tearin' in, tellin' Archer to tag Marsans. So Jim walks over and tags the Cuban, who was brushin' off his uniform.

"You're out!" says Klem. "You never touched the plate."

I guess Marsans knowed the umps was right because he didn't make much of a holler. But Speed sure got a pannin' in the clubhouse.

"I suppose you knowed he was goin' to miss the plate!" says Hank sarcastic as he could.

Everybody on the club roasted him, but it didn't do no good.

Well, you know what happened to me. I only got into one game with the Cubs—one afternoon when Leach was sick. We was playin' the Boston bunch and Tyler was workin' against us. I always had

---

◆ *Clarke*—Thomas Aloysius Clarke (1888–1945), the Reds catcher from 1909 to 1917, and one of the game's leading pinch hitters. Including one game with the Cubs in 1918, Clarke hit .265 in 671 games in ten seasons. See Jack Kavanagh, "Tommy Clarke," *The Ballplayers*, p. 194.

◆ *Latonia*—A Kentucky suburb five miles south of Cincinnati.

◆ *Marsans*—Armando Marsans (1887–1960), a utility player with the Reds from 1911 until mid-1914, when he jumped to St. Louis of the Federal League. Subsequently, he played for the Browns and Yankees, ending his major league career in 1918. In 655 games, mainly in the outfield, Marsans hit .269. A Cuban, he was an early Latin American player in American baseball. See A. D. Suehsdorf, "Armando Marsans," *The Ballplayers*, pp. 671–72.

◆ *Tyler*—George Albert Tyler (1889–1953), the Braves' ace lefthander, who with Dick Rudolph and Seattle Bill James was to pitch the team to the 1914 pennant. Pitching for the Braves from 1910 to 1917 and for the Cubs from 1918 to 1921, Tyler won 125 and lost 119. He was also a good hitter, making nine pinch hits in 39 attempts. See Norman L. Macht, "Lefty Tyler," *The Ballplayers*, p. 1106.

trouble with lefthanders and this was one of his good days. I couldn't see what he throwed up there. I got one foul durin' the afternoon's entertainment; and the wind was blowin' a hundred-mile gale, so that the best outfielder in the world couldn't judge a fly ball. That Boston bunch must of hit fifty of 'em and they all come to my field.

If I caught any I've forgot about it. Couple o' days after that I got notice o' my release to Indianapolis. ◆

Parker kept right on all season doin' the blamedest things you ever heard of and gettin' by with 'em. One o' the boys told me about it later. If they was playin' a double-header in St. Louis, with the thermometer at 130 degrees, he'd get put out by the umps in the first innin' o' the first game. If he started to steal the catcher'd drop the pitch or somebody'd muff the throw. If he hit a pop fly the sun'd get in somebody's eyes. If he took a swell third strike with the bases full the umps would call it a ball. If he cut first base by twenty feet the umps would be readin' the mornin' paper.

Zimmerman's leg mended, so that he was all right by June; and then Saier got sick and they tried Speed at first base. He'd never saw the bag before; but things kept on breakin' for him and he played it like a house-afire. The Cubs copped the pennant and Speed got in on ◆ the big dough, besides playin' a whale of a game through the whole serious.

Speed and me both went back to Ishpeming to spend the winter—though the Lord knows it ain't no winter resort. Our homes was there; and besides, in my case, they was a certain girl livin' in the old burg.

Parker, o' course, was the hero and the swell guy when we got home. He'd been in the World's Serious and had plenty o' dough in his kick. I come home with nothin' but my suitcase and a hard-luck story, which I kept to myself. I hadn't even went good enough in Indianapolis to be sure of a job there again.

That fall—last fall—an uncle o' Speed's died over in the Soo and left him ten thousand bucks. I had an uncle down in the Lower Peninsula who was worth five times that much—but he had good health!

This girl I spoke about was the prettiest thing I ever see. I'd went with her in the old days, and when I blew back I found she was still

---

◆ *Indianapolis*—A club of the Class AA American Association.

◆ *the Cubs copped the pennant*—After 1910 the Cubs won no pennants until 1918. The Giants won the 1912 pennant.

strong for me. They wasn't a great deal o' variety in Ishpeming for a girl to pick from. Her and I went to the dance every Saturday night and to church Sunday nights. I called on her Wednesday evenin's, besides takin' her to all the shows that come along—rotten as the most o' them was.

I never knowed Speed was makin' a play for this doll till along last Feb'uary. The minute I seen what was up I got busy. I took her out sleigh-ridin' and kept her out in the cold till she'd promised to marry me. We set the date for this fall—I figured I'd know better where I was at by that time.

Well, we didn't make no secret o' bein' engaged; down in the poolroom one night Speed come up and congratulated me. He says:

"You got a swell girl, Dick! I wouldn't mind bein' in your place. You're mighty lucky to cop her out—you old Horseshoes, you!"

"Horseshoes!" I says. "You got a fine license to call anybody Horseshoes! I suppose you ain't never had no luck?"

"Not like you," he says.

I was feelin' too good about grabbin' the girl to get sore at the time; but when I got to thinkin' about it a few minutes afterward it made me mad clear through. What right did that bird have to talk about me bein' lucky?

Speed was playin' freeze-out at a table near the door, and when I started home some o' the boys with him says:

"Good night, Dick."

I said good night and then Speed looked up.

"Good night, Horseshoes!" he says.

That got my nanny this time.

"Shut up, you lucky stiff!" I says. "If you wasn't so dam' lucky you'd be sweepin' the streets." Then I walks on out.

I was too busy with the girl to see much o' Speed after that. He left home about the middle o' the month to go to Tampa with the Cubs. I got notice from Indianapolis that I was sold to Baltimore. I didn't care much about goin' there and I wasn't anxious to leave home under the circumstances, so I didn't report till late.

When I read in the papers along in April that Speed had been traded to Boston for a couple o' pitchers I thought: "Gee! He must of lost his rabbit's foot!" Because, even if the Cubs didn't cop again, they'd have a city serious with the White Sox and get a bunch o' dough that way. And they wasn't no chance in the world for the Boston Club to get nothin' but their salaries.

It wasn't another month, though, till Shafer, o' the Giants, quit◆◇ baseball and McGraw was up against it for a third baseman. Next thing I knowed Speed was traded to New York and was with another winner—for they never was out o' first place all season.

I was gettin' along all right at Baltimore and Dunnie liked me; so I ◆ felt like I had somethin' more than just a one-year job—somethin' I could get married on. It was all framed that the weddin' was comin' off as soon as this season was over; so you can believe I was pullin' for October to hurry up and come.

One day in August, two months ago, Dunnie come in the clubhouse and handed me the news.

"Rube Oldring's busted his leg," he says, "and he's out for the rest ◆ o' the season. Connie's got a youngster named Joyce that he can stick in there, but he's got to have an extra outfielder. He's made me a good proposition for you and I'm goin' to let you go. It'll be pretty soft for you, because they got the pennant cinched and they'll cut you in on the big money."

"Yes," I says; "and when they're through with me they'll ship me to Hellangone, and I'll be draggin' down about seventy-five bucks a month next year."

"Nothin' like that," says Dunnie. "If he don't want you next season

◇ *Shafer*—Drawing of Tillie Shafer by Lawrence Semon. (National Baseball Library, Cooperstown, New York)

◆ *Shafer*—Arthur Joseph "Tillie" Shafer (1889–1962), mainly an infielder, as stated, and a third baseman for the Giants from 1909 to 1913. In 283 games Shafer hit .273. In his best season, 1913, he hit .287. He did, in fact, quit baseball after that season. A University of Santa Clara alumnus, he became a successful real estate operator in Los Angeles and a prominent local amateur golfer.

◆ *Dunnie*—John Joseph "Jack" Dunn (1872–1928), "the McGraw of the Minors," owner and manager of the Baltimore Orioles of the International League. In a playing career of eight seasons with Brooklyn, Philadelphia, and New York of the National League and Baltimore of the American spanning the period 1897–1904, Dunn had hit .245 in 490 games, mainly in the infield, but he also pitched to a record of 64–59. After leaving the Giants, following the 1904 season, Dunn became manager at Providence in 1905, and moved to Baltimore in 1907. There his principal achievement was winning seven consecutive International League pennants, from 1919 to 1925. Except that these clubs typically lacked good catchers, they would have been competitive with the major league teams of the period; Connie Mack, in particular, purchased many of Dunn's best players, including Lefty Grove. Dunn's descendants continued in control of the team until Baltimore reentered the American League in 1953, and remained active in the administration of the major league club. See Norman L. Macht, "Jack Dunn," *The Ballplayers*, p. 298.

◆ *Rube Oldring's busted his leg*—Oldring did break his leg, but in 1910, on the eve of the World Series.

◇ *Johnson*—Walter Johnson at the plate in 1926. The year before he had hit .433 with 20 RBIs (see footnote, p. 46). (National Baseball Library, Cooperstown, New York)

he's got to ask for waivers; and if you get out o' the big league you come right back here. That's all framed."

So that's how I come to get with the Ath-a-letics. Connie give me a nice, comf'table seat in one corner o' the bench and I had the pleasure o' watchin' a real ball club perform once every afternoon and sometimes twice.

Connie told me that as soon as they had the flag cinched he was goin' to lay off some o' his regulars and I'd get a chance to play.

Well, they cinched it the fourth day o' September and our next engagement was with Washin'ton on Labor Day. We had two games and I was in both of 'em. And I broke in with my usual lovely luck, because the pitchers I was ast to face was Boehling, a nasty lefthander, and this guy Johnson. ◇

The mornin' game was Boehling's and he wasn't no worse than some o' the rest of his kind. I only whiffed once and would of had a triple if Milan hadn't run from here to New Orleans and stole one off me.

I'm not boastin' about my first expereince with Johnson though. They can't never tell me he throws them balls with his arm. He's got a gun concealed about his person and he shoots 'em up there. I was leadin' off in Murphy's place and the game was a little delayed in ◆ startin', because I'd watched the big guy warm up and wasn't in no hurry to get to that plate. Before I left the bench Connie says:

"Don't try to take no healthy swing. Just meet 'em and you'll get along better."

So I tried to just meet the first one he throwed; but when I stuck out my bat Henry was throwin' the pill back to Johnson. Then I ◆ thought: Maybe if I start swingin' now at the second one I'll hit the third one. So I let the second one come over and the umps guessed it was another strike, though I'll bet a thousand bucks he couldn't see it no more'n I could.

While Johnson was still windin' up to pitch again I started to swing—and the big cuss crosses me with a slow one. I lunged at it twice and missed it both times, and the force o' my wallop throwed me clean back to the bench. The Ath-a-letics was all laughin' at me and I laughed too, because I was glad that much of it was over.

McInnes gets a base hit off him in the second innin' and I ast him how he done it.

"He's a friend o' mine," says Jack, "and he lets up when he pitches to me."

I made up my mind right there that if I was goin' to be in the league next year I'd go out and visit Johnson this winter and get acquainted.

I wished before the day was over that I was hittin' in the catcher's

---

◆ *Murphy's place*—Probably John Edward "Honest Eddie" Murphy (1891–1969), the Athletics' regular rightfielder. In 1913 Murphy was having his best season, hitting .295 in 136 games. Murphy came to the White Sox in mid-1915 and was a reserve outfielder on the 1917 and 1919 championship teams. He was active with the White Sox until 1921, and then played 16 games for the Pirates in 1926. Overall, he hit .287 in 760 games. See Jack Kavanagh, "Eddie Murphy," *The Ballplayers*, p. 775.

Alternatively, the reference may be to Daniel Francis Murphy (1876–1955), a veteran outfielder for the Athletics who played only 40 games in 1913, his last season with the club. After two seasons with the Giants, Danny Murphy had played with the Athletics since 1902. He closed his career with two seasons for the Brooklyn Federals. Because the player is treated as the regular leadoff man, it is apparently Eddie Murphy who is indicated. See Jack Kavanagh, "Danny Murphy," *The Ballplayers*, p. 775.

◆ *Henry*—John Park Henry (1888–1941), Washington's regular catcher. Henry was a weak hitter, but a good receiver—an important asset in consideration of Johnson's speed. With the Senators from 1910 to 1917 and the Braves in 1918, Henry hit only .207 in 683 games. An alumnus of Amherst, Henry later coached at Cornell. See Jack Kavanagh, "John Henry," *The Ballplayers*, p. 464.

◇ *I sent her a kind o' sassy letter sayin' I guessed it was up to me to name the day*—Drawing by F. R. Gruger for the *The Saturday Evening Post,* August 15, 1914.

place, because the fellers down near the tail-end of the battin' order only had to face him three times. He fanned me on three pitched balls again in the third, and when I come up in the sixth he scared me to death by pretty near beanin' me with the first one.

"Be careful!" says Henry. "He's gettin' pretty wild and he's liable to knock you away from your uniform."

"Don't he never curve one?" I ast.

"Sure!" says Henry. "Do you want to see his curve?"

"Yes," I says, knowin' the hook couldn't be no worse'n the fast one.

So he give me three hooks in succession and I missed 'em all; but I felt more comf'table than when I was duckin' his fast ball. In the ninth he hit my bat with a curve and the ball went on the ground to McBride. He booted it, but throwed me out easy—because I was so surprised at not havin' whiffed that I forgot to run!

Well, I went along like that for the rest o' the season, runnin' up against the best pitchers in the league and not exactly murderin' 'em.

Everything I tried went wrong, and I was smart enough to know that if anything had depended on the games I wouldn't of been in there for two minutes. Joyce and Strunk and Murphy wasn't jealous o' me a bit; but they was glad to take turns restin', and I didn't care much how I went so long as I was sure of a job next year.

I'd wrote to the girl a couple o' times askin' her to set the exact date for our weddin'; but she hadn't paid no attention. She said she was glad I was with the Ath-a-letics, but she thought the Giants was goin' to beat us. I might of suspected from that that somethin' was wrong, because not even a girl would pick the Giants to trim that bunch of ourn. Finally, the day before the serious started, I sent her a kind o' sassy letter sayin' I guessed it was up to me to name the day, and askin' whether October twentieth was all right. I told her to wire me yes or no.

I'd been readin' the dope about Speed all season, and I knowed he'd had a whale of a year and that his luck was right with him; but I never dreamed a man could have the Lord on his side as strong as Speed did in that World's Serious! I might as well tell you all the dope, so long as you wasn't there.

The first game was on our grounds and Connie give us a talkin' to in the clubhouse beforehand.

"The shorter this serious is," he says, "the better for us. If it's a long serious we're goin' to have trouble, because McGraw's got five pitchers he can work and we've got about three, so I want you boys to go at 'em from the jump and play 'em off their feet. Don't take things easy, because it ain't goin' to be no snap. Just because we've licked 'em before ain't no sign we'll do it this time."

Then he calls me to one side and ast me what I knowed about Parker.

"You was with the Cubs when he was, wasn't you?" he says.

"Yes," I says; "and he's the luckiest stiff you ever seen! If he got stewed and fell in the gutter he'd catch a fish."

◆ *McGraw's got five pitchers he can work*—Presumably Christy Mathewson (25–11), Rube Marquard (23–10), Jeff Tesreau (22–13), Al Demaree (13–4), and Art Fromme (10–6).

◆ *we've got about three*—This is an odd statement to attribute to Mack. In 1913 he had a staff consisting of Chief Bender (21–10), Eddie Plank (18–10), Boardwalk Brown (17–11), Bullet Joe Bush (14–6), Byron Houck (14–6), and the young Bob Shawkey (8–5).

◆ *we've licked 'em before*—The Athletics had defeated the Giants in the 1911 World Series, four games to two.

◇ *Plank*—Eddie Plank warming up in the road uniform of the 1913–14 Athletics. (National Baseball Library, Cooperstown, New York)

"I don't like to hear a good ball player called lucky," says Connie. "He must have a lot of ability or McGraw wouldn't use him regular. And he's been hittin' about .340 and played a bang-up game at third base. That can't be all luck."

"Wait till you see him," I says; "and if you don't say he's the luckiest guy in the world you can sell me to the Boston Bloomer Girls. He's so lucky," I says, "that if they traded him to the St. Louis Browns they'd have the pennant cinched by the Fourth o' July."

And I'll bet Connie was willin' to agree with me before it was over.

Well, the Chief worked against the Big Rube in that game. We beat ◆ 'em, but they give us a battle and it was Parker that made it close. We'd

---

◆ *Well, the Chief worked against the Big Rube in that game.*—In the actual first game of the 1913 World Series, Bender did work against Marquard, winning 6–4. As stated, Baker hit a home run at the Polo Grounds.

gone along nothin' and nothin' till the seventh, and then Rube walks Collins and Baker lifts one over that little old wall. You'd think by this time them New York pitchers would know better than to give that guy anything he can hit.

In their part o' the ninth the Chief still had 'em shut out and two down, and the crowd was goin' home; but Doyle gets hit in the sleeve with a pitched ball and it's Speed's turn. He hits a foul pretty near straight up, but Schang misjudges it. Then he lifts another one and this time McInnes drops it. He'd ought to of been out twice. The Chief tries to make him hit at a bad one then, because he'd got him two strikes and nothin'. He hit at it all right—kissed it for three bases between Strunk and Joyce! And it was a wild pitch that he hit. Doyle scores, o' course, and the bugs suddenly decide not to go home just yet. I fully expected to see him steal home and get away with it, but Murray cut into the first ball and lined out to Barry. ◆

Plank beat Matty two to one the next day in New York, and again ◆◇ Speed and his rabbit's foot give us an awful argument. Matty wasn't so good as usual and we really ought to of beat him bad. Two different times Strunk was on second waitin' for any kind o' wallop, and both times Barry cracked 'em down the third base line like a shot. Speed stopped the first one with his stomach and extricated the pill just in time to nail Barry at first base and retire the side. The next time he throwed his glove in front of his face in self-defense and the ball stuck in it.

◇ *Plank*—The Edward S. Plank plaque at the National Baseball Hall of Fame and Museum, Cooperstown, New York.

◆ *Murray*—John Joseph "Red" Murray (1884–1958), the Giants rightfielder. A relatively weak member of an extremely strong team, Murray hit .267 in 1913. Murray broke in with the Cardinals in 1906, came to the Giants in 1909, played 51 games for the Cubs in 1915, and finished his major league service with the Giants in 1917. In 11 seasons he hit .270 in 1,263 games. See Cappy Gagnon, "Red Murray," *The Ballplayers*, p. 777.

◆ *Plank*—Edward Stewart Plank (1875–1926), the leading lefthander of the early twentieth century. Plank pitched for the Athletics from 1901 to 1914, for the St. Louis Federals in 1915, and for the Browns in 1916–17. His 327 victories (306 in the American League) and eight 20-game seasons (seven in the American League) were records for a lefthanded pitcher until broken by Warren Spahn. Plank's 69 shutouts remain the record for a lefthander.

Plank, a graduate of Gettysburg College, was in some respects a lefthanded counterpart of Mathewson, an alumnus of Bucknell. They met in World Series play three times, Mathewson winning twice and Plank once. In the second game of the 1913 Series, Plank did face Mathewson, but Mathewson won, 3–0 in ten innings.

Plank became a member of the Baseball Hall of Fame in 1946. See Joseph Lawler, "Edward Stewart Plank," *Biographical Dictionary of American Sports: Baseball*, pp. 450–51.

In the sixth innin' Schang was on third base and Plank on first, and two down, and Murphy combed an awful one to Speed's left. He didn't have time to stoop over and he just stuck out his foot. The ball hit it and caromed in two hops right into Doyle's hand on second base before Plank got there. Then in the seventh Speed bunts one and Baker trips and falls goin' after it or he'd of threw him out a mile. They was two gone; so Speed steals second, and, o' course, Schang has to make a bad peg right at that time and lets him go to third. Then Collins boots one on Murray and they've got a run. But it didn't do 'em no good, because Collins and Baker and McInnes come up in the ninth and walloped 'em where Parker couldn't reach 'em.

Comin' back to Phily on the train that night, I says to Connie:

"What do you think o' that Parker bird now?"

"He's lucky, all right," says Connie smilin'; "but we won't hold it against him if he don't beat us with it."

"It ain't too late," I says. "He ain't pulled his real stuff yet."

The whole bunch was talkin' about him and his luck, and sayin' it was about time for things to break against him. I warned 'em that they wasn't no chance—that it was permanent with him.

Bush and Tesreau hooked up next day and neither o' them had ◆ much stuff. Everybody was hittin' and it looked like anybody's game right up to the ninth. Speed had got on every time he come up—the wind blowin' his fly balls away from the outfielders and the infielders bootin' when he hit 'em on the ground.

When the ninth started the score was seven apiece. Connie and McGraw both had their whole pitchin' staffs warmin' up. The crowd was wild, because they'd been all kinds of action. They wasn't no danger of anybody's leavin' their seats before this game was over.

Well, Bescher is walked to start with and Connie's about ready to ◆

◆ *Bush*—Leslie Ambrose "Bullet Joe" Bush (1892–1974), a fastballing right-hander who pitched for the Athletics from 1912 to 1917. Another player who would move in both of the mass liquidations of the time, Bush went to the Red Sox in 1918 and to the Yankees in 1922. His best season was 26–7 in 1922. He went to the Browns in 1925, where he had his last strong season, 14–14. Subsequently, he pitched briefly for the Senators, Pirates, and Giants, ending his career with the Athletics in 1928. In 17 seasons he won 196 and lost 181. A good hitter, he had a lifetime batting average of .253, and after his major league service played a season as an outfielder in the Pacific Coast League. See Jack Kavanagh, "Joe Bush," *The Ballplayers*, pp. 141–42.

◆ *Bescher*—Robert Henry Bescher (1884–1942), an outfielder who spent only the 1914 season with the Giants. In 1913 Bescher was with the Reds, for whom he had played since 1908. From 1915 to 1917 he played for the Cardinals, and in

give Bush the hook; but Doyle pops out tryin' to bunt. Then Speed gets two strikes and two balls, and it looked to me like the next one was right over the heart; but Connolly calls it a ball and gives him ◆◇ another chance. He whales the groove ball to the fence in left center and gets round to third on it, while Bescher scores. Right then Bush comes out and the Chief goes in. He whiffs Murray and has two strikes on Merkle when Speed makes a break for home—and, o' course, that was the one ball Schang dropped in the whole serious!

They had a two-run lead on us then and it looked like a cinch for them to hold it, because the minute Tesreau showed a sign o' weakenin' McGraw was sure to holler for Matty or the Rube. But you know how quick that bunch of ourn can make a two-run lead look sick. Before McGraw could get Jeff out o' there we had two on the bases.

Then Rube comes in and fills 'em up by walkin' Joyce. It was Eddie's turn to wallop and if he didn't do nothin' we had Baker comin' up next. This time Collins saved Baker the trouble and whanged one clear to the woods. Everybody scored but him—and he could of, too, ◆ if it'd been necessary.

In the clubhouse the boys naturally felt pretty good. We'd copped three in a row and it looked like we'd make it four straight, because we had the Chief to send back at 'em the followin' day.

"Your friend Parker is lucky," the boys says to me, "but it don't look like he could stop us now."

I felt the same way and was consultin' the time-tables to see whether I could get a train out o' New York for the West next evenin'. But do you think Speed's luck was ready to quit? Not yet! And it's a wonder we didn't all go nuts durin' the next few days. If words could kill, Speed would of died a thousand times. And I wish he had!

◇ *Connolly*—Umpire Tom Connolly, probably taken in the 1920's. (National Baseball Library, Cooperstown, New York)

◇ *Connolly*—The Thomas Henry Connolly plaque at the National Baseball Hall of Fame and Museum, Cooperstown, New York.

(*continued from page 412*)
1918, for the Indians. In 1,228 games, he hit only .258, but stole 427 bases. A former football player at Wittenberg College, he led the National League in stolen bases annually from 1909 to 1912, stealing 80 in 1911. See Cappy Gagnon, "Bob Bescher," *The Ballplayers*, p. 75.

◆ *Connolly*—Thomas Henry Connolly (1870–1961), an umpire in the American League from literally its first game in 1901 to 1931, and the circuit's supervising umpire until 1953. See David L. Porter, "Thomas Henry Connolly," *Biographical Dictionary of American Sports: Baseball*, pp. 109–11.

◆ *Everybody scored but him—and he could of, too, if it'd been necessary.*—In the third game at New York on October 9, Bush easily beat Tesreau, 8–2. Collins did win the game with three hits and three runs batted in, but Wally Schang, not Collins, hit a home run. Doc Crandall, not Rube Marquard, relieved Tesreau in the seventh inning.

They wasn't no record-breakin' crowd out when we got to the Polo ◆ Grounds. I guess the New York bugs was pretty well discouraged and the bettin' was eight to five that we'd cop that battle and finish it. The Chief was the only guy that warmed up for us and McGraw didn't have no choice but to use Matty, with the whole thing dependin' on this game.

They went along like the two swell pitchers they was till Speed's innin', which in this battle was the eighth. Nobody scored, and it didn't look like they was ever goin' to till Murphy starts off that round with a perfect bunt and Joyce sacrifices him to second. All Matty had to do then was to get rid o' Collins and Baker—and that's about as easy as sellin' silk socks to an Eskimo.

He didn't give Eddie nothin' he wanted to hit, though; and finally he slaps one on the ground to Doyle. Larry made the play to first base and Murphy moved to third. We all figured Matty'd walk Baker then, and he done it. Connie sends Baker down to second on the first pitch to McInnes, but Meyers don't pay no attention to him—they was playin' for McInnes and wasn't takin' no chances o' throwin' the ball away.

Well, the count goes to three and two on McInnes and Matty comes with a curve—he's got some curve too; but Jack happened to meet it and—Blooie! Down the left foul line where he always hits! I never seen a ball hit so hard in my life. No infielder in the world could of stopped it. But I'll give you a thousand bucks if that ball didn't go kerplunk right into the third bag and stop as dead as George Washington! It was child's play for Speed to pick it up and heave it over to Merkle before Jack got there. If anybody else had been playin' third base the bag would of ducked out o' the way o' that wallop; but even the bases themselves was helpin' him out.

The two runs we ought to of had on Jack's smash would of been just enough to beat 'em, because they got the only run o' the game in their half—or, I should say, the Lord give it to 'em.

Doyle'd been throwed out and up come Parker, smilin'. The minute I seen him smile I felt like somethin' was comin' off and I made the remark on the bench.

Well, the Chief pitched one right at him and he tried to duck. The

---

◆ *the Polo Grounds*—Home park of the Giants from its opening in 1891 until the team moved to San Francisco after the 1957 season. The permanent steel-and-concrete stands were built following a fire in 1911. The New York Mets played at the Polo Grounds from their founding in 1962 until Shea Stadium was available to them in 1964.

ball hit his bat and went on a line between Jack and Eddie. Speed didn't know he'd hit it till the guys on the bench wised him up. Then he just had time to get to first base. They tried the hit-and-run on the second ball and Murray lifts a high fly that Murphy didn't have to move for. Collins pulled the old bluff about the ball bein' on the ground and Barry yells, "Go on! Go on!" like he was the coacher. Speed fell for it and didn't know where the ball was no more'n a rabbit; he just run his fool head off and we was gettin' all ready to laugh when the ball come down and Murphy dropped it!

If Parker had stuck near first base, like he ought to of done, he couldn't of got no farther'n second; but with the start he got he was pretty near third when Murphy made the muff, and it was a cinch for him to score. The next two guys was easy outs; so they wouldn't of had a run except for Speed's boner. We couldn't do nothin' in the ninth and we was licked. ◆

◇ *Demaree*—Drawing of Al Demaree by Lawrence Semon. (National Baseball Library, Cooperstown, New York)

Well, that was a tough one to lose; but we figured that Matty was through and we'd wind it up the next day, as we had Plank ready to send back at 'em. We wasn't afraid o' the Rube, because he hadn't never bothered Collins and Baker much.

The two lefthanders come together just like everybody'd doped it and it was about even up to the eighth. Plank had been goin' great and, though the score was two and two, they'd got their two on boots and we'd hit ourn in. We went after Rube in our part o' the eighth and knocked him out. Demaree stopped us after we'd scored two ◆◇ more.

"It's all over but the shoutin'!" says Davis on the bench. ◆

◆ *we was licked*—In the actual fourth game Bender beat Al Demaree, 6–5, on October 10 at Philadelphia.

◆ *Demaree*—Albert Wentworth Demaree (1886–1962), a righthanded pitcher for the Giants from 1912 to 1914 and again in 1917–18, with intervening years playing for the Phillies and Cubs. He finished his career with the Braves in 1919, completing a lifetime record of 81–72. Demaree had an unusual and highly successful post-baseball career as a sports cartoonist. See Norman L. Macht, "Al Demaree," *The Ballplayers*, p. 267.

◆ *Davis*—Harry H. Davis (1873–1947), coach of the Athletics. Davis had played for several National League teams in the late 1890's, then for the Athletics from 1901 to 1911. He managed the Cleveland Naps in 1912 and returned to the Athletics as a coach in the following year. A first baseman, he played occasionally for the team as late as 1917. In 22 seasons he hit .277 in 1,757 games and hit the then-impressive total of 74 home runs. A native Philadelphian, Davis later served in the city council. See Morris A. Eckhouse and Jack Kavanagh, "Harry Davis," *The Ballplayers*, p. 257.

"Yes," I says, "unless that seventh son of a seventh son gets up there again."

He did, and he come up after they'd filled the bases with a boot, a base hit and a walk with two out. I says to Davis:

"If I was Plank I'd pass him and give 'em one run."

"That wouldn't be no baseball," says Davis—"not with Murray comin' up."

Well, it mayn't of been no baseball, but it couldn't of turned out worse if they'd did it that way. Speed took a healthy at the first ball; but it was a hook and he caught it on the handle, right up near his hands. It started outside the first-base line like a foul and then changed its mind and rolled in. Schang run away from the plate, because it looked like it was up to him to make the play. He picked the ball up and had to make the peg in a hurry.

His throw hit Speed right on top o' the head and bounded off like it had struck a cement sidewalk. It went clear over to the seats and before McInnes could get it three guys had scored and Speed was on third base. He was left there, but that didn't make no difference. We ◆ was licked again, and for the first time the gang really begun to get scared.

We went over to New York Sunday afternoon and we didn't do no singin' on the way. Some o' the fellers tried to laugh, but it hurt 'em. Connie sent us to bed early, but I don't believe none o' the bunch got much sleep—I know I didn't; I was worryin' too much about the serious and also about the girl, who hadn't sent me no telegram like I'd ast her to. Monday mornin' I wired her askin' what was the matter and tellin' her I was gettin' tired of her foolishness. O' course I didn't make it so strong as that—but the telegram cost me a dollar and forty cents.

Connie had the choice o' two pitchers for the sixth game. He could use Bush, who'd been slammed round pretty hard last time out, or the Chief, who'd only had two days' rest. The rest of 'em—outside o' Plank—had a epidemic o' sore arms. Connie finally picked Bush, so's

---

◆ *We was licked again*—In the fifth game at New York on October 11, Plank ended the Series with one of his most memorable performances, defeating Mathewson, 3–1, and allowing the Giants only two hits. He faced only 29 men. All of the runs of both teams came as the result of errors. The Athletics won the Series, four games to one. Accordingly, the accounts of a sixth and a seventh game, below, are entirely fictional.

he could have the Chief in reserve in case we had to play a seventh game. McGraw started Big Jeff and we went at it.

It wasn't like the last time these two guys had hooked up. This time they both had somethin', and for eight innin's runs was as scarce as Chinese policemen. They'd been chances to score on both sides, but the big guy and Bush was both tight in the pinches. The crowd was plumb nuts and yelled like Indians every time a fly ball was caught or a strike called. They'd of got their money's worth if they hadn't been no ninth; but, believe me, that was some round!

They was one out when Barry hit one through the box for a base. Schang walked, and it was Bush's turn. Connie told him to bunt, but he whiffed in the attempt. Then Murphy comes up and walks—and the bases are choked. Young Joyce had been pie for Tesreau all day or else McGraw might of changed pitchers right there. Anyway he left Big Jeff in and he beaned Joyce with a fast one. It sounded like a tire blowin' out. Joyce falls over in a heap and we chase out there, thinkin' he's dead; but he ain't, and pretty soon he gets up and walks down to first base. Tesreau had forced in a run and again we begun to count the winners' end. Matty comes in to prevent further damage and Collins flies the side out.

"Hold 'em now! Work hard!" we says to young Bush, and he walks out there just as cool as though he was goin' to hit fungoes.

McGraw sends up a pinch hitter for Matty and Bush whiffed him. Then Bescher flied out. I was prayin' that Doyle would end it, because Speed's turn come after hisn; so I pretty near fell dead when Larry hit safe.

Speed had his old smile and even more chest than usual when he come up there, swingin' five or six bats. He didn't wait for Doyle to try and steal, or nothin'. He lit into the first ball, though Bush was tryin' to waste it. I seen the ball go high in the air toward left field, and then I picked up my glove and got ready to beat it for the gate. But when I looked out to see if Joyce was set, what do you think I seen? He was lyin' flat on the ground! That blow on the head had got him just as Bush was pitchin' to Speed. He'd flopped over and didn't no more know what was goin' on than if he'd croaked.

Well, everybody else seen it at the same time; but it was too late. Strunk made a run for the ball, but they wasn't no chance for him to get near it. It hit the ground about ten feet back o' where Joyce was lyin' and bounded way over to the end o' the foul line. You don't have to be told that Doyle and Parker both scored and the serious was tied up.

We carried Joyce to the clubhouse and after a while he come to. He cried when he found out what had happened. We cheered him up all we could, but he was a pretty sick guy. The trainer said he'd be all right, though, for the final game.

They tossed up a coin to see where they'd play the seventh battle and our club won the toss; so we went back to Philly that night and cussed Parker clear across New Jersey. I was so sore I kicked the stuffin' out o' my seat.

You probably heard about the excitement in the burg yesterday mornin'. The demand for tickets was somethin' fierce and some of 'em sold for as high as twenty-five bucks apiece. Our club hadn't been lookin' for no seventh game and they was some tall hustlin' done round that old ball park.

I started out to the grounds early and bought some New York papers to read on the car. They was a big story that Speed Parker, the Giants' hero, was goin' to be married a week after the end o' the serious. It didn't give the name o' the girl, sayin' Speed had refused to tell it. I figured she must be some dame he'd met round the circuit somewheres.

They was another story by one o' them smart baseball reporters sayin' that Parker, on his way up to the plate, had saw that Joyce was about ready to faint and had hit the fly ball to left field on purpose. Can you beat it?

I was goin' to show that to the boys in the clubhouse, but the minute I blowed in there I got some news that made me forget about everything else. Joyce was very sick and they'd took him to a hospital. It was up to me to play!

Connie come over and ast me whether I'd ever hit against Matty. I told him I hadn't, but I'd saw enough of him to know he wasn't no worse'n Johnson. He told me he was goin' to let me hit second—in Joyce's place—because he didn't want to bust up the rest of his combination. He also told me to take my orders from Strunk about where to play for the batters.

"Where shall I play for Parker?" I says, tryin' to joke and pretend I wasn't scared to death.

"I wisht I could tell you," says Connie. "I guess the only thing to do when he comes up is to get down on your knees and pray."

The rest o' the bunch slapped me on the back and give me all the encouragement they could. The place was jammed when we went out on the field. They may of been bigger crowds before, but they never was packed together so tight. I doubt whether they was even room enough left for Falkenberg to sit down. ◆

The afternoon papers had printed the stuff about Joyce bein' out of it, so the bugs was wise that I was goin' to play. They watched me pretty close in battin' practice and give me a hand whenever I managed to hit one hard. When I was out catchin' fungoes the guys in the bleachers cheered me and told me they was with me; but I don't mind tellin' you that I was as nervous as a bride.

They wasn't no need for the announcers to tip the crowd off to the pitchers. Everybody in the United States and Cuba knowed that the Chief'd work for us and Matty for them. The Chief didn't have no trouble with 'em in the first innin'. Even from where I stood I could see that he had a lot o' stuff. Bescher and Doyle popped out and Speed whiffed.

Well, I started out makin' good, with reverse English, in our part. Fletcher booted Murphy's ground ball and I was sent up to sacrifice. ◆ I done a complete job of it—sacrificin' not only myself but Murphy with a pop fly that Matty didn't have to move for. That spoiled whatever chance we had o' gettin' the jump on 'em; but the boys didn't bawl me for it.

"That's all right, old boy. You're all right!" they said on the bench—if they'd had a gun they'd of shot me.

I didn't drop no fly balls in the first six innin's—because none was hit out my way. The Chief was so good that they wasn't hittin' nothin'

◆ *Falkenberg*—Frederick Peter Falkenberg (1880–1961), a much-traveled right-handed pitcher who had recorded his best season, 23–10, in 1913, with Cleveland in the American League. Variously with the Pirates, Senators, Indians, Athletics, and Indianapolis/Newark and Brooklyn of the Federal League, Falkenberg won 130 and lost 123 between 1903 and 1917. He was 6′5″ and weighed only 180. See Jack Kavanagh, "Cy Falkenberg," *The Ballplayers*, p. 324.

◆ *Fletcher*—Arthur Fletcher (1885–1950), shortstop of the Giants from 1909 to 1920. Upon finishing his career with the Phillies in 1922, Fletcher had hit .277 in 1,529 games. An intelligent and serious-minded man, Fletcher was an obvious managerial prospect. Managing weak Phillies teams from 1923 to 1926, he developed a dislike of managerial life, and in 1927 accepted the third-base coaching job with the Yankees, a position he was to hold through 1945. He managed the Yankees for 11 games at the end of the 1929 season upon the death of Miller Huggins, but declined the permanent managership, even though he evaluated it as the best job in baseball. He also declined managerships of the White Sox, Tigers, and Browns during his long tenure with the Yankees. See Horace R. Givens, "Arthur 'Art' Fletcher," *Biographical Dictionary of American Sports: 1989–1992 Supplement*, p. 55.

out o' the infield. And we wasn't doin' nothin' with Matty, either. I led off in the fourth and fouled the first one. I didn't molest the other two. But if Connie and the gang talked about me they done it internally. I come up again—with Murphy on third base and two gone in the sixth, and done my little whiffin' specialty. And still the only people that panned me was the thirty thousand that had paid for the privilege!

My first fieldin' chance come in the seventh. You'd of thought that I'd of had my nerve back by that time; but I was just as scared as though I'd never saw a crowd before. It was just as well that they was two out when Merkle hit one to me. I staggered under it and finally it hit me on the shoulder. Merkle got to second, but the Chief whiffed the next guy. I was gave some cross looks on the bench and I shouldn't of blamed the fellers if they'd cut loose with some language; but they didn't.

They's no use in me tellin' you about none o' the rest of it—except what happened just before the start o' the eleventh and durin' that innin', which was sure the big one o' yesterday's pastime—both for Speed and yours sincerely.

The scoreboard was still a row o' ciphers and Speed'd had only a fair amount o' luck. He'd made a scratch base hit and robbed our bunch of a couple o' real ones with impossible stops.

When Schang flied out and wound up our tenth I was leanin' against the end of our bench. I heard my name spoke, and I turned round and seen a boy at the door.

"Right here!" I says; and he give me a telegram.

"Better not open it till after the game," says Connie.

"Oh, no; it ain't no bad news," I said, for I figured it was an answer from the girl. So I opened it up and read it on the way to my position. It said:

"Forgive me, Dick—and forgive Speed too. Letter follows."

Well, sir, I ain't no baby, but for a minute I just wanted to sit down and bawl. And then, all of a sudden, I got so mad I couldn't see. I run right into Baker as he was pickin' up his glove. Then I give him a shove and called him some name, and him and Barry both looked at me like I was crazy—and I was. When I got out in left field I stepped on my own foot and spiked it. I just had to hurt somebody.

As I remember it the Chief fanned the first two of 'em. Then Doyle catches one just right and lams it up against the fence back o' Murphy. The ball caromed round some and Doyle got all the way to third base. Next thing I seen was Speed struttin' up to the plate. I run clear in from my position.

"Kill him!" I says to the Chief. "Hit him in the head and kill him, and I'll go to jail for it!"

"Are you off your nut?" says the Chief. "Go out there and play ball—and quit ravin'."

Barry and Baker led me away and give me a shove out toward left. Then I heard the crack o' the bat and I seen the ball comin' a mile a minute. It was headed between Strunk and I and looked like it would go out o' the park. I don't remember runnin' or nothin' about it till I run into the concrete wall head first. They told me afterward and all the papers said that it was the greatest catch ever seen. And I never knowed I'd caught the ball!

Some o' the managers have said my head was pretty hard, but it wasn't as hard as that concrete. I was pretty near out, but they tell me I walked to the bench like I wasn't hurt at all. They also tell me that the crowd was a bunch o' ravin' maniacs and was throwin' money at me. I guess the ground-keeper'll get it.

The boys on the bench was all talkin' at once and slappin' me on the back, but I didn't know what it was about. Somebody told me pretty soon that it was my turn to hit and I picked up the first bat I come to and starts for the plate. McInnes come runnin' after me and ast me whether I didn't want my own bat. I cussed him and told him to mind his own business.

I didn't know it at the time, but I found out afterward that they was two out. The bases was empty. I'll tell you just what I had in my mind: I wasn't thinkin' about the ball game; I was determined that I was goin' to get to third base and give that guy my spikes. If I didn't hit one worth three bases, or if I didn't hit one at all, I was goin' to run till I got round to where Speed was, and then slide into him and cut him to pieces!

Right now I can't tell you whether I hit a fast ball, or a slow ball, or a hook, or a fader—but I hit somethin'. It went over Bescher's head like a shot and then took a crazy bound. It must of struck a rock or a pop bottle, because it hopped clear over the fence and landed in the ◆ bleachers.

Mind you, I learned this afterward. At the time I just knowed I'd hit one somewheres and I starts round the bases. I speeded up when

◆ *it hopped clear over the fence and landed in the bleachers.*—A ball that bounced over the fence was considered a home run until 1930 in the American League and until 1931 in the National, when it became a ground-rule double.

I got near third and took a runnin' jump at a guy I thought was Parker. I missed him and sprawled all over the bag. Then all of a sudden, I come to my senses. All the Ath-a-letics was out there to run home with me and it was one o' them I'd tried to cut. Speed had left the field. The boys picked me up and seen to it that I went on and touched the plate. Then I was carried into the clubhouse by the crazy bugs.

Well, they had a celebration in there and it was a long time before I got a chance to change my clothes. The boys made a big fuss over me. They told me they'd intended to give me five hundred bucks for my divvy, but now I was goin' to get a full share.

"Parker ain't the only lucky guy!" says one of 'em. "But even if that ball hadn't of took that crazy hop you'd of had a triple."

A triple! That's just what I'd wanted; and he called me lucky for not gettin' it!

The Giants was dressin' in the other part o' the clubhouse; and when I finally come out there was Speed, standin' waitin' for some o' the others. He seen me comin' and he smiled. "Hello, Horseshoes!" he says.

He won't smile no more for a while—it'll hurt too much. And if any girl wants him when she sees him now—with his nose over shakin' hands with his ear, and his jaw a couple o' feet foul—she's welcome to him. They won't be no contest!

Grimes leaned over to ring for the waiter.

"Well," he said, "what about it?"

"You won't have to pay my fare," I told him.

"I'll buy a drink anyway," said he. "You've been a good listener—and I had to get it off my chest."

"Maybe they'll have to postpone the wedding," I said.

"No," said Grimes. "The weddin' will take place the day after tomorrow—and I'll bat for Mr. Parker. Did you think I was goin' to let him get away with it?"

"What about next year?" I asked.

"I'm goin' back to the Ath-a-letics," he said. "And I'm goin' to hire somebody to call me 'Horseshoes!' before every game—because I can sure play that old baseball when I'm mad."

Back to Baltimore

Well, boys, I'm goin' right through to Pittsburgh with you if you don't ◆ mind, and I aint been traded to your bunch nor the Pirates neither. It'll be in all the papers to-night or to-morrow mornin', so they aint no use o' me keepin' it a secret. I've jumped to the Baltimore Feds, and whether Knabe is figurin' on usin' me regular or settin' me on the ◆◇ bench or givin' me a job washin' undershirts, I don't know or I don't givadam. I couldn't be no worse off than I was up there.

Managin' a club may be all O. K. if the directors is all bachelors and has all o' them tooken a oath not to never get married. But when a

---

"Back to Baltimore" was published in *The Red Book Magazine*, XXIV (November 1914), 29–41. The late Charlie Deal (1891–1979), the last surviving man who played for the Braves in the 1914 World Series, was extremely helpful in sorting out actual from fictional characters in this story.

◆ *Well, boys,*—Apparently the Chicago Cubs en route east. The story is set on the Boston Braves of 1914. The actual Braves of 1914 won the pennant, as distinct from the performance of Lardner's fictional version.

◆ *Knabe*—Franz Otto Knabe (1884–1961), manager of the Baltimore Terrapins of the Federal League. After a brief trial with the Pirates in 1905, Knabe was the regular second baseman for the Phillies from 1907 to 1913. He managed Baltimore to third- and eighth-place finishes in the two seasons of the Federal League, and then returned to the National League for a final season with the Pirates and Cubs in 1916. Knabe hit .247 in 1,284 games. See Joseph Lawler, "Otto Knabe," *The Ballplayers*, p. 579.

◇ *Knabe*—Otto Knabe, manager of the Baltimore Terrapins of the Federal League, shown in the uniform of the 1913 Philadelphia Phillies. (National Baseball Library, Cooperstown, New York)

man's got a wife, they aint no tellin' when he's goin' to die, and when he dies and she gets a hold o' the ball club, *good night*. If they ever is a skirt elected President o' the United States, I'll move to Paris or Europe or somewheres, if I have to walk.

As for this here Mrs. Hayes, the dope about her lettin' the directors ◆

◆ *Mrs. Hayes*—A fictional character, probably based on Helen Britton, who became president of the St. Louis Cardinals before the 1911 season. The daughter of the Cleveland traction magnate Frank De Haas Robison, Mrs. Britton inherited control of the Cardinals upon the death of her uncle, M. Stanley Robison. She was 32 at the time, and had two children.

run the club was all bunk. She's been the boss ever since the old bird croaked, or else I'd of stuck there and finished higher with that gang ◇ than they finished since Frank Selee had 'em. ◆

Well, sir, I'm canned out of a managin' job, and I'm through with the big league, I guess, and I'm goin' back where I started in at— Baltimore. But you don't need to waste no sympathy on me. I'm gettin'

◇ *that gang*—The Boston Braves of 1914. *Bottom row:* Joe Connolly, Fred Mitchell, Willie Connors (mascot), Dick Rudolph, Rabbit Maranville, Dick Crutcher, Bill Martin, Johnny Evers. *Middle row:* George Whitted, Oscar Dugey, George Tyler, Paul Strand, Josh Devore, Larry Gilbert, Carlisle Smith, Herb Moran. *Top row:* Seattle Bill James, Ted Cather, Charlie Deal, George Davis, Ensign Cottrell, Gene Cocreham, Otto Hess, Les Mann, Hank Gowdy, Charley Schmidt, Bert Whaling. (National Baseball Library, Cooperstown, New York)

◆ *Frank Selee*—Frank Gibson Selee (1859–1909), manager of the Boston National League club from 1890 to 1901. Selee, who never played major league baseball, won pennants for the club in 1891, 1892, 1893, 1897, and 1898. He managed the Cubs from 1902 until late in the 1905 season, when, suffering from tuberculosis, he turned the team over to Frank Chance. Selee was, however, largely responsible for assembling the personnel of the Cub championship teams of 1906–08 and 1910. His managerial percentage of .598 trails only Joe McCarthy, Jim Mutrie, and Charles A. Comiskey. See A. D. Suehsdorf, "Frank Selee," *The Ballplayers*, pp. 984–85.

as much dough as they give me up there, and they wont be no chancet o' me bein' drove crazy by a skirt. Them Baltimore people used to like me O. K. when Dunnie had me, and I guess I aint did nothin' since to make 'em sore. I'll give 'em the best I got, and I'll let Knabe do all the worryin'. I'm off'n that stuff, and if any boob ever offers me another managin' job, I'll bean him with a crowbar or somethin'.

I bet you'll see in a few days where Mrs. Hayes gets through bein' a widow, and her next name's goin' to be Mrs. William Baker Junior. ◆ They aint no danger o' me forgettin' that name. The guy that owns it is a ball player, but the only thing alike about he and the Baker Connie Mack's got is that they both listen with their ears. You fellas didn't never get a look at this bird because he was so good that we didn't only play him in one game, and that was against the Philly club. If him and her does hook up, he wont need to play no more. With them runnin' the team together, they'll be enough comedy without him puttin' on a uniform any more.

You knowed Old Man Hayes, o' course. He was a good old scout, but ◆ he pulled a lot o' boners, one o' which was him marryin' this doll. She's a handsome devil all right; I'll slip her that much. But he should ought to of knew that he didn't cop her because she was a-stuck on him. She had it doped that he was about all in, and it wouldn't be long till the dough was all hern. His heart was bad, and they was two or three other things the matter with him, and havin' her round didn't make him no healthier. At that, he'd of croaked sooner or later without no female help.

He was sure nuts over his ball club, and it hurt him every time we lose a game. You can see where he was hurt pretty often last year. At that, Bill Fox was gettin' by all right with the managin' job, when you ◆ figure the bunch he had. But finishin' seventh didn't make no hit with the old man, even if we thought we done pretty well to stay in the league and not get arrested. Anyway, Bill got canned and the job was gave to me. If I hadn't 've needed the money pretty bad, I wouldn't never 've tooken it.

◆ *William Baker Junior*—A fictional character.

◆ *Old Man Hayes*—A fictional character. The president of the Braves from 1912 to 1915 was James E. Gaffney.

◆ *Bill Fox*—A fictional character. The manager of the Braves in 1913 was George Stallings, who brought the team to a fifth-place finish.

Them deals I made last winter helped us a whole lot, and when we got down South this spring, we wasn't a bad lookin' club, barrin' one or two positions. We was such a improvement over the old gang that the old man lost his needle and was countin' the world's serious receipts along in March. He kept a-askin' me who did I think would be in the race with us. If I had of told him the truth and says we couldn't win no pennant unless your bunch and the New York club was killed in a railroad wreck, he'd of canned me. So what was I to do but tell him we had a good fightin' chancet to cop, when we didn't have no more chancet than a rabbit or somethin'. I says the luck would have to be with us and if it was, we might surprise everybody. That luck stuff was to be my alibi when we landed where we belonged.

The season opened and we got away good. McGraw's pitchers was ◆ in no shape, and we skun 'em three out o' the first four. We broke even with Philly and give Brooklyn a good lickin'. We was right out in front along with you fellas. Then we struck a slump, and you guys and Philly both goes ahead of us. The old man called me in and ast me why didn't we stay in first place. I might of told him it was because we knowed we didn't have no business there. But I stalled and says I didn't want to have my club go too fast at first or they might maybe get tired out.

Then we come West in May, and the old boy come along with us. We opened up in Cincy and broke even with 'em, though they looked ◆ like the worst club in the world. The old man wasn't feelin' well, and a doctor told him he should ought to go home, but he says he would go to St. Louis with us. Higgins trimmed us four straight, and that ◆◇ finished the boss. He grabbed a train for home, but croaked on the way there.

◇ *Higgins*—The Miller James Huggins plaque at the National Baseball Hall of Fame and Museum, Cooperstown, New York.

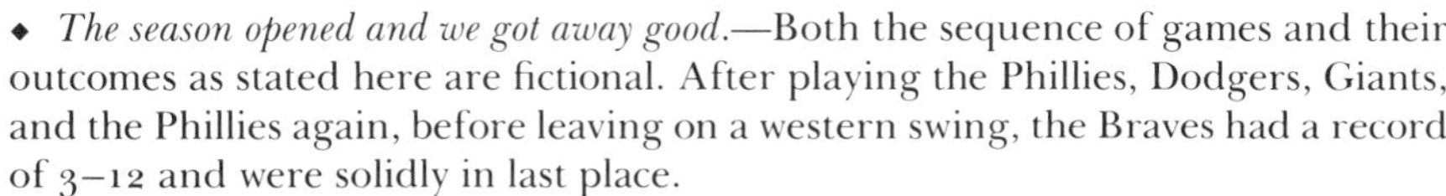

◆ *The season opened and we got away good.*—Both the sequence of games and their outcomes as stated here are fictional. After playing the Phillies, Dodgers, Giants, and the Phillies again, before leaving on a western swing, the Braves had a record of 3–12 and were solidly in last place.

◆ *they looked like the worst club in the world*—Again, these results are fictional. The western tour began in Pittsburgh, whence the Braves proceeded to Cincinnati, where they lost all three games of their series there. The 1914 Reds could hardly be said to look like the worst team in the world at that time, but they did prove to be a pitiful outfit, finishing last, 34½ games out of first place, and nine games out of seventh.

◆ *Higgins*—Miller James Huggins (1879–1929), manager of the Cardinals, from 1913 to 1917, and the Yankees, from 1918 until immediately before his death on September 25, 1929. Although he finished no higher than third in St. Louis, he led the Yankees to the pennants of 1921, 1922, 1923, 1926, 1927, and 1928. As a player, Huggins had played second base for the Reds from 1904 to 1909 and for

It was gave out in the papers that young Mrs. Hayes would be president o' the club, but I didn't take no stock in that till we come in off'n the road. I was like everybody else; I figured that Williams, the ◆ vice president, and them other directors would run things.

But when we got home, after a rotten trip, she ast me to come and see her at the office. I goes, and there she is, walkin' up and down the rug just like her husband was always doin'. When we had shooken hands, she says:

"Well, Mr. Dixon, you didn't have no success in the West."

"No," I says. "We run into some tough luck."

Then she ast me was it tough luck or rotten ball playin', and I says it was some o' both. Then she says:

"We'll try and stren'then your team. I and Mr. Williams, the vice president, has decided we got to spend some dough for new players. I have gave Mr. Sullivan orders to go scoutin' round the colleges." ◆

"Lay off'n the colleges," I says. "We don't need no more ornaments. What we should ought to have is some ball players. Besides that, you can't buy no men off'n the colleges. They don't sell 'em."

She says: "I guess we can get a hold of 'em if we slip 'em big sal'ries." Then she says: "I'd like to make this here club a team of gentlemen, and they're more gentlemen in the colleges than anywheres else."

They was nuthin' for me to do then but beat it out o' the office and get a drink o' brandy.

We kept on playin' our best, and that was about good enough to get us beat oftener than we win. But I was satisfied with the way we was goin'. I knowed we wasn't topheavy with class. Sullivan came in from scoutin', and I ast him where was his collegers. He says:

(*continued from page 427*)
the Cardinals from 1910 to 1916, hitting .265 in 1,585 games. A graduate of the University of Cincinnati law school, he was a member of the Ohio bar. Huggins was elected to the Baseball Hall of Fame in 1964 for his managerial accomplishments. See Frank J. Olmsted, "Miller James Huggins," *Biographical Dictionary of American Sports: Baseball*, pp. 268–69.

◆ *Williams*—Apparently a fictional character.

◆ *Sullivan*—This is probably a reference to Ted Sullivan, who did a great deal of free-lance scouting in his career, although there is no evidence he did so for the Braves in this period. The team's full-time scout in 1911 during Lardner's tenure in Boston was Billy Hamilton, but newspaper accounts of the team in the period of the story do not indicate that the club employed one. Because Sullivan is the most common surname in Boston, one cannot rule out the possibility that this is a reference to a local figure.

"I've been everywhere in the rah-rah circuit, and I aint saw no ball player that could carry bats in the Japanese League."

So I figured we wasn't goin' to be pestered with none o' them there birds that does nothin' but kick the ball round because they got the habit playin' football.

The skirt had been travelin' a lot and hadn't gave me no bother to speak of. But when she come back, my troubles begin. She come out to the games and set in a box clos't up to our bench. We was playin' Brooklyn one day, and Rucker was good. We was a couple o' runs ◆ behind along in the eighth and no hope o' catchin' up, with him goin' that way. They was two of us out, and then Rucker walks somebody and Red Smith boots one, so they was two on when it come my turn ◆ to hit. I starts up, but she calls me over to the box.

"Mr. Dixon," she says, "this would be a good place for a home run."

I says: "Yes, this is the right spot. I s'pose you'd like to see me hit one."

"You bet I would," she says.

"Well," I says, "which fence do you think I should ought to hit it over?"

"I don't care which fence," she says.

Well, I goes up there and done my best to obey orders. Nobody never swung no harder'n me, and the way I was wallopin' at 'em, I'd of knocked one o' them walls down if I had of connected. But I missed three and we didn't score.

Do you remember the day you fellas give us that awful beatin'—twelve to nothin'? Cheney worked for you and we didn't never have a look-in. What do you think she pulled after that game? She waited for me outside o' the park and says she wished I'd tell Mr. O'Day not to never let Cheney pitch there no more.

I says: "It wouldn't hurt my feelin's if he never pitched nowheres."

◆ *Rucker*—George Napoleon "Nap" Rucker (1884–1970), lefthanded pitcher for the Dodgers since 1907. He had never won less than 13 games in a season and peaked with 22–18 in 1911. After 1913 he was ineffective, and in 1914 recorded only a 7–6 season. He played through 1916, winning 135 and losing 136. See Jack Kavanagh, "Nap Rucker," *The Ballplayers*, p. 943.

◆ *Red Smith*—James Carlisle Smith (1890–1966), the Dodgers third baseman, who was sold to the Braves on August 13, 1914. Active from 1911 to 1919 with the Dodgers and Braves, Smith hit .278 in 1,117 games. He was a major figure in the Braves' pennant drive, but broke his leg in the last game of the season, and thus missed the Braves' sweep of the World Series. He was replaced by Charlie Deal. See Jack Kavanagh, "Red Smith," *The Ballplayers*, p. 1015.

◇ *Hub*—Hub Perdue in the Braves uniform of 1913 or 1914 (see footnote, p. 351). (George E. Brace collection)

"Well," she says, "I hope you'll see to it, because my doctor tells me the spitball aint sanitary."

Then, one day, she ast me what made Hub's cheek bulge out so◆◇ when he worked. I told her he had a ulcer on his teeth. She ast why his face was swole up that way only when he was pitchin', and I told her I didn't never work him only on days when his teeth was pretty

◆ *Hub*—Perdue, after nine games with the Braves, in which he posted a 2–5 record, was traded to the Cardinals for Ted Cather and George Whitted on June 27, 1914. This and the reference to Red Smith immediately above are consistent with a presumption that Lardner wrote the story in mid-season of 1914. As noted below, Lardner mentions Josh Devore, who was acquired on July 3, as playing for the club. More generally, he treats the Braves as a weak team. As is well known, they were indeed in last place on July 4, but in the second half of a season customarily described as miraculous, won the pennant by 10½ games.

sore, so's the batters'd feel sorry for him. She must of knew I was kiddin', but she never called me for it.

She had me worried to death with stuff like that. She wanted the suits sent to the laundry after all the games and says all of us should ought to quit slidin' because it dirtied us up so much. I got so's I stuck in the club-house a couple of hours after the games, so's to be sure and not run into her when I come out.

Well, she goes down to Yale college on some party or somethin', and when she come back, we was just finishin' up with the Western clubs. We was out in practice one day when I seen her beckonin' to me. I goes over to where she was settin', and she says:

"I've got you a new player."

"Who is he?" I says.

She says: "His name is Mr. Baker, and he has just went through ◆ Yale. He will meet you in New York."

Then I ast her what position did he play, and she says: "He aint made up his mind yet. He has been busy learnin' his lessons."

Then I ast her wasn't he on the Yale team, and she says: "No, but he could of been if he had of wanted to. The coach told him so, but he didn't have no time to play. You could tell the minute you seen him that he was a born ath-a-lete and he's a gentleman too, and I b'lieve he will help you in more ways than just one way."

"Well," I says, "they's only one way he could help us and that is to get in there and play ball. If he can do that, I don't care if he's a gentleman or a policeman."

Then I ast her what sal'ry was he goin' to get.

"Oh," she says, "you wont need to bother about that. I've already fixed that up already. I have gave him a contract for five thousand."

I ast her did she mean five thousand for five years, and she says: "No, I meant five thousand for this year."

Then I says: "That's as much as I'm gettin', and this here guy aint even made good yet."

"He'll make good all right," she says. "You can tell that from just lookin' at him, and he comes off'n a good fam'ly."

* * *

◆ *Mr. Baker*—A fictional character.

Well, we goes to New York, and I was waitin' round the lobby o' the hotel for the baggage to come in, when Kelly, the secretary, calls me ◆ over to the desk. He pointed out a name on the hotel book and ast me who was it, because the guy was registered as belongin' to us. "William Baker Junior, Boston Baseball Nine," was what it says. Do you get that? "Boston Baseball Nine!" Before I ever seen him, I knowed just what he was goin' to look like, and when I seen him, he looked just like I knowed he was goin' to. But he was a big bird—so big he couldn't get no clo'es big enough. He looked like as if he was goin' to bust right through 'em. His hair was plastered back off'n his forehead, and his shirt and tie would've made a rainbow jealous.

He come up to me and says: "Is this the head coach?"

I says: "Yes, whetever that is, I'm it."

"What time does the game start?" he says.

"Three-thirty," I says, "but we get out there about a quarter after two."

Then he ast me couldn't they start it some other time because he had a engagement. I says I would excuse him, and he says: "Thanks." Then I says: "I'll excuse you all the time if you say the word." But he says no, that wouldn't be right, because he felt like as if he should ought to do some work oncet in a while to earn his pay. Then he says he was pleased to of met me and walked away.

I guess he must of kept his date at a soda fountain or wherever it was he had a date at, because he didn't show up out to the park and I never seen no more of him till the next mornin'. Then he come to see me while I was writin' a letter and ast me could he have six passes to the game. I says: "You'd better take ten," and I writes out a pass for ten on one o' the hotel letter-heads, and I signs Otto Hess' name to it. ◆

◆ *Kelly*—Peter F. Kelley (1870–1944), secretary of the Braves from 1909 to 1912. Kelley had held the office during Lardner's season of covering the team for the Boston *American* in 1911. The post was in fact held by Herman Nickerson in 1914. At other times in his career, Kelly was a sportswriter for the *American* and other Boston newspapers. Notably, he had been responsible for the official adoption of the Boston American League club's nickname of "Red Sox" in 1908.

◆ *Otto Hess*—Otto C. Hess (1878–1926), an erratic lefthanded pitcher nearing the end of his career. Hess had pitched for the Cleveland Naps from 1902 to 1908, winning 20 games in 1906, and for the Braves from 1912 to 1915. In ten seasons in the major leagues, he won 69 and lost 91. He had a reputation for having a bad inning per game. He was unusual among major leaguers for having been born in Switzerland. See Norman L. Macht, "Otto Hess," *The Ballplayers*, p. 470.

He says "Thanks," and walked away. If I'd of signed President Bryan's name, he'd of thanked me just the same. And the pass would of been just as good.

I come out o' the hotel about one o'clock and starts for the elevated, but the colleger was standin' on the sidewalk and he hollered at me. He ast me was I goin' out and I says yes, I thought I would, because I didn't have no other date. Then he ast me would I ride out with him because he'd ordered a taxi. They wasn't none o' my ball players had ever tooken me to the park in a taxi before, but I didn't have no objection, so I and him piled in, and out we goes together.

When we got through ridin', I says, "You better let me split with you," but he says, "They aint no splittin' to be did. It's in my contract that I use cabs to and from the grounds," and he tells the driver to charge it to the club. Well, I butts in and says, "Here! You can't get by with that stuff. If you're out to give the club a trimmin', you better pull it when I aint round." Then what does he do but pull his contract out of his pocket and show it to me, and there it was, in black and white, that he was to be gave rides on the club to and from the parks where we played. Can you beat that?

We come into the grounds and I took him in the club-house and had Doc give him a unie. He made a holler because they wasn't no feet in the stockin's and I told him he was supposed to wear socks besides the stockin's. So he leaves on the reg'lar socks he'd wore with his street clo'es, and they was purple!

I wisht you could of heard the ball players ride him. They pulled some awful raw stuff, and if he hadn't of been such a boob, he'd of lost his temper and tried to lick somebody. But I don't b'lieve he never wised up that he was gettin' kidded. Even when Hub called him "Gertie," it didn't seem to make no difference to him.

We goes out to warm up and I notice that he don't have no cap on. I was goin' to tell him about it, but the boys says: "No. Let him play bareheaded and give the crowd a treat." They wasn't much practicin' done. The New York bunch come over round our bench so's they

---

◆ *President Bryan*—William Jennings Bryan (1860–1925), the losing Democratic presidential candidate in 1896, 1900, and 1908.

◆ *Doc*—James B. Neary (1878–1944). A well-known local runner, Neary was hired by owner George B. Dovey in 1909 to instruct the players in techniques of sprinting. He continued with the Braves as trainer until he retired in 1941. He also served as track coach at Vermont Academy and Bellows Military Academy.

wouldn't miss nothin'. I give him a ball and a catcher's glove and told Tyler to throw him a few. George just lobbed one at him and he got it on the meat hand. He raised a holler and tells Tyler he shouldn't ought to throw so hard. I yells at him to use his mitt, but he says the ball stung his hand right through it, and after tryin' all the wrong ways they is o' catchin' a ball, he quit and set down on the bench. McGraw calls me over and ast was I startin' a chorus or what. I told him how I happened to get a-hold o' the bird, and then I ast him did he want to make a trade. He says:

"What'll you take for him?"

I says: "Oh, I'll give him to you for Matty and a piece o' money."

"No," he says, "I don't want to cheat you. Take the grandstand and a chew o' tobacco."

Well, I sends him up to take his turn in battin' practice, and he acted like as if the bat was as heavy as one o' these here steel rails. Hess slops a slow one up to him, and instead o' swingin', he ducks out o' the way and tells me he aint used to battin' at such swift balls. Hess hears him pull that and the next one he throwed was a fast one, just as fast as he could throw it. Mr. Baker turns white as a sheet and drops his bat and walks to the bench.

I stuck him in the outfield in fieldin' practice, but he looked so rotten that I took him out o' there for fear o' gettin' him killed. I called him in and says:

"You've did enough for one day, so go in and change your clo'es and you can watch the game from the stand. Maybe you'll run acrost that crowd I give you the passes for."

He was willin' to quit, all right, and the fun was over for the day. After the game, I send a long telegram to Williams, the vice president, and tells him what a joke our new player was and that it was throwin' money away to even pay his board, let alone that Fed'ral League sal'ry he was gettin'. I didn't get no answer from Williams, but a letter come from the skirt. She give me a call for not sendin' the telegram to her instead o' Williams and ast me how could I judge if a man was a ball player when I hadn't only saw him one day.

Well, I wires to Williams that I was through, because I'd signed to manage a ball club and not to run no burlesque show, but he jumps on a train and comes over to New York to see me. He says they was tryin' to get her to sell out her stock and that him and the other directors appreciated what I'd did for the club and wanted me to stick.

So I stuck and went along the best I could. I didn't pay no more attention to "Gertie" except to tell him to beat it to the club-house before the games started. He kept on comin' out to the park, wherever we was playin', and puttin' on his unie, without no cap, and settin' on the bench till the practice was over. Then he'd go in and put on one of his eight or nine different suits o' clo'es, and go up in the stand and watch the game from there or else go to the matinée or somewheres.

I didn't hardly ever say nothin' to him, but I couldn't make the rest o' the bunch lay off. They tipped their hats whenever they seen him. While he was settin' on the bench, they'd take a shot at him with the ball, and oncet or twicet they hit him, but not wheres it hurt him bad. He thought it was a accident when he got hit, but I knowed better. Every oncet in a while, somebody'd happen to step on his feet with their spikes, and then they'd beg his pardon. Some o' them left their caps off while they was practicin' and hollered "Ouch!" when they catched the ball. And on the train they'd get together and give college yells. He didn't never get sore, and I don't s'pose I would of neither if I'd been gettin' five thousand for changin' my clo'es a couple o' times a day.

They tried to get him in the poker game, but they wasn't nothin' doin'. He says he liked to play bridge w'ist but that was all the cards he knowed. When we was on trains, he spent the time lookin' at the scenery or readin' magazines.

I remember one night when we was goin' to Philly and he was settin' ◇ acrost the aisle from I and Hub. He was readin', and pretty soon he looks up from off of his magazine and says:

"You guys should ought to read this here story in here. It's a baseball story and it's about two teams bein' tied for the pennant on the last day o' the season, and one o' the teams had a star pitcher that was sure to win the decidin' game if nothin' didn't happen to him, so they stuck him in to pitch but in the first innin' he strained his arm so it hurt him every ball he throwed but he didn't say nothin' about it, but kept on pitchin' and win his game and the pennant, though he was sufferin' terrible pain all the while. I call that nerve!"

"Nerve!" says Hub. "Say, that wasn't nothin' to what I seen come off in the Southern League the last year I was down there. The Nashville club that I was with and the New Orleans club was tied for ◆

◆ *The Nashville club that I was with*—As stated, Perdue had spent his most recent year in the minor leagues with Nashville of the Southern Association in 1910, with a 12–17 record. Because Lardner was particularly fond of Perdue, there is reason

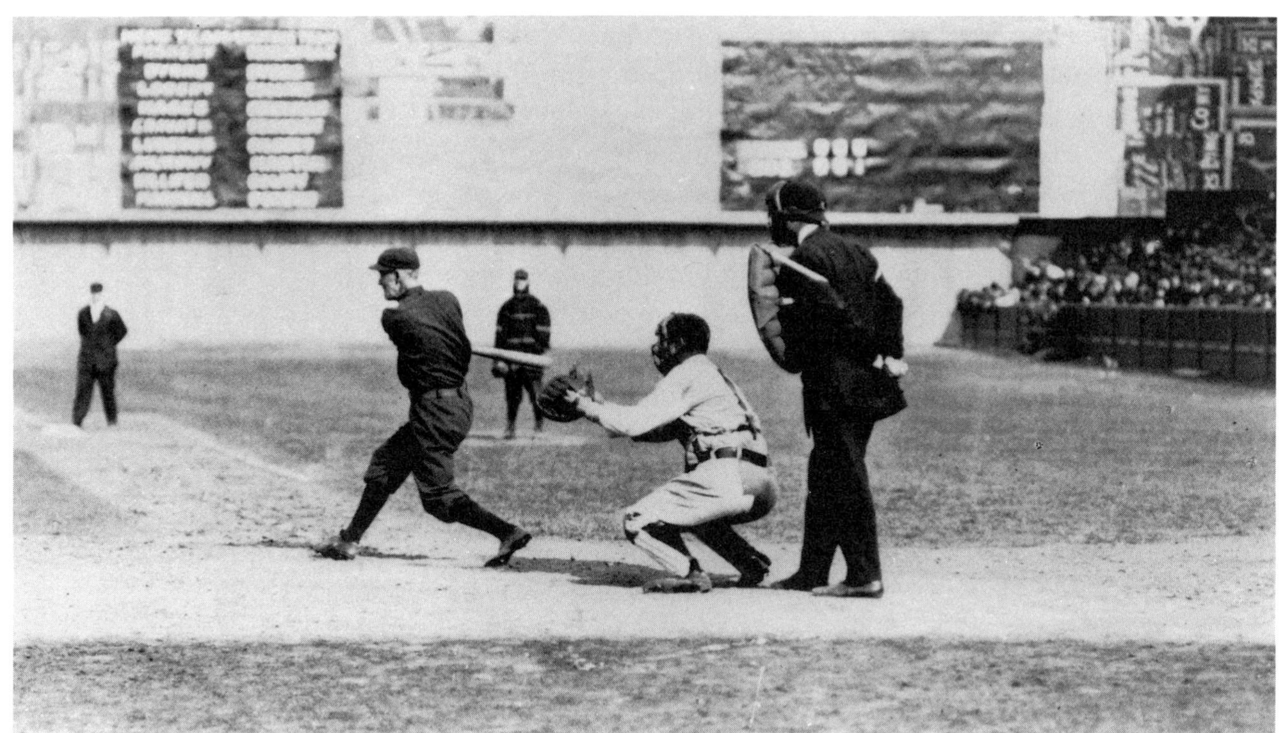

◇ *we was goin' to Philly*—Johnny Evers at bat for the Braves in Baker Bowl in 1914. The Phillies' catcher is Bill Killefer. (National Baseball Library, Cooperstown, New York)

first place, and we had to play a extra game to settle it. We had a first sacker named Smith that was the greatest I ever see. Up to the first of ◆ August he was battin' .600 and it got so's the pitchers wouldn't give him nothin' more to hit but walked him every time he come up. He offered to bat with one hand if they'd pitch strikes to him, but they wouldn't take a chancet, and finally the umps'd just give him his base every time he come up without waitin' for the four balls to be throwed.

"Well, it come time for this final game and we knowed we had it won if Smith was all right. The New Orleans club knowed it too, and they was out to get him. So when he got on in the first innin' on a base on balls, their first baseman deliberately stepped on his foot and spiked him somethin' awful. He couldn't walk on that foot no more, but he wouldn't quit, and after he'd drawed one of his bases on balls, every so often, he stole all the rest o' the bases hoppin' on his good foot.

(*continued from page 435*)
to believe that this is an accurate rendition of his speech habits. Perdue was among the players most lacking in formal education.

◆ *Smith*—It hardly need be said that Smith is a fictional character.

"It come along the twenty-first innin' and the score was six to six. He'd scored every one of our six runs by walkin' to first and then hoppin' the rest o' the way. Well, he walked in the twenty-first and starts hoppin' to second. The catcher knowed they was no use to throw to second or to third neither, because Smith was so fast, even on one foot, that he was bound to beat it. So the catcher just kept a hold o' the ball, knowin' Smith wouldn't never stop till he got clear home. Along come Smith, hoppin' for the plate, and the catcher run out to meet him, but he hopped clean over the catcher's head and scored the run that beat 'em and won us the pennant. They was about sixty thousand people out there, and they tried to carry Smith off o' the field on their shoulders, but he hopped into the club-house before they could catch him. And when he took off his shoe, two toes dropped out!"

"My!" says the colleger, with his mouth wide open. "I should say that was nerve. And didn't this here Smith never get into the big league?"

"No," says Hub. "He got blood-poisonin' in that foot and they had to cut his whole leg off, and the National Commission's got a rule that you can't play in neither big league unless you got two legs."

After that, Baker and Hub hung round together all the time. He fell for everything Hub told him, no matter how raw. He was givin' Hub a good time, and it'd 've been all right if we could of stayed on the road all the while, but I knowed when we got home, the doll'd ast me why wasn't I playin' him and then the trouble'd start.

Sure enough, when we come in off o' the trip, she called me to the office and put it up to me.

"Well," I says, "I don't think he's got enough experience yet. You just let me handle him and keep him on the bench awhile, and maybe he'll develop into a pretty fair ball player."

I suppose I should ought not to of gave her no encouragement about him, but I was figurin' all the time that she'd be boughten out o' the club pretty soon, and then I could can him. At that, I didn't have no objections to keepin' him except that I knowed he was cheatin' the club out of about two hundred bucks every first and fifteenth. If I had to let him go, the gang'd of missed him, especially Hub.

I run into Williams one day and ast him when was the skirt goin' to sell out, and he says they'd tried hard to get her stock away from her, but she'd made up her mind to stick it out till the end o' the season, but that Williams and the other directors was thinkin' about takin' it up with the rest o' the league and tryin' to force her out, but she'd gave 'em her promise that she'd sell in the fall if they still thought she should ought to. So they was nothin' for me to do but make as good a showin' as I could and figure on next year.

It was after the mornin' game on the Fourth o' July that she horned in again. She tells me that her brother and bunch of his friends from Yale college is comin' to the afternoon game, and they want to see their pal perform. I says I'd let him practice and they could watch him if they come out early enough, but she says, no, that wouldn't do; some o' them boys was sayin' that they didn't b'lieve he could play ball, and she wanted to show 'em that he could.

Well, I thought awhile, and then I made up my mind that if he had to be gave some position, he might as well have mine and I could take a rest. So I tells the umps about the change and then I goes back to the bench and sits in a corner where they wasn't nobody could see me.

I wisht you could of been there. The papers had a lot o' stuff about it, but they didn't tell more'n half. Hub was pitchin' and we was playin' Philly. He got the first two of 'em out, and then Cravath hits one down to the colleger on a perfect hop. I was lookin' for him to throw it wild after he got it, but Pat Moran was coachin' at first base, and he hollers to him to throw it to second. So what does he do but just like Pat tells ◇ him to and naturally Maranville wasn't there to cover because they wasn't no play. So the ball goes out in the outfield, and Cravath got clear round to third base. Then Magee busts one, and they got a run. I thought Hub'd be sore, but he wasn't. When he come in to the bench, he was laughin' his head off, and he says:

"Don't never take me out o' this game. This is one battle I want to see all the way through."

Well, Devore leads off for us, and he walks. The colleger's up next, ◆ and I tells him to bunt. The first two Rixey throwed him was a mile outside, but he bunts at 'em just the same. Then Rixey curves one, and he tries to duck, but he can't get out o' the way. The ball hit him in the sleeve or somewheres, and Rigler tells him to take his base, but he wouldn't move.

◆ *Devore*—Joshua "Josh" Devore (1887–1954), a veteran outfielder picked up by the Braves from the Phillies on July 3, 1914. Previously with the Giants and Reds since 1908, Devore was to end his career in 1914, hitting .277 in 601 games. The reference is inconsistent with the treatment of Perdue, for Devore was acquired four days after Perdue was dealt to the Cardinals. See Norman L. Macht, "Josh Devore," *The Ballplayers*, p. 272.

◇ *throw it to second*—The Braves' infield of 1914. From the left, shortstop Rabbit Maranville, second baseman Johnny Evers, third baseman Charlie Deal, and first baseman Charley Schmidt. The photograph was probably taken in 1925, when Maranville played for the Cubs. (National Baseball Library, Cooperstown, New York)

"What's the matter?" says Rig. "Why don't you take your base? Are you hurt?"

"No," says the colleger, "but the manager says I was to bunt."

Well, we had to drive him to first base, and then he steals second, or tries to, with Devore standin' right there. Devore don't move off'n the bag, so they tagged "Gertie" out. When he comes in, I ast him what was he tryin' to pull off. He says Luderus had told him to steal. Then I says:

"Don't never pay no attention to what them Philly guys tells you. If I want you to steal a base, I'll send you a night letter."

We didn't score, and nobody hit nothin' at him in their half o' the second, though they was all tryin' to. Hub was tryin' to let 'em, too.

The third innin' was a bear. Dooin hits one at him, and he jumps out o' the way. Rixey struck out, and then Dooin starts to steal. I'd told Maranville to take all the pegs, but he thought it'd be more fun to leave 'em to "Gertrude." So he hollers to him to cover. Whalin ◆

◆ *Whalin*—Albert James "Bert" Whaling (1888–1965), second-string catcher for the Braves from 1913 to 1915. In 211 games, Whaling hit .225.

makes a perfect peg, and the colleger surprises everybody by catchin' it. But when he'd catched it, he steps on the bag instead of tryin' to tag Red. Then Red says to him:

"I bet I can beat you to third base."

Red starts runnin' with the ball right in Baker's hands, and instead o' throwin' it, he holds right on to it and goes after Red. He wasn't no slouch runner at that, and he made it a clos't race, but Red beat him. The bugs was a-hollerin' their heads off, and most o' the ball players was so sick from laughin' that they couldn't do nothin'. Rig' kept lookin' over at me to see if I wasn't goin' to take the bird out o' the game, but I didn't have no stren'th left to shake my head, even.

After the sprintin' race, they took the ball away from him and throwed it back to Hub. Byrne hits one at Hub, but he jumps out o' ◆ the way so our "star" can get it, and he goes over and sticks his feet in front o' the ball and it stops right clost to him. Byrne kept on runnin' past first base and yelled at him to leave the ball lay, so he left it lay and Byrne goes all the way home. After that, when anybody got a hold o' the ball, they'd throw it to him and he catched one or two o' the throws, but most o' them he got out o' the way of, and even when he catched 'em, he held onto the ball till everybody'd scored. They made twelve runs in that one innin', and we wouldn't never of got the side out if it hadn't only of been for the umpires. They was tired from workin' the mornin' game and this one, too, so they pulled a couple o' raw ones and wound it up.

Rig' come over to me between innin's and ast me did I think this was a joke. I told him it wasn't no fault o' mine, and explained how it had came off.

"Well," he says, "I've got to catch the midnight train for New York, and we won't never get through in time if this keeps up."

"I can't help it," I says.

Then he says: "I can," and he goes back to his position.

The colleger's turn to bat come in our half, and Rixey rolls one up to him on the ground. Rig' calls it a strike, tryin' to get Baker sore, but he don't never even look round. It'd of been O. K. with him if

---

◆ *Byrne*—Robert Mathew Byrne (1884–1964), a career third baseman who was playing second base for the Phillies in 1914 in the wake of Otto Knabe's defection to the Federal League. Byrne played for the Cardinals from 1907 to 1909, the Pirates from 1909 to 1913, and the Phillies from 1913 to 1917, and ended his career with one game for the champion White Sox of 1917. He hit .254 in 1,282 games. See Jack Kavanagh, "Bobby Byrne," *The Ballplayers,* p. 144.

they'd called a strike before the ball was throwed. Rixey rolled another one up, and Rig' calls it another strike. Then before Baker could say a word, and he wasn't goin' to say nothin' neither, Rig' puts him out of the game for kickin'. Most o' the crowd started home when they seen the show was over, but I didn't blame the umps none—I'd of did the same if I'd of been in their place. We finished up pretty fast after that, because they wasn't no chancet for us to ever come near catchin' up.

After I dressed, I forgot what I was doin' and walked right out o' the club-house without givin' the doll a chancet to make a get-away. There she was, layin' for me.

"What did you take him out o' the game for?" she says.

"I didn't take him out o' no game," I says. "The umps didn't like his language."

Then she ast me what was the matter with his language, and I says I didn't think the umps could understand it right.

"Well," she says, "if a umpire can't understand plain English, he should not ought to be no umpire, and I will write to the president o' the league and have both o' these here men discharged." Then she says: "Mr. Baker was doin' splendid and would of did still better if he had of been left in longer. He didn't catch all them balls that was throwed to him, but that's because he aint had no practice." Then she says: "I am goin' out of town to-night, but I want you to keep on lettin' Mr. Baker play every day, and I'll watch the papers, and if I see where he aint playin', you'll hear from me."

Well, I couldn't see no joke in it when I got home that night. The ball players was wise and knowed it wasn't my fault. But I was a-scared that the bugs and these here reporters would get after me if I let the boob play every day. And I was a little bit proud o' the work we'd did and didn't want to have it all wasted. I figured it all out, the way I was goin' to get rid of him. I was goin' to have one o' the pitchers hit him with the ball in battin' practice—not hard enough to kill him, but just so's it would scare him out of baseball. I thought he couldn't stand the gaff and would quit in a minute.

I gets out there early the next mornin' for practice and frames it up with Young, a big busher we had that was fast as a streak and hog ◆

◆ *Young*—Apparently a fictional character.

wild. I sends him out to pitch to us and then tells the colleger to go up there and swing till he learned how to bat. It was prob'ly a dirty trick, but I couldn't think o' no other way.

Well, I pulled a boner when I says anything to this here Young. What I should ought to of did was say nothin', but just stick him in there to pitch natural, and then he'd of hit the bird by accident. But when he was tryin' to hit him, he couldn't even come clost. He was tryin' to be wild, and he pitched more strikes than he ever done before in his life. Gertrude didn't hit nothin', and nothin' hit him. So fin'lly I give up and sent Young to the club-house and started the reg'lar practice.

Fallin' down on that made me meaner'n ever, and I doped out something else. I tells the colleger he stood too far from the plate when he swung at a ball. I says: "When you go up to bat in the game, keep one foot on the plate," figurin' that the guy that pitched for Philly would try to drive him away and either wound him or scare him to death.

Alexander worked for them, and Baker stood right on top o' the plate. Dooin called the umps' attention, and the umps warned him, but he wouldn't move. Fin'lly Alexander shot one up there and he didn't duck in time. It catched him in front o' the ear, and he dropped like as if he was shot. I bet I was the most scared guy in the world. For a minute I felt like a murderer, and I wasn't never so glad in my life as when I seen him get up. He staggered round a little, and I had 'em bring him over to the bench. I stuck myself in to run for him, and some o' the boys took him in the club-house and got him fixed up. He wasn't hurt bad, though he got a mean lookin' bump.

We was startin' West again that night and I didn't never expect him to show up for no trip. But there he was, down to the train, with his wagonload o' scenery.

"Well," I says, "you got your nerve."

"Yes," he says, "I'm goin' to show Hub that they's more'n one game ball player in the world."

He was still thinkin' about that one-legged guy in the Southern League.

We opened up in Pittsburgh, and I kept him on the bench. I knowed Mrs. Hayes would wire and ask me why wasn't he playin', and when she did, I wrote to her sayin' he was hurt by that there blow on the head. But that alibi wouldn't get by very long, and I figured I'd have to frame somethin' new.

The first night in St. Louis, I thought up somethin' and got Doc, the trainer, to help me pull it. I buys two tickets to a show and gives 'em to Doc with instructions to ask the colleger to go along. After the show, they was to go to Tony's for lunch. He was to order two beers, ◆ and then I was to drop in and catch Baker with a big stein in front of him. Then I was to swell up and suspend him for drinkin'. Doc done his best, but the bird says beer made him sick and he wouldn't have nothin' to do with it. So when I come in, he was eatin' some kind o' fancy sandwich and lappin' up a lemonade or somethin'.

He ast me the next afternoon why didn't I let him play, and I says:

"You aint no ball player and you wouldn't be no ball player if you kept at it a thousand years. You should ought to be trimmin' hats."

"Mrs. Hayes thinks I'm all O. K.," he says.

"Yes," I says, "and you could start one o' these here Carnegie liberries with what she don't know about baseball." I says: "Why don't you quit?"

Then he says: "I can't quit because I can't afford to lose this here sal'ry."

I says: "What do you mean, you can't afford? You had plenty o' clo'es when you joined us," I says, "and you must of had money o' your own or you couldn't of boughten them clo'es."

Then he says his old man give him a allowance of a hundred a month and he spent all o' that on his clo'es, and that the old man had told him he would double this here allowance if the boy showed he could earn five thousand bucks a year when he got out o' college, and the old man didn't care how he earned it. So he'd told Mrs. Hayes the whole story and she'd tooken pity on him and give him the job. I ast him wasn't they no other way he could "earn" the money, and he says he s'posed they was lots o' ways, only this here way was easiest.

I says: "Yes, but you aint earnin' nothin' here. You might just as well stick fellas up on the street as draw a sal'ry as a ball player. You're stealin' it either way."

He just laughed, and then I says:

"Don't your old man care if you mix up with us tough guys?"

"No," he says, "the old man don't care, but the old lady does. I told her you was a nice, polite bunch o' fellas and she fell for it, or else she'd of made me cut this out and come home."

◆ *Tony's*—Probably Tony Faust's Restaurant on Broadway near Elm, one of the principal restaurants of downtown St. Louis, but possibly John Tony's Restaurant at 613 South Second Street.

The hunch come to me all of a sudden, and I says:

"What's your old lady's name and where does she live at?"

He told me, and I couldn't hardly wait till I got back to the hotel.

I don't know now just what I wrote, but it was some letter. I told her we was a bunch o' stews and that when we wasn't lushin' beer or playin' poker, we was going to burlesque shows. I says her son was pickin' up a awful bunch o' language and drinkin' his fool head off. I says he was stuck on a burlesque queen and was spendin' all his dough on her. And I wound it up by sayin' that Dixon, the manager, had killed his wife and they wasn't no tellin' when he'd cut loose and kill somebody else. I didn't sign no name, but just put "From a Friend in Need" down at the bottom.

It was in your town that he heard from her, and he showed me the letter. She says he was to come home at oncet and that she'd made the old man promise to come through with a extra allowance without makin' him do no work for it. But if he didn't cut out the ball playin' and beat it for home he wouldn't never get another nickel out o' none o' them. She hadn't gave no reason for writin' this way, and he was up in the air. I told him we was sorry to lose him, but maybe it was best for him to quit playin' ball, even if he hadn't never started. He left us the second night in Chi. Hub was good and sore at me. He says I'd spoiled the season for him.

I felt so good about gettin' him off'n my hands that I went out there and played like Cobb or somebody the rest o' the trip. Maybe you fellas remember how I hit ag'in' you them last two days. I done even better'n that in Cincinnati and New York. It was the best trip we'd made in a good many years, and the bugs at home went crazy over us. They was ten thousand out to the first game of our serious at home with St. Louis—on a Thursday, at that.

O' course I knowed they'd be a argument with the skirt. Our winnin' streak wouldn't make her forget to ask me what had become o' Baker. When she ast me, I sprung the stuff about him gettin' a letter from his mother, but I didn't tell her nothin' about the letter I'd wrote. She didn't say nothin', but she looked pretty sore, and she forgot all about givin' me the glad hand for what we'd did in the West.

We done pretty well at home ag'in' St. Louis and Pittsburgh. Then ◇ you fellas come along and I guess I don't need to tell you that we was goin' good. I was beginnin' to think we maybe might keep it up and throw a scare into some o' you birds.

She didn't never come out to yesterday's game, but I didn't suspect

nothin' wrong till Kelly, the secretary, come into the club-house after me. He tells me that she wants to see me down to the down-town office.

"All right," I says. "I'll beat it down there right after the game."

"No," says Kelly, "she wants you right now."

So I took my unie off and beat it down there in a taxi. The girl in the front office told me to go right on in, and in I went. There was the dame, settin' at the desk where poor old Hayes used to set. And they was two big coppers with her. Without sayin' "How d'ya do" or nothin', she opens right up on me and says:

"These here officers is here to protect me. If you start somethin', you'll get nothin' but the worst of it." Then she pulls a letter out o' the desk and says: "This here letter is from Mr. Baker's mother, and in it she tells me why she made her boy come home. Somebody has tooken the trouble to tell her some fac's about this here ball club—*my* ball club that I was proud of! But I aint proud of it no more. I aint proud o' no gang o' hoodlums that don't do nothin' but gamble and drink and run round with actresses and lead young men astray."

◇ *We done pretty well at home*—Home park for the Braves in 1914 was South End Grounds, in its final season of use; the management was to build its modern Braves Field for the 1915 season. This view, taken in the 1890's, shows the Grounds' short right-field line, only 255 feet long. The left-field line was even shorter, at 250 feet. Oddly, the park had Boston's only double-deck grandstand. (National Baseball Library, Cooperstown, New York)

"Is that all?" I says.

"No," she hollers, "that aint all. Mr. Dixon, you killed your wife!"

"That's a whole lot o' bunk," I says. "I didn't never have no wife, so how could I kill my wife when I didn't never have none?"

"Don't lie to me!" she says. "Even if you didn't never have no wife, you killed somebody, maybe a innocent girl that was wronged."

"Cut the comedy," I says. "They's nothin' to that stuff. Somebody's went and gave the old lady a bum steer."

"What for?" she ast.

"Prob'ly," I says, "because somebody was tired o' having that boob on the ball club and figured that was the best way to get rid of him."

"We wont discuss it no fu'ther," she says. "I called you up to tell you you aint managin' the club no longer. You can stay here under the terms o' your contract and play ball if you want to, but maybe you wouldn't want to work for the new manager."

"Who is it?" I says.

"That's none o' your business," she says. "I will tell you when the proper time comes."

Then I says: "Is the seamstress comin' back?"

"The *who?*" she hollers.

"That there colleger," I says. "If I was you, I'd get him back, because you and him is certainly a grand combination. It's hard to tell which one o' you knows the most about baseball, you or that bird. Even if you couldn't use him as no ball player, you could chop up his head and build a new grandstand."

"He was smart enough to go through Yale college," she says.

"No," says I. "He didn't never go through no Yale college. If they was any college that he went through, it was this here Wellesley college."

Then I turns and beats it for the door.

Well, sir, they aint nothin' more to tell except one thing. When I come out o' the door into the outside office, I bumped right square into "Gertie." He was smilin' like a big kid, and he says: "Hello, there!" Well, I didn't say nothin' to him, but I give him a good kick in the shin, and I stepped all over his patent-leather shoes. Then I went on about my business.

I wired Knabe, and they wasn't nothin' to it. He told me to come on and join 'em in Pittsburgh, and I just had time to get my stuff together and catch this train.

I guess she wont try and get no injunction out agin' me. But I wisht she would. I'd like to tell my story to a judge, provided the judge wasn't no woman.

You know who's goin' to manage that club, don't you? And you know who's going to be president of it. Well, sir, I'll bet you anything you want to bet that they wont even finish in Mass'chusetts.

Alibi Ike

I

His right name was Frank X. Farrell, and I guess the X stood for "Excuse me." Because he never pulled a play, good or bad, on or off the field, without apologizin' for it.

"Alibi Ike" was the name Carey wished on him the first day he ◆ reported down South. O' course we all cut out the "Alibi" part of it right away for the fear he would overhear it and bust somebody. But we called him "Ike" right to his face and the rest of it was understood by everybody on the club except Ike himself.

"Alibi Ike" was published in *The Saturday Evening Post*, CLXXXVIII (July 31, 1915), 16–18, 30.

◆ *Carey*—One of numerous fictional characters. Beginning with this story, Lardner forsook his practice of setting the scene on actual teams with genuine players as teammates of the fictional characters. The team in this story, which appears also in "The Poor Simp" and "Where Do You Get That Noise?" is not identified, except as a western team. Its opponents are all of the National League clubs except the Chicago Cubs. Accordingly, it is a Cub team with fictional personnel.

Carey is not Max Carey, star outfielder of the Pittsburgh Pirates; the Pirates are explicitly mentioned as an opposing team.

Beyond this point, all characters will be presumed fictional, and will not be identified as such unless they appear in ambiguous contexts, interspersed with actual persons. Actual figures will continue to be identified.

He ast me one time, he says:

"What do you all call me Ike for? I ain't no Yid."

"Carey give you the name," I says. "It's his nickname for everybody he takes a likin' to."

"He mustn't have only a few friends then," says Ike. "I never heard him say 'Ike' to nobody else."

But I was goin' to tell you about Carey namin' him. We'd been workin' out two weeks and the pitchers was showin' somethin' when this bird joined us. His first day out he stood up there so good and took such a reef at the old pill that he had everyone lookin'. Then him and Carey was together in left field, catchin' fungoes, and it was after we was through for the day that Carey told me about him.

"What do you think of Alibi Ike?" ast Carey.

"Who's that?" I says.

"This here Farrell in the outfield," says Carey.

"He looks like he could hit," I says.

"Yes," says Carey, "but he can't hit near as good as he can apologize."

Then Carey went on to tell me what Ike had been pullin' out there. He'd dropped the first fly ball that was hit to him and told Carey his glove wasn't broke in good yet, and Carey says the glove could easy of been Kid Gleason's gran'father. He made a whale of a catch out o' the next one and Carey says "Nice work!" or somethin' like that, but Ike says he could of caught the ball with his back turned only he slipped when he started after it and, besides that, the air currents fooled him.

"I thought you done well to get to the ball," says Carey.

"I ought to been settin' under it," says Ike.

"What did you hit last year?" Carey ast him.

"I had malaria most o' the season," says Ike. "I wound up with .356."

"Where would I have to go to get malaria?" says Carey, but Ike didn't wise up.

I and Carey and him set at the same table together for supper. It took him half an hour longer'n us to eat because he had to excuse himself every time he lifted his fork.

"Doctor told me I needed starch," he'd say, and then toss a shovelful o' potatoes into him. Or, "They ain't much meat on one o' these chops," he'd tell us, and grab another one. Or he'd say: "Nothin' like onions for a cold," and then he'd dip into the perfumery.

"Better try that apple sauce," says Carey. "It'll help your malaria."

"Whose malaria?" says Ike. He'd forgot already why he didn't only hit .356 last year.

I and Carey begin to lead him on.

"Whereabouts did you say your home was?" I ast him.

"I live with my folks," he says. "We live in Kansas City—not right down in the business part—outside a ways."

"How's that come?" says Carey. "I should think you'd get rooms in the post office."

But Ike was too busy curin' his cold to get that one.

"Are you married?" I ast him.

"No," he says. "I never run round much with girls, except to shows onct in a wile and parties and dances and roller skatin'."

"Never take 'em to the prize fights, eh?" says Carey.

"We don't have no real good bouts," says Ike. "Just bush stuff. And I never figured a boxin' match was a place for the ladies."

Well, after supper he pulled a cigar out and lit it. I was just goin' to ask him what he done it for, but he beat me to it.

"Kind o' rests a man to smoke after a good work-out," he says. "Kind o' settles a man's supper, too."

"Looks like a pretty good cigar," says Carey.

"Yes," says Ike. "A friend o' mine give it to me—a fella in Kansas City that runs a billiard room."

"Do you play billiards?" I ast him.

"I used to play a fair game," he says. "I'm all out o' practice now—can't hardly make a shot."

We coaxed him into a four-handed battle, him and Carey against Jack Mack and I. Say, he couldn't play billiards as good as Willie ◆ Hoppe, not quite. But to hear him tell it, he didn't make a good shot all evenin'. I'd leave him an awful-lookin' layout and he'd gather 'em up in one try and then run a couple o' hundred, and between every carom he'd say he'd put too much stuff on the ball, or the English didn't take, or the table wasn't true, or his stick was crooked, or somethin'. And all the time he had the balls actin' like they was Dutch soldiers and him Kaiser William. We started out to play fifty points, but we had to make it a thousand so as I and Jack and Carey could try the table.

The four of us set round the lobby a wile after we was through playin', and when it got along toward bedtime Carey whispered to me and says:

◆ *Willie Hoppe*—William F. Hoppe (1887–1959), the world's foremost billiard player, champion of various classes of balk-line and three-cushion billiards at various times from 1906 to 1941.

"Ike'd like to go to bed, but he can't think up no excuse."

Carey hadn't hardly finished whisperin' when Ike got up and pulled it.

"Well, good night, boys," he says. "I ain't sleepy but I got some gravel in my shoes and it's killin' my feet."

We knowed he hadn't never left the hotel since we'd came in from the grounds and changed our clo'es. So Carey says:

"I should think they'd take them gravel pits out o' the billiard room."

But Ike was already on his way to the elevator, limpin'.

"He's got the world beat," says Carey to Jack and I. "I've knew lots o' guys that had an alibi for every mistake they made; I've heard pitchers say that the ball slipped when somebody cracked one off'n 'em; I've heard infielders complain of a sore arm after heavin' one into the stand, and I've saw outfielders tooken sick with a dizzy spell when they've misjudged a fly ball. But this baby can't even go to bed without apologizin', and I bet he excuses himself to the razor when he gets ready to shave."

"And at that," says Jack, "he's goin' to make us a good man."

"Yes," says Carey, "unless rheumatism keeps his battin' average down to .400."

Well, sir, Ike kept whalin' away at the ball all through the trip till everybody knowed he'd won a job. Cap had him in there regular the last few exhibition games and told the newspaper boys a week before the season opened that he was goin' to start him in Kane's place.

"You're there, kid," says Carey to Ike, the night Cap made the 'nnouncement. "They ain't many boys that wins a big league berth their third year out."

"I'd of been up here a year ago," says Ike, "only I was bent over all season with lumbago."

II

It rained down in Cincinnati one day and somebody organized a little game o' cards. They was shy two men to make six and ast I and Carey to play.

"I'm with you if you get Ike and make it seven-handed," says Carey.

So they got a hold of Ike and we went up to Smitty's room.

"I pretty near forgot how many you deal," says Ike. "It's been a long wile since I played."

I and Carey give each other the wink, and sure enough, he was just as ig'orant about poker as billiards. About the second hand, the pot was opened two or three ahead of him, and they was three in when it come his turn. It cost a buck, and he throwed in two.

"It's raised, boys," somebody says.

"Gosh, that's right, I did raise it," says Ike.

"Take out a buck if you didn't mean to tilt her," says Carey.

"No," says Ike, "I'll leave it go."

Well, it was raised back at him and then he made another mistake and raised again. They was only three left in when the draw come. Smitty'd opened with a pair o' kings and he didn't help 'em. Ike stood pat. The guy that'd raised him back was flushin' and he didn't fill. So Smitty checked and Ike bet and didn't get no call. He tossed his hand away, but I grabbed it and give it a look. He had king, queen, jack and two tens. Alibi Ike he must have seen me peekin', for he leaned over and whispered to me.

"I overlooked my hand," he says. "I thought all the wile it was a straight."

"Yes," I says, "that's why you raised twice by mistake."

They was another pot that he come into with tens and fours. It was tilted a couple o' times and two o' the strong fellas drawed ahead of Ike. They each drawed one. So Ike throwed away his little pair and come out with four tens. And they was four treys against him. Carey'd looked at Ike's discards and then he says:

"This lucky bum busted two pair."

"No, no, I didn't," says Ike.

"Yes, yes, you did," says Carey, and showed us the two fours.

"What do you know about that?" says Ike. "I'd of swore one was a five spot."

Well, we hadn't had no pay day yet, and after a wile everybody except Ike was goin' shy. I could see him gettin' restless and I was wonderin' how he'd make the get-away. He tried two or three times. "I got to buy some collars before supper," he says.

"No hurry," says Smitty. "The stores here keeps open all night in April."

After a minute he opened up again.

"My uncle out in Nebraska ain't expected to live," he says. "I ought to send a telegram."

"Would that save him"? says Carey.

"No, it sure wouldn't," says Ike, "but I ought to leave my old man know where I'm at."

"When did you hear about your uncle?" says Carey.

"Just this mornin'," says Ike.

"Who told you?" ast Carey.

"I got a wire from my old man," says Ike.

"Well," says Carey, "your old man knows you're still here yet this afternoon if you was here this mornin'. Trains leavin' Cincinnati in the middle o' the day don't carry no ball clubs."

"Yes," says Ike, "that's true. But he don't know where I'm goin' to be next week."

"Ain't he got no schedule?" ast Carey.

"I sent him one openin' day," says Ike, "but it takes mail a long time to get to Idaho."

"I thought your old man lived in Kansas City," says Carey.

"He does when he's home," says Ike.

"But now," says Carey, "I s'pose he's went to Idaho so as he can be near your sick uncle in Nebraska."

"He's visitin' my other uncle in Idaho."

"Then how does he keep posted about your sick uncle?" ast Carey.

"He don't," says Ike. "He don't even know my other uncle's sick. That's why I ought to wire and tell him."

"Good night!" says Carey.

"What town in Idaho is your old man at?" I says.

Ike thought it over.

"No town at all," he says. "But he's near a town."

"Near what town?" I says.

"Yuma," says Ike.

Well, by this time he'd lost two or three pots and he was desperate. We was playin' just as fast as we could, because we seen we couldn't hold him much longer. But he was tryin' so hard to frame an escape that he couldn't pay no attention to the cards, and it looked like we'd get his whole pile away from him if we could make him stick.

The telephone saved him. The minute it begun to ring, five of us jumped for it. But Ike was there first.

"Yes," he says, answerin' it. "This is him. I'll come right down."

And he slammed up the receiver and beat it out o' the door without even sayin' good-by.

"Smitty'd ought to locked the door," says Carey.

"What did he win?" ast Carey.

We figured it up—sixty-odd bucks.

"And the next time we ask him to play," says Carey, "his fingers will be so stiff he can't hold the cards."

Well, we set round a wile talkin' it over, and pretty soon the telephone rung again. Smitty answered it. It was a friend of his'n from Hamilton and he wanted to know why Smitty didn't hurry down. He was the one that had called before and Ike had told him he was Smitty.

"Ike'd ought to split with Smitty's friend," says Carey.

"No," I says, "he'll need all he won. It costs money to buy collars and to send telegrams from Cincinnati to your old man in Texas and keep him posted on the health o' your uncle in Cedar Rapids, D. C."

III

And you ought to heard him out there on that field! They wasn't a day when he didn't pull six or seven, and it didn't make no difference whether he was goin' good or bad. If he popped up in the pinch he should of made a base hit and the reason he didn't was so-and-so. And if he cracked one for three bases he ought to had a home run, only the ball wasn't lively, or the wind brought it back, or he tripped on a lump o' dirt, roundin' first base.

They was one afternoon in New York when he beat all records. Big Marquard was workin' against us and he was good.

In the first innin' Ike hit one clear over that right field stand, but it was a few feet foul. Then he got another foul and then the count come to two and two. Then Rube slipped one acrost on him and he was called out.

"What do you know about that!" he says afterward on the bench. "I lost count. I thought it was three and one, and I took a strike."

"You took a strike all right," says Carey. "Even the umps knowed it was a strike."

"Yes," says Ike, "but you can bet I wouldn't of took it if I'd knew it was the third one. The score board had it wrong."

"That score board ain't for you to look at," says Cap. "It's for you to hit that old pill against."

"Well," says Ike, "I could of hit that one over the score board if I'd knew it was the third."

"Was it a good ball?" I says.

"Well, no, it wasn't," says Ike. "It was inside."

"How far inside?" says Carey.

"Oh, two or three inches or half a foot," says Ike.

"I guess you wouldn't of threatened the score board with it then," says Cap.

"I'd of pulled it down the right foul line if I hadn't thought he'd call it a ball," says Ike.

Well, in New York's part o' the innin' Doyle cracked one and Ike run back a mile and a half and caught it with one hand. We was all sayin' what a whale of a play it was, but he had to apologize just the same as for gettin' struck out.

"That stand's so high," he says, "that a man don't never see a ball till it's right on top o' you."

"Didn't you see that one?" ast Cap.

"Not at first," says Ike; "not till it raised up above the roof o' the stand."

"Then why did you start back as soon as the ball was hit?" says Cap.

"I knowed by the sound that he'd got a good hold of it," says Ike.

"Yes," says Cap, "but how'd you know what direction to run in?"

"Doyle usually hits 'em that way, the way I run," says Ike.

"Why don't you play blindfolded?" says Carey.

"Might as well, with that big high stand to bother a man," says Ike. "If I could of saw the ball all the time I'd of got it in my hip pocket."

Along in the fifth we was one run to the bad and Ike got on with one out. On the first ball throwed to Smitty, Ike went down. The ball was outside and Meyers throwed Ike out by ten feet.

You could see Ike's lips movin' all the way to the bench and when he got there he had his piece learned.

"Why didn't he swing?" he says.

"Why didn't you wait for his sign?" says Cap.

"He give me his sign," says Ike.

"What is his sign with you?" says Cap.

"Pickin' up some dirt with his right hand," says Ike.

"Well, I didn't see him do it," Cap says.

"He done it all right," says Ike.

Well, Smitty went out and they wasn't no more argument till they come in for the next innin'. Then Cap opened it up.

"You fellas better get your signs straight," he says.

"Do you mean me?" says Smitty.

"Yes," Cap says. "What's your sign with Ike?"

"Slidin' my left hand up to the end o' the bat and back," says Smitty.

"Do you hear that, Ike?" ast Cap.

"What of it?" says Ike.

"You says his sign was pickin' up dirt and he says it's slidin' his hand. Which is right?"

"I'm right," says Smitty. "But if you're arguin' about him goin' last innin', I didn't give him no sign."

"You pulled your cap down with your right hand, didn't you?" ast Ike.

"Well, s'pose I did," says Smitty. "That don't mean nothin'. I never told you to take that for a sign, did I?"

"I thought maybe you meant to tell me and forgot," says Ike.

They couldn't none of us answer that and they wouldn't of been no more said if Ike had of shut up. But wile we was settin' there Carey got on with two out and stole second clean.

"There!" says Ike. "That's what I was tryin' to do and I'd of got away with it if Smitty'd swang and bothered the Indian."

"Oh!" says Smitty. "You was tryin' to steal then, was you? I thought you claimed I give you the hit and run."

"I didn't claim no such a thing," says Ike. "I thought maybe you might of gave me a sign, but I was goin' anyway because I thought I had a good start."

Cap prob'ly would of hit him with a bat, only just about that time Doyle booted one on Hayes and Carey come acrost with the run that tied.

Well, we go into the ninth finally, one and one, and Marquard walks McDonald with nobody out.

"Lay it down," says Cap to Ike.

And Ike goes up there with orders to bunt and cracks the first ball into that right-field stand! It was fair this time, and we're two ahead, but I didn't think about that at the time. I was too busy watchin' Cap's face. First he turned pale and then he got red as fire and then he got blue and purple, and finally he just laid back and busted out laughin'. So we wasn't afraid to laugh ourselfs when we seen him doin' it, and when Ike come in everybody on the bench was in hysterics.

But instead o' takin' advantage, Ike had to try and excuse himself. His play was to shut up and he didn't know how to make it.

"Well," he says, "if I hadn't hit quite so quick at that one I bet it'd of cleared the center-field fence."

Cap stopped laughin'.

"It'll cost you plain fifty," he says.

"What for?" says Ike.

"When I say 'bunt' I mean 'bunt,'" says Cap.

"You didn't say 'bunt,'" says Ike.

"I says 'Lay it down,'" says Cap. "If that don't mean 'bunt,' what does it mean?"

"'Lay it down' means 'bunt' all right," says Ike, "but I understood you to say 'Lay on it.'"

"All right," says Cap, "and the little misunderstandin' will cost you fifty."

Ike didn't say nothin' for a few minutes. Then he had another bright idear.

"I was just kiddin' about misunderstandin' you," he says. "I knowed you wanted me to bunt."

"Well, then, why didn't you bunt?" ast Cap.

"I was goin' to on the next ball," says Ike. "But I thought if I took a good wallop I'd have 'em all fooled. So I walloped at the first one to fool 'em, and I didn't have no intention o' hittin' it."

"You tried to miss it, did you?" says Cap.

"Yes," says Ike.

"How'd you happen to hit it?" ast Cap.

"Well," Ike says, "I was lookin' for him to throw me a fast one and I was goin' to swing under it. But he come with a hook and I met it right square where I was swingin' to go under the fast one."

"Great!" says Cap. "Boys," he says, "Ike's learned how to hit Marquard's curve. Pretend a fast one's comin' and then try to miss it. It's a good thing to know and Ike'd ought to be willin' to pay for the lesson. So I'm goin' to make it a hundred instead o' fifty."

The game wound up 3 to 1. The fine didn't go, because Ike hit like a wild man all through that trip and we made pretty near a clean-up. The night we went to Philly I got him cornered in the car and I says to him:

"Forget them alibis for a wile and tell me somethin'. What'd you do that for, swing that time against Marquard when you was told to bunt?"

"I'll tell you," he says. "That ball he throwed me looked just like the one I struck out on in the first innin' and I wanted to show Cap what I could of done to that other one if I'd knew it was the third strike."

"But," I says, "the one you struck out on in the first innin' was a fast ball."

"So was the one I cracked in the ninth," says Ike.

IV

You've saw Cap's wife, o' course. Well, her sister's about twict as good-lookin' as her, and that's goin' some.

Cap took his missus down to St. Louis the second trip and the other one come down from St. Joe to visit her. Her name is Dolly, and some doll is right.

Well, Cap was goin' to take the two sisters to a show and he wanted a beau for Dolly. He left it to her and she picked Ike. He'd hit three on the nose that afternoon—off'n Sallee, too.

They fell for each other that first evenin'. Cap told us how it come off. She begin flatterin' Ike for the star game he'd played and o' course he begin excusin' himself for not doin' better. So she thought he was modest and it went strong with her. And she believed everything he said and that made her solid with him—that and her make-up. They was together every mornin' and evenin' for the five days we was there. In the afternoons Ike played the grandest ball you ever see, hittin' and runnin' the bases like a fool and catchin' everything that stayed in the park.

I told Cap, I says: "You'd ought to keep the doll with us and he'd make Cobb's figures look sick."

But Dolly had to go back to St. Joe and we come home for a long serious.

Well, for the next three weeks Ike had a letter to read every day and he'd set in the clubhouse readin' it till mornin' practice was half over. Cap didn't say nothin' to him, because he was goin' so good. But I and Carey wasted a lot of our time tryin' to get him to own up who the letters was from. Fine chanct!

"What are you readin'?" Carey'd say. "A bill?"

"No," Ike'd say, "not exactly a bill. It's a letter from a fella I used to go to school with."

"High school or college?" I'd ask him.

"College," he'd say.

"What college?" I'd say.

Then he'd stall a wile and then he'd say:

"I didn't go to the college myself, but my friend went there."

"How did it happen you didn't go?" Carey'd ask him.

"Well," he'd say, "they wasn't no colleges near where I lived."

"Didn't you live in Kansas City?" I'd say to him.

One time he'd say he did and another time he didn't. One time he says he lived in Michigan.

"Where at?" says Carey.

"Near Detroit," he says.

"Well," I says, "Detroit's near Ann Arbor and that's where they got the university."

"Yes," says Ike, "they got it there now, but they didn't have it there then."

"I come pretty near goin' to Syracuse," I says, "only they wasn't no railroads runnin' through there in them days."

"Where'd this friend o' yours go to college?" says Carey.

"I forget now," says Ike.

"Was it Carlisle?" ast Carey.

"No," says Ike, "his folks wasn't very well off."

"That's what barred me from Smith," I says.

"I was goin' to tackle Cornell's," says Carey, "but the doctor told me I'd have hay fever if I didn't stay up North."

"Your friend writes long letters," I says.

"Yes," says Ike; "he's tellin' me about a ball player."

"Where does he play?" ast Carey.

"Down in the Texas League—Fort Wayne," says Ike.

"It looks like a girl's writin'," Carey says.

"A girl wrote it," says Ike. "That's my friend's sister, writin' for him."

"Didn't they teach writin' at this here college where he went?" says Carey.

"Sure," Ike says, "they taught writin', but he got his hand cut off in a railroad wreck."

"How long ago?" I says.

"Right after he got out o' college," says Ike.

"Well," I says, "I should think he'd of learned to write with his left hand by this time."

"It's his left hand that was cut off," says Ike; "and he was left-handed."

"You get a letter every day," says Carey. "They're all the same writin'. Is he tellin' you about a different ball player every time he writes?"

"No," Ike says. "It's the same ball player. He just tells me what he does every day."

"From the size o' the letters, they don't play nothin' but double-headers down there," says Carey.

We figured that Ike spent most of his evenin's answerin' the letters from his "friend's sister," so we kept tryin' to date him up for shows and parties to see how he'd duck out of 'em. He was bugs over spaghetti, so we told him one day that they was goin' to be a big feed of it over to Joe's that night and he was invited.

"How long'll it last?" he says.

"Well," we says, "we're goin' right over there after the game and stay till they close up."

"I can't go," he says, "unless they leave me come home at eight bells."

"Nothin' doin'," says Carey. "Joe'd get sore."

"I can't go then," says Ike.

"Why not?" I ast him.

"Well," he says, "my landlady locks up the house at eight and I left my key home."

"You can come and stay with me," says Carey.

"No," he says, "I can't sleep in a strange bed."

"How do you get along when we're on the road?" says I.

"I don't never sleep the first night anywheres," he says. "After that I'm all right."

"You'll have time to chase home and get your key right after the game," I told him.

"The key ain't home," says Ike. "I lent it to one o' the other fellas and he's went out o' town and took it with him."

"Couldn't you borry another key off'n the landlady?" Carey ast him.

"No," he says, "that's the only one they is."

Well, the day before we started East again, Ike come into the clubhouse all smiles.

"Your birthday?" I ast him.

"No," he says.

"What do you feel so good about?" I says.

"Got a letter from my old man," he says. "My uncle's goin' to get well."

"Is that the one in Nebraska?" says I.

"Not right in Nebraska," says Ike. "Near there."

But afterwards we got the right dope from Cap. Dolly'd blew in from Missouri and was goin' to make the trip with her sister.

V

Well, I want to alibi Carey and I for what come off in Boston. If we'd of had any idear what we was doin', we'd never did it. They wasn't nobody outside o' maybe Ike and the dame that felt worse over it than I and Carey.

The first two days we didn't see nothin' of Ike and her except out to the park. The rest o' the time they was sight-seein' over to Cambridge and down to Revere and out to Brook-a-line and all the other places where the rubes go.

But when we come into the beanery after the third game Cap's wife called us over.

"If you want to see somethin' pretty," she says, "look at the third finger on Sis's left hand."

Well, o' course we knowed before we looked that it wasn't goin' to be no hangnail. Nobody was su'prised when Dolly blew into the dinin' room with it—a rock that Ike'd bought off'n Diamond Joe the first trip to New York. Only o' course it'd been set into a lady's-size ring instead o' the automobile tire he'd been wearin'.

Cap and his missus and Ike and Dolly ett supper together, only Ike didn't eat nothin', but just set there blushin' and spillin' things on the tablecloth. I heard him excusin' himself for not havin' no appetite. He says he couldn't never eat when he was clost to the ocean. He'd forgot about them sixty-five oysters he destroyed the first night o' the trip before.

He was goin' to take her to a show, so after supper he went upstairs to change his collar. She had to doll up, too, and o' course Ike was through long before her.

If you remember the hotel in Boston, they's a little parlor where the piano's at and then they's another little parlor openin' off o' that. Well, when Ike come down Smitty was playin' a few chords and I and Carey was harmonizin'. We seen Ike go up to the desk to leave his key and we called him in. He tried to duck away, but we wouldn't stand for it.

We ast him what he was all duded up for and he says he was goin' to the theayter.

"Goin' alone?" says Carey.

"No," he says, "a friend o' mine's goin' with me."

"What do you say if we go along?" says Carey.

"I ain't only got two tickets," he says.

"Well," says Carey, "we can go down there with you and buy our own seats; maybe we can all get together."

"No," says Ike. "They ain't no more seats. They're all sold out."

"We can buy some off'n the scalpers," says Carey.

"I wouldn't if I was you," says Ike. "They say the show's rotten."

"What are you goin' for, then?" I ast.

"I didn't hear about it bein' rotten till I got the tickets," he says.

"Well," I says, "if you don't want to go I'll buy the tickets from you."

"No," says Ike, "I wouldn't want to cheat you. I'm stung and I'll just have to stand for it."

"What are you goin' to do with the girl, leave her here at the hotel?" I says.

"What girl?" says Ike.

"The girl you ett supper with," I says.

"Oh," he says, "we just happened to go into the dinin' room together, that's all. Cap wanted I should set down with 'em."

"I noticed," says Carey, "that she happened to be wearin' that rock you bought off'n Diamond Joe."

"Yes," says Ike. "I lent it to her for a wile."

"Did you lend her the new ring that goes with it?" I says.

"She had that already," says Ike. "She lost the set out of it."

"I wouldn't trust no strange girl with a rock o' mine," says Carey.

"Oh, I guess she's all right," Ike says. "Besides, I was tired o' the stone. When a girl asks you for somethin', what are you goin' to do?"

He started out toward the desk, but we flagged him.

"Wait a minute!" Carey says. "I got a bet with Sam here, and it's up to you to settle it."

"Well," says Ike, "make it snappy. My friend'll be here any minute."

"I bet," says Carey, "that you and that girl was engaged to be married."

"Nothin' to it," says Ike.

"Now look here," says Carey, "this is goin' to cost me real money if I lose. Cut out the alibi stuff and give it to us straight. Cap's wife just as good as told us you was roped."

Ike blushed like a kid.

"Well, boys," he says, "I may as well own up. You win, Carey."

"Yatta boy!" says Carey. "Congratulations!"

"You got a swell girl, Ike," I says.

"She's a peach," says Smitty.

"Well, I guess she's O. K.," says Ike. "I don't know much about girls."

"Didn't you never run round with 'em?" I says.

"Oh, yes, plenty of 'em," says Ike. "But I never seen none I'd fall for."

"That is, till you seen this one," says Carey.

"Well," says Ike, "this one's O. K., but I wasn't thinkin' about gettin' married yet a wile."

"Who done the askin'—her?" says Carey.

"Oh, no," says Ike, "but sometimes a man don't know what he's gettin' into. Take a good-lookin' girl, and a man gen'ally almost always does about what she wants him to."

"They couldn't no girl lasso me unless I wanted to be lassoed," says Smitty.

"Oh, I don't know," says Ike. "When a fella gets to feelin' sorry for one of 'em it's all off."

Well, we left him go after shakin' hands all round. But he didn't take Dolly to no show that night. Some time wile we was talkin' she'd came into that other parlor and she'd stood there and heard us. I don't know how much she heard. But it was enough. Dolly and Cap's missus took the midnight train for New York. And from there Cap's wife sent her on her way back to Missouri.

She'd left the ring and a note for Ike with the clerk. But we didn't ask Ike if the note was from his friend in Fort Wayne, Texas.

VI

When we'd came to Boston Ike was hittin' plain .397. When we got back home he'd fell off to pretty near nothin'. He hadn't drove one out o' the infield in any o' them other Eastern parks, and he didn't even give no excuse for it.

To show you how bad he was, he struck out three times in Brooklyn one day and never opened his trap when Cap ast him what was the matter. Before, if he'd whiffed oncet in a game he'd of wrote a book tellin' why.

Well, we dropped from first place to fifth in four weeks and we was still goin' down. I and Carey was about the only ones on the club that spoke to each other, and all as we did was remind ourself o' what a boner we'd pulled.

"It's goin' to beat us out o' the big money," says Carey.

"Yes," I says. "I don't want to knock my own ball club, but it looks like a one-man team, and when that one man's dauber's down we couldn't trim our whiskers."

"We ought to knew better," says Carey.

"Yes," I says, "but why should a man pull an alibi for bein' engaged to such a bearcat as she was?"

"He shouldn't," says Carey. "But I and you knowed he would or we'd never started talkin' to him about it. He wasn't no more ashamed o' the girl than I am of a regular base hit. But he just can't come clean on no subjec'."

Cap had the whole story, and I and Carey was as pop'lar with him as an umpire.

"What do you want me to do, Cap?" Carey'd say to him before goin' up to hit.

"Use your own judgment," Cap'd tell him. "We want to lose another game."

But finally, one night in Pittsburgh, Cap had a letter from his missus and he come to us with it.

"You fellas," he says, "is the ones that put us on the bum, and if you're sorry I think they's a chancet for you to make good. The old lady's out to St. Joe and she's been tryin' her hardest to fix things up. She's explained that Ike don't mean nothin' with his talk; I've wrote and explained that to Dolly, too. But the old lady says that Dolly says that she can't believe it. But Dolly's still stuck on this baby, and she's pinin' away just the same as Ike. And the old lady says she thinks if you two fellas would write to the girl and explain how you was always kiddin' with Ike and leadin' him on, and how the ball club was all shot to pieces since Ike quit hittin', and how he acted like he was goin' to kill himself, and this and that, she'd fall for it and maybe soften down. Dolly, the old lady says, would believe you before she'd believe I and the old lady, because she thinks it's her we're sorry for, and not him."

Well, I and Carey was only too glad to try and see what we could do. But it wasn't no snap. We wrote about eight letters before we got one that looked good. Then we give it to the stenographer and had it wrote out on a typewriter and both of us signed it.

It was Carey's idear that made the letter good. He stuck in somethin' about the world's serious money that our wives wasn't goin' to spend unless she took pity on a "boy who was so shy and modest that he was afraid to come right out and say that he had asked such a beautiful and handsome girl to become his bride."

That's prob'ly what got her, or maybe she couldn't of held out much longer anyway. It was four days after we sent the letter that Cap heard from his missus again. We was in Cincinnati.

"We've win," he says to us. "The old lady says that Dolly says she'll give him another chancet. But the old lady says it won't do no good for Ike to write a letter. He'll have to go out there."

"Send him to-night," says Carey.

"I'll pay half his fare," I says.

"I'll pay the other half," says Carey.

"No," says Cap, "the club'll pay his expenses. I'll send him scoutin'."

"Are you goin' to send him to-night?"

"Sure," says Cap. "But I'm goin' to break the news to him right now. It's time we win a ball game."

So in the clubhouse, just before the game, Cap told him. And I certainly felt sorry for Rube Benton and Red Ames that afternoon! I ◆

◆ *Red Ames*—Leon Kessling Ames (1882–1936), a veteran righthander, with Cincinnati since 1913 after a decade with the Giants. In New York he had been a member of the starting rotation with Christy Mathewson and Joe McGinnity. Ames was to go to the Cardinals in mid-season of 1915 and would remain there until 1919, when he would close out his major league career with three games for the Phillies. He lost 23 games in 1914, but was already establishing himself as an effective relief pitcher. In 17 seasons, Ames won 183 and lost 167 in 532 appearances. See Jack Kavanagh, "Red Ames," *The Ballplayers*, p. 22.

and Carey was standin' in front o' the hotel that night when Ike come out with his suitcase.

"Sent home?" I says to him.

"No," he says, "I'm goin' scoutin'."

"Where to?" I says. "Fort Wayne?"

"No, not exactly," he says.

"Well," says Carey, "have a good time."

"I ain't lookin' for no good time," says Ike. "I says I was goin' scoutin'."

"Well, then," says Carey, "I hope you see somebody you like."

"And you better have a drink before you go," I says.

"Well," says Ike, "they claim it helps a cold."

Harmony

Even a baseball writer must sometimes work. Regretfully I yielded my seat in the P. G., walked past the section where Art Graham, Bill Cole, ◆ Lefty Parks and young Waldron were giving expert tonsorial treatment to "Sweet Adeline," and flopped down beside Ryan, the manager.

"Well, Cap," I said, "we're due in Springfield in a little over an hour ◆ and I haven't written a line."

"Don't let me stop you," said Ryan.

"I want you to start me," I said.

"Lord!" said Ryan. "You oughtn't to have any trouble grinding out stuff these days, with the club in first place and Young Waldron gone crazy. He's worth a story any day."

"That's the trouble," said I. "He's been worked so much that there's

---

"Harmony" was published in *McClure's Magazine*, XLV (August 1915), 20–22, 56–57.

◆ *P. G.*—Poker game.

◆ *Cap*—Once again, the characters are fictional. The team is not identified, but even though the manager is again identified as "Cap," the team is apparently not the fictional version of the Chicago Cubs introduced in "Alibi Ike." The personnel mentioned do not accord with those in "Alibi Ike." A later reference to the railroad service to Minneapolis places the team in Chicago, however, and Lardner mentions that the team plays in Detroit. Accordingly, the team plays in the American League, and may be taken as a fictional version of the White Sox.

nothing more to say about him. Everybody in the country knows that he's hitting .420, that he's made nine home runs, twelve triples and twenty-some doubles, that he's stolen twenty-five bases, and that he can play the piano and sing like *Carus'*. They've run his picture ◆ oftener than Billy Sunday and Mary Pickford put together. Of course, ◆ you might come through with how you got him."

"Oh, that's the mystery," said Ryan.

"So I've heard you say," I retorted. "But it wouldn't be a mystery if you'd let me print it."

"Well," said Ryan, "if you're really hard up I suppose I might as well come through. Only there's really no mystery at all about it; it's just what I consider the most remarkable piece of scouting ever done. I've been making a mystery of it just to have a little fun with Dick Hodges. You know he's got the Jackson club and he's still so sore about ◆ my stealing Waldron he'll hardly speak to me.

"I'll give you the dope if you want it, though it's a boost for Art Graham, not me. There's lots of people think the reason I've kept the thing a secret is because I'm modest.

"They give me credit for having found Waldron myself. But Graham is the bird that deserves the credit and I'll admit that he almost had to get down on his knees to make me take his tip. Yes, sir, Art Graham was the scout, and now he's sitting on the bench and the boy he recommended has got his place."

"That sounds pretty good," I said. "And how did Graham get wise?"

"I'm going to tell you. You're in a hurry; so I'll make it snappy.

"You weren't with us last fall, were you? Well, we had a day off in Detroit, along late in the season. Graham's got relatives in Jackson; so he asked me if he could spend the day there. I told him he could and

---

◆ *Carus'*—Enrico Caruso (1873–1921), leading operatic tenor of the early twentieth century.

◆ *Billy Sunday*—William Ashley Sunday (1862–1935), the best-known evangelist preacher of the time. Sunday had been a fast outfielder for Chicago, Pittsburgh, and Philadelphia of the National League, but he was converted to evangelical Christianity. As a player, Sunday hit .248 in 499 games; as an evangelist, he was a conspicuous figure in the Prohibition movement and in efforts to prohibit Sunday baseball. See William Gerald McLoughlin, *Billy Sunday Was His Real Name* (Chicago: University of Chicago Press, 1955).

Mary Pickford—Stage name of Gladys Smith Moore (1893–1979), the leading film actress of the day, a specialist in roles of young girls. Later she was a successful producer.

◆ *Jackson*—Jackson, Mich., as usual a club in the Class C Southern Michigan Association. Dick Hodges is a fictional character; the president of the club was Winthrop Withington.

asked him to keep his eyes peeled for good young pitchers, if he happened to go to the ball game. So he went to Jackson and the next morning he came back all excited. I asked him if he'd found me a pitcher and he said he hadn't, but he'd seen the best natural hitter he'd ever looked at—a kid named Waldron.

"'Well,' I said, 'you're the last one that ought to be recommending outfielders. If there's one good enough to hold a regular job, it might be your job he'd get.'

"But Art said that didn't make any difference to him—he was looking out for the good of the club. Well, I didn't see my way clear to asking the old man to dig up good money for an outfielder nobody'd ever heard of, when we were pretty well stocked with them, so I tried to stall Art; but he kept after me and kept after me till I agreed to stick in a draft for the kid just to keep Art quiet. So the draft went in and we got him. Then, as you know, Hodges tried to get him back, and that made me suspicious enough to hold onto him. Hodges finally came over to see me and wanted to know who'd tipped me to Waldron. That's where the mystery stuff started, because I saw that Hodges was all heated up and wanted to kid him along. So I told him we had some mighty good scouts working for us, and he said he knew our regular scouts and they couldn't tell a ball-player from a torn ligament. Then he offered me fifty bucks if I'd tell him the truth and I just laughed at him. I said: 'A fella happened to be in Jackson one day and saw him work. But I won't tell you who the fella was because you're too anxious to know.' Then he insisted on knowing what day the scout had been in Jackson. I said I'd tell him that if he'd tell me why he was so blame curious. So he gave me his end of it.

"It seems his brother, up in Ludington, had seen this kid play ball ◆ on the lots and had signed him right up for Hodges and taken him to Jackson, and of course, Hodges knew he had a world beater the minute he saw him. But he also knew he wasn't going to be able to keep him in Jackson, and naturally he began to figure how he could get the most money for him. It was already August when the boy landed in Jackson; so there wasn't much chance of getting a big price last season. He decided to teach the kid what he didn't know about baseball and to keep him under cover till this year. Then everybody would be

---

◆ *Ludington*—A town (pop. 10,367 in 1910) on the west coast of the Lower Peninsula of Michigan, notable as the terminus of the cross-lake railroad-car ferries of the Pere Marquette Railway and its successors.

touting him and there'd be plenty of competition. Hodges could sell to the highest bidder.

"He had Waldron out practising every day, but wouldn't let him play in a game, and every player on the Jackson club had promised to keep the secret till this year. So Hodges wanted to find out from me which one of his players had broken the promise.

"Then I asked him if he was perfectly sure that Waldron hadn't played in a game, and he said he had gone in to hit for somebody just once. I asked him what date that was and he told me. It was the day Art had been in Jackson. So I said:

"'There's your mystery solved. That's the day my scout saw him, and you'll have to give the scout a little credit for picking a star after seeing him make one base hit.'

"Then Hodges said:

"'That makes it all the more a mystery. Because, in the first place, he batted under a fake name. And, in the second place, he didn't make a base hit. He popped out.'

"That's about all there is to it. You can ask Art how he picked the kid out for a star from seeing him pop out once. I've asked him myself, and he's told me that he liked the way Waldron swung. Personally, I believe one of those Jackson boys got too gabby. But Art swears not."

"That *is* a story," I said gratefully. "An old outfielder who must know he's slipping recommends a busher after seeing him pop out once. And the busher jumps right in and gets his job."

I looked down the aisle toward the song birds. Art Graham, now a bench warmer, and young Waldron, whom he had touted and who was the cause of his being sent to the bench, were harmonizing at the tops of their strong and not too pleasant voices.

"And probably the strangest part of the story," I added, "is that Art doesn't seem to regret it. He and the kid appear to be the best of friends."

"Anybody who can sing is Art's friend," said Ryan.

I left him and went back to my seat to tear off my seven hundred words before we reached Springfield. I considered for a moment the advisability of asking Graham for an explanation of his wonderful bit of scouting, but decided to save that part of it for another day. I was in a hurry and, besides, Waldron was just teaching them a new "wallop," and it would have been folly for me to interrupt.

"It's on the word 'you,'" Waldron was saying. "I come down a tone; Lefty goes up a half tone, and Bill comes up two tones. Art just sings it like always. Now try her again," I heard him direct the song birds. They tried her again, making a worse noise than ever:

> "I only know I love you;
> Love me, and the world (the world) is mine (the world is mine)."

"No," said Waldron. "Lefty missed it. If you fellas knew music, I could teach it to you with the piano when we get to Boston. On the word 'love,' in the next to the last line, we hit a regular F chord. Bill's singing the low F in the bass and Lefty's hitting middle C in the baritone, and Art's on high F and I'm up to A. Then, on the word 'you,' I come down to G, and Art hits E, and Lefty goes up half a tone to C sharp, and Cole comes up from F to A in the bass. That makes a good wallop. It's a change from the F chord to the A chord. Now let's try her again," Waldron urged.

They tried her again:

> "I only know I love you—"

"No, no!" said young Waldron. "Art and I were all right; but Bill came up too far, and Lefty never moved off that C. Half a tone up, Lefty. Now try her again."

We were an hour late into Springfield, and it was past six o'clock when we pulled out. I had filed my stuff, and when I came back in the car the concert was over for the time, and Art Graham was sitting alone.

"Where are your pals?" I asked.

"Gone to the diner," he replied.

"Aren't you going to eat?"

"No," he said, "I'm savin' up for the steamed clams." I took the seat beside him.

"I sent in a story about you," I said.

"Am I fired?" he asked.

"No, nothing like that."

"Well," he said, "you must be hard up when you can't find nothin' better to write about than a old has-been."

"Cap just told me who it was that found Waldron," said I.

"Oh, that," said Art. "I don't see no story in that."

"I thought it was quite a stunt," I said. "It isn't everybody that can pick out a second Cobb by just seeing him hit a fly ball."

Graham smiled.

"No," he replied, "they's few as smart as that."

"If you ever get through playing ball," I went on, "you oughtn't to have any trouble landing a job. Good scouts don't grow on trees."

"It looks like I'm pretty near through now," said Art, still smiling. "But you won't never catch me scoutin' for nobody. It's too lonesome a job."

I had passed up lunch to retain my seat in the card game; so I was hungry. Moreover, it was evident that Graham was not going to wax garrulous on the subject of his scouting ability. I left him and sought the diner. I found a vacant chair opposite Bill Cole.

"Try the minced ham," he advised, "but lay off'n the sparrow-grass. It's tougher'n a double-header in St. Louis."

"We're over an hour late," I said.

"You'll have to do a hurry-up on your story, won't you?" asked Bill. "Or did you write it already?"

"All written and on the way."

"Well, what did you tell 'em?" he inquired. "Did you tell 'em we had a pleasant trip, and Lenke lost his shirt in the poker game, and I'm goin' to pitch to-morrow, and the Boston club's heard about it and hope it'll rain?"

"No," I said. "I gave them a regular story to-night—about how Graham picked Waldron."

"Who give it to you?"

"Ryan," I told him.

"Then you didn't get the real story," said Cole, "Ryan himself don't know the best part of it, and he ain't goin' to know it for a w'ile. He'll maybe find it out after Art's got the can, but not before. And I hope nothin' like that'll happen for twenty years. When it does happen, I want to be sent along with Art, 'cause I and him's been roomies now since 1911, and I wouldn't hardly know how to act with him off'n the club. He's a nut all right on the singin' stuff, and if he was gone I might get a chanct to give my voice a rest. But he's a pretty good guy, even if he is crazy."

"I'd like to hear the real story," I said.

"Sure you would," he answered, "and I'd like to tell it to you. I will tell it to you if you'll give me your promise not to spill it till Art's gone. Art told it to I and Lefty in the club-house at Cleveland pretty near a month ago, and the three of us and Waldron is the only ones that knows it. I figure I've did pretty well to keep it to myself this long, but it seems like I got to tell somebody."

"You can depend on me," I assured him, "not to say a word about it till Art's in Minneapolis, or wherever they're going to send him."

"I guess I can trust you," said Cole. "But if you cross me, I'll shoot my fast one up there in the press coop some day and knock your teeth loose."

"Shoot," said I.

"Well," said Cole, " I s'pose Ryan told you that Art fell for the kid after just seein' him pop out."

"Yes, and Ryan said he considered it a remarkable piece of scouting."

"It was all o' that. It'd of been remarkable enough if Art'd saw the bird pop out and then recommended him. But he didn't even see him pop out."

"What are you giving me?"

"The fac's," said Bill Cole. "Art not only didn't see him pop out, but he didn't even see him with a ball suit on. He wasn't never inside the Jackson ball park in his life."

"Waldron?"

"No. Art I'm talkin' about."

"Then somebody tipped him off," I said, quickly.

"No, sir. Nobody tipped him off, neither. He went to Jackson and spent the ev'nin' at his uncle's house, and Waldron was there. Him and Art was together the whole ev'nin'. But Art didn't even ask him if he could slide feet first. And then he come back to Detroit and got Ryan to draft him. But to give you the whole story, I'll have to go back a ways. We ain't nowheres near Worcester yet, so they's no hurry, except that Art'll prob'ly be sendin' for me pretty quick to come in and learn Waldron's lost chord.

"You wasn't with this club when we had Mike McCann. But you must of heard of him; outside his pitchin', I mean. He was on the stage a couple o' winters, and he had the swellest tenor voice I ever heard. I never seen no grand opera, but I'll bet this here C'ruso or McCormack or Gadski or none o' them had nothin' on him for a pure ◆ tenor. Every note as clear as a bell. You couldn't hardly keep your eyes dry when he'd tear off 'Silver Threads' or 'The River Shannon.'

"Well, when Art was still with the Washin'ton club yet, I and Lefty and Mike used to pal round together and onct or twict we'd hit up

---

◆ *McCormack*—John MacCormack (1884–1945), a leading Irish operatic and concert tenor.

Gadski—Johanna Gadski (1872–1932), a German soprano, a specialist in Wagner.

some harmony. I couldn't support a fam'ly o' Mormons with my voice, but it was better in them days than it is now. I used to carry the lead, and Lefty'd hit the baritone and Mike the tenor. We didn't have no bass. But most o' the time we let Mike do the singin' alone, 'cause he had us outclassed, and the other boys kept tellin' us to shut up and give 'em a treat. First it'd be 'Silver Threads' and then 'Jerusalem' and then 'My Wild Irish Rose' and this and that, whatever the boys ast him for. Jake Martin used to say he couldn't help a short pair if Mike wasn't singin'.

"Finally Ryan pulled off the trade with Griffith, and Graham come on our club. Then they wasn't no more solo work. They made a bass out o' me, and Art sung the lead, and Mike and Lefty took care o' the tenor and baritone. Art didn't care what the other boys wanted to hear. They could holler their heads off for Mike to sing a solo, but no sooner'd Mike start singin' than Art'd chime in with him and pretty soon we'd all four be goin' it. Art's a nut on singin', but he don't care nothin' about list'nin', not even to a canary. He'd rather harmonize than hit one past the outfielders with two on.

"At first we done all our serenadin' on the train. Art'd get us out o' bed early so's we could be through breakfast and back in the car in time to tear off a few before we got to wherever we was goin'.

"It got so's Art wouldn't leave us alone in the different towns we played at. We couldn't go to no show or nothin'. We had to stick in the hotel and sing, up in our room or Mike's. And then he went so nuts over it that he got Mike to come and room in the same house with him at home, and I and Lefty was supposed to help keep the neighbors awake every night. O' course we had mornin' practice wile we was home, and Art used to have us come to the park early and get in a little harmony before we went on the field. But Ryan finally nailed that. He says that when he ordered mornin' practice he meant baseball and not no minstrel show.

"Then Lefty, who wasn't married, goes and gets himself a girl. I met her a couple o' times, and she looked all right. Lefty might of married her if Art'd of left him alone. But nothin' doin'. We was home all through June onct, and instead o' comin' round nights to sing with us, Lefty'd take this here doll to one o' the parks or somewheres. Well, sir, Art was pretty near wild. He scouted round till he'd found out why Lefty'd quit us and then he tried pretty near everybody else on the club to see if they wasn't some one who could hit the baritone. They wasn't nobody. So the next time we went on the road, Art give

Lefty a earful about what a sucker a man was to get married, and looks wasn't everything and the girl was prob'ly after Lefty's money and he wasn't bein' a good fella to break up the quartette and spoil our good times, and so on, and kept pesterin' and teasin' Lefty till he give the girl up. I'd of saw Art in the Texas League before I'd of shook ◆ a girl to please him, but you know these left-handers.

"Art had it all framed that we was goin' on the stage, the four of us, and he seen a vaudeville man in New York and got us booked for eight hundred a week—I don't know if it was one week or two. But he sprung it on me in September and says we could get solid bookin' from October to March; so I ast him what he thought my Missus would say when I told her I couldn't get enough o' bein' away from home from March to October, so I was figurin' on travelin' the vaudeville circuit the other four or five months and makin' it unanimous? Art says I was tied to a woman's apron and all that stuff, but I give him the cold stare and he had to pass up that dandy little scheme.

"At that, I guess we could of got by on the stage all right. Mike was better than this here Waldron and I hadn't wore my voice out yet on the coachin' line, tellin' the boys to touch all the bases.

"They was about five or six songs that we could kill. 'Adeline' was our star piece. Remember where it comes in, 'Your fair face beams'? Mike used to go away up on 'fair.' Then they was 'The Old Millstream' and 'Put on Your Old Gray Bonnet.' I done some fancy work in that one. Then they was 'Down in Jungle Town' that we had pretty good. And then they was one that maybe you never heard. I don't know the name of it. It run somethin' like this."

Bill sottoed his voice so that I alone could hear the beautiful refrain:

"'Years, years, I've waited years
Only to see you, just to call you 'dear.'
Come, come, I love but thee,
Come to your sweatheart's arms; come back to me.'

"That one had a lot o' wallops in it, and we didn't overlook none o' them. The boys used to make us sing it six or seven times a night. But 'Down in the Cornfield' was Art's favor-ight. They was a part in that where I sung the lead down low and the other three done a banjo stunt. Then they was 'Castle on the Nile' and 'Come Back to Erin' and a whole lot more.

◆ *I'd of saw Art in the Texas League*—This is probably a reference to the oppressive heat characteristic of the cities in the Texas League in an era when all games were played by day.

"Well, the four of us wasn't hardly ever separated for three years. We was practisin' all the w'ile like as if we was goin' to play the big time, and we never made a nickel off'n it. The only audience we had was the ball players or the people travelin' on the same trains or stoppin' at the same hotels, and they got it all for nothin'. But we had a good time, 'specially Art.

"You know what a pitcher Mike was. He could go in there stone cold and stick ten out o' twelve over that old plate with somethin' on 'em. And he was the willin'est guy in the world. He pitched his own game every third or fourth day, and between them games he was warmin' up all the time to go in for somebody else. In 1911, when we was up in the race for aw'ile, he pitched eight games out o' twenty, along in September, and win seven o' them, and besides that, he finished up five o' the twelve he didn't start. We didn't win the pennant, and I've always figured that them three weeks killed Mike.

"Anyway, he wasn't worth nothin' to the club the next year; but they carried him along, hopin' he'd come back and show somethin'. But he was pretty near through, and he knowed it. I knowed it, too, and so did everybody else on the club, only Graham. Art never got wise till the trainin' trip two years ago this last spring. Then he come to me one day.

" 'Bill,' he says, 'I don't believe Mike's comin' back.'

" 'Well,' I says, 'you're gettin's so's they can't nobody hide nothin' from you. Next thing you'll be findin' out that Sam Crawford can hit.'

" 'Never mind the comical stuff,' he says. 'They ain't no joke about this!'

" 'No,' I says, 'and I never said they was. They'll look a long w'ile before they find another pitcher like Mike.'

" 'Pitcher my foot!' says Art. 'I don't care if they have to pitch the bat boy. But when Mike goes, where'll our quartette be?'

" 'Well,' I says, 'do you get paid every first and fifteenth for singin' or for crownin' that old pill?'

" 'If you couldn't talk about money, you'd be deaf and dumb,' says Art.

" 'But you ain't playin' ball because it's fun, are you?'

" 'No,' he says, 'they ain't no fun for me in playin' ball. They's no fun doin' nothin' but harmonizin', and if Mike goes, I won't even have that.'

" 'I and you and Lefty can harmonize,' I says.

" 'It'd be swell stuff harmonizin' without no tenor,' says Art. 'It'd be like swingin' without no bat.'

"Well, he ast me did I think the club'd carry Mike through another season, and I told him they'd already carried him a year without him bein' no good to them, and I figured if he didn't show somethin' his first time out, they'd ask for waivers. Art kept broodin' and broodin' about it till they wasn't hardly no livin' with him. If he ast me onct he ast me a thousand times if I didn't think they might maybe hold onto Mike another season on account of all he'd did for 'em. I kept tellin' him I didn't think so; but that didn't satisfy him and he finally went to Ryan and ast him point blank.

"'Are you goin' to keep McCann?' Art ast him.

"'If he's goin' to do us any good, I am,' says Ryan. "If he ain't, he'll have to look for another job.'

"After that, all through the trainin' trip, he was right on Mike's heels.

"'How does the old souper feel?' he'd ask him.

"'Great!' Mike'd say.

"Then Art'd watch him warm up, to see if he had anything on the ball.

"'He's comin' fine,' he'd tell me. 'His curve broke to-day just as good as I ever seen it.'

"But that didn't fool me, or it didn't fool Mike neither. He could throw about four hooks and then he was through. And he could of hit you in the head with his fast one and you'd of thought you had a rash.

"One night, just before the season opened up, we was singin' on the train, and when we got through, Mike says:

"'Well, boys, you better be lookin' for another C'ruso.'

"'What are you talkin' about?' says Art.

"'I'm talkin' about myself,' says Mike. 'I'll be up there in Minneapolis this summer, pitchin' onct a week and swappin' stories about the Civil War with Joe Cantillon.'

"'You're crazy,' says Art. 'Your arm's as good as I ever seen it.'

"'Then,' says Mike, 'you must of been playin' blindfolded all these years. This is just between us, 'cause Ryan'll find it out for himself; my arm's rotten, and I can't do nothin' to help it.'

"Then Art got sore as a boil.

"'You're a yellow, quittin' dog,' he says. 'Just because you come round a little slow, you talk about Minneapolis. Why don't you resign off'n the club?'

"'I might just as well,' Mike says, and left us.

"You'd of thought that Art would of gave up then, 'cause when a ball player admits he's slippin', you can bet your last nickel that he's through. Most o' them stalls along and tries to kid themself and everybody else long after they know they're gone. But Art kept talkin' like they was still some hope o' Mike comin' round, and when Ryan told us one night in St. Louis that he was goin' to give Mike his chanct, the next day, Art was as nervous as a bride goin' to get married. I wasn't nervous. I just felt sorry, 'cause I knowed the old boy was hopeless.

"Ryan had told him he was goin' to work if the weather suited him. Well, the day was perfect. So Mike went out to the park along about noon and took Jake with him to warm up. Jake told me afterwards that Mike was throwin', just easy like, from half-past twelve till the rest of us got there. He was tryin' to heat up the old souper and he couldn't of ast for a better break in the weather, but they wasn't enough sunshine in the world to make that old whip crack.

"Well, sir, you'd of thought to see Art that Mike was his son or his brother or somebody and just breakin' into the league. Art wasn't in the outfield practisin' more than two minutes. He come in and stood behind Mike w'ile he was warmin' up and kept tellin' how good he looked, but the only guy he was kiddin' was himself.

"Then the game starts and our club goes in and gets three runs.

" 'Pretty soft for you now, Mike,' says Art, on the bench. 'They can't score three off'n you in three years.'

"Say, it's lucky he ever got the side out in the first innin'. Everybody that come up hit one on the pick, but our infield pulled two o' the greatest plays I ever seen and they didn't score. In the second, we got three more, and I thought maybe the old bird was goin' to be lucky enough to scrape through.

"For four or five innin's, he got the grandest support that was ever gave a pitcher; but I'll swear that what he throwed up there didn't have no more on it than September Morning. Every time Art come to the bench, he says to Mike, 'Keep it up, old boy. You got more than you ever had.'

"Well, in the seventh, Mike still had 'em shut out, and we was six runs to the good. Then a couple o' the St. Louis boys hit 'em where they couldn't nobody reach 'em and they was two on and two out. Then somebody got a hold o' one and sent it on a line to the left o' second base. I forgot who it was now; but whoever it was, he was supposed to be a right field hitter, and Art was layin' over the other way for him. Art started with the crack o' the bat, and I never seen a

◇ *"I ought to caught it in my pants pocket"*—Drawing by Arthur William Brown for *McClure's Magazine*, August 1915.

man make a better try for a ball. He had it judged perfect; but Cobb or Speaker or none o' them couldn't of catched it. Art just managed to touch it by stretchin' to the limit. It went on to the fence and everybody come in. They didn't score no more in that innin'.

"Then Art come in from the field and what do you think he tried to pull?

"'I don't know what was the matter with me on that fly ball,' he says. 'I ought to caught it in my pants pocket. But I didn't get started till it ◇ was right on top o' me.'

"'You misjudged it, didn't you?' says Ryan.

"'I certainly did,' says Art without crackin'.

"'Well,' says Ryan, 'I wisht you'd misjudge all o' them that way. I never seen a better play on a ball.'

"So then Art knowed they wasn't no more use trying to alibi the old boy.

"Mike had a turn at bat and when he come back, Ryan ast him how he felt.

"'I guess I can get six more o' them out,' he says.

"Well, they didn't score in the eighth, and when the ninth come Ryan sent I and Lefty out to warm up. We throwed a few w'ile our club was battin'; but when it come St. Louis' last chanct, we was too much interested in the ball game to know if we was throwin' or bakin' biscuits.

"The first guy hits a line drive, and somebody jumps a mile in the air and stabs it. The next fella fouled out, and they was only one more to get. And then what do you think come off? Whoever it was hittin' lifted a fly ball to center field. Art didn't have to move out of his tracks. I've saw him catch a hundred just like it behind his back. But you know what he was thinkin'. He was sayin' to himself, 'If I nail this one, we're li'ble to keep our tenor singer a w'ile longer.' And he dropped it.

"Then they was five base hits that sounded like the fourth o' July, and they come so fast that Ryan didn't have time to send for I or Lefty. Anyway, I guess he thought he might as well leave Mike in there and take it.

"They wasn't no singin' in the clubhouse after that game. I and Lefty always let the others start it. Mike, o' course, didn't feel like no jubilee, and Art was so busy tryin' not to let nobody see him cry that he kept his head clear down in his socks. Finally he beat it for town all alone, and we didn't see nothin' of him till after supper. Then he got us together and we all went up to Mike's room.

"'I want to try this here "Old Girl o' Mine,"' he says.

"'Better sing our old stuff,' says Mike. 'This looks like the last time.'

"Then Art choked up and it was ten mintues before he could get goin'. We sung everything we knowed, and it was two o'clock in the mornin' before Art had enough. Ryan come in after midnight and set a w'ile listenin', but he didn't chase us to bed. He knowed better'n any of us that it was a farewell. When I and Art was startin' for our room, Art turned to Mike and says:

"'Old boy, I'd of gave every nickel I ever owned to of caught that fly ball.'

"'I know you would,' Mike says, 'and I know what made you drop it. But don't worry about it, 'cause it was just a question o' time, and if I'd of got away with that game, they'd of murdered some o' the infielders next time I started.'

"Mike was sent home the next day, and we didn't see him again. He was shipped to Minneapolis before we got back. And the rest o' the season I might as well of lived in a cemetery w'ile we was on the road. Art was so bad that I thought onct or twict I'd have to change roomies. Onct in a w'ile he'd start hummin' and then he'd break off short and growl at me. He tried out two or three o' the other boys on the club to see if he couldn't find a new tenor singer, but nothin' doin'. One night he made Lefty try the tenor. Well, Lefty's voice is bad enough down low. When he gets up about so high, you think you're in the stockyards.

"And Art had a rotten year in baseball, too. The old boy's still pretty near as good on a fly ball as anybody in the league; but you ought to saw him before his legs begin to give out. He could cover as much ground as Speaker and he was just as sure. But the year Mike left us, he missed pretty near half as many as he got. He told me one night, he says:

"'Do you know, Bill, I stand out there and pray that nobody'll hit one to me. Every time I see one comin' I think o' that one I dropped for Mike in St. Louis, and then I'm just as li'ble to have it come down on my bean as in my glove.'

"'You're crazy,' I says, 'to let a thing like that make a bum out o' you.'

"But he kept on droppin' fly balls till Ryan was talkin' about settin' him on the bench where it wouldn't hurt nothin' if his nerve give out. But Ryan didn't have nobody else to play out there, so Art held on.

"He come back the next spring—that's a year ago—feelin' more cheerful and like himself than I'd saw him for a long w'ile. And they was a kid named Burton tryin' out for second base that could sing pretty near as good as Mike. It didn't take Art more'n a day to find this out, and every mornin' and night for a few days the four of us would be together, hittin' her up. But the kid didn't have no more idea o' how to play the bag than Charley Chaplin. Art seen in a minute ◆ that he couldn't never beat Cragin out of his job, so what does he do but take him out and try and learn him to play the outfield. He wasn't no worse there than at second base; he couldn't of been. But before he'd practised out there three days they was bruises all over his head and shoulders where fly balls had hit him. Well, the kid wasn't with us long enough to see the first exhibition game, and after he'd went, Art was Old Mam Grump again.

"'What's the matter with you?' I says to him. 'You was all smiles the day we reported and now you could easy pass for a undertaker.'

"'Well,' he says, 'I had a great winter, singin' all the w'ile. We got a

---

◆ *Charley Chaplin*—Sir Charles Spencer Chaplin (1889–1977), British-born comedian, and the most popular male figure in the motion pictures of the time. Chaplin produced a long series of films as actor, author, composer, and director, from his debut in 1914 to the 1950's.

good quartette down home and I never enjoyed myself as much in my life. And I kind o' had a hunch that I was goin' to be lucky and find somebody amongst the bushers that could hit up the old tenor.'

"'Your hunch was right,' I says. 'That Burton kid was as good a tenor as you'd want.'

"'Yes,' he says, 'and my hunch could of played ball just as good as him.'

"Well, sir, if you didn't never room with a corpse, you don't know what a whale of a time I had all last season. About the middle of August he was at his worst.

"'Bill,' he says, 'I'm goin' to leave this old baseball flat on its back if somethin' don't happen. I can't stand these here lonesome nights. I ain't like the rest o' the boys that can go and set all ev'nin' at a pitcher show or hang round them Dutch gardens. I got to be singin' or I am mis'rable.'

"'Go ahead and sing,' says I. 'I'll try and keep the cops back.'

"'No,' he says, 'I don't want to sing alone. I want to harmonize and we can't do that 'cause we ain't got no tenor.'

"I don't know if you'll believe me or not, but sure as we're settin' here he went to Ryan one day in Philly and tried to get him to make a trade for Harper.

"'What do I want him for?' says Ryan.

"'I hear he ain't satisfied,' says Art.

"'I ain't runnin' no ball players' benefit association,' says Ryan, and Art had to give it up. But he didn't want Harper on the club for no other reason than because he's a tenor singer!

"And then come that Dee-troit trip, and Art got permission to go to Jackson. He says he intended to drop in at the ball park, but his uncle wanted to borry some money off'n him on a farm, so Art had to drive out and see the farm. Then, that night, this here Waldron was up to call on Art's cousin—a swell doll, Art tells me. And Waldron set down to the py-ana and begin to sing and play. Then it was all off; they wasn't no spoonin' in the parlor that night. Art wouldn't leave the kid get off'n the py-ana stool long enough to even find out if the girl was a blonde or a brunette.

"O' course Art knowed the boy was with the Jackson club as soon as they was interduced, 'cause Art's uncle says somethin' about the both o' them bein' ball players, and so on. But Art swears he never thought o' recommendin' him till the kid got up to go home. Then he ast him what position did he play and found out all about him, only o' course Waldron didn't tell him how good he was 'cause he didn't know himself.

"So Art ast him would he like a trial in the big show, and the kid says he would. Then Art says maybe the kid would hear from him, and then Waldron left and Art went to bed, and he says he stayed awake all night plannin' the thing out and wonderin' would he have the nerve to pull it off. You see he thought that if Ryan fell for it, Waldron'd join us as soon as his season was over and then Ryan'd see he wasn't no good; but he'd prob'ly keep him till we was through for the year, and Art could alibi himself some way, say he'd got the wrong name or somethin'. All he wanted, he says, was to have the kid along the last month or six weeks, so's we could harmonize. A nut? I guess not.

"Well, as you know, Waldron got sick and didn't report, and when Art seen him on the train this spring he couldn't hardly believe his eyes. He thought surely the kid would of been canned durin' the winter without no trial.

"Here's another hot one. When we went out the first day for practice, Art takes the kid off in a corner and tries to learn him enough baseball so's he won't show himself up and get sent away somewheres before we had a little benefit from his singin'. Can you imagine that? Tryin' to learn this kid baseball, when he was born with a slidin' pad on.

"You know the rest of it. They wasn't never no question about Waldron makin' good. It's just like everybody says—he's the best natural ball player that's broke in since Cobb. They ain't nothin' he can't do. But it *is* a funny thing that Art's job should be the one he'd get. I spoke about that to Art when he give me the story.

"'Well,' he says, 'I can't expect everything to break right. I figure I'm lucky to of picked a guy that's good enough to hang on. I'm in stronger with Ryan right now, and with the old man, too, than when I was out there playin' every day. Besides, the bench is a pretty good place to watch the game from. And this club won't be shy a tenor singer for nine years.'

"'No,' I says, 'but they'll be shy a lead and a baritone and a bass before I and you and Lefty is much older.'

"'What of it?' he says. 'We'll look up old Mike and all go somewheres and live together.'"

We were nearing Worcester. Bill Cole and I arose from our table and started back toward our car. In the first vestibule we encountered Buck, the trainer.

"Mr. Graham's been lookin' all over for you, Mr. Cole," he said.

"I've been rehearsin' my part," said Bill.

We found Art Graham, Lefty, and young Waldron in Art's seat. The kid was talking.

"Lefty missed it again. If you fellas knew music, I could teach it to you on the piano when we get to Boston. Lefty, on the word 'love,' in the next to the last line, you're on middle C. Then, on the word 'you,' you slide up half a tone. That'd ought to be a snap, but you don't get it. I'm on high A and come down to G and Bill's on low F and comes up to A. Art just sings the regular two notes, F and E. It's a change from the F chord to the A chord. It makes a dandy wallop and it ought to be a—"

"Here's Bill now," interrupted Lefty, as he caught sight of Cole.

Art Graham treated his roommate to a cold stare.

"Where the h—l have you been?" he said angrily.

"Lookin' for the lost chord," said Bill.

"Set down here and learn this," growled Art. "We won't never get it if we don't work."

"Yes, let's tackle her again," said Waldron. "Bill comes up two full tones, from F to A. Lefty goes up half a tone, Art sings just like always, and I come down a tone. Now try her again."

Two years ago it was that Bill Cole told me that story. Two weeks ago Art Graham boarded the evening train on one of the many roads that ◆ lead to Minneapolis.

The day Art was let out, I cornered Ryan in the club-house after the others had dressed and gone home.

"Did you ever know," I asked, "that Art recommended Waldron without having seen him in a ball suit?"

"I told you long ago how Art picked Waldron," he said.

"Yes," said I, "but you didn't have the right story."

So I gave it to him.

"You newspaper fellas," he said when I had done, "are the biggest suckers in the world. Now I've never given you a bad steer in my life.

◆ *the evening train on one of the many roads that lead to Minneapolis.*—This passage places the story in Chicago; from no other city would there be many roads to Minneapolis running evening trains. The Milwaukee Road, Chicago & North Western, Soo Line (Wisconsin Central), Burlington Route, Chicago Great Western, Rock Island, and Illinois Central–Minneapolis & St. Louis all ran night trains from Chicago to the Twin Cities with dinner-hour departures.

But you don't believe what I tell you and you go and fall for one of Bill Cole's hop dreams. Don't you know that he was the biggest liar in baseball? He'd tell you that Walter Johnson was Jack's father if he thought he could get away with it. And that bunk he gave you about Waldron. Does it sound reasonable?"

"Just as reasonable," I replied, "as the stuff about Art's grabbing him after seeing him pop out."

"I don't claim he did," said Ryan. "That's what Art told me. One of those Jackson ball players could give you the real truth, only of course he wouldn't, because if Hodges ever found it out he'd shoot him full of holes. Art Graham's no fool. He isn't touting ball players because they can sing tenor or alto or anything else."

Nevertheless, I believe Bill Cole; else I wouldn't print the story. And Ryan would believe, too, if he weren't in such a mood these days that he disagrees with everybody. For in spite of Waldron's wonderful work, and he is at his best right now, the club hasn't done nearly as well as when Art and Bill and Lefty were still with us.

There seems to be a lack of harmony.

The Poor Simp

My head ain't so heavy with brains that I walk stooped over. But I do claim to have more sense than the most o' them that's gettin' by in this league, and when I get the can it won't be because I don't know what I'm doin' out there. Ask anybody in the business what kind of a ball player I am. Some o' them will say I'm pretty fair, and some o' them may say I'm rotten' but they'll all say I'm smart.

I've made my share of errors and I've hit many a perpendicular home run in the pinch, but I never lost a game by peggin' to the wrong base or by not knowin' how many was out. They ain't many can claim a record like that without gettin' called on it.

Well, that record won't buy me no round steaks when I get through here, and when I think o' the things that's happened to me and the things that's happened to fellas that didn't hardly know which was right field, I feel like I'd been better off if I'd just been born from my neck down.

Look at Jack Andrews! Bill Garwood, that batted right ahead of him, told me onct that the calves of his legs was all spike wounds, where Jack had slid into him from behind. It got so finally that every

---

"The Poor Simp" was published in *The Saturday Evening Post*, CLXXXVIII (September 11, 1915), 16–18, 61–62.

time Bill was on second and Jack on first Bill'd steal third to keep from bein' cut down. And Bill'd try to stretch every hit he made into a double so's to be two bases ahead o' Jack. And now Jack's runnin' a halfway house outside o' Chicago and it's a dull night when he don't take in a hundred bucks!

Then look at Red Burns!

Red never knowed how the game come out till he seen the paper next mornin', and they had to page him when it was his turn to hit. And now he's in the contractin' business in Cleveland and the hardest work he does is addin' up the month's profits.

And then look at me! S'posed to be one o' these here brainy ball players that never pulls a bone. Playin' my seventh year in fast company. Only gettin' forty-five hundred right now, because I never jumped a contract or spiked an umpire. And when they're through with me I can starve to death or pick up some nice, soft snap in a foundry.

I read the other day where some doctor says everybody should ought to have their appendixes and their tonsils and their adenoids cut out when they're still a baby yet. Well, them things didn't never give me no trouble. But I wisht I'd of had my brains removed before I ever learned to use 'em. They're the worst handicap a man can have in this business.

The less a guy knows, so much the sooner he can retire and live on his income.

You think I'm just talkin' against time? No, sir; you're listenin' to the truth now. And if you don't believe me ask Carey. Ask him to tell you about Skull Scoville. Or if you ain't too sleepy I'll tell you about him myself.

II

It takes Carey to spot these boobs, and Carey wasn't with us on the ◆ spring trip last year. If you'll remember he was coachin' a college team down in Ohio and got permission to report late. Skull was with us all the wile, but I was too busy gettin' myself in shape to pay much attention to the new ones. All as I noticed about him was that he done a lot of struttin' and acted like he was more anxious to look pretty than to make good.

◆ *Carey*—The mention of Carey identifies the team as the fictional version of the Chicago Cubs introduced in "Alibi Ike."

But Carey hadn't been round more'n a day when he braced me about Skull.

"When did we sign Francis X. Bushman?" he says.

"That's Scoville," I told him. "Skull Scoville."

"Some jealous cat must of gave him that nickname," says Carey.

"It's what they called him last year in the Carolina League," I says.

"Is he goin' back there?" ast Carey.

"I haven't been watchin' him much," I says.

"I hope he sticks," says Carey. "All our club needs is looks."

"You don't care nothin' about his looks," I says. "You're scoutin' for somebody to pick on."

"Maybe you're right," says Carey. "I wisht I could stay with them college boys all year. A couple o' them fell for all the old junk I could remember. I run out o' stale stuff finally and was goin' to write to you."

"Thanks," I says.

"But this here Skull does look promisin'," says Carey, "and I guess we'll have to try him out."

So Carey went over to where the kid was warmin' up and started in on him. After a wile he come back.

"I guess I can't pick 'em," he says. "When they get waivers on me I'm goin' scoutin'—not for no ball club, but for some circus that's shy o' clowns."

"What did you pull on him?" I ast.

"Just a couple o' feelers," says Carey. "I ast him what league he come from and he says the Carolina League. I says: 'Oh, yes. Milwaukee won the pennant, didn't they?' 'No,' he says; 'Columbia.' 'Oh, yes,' I says. 'I got it mixed up with the Utah League, where the women manages the teams.' 'Where's that league at?' he says. 'The Utah League?' I says. 'You take a westbound Hodiamont car in St. Louis

---

◆ *Francis X. Bushman*—Francis Xavier Bushman (1883–1966), the most popular romantic leading man of the motion pictures of the day.

◆ *Carolina League*—Presumably the Carolina Baseball Association, which operated from 1908 through 1912 as a Class D league of six teams: Anderson, Charlotte, Greensboro, Greenville, Spartanburg, and Winston-Salem. Columbia was not a member. The extant Class A Carolina League dates only from 1945. For the identification of minor leagues and their members, see Robert Obojski, *Bush League: A History of Minor League Baseball* (New York: Macmillan Publishing Co., 1975); Lloyd Johnson and Miles Wolff, eds., *The Encyclopedia of Minor League Baseball* (Durham: Baseball America, Inc., 1993).

◆ *Hodiamont car*—An actual streetcar line in St. Louis. It was the last line in the city to be converted to buses, on May 21, 1966.

and transfer twict, and then walk a block down to the wharf and get on the steamer goin' to Michigan City, only you get off when they come to Shreveport, and you can see it from there.' "

"You're goin' to have a good season," I says.

"No, it can't last," says Carey. "Some day Cap'll stick him in there and then it'll be back to the Carolina you love."

But Carey had it doped wrong. Cap give Skull a chance the second serious with the Cardinals, up home, and he got by nice. He was a little wild, but it helped him, because his fast one was fast enough to have 'em scared. They was swingin' with one foot in the bucket. Bill handled him good and Cap was tickled to death with his showin'.

"What do you think of him?" Cap ast Carey.

"Best young pitcher I've looked at in a long wile," says Carey. "You'll make a big mistake if you leave him go."

"I ain't goin' to leave him go," says Cap.

"You'd be a sucker if you did," says Carey. "But if I was you I wouldn't work him too of'en for a wile. He's nothin' but a kid and you ought to give him time to get his bearin's."

You see Carey was afraid that Skull wouldn't look as good the next time out, and he was crazy to have him stick on the club so's we could enjoy him. They wasn't no need of him bein' afraid, though, because Skull kept right on mowin' 'em down. He had everything but a noodle, and a man don't need to know nothin' about pitchin' with Bill behind that bat.

III

It come along May and we was goin' East. Brooklyn was the first place we was scheduled and we was leavin' home on the five-thirty, right after a game.

Well, the first thing Carey done when we got on the train was to tell the dinge to make up two berths. Then he took off his coat and collar like he was gettin' ready to undress. Some o' the boys went right into the diner and Skull was goin' to follow 'em when Carey nailed him.

"Where are you goin', kid?" he says.

"To get my supper," says Skull.

"Take a tip from me and stay where you are," says Carey. "Them other fellas ain't goin' to have nothin' to eat. They're tryin' to stall you."

"What's the idear?" says Skull.

"It's old stuff," says Carey, "but I'll explain it to you. This car ain't only got twelve lowers and they's twenty-four of us on the trip. That means they can't only twelve of us have lowers and the rest gets uppers. But the first twelve in bed gets the lowers."

"Yes," says Skull, "but the secretary give me a piece o' paper that says I'm to have a lower."

"Well," says Carey, "can you knock somebody out o' bed with that piece of paper? I'm tellin' you, kid. The paper don't make no difference; it's the fellas that gets there first."

"Are you goin' to bed yourself?" says Skull.

"You bet I am," says Carey.

"But you won't get no supper," says Skull.

"Supper!" says Carey. "I'd rather go without twenty suppers than ride in a upper through them Indiana mountains. These other birds is tryin' to put somethin' over. They'll wait till the dinge gets a couple o' berths made up and then they'll race fer 'em. He's makin' up two right now and you can bet that one is goin' to be mine."

Pretty soon Skull was peelin' his coat.

"Keep some loose change under your pillow," says Carey. "You're liable to be awake when we go through Fall River and you can send the porter out for a sandwich."

Well, Carey hid behind the curtains of his berth and waited till Skull was all set for the night. Then he put his collar and coat back on and come into the diner and told us about it. Only o' course he didn't tell Cap.

I was back in our car when Cap come in. He seen the two berths made up and got curious. First he peeked into the one Carey's been settin' in and they wasn't nobody there. Then he looked in at Skull.

"What's the matter?" he says. "Sick?"

"No, I ain't sick," says Skull.

"Been drinkin' somethin'?" says Cap.

"No," says Skull.

"Well," says Cap, "you go to bed nights after this and you won't be all in in the middle o' the afternoon."

I snuck down to Skull's berth.

"Just lay low in there," I says. "He was tryin' to get you out because he wants that berth. It's the best spot in the car—right over the front wheels. You hold on to it."

Along about nine o'clock all the berths was made up but one, the seat where the boys was playin' cards. I and Carey was up in the buffet car, but Smitty told us what come off.

Skull stuck his head out between the curtains and seen the card game. Smitty seen him lookin'.

"Ain't you goin' to bed?" says Skull.

"We can't," says Smitty. "All the lowers is gone."

"I'll set up a wile if you want to lay here," says Skull.

"Off o' that noise!" says Smitty. "Cap would fine us a hundred apiece if he catched us tradin' berths."

So Skull laid back, but pretty soon he peeked out again and ast for the porter.

"He got sore and quit at South Bend," says Smitty.

"Have we came to Fall River yet?" ast Skull. ◆

"No, and we ain't goin' to," says Smitty.

"Why not?" says Skull.

"They's a big storm there," says Smitty. "So we're goin' round the other way, through Evanston."

"Can a man get a sandwich there?"

"Not a sandwich," says Smitty. "But they's a old lady meets this train every night with a basket o' fried chicken and mashed potatoes—four bits a throw."

"What time do we get to Evanston?"

"Can't tell; it ain't on the regular schedule," says Smitty. "But you'll know when we're pullin' in—the engine'll give one long whistle."

"They done that a wile ago," says Skull.

"Yes," says Smitty. "The engineer thought it was Evanston, but it ◆ wasn't. His mistake."

Smitty come up afterward and joined us in the buffet car. We was all back and undressin' when we slowed up for Toledo. Carey spoke up loud.

"This must be Evanston," he says.

Skull popped out of his berth.

"Where'll I find that woman?" he says to Smitty.

"Up at the head end," says Smitty. "She's the fireman's mother-in-law."

Skull started up the aisle.

◆ *Fall River*—A textile town south of Boston, notable in transportation chiefly as the port for changing between the Fall River Line steamers and the New Haven Railroad's boat trains to and from Boston. Fall River, obviously, was not on the New York Central main line, on which the train is traveling.

◆ *Evanston*—As the first suburb north of Chicago, Evanston's serving as a way-point would have required the train to cross Lake Michigan.

"Here," I says, "you can't go callin' in your nightgown."

"You won't have time to dress," says Smitty. "We're only here two minutes."

"You better forget eatin'," says Carey. "I got hungry at Elkhart and wile I was scoutin' I lost my berth."

Skull turned to me.

"Go out and find her for me, will you?" he says. "Get two orders, one for you and one for me, and I'll pay you for the both."

"I ain't hungry," I says. "I had a pretty good dinner—soup and lake trout and a porterhouse with mushrooms and hashed brown potatoes and poached eggs and salad and apple pie and coffee."

"I'll go out for you," says Carey; "but if I get left you'll have to pay my fare from here to New York."

So Carey went out in the vestibule and stalled round till the train started up again. Then he come back, pantin' like he'd ran a mile.

"That's fine luck!" he says. "She'd just gave me the stuff when the train began to pull out. If I hadn't ran clear back here I'd of got left; they wasn't no other door open. And wile I was runnin' I dropped your supper."

Well, I don't know how much more sleep Skull got that night, but I'll bet he was No. 1 in the diner next mornin'. And I'll bet when the chef seen the order he wondered where Jess Willard got on at.

IV

It rained the first two days we was East. The sun was out the third mornin' and I and Carey was standin' in front o' the hotel when Skull showed up.

"Swell day," he says.

"Yes," says Carey, "and you know what it means, don't you? It means we'll have to beat it for Brooklyn as soon as we digest our breakfast. Three games."

"Three games," says Skull. "They won't play 'em all to-day, will they?"

"They're liable to," says Carey. "You can't never tell about Brooklyn."

"I ain't had no breakfast yet," says Skull.

"You better hurry it up, then," says Carey. "We was just goin' to start."

"Wait for me, will you?" says Skull.

"Not a chancet," says Carey. "I got to be there early to help direct the practice."

◇ *Robbie*—Wilbert Robinson in a Dodger uniform, at right, with John McGraw of the Giants, in 1922 or 1924. (National Baseball Library, Cooperstown, New York)

"You'll have to go alone," I says. "All the rest o' the boys will be gone before you're through your breakfast."

"How do I get there?" says Skull.

"They'll be a taxi to take you," says Carey. "You just come out here and look round and when you see a driver lookin' at you, hop in his car and tell him where you want to go. The club'll settle for it."

Well, as soon as Skull had went in to breakfast, Carey tipped off the rest o' the gang to keep out o' sight for a wile. I and him went over in the park acrost the street and watched for Skull to come out. Finally he come and they was two taxis standin' there. He hopped into the nearest one, told the driver to take him to the Brooklyn ball park, and off they went. It wasn't much of a trip—only from Eighty-first and Columbus to hellangone.

I s'pose he landed there about ten or ten-thirty. When we come, at a quarter to two, he was out in a suit, practicin' with the Brooklyn bunch.

Robbie seen us and came over. ◆◇

"What are you fellas pullin'?" he says. "Tryin' to get our signs? This bird's been here all day; landed in a taxi this mornin'. And he had a

◆ *Robbie*—Wilbert Robinson (1863–1934), manager of the Dodgers. After a playing career spanning the years 1886 to 1902, mainly with the Baltimore Orioles (but also with Philadelphia of the American Association and the St. Louis Cardinals), Robinson, in spite of very limited formal education, became one of the most notable managers of the era of Lardner's stories. Robinson replaced John McGraw

big brawl with the chauffeur about who was goin' to settle. Finally the chauffeur said he'd have him pinched and then the guy come acrost. But he told me that your club was payin' for the rig and he'd collect back from your secretary. Then he ast me if we was goin' to play three games to-day and I says, No, the first two had been called off. So he's been out monkeyin' with my crowd ever since. I thought at first he was lit up, but afterward I seen he wasn't."

"We was tryin' to do you a favor," says Carey. "A fella that's managin' a club in Brooklyn deserves a treat oncet in a wile. We're doin' the best we can for you, and we'll call it square if you don't pitch Rucker against us."

"But what's this bird's name?" says Robbie.

"That's Scoville," I says, "the boy that's been doin' all our winnin'."

"I'm too old to be kidded," says Robbie. "That fella's too handsome to be a good pitcher."

"If you think he can't pitch, you ain't too old to make a mistake," I says.

"It's a part of his system," says Carey, "to visit all mornin' with the club he's goin' to work against. He figures he'll do better if he knows the batters."

Well, sir, Skull pitched the game and Rucker pitched against him. Rucker outpitched him about two to one, but Skull copped.

"What do you think o' the visitin' system?" I says to Robbie, goin' out.

But he didn't have no comeback.

I and Carey and Skull rode back to the hotel together.

"Too bad you went over this mornin' for nothin'," says Carey. "As soon as we got there and found out they wasn't only goin' to play one game, we called you up to tell you about it, but you'd already left."

"I didn't go over for nothin'," says Skull. "It was eight dollars and seventy-five cents. But o' course the club'll give it back to me."

◇ *Robbie*—Drawing of Wilbert Robinson by Lawrence Semon. (National Baseball Library, Cooperstown, New York)

(*continued from page 492*)
as manager of the Orioles in 1902 when McGraw made his famous defection to the Giants. Robinson brought the team in last and did not again manage until he assumed command of the Dodgers in 1914. He managed the team through 1931, winning 1,397 and losing 1,395. He won the 1916 and 1920 pennants and was chosen for the Baseball Hall of Fame for his managerial accomplishments in 1945. As a player he had hit .273 in 1,371 games, mainly as a catcher. See William A. Borst, "Wilbert Robinson," *Biographical Dictionary of American Sports: Baseball*, pp. 481–82.

Carey seen where he was liable to get into trouble.

"Don't say nothin' to them about it," he says. "I'll go to the front for you. I know the sec. better'n you do and I can handle him."

So after supper, Carey found Skull again and broke the news to him.

"I seen the sec.," he says, "but they was nothin' doin'. If you'll remember, two taxis was settin' out there when you got ready to go, and you took the wrong one. The other one was already paid for. So you'll have to stand for it. That's what you get for bein' with a cheap club."

Skull swallowed his medicine without a whimper. But after that you couldn't get him into a taxi, not if he seen you pay for it in advance.

V

The mornin' o' the first day o' the New York serious he set with us at breakfast.

"You want to get up to the Polo Grounds early," says Carey. "Maybe you'll see part o' the polo game." ◆

"Are you fellas goin' early?" he says.

"No," says Carey, "we've saw polo played already, and they won't let a man in twicet. They're afraid he'd learn the secrets o' the game."

"How do you get there without goin' in no taxi?" ast Skull.

I guess I already told you where we was stoppin'—Eighty-first and Columbus. I was just goin' to tell him to jump on the Elevated and stay on to the end o' the line, but Carey flagged me.

"Go out here on the corner," he says, "and take a car goin' south. If the motorman don't make no mistake, it'll keep goin' till it gets way down to the Battery—that's where the pitchers and catchers all starts from. But if you don't see no pitchers and catchers that you know, ask a policeman where the Sixth Avenue Elevated is, and then get on a Harlem train. Ride forward and hold on round the curves. Set near a window if you can, only don't catch cold in your arm. Better be readin' a paper, if you can find one in the train; then they won't no girls talk

---

◆ *the polo game*—No polo game was ever played at the Polo Grounds. The ballpark bore the name of an actual polo ground owned by the publisher James Gordon Bennett. Situated at 110th Street and Fifth Avenue, it was the park where the Giants had played following their transfer from Troy, N.Y., in 1883. See Lowell Reidenbaugh, *Take Me Out To The Ball Park* (St. Louis: The Sporting News Publishing Co., 1983), pp. 166–76.

to you. They's a couple o' girls here in New York that'd pick your pockets if they got a chancet. Your looks wouldn't save you. And get off when you get to the Polo Grounds."

"How'll I know when I'm there?" ast Skull.

"You'll hear a lot o' yellin'," says Carey, "the Giants practicin' what they're goin' to say to Klem."

Skull got lost somewheres, 'way down town; he couldn't tell us just where. It was afternoon when he finally got to the Polo Grounds, and o' course the polo game was all over.

"You seen the town, though, didn't you?" says Carey.

"What town?" says Skull.

"Ishpeming," says Carey.

"No," says Skull, "I was right here in New York all the wile."

He made earlier starts the next two mornin's, but he never did manage to get there in time for polo. He was to pitch the third game and he was restin' in the club house when I and Carey come in.

"You work to-day, don't you?" says Carey.

"Yes," he says.

"I got a message for you from Cap," says Carey. "He had to go back to the hotel after the bag o' close decisions, and he wanted me to be sure and tell you to have a long talk with McGraw before the game."

"What should I talk to him about?" says Skull.

"Ask him a lot o' questions," says Carey. "He's a grand fella for a young pitcher to talk to. He'll help you a lot. Ask him what his men can hit and what they can't hit, and who's goin' to work for them. Ask him anything you can think of, and try and remember everything he tells you."

Skull got right up and went out to look for McGraw. When we was dressed and come on the field, he was over by their bench, obeyin' instructions. I don't know what Mac thought of him; probably didn't think much of anything. Mac's saw so many nuts that they don't excite him no more.

Pretty soon Skull come struttin' back to where we was.

"What'd you learn?" I ast him.

"He told me Mathewson or Marquard or Tesreau was goin' to pitch," says Skull. "Then I ast him what his men could hit and he says they can't hit nothin'. So I ast him what they couldn't hit and he says everythin'. Then he ast me what I done for my complexion and I told him I didn't do nothin' for it. And I couldn't think o' nothin' more to ask him, so I come away."

Well, after a wile, Cap showed up and Carey stuck round to change the subject if Skull begun tellin' about his interview with McGraw. They wasn't nothin' said till it was time for their fieldin' practice.

"You work, Scoville," says Cap.

"All right," says Skull.

"Well, warm up with somebody," says Cap.

"I won't need much warmin' up," says Skull.

"Why not?" says Cap.

"These fellas can't hit nothin'," says Skull.

"Who told you so?" ast Cap.

"McGraw," says Skull. "He's their manager."

"Is he?" says Cap. "I thought it was George Cohan." ◆

"No," says Skull. "It's McGraw."

"When was you talkin' with him?" ast Cap.

Then Carey horned in. "Mac was kiddin' you," he says. "He's got a good hittin' club."

"You bet he has!" says Cap. "You get that other idear out o' your head."

"What would he kid me for?" says Skull.

"Get out there and warm up!" says Cap. "McGraw's got three of 'em doin' it."

"Yes," says Skull. "He's goin' to work Mathewson or Marquard or Tesreau."

"I don't see how you can guess so good," says Cap.

"No," says Skull. "It's one o' them three."

Well, McGraw'd either been kiddin' him or he was mistaken about his own ball club. Skull didn't know which. But he knowed before he went to the shower that they could hit.

VI

Skull pitched a one-hit game over in Philly. But he wasn't in there a whole innin'. He pitched to six men and the other five got bases on balls.

He went better up in Boston. He had two men out before Cap yanked him.

"What time can you get a train for Carolina?" says Carey.

"You goin' down there?" ast Skull.

◆ *George Cohan*—George Michael Cohan (1878–1942), the most famous musical actor of the period, and the author and producer of numerous musical comedies.

"No," says Carey. "I thought maybe you was goin'."

"Oh, no," says Skull. "I'm gettin' more money up here."

"Did you get your pockets picked in New York?" says Carey.

"I guess not," says Skull.

"Just plain lost it, huh?" says Carey.

"Lost what?" ast Skull.

"Your control," says Carey.

"What's that?" says Skull.

"You had swell control in New York," says Carey. "You was hittin' their bats right in the middle. But the way you've went the last two games, you've got us all guessin'. We don't know whether you're goin' to hit the coacher at third base or kill a reporter. Pretty soon you'll have the field umpire wearin' a mask and protector. Is your arm sore?"

"No," says Skull.

"I didn't think it could be," says Carey, "on account o' the distance you get. But if your arm ain't sore, what's the matter?"

"Matter with who?" says Skull.

"You," says Carey. "You don't think the umpire's missin' 'em all, do you?"

"I'm wild," says Skull.

"Oh, that's it!" says Carey. "I've been puzzlin' my brains to find out what it was. But I see now; you're wild. And what do you s'pose makes you wild?"

"I can't pitch where I'm aimin'," says Skull. "I can't pitch no strikes. I keep givin' bases on balls."

"Funny I didn't think of that," says Carey. "I knowed they was somethin' the matter, but I couldn't put my finger right on it. I'll tell Cap and maybe we can get them to enlarge the plate."

"They wouldn't do that, would they?" says Skull.

"Well," says Carey, "they probably wouldn't in most o' the towns. But they can't stop us from doin' it on our own grounds. It's our own plate there, and I guess we can have any size we want to."

"But if I kept pitchin' too high or too low, the size o' the plate wouldn't make no difference," says Skull.

When we was through at Boston we made the cute little jump to St. ◆ Louis, and Carey was ridin' him all the way.

◆ *the cute little jump to St. Louis*—Boston–St. Louis was the longest trip the schedule required in the days of eight-team leagues and train travel. Players looked upon it as particularly tedious and unrelieved. On the fastest direct train, the New York

"This line," he told him, "is the one the James Boys works on. You see one o' the Jameses pitches for Boston and another pitches for St. ◆ Louis in the other league. And the ones that ain't ball players works back and forth between the two towns. Somebody has to set up all night and keep watch. I've been picked to set up the first night because I can shoot so good. To-morrow mornin' we'll draw lots to see who sets up to-morrow night. But if you got somethin' you don't want to lose you better sleep with one eye open and keep your suitcase right in the berth with you. O' course it's too late for 'em to steal your control, but they might get your fast ball and then you wouldn't have nothin' but your complexion."

"Oh, yes, I would," says Skull. "I got a little money and a watch and some clo'es."

"Shut up!" says Carey. "Don't be boastin' o' what you got. Maybe one o' them Jameses is right in this car now. You can't never tell where they're hidin'."

Well, the next mornin' we all ast Carey what kind of a night he had and did he see anything suspicious, and so forth. He told us he had one bad scare. Somebody come through the car with a mask on. But as soon as he seen the mask he knowed it wasn't one o' the James Boys, because they wasn't none of them catchers.

"Who was it?" I says.

(*continued from page 497*)
Central System's Southwestern Limited and its connections, the trip was 28 hours and 50 minutes over a distance of 1,126 miles.

◆ *one o' the Jameses pitches for Boston*—William Lawrence "Seattle Bill" James (1892–1971), one of the three pitchers who had pitched the Braves to the World Championship of 1914. James is usually cited as the most extreme example of a one-year wonder in the history of baseball. In 1913 he produced a 6–10 record, but in 1914 won 26 and lost 7, leading the league with a winning percentage of .788. He also won two of the Braves' four victories in the World Series. His record in 1915 was just 5–4, and he had no decision in one appearance for the Braves in 1919. See Jack Kavanagh, "Bill James," *The Ballplayers*, p. 519.

another pitches for St. Louis in the other league.—William Henry "Big Bill" James (1888–1942), a journeyman righthander who pitched for the Browns in 1914 and most of 1915. He had been with Cleveland in 1911 and 1912. Subsequently, from 1915 to 1919, he was with Detroit. Finally, after 13 games with the Red Sox, James went to the White Sox as one of the several pitchers whom Comiskey acquired in his effort to patch up his pitching staff sufficiently to clinch the 1919 pennant. It was James's melancholy duty to relieve Claude Williams after Williams' successful throwing of the final game of the 1919 World Series. In eight seasons, James pitched in 203 games, winning 65 and losing 71. See Jack Kavanagh, "Bill James," *The Ballplayers*, p. 519. (Kavanagh's piece on "Seattle Bill" James—see the preceding note—is on the same page.)

"Some society fella," he says, "goin' to the masquerade ball up in the day coach."

We drawed lots right after we was through breakfast. They was supposed to be all our names wrote on pieces o' paper and dropped into a hat. Then the fella that drawed his own name was to keep watch the second night.

Skull was the baby. All the rest of us drawed his name, too, only o' course he didn't know that.

"Well," says Carey, "it looks like it's up to you. And you don't want to take it as a joke. Whether we get by or not depends on how you work. You'll have to take my gun; I'll show you how it handles. If you see some stranger come into the car, shoot! Don't throw a baseball at him or you might wound the engineer. You better set up in the washroom all night with the porter, and if he asks you to help him shine shoes you go ahead and help him. Some o' these here porters is in with the James Boys and if they get sore it's good night. And be sure and don't let the robbers get the first shot."

Skull tried to sleep a little durin' the day. But he was too nervous.

"Who's keepin' watch now?" he ast Carey.

"Nobody, in the daytime," says Carey. "They're afraid of bein' seen by scouts, because, as I say, one o' them's with the Braves and another with the Browns, and the next one that gets caught might be hung or sent to the Carolina League."

Carey had to borry a gun off'n the conductor.

"I'll be sure it's empty before I leave the bird have it," he says. "He's dangerous enough with a baseball in his hand, let alone a loaded gat."

Well, sir, I wisht you'd saw the porter when Skull and the gun went on watch at eleven that night. We had to call him out and put him wise or he'd of dove off the train. He told us he never seen a guy as restless as Skull. All night long he was movin' round—out on the platform, then back in the washroom, then through to the other end o' the car and then out on the platform again. And jumpin' sideways at every noise.

"Nothin' doin', eh?" says Carey in the mornin'. "Not a sign o' 'em?"

"Not a sign," says Skull.

"And ain't you sleepy?" says Carey.

"Yes, I am," says Skull. "I hope I don't have to work this afternoon."

"What if you do?" says Carey. "It won't keep you up more'n ten minutes."

VII

Skull didn't pitch that afternoon. He didn't pitch the next day neither, but he was in there tryin'. Rigler could of umpired with his right arm cut off. They wasn't no strikes to call.

When he'd throwed fourteen without gettin' one clost, Cap took him out.

"I'd leave you go through with it," says Cap, "only the public likes to see some hittin'. Did you think just because this is a bad ball town you couldn't pitch nothin' but bad balls?"

"I'm wild," says Skull. "I can't get 'em over."

"I'd of guessed it in a few more minutes," says Cap. "Did you ever try pitchin' left-handed?"

"Left-handed?" says Skull. "Why, I wouldn't know where a ball was goin' if I throwed it left-handed."

"Then you must be equally good with both hands," says Cap.

Waivers was ast on Skull before we left St. Louis.

"They's no use foolin' along with him," Cap told us. "He don't look like he'd ever get a man out, and even if his control come back you couldn't never learn him nothin'."

"I knowed it," says Carey. "I knowed we'd never have him the whole year."

"It's better for you this way," I says. "Your brains would be wore out before fall."

We went back home and the third day we was there Cap told us that everybody'd waived.

"The next thing's placin' him," he says. "The newspaper boys has advertised him so good that every hick town in the country is wise to him. If I can't make no deal within a couple o' weeks I'll leave him go outright."

The two weeks was pretty near up when Carey put over his last one on the poor simp. I and Carey was throwin' in front o' the stand when a couple o' girls was showed into a box right clost to us. They was in black from head to foot; pretty as a picture too. But their clo'es was the kind that you don't see no city-broke dames wearin' in a ball orchard.

"Come to town just for the day?" says Carey, but they didn't pay no attention.

Carey come over to me.

"Uncle Zeke died and left 'em three hundred iron men," he says, "and they're goin' to blow it all in one grand good time. I bet they'll be dancin' in Dreamland to-night; they're dressed for it already."

"The blonde's a bearcat," I says.

"Yes," says Carey, "and you can figure the other one's the class o' the pair. That's the way it always breaks."

Skull had been shaggin' in the outfield. Carey spotted him as he was struttin' back to the bench, and it was all off.

"You lucky stiff!" says Carey.

"What do you mean?" says Skull.

"I guess you know what I mean," says Carey. "What did you come in for?"

"I'm tired," says Skull.

"Oh, yes," says Carey. "I s'pose you didn't see them dolls lookin' you over."

"What dolls?" ast Skull.

"Them two in the box," says Carey.

Skull give 'em the double-o.

"Who are they?" he says.

"You don't know who they are?" says Carey. "That's Lizzie Carnegie and her sister-in-law, and they's a movin' van outside with their pocketbooks in it."

"Well," says Skull, "that don't get me nothin'."

"Don't get you nothin' when the richest girl in the country wants to meet you?" says Carey.

"How do you know she wants to meet me?" says Skull.

"Didn't she call me over and tell me?" says Carey. "She says: 'Who's that handsome bird shaggin' fungoes in the outfield?' So I told her who you was. Then she ast if you was married and I says you wasn't. Then she ast how she could get to talk to you, and I told her I'd find out if you was engaged after the game, and if you wasn't you'd probably be glad to give her a minute's time. So all as you have to do now is go over there and make the date."

"Which is Lizzie?" ast Skull.

"The one with the earrings," says Carey.

They both was wearin' 'em.

Well, sir, Skull started over toward the box.

"He's liable to get pinched," I says.

"If he does I'll fix it," says Carey.

Skull didn't get pinched. He got two nice smiles, and Cap had to send me over to drag him away when the game started. And I and Carey came out o' the club-house after the game just in time to see Skull and the pair o' them hikin' for the exit.

When we got to mornin' practice next day, Skull had been let out already.

"I told him he was free to sign wherever he wanted to go," says Cap. "I told him to get a catcher somewheres and practice till he could pitch one or two strikes per innin'. I told him maybe he could land in the Federal. He says he guessed he would try the Utah League, where the women manages the clubs. He says women almost always gen'ally took a fancy to him."

"Yes," says Carey, "most o' them likes a good-lookin' fella all the better if he's a little wild."

We didn't see no more o' Skull till we got in from Cincinnati, the day before the Fourth o' July. He was standin' in the station, holdin' two suit cases.

"Hello there, boy," says Carey. "Where are you headin'?"

"Just downstate a ways," he says.

"Joinin' some club?" says Carey.

"No," says Skull. "I'm goin' to get married."

"Good night!" says Carey. "And who's the defendant?"

"That there blond girl," says Skull. "The girl that was out to the park that day with the other girl. Only you had her name wrong. Her name's Conahan. Mary Conahan. And the other one ain't her sister-in-law, but just a friend o' her'n."

"I must of had 'em mixed up," says Carey.

"Yes," says Skull, "you mistook 'em for somebody else. But you had one thing right: She's got the old kale."

"A lot of it?" says Carey.

"A plenty," says Skull. "Her old man makes this here Silver Tip ◆ beer; maybe you've drank it already."

"And I s'pose you're goin' to drive a wagon," says Carey.

"No," says Skull. "The old man's been feelin' bad for the last year and I'm goin' to kind-a look after the business."

"And," I says, "I bet you know just as much about brewin' beer as you do about pitchin'."

"Oh, no," says Skull. "Nowheres near."

◆ *Silver Tip beer*—A fictional brand, probably a corruption of Silver Top, a label of the Duquesne Brewing Co. of Pittsburgh.

"But you pick things up quick," says Carey.

Skull's train was gettin' ready to start.

"Well," he says, "good luck to you, and tell the boys I hope they win the pennant."

"No chancet now," says Carey.

We went over to the gate with him.

"Where to?" says the guy. "Show your ticket!"

"By cracky, I forgot about a ticket."

"I s'pose you thought the secretary'd tend to that," says Carey.

"Too late now," I says. "You'll have to pay on the train."

"You won't have no trouble," says Carey. "They's lady conductors on this road."

We persuaded the gateman to leave him through.

"Now," says Carey, "let's I and you get good and drunk."

"Yes," I says; "but let's go to a place where they keep Silver Tip, so's to help out old Skull."

"Help him out!" says Carey. "We're the ones that need help—us smart Alecks!"

Where Do You Get That Noise?

The trade was pulled wile the Phillies was here first trip. Without ◆ knockin' nobody, the two fellas we give was worth about as much as a front foot on Main Street, Belgium. And the fella we got had went better this spring than any time since he broke in. So when the news o' the deal come out I says to Dode, I says: ◆◇

"What's the matter with Pat tradin' Hawley? What's he goin' to do ◆ with them two he's gettin'—make ticket takers out of 'em? What's the idear?"

"It does look like a bad swap for us," says Dode. "Hawley's worth six like them you're givin' us, and he ain't only twenty-seven years old."

"That's what I'm tellin' you," I says. "The deal looks like you was tryin' to help us out."

"We are," says Dode. "Didn't we just get through helpin' you out o' the first division?"

"Where Do You Get That Noise?" was published in *The Saturday Evening Post*, CLXXXVIII (October 23, 1915), 10–12, 40–41.

◆ *wile the Phillies was here*—The team is again the fictional version of the Chicago Cubs introduced in "Alibi Ike."

◆ *Dode*—Dode Paskert, centerfielder for the Phillies.

◆ *Pat*—Pat Moran. This reference places the story in 1915, Moran's first year as manager of the Phillies.

◇ *Dode*—Dode Paskert in a Phillies uniform, probably about 1916 (see footnote, pp. 370–71). (George E. Brace collection)

"Save that for the minstrels," I says. "Give me the inside on this business: Is they somethin' the matter with him? The trade's made now already and it won't hurt you none to come clean. Didn't him and Pat get along?"

"Sure! Why not?" says Dode. "Did you ever see a guy that Pat couldn't get along with him?"

"Well then," says I, "what's the answer? Don't keep me in suspenders."

"I ain't sure myself," says Dode, "but I and Bobby was talkin' it over and we figured that Pat just plain got sick o' hearin' him talk."

"Feed that to the goldfish," I says. "If Pat couldn't stand conversation he wouldn't of never lasted this long."

"Conversation, yes," Dode says; "but it's a different thing when a bird makes an argument out of everything that's said. They wasn't a day passed but what Hawley just as good as called everybody on the club a liar. And it didn't make no difference whether you was talkin' to him or not. If I happened to be tellin' you that my sister was the champion chess player o' Peanut County, he'd horn right in and say she wasn't no such a thing; that So-and-So was the champion. And they wouldn't be no use to argue with him because you couldn't even get a draw. He'd say he was born in the county seat o' Peanut County and empired all the chess tournaments there. They wasn't no subject that he didn't know all about it better'n anybody else. They wasn't no town he wasn't born and brought up in. His mother or his old man is first cousins to everybody in the United States. He's been operated on for every disease in the hospital. And if he's did all he says he's did he'll be eight hundred and twenty-two years old next Halloween."

"They's lots o' fellas like that," I says.

"You think so?" says Dode. "You wait a wile. Next time I see you, if you don't say he's all alone in the Argue League I'll give you my bat."

"If he's that good," I says, "he'll be soup for Carey."

"He will at first, maybe," says Dode; "but Carey'll get sick of him, just like Pat and all the rest of us did."

II

I didn't lose no time tellin' Carey about Dode's dope, and Carey didn't lose no time tryin' it out. It was the second day after Hawley joined us. It looked like rain, as usual, and we was stallin' in the clubhouse, thinkin' they'd maybe call it off before we had to dress.

"I see in some paper," says Carey, "where the heavy artillery fire over in Europe is what makes all this duck weather."

He didn't get no rise; so he wound up again.

"It seems like it must be somethin' that does it because they wasn't never no summer like this before," he says.

"What do you mean—no summer like this?" says Hawley.

"No summer with so much rain as they's been this summer," Carey says.

"Where do you get that stuff?" says Hawley. "This here summer's been dry, you might say."

"Yes," says Carey; "and you might say the Federals done well in ◆ Newark."

◆ *the Federals done well in Newark*—Newark is an odd choice by which to delineate the failure of the Federal League. The weakest franchises were Kansas City and Buffalo, both of which announced that they were unable to continue into 1916. Brooklyn was thought to be the heaviest loser, but it was owned by the Ward

"I mean," says Hawley, "that this here summer's been dry compared to other summers."

"I s'pose," says Carey, "they wasn't never such a dry summer?"

"They's been lots of 'em," Hawley says. "They's been lots o' summers that was drier and they's been lots o' summers when they was more rain."

"Not in the last twenty years," says Carey.

"Yes, in the last twenty years too," says Hawley. "Nineteen years ago this summer made this here one look like a drought. It come up a storm the first day o' May and they wasn't a day from then till the first o' September when it didn't rain one time or another.""

"You got some memory," says Carey—"goin' back nineteen years."

"I guess I ought to remember it," says Hawley. "That was the first year my old man left me go to the ball games alone, and they wasn't no games in our town from April till Labor Day. They wasn't no games nowheres because the railroads was all washed out. We lived in Cleveland and my old man was caught in New York when the first o' the floods come and couldn't get back home for three months."

"Couldn't he hire a canoe nowheres?" says Carey.

"Him and some others was thinkin' about tryin' the trip on a raft," says Hawley, "but my old lady was scared to have him try it; so she wrote and told him to stay where he was."

"She was lucky to have a carrier pigeon to take him the letter," says Carey. "Or did you swim East with it?"

"Swim!" Hawley says. "Say, you wouldn't talk about swim if you'd saw the current in them floods!"

"I'm sorry I missed it," says Carey. "I was still over in Portugal yet that year."

"It dried up in time for the world serious," says Hawley.

"The world serious between who?" ast Carey.

"The clubs that won out in the two leagues," says Hawley.

"I didn't know they was two leagues in '96," says Carey. "Who did ◆ they give the pennants to—the clubs that was ahead when it begin to sprinkle?"

(continued from page 506)
baking interests and was relatively well financed. Newark, which was owned by the oilman Harry F. Sinclair, lost money in 1915, but the management expressed an intention of continuing in 1916.

◆ *I didn't know they was two leagues in '96*—There were not. The American Association disbanded after the 1891 season, and there was no second major league until the American League announced major league status in 1901.

"Sprinkle!" says Hawley. "Say, you'd of called it a sprinkle if you'd saw it. Sprinkle! Say, I guess that was some sprinkle!"

"I guess it must of been some sprinkle!" says Carey. "It must of made this summer look like a sucker."

"No," says Hawley; "this summer's been pretty bad."

"But nowheres near like nineteen year ago," says Carey.

"Oh, I guess they's about the same rainfall every year," Hawley says. "But, still and all, we've had some mighty wet weather since the first o' May this year, and I wouldn't be su'prised if the heavy artillery fire in Europe had somethin' to do with it."

"That's ridic'lous," says Carey.

"Ridic'lous!" says Hawley. "Where do you get that stuff?" Don't you know that rain can be started with dynamite? Well, then, why wouldn't all that shootin' affect the weather? They must be some explanation."

"Did you make him?" says Carey to me afterward. "He trimmed me both ways. Some day he'll single to right field and throw himself out at first base. I seen I was in for a lickin', so I hedged to get a draw, and the minute I joined his league he jumped to the outlaws. But after this I'm goin' to stick on one side of it. He goes better when he's usin' his own stuff."

III

In battin' practice the next day Carey hit one up against them boards in right center on a line.

"Good night!" says Smitty. "I bet that's the hardest wallop that was ever made on these grounds."

"I know I didn't never hit one harder here," says Carey. "I don't never hit good in this park. I'd rather be on the road all the wile. I hit better on the Polo Grounds than anywheres else. I s'pose it's on account o' the background."

"Where do you get that stuff?" says Hawley. "Everybody hits better in New York than they do here. Do you want to know why? Because it's a clean town, without no dirt and cinders blowin' in your eyes. This town's all smoke and dirt, and it ain't no wonder a man's handicapped. The fellas that's with clubs in clean towns has got it all over us. Look at Detroit—one o' the cleanest towns in the country! And look how Cobb and Crawford hit! A man in one o' these smoke holes can't never pile up them big averages, or he can't last as long, neither."

"No," says Carey; "and that accounts for Wagner's rotten record in Pittsburgh."

Do you think that stopped him? Not him!

"Yes," he says; "and how much would Wagner of hit if he'd been playin' in New York or Detroit all the wile? He wouldn't never been below .500. And he'd of lasted just twicet as long."

"But on account of him landin' in Pittsburgh," says Carey, "the poor kid'll be all through already before he's fairly started yet. It's a crime and the grand jury should ought to take steps."

"Have you ever been to Washington?" says I.

"Have I ever been to Washington?" says Hawley. "Say, I know Washington like a book. My old man's brother's a senator there in Congress. You must of heard o' Senator Hawley." ◆

"Oh, yes," says Carey; "the fella that made the speech that time."

"That's the fella," says Hawley. "And a smart fella too. Him and Woodruff Wilson's just like brothers. They're always to each other's houses. That's where I met Wilson—was at Uncle Zeke's. We fanned together for a couple hours. You wouldn't never know he was the President. He don't let on like he was any better than I or you."

"He ain't as good as you; that's a pipe!" says Carey.

"Where does your cousin live?" says Smitty.

"Cousin Zeke's got the swellest apartment in Washington," says Hawley. "Right next to the Capitol, on Pennsylvania Street."

"I wisht I could live there," I says. "It's the best town in the country for my money. And it's the cleanest one too."

"No factories or smoke there," says Carey.

"I wonder how it comes," I says, "that most o' the fellas on the Washington Club, playin' in the cleanest town in the country most o' the wile, can't hardly foul a ball—let alone hit it."

"Maybe the silver dust from the mint gets in their eyes," says Carey.

"Where do you get that noise?" says Hawley. "The mint ain't nowheres near the ball orchard."

"Well then," I says, "how do you account for the club not hittin'?"

"Say," says Hawley, "it ain't no wonder they don't hit in that town. We played a exhibition game there last spring and we didn't hit, neither."

"Who pitched against you—Johnson?" I ast him.

"Yes; Johnson," says Hawley.

◆ *Senator Hawley*—Willis Chatman Hawley (1864–1941), U.S. Senator from Oregon, chairman of the Joint Committee on Internal Revenues and co-sponsor of the Smoot-Hawley Tariff Act of 1930.

"But that don't explain why the Washington bunch can't hit," says Carey. "He ain't mean enough to turn round and pitch against his own club."

"They won't nobody hit in that town," says Hawley, "and I don't care if it's Johnson pitchin' or the mayor."

"What's the trouble?" I says.

"The heat gets 'em!" says Carey.

"No such a thing!" says Hawley. "That shows you don't know nothin' about it. It's the trees."

"The trees!" I says. "Do they play out in the woods or somewheres?"

"No," says Hawley. "If they did they'd be all right. Their ball park's just like any ball park; they ain't no trees in it. But they's trees all over the rest o' the town. It don't make no difference where you go, you're in the shade. And then, when you get to the ball park you're exposed to the sun all of a sudden and it blinds you."

"I should think it would affect their fieldin' too," says Carey.

"They wear goggles in the field," says Hawley.

"Do the infielders wear goggles?" ast Carey.

"No; but most o' the balls they got to handle comes on the ground. They don't have to look up for 'em," says Hawley.

"S'pose somebody hits a high fly ball that's comin' down right in the middle o' the diamond," says Carey. "Who gets it?"

"It ain't got," says Hawley. "They leave it go and it gen'ally almost always rolls foul."

"If I was Griffith," says Carey, "I'd get the Forestry Department to cut away the trees in some part o' town and then make all my ball players live there so's they'd get used to the sun."

"Or he might have a few big maples planted round the home plate some Arbor Day," I says.

"Yes," says Carey; "or he might trade Johnson to the Pittsburgh Federals for Oakes."

"He'd be a sucker to trade Johnson," says Hawley.

IV

Well, we played down in Cincy one Saturday to a crowd that might of all came out in the one street car without nobody ridin' in the motorman's vest pocket. We was discussin' it that night at supper.

"It's no more'n natural," I says. "The home club's been goin' bad and you can't expect the whole population to fight for a look at 'em."

"Yes," says Carey; "but it ain't only here. It's everywheres. We didn't hardly draw our breath at St. Louis and the receipts o' that last double-header at home with Pittsburgh wouldn't buy enough shavin' soap to lather a gnat. All over the circuit it's the same way, and in the other leagues too. It's a off year, maybe; or maybe they's reason for it that we ain't doped out."

"Well," I says, "the war's hurt business, for one thing, and people ain't got no money to spend on box seats. And then golf's gettin' better all the wile. A man'd naturally rather do some exercisin' himself than watch somebody else do it. Besides that, automobiles has got so cheap that pretty near everybody can buy 'em, and the people that owns 'em takes their friends out in the country instead o' comin' to the ball yard. And besides that," I says, "they's too much baseball and the people's sick of it."

Hawley come in and set down with us wile I was still talkin' yet.

"What's the argument?" he says.

"We was tryin' to figure out why we can't get a quorum out to the games no more," says Carey.

"Well," says Hawley, "you know the real reason, don't you?"

"No," says Carey; "but I bet we're goin' to hear it. I bet you'll say it's on account o' the Gulf Stream."

"Where do you get that noise?" says Hawley. "If you want to know the real reason, the war's the real reason."

"That's what I was sayin'," says I. "The war's hurt business and people ain't got no money to blow on baseball."

"That shows you don't know nothin' about it," says Hawley.

"Then I got you tied," I says, "because you just sprung the same thing yourself."

"No such a thing!" says Hawley. "You're talkin' about the war hurtin' business and I'm talkin' about the war hurtin' baseball."

"What's the difference?" I says.

"All the difference in the world," says Hawley. "If everybody was makin' twicet as much money durin' the war as they made before the war started yet, the baseball crowds wouldn't be no bigger than they have been."

"Come acrost with the answer," says Carey. "The strain's somethin' awful."

"Well, boys," says Hawley, "they ain't nobody in this country that ain't pullin' for one side or the other in this here war. Is that right or wrong?"

"Which do you say it is?" says Carey.

"I say it's right because I know it's right," says Hawley.

FOOD FOR FANS

EDITOR GEO. L. MORELAND STATISTICIAN

SPORTING RECORDS

Published Daily Except Sunday

Yearly Subscription $31.20

By The Sporting Records Publishing Company, 333 South Dearborn Street, Chicago, Ill.
General Business Office, 2456 Jackson Boulevard, Chicago, Ill.

Copyright 1915

Vol. 1. MONDAY, AUG. 2, 1915 No. 106

Cincinnati, N. L.
SEASON 1915

1. Rapp, c.
2. Trombley, outfielder.
3. Wagner, infielder.
4. Killifer, outfielder.
5. Wingo, c.
6. Dodin, c, released to New York.
7. Brown, p.
8. Benton, p.
9. Gonzales, c, Released to St. L.
10. Ames, p.
11. Clark, c.
13. Herzog, ss. and Manager.
14. Douglass, Released to Brooklyn.
15. Molwitz, infielder.
16. Dale, p.
17. Schneider, p.
18. Lear, p.
19. Von Kolwitz, outfielder.
20. Griffith, outfielder.
21. Groh, infielder.
22. Fittery, p.
23. Leach, outfielder.

RECORD OF REDS SINCE 1876

Year	Games	Won	Lost	Pct.	Pos.
1876	65	9	56	135	8
1877	72	19	53	268	6
1878	60	37	23	617	2
1879	74	38	36	544	5
1880	80	21	59	263	8
1890	133	78	55	586	4
1891	137	56	81	409	7
1892	150	82	68	547	5
1893	128	65	63	508	6
1894	129	54	75	419	10
1895	130	66	64	508	8
1896	127	77	50	606	3
1897	132	76	56	576	4
1898	152	92	60	605	3
1899	150	83	67	553	6
1900	139	62	77	446	7
1901	139	52	87	374	8
1902	140	70	70	500	4
1903	139	74	65	532	4
1904	153	88	65	575	3
1905	153	79	74	516	5
1906	151	64	87	424	6
1907	153	66	87	431	6
1908	154	73	81	474	5
1909	153	77	76	504	4
1910	154	75	79	487	5
1911	153	70	83	458	6
1912	153	75	78	490	4
1913	153	64	89	418	7
1914	157	60	94	390	8

◇ *here in Cincinnati*—The Cincinnati Reds of 1915. (National Baseball Library, Cooperstown, New York)

"Well then," says Carey, "don't ask us boobs."

"No matter what a man says about he bein' neutral," says Hawley, "you can bet that down in his heart he's either for the Dutchmen or the Alleys; I don't care if he's Woodruff Wilson or Bill Klem. We all got our favorites."

"Who's yours?" I says.

"Don't you tell!" says Carey. "It wouldn't be fair to the other side."

"I don't mind tellin'," says Hawley. "I'd be a fine stiff to pull for the Dutchmen after all King George done for my old man."

"What did he do for him?" says Carey.

"Well, it's a long story," says Hawley.

"That's all right," says Carey. "They's only one game to-morrow."

"I'll give it to you some other time," Hawley says.

"I hope you don't forget it," says Carey.

"Forget it!" says Hawley. "When your old man's honored by the royalties you ain't liable to forget it."

"No," says Carey; "but you could try."

"Here!" I says. "I'm waitin' to find out how the war cuts down the attendance."

"I'm comin' to that," says Hawley. "When you figure it out they couldn't nothin' be simpler."

"It does sound simple, now it's been explained," says Carey.

"It ain't been explained to me," I says.

"You're in too big a hurry," Hawley says. "If you wouldn't interrupt a man all the wile you might learn somethin'. You admit they ain't nobody that's neutral. Well then, you can't expect people that's for the Alleys to come out to the ball park and pull for a club that's mostly Dutchmen, and you can't expect Dutchmen to patronise a club that's got a lot o' fellas with English and French names."

"Wait a minute!" says Carey. "I s'pose they ain't no Germans here ◇ in Cincinnati, is they?"

"Sure!" says Hawley. "The place is ran over with 'em."

"Then," says Carey, "why don't they break all records for attendance at this park, with Heine Groh and Fritz Mollwitz and Count Von ◆ Kolnitz and Wagner and Schneider and Herzog on the ball club?" ◆◇

"Because they's others on the team that offsets 'em," says Hawley. "We'll say they's a Dutchman comes out to the game to holler for some o' them boys you mentioned. We'll say that Groh kicks a ground ball and leaves three runs score and puts the club behind. And then we'll

---

◆ *Fritz Mollwitz*—Frederick August Mollwitz (1890–1967), a genuine German, born at Kolberg on the Baltic seacoast. A journeyman first baseman, Mollwitz played for the Cubs, Reds, Pirates, and Cardinals from 1913 to 1919, hitting .241 in 534 games. In 1915 Mollwitz was the regular first baseman of the Reds, hitting .259 in 153 games. See Art Ahrens, "Fritz Mollwitz," *The Ballplayers*, p. 752.

Count Von Kolnitz—Alfred Holmes "Fritz" von Kolnitz (1893–1948), the Reds' utility infielder and part-time catcher. Von Kolnitz played in 41 games for the Reds in 1914, 50 in 1915, and 24 for the White Sox in 1916, hitting .212 overall.

◆ *Wagner*—Joseph Bernard Wagner (1889–1948), another utility infielder of the Reds. In 1915, his only season in the major leagues, Wagner played 75 games in the Reds' infield, hitting .178.

Schneider—Peter Joseph Schneider (1895–1957), a righthanded pitcher who was to lead the league in losses in 1915 with a 13–19 record. He had his best season, 20–19, in 1917. Including one loss with the Yankees in 1919, Schneider won 57 and lost 86 in six seasons. On returning to the minors he became an outfielder in the Pacific Coast League. See L. Robert Davids, "Pete Schneider," *The Ballplayers*, p. 972.

Herzog—Charles Lincoln "Buck" Herzog (1885–1953), an infielder who spent 13 seasons with the Giants, Braves, Reds, and Cubs from 1908 to 1920, hitting .259 in 1,493 games. Herzog managed the Reds from 1914 until mid-1916, when he was replaced by Christy Mathewson. An alumnus of the University of Maryland,

◇ *Herzog*—Buck Herzog as a Cincinnati Red, around 1915. (National Baseball Library, Cooperstown, New York)

say that Clarke comes up in the ninth innin' and wins the game for ◆ Cincinnati with a home run. That makes the Dutchman look like a rummy, don't it? Or we'll say Schneider starts to pitch a game and gets knocked out, and then Dale comes in and they can't foul him. Your ◆

◇ *Herzog*—Drawing of Buck Herzog by Lawrence Semon. (National Baseball Library, Cooperstown, New York)

(*continued from page 513*)
Herzog, following his playing career, was athletic-passenger agent for the Baltimore & Ohio Railroad. See Jack Kavanagh, "Buck Herzog," *The Ballplayers*, p. 469.

◆ *Clarke*—Thomas Aloysius Clarke (1888–1945), catcher for the Reds from 1909 to 1917. Including a single game for the Cubs in 1918, he played 671 games, made 453 hits, and batted .265. He was a coach for the Giants from 1932 to 1935, and again in 1938. See Jack Kavanagh, "Tommy Clarke," *The Ballplayers*, p. 194.

◆ *Dale*—Emmett Eugene Dale (1889–1958), a righthander having his only strong season for the Reds, 18–17 in 1915. Previously, he had pitched briefly for the Cardinals in 1911 (1–2) and 1912 (0–5). In 1916, after running up a 3–4 record early in the season, he was suspended by the Reds and left baseball. See Norman L. Macht, "Gene Dale," *The Ballplayers*, p. 248.

German friend wishes he had of stayed home and washed part o' the dashhound."

"Yes," says Carey; "but wouldn't he want to come to the game again the next day in hopes he'd get his chancet to holler?"

"No," says Hawley; "because, whatever happened, they'd be somethin' about it he wouldn't like. If the Reds win the Alleys on the club'd feel just as good as the Dutchmen, and that'd make him sore. And if they lost he'd be glad on account o' the Alleys; but he'd feel sorry for the Germans."

"Then they's only one thing for Garry Herrmann to do," I says: "he ◆◇ should ought to trade off all his Alleys for Dutch."

"That'd help the attendance at home," says Hawley; "but when his club played in Boston who'd go out to see 'em?"

"Everybody that could borrow a brick," says Carey.

"Accordin' to your dope," I says, "they's only one kind of a club that'd draw everywheres, and that's a club that didn't have no Dutchmen or Alleys—neither one."

"That's the idear," says Hawley: "a club made up o' fellas from countries that ain't got nothin' to do with the war—Norwegians, Denmarks, Chinks, Mongrels and them fellas. A guy that had brains enough to sign up that kind of a club would make a barrel o' money."

"A guy'd have a whole lot o' trouble findin' that kind of a club," I says.

"He'd have a whole lot more trouble," says Carey, "findin' a club they could beat."

◇ *Garry Herrmann*—August Herrmann, owner of the Cincinnati Reds and chairman of the National Commission, the triumvirate that ruled baseball in the period of these stories. (National Baseball Library, Cooperstown, New York)

V

Smitty used to get the paper from his home town where his folks lived at, somewheres near Lansing, Michigan. One day he seen in it where his kid brother was goin' to enter for the state golf championship.

"He'll just about cop it too," says Smitty. "And he ain't only seventeen years old. He's been playin' round that Wolverine Country Club, in ◆ Lansing, and makin' all them birds like it."

◆ *Garry Herrmann*—August Herrmann (1859–1931), owner of the Cincinnati Reds from 1902 to 1927 and chairman of the National Commission, the ruling body of baseball, from 1903 to 1920. See Bob Carroll, "Garry Herrmann," *The Ballplayers*, pp. 468–69.

◆ *Wolverine Country Club, in Lansing*—Apparently a fictional enterprise.

"The Wolverine Club, in Lansing?" says Hawley.

"That's the one," Smitty says.

"That's my old stampin' grounds," says Hawley. "That's where I learned the game at."

"The kid holds the record for the course," says Smitty.

"He don't no such a thing!" says Hawley.

"How do you know?" says Smitty.

"I guess I'd ought to know," Hawley says. "The guy that holds that record is talkin' to you."

"What's your record?" says Smitty.

"What'd your brother make?" says Hawley.

"Plain seventy-one," says Smitty; "and if you ever beat that you can have my share o' the serious money."

"You better make a check right now," says Hawley. "The last time I played at that club I rolled up seventy-three."

"That beats me," Smitty says.

"If you're that good," says Carey, "I'd like to take you on sometime. I can score as high as the next one."

"You might get as much as me now because I'm all out o' practice," says Hawley; "but you wouldn't of stood no show when I was right."

"What club was you best with?" ast Carey.

"A heavy one," says Hawley. "I used to play with a club that they couldn't hardly nobody else lift."

"An iron club?" says Smitty.

"Well," says Hawley, "it felt like they was iron in it."

"Did you play all the wile with one club?" ast Carey.

"You bet I did," Hawley says. "I paid a good price and got a good club. You couldn't break it."

"Was it a brassie?" says Smitty.

"No," says Hawley. "It was made by some people right there in Lansing."

"I'd like to get a hold of a club like that," says Carey.

"You couldn't lift it," Hawley says; "and even if you could handle it I wouldn't sell it for no price—not for twicet what it cost."

"What did it cost?" Smitty ast him.

"Fifty bucks," says Hawley; "and it'd of been more'n that only for the people knowin' me so well. My old man used to do 'em a lot o' good turns."

"He must of stood in with 'em," says Carey, "or they wouldn't of never left go of a club like that for fifty."

"They must of sold it to you by the pound," I says—"about a dollar a pound."

"Could you slice a ball with it?" says Carey.

"That was the trouble—the balls wouldn't stand the gaff," Hawley says. "I used to cut 'em in two with it."

"How many holes did they have there when you was playin'?" Smitty ast.

"Oh, three or four," he says; "but they didn't freeze me."

"They got eighteen now," says Smitty.

"They must of left the course run down," Hawley says. "You can bet they kept it up good when my old man was captain."

"Has your brother ever been in a big tourney before?" I says to Smitty.

"He was in the city championship last summer," says Smitty.

"How'd he come out?" Hawley ast.

"He was second highest," says Smitty. "He'd of win, only he got stymied by a bumblebee."

"Did they cauterize it?" says Carey.

"Where do you get that noise?" says Hawley. "They ain't no danger in a bee sting if you know what to do. Just slip a piece o' raw meat on it."

"Was you ever stymied by a bee?" says Carey.

"Was I!" says Hawley. "Say, I wisht I had a base hit for every time them things got me. My old lady's dad had a regular bee farm down in Kentucky, and we'd go down there summertimes and visit and help gather the honey. I used to run round barefooted and you couldn't find a square inch on my legs that wasn't all et up."

"Must of kept your granddad broke buyin' raw meat," says Carey.

"Meat wasn't so high in them days," says Hawley. "Besides he didn't have to buy none. He had his own cattle."

"I should think the bees would of stymied the cattle," says Carey.

"Cattle's hide's too tough; a bee won't go near 'em," says Hawley.

"Why didn't you hire a cow to go round with you wile you collected honey?" says Carey.

"What'd you quit golf for?" ast Smitty.

"A fella can't play golf and hit good," says Hawley.

"I should think it'd help a man's hittin'," Carey says. "A golf ball's a whole lot smaller than a baseball, and a baseball should ought to look as big as a balloon to a man that's been playin' golf."

"Where do you get that noise?" says Hawley. "Golf's bad for a man's battin'; but it ain't got nothin' to do with your swing or your eye or the size o' the ball."

"What makes it bad, then?" I ast him.

"Wait a minute and I'll tell you," he says. "They's two reasons: In the first place they's genally almost always some people playin' ahead o' you on a golf course and you have to wait till they got out o' reach. You get in the habit o' waitin' and when you go up to the plate in a ball game and see the pitcher right in front o' you and the infielders and baserunners clost by, you're liable to wait for 'em to get out o' the way for the fear you'll kill 'em. And wile you're waitin' the pitcher's liable to slip three over in the groove and you're struck out."

"I wasn't never scared o' killin' no infielder," says Carey.

"And what's the other reason?" I says.

"The other reason," says Hawley, "is still better yet than the one I give you."

"Don't say that!" says Smitty.

"When you're playin' golf you pay for the balls you use," says Hawley; "so in a golf game you're sort of holdin' back and not hittin' a ball as far as you can, because it'll cost you money if you can't find it. So you get used to sort o' holdin' back; and when you get up there to the plate you don't take a good wallop for the fear you'll lose the ball. You forget that the balls is furnished by the club."

"And besides that," says Carey, "you're liable to get to thinkin' that your bat cost fifty bucks, the same as your golf racket, and you don't swing hard because you might break it."

"You don't know nothin' about it," says Hawley.

VI

Now I don't care how big a goof a man is, he'd ought to know better than get smart round a fella that's slumped off in his battin'. Most o' the time they ain't no better-natured fella in the world than Carey; but when him and first base has been strangers for a wile, lay offen him!

That's how Hawley got in bad with Carey—was talkin' too much when the old boy wasn't in no mood to listen.

He begin to slump off right after the Fourth o' July double-header. In them two games a couple o' the boys popped out when they was sent up to sacrifice. So Cap got sore on the buntin' game and says we'd hit and run for a wile. Well, the first innin', every day for the next three days, Bishop led off with a base on balls and then started down when he got Carey's sign. And all three times Carey cracked a line drive right at somebody and they was a double play. After the last time he come in to the bench tryin' to smile.

"Well," he says, "I guess that's about a record."

"A record! Where do you get that stuff?" says Hawley. "I come up four times in Philly in one game and hit into four double plays."

"You brag too much!" says Carey; but you could see he didn't want to go along with it.

Well, that last line drive seemed to of took the heart out of him or somethin', because for the next week he didn't hardly foul one—let alone gettin' it past the infield.

When he'd went through his ninth game without a blow Hawley braced him in the clubhouse. "Do you know why you ain't hittin'?" he says.

"Yes," says Carey. "It's because they don't pitch where I swing."

"It ain't no such a thing!" says Hawley. "It's because you don't choke up your bat enough."

"Look here!" says Carey. "I been in this league longer'n you and I've hit better'n you. When I want advice about how to hold my bat I'll get you on the wire."

You knew how clost the clubs was bunched along in the middle o' July. Well, we was windin' up a series with Brooklyn and we had to cop the last one to break even.

We was tied up in the ninth and one out in their half when Wheat ◆◇ caught a-hold o' one and got three bases on it. Cutshaw raised one a ◆ little ways back o' second base and it looked like a cinch Wheat couldn't score if Carey got her. Well, he got her all right and Wheat come dashin' in from third like a wild man.

Now they ain't no better pegger in the league than this same Carey

---

◆ *Wheat*—Zachariah Davis "Zack" Wheat (1888–1972), the Dodger's all-time leading outfielder. With the Dodgers from 1909 to 1926 and the Athletics for a final season in 1927, Wheat played in 2,410 games, made 2,884 hits, and batted .317. He was batting champion of the National League in 1918 with a .335 average, and in both 1923 and 1924 recorded a .375 average. Wheat was elected to the Baseball Hall of Fame in 1959. See Arthur F. McClure, "Zachariah David [sic] Wheat," *Biographical Dictionary of American Sports: Baseball*, pp. 601–2.

◆ *Cutshaw*—George William Cutshaw (1887–1973), the Dodgers second baseman from 1912 to 1917. Later he played for Pittsburgh, from 1918 to 1921, and for Detroit, in 1922 and 1923. In 1,516 games in 12 seasons, Cutshaw hit .265. He was the outstanding defensive second baseman of his era, an excellent baserunner, and one of the most difficult batters to strike out. See Cappy Gagnon, "George Cutshaw," *The Ballplayers*, pp. 244–45.

◇ *Wheat*—Zack Wheat in the Dodgers uniform of 1925. (National Baseball Library, Cooperstown, New York)

and I'd of bet my life Wheat was runnin' into a double play. I thought he was a sucker for makin' the try. But Carey throwed her twenty feet to one side o' the plate. The run was in and the game was over.

Hawley hadn't hardly got in the clubhouse before he started in.

"Do you know what made you peg bad?" he says.

"Shut up!" says Smitty. "Is that the first bad peg you ever seen? Does they have to be a reason for all of 'em? He throwed it bad because he throwed it bad."

"He throwed it bad," says Hawley, "because he was in center field instead o' left field or right field. A center fielder'll peg wide three times to the others' oncet. And you know why it is, don't you?"

Nobody answered him.

"I'll tell you why it is," he says: "They's a foul line runnin' out in right field and they's a foul line runnin' out in left field, and them two lines gives a fielder somethin' to guide his throw with. If they was a

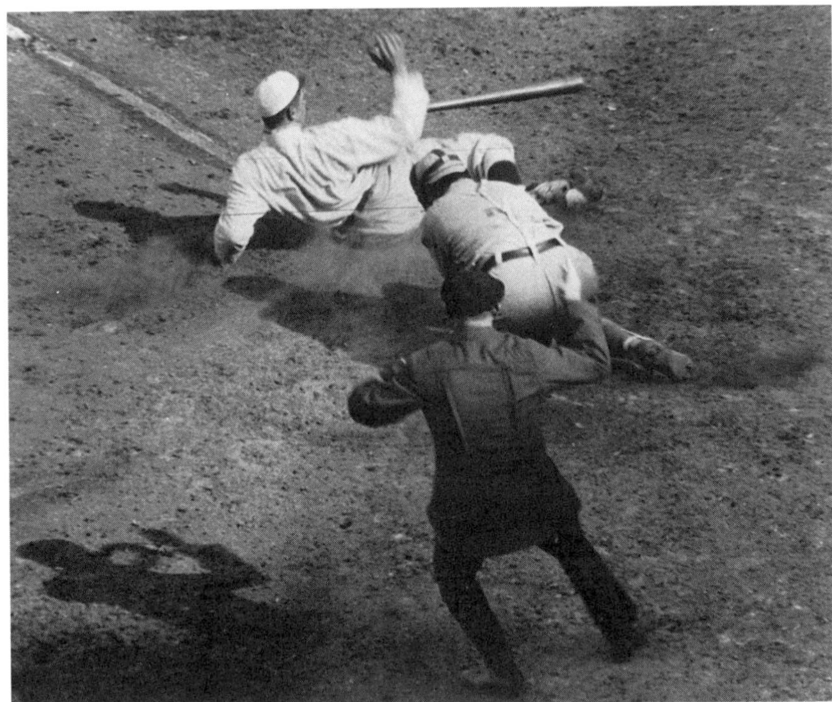

◇ *Wheat*—Zack Wheat of the Dodgers out at home in a game against the Giants in 1914. (National Baseball Library, Cooperstown, New York)

white line runnin' from home plate through second base and out in center field you wouldn't see so many bad pegs from out there.

"But that ain't the only reason," says Hawley. "They's still another reason: The old boy ain't feelin' like hisself. He's up in the air because he ain't hittin'."

That's oncet where Hawley guessed right. But Carey didn't say a word—not till we was in the Subway.

"I know why I ain't hittin' and why I can't peg," he told me. "I'm so sick of this Wisenheimer that I can't see. I can't see what they're pitchin' and I can't see the bases. I'm lucky to catch a fly ball."

"Forget him!" I says. "Let him rave!"

"I can't stop him from ravin'," says Carey; "but he's got to do his ravin' on another club."

"What do you mean?" I says. "You ain't manager."

"You watch me!" says Carey. "I ain't goin' to cripple him up or nothin' like that, but if he's still with us yet when we come offen this trip I'll make you a present o' my oldest boy."

"Have you got somethin' on him?"

"No," says Carey; "but he's goin' to get himself in wrong. And I think he's goin' to do it to-night."

VII

He done it—and that night too.

I guess you know that, next to winnin', Cap likes his missus better'n anything in the world. She is a nice gal, all right, and as pretty as they make 'em.

Cap's as proud of her as a colleger with a Charlie Chaplin mustache. When the different papers would print Miss So-and-So's pitcher and say she was the handsomest girl in this, that or the other place, Cap'd point it out to us and say: "My gal makes her look like a bad day outdoors."

Cap's wife's a blonde; and—believe me, boy—she dresses! She wasn't with us on this trip I'm speakin' of. She hasn't been with us all season, not since the trainin' trip. I think her mother's sick out there in St. Joe. Anyway, Hawley never seen her—that is, to know who she was.

Well, Carey framed it up so's I and him and Cap went in to supper together. Hawley was settin' all alone. Carey, brushin' by the head waiter, marches us up to Hawley's table and plants us. Carey's smilin' like he didn't have a care in the world. Hawley noticed the smile.

"Yattaboy!" he says. "Forget the base hits and cheer up!"

"I guess you'd cheer up, too, if you'd seen what I seen," says Carey. "Just lookin' at her was enough to drive away them Ockaway Chinese blues."

"That ain't no way for a married man to talk," says Cap.

"Well," says Carey, "gettin' married don't mean gettin' blind."

"What was she like?" ast Cap.

"Like all the prettiest ones," says Carey. "She was a blonde."

"Where do you get that noise?" says Hawley, buttin' in. "I s'pose they ain't no pretty dark girls?"

"Oh, yes," says Carey, "octoroons and them."

"Well," says Hawley, "I never seen no real pretty blondes. They ain't a blonde livin' that can class up with a pretty brunette."

"Where do you get that noise?" says Carey.

"Where do I get it!" says Hawley. "Say, I guess I've saw my share o' women. When you seen as many as I seen you won't be talkin' blonde."

"I seen one blonde that's the prettiest woman in this country," says Carey.

"The one you seen just now?" says Hawley.

"No, sir; another one," says Carey.

"Where at?" Hawley ast him.

"She's in Missouri, where she first come from," says Carey; "and she's the prettiest girl that was ever in the state."

"That shows you don't know what you're talkin' about," Hawley says. "I guess I ought to know the prettiest girl in Missouri. I was born and raised there, and the prettiest girl in Missouri went to school with me."

"And she was a blonde?" says Carey.

"Blonde nothin'!" says Hawley. "Her hair was as black as Chief Meyers'. And when you see a girl with black hair you know it's natural color. Take a blonde and you can't tell nothin' about it. They ain't one in a thousand of 'em that ain't dyed their hair."

Cap couldn't stand it no longer.

"You talk like a fool!" he says. "You don't know nothin' about women."

"I guess I know as much as the next one," says Hawley.

"You don't know nothin'!" says Cap. "What was this girl's name?"

"What girl's name?" says Hawley.

"This black girl you're talkin' about—this here prettiest girl in Missouri," says Cap.

"I forget her name," says Hawley.

"You never knowed her name," says Cap. "You never knowed nothin'! We traded nothin' to get you and we got stung at that. If you want your unconditional release, all you got to do is ask for it. And if you don't want it I'll get waivers on you and send you down South where you can be amongst the brunettes. We ain't got no room on this club for a ball player that don't know nothin' on no subject. You're just as smart about baseball as you are about women. It's a wonder your head don't have a blow-out! If a torpedo hit a boat you was on and you was the only one drownded, the captain'd send a wireless: 'Everybody saved!' "

Cap broke a few dishes gettin' up from the table and beat it out o' the room.

Hawley was still settin', with his mouth wide open, lookin' at his prunes. After a wile I and Carey got up and left him.

"He ain't a bad fella," I says when we was outside. "He don't mean nothin'. It looks to me like a raw deal you're handin' him.."

"I don't care how it looks to you or anybody else," says Carey. "I still got a chancet to lead this league in hittin' and I ain't goin' to be talked out of it."

"Do you think you'll hit when he's gone?"

"You bet I'll hit!" says Carey.

Cap ast for waivers on Hawley, and Pittsburgh claimed him.

"I wisht it had of been some other club," he says to me. "That's another o' them burgs where the smoke and cinders kills your battin'."

But I notice he's been goin' good there and he should ought to enjoy hisself tellin' Wagner how to stand up to the plate.

The day after he'd left us I kept pretty good track o' Carey. He popped out twicet, grounded out oncet and hit a line drive to the pitcher.

Good for the Soul

Before me, a member of the Baseball Writers' Association of America, ◆ appeared this first day of February, 1916, one Robert Frederick Warner, alias Buck Warner, lately a professional player of the game known ◆ as baseball and now part owner of an automobile garage in Hopsboro, ◆ a suburb of Cincinnati, and voluntarily and without threat or coercion did dictate a confession, the full text of which follows:

I

The wife says that if I didn't quit grouchin' round the house she'd just plain leave me and go and live with her Aunt Julia. Well, the wife's a good scout and Aunt Julia's home is a farm twelve miles from Dayton, so I promised I'd try and cheer up.

"Good for the Soul" was published in *The Saturday Evening Post*, CLXXXVIII (March 25, 1916), 20–23, 78, 81–82.

◆ *Baseball Writers' Association of America*—The professional organization of baseball journalists, founded in New York on October 10, 1908, and from the outset the most prestigious association in sportswriting.

◆ *Buck Warner*—A fictional character. As far as is known, all characters in this story are fictional. The story is set on a mythical Federal League team in Indianapolis in 1915. The actual Indianapolis Federal League team played only in 1914 and, as noted earlier, shifted to Newark for the 1915 season.

◆ *Hopsboro*—Apparently a fictional community.

"Yes, but you promised the same thing before," says Ethel; that's the wife's name. "You promised the same thing before and that's all the good it done," she says. "It's your crazy old conscience that's botherin' you. You'd ought to go to the hospital and have it took out."

"Operations costs money," I says.

"Well," says Ethel, "I'd rather be broke than have old Sidney Gloom for a husband."

"I'll try and cheer up," I says again.

"You're the world's greatest tryer," says she, "but your attempts to make everybody miserable is the only ones that's successful."

It was at breakfast yesterday mornin' that she was payin' me these compliments. At supper she pointed out a piece in the evenin' paper and told me I should read it.

Seems like some old bird about seventy, worth a couple o' millions, had been a clerk in a grocery store when he was a kid, and one day he helped himself to twenty dollars out o' the till, and he was scared to death they'd learn who done it and send him over, but for some reason it wasn't never found out. So, as I say, he finally got rich and had everything that's supposed to make a man happy, but he hadn't been able to sleep good for several years on account o' thinkin' about his crime. So the minister o' the church where he attended at preached a sermon on what a good thing confession was for sinners, and the old boy couldn't even sleep through the sermon, so he got the drift and made up his mind to see if a confession would cure his insomnia and not bein' able to sleep. So he wrote one out, describin' what he'd did, and sent it to the minister to be read out loud in church, and that night he slept like a horse.

"Well," I says, when I was through readin', "what about it?"

"It's worth a try," says Ethel.

"You go in town to-morrow and find somebody that'll listen, and tell 'em all about your horrible crime. And then see if you can't come home to me smilin'."

"That'll be easy," I says, "if you'll leave me drink a couple o' beers."

"You can do that too," she says, "if you think it'll wash away the blues."

I thought she was kiddin' at first; I mean about the confessin'. But she made me understand she was serious.

"But I'd have to bring in the names of others that ain't entirely innocent," I says.

"Go as far as you like," says she. "You certainly don't think they're worth shieldin'; 'specially Carmody."

So here I am and she says I was to tell it all and not keep nothin' back.

It won't be necessary to start with where I was born and so forth. A year ago last August is where it really begins. Before that I'd been in the National League six years, and if they'd left me stick to shortstop all the time, they wouldn't of nobody had me beat. But they found out I could play anywheres they put me and they kept shiftin' me round like a motorcycle cop.

In the six years I'd did even worse than not save no money. I'd piled up pretty near four thousand dollars' worth o' debts. The biggest part of it I owed to fellas on the club that'd came through for me when I made a flivver out of a billiard hall in Brooklyn.

So, as I say, a year ago last August found me four thousand to the bad and that's when I met Ethel. We was playin' in Pittsburgh and she was visitin' some people I know there. She had eye trouble and liked me the first time she seen me. But she didn't like me nowheres near as much as I liked her. We both fell pretty hard, though, and the third evenin' we was together we got engaged to be married.

"I wisht I had more to offer you," I told her. "I'm flat outside o' my salary and I owe a plain four thousand."

"I don't care how much or how little you've got," she says. "Your salary'll keep us all right. But I don't want to marry you till you're clear o' debt."

"We'll do some waitin' then," I says. "A year from this fall is the best I can promise. I'll live on nothin' this winter and I won't spend nothin' next summer and I think I can just about get cleaned up. It'll be somethin' new for me to try and save, but you're worth starvin' for."

"And you're worth waitin' for," says she.

So we says good-by and I went to Chicago with the club. And the second day there I slipped roundin' first base and throwed my knee pretty near out o' my stockin'.

It wasn't no common sprain or strain. The old bird just simply flew out of his cage and flew out to stay. I seen two doctors there and two more back home. They all says the same thing; that I was through playin' ball.

"After it's had a rest," they told me, "just walkin' on it won't hurt nothin'. But the minute you run you're liable to get crippled up good and proper. And if you stooped quick or made a quick turn or if your leg got bumped into, you might serve a good long sentence on the old hair mattress."

I didn't want Ethel to find out how bad it was, so all that come out in the paper was that I had a Charley horse. Mac, o' course, knowed the truth, but he couldn't do nothin' except feel sorry for me. He knowed about the girl too.

"I wisht I had a place for you," he says, "but you wouldn't be satisfied scoutin', and with the low player limit we can't carry no men that ain't goin' to do us some good. You'll get paid, o' course, up to the end o' the season. But I can't offer you no contract for next year."

"That's all right," I says. "I just want it kept quiet till I find somethin' I can do."

And w'ile I was still half dazed over the shock of it I got a letter from the girl. She had some big news, she says. Her Aunt Julia'd been told about I and her bein' engaged and had promised her a present o' $2500 on the day we was married. And we was to put this money with another $2500 that her brother, Paul, was goin' to save up, and I and her brother was goin' to buy a garage in Hopsboro from a fella that'd promised Paul he'd sell it to him in a year.

And it was the only garage in Hopsboro and done a whale of a business. And Paul was a swell mechanic and I'd take care o' the business end. And I could quit playin' ball and never be away from home. It sounded mighty good to me just then. But they was still a little trifle o' four thousand that'd have to be took care of.

I'd just mailed back an answer, as cheerful as I could write, when a call come over the phone that Mr. A. T. Grant wanted to see me at the Kingsley Hotel. I'd saw his name mentioned in connection with a club in the new league, but I didn't know if he'd bought it or not.

Well, I went down there in a taxi and was showed right up to his room.

He shook hands with me and then ast me if I was signed up for next year. I told him I wasn't.

"I've just bought the club I was after," he says. "I wanted to know if you'd consider an offer."

I done some tall thinkin'. I made up my mind that it wouldn't do no harm to sign. If I found I couldn't play nobody'd be hurt. But if the old knee wasn't as bad as the doctors thought I'd probably get a better job here than anywheres else.

"Who's goin' to be your manager?" I ast him.

"Billy Carmody," he says. "He was the shortstop on the club this year."

"I never met him, but o' course I've heard of him," I says.

Then I done some more thinkin'.

"What's your offer?" I says.

"Five thousand," says Mr. Grant.

"Where would you want me to play?" I ast him.

"Where would you want to play?" says he.

That give me a hunch. I'd heard they was one or two short fences in the league. Maybe I could play an outfield position even if my legs wouldn't stand the infield strain.

"In the outfield," I told him.

"Which field?" he says, and then I knowed he was a bug.

"Right field," says I.

"That suits me," he says, and he sent for his secretary to fix up a contract.

So I signed to play right field, and nowheres else, for Mr. Grant's club for one year at $5000.

"This business is new to me," he says, "but I believe I'll get a lot o' pleasure out of it."

"What other men have you got signed?" I ast him.

"I'm not at liberty to tell you," he says. "But I may tell you that most o' them is young men that's as new to professional ball as I am. I believe in gettin' young fellas, for enthusiasm's more valuable than experience in a sport o' this kind."

"Oh, easy," I says.

Then we shook hands again and I beat it to a train for Dayton, where the girl was stayin'. And when I seen her I give her the whole story. It looked now like they was a little bit o' hope.

II

The papers I'd saw durin' the winter hadn't wasted no space on our club and I didn't know exactly who was my teammates till I blowed into Dixie Springs, the first week in March. ◆

I landed in the forenoon. The clerk at the hotel told me the gang was all out to the grounds, practicin'. So I planted my baggage and washed up, and then set out on the porch, waitin' for the boys to come back. The beanery was on the main street, but from the number o' people that went past you'd of thought our trainin' camp had been

---

◆ *Dixie Springs*—The only place of this name in the United States at the time was a point of no reported population on the Southern Railway in the vicinity of Parish, Walker County, Alabama. It appears to be too insignificant even for the role attributed to it in this story.

picked out by Robinson Caruso. About one bell I got sick o' lookin' at mud puddles and woke up the clerk again.

"What do you s'pose is keepin' 'em so long?" I ast him.

"They don't never show up till after four," he says.

"Don't they come back for lunch?" I ast.

"No," he says. "You see the ball grounds is over a quarter of a mile from here and Mr. Grant, who's the proprietor o' the nine, figured it would wear his men out to make the trip four times a day."

"So they don't eat at noon?" I says.

"Oh, yes," says the clerk. "We put up a nice lunch here and send it to 'em."

"I hope you don't send 'em nothin' that's hard to chew," I says. After a w'ile I got up nerve enough to attemp' the killin' journey to the orchard.

It was an old fairgrounds or somethin', just on the edge o' what you'd call the town if you was good-natured. Waivers had been ast on a lot o' the boards on the fence and they was plenty o' places where a brewer could of walked through sideways. I was goin' in at the gate because it was handiest, but I found it locked. I give it a kick and it was opened from inside by a barber hater.

"You can't come in," he says through the shrubbery.

"Why not?" says I.

"I've got orders," he says.

"I don't wonder," I says. "You're liable to get anything in them dragnets."

"I'll fix you if you try to come in," he says.

"What'll you do?" says I. "Tickle me to death with them plumes?"

"Mr. Grant don't want no spies hangin' round," says Whiskers. ◇

"O' course not," says I. "But I'm one of his ball players."

"Oh, no, you aint," says the Old Fox. "If you was you'd be wearin' one o' them get-ups with the knee pants and the spellin' on the blouse."

"Look here," I says. "I don't want to cut my way through the undergrowth; they's too much danger of infection. You run along and tell Mr. Grant his star performer has arrived, and when you come back I'll give you thirty-five cents to'rds a shave."

So the old boy slammed the gate shut and locked her again and the minute it was locked I went to the nearest gap in the fence and eased in.

They was a game o' ball goin' on and I started over to where they was playin' to see if I recognized anybody. But I hadn't went more'n

◇ *"Mr. Grant don't want no spies hangin' round," says Whiskers*— Drawing by M. L. Blumenthal for *The Saturday Evening Post*, March 25, 1916.

a step or two when Whiskers come dashin' up to me with Mr. Grant followin'.

"This is the man!" yells Whiskers. "And my suspicions was right or he wouldn't of snuck in."

Mr. Grant was gaspin' too hard to talk at first; when he catched his breath he lit into me. "A spy, eh!" he says. "Tryin' to learn our secrets, eh! That's a fine job for a big man like you! Whose stool pigeon are you?" he says. "Stop the game!" he says to Whiskers. "Don't let 'em show nothin' in front o' this sneak!"

But they wasn't no need of him givin' that order, because when the boys heard the rumpus they quit o' their own accord and come runnin' over to be in on it.

Leadin' the pack was Jimmy Boyle, that I'd busted into the game with, out in Des Moines. I'd noticed from the box scores the summer before that they was a Boyle in this league, but I hadn't never thought of it bein' Jimmy. In fac', till I seen him sprintin' to'rds me, I'd forgot they was such a guy. It was nine years since I'd saw him.

"Hello, Buck!" he hollers.

"Buck!" says Mr. Grant. "You ain't Buck Warner, are you?"

"That's me," I says, "and I guess if it hadn't been for Jimmy recognizin' me you'd of had me shot for a spy."

The Old Boy looked like he was gettin' ready to cry.

"I certainly owe you my apologies," he says. "I don't remember faces as good as I used to and besides, you're dressed different than when you and me met."

"Yes," I says, "I've changed my clo'es twice since September."

"I hope you'll forgive me," says Mr. Grant.

"I'll think it over," I says.

By this time the whole bunch was gathered round and I had a chance to see who was who. Outside o' Jimmy Boyle they wasn't only four out o' more'n two dozen that I knowed by sight. One o' the four, o' course, was Billy Carmody. Him and I hadn't never met; he'd always been in the American till he jumped. But I'd saw his picture of'en enough to spot him. Then they was Hi Boles that I'd knew in the Association. And they was Charley Wade that the Boston club had for w'ile, and Red Fulton, that had been with Philly. The rest o' them was all strangers to me and most o' them looked about as much like ball players as Mary Pickford.

I shook hands with Red and Charley and Jimmy and Hi Boles, and Mr. Grant introduced me to the gang.

"Now," he says, "I wisht you'd shake with me to show you don't bear no grudge. I wouldn't of had this thing happen for the world."

"I don't blame you at all, sir," I says. "A club owner's got to be careful these days, because if other owners will go as far as stealin' your ball players, they certainly wouldn't hesitate at hirin' spies to try and cop your club's hit-and-run signs. But," I says, "I think you're foolish not to plug them holes in the fence. A scout with a strong glass could stand way out there behind center field and find out how many fingers your catchers used to signal for a curve ball."

"Yes," he says, winkin', "but the signals we use now and the signals we're goin' to use when the season opens up is two different things."

"Oh! Deep stuff, eh!" says I. "Well, if that's the way you're workin' it you'd ought not to be scared of outsiders swipin' information. Leave as many of 'em as wants to come and look us over, and the more bum dope they take back home, the easier we'll beat 'em when we meet 'em."

"But I don't want nobody to even know my line-up," says Mr. Grant, "not till the boys runs out on the field for the openin' game. If they don't know who we got or what we got or our battin' order or nothin', they can't prepare for us, can they?"

"Ain't they no reporters along?" I ast him.

"I wouldn't have 'em," says Mr. Grant. "I don't want to have no advance news get out about this club. Takin' your enemies by su'prise is more'n half the battle."

"Yes," says I, "but after the first day they won't be no more su'prise. The whole country'll know who we are."

"But we'll be leadin' the league," he says. "They can't take that away from us."

"Not for twenty-four hours," says I.

By this time, Carmody'd took his men back to their practice. I wanted to see 'em in action and made a move to go over to where they was at, but the Old Boy flagged me.

"They'll be through in five minutes," he says. "You must be wore out with your long trip, so let's you and I walk back to the hotel and set and rest till the boys comes in. I want you to be fresh to-morrow."

So we come away together and the last thing I seen at the grounds was Whiskers. He had the gate open far enough so's his head could stick out and he could see the whole length o' the main street. They wasn't a chance for a spy to catch him off guard, unless the spy used unfair tactics and snuck up from some other direction.

"What do you think of our club?" says Mr. Grant.

"I don't know nothin' about it," I says. "Most o' them boys is strangers to me."

"But ain't they nice lookin' boys?" he says.

"Sure," says I, "but some o' the best ball players I ever seen was homelier than muskrats."

"But their bein' homely didn't make 'em good ball players," says he.

"No," I says, "but it helped 'em keep in the pink. They couldn't go girl-crazy and stay out all hours o' the night dancin'; they wasn't no girls that'd dance with 'em or be seen with 'em. And they couldn't lay against the mahogany all evenin', because all bars has got mirrors back o' them, and if a man didn't never open his eyes they'd think you'd fell asleep and throw you out."

"Your arguments may be all right for some teams," says Mr. Grant, "but they don't hold as far as we're concerned. Bein' handsome won't hurt my boys, because they can't run round nights or drink neither one."

"Why not?" I ast him.

"Because they's a club rule against it," he says.

"Oh!" I says. "O' course that makes it different. How'd you ever happen to think o' makin' a rule like that? I bet when the other club owners hears about it, they'll follow suit and thank you for originatin' the idear."

"I hope they do follow suit," he says. "It's one o' my ambitions to perjure baseball of its evils."

"I wish you luck," says I.

"And another one," he says, "is to win the pennant, and between you and I, I believe I'm goin' to realize it."

"What year?" I says.

"This year," says my boss.

"Well," I says, "I'm new in the league and I don't know what it takes to win. But from what I seen of your club and from what I read about Chicago and St. Louis and some o' the rest, I'd say you had to ◆ strengthen some."

"I'm afraid you're pessimistical, Warner," he says. "I've got the winnin' combination—yourself and Carmody and Fulton and Wade and Boles and Boyle for experience and balance, and those youngsters o' mine for speed and spirit. We'll take the League off'n their feet."

"What does Carmody think about it?"

"The same as me," he says. "And he's a great manager."

"He must be," says I.

Well, when the crowd come in, Jimmy Boyle chased up to the clerk o' the hotel and had it fixed for me to room with him.

"They had me paired with one o' the kids," he says, "but I got to have somebody to laugh with. This is goin' to be the greatest season you ever went through. I don't know what I'll hit, but I bet I giggle .380."

"What is they to laugh at?" I says.

"What ain't they to laugh at?" says Jimmy. "Wait till you get acquainted wiht the old man! Wait till you've saw our gang in action!

◆ *Chicago and St. Louis*—Chicago and St. Louis finished first and second, respectively, in the Federal League in 1915.

Wait till you watch Carmody managin'! Dutch Schaefer couldn't of ◆ got up a better club than this."

"What have we got, outside o' you and the other fellas I know?" I ast him.

"Say, if I told you, you wouldn't believe it," says Jimmy. "In the first place, there's old Grant. If he ain't got no relatives the county'd ought to look after him. He's goin' to keep us a secret till the season opens and then we're goin' to win the first game by su'prise. And somebody tipped him off that the club that wins the first game has got the best chance for the pennant. O' course they's eight clubs in the league and four o' them'll prob'ly win their first games, but he never thought o' that. And besides, the only chance we got o' winnin' the first game or any other game is to have the other club look at us and die laughin'."

"Ain't they no stuff in them kids?" I ast.

"Just one o' them," says Boyle. "They's a boy named Steele that must of took his name from his right arm. He can whizz 'em through there faster'n Johnson. He could win with any club in the world but our'n."

"Who's the other pitchers?" I ast him.

"They ain't none," says Boyle, "none that counts. All told, we got three right-handers and three cockeyes, but outside o' Steele, I'd go up there and catch any one o' them without a mask or glove or protector or nothin'. When the balls they throw don't hit the screen on the fly they'll hit the fence on the first hop."

"Where'd he get 'em all?" says I.

"He must of bought 'em off'n Pawnee Bill," says Jimmy. ◆

"We seem to be long on catchers," I says.

"Wade and Fulton and myself," says Jimmy, "but some of us is goin' to get switched before the season's a week old. As I say, when Steele ain't pitchin' the club don't need no catcher, and it sure does need other things. Carmody's playin' short and Boles is the first sacker and you'll be somewheres in the outfield. That only leaves four positions without nobody to fill 'em. So I and Red and Charley's wonderin' which one of us'll be elected first. I wouldn't mind tacklin' right field; they's some short fences in the league. But Carmody's just crazy enough to stick me at third base where a man don't have time to duck."

◆ *Dutch Schaefer*—Apparently Germany Schaefer. He never managed, and given his reputation as a comedian, he was a most unlikely choice for the responsibility.
◆ *Pawnee Bill*—Major Gordon William Lillie (1860–1942), proprietor of one of the principal Wild West shows of the day.

"You lay off'n right field," I says. "I got a lien on that bird."

"You'll play where Carmody puts you," says Jimmy.

"You're delirious," says I. "You ain't seen my contract. I signed to play right field and nowheres else, and you couldn't get me out o' there with a habeas corpus."

"Mr. Fox, eh?" says Boyle.

"You know it," I says, "and between you and I, they's a reason. I'd just as soon tell you because they ain't no danger o' you spillin' it. My right knee slipped out on me last August, and when it went, it went for good. All the doctors I seen give me the same advice—to get out o' baseball. And I had my mind all made up to quit when old Grant stepped in with his offer. I took it, knowin' all the w'ile that it was grand larceny."

"Don't you worry about that," says Jimmy. "They'll be only one guy on this club that ain't a burglar. That's young Steele. The rest of us, includin' the M.G.R., is a bunch o' bandits. But I'm not frettin' over it. I figure that if he wasn't givin' me this dough somebody else'd be gettin' it, maybe somebody without as much license to it as me. If they wasn't nobody dependin' on me I might feel ashamed. But when you got a wife and two kids, and an old bug comes along and slips you a contract for three times what you're worth, it'd be cheatin' your folks to not take it."

"I ain't got no folks," I says.

"But you can't never tell," says Boyle.

"I can tell," I says, "if you'll listen. I met a little lady the middle o' last July. The first week in August we got engaged. And the second week in August Mr. Knee blowed out. So when Grant come after me, along in September, I begin to believe in angels. But I ain't never felt right about it."

"How bad is the old dog?" says Jimmy. "Can you run on it at all?"

"I can run on it," I says, "but I can't get up no speed. And I don't know when she's goin' to slip again. I can't start quick. And I'm scared to stoop."

"You won't need to stoop; not with our pitchers," says Jimmy. "All that'll come out your way is line drives or high boys over the wall."

"And if I turn sudden, I'm gone," says I.

"That's easy," says Boyle. "Rest your spine against them boards and do all your runnin' to'rds the infield. You won't be the first outfielder that played that system."

"Carmody'll wise up to me," I says.

"You should worry your head off about Carmody," says Boyle. "He's pretendin' to take his job serious, but down in his heart he knows he's a thief. He's got just as much right to manage a ball club as that girl o' yours. You just stick it out and draw the old check every first and fifteenth, and remember that you got plenty o' company. Even if your two legs was cut off at the waist you'd be worth five times as much as some of us."

"Careful there, Jim," I says.

"You can hit, can't you?" he says. "And you can catch fly balls, and you can throw. There's three things you can do, and that's three more things than most of our gang can do. No, I'll take that back. They's one thing they can all do."

"What's that?" I ast him.

"Eat," says Jimmy, "and if you don't believe it come down in the dinin' room. The doors is supposed to open for supper at five-thirty, but after the first day we was here, the manager seen that the only way to save the doors was to keep 'em open all the w'ile. All the other ball clubs I was ever with talked about their hittin' and their bad luck, and all that. But this bunch don't talk nothin' but meats and groceries, and when they ain't talkin' about 'em it's because they got so many o' them in their mouth that they can't talk. The kid that was roomin' with me put what he couldn't eat in his pockets or inside his shirt, and after every meal he'd come straight to the room and unload on top o' the bureau. And if I went near his storehouse to brush my hair or look in the glass, he'd growl like a dog. He had himself trained so's he wouldn't sleep more'n three hours in a row. He'd go to bed at nine and get up at twelve and three for refreshments. But no matter how hungry he was at three, he always managed to save a piece o' cold hamburger or a little fricasseed veal for when he woke up in the mornin', so's he wouldn't have to go down to breakfast in his night-gown. Our second day here it was rainin' when I rolled out o' bed. Griffin, the kid I'm tellin' you about, was puttin' on his clo'es with one hand and feedin' himself with the other. 'Well, boy,' I says to him, 'it looks like we'd loaf to-day.' He must of thought I'd mentioned veal loaf or a loaf o' bread, because all the answer I got was more things to eat. 'Fruit and cereal,' he says, 'prunes and oranges and oatmeal, bacon and eggs straight up, small tenderloin medium, sausage and cakes, buttered toast, some o' them rolls, and a pot o' coffee.' 'Well,' I says, 'your dress rehearsal goes off all right; if you don't get scared and forget your lines in front o' the waiter, you'll be the hit o' the show.' But I might as well of been talkin' to a post hole. He didn't know I was speakin' unless I spoke like a bill o' fare."

"What position does he play?" I ast.

"Third base," says Jimmy, "and for the fear everybody won't know it, he always keeps one foot on the bag. But don't get the idear that he's a bigger eater than the rest o' them. They ain't no more difference in their appetites than in their ball playin'. When they got their noses in the feed-trough, though, they look like they was at home. And when they're out there on the field, you'd think they was It for blindman's buff."

I ast him about the Old Man havin' their lunch sent out.

"Even Carmody laughed at that," he says; "but Carmody's figured that the way to get along with old Grant is to agree with him in everything. So we're relieved from two changes o' clo'es, and a half mile walk that might help some of us get down to weight."

"Is it a regular lunch?" I ast him.

"All but the tools," says Jimmy. "And that makes it the favorite meal with Griffin and them. They can throw it in faster and without near as much risk. And all you have to do to start a riot is drop a bone or part of a potato on the grass."

"How is the grounds?" I says.

"Just as good as the club," says Boyle.

"Who picked out this joint?" says I.

"The same old bug that picked up these ball players," says Jimmy. "He was lookin' for a quiet place and he got it. The burg's supposed to have a population o' twelve hundred, but I haven't even saw the twelve. Dixie Springs they call it, but the only springs is in Carmody's bed. The town and the grounds is both jokes. The hotel's all right outside o' the rooms. I'll own up the eatin's good, but that's the one thing that don't make no difference to this bunch of our'n. They'd go to it just the same if it was raw mule chops."

"How much longer do we stick?" I ast him.

"Plain five weeks," says Jimmy. "We don't play no exhibitions nowheres because they might be spies from the other clubs watchin' us. We stay right here and do all our practicin' in a park that was laid out by a steeplechase fan, and then we go straight home and win the openin' game and the pennant by su'prise. You're lucky you come a week late. If I'd knew the dope in advance I wouldn't of never reported till the day o' the big su'prise party. But leave us hurry downstairs or it'll be too late for you to get a look at a fine piece of American scenery."

"What's that?" I ast.

"The Royal Gorge," says Jimmy.

Well, he hadn't lied when he told me about their eatin'. It was just like as if they knowed the league wasn't only goin' to last this one more season, and they all o' them expected to live to be over ninety, and was tryin' to get fixed up in a year for the next sixty-five. You remember how them waiters down South come one-steppin' in with their trays balanced on their thumb a mile over their head? Well, they didn't pull that stunt with the orders these here boys give 'em. Each fella's meal took two pallbearers, with a couple o' mourners followin' along behind to pick up whatever floral pieces fell off when the casket listed.

I and Boyle and Fulton and Hi Boles had a table to ourself, and you ought to saw them Ephs quarrel over who'd wait on us. Besides our four orders together not bein' as big as one o' them other guys', we wasn't so exhausted at the end o' the meal that we couldn't dig down in our pocket and get a dime. Mr. Grant and Carmody and the secretary set next to our table and it seemed to worry the Old Boy that our appetites was so poor. He'd say:

"Warner, I'm afraid you ain't feelin' good. You don't eat hardly nothin'."

"I'm all right," I'd tell him; "but eatin' ain't no new experience for me. I ett for several years before I broke into baseball and I been gettin' regular meals ever since."

The lunch served out to the grounds was worth travelin' south just to look at it. It always come prompt at twelve, and for a half hour before that time every ground ball was a base hit because the fielders was all lookin' up at the sun. And when the baskets full o' nourishment was drug in, no matter if we was right in the middle of an innin', everybody'd throw away their bats and gloves and race for the front. Carmody'd follow along smilin', like it was a good joke.

I was hungry my first day out. I told Jimmy I felt like eatin' a big meal.

"Well," he says, "I bet you don't eat it when you see it."

He win his bet. I was the last fella up to the baskets. They was a couple o' sandwiches and one or two pieces o' fried chicken left, but it'd all been pawed over by the early birds, and amongst the other things the grounds was shy of was a place to wash your hands. Even if they'd been one, nobody'd of had time to use it.

So that day and the rest o' the time we was there I set out on the sidelines with Hi and Jimmy and Red durin' the noon hour, and watched the performance.

"This mayn't be a big league," says Jimmy, "but our club'll be big if they don't all get lockjaw."

"It'll take two engines to pull us home," says Red.

"If them boys could hit, they'd be heavy hitters," says Hi.

Well, they couldn't hit or they couldn't field; that is, the most o' them couldn't. They was a couple that had the stuff to make pretty fair ball players if they'd knew anything. Carmody couldn't learn 'em because he didn't know nothin' himself. I done what I could to help 'em, partly because I'm kind-hearted, and partly so's I'd be doin' somethin' else besides riskin' my life in that outfield. It was rough enough so's a fella with two good legs would be scared to take a chance, and it wasn't no place for a cripple to frolic round in.

We put on two ball games a day between the regulars and yannigans. The only reason for callin' our team the regulars was on account o' Carmody playin' with us. We was licked most o' the time because young Steele done most o' the pitchin' against us. He sure could buzz 'em through and he had as good control as I ever seen in a kid. He was workin' the day that I and Carmody had our first and last argument. Carmody's whole idear o' baseball was "take two strikes." That was his instructions to everybody that went up to hit. It was all right when the other fellas was pitchin' because they was all o' them pretty near sure to walk you. But I couldn't see no sense doin' it against Steele; it just helped him get you in a hole.

This day it come up to the seventh innin' and Steele had us beat four to nothin'. We was all ordered to take two strikes and most of us was addin' one onto the order. But in the seventh, one o' the kids happened to get a base hit and they was a couple o' boots, and when it was my turn to go up there, the bases was choked and two out.

"Take two strikes," yells Carmody.

"Yes," I says to myself, "I'll take two strikes."

So Steele, thinkin' I'd obey orders, laid the first one right over in my groove and I busted it out o' the ball park.

When I come in to the bench Carmody was layin' for me.

"What kind o' baseball is that?" he says.

"It's real baseball," I says. "If you think it ain't you're crazy. When a pitcher's got as good control as him, and we're four runs behind and the bases is full, I'm goin' to crack the first ball I can reach."

He called me over away from the gang.

"It's a bad example," he says, "for you to not follow instructions."

"Maybe it is," says I, "but when the instructions is ridic'lous I'm goin' to forget 'em."

"I'm managin' this ball club," he says.

"You're doin' a grand job," says I. "When you take money for managin', it's plain highway robbery."

"I suppose you're earnin' yourn," says Carmody. "I suppose you got two good legs."

That kind o' shook me up.

"Listen," he says, "I got just as much license to draw a manager's salary as you have for takin' a ball player's. You're liable to be on crutches before the middle of April. But if I don't make no crack to Grant he won't know you was crippled when you signed; he'll think, when your knee goes back on you, that it's the first time and just an accident. So," he says, "if I was you I'd play the way the manager told me and not make no fuss."

"You win," says I. "But have a heart and forget once in a w'ile to give me orders. I don't mind if the rest o' the league knows I got a bum leg, but I don't want 'em to think my head's cut off."

They wasn't never such a long five weeks as I put in down to this excuse for a trainin' camp. After the first few days I got sick o' laughin' and sleepin' and everything else. I'd promised the girl I wouldn't take a drink, but all that kept me from breakin' the promise was lack of opportunity. The burg didn't even have a soda foundry.

Nights afrter supper I'd write a long letter to the future Missus and then I and Boyle'd set up in the room and wish we was somewheres else. Once or twice old Grant called on us and raved about our chances to win the pennant.

"If you boys finish on top," he says, "and if the European war's over by that time, I might give you all a trip acrost the pond next fall."

When he'd went out and left us after spillin' that great piece o' news, we was as excited as a couple o' draft horses.

"I wonder what they soak a man for a steamer trunk," says Jimmy. "It'd be a grand honeymoon for you," he says. "The lady'll love you better'n ever when she knows you're goin' to take her to see the Tower o' London and the Plaster o' Paris."

"I hope," says I, "that they'll be sure and have all the dead removed before we get there."

"We'll be right to home in the trenches after practicin' all spring on these grounds," says Jimmy.

Well, the time went by one way and another and the happiest day o' my life, bar one, was when us Wellfeds clumb aboard a rattler headed north. Our trainin' season was over and we was in every bit as good shape as if we'd just left the operatin' table. Our team was picked and they was ball players in every position except two, but Carmody and Wade was the only ones in the lot that was playin' where they belonged. The two kids that acted like they had a little ability was in the outfield with me. Jimmy Boyle'd been tried at second base and third base, but he was lost both places, so they'd stuck him on first and shifted Hi Boles, a first sacker, to third. Red Fulton, another catcher, was pretendin' to play second base. Carmody was at shortstop and it looked like Charley Wade was elected to catch whenever it didn't rain. That was the club that was goin' to take the pennant by su'prise and spend the winter in Monte Carlo.

But I was too happy over leavin' Dixie Springs to be worryin' about how rotten we looked.

"Lord!" I says to Charley Wade, "I guess it won't seem great to be in a real town!"

"I don't know," he says, "I'm afraid I'll be nervous when I get where they's people."

III

They wasn't enough people in the park the day we opened to bother Charley Wade or anybody else. Old Grant had made such a success o' keepin' us a secret that only about eight hundred knowed we was goin' to perform; anyway, that's all that come out to watch us, and in his great, big new stands, they looked like a dozen fleas on a flat car.

It was a crime, too, that we didn't have a crowd, because we win the ball game. The records will show that; you don't have to take my word. The Old Boy had predicted a su'prise and his prophecy come true. And the ones that was most su'prised was us and the fellas we beat.

When that Buffalo bunch first come out and seen our line-up in ◆ battin' practice, they laughed themself hoarse. But they didn't do no laughin' after the game started and they got a sample o' Steele's stuff. The weather was twice as cold as any we'd ran into down South, but it didn't seem to make no difference to him. He was lightnin' fast and steady as Matty. He didn't give 'em one real chance to score.

We trimmed 'em two to nothin' and I drove in the both of our runs. Along with that I was lucky enough to make quite a catch o' the only ball they hit hard off o' Steele.

When we got in the clubhouse afterwards, Mr. Grant was there, actually cryin' for joy. He throwed his arms round Steele and was goin' to do the same to me, but I backed off and told him I was engaged.

◆ *that Buffalo bunch*—Buffalo was to finish sixth in the Federal League in 1915.

O' course they was reporters lookin' us over this time and the next mornin' the population was informed that Grant and Carmody'd made quite a ball club out of a bunch of misfits. So when she started that afternoon, the stands was pretty near filled.

Our whole pitchin' staff, except Steele, was in there at one time or another. The Buffalo club hadn't been able to hit Steele. They didn't have to hit these other babies. I don't know how many bases on balls was gave, but I bet it was a world's record. Charley Wade, back o' the bat, did more shaggin' than all the outfielders. When Buffalo was battin' the umps could of left his right arm in the checkroom. Fourteen to nothin' it wound up and they was no comin' in the clubhosue after the game.

Steele was beat his next time out, but win his third start. And one o' the cockeyes come acrost with a win in the second series, gettin' some valuable help from an umpire that'd been let out o' the Association for bein' stone blind. I think altogether we copped four games in April. Along the last part o' May or the first o' June we grabbed two in succession, but the streak was broke up when Jimmy dropped three pegs in the eighth and ninth innin's o' the third game.

Durin' the home series in May, four or five hundred people that was fond o' low comedy come out every afternoon to get our stuff. But we pulled the same gags so often that they quit us after a w'ile. We went round the western half o' the circuit in June and our split o' the gate wouldn't of tipped the porters. Then we come home again and was welcomed by thirty-seven paid admissions, five ushers and two newspaper men.

The Old Boy cut the price to a dime for the bleachers. The ticket takers slept peaceful all afternoon. Then he hired a band to give a concert every day, so for a w'ile we was sure of an attendance o' thirty, except when the piccolo player got piccoloed.

When August come I was leadin' the league in hittin' and Mr. Grant thought I was the most valuable man he had. He overlooked a few things about my record that would of wised up any real baseball man. For instance, though I was battin' .420, my total o' stolen bases was three, and all three o' them was steals o' second that'd been made in double steals with Hi Boles goin' from second to third. And I didn't only have about ten extra base hits, o' which five was home run drives out o' the park. In other words, I wasn't doin' no more runnin' than I had to, and I didn't try to get nowheres where they was a chance that I'd have to slide. And under this kind o' treatment, Mr. Leggo had held up good. I'd felt him wabble two different times when I was chasin' fly balls, but he'd popped back into place without me even coaxin' him.

Then, in the middle of August, everything happened at once. Charley Wade broke an ankle, Carmody's right arm went dead, and the girl had a brawl with Aunt Julia.

We was in Indianapolis. We'd just got through carryin' Charley into the clubhouse when a boy come down to the bench and handed me a telegram. It says I was to come at once; she must see me.

"Carmody," I says, "I got to run down to Dayton to-night."

"What for?" he says.

"Somebody wants me," I told him.

"Not as bad as I do," he says.

"Well," says I, "it's somebody that makes more difference than you do."

"I'll talk to you after the game," he says.

It was our last bats and it didn't take 'em long to get us out.

"Now," says Carmody, "you can go to Dayton to-night if you'll promise to be back in time to play to-morrow."

"I can't make no promise," I says.

"Then you can't go," says Carmody.

"What's the matter with you?" I says. "Can't you stick a pitcher or one o' them kids in right field for one day?"

"You ain't goin' to play right field no more," he says.

"I ain't goin' to play nowheres else," says I. "Do you think I'm goin' to catch in Charley's place?'"

"No," he says. "I'm goin' to put Boyle back there."

"And me go to first?" I says.

"No," says Carmody. "I'm goin' there myself and you're goin' to take my place at shortstop."

"You're maudlin," I says. "I signed a contract to play right field and that's where I'm goin' to stick. I'm awkward enough out there; I'd be a holy show on the infield. Besides, you never played first base in your life and one o' the pitchers or that big Griffin kid could do as good as you. What's the use o' breakin' up your whole combination just because one fella's hurt?"

"We couldn't make no change that'd be for the worse," says Carmody. "But I'll come clean with you and tell you where I'm at. I'm gettin' $1800 a month for this job. But my contract says I got to play the whole season out or he can cut $2500 off'n my year's salary."

"Well," I says, "what's the difference if you play first base or stay where you're at?"

"I can't stay where I'm at," he says. "My souper's deader'n that place we trained. She quit on me in the seventh innin' to-day. I couldn't stand on the foul line and throw to fair ground."

"You hurt it in action, didn't you?" I says.

"Yes, but he's sore at me," says Carmody, "on account of our swell showin'. And the way my contract reads, he could keep my dough if he wanted to."

"But you'll have to throw when you're playin' first base," says I.

"No, I won't," he says. "You watch me and see. If I've got the ball and they's a play to make anywheres, you'll see the old pill slip right out o' my hand and lay there on the ground."

"But I don't see why you should pick on me," I says. "Boles or Red Fulton or one o' them kids could do a whole lot better job o' short-stoppin' than me."

"Boles and Fulton is bad enough where they're at," he says, "without wishin' a new bunch o' trouble on 'em. You've played there and you'd know what you was doin' even if you couldn't stoop over or cover no ground. Besides," he says, "old Grant wants you to tackle it."

"When was you talkin' to him?" I says. "You ain't seen him since Charley got hurt and your arm went."

"That's more secrets," says Carmody. "Between you and I, my arm's been bad a long w'ile and I had the hunch it was goin' to do just what it done. So I told him a little story a couple o' weeks ago. I told him I wasn't satisfied with the way Boyle was playin' first base and I told him I was a pretty good first sacker myself and thought I'd move over there. So he ast me who'd play shortstop and I told him you'd make the best man and he says he thought so, too, but your contract read that you'd only play right field. So I told him maybe he could coax you to switch."

"It must be hard for you to shave with all that cheek," I says. "You can go and tell him now that you ast me would I play shortstop and I told you No, I wouldn't. So that's settled, and now I'm goin' to catch a train. If I can get back to-morrow I will. And if I do get back, I'll be in right field."

I left him bawlin' me out, but I knowed he couldn't do nothin' to me. I had as much on him as he had on me.

I run into a flood in Dayton, but it was salt water this time. The girl ◆

◆ *a flood in Dayton*—The reference is to a flood of March 26, 1913, which ravaged most of Ohio and Indiana. The inundation was worst at Dayton, where the Great

cried for two hours after I got there and couldn't quit long enough to tell me what it was about. I finally made like I was goin' away disgusted. Then she come through.

They wasn't goin' to be no $2500 from Aunt Julia. Aunt Julia'd fell in love with a G. A. R. that hadn't did nothin' since '65 but celebrate his team's victory. So Ethel, instead o' usin' her head, lost it, and ast Aunt Julia what she meant by tyin' up with a bird twenty years older than herself that hadn't shaved since Grant took Richmond. So they broke up in a riot and all bets was off.

"Well," I says, "maybe she'll get over it."

"No, she won't," says Ethel, "and even if she did, I wouldn't take her old money."

"Any high-class bank would give you new money for it," I says.

"It ain't no time for jokin'," she says. "Everything's all over. We can't get married this year; maybe not for ten years; maybe never."

"I don't have to pay all them debts right away," I says. "I can hold out $2500 and give it to Paul. The boys have waited this long for their dough; I guess they can wait a w'ile longer."

"You know what I've told you," she says. "We won't be married one minute before you're out o' debt."

"Well," I says, "it looks like they was no hurry about gettin' a license. They ain't goin' to be no post-season money for us guys."

"We'll just have to wait then," says the girl. "You'll have to save every cent o' your next year's pay."

"They ain't goin' to be no next year's pay," says I. "This league'll be past history in another season. And I couldn't carry bats anywheres else."

The more we talked the bluer things looked and I guess I'd of been cryin' myself in another minute if the big idear hadn't came to me.

"Wait a minute!" I says. "They's a chance that we can get out o' this all right."

"What's the dope?" she ast me.

But I couldn't tell her; it wasn't clear in my own mind yet and I didn't want to say nothin' till I'd schemed it out.

"I'm goin' right back, back, back to Indiana," I says. "You'll get a

---

(*continued from page 545*)
Miami River killed 83 people in the central area and did some $100 million in property damage.

wire from me to-morrow night. Maybe it'll be good news and maybe it won't. But you'll know pretty near as soon as I do."

I was up in Carmody's room at seven o'clock the next mornin'. I ast him if he'd said anything to Mr. Grant about me refusin' to play shortstop.

"No," he says. "I was hopin' you'd change your mind."

"Maybe I will," I says, "but not without he coaxes me."

Carmody didn't ask me what I was gettin' at. He dressed and went downstairs to find the Old Boy. And at half-past eight, in the dinin' room, the coaxin' commenced.

"Warner," says Mr. Grant, "Carmody's thinkin' about makin' a few changes in the team."

"Is that so?" I says. "What are they?"

"Well," he says, "he ain't satisfied with the way Boyle plays first base. And besides, now that Wade's hurt, he thinks Boyle should ought to go back and catch again. And he wants to try first base himself. So that would leave shortstop open."

"Maybe you could get a hold o' some semi-pro shortstopper," I says.

"I don't want none," he says. "I want a man that's had big league experience. I believe that with Carmody on first base and a good man at shortstop we could finish seventh yet. What do you think?"

"Very likely," I says, knowin' that they wasn't a chance in the world.

"I'd give a good deal to pull out o' last place," says he.

"Well," I says, "I'll see if I can't think o' some good shortstop that ain't tied up."

"You don't have to try and think o' one," says Mr. Grant. "I've got one in mind."

"Who's that?" I says.

"Yourself," he says. I pretended like I was too su'prised to speak.

"You can play the position, can't you?" he ast.

"Sure," says I. "That's where I was born and brought up."

"Well, then," he says, rubbin' his hands.

"Well, nothin'," I says. "I'm signed as a right fielder."

"We could make a new contract," he says.

"But listen, Mr. Grant," I says. "W'ile I know shortstop like a book, I don't want to play it. It's too hard. It keeps a man thinkin' and workin' every minute. One season at shortstop is pretty near as wearin' as two in the outfield. That's why I insisted on right field. I wanted to take things a little easier this year. That's why I was willin' to sign with you for $5000."

"What would you of wanted to play short?" he ast me.

"Oh," I says. "I wouldn't of thought of it for less than $9000."

He didn't say nothin' for a minute; a good long minute too. Finally he says:

"Well, Warner, they's only about six more weeks to go. But I'm wild to get out o' last place and I'll spend some money to do it, though spendin' money has been my chief business all season. I want to be fair with you, so if you'll finish out the season at shortstop I'll give you $2500 extra."

This time it was me that wanted to hug him. But I played safe. I considered and considered and considered and finally I give in.

"I'll do it, Mr. Grant," I says. "As a favor to you, I'll do it."

Out in the lobby Carmody was waitin' for me.

"It's fixed," I says. "He's a pretty good coaxer."

"What did you get?" he ast me.

"A November weddin'," says I.

I'd promised to wire Ethel by night, but the thing had been pulled a whole lot quicker'n I'd hoped for. I run right from Carmody to the telegraph office.

"All fixed," I says in my message. "I got $2500 extra."

At lunch time her answer come back:

"Good old boy. Did you hold somebody up?"

Well, sir, believe me or not, I hadn't thought of it that way before. But when I read her wire I had to admit to myself that she'd pretty near called the turn.

The less said about them last six weeks the better. I don't know how many games we was beat, but five was what we win. I felt worst about poor Steele. There he was, working' his head off two to four games a week, worth four times as much as all the rest of us together, and drawin' a salary o' $400 a month. He's with a real club this year and you watch him go!

The Crook

To-morrow mornin' you'll see a statement in the papers, signed by Ban, sayin' that it's been learned that they was some excuse for Bull doin' what he done, and that the charge of him bein' pickled on the field wasn't true, and that he's been took back on the staff. But they won't be nothin' printed about who was the dandy little fixer; my part in it is a secret between you and I and one or two others.

I don't suppose they's a ball player in the League that Bull's chased ◆ as often as me. I don't suppose they's anybody he's pulled as much of his stuff on. I can't count the times I've got cute with him, but the times I got the best o' the repartee I can count 'em on the fingers of a catcher's mitt. Just the same, it was me that went to Ban with the real dope and was the cause of him gettin' rehired, and it was me that got him his girl back, though he don't know about that yet.

I wouldn't of took no trouble in the case if it was any other umps but Bull. But I come as near likin' him as a man could like a guy that never give a close one any way but against you. And he's a good umps, too; he guesses about a third of 'em right, where the rest o' Ban's

---

"The Crook" was published in *The Saturday Evening Post*, CLXXXVIII (June 24, 1916), 18–20, 52–53.

◆ *I don't suppose they's a ball player in the League that Bull's chased as often as me.*— The narrator is first baseman on a fictional version of the White Sox.

◇ *Duff Lewis . . . Cady*—Duffy Lewis, at left, and Hick Cady, at right, flank catcher Chester Thomas in Red Sox uniforms at the time of the story. (National Baseball Library, Cooperstown, New York)

School for the Blind don't see one in ten. And another thing: I felt sorry for him when he told me the deal he got. And besides that, he's gave me too many good laughs for me to stand by and see him canned out o' the League. Many's the time I've made a holler just to hear what he'd say, and he always said somethin' worth hearin', even if it stung; that is, up to day before yesterday, when the blow-off come.

I noticed he wasn't himself when I was throwed out at the plate in the second innin'. I wanted to stop at third, but Jack made me keep ◆ goin', and Duff Lewis all ready to shoot with that six-inch howitzer he ◆◇

◆ *Jack*—Probably Jack Lapp, who caught 34 games for the White Sox in 1916. Lapp was the sort of veteran player who was so often assigned to coaching in the period. Specialized coaching staffs of the modern sort date mainly from the 1920's.

◆ *Duff Lewis*—George Edward "Duffy" Lewis (1888–1979), a fine defensive outfielder and a fixture in left field for the Red Sox since 1910. Active for the Red Sox through 1917, the Yankees in 1919 and 1920, and finally the Senators in 1921, Lewis hit .284 in 1,459 games. He achieved his greatest fame in the Lewis-Speaker-Hooper outfield of the Red Sox championship team of 1912—one of the common choices among the best outfields of all time—and he was never so effective after his wartime service as he had been earlier. After managing in the minor leagues, he was appointed coach for the Braves in 1931, and became the team's traveling secretary in 1936, a post he held both in Boston and Milwaukee until 1961. See Ellery H. Clark, Jr., "Duffy Lewis," *The Ballplayers*, p. 621.

wears in his right sleeve. Cady and the ball strolled out to see me and ◆ I couldn't get past 'em.

"You're out!" says Bull.

"He didn't tag me," I says.

And Bull didn't say a word.

In the fourth innin' Hooper was on third base and somebody hit a fly ball to Shano. Hooper scored after the catch and big Cahill run out ◆ from the bench and made a holler that he'd left the bag too quick. The ball was throwed over to third base, but Tommy wouldn't allow ◆ the play. Then Cahill went to Bull and ast him hadn't he saw it. O' course Bull says he hadn't.

"No, I guess not!" says Cahill. "Us burglars stick together." And then, on the way back to the bench, he turned to Bull and says: "You're so crooked you could sleep in a French horn."

Bull was just puttin' on his mask, but he throwed it on the ground and tore after Cahill. He nailed him right on the edge o' the dugout, and what a beatin' he give him! It took eight or nine of us to drag him off, and he managed to wallop everybody at least once durin' the action. Some o' the boys picked Cahill up and carried him to the clubhouse. He was a wreck. Bull stood there a minute, starin' at nothin'; then he turned and faced the grand stand.

"Anybody else," he yelled—"anybody else that thinks I'm a crook can come down and get a little o' the same."

Well, they wasn't no need of extra police to keep the crowd back. But Ban was settin' in the stand and o' course he wasn't goin' to just set there and not do nothin'. It was too raw. So he give orders for the cops to grab Bull and get him out o' the way before he committed murder. They led him to his dressin' room and stuck with him w'ile he changed clo'es. Then they called the wagon and give him a ride. Tommy handled the rest o' the game alone and we was beat just as bad as if nothin' had happened.

Right after the game the witnesses was examined. Cahill's lips was so swelled he couldn't hardly talk. But several of us had heard the whole thing and could testify they hadn't been no profanity. Cahill

---

◆ *Cady*—Forrest LeRoy "Hick" Cady (1886–1946), the Red Sox' second-string catcher. Cady never achieved first-string status, but played with the Red Sox from 1912 to 1917, the Indians in 1918, and the Phillies in 1919, hitting .240 in 355 games.

◆ *Cahill*—A fictional character.

◆ *Tommy*—The umpire Tom Connolly.

hadn't no license to call Bull crooked, but if an umps was goin' to fight for a little thing like that, every ball game'd wind up in a holycaust. Besides, "a crook" was one o' the mildest things Bull'd ever been called, and till this time nobody'd ever knew him to lose his temper.

As I say, his specialty was conversation. When they was a kick made, he'd generally always pull some remark that go a laugh from everybody but the fella that was crabbin', and sometimes from he himself. He'd canned plenty o' guys out o' the ball game for tryin' too hard to show him up, but he'd did it as part o' the day's work and without displayin' any venoms. I'd heard 'em tell him he was yellow, and blind, and a jellyfish, and a "homer," and a thief, and a liar; and that he'd steal the ◆ cream off'n his mother's coffee; and that his backbone was all above the neck. I'd heard 'em call him fightin' names and saw him take it smilin'. And now, because a fella made an innocent remark about him bein' crooked, and no naughty words along with it, he'd went off his bean and all but destroyed a good Irish citizen, besides intimidatin' five or six thousand o' the unemployed.

It wasn't no wonder everybody thought what they thought, though Bull hadn't never been known to touch a drop between April and October.

"I'll uphold my umpires when they're right," Ban says to the reporters; "but when they're wrong, they got to suffer for it. They's only just the one explanation for Bull's actions. So he's discharged from the staff."

"What about Cahill?" ast somebody. "Goin' to suspend him?"

"No," says Ban. "Bull saved me the trouble."

Well, Tommy fixed it up to have Bull let out o' jail and took him back to the hotel where the two o' them was stoppin'. When Tommy told him he was canned he didn't make no comments only to say that they was one good thing about the umpirin' job—you didn't feel bad if you lost it.

On my way home from the game I got to thinkin' about Bull and what a shame it was to have him let out for just the one slip, and wonderin' what he'd do with himself, and so on. So when I'd had supper I rode down to the umps' beanery to try and find him, and maybe cheer him up.

◆ *homer*—An umpire who systematically favors the home team to minimize the hostility of the crowd. Calling an umpire a homer is usually grounds for immediate ejection from the game.

He'd went out. Tommy told me he'd disappeared after askin' for his mail and not gettin' none.

"He'll come back with a fine package," says Tommy.

"Do you know what made him fall off?" I says.

"He didn't fall off," says Tommy. "That's the funny part of it. I and him was right up in my room readin' the papers all mornin'; then we had lunch and went out to the park together and got dressed and went on the field. I noticed he was grouchin', but I was with him every minute o' the day up to game time and I know for a fact that he didn't have nothin' to drink only his coffee at breakfast. Somethin's happened to him, but I don't like to get inquisitive because we haven't only been teamin' together a couple o' weeks."

I and Tommy didn't have nothin' else to do, so we set down in the writin' room and chinned. Bull, o' course, was the subject o' the conversation. You could talk about him all week and not tell half o' the stuff.

The first game he umpired in our League was openin' day in Chi, four or five years ago. It was our club and St. Louis. I guess he was about twenty-six years old then, but he didn't look more'n twenty. So the boys was inclined to ride him. Arnold, the St. Louis catcher, started ◆ on him in the first innin'.

"Did you ever see a ball game, kid?" he ast him.

"No," says Bull, "but if I make good these four days, I'm goin' to stay here for the Detroit series."

Arnold come up with the bases full and two out in the fourth or fifth. He took three healthy lunges and fanned. I led off in our half and Bull called the first one a ball. It was pretty close and Arnold, peeved about strikin' out in the pinch, slammed the pill on the ground.

"You're a fine umpire!" he says.

"I can't be right all the time," says Bull. "Even the best of us misses 'em sometimes. But I'll have to miss the next two in succession to tie your score."

We was one run ahead when the ninth begin. We got two o' them out and then Hank Douglas made a base hit and stole second. The ◆ next fella made another base hit, but Shano fielded it clean and Hank was called out at the plate.

"That's right," he says to Bull. "Favor the home team. You wouldn't be umpirin' in this league if you wasn't yellow."

◆ *Arnold . . . Hank Douglas*—Fictional characters.

"No," says Bull, walkin' away, "and you wouldn't be in the League at all if you wasn't a Brown."

In one o' the Detroit games Cobb was on second base with a man out and Crawford hit a slow ground ball between short and third. The ball was fielded to first base and Cobb kept right on for home. Parker was catchin' for us and he was a little spike-shy, especially with ◆ Cobb. So when the ball was relayed to him from first base he backed off in an alley somewheres and give Tyrus the right o' way. Somebody hollered from the bench that Cobb hadn't touched third.

"Yes, I seen it," says Parker to Bull, lookin' for an alibi. "He cut third base."

"I don't know about that," Bull says, "but it's a safe bet that he'll never cut you."

Bull went with us for our first series in Cleveland that year. They was a fly-ball hit to Lawton in the third and he muffed it square, lettin' ◆ in a couple o' runs. As soon as he'd dropped the ball he looked up in the sky and then stopped the game till he'd ran in and got his glasses, though it was so cloudy that we was hurryin' to beat the rain. Right afterward, when Lawton come to bat, Bull called a strike on him.

"Too high! Too high!" says Lawton.

"Maybe it was," says Bull, "I lost it in the sun."

A little w'ile later the Cleveland club had a chance to tie us up. It was some left-hand batter's turn to hit, but they was a cockeye pitchin' for us, so they sent up a kid named Brodie, a right-hander, to pinch ◆ hit. He swung at the first one and missed it. The next one was called a strike, and w'ile he was turned round, arguin' with Bull about it, another one come whizzin' over and Bull says:

"You're out!"

"It wasn't a legal delivery," says Brodie.

"Why not?" says Bull. "His feet was on the slab and you wasn't out o' your box."

"You got a lot to learn about baseball," says Brodie.

"I'm learnin' fast," says Bull. "I just found out why they call your club the Naps."

He didn't put nobody out of a game till along in the middle o' that season. We was playin' Washin'ton and Kennedy was in a battin' slump. ◆ He was sore at the world and tryin' to take it out on the umps. He'd throwed his glove all over the field and tossed his cap in the air and

---

◆ *Parker . . . Lawton . . . Brodie . . . Kennedy*—All fictional characters.

beefed on every decision, if it was close or not. He struck out twice, and when Bull called a strike on him his third time up, he stooped over and grabbed a handful o' dirt.

"A yard outside!" he says, and tossed the dirt to'rds Bull.

"Well, Mr. Kennedy," Bull says, "if there is a yard outside, that's where you better spend the rest o' the afternoon."

"Am I out o' the game?" says Kennedy.

"Hasn't nobody told you?" says Bull. "You been out of it pretty near two weeks."

"You're about as funny as choppin' down trees," says Kennedy.

"Go in and dress," Bull told him. "Maybe you'll find your battin' eye in your street clo'es."

The next day Bull was umpirin' the bases. Kennedy didn't get suspended, and when he come to bat in the first innin' and seen that Bull had switched, he yelled to him: "Congratulations! You ought to do better out there. It's a cinch you couldn't do worse."

"Walter," says Bull to Johnson, who was pitchin', "give Kennedy a base on balls. I want to talk to him."

In the last game o' the series Kennedy finally did get a hold o' one and hit it for two bases.

"Now it's my turn to congratulate you," Bull says to him.

"Oh," says Kennedy, "I can hit 'em all right when they's a good umps behind that plate."

W'ile he was still talkin', whoever was pitchin' wheeled round and catched him a mile off'n the bag. Bull waved him out and he started to crab.

"Go on in to the bench, Kennedy," says Bull. "The game must look funny to you from here anyway."

Big Johnson worked against us in Chi one day and he had more stuff than I ever seen him have. Poor little Weber, facin' him for the ◆ first time, was scared stiff. He just stood there and took three. Next time, he struck at one and let the next two come right over. Bull, who was back o' the plate, couldn't help from laughin' and the kid got sore.

"Why don't you call 'em all strikes!" he says.

"I would," Bull says, "only they's just a few o' them I can see."

Well, Weber's third trip up there was just like his first one. He didn't even swing. And after Bull had called him out for the third time, he says:

◆ *Weber*—Fictional character.

"Fine work, umps! You ought to go to an oculist and get the dust took out o' your eyes."

"Yes," says Bull, "and you ought to go to a surgeon and have the bat removed from your shoulder."

One afternoon Jennin's started a kid named Sawyer against us. He ◆ was hog wild and he throwed ten balls without gettin' a strike.

"It looks like a tough day for us, Bull," says Stanage.

"Well, anyway," Bull says, "my right arm needs a good rest."

When two fellas had walked and they was two balls on the next one, Sawyer pitched a ball that you could of called either way. Bull called it a ball.

"What was the matter with that one?" says Sawyer.

"You pitched it," says Bull.

He was base umpire once when Walsh caught Carney flat-footed ◆ off o' third base. It was in the ninth innin' and they was only the one run behind us, so Carney begin to whine.

"Kind o' drowsy, eh?" says Bull. "I'll bet your mother was up all night with you."

Before the end of his first season he had the boys pretty well scared o' that tongue of his'n and they weren't none o' them sayin' much to him. But o' course, durin' the winter, they forgot how he could lash 'em, and when spring come again he was as good as ever. It's been that way every season since. Along about this time, and up to July, they're layin' themself wide open and takin' all he can give. Then, from July on, they're tired o' being' laughed at and they see they can't get the best of him, so they lay off.

Not me, though. I beef on every decision he makes against me all season long. I can get as good a laugh when it's me that's the goat as when it's somebody else.

He's pulled some pippins on me. I wisht I'd wrote down even half o' them, but anyway they don't sound as good when I tell 'em as when he sprung 'em on me.

I remember we was playin' our last series with the Boston club in 1912. They'd cinched the pennant already and nobody cared a whole lot how our games come out. I've got plenty o' friends in Boston, and the first night we was there I neglected to go to bed. So the next afternoon I was kind o' logy.

◆ *Sawyer . . . Carney*—Fictional characters.

I dropped a couple o' thrown balls at first base and was off the bag ◆ once when I had all the time in the world to find it. Well, Bull had three or four close ones to guess and he guessed 'em all against us.

"Are you goin' to work in the World's Series?" I ast him.

"I haven't heard," he says.

"If you do," I says, "I'm goin' to bet my season's pay on the Red Sox."

"If you're lookin' for easy money," says Bull, "why don't you go ahead and bet your season's pay on the Red Sox, and then sign with the Giants to play first base?"

In 1914 I'd been havin' a long spell o' bad luck with my hittin' and they was just gettin' ready to bench me when one day, in St. Louis, I got one safe. I tried to make two bases on it, but overslid the bag and Bull called me out.

"Oh, Bull!" I says. "Have a heart."

"They won't bawl you for this," says Bull. "You ain't been here in so long it's no wonder you forgot where the station was. I think you done pretty well to remember my name. I been umpirin' the bases for two weeks."

Then they was once in Boston, just last year. We still had a chance yet and we was crazy to take a fall out o' that bunch. I was overanxious, I guess. Anyway, it was a tight game and in the sixth or seventh innin' I got caught off o' first. "Bull," I says, "if you're with the home club, why don't you wear a white suit?"

"Larry," says he, "you ought to play ball in your pyjamas."

And in New York one day I give somebody the hit and run, and the ball fooled me and I didn't swing. The fella was throwed out at second base, and Bull called it a strike on me.

"Why, Bull!" I says. "He was wastin' that ball."

"Sure he was," says Bull. "All the good balls is wasted on you."

And once in Washin'ton, we was two runs to the good in the ninth and had two men out and it looked all over. The next man—Milan, I think it was—hit a fly ball straight up and I hollered I was goin' to take it. Well, it just missed beanin' me and Milan pulled up at second base. The next fella hit a ground ball between I and the bag. I missed it clean. Milan scored and the other fella stopped at second. Then

◆ *I dropped a couple o' thrown balls at first base*—The actual first baseman of the White Sox in 1912 was Rollie Zeider.

somebody made a three-base hit. The score was tied and the winnin' run was on third base.

A slow ground ball was hit down to'rds me. I seen that Doran, who ◆ was pitchin', was goin' for the ball instead o' the bag and I seen that the ball was mine and I'd have to get it and chase back with it myself. I done it as fast as I could and the play was mighty close. Bull called the man safe. It meant the game and we was all sore, but me especially, on account o' them two flivvers.

"You blind owl!" I says to Bull. "Who told you you could umpire?"

"Who recommended you to Griffith?" says Bull.

That's the way he was. You could set up all night and figure out what you was goin' to say to him next day, and then when you said it, he'd come back with somethin' that made you wish you hadn't. That is, unless you was like me and kept after him just for the laughs he give you.

I and Tommy set there talkin' till pretty close to midnight. Then we decided they wasn't no more use waitin' for Bull. So Tommy went up to his room and I moseyed out the front door and onto the walk. I hadn't took more'n a couple o' steps when I seen the guy we'd been fannin' about. He was just goin' in to the hotel bar. I followed him.

"Hello, Bull!" I says, when we was both inside.

"What's the idear?" he says. "Did you come clear down here to tell me that Cady didn't tag you?"

"No," I says. "He tagged me all right. But I'm taggin' you to find out what's got into you."

"I guess I got plenty into me now," says he. "When a man that's cold sober gets fired from his job for bein' lit, they's only the one thing to do. I've been tryin' my best all evenin' to deserve the reputation they've wished on me."

I give him the double O. He could walk straight and he could talk straight. But he was kind of owl-eyed and his face looked like a royal flush o' diamonds.

"Let's have somethin'," he says.

"You've had enough," says I.

"That's no sign I ain't goin' to have more," he says.

"You better go to bed," I says.

◆ *Doran*—A fictional character, but the name is an adaptation of George H. Doran, publisher of the first book edition of *You Know Me Al*.

"What for?" says he. "I got nothin' to do to-morrow or any other to-morrow. I'm through."

"They's other leagues," says I. "You won't have no trouble gettin' a job."

"I don't want no job," says Bull. "I haven't no use for a job."

"What are you goin' to live on?" I ast him.

"I don't want to live," he says.

"Aw, piffle!" says I. "You'll feel better for a good night's sleep."

"Well," says Bull, "they's just as much chance o' me gettin' a good night's sleep as they is o' them playin' part o' the World's Series in Peoria."

"Bull," I says. "I believe they's somethin' botherin' you outside o' losin' your job."

"You're too smart to be playin' ball," he says.

O' course I knowed then that Tommy'd been right—that the old boy had had a blow o' some kind. And I was mighty curious to learn what'd came off. But I realized it wouldn't get me nothin' to ask.

We h'isted three or four together without exchangin' a word. Then, all of a sudden, I seen a big tear streakin' down Bull's cheek and in another minute I was listenin' to his story.

Bull's parents is both dead—been dead five or six years. He never had no brothers or sisters or aunts or uncles or nothin'. He was born down South somewheres and didn't have no use for cold weather, but his old man moved to Buffalo when Bull was about sixteen, so from that time till his mother and father died he spent his winters, and the summers before he went to umpirin', up North. They wasn't no reason why he shouldn't suit himself after the old people passed out, so back South he went for his winters. He stayed in New Orleans the first couple o' years, but it cost him a pile o' money. Then he tried Montgomery, and that's where he met the lady.

Her name's Maggie, Maggie Gregory. Bull described her as the prettiest thing he ever seen, and so on. The Gregorys didn't have so much dough that they didn't know how to spend it. In fact, they was kind o' hard up. The head o' the house worked in a hardware store for somethin' like fifteen a week. He had a son named Martin; yes, sir, the same Martin Gregory that Connie Mack let go last week and ◆ we got signed up now.

◆ *Martin Gregory*—A fictional character.

Martin and Maggie was twins. Maggie was learnin' the milliner trade, but at the time Bull met 'em Martin wasn't workin' at all, except durin' meals. He was one o' the kind o' guys that'd rather go to the electric chair, where he could be sure o' settin' down, than attend the theater and take a chance o' havin' to stand up w'ile they played the Star-Spangled Banner. If he'd lived in a town where they wasn't no letter carriers he wouldn't never got no mail. He'd of starved to death in a cafeteria with a pocket full o' money.

He treated the whole of his family like they was waiters, and they treated him like he was the Kaiser. His mother was crazy over him, and Maggie used to split fifty-fifty with him on her princely salary. The old man never called him, and seemed to just take it for granted that Martin was born to have the best of it.

Bull landed in Montgomery the same time that the Gregorys made up their mind to take a boarder. They put an ad. in the paper and Bull answered it. He answered it in the evenin', when Maggie was home. After gettin' a look at her, he'd of stayed there if they made him sleep in the sink and give him nothin' to eat but catnip.

Maggie and Martin was eighteen then. They ain't no use o' me tryin' to give you Bull's description of her. Martin, accordin' to Bull, was a handsome kid and had the best clo'es his sister's money could buy. He was built like an ath-a-lete and his features was enough like the girl's to make him good-lookin'. Bull fell for him this first night; he didn't know nothin' then about the feud between Martin and Work.

Well, they all treated Bull like he was an old friend and made him feel more like it was his own house than just a place to board. Maggie smiled at him every time she seen him, though it wasn't no case o' love at first sight on her part; she was just tryin' to be friendly. The old lady worried if he didn't take nine or ten helpin's o' whatever was on the table, and kept his room as neat and clean as Martin's. The old man played rummy with him three or four times a week and give Bull good laughs on all his quick stuff. And Martin took kindly to him, too, figurin' probably that the dough Bull paid for board would mean more dude clo'es in the wardrobe. Bull says he never knowed what this here Southern hospitality was till he went to live with the Gregorys.

It wasn't till Bull had been there about three weeks that he told 'em what he done for a livin'. Well, the old people and Maggie didn't know nothin' about baseball except that Martin, when he was a kid, had been the best player in the school where he attended at. He'd told 'em so. But Martin himself, it turned out, was a nut on the national pastime. He knowed who Cobb was and who Matty was and their records, right down to little bits o' fractions. Not only that, but he went to see the Montgomery bunch perform whenever they had the courage to face the home crowd. So Bull was a hero to him, in spite of his profession.

At meals, Martin wouldn't talk nothin' but baseball, and Bull had to talk it with him. I suppose the proud parents and Maggie felt kind o' sorry for Bull, figurin' that the kid, bein' perfect, was gettin' all the best of him in the arguments. The old boy was foxy enough to see that the easiest way to win Maggie was by helpin' to make Martin look good. So when they'd got about so far in a fannin' bee, Bull'd stop dead and say, "By George! You're right," even if Martin was arguin' that Walter Johnson ought to learn to throw left-handed and play third base.

Bull thought he was just a fresh kid. He thought the reason he wasn't workin' was probably because he'd lost a job and hadn't found another. He liked Martin O. K. till he begin to suspect that he was too proud to toil. It was the old lady that give him the hunch, when she says somethin' about the kid's delicate health.

"Yes," Bull says to himself, "he's awful delicate lookin', like Frank ◆ Gotch."

Before the winter was half over, Bull was givin' 'em the time o' their lives, takin' 'em somewheres every other night. It was a pipe that Maggie liked him, and it was a bigger pipe that she had him on her reserve list, with no chance to get away. But he was too shy to talk to her about anything but the climate; he says she was the first girl he was ever scared of.

Along in March, some o' the Montgomery ball players showed up ◆ for their trainin'. Bull always took some work in the spring to get himself hard and fix up his wind pipes, so that year he joined the local bunch and done stunts with them. Martin ast to go along with him the third or fourth day. So out they went together to the Montgomery orchard and Bull got the biggest su'prise of his life.

Instead o' settin' up in the stand and lookin' on, Martin peeled down to his shirtsleeves and busted right into the practice. He tackled

---

◆ *Frank Gotch*—Frank Alvin Gotch (1878–1917), the leading professional wrestler of the period. Except briefly in 1906, Gotch was world's heavyweight professional wrestling champion from 1905 until his retirement in 1913.

◆ *Montgomery*—Montgomery, Ala., had a franchise in the Class C South Atlantic League in 1916, but the team withdrew on June 21. The city had no club in 1915, but had been in the Southern Association previously.

the high-low game first, and Bull says to see him at it you wouldn't of ◆ never believed it was the same boy that wouldn't drink coffee unless you held the cup to his mush. Baseball wasn't work to him—it was fun. And that made the whole difference.

Well, Martin showed so much life the first day that Bull borrowed a suit for him and fixed it with the Montgomery gang to leave him frolic round their park as much as he liked. And he wasn't no joke with the ath-a-letes. He didn't know nothin', but he had as much mechanical ability as you ever see in a kid. He could whip the ball round like a shot, and he was good on ground balls and he swung the old stick like it was a lath. Bull give him a lot o' pointers and so did the rest o' the boys, and by the time Bull was ready to go North, Martin was good enough to hold down an infield job somewhere in the brush.

Maggie and old Gregory was as proud as peacocks. The old woman was proud, too, but she was scared to death that the pet would get beaned or stepped on and killed. Bull finally convinced her that baseball was as safe as ridin' in a rockin-chair, and Martin was allowed to keep on with the only exercise he'd took in years, outside o' puttin' on his pyjamas at night and pullin' 'em off in the mornin'.

Bull left Montgomery with the understandin' that he could have his room when he come back in the fall. Maggie squeezed his hand when she told him good-by, and that, Bull says, along with the post cards she sent him, was all that kept him alive that summer.

In June the Gregorys sent him a clippin' from a Montgomery paper. Martin had been signed by the Montgomery club to play second base, and he looked like the best thing that had broke into the Southern League in years.

The second off-season that Bull spent with the Gregorys he was still too shy yet to make any play for the lady, outside o' blowin' all his loose change in showin' she and her folks a time. But last fall, after they'd gave him his bit for workin' in the big series, and he felt like he had enough financial backin' to justify the plunge, he wired her to meet his train and he pulled his speech on her w'ile his nerve was still with him.

She didn't say yes or she didn't say no. She told him she liked him a whole lot bettern'n anybody except Brother Martin, and she appreciated his kindness to all o' them, and so on. But it would take a lot o'

◆ *the high-low game*—A fielding drill in which the ball is thrown alternately high and low to prepare infielders for batted and thrown balls in the game to follow. See *Dickson's Baseball Dictionary*, p. 200.

thinkin' to decide the question, and could he wait? So he says he could do anything for her and they left it go at that.

As soon as they was off'n the subject, she begin to talk about Martin and what he'd been doin' in baseball. She admitted that he was the greatest ball player south of Alaska, but o' course the Montgomery club didn't give him a fair show on account o' bein' jealous, and the manager kept him on the bench half the time for the fear some big league scout'd see him and steal him away from Montgomery. What she wanted Bull to do was tell some manager in our league about him, and have him bought. Martin would do the rest; he'd show 'em if he ever got the chance.

Well, Bull told her it was against the rules for an umps to recommend ◆ a ball player to a club in his own league. It wouldn't be fair to the Boston club, for instance, if Bull give Detroit first whack at a second Cobb. O' course Bull knowed that plenty o' scouts must of saw Martin and passed him up, and that the Montgomery club wasn't tryin' to conceal a man for who they could get a big price.

She ast him if he couldn't get some friend to do the recommendin' if he couldn't do it himself. He told her he was scared his part in it would be found out. Then she says that he must care a lot about her if he was afraid to take a little risk like that. He told her he'd try and think of a way to swing it, but she must give him time.

He found Martin more of a dude than ever and as modest as a wrestler. He couldn't talk about nothin' but how much better he was than the Southern League, and it was easy to see from his clo'es that he wasn't contributin' nothin' to the family except conversation and his personal attendance at meals.

Hatin' yourself, though, ain't nothin' against a ball player. Take most any real star and when the dialogue ain't about him he's bored to death, and if he has a bad day, pitchin' or hittin' or whatever it is he does, it's plain tough luck or rotten umpirin'.

So Bull didn't think none the less o' Martin's ability on account o' the size of his chest, even if he did get good an' sick o' hearin' nothin' but Martin, Martin, Martin, all day and half the night.

Bull would of gave anything if Maggie and the rest o' them had

◆ *it was against the rules for an umps to recommend a ball player to a club in his own league.*—This rule, which dates from 1913, stems from the outcry against Cy Rigler's recommending Eppa Rixey to the Phillies in 1912. At present, Rule 28:04 of the National Agreement merely prohibits an umpire from accepting compensation for such recommendations; it does not literally prohibit the recommendation itself.

forgot their scheme to land the pet in the big menagerie. But they wasn't a chance. When he'd rather of been hearin' that she cared somethin' about him, she was eggin' him on to hurry up and think of a way to bring Brother to the attention o' the real people.

In December Bull read in the paper that Ted Pierce, the manager ◆ o' the Montgomery club, was in town. He made a date to meet him and find out just how good Martin was.

"He's just good enough to of pretty near drove me wild," Ted told him. "If we're ten runs ahead and he comes up with the bases full, he'll hit one from here to Nashville. Or if we're fifteen runs behind in the last half o' the ninth with two out, it's fifty to one that he'll get to first base. But put him up to that plate when everything depends on him and you'd think he had paralysis o' the arms. He'll take three in the groove and then holler murder at the umps."

"Plain yellow, eh?" says Bull.

"I don't like to say that about nobody," Ted says. "But if the old U. S. called for volunteers, I'd bet on Benedict Arnold to beat him to the front."

"Ain't they no chance of him gettin' over it?" ast Bull.

"I've tried everything," says Ted. "I've called him all the names I could think of. I've tried to jolly him too: I've told him the pitchers was all scared of him and all he'd have to do was swing that club. But he's just as bad as when he broke in."

"He's a kid yet," says Bull. "It may be just stage fright."

"It may be," says Ted. "He certainly is cocky enough most o' the time; it's only in a pinch that he loses it."

"I'm a friend of his family," says Bull. "I'd like awful well to see him move up."

"You wouldn't like it no better'n me," says Ted. "I'd like to see him move anywheres. I'm sick o' lookin' at him. If you can sell him for any kind of a price, I'll give you half of it."

"You know I couldn't sell him," says Bull. "But if somebody else recommended him to somebody and I was ast about him, I'd do my best."

"Well," says Ted, "I ain't goin' to recommend him, nowheres, unless it's to a fella I got no use for. I'm goin' to try again in the spring, and if he don't quit chokin' to death every time he's got a chance to be a

---

◆ *Ted Pierce*—Apparently a fictional character. Montgomery's manager in 1914, its most recent year in the Southern Association, was Robert James Gilks.

hero, I'll tie a can on him whether he's a friend o' yours or Woodrow Wilson's."

"Outside o' that, he's a good ball player, is he?" says Bull.

"They ain't no man I ever seen with more natural advantages," Ted told him. "His record shows that he hit .329 and stole thirty-two bases and fielded as good as any second baseman in the league. But he didn't make none o' those base hits when we'd of gave a thousand dollars apiece for 'em, and when he could of pulled a pitcher out of a hole with a swell piece o' fieldin' he simply booted the ball all over the infield."

"They's just the one hope for him, then," says Bull, "and that's to go out and get some o' the old nervine."

"If you can make him do that," says Ted, "I'll guarantee to sell him to any club you name."

So Bull, that night, told Maggie that Martin was still shy of experience and needed at least another year in minor league ball before he could hope to stick up with the E-light. He figured that he could work on the kid all the rest o' the winter and maybe succeed in stingin' him enough with hot conversation to get that streak out of him.

But Maggie right away wanted to know where Bull'd got his information and Bull had to tell her.

"No wonder!" says Maggie. "Pierce never did have a good word for him. Him and all the rest o' them's jealous."

"You're mistaken," says Bull. "Pierce wouldn't like nothin' better than to sell him for a good price."

"All right," says Maggie, "if you think I'm mistaken, that shows you don't care nothin' about me."

So Bull didn't have no answer to that swell argument only to beg her pardon and say she was probably right.

Well, it finally come to a kind of a showdown; Bull was either to see that Martin got his chance this spring or he'd have to worry along without Maggie. She didn't come right out and say that the way I've put it, but she made it plain enough so's they wasn't much chance to misunderstand.

Bull kicked the sheets round for a few nights and then got his idear. O' course the first thing was to pick a club that was tryin' to build up, and if possible to pick one that had a manager who'd pay the right kind of attention to a kid. Bull chose Connie as the best bet. The next thing was to persuade Connie to give Martin his trial. Bull wanted to be perfectly square, as you'll see by the deal he put through. He got a fella there in Montgomery with a good Irish name to write to Connie and recommend the boy, and if Connie didn't believe Martin was a good prospect he was to ask Bull about him, and if Martin didn't make good he wouldn't cost Connie nothin', not even his railroad fare to the trainin' camp and back. Bull framed it up with Ted Pierce as a matter o' friendship to leave the boy go on trial, and if he did su'prise 'em all and make good, the Montgomery club was to get whatever Connie was willin' to pay.

Well, the letter was sent and Connie wrote back to Bull, and says a boy named Gregory had been mentioned to him, and ast Bull was he worth a trial. Bull answered that Gregory was a kid with great natural ability and one or two faults that'd have to be overcome. Then Connie fixed it with the Montgomery club, and Bull thought he'd finished his job.

But he found out different. W'ile Maggie consented to becomin' engaged, she wasn't in no hurry to get married. She says her parents was gettin' old and she didn't want to leave 'em all summer, and besides, she didn't have no clo'es, and besides, it would be a whole lot nicer to wait till fall and spend the honeymoon where they'd first met each other and when Bull was just startin' his vacation instead of endin' it. Bull coaxed and coaxed, but her rules was just like his'n—she couldn't change a decision on a question o' judgment.

In the three weeks before Martin was to report in Jacksonville, Bull ◆ done nothin' but try and shoot him full o' confidence.

"The pitchers down here have got everything you'll see in the big league," he told him. "You don't need to be afraid o' none o' them. A man that handles a bat the way you do can hit anything in the world if he'll just swing. Connie or any other manager don't care how many times you strike out in the pinch, provided you strike out tryin'. You got the stuff in you to make Cobb and Baker and them look like a rummy. Don't get scared; that's all."

Bull pulled that talk on him right up to the day the kid left Montgomery. Down at the train, Bull says to him:

"Remember, they's nothin' to be scared of. Make us all proud o' you! Make good!"

"I'll make good if they give me a square deal," he says.

"Yes," Bull says to himself, "it's a cinch it'll be somebody else's fault if he falls down. It always is."

◆ *Martin was to report in Jacksonville*—The Athletics trained in 1916 at Jacksonville, Florida.

Well, in a little w'ile it come time for Bull to leave, too. And here's what the girl sprung on him at the partin':

"You'll help him all you can, won't you?" she says.

"They's not a chance for me to help him," says Bull. "A man in my place can't favor nobody."

"A man could," she says, "if a man knowed it would please the girl he was stuck on."

Now if it'd of been me that she made that remark to, I'd of ast for waivers. But you know what they say about love bein' blind. And when it's a combination o' love and an umpire—well, how can you beat it!

Bull kept close tab on the papers and he seen that Martin was at second base in the lineup o' the Ath-a-letics' regular club. This was w'ile they was still South. Then, in one o' their last exhibitions before the season started, Martin's name was left out. He wrote to the kid and he wrote to Maggie, tryin' to find out what was doin'. Maggie wrote back that she didn't know and Martin didn't answer at all.

The season begin and Bull was workin' in the West. Every mornin' he grabbed the papers and looked to see if Martin was back in. Four times in three weeks the kid went up to bat for somebody, but without doin' no good. Then come the second week in this month and the first series between the Eastern clubs and us.

Bull had the Detroit-Philadelphia series. Just before the first game he run into Connie outside o' the park. They shook hands and then Bull says:

"Didn't you ask me about a ball player this winter?"

"Yes," says Connie, "a boy named Gregory."

"How's he comin'?" says Bull.

"I don't think he's comin'," says Connie. "I think he's just gettin' ready to go."

"What's the trouble?" ast Bull.

"Well," says Connie, "once in a w'ile our club happens to not be ◆ more'n two or three runs behind, happens to have a chance to tie or win. Gregory's one o' the kind o' ball players that spoils them chances.

◆ *once in a w'ile our club happens to not be more'n two or three runs behind, happens to have a chance to tie or win.*—The Athletics of 1916, the year of the story, are the usual choice as the worst team in the modern history of baseball. They finished last with a 36–117 record, for a .235 percentage, lowest of the twentieth century. The team finished 40 games out of seventh place. See George Robinson and Charles Salzberg, *On a Clear Day They Could See Seventh Place: Baseball's Worst Teams* (New York: Dell Publishing Group, 1991), pp. 65–91.

In practice down South he looked like a find. He hit everything and fielded all over the place. But we got into some tight exhibitions on the way up and when the opportunities come to him to do somethin' big he faded away. He ain't there in a pinch; that's all."

"Is he with you yet?" Bull ast him.

"He's with us," says Connie; "he's with us for one more trial. If they's a place in this series where I can use a substitute hitter, Gregory's goin' to be the man. And if he don't swing that club the way he can swing it when it don't mean nothin', I'll hand him his transportation back to Montgomery."

"Does the kid know that?" ast Bull.

"Yes," says Connie, "and if they's any stuff in him the knowledge that this is his last chance should ought to bring it out."

"You mean," says Bull, "that if he strikes out again in a pinch he's through?"

"No, I don't," says Connie. "I mean he's through if he doesn't try to murder that ball. I don't care if he strikes out on three pitches, just so he swings."

"But suppose," says Bull—"suppose they don't throw him nothin' he can hit; suppose they walk him."

"O' course," says Connie, "if the count gets down to two and three, I'd want him to pass the ball up if it was bad. But if it was where he could reach it, I'd want him to take a wallop, just to show me he ain't scared."

So that's how Martin stood with Connie at the beginnin' o' this series between the Ath-a-letics and Detroit.

The thing didn't happen the first day. The game wasn't close and Martin watched it all from the bench. Bull talked to him, but didn't get what you could call a cordial welcome. Bull wasn't su'prised at that; they ain't no ball player that'll kid with an umps when his dauber's down. He refused Bull's invitation to come round to the hotel that night and have supper with him. And Bull decided that the best play was to leave him alone.

They was a letter from the girl waitin' for Bull that evenin'. She'd heard from her brother and she knowed that he wasn't burnin' up the League; but he'd confessed that Connie hadn't treated him good and the umpires had robbed him blind. She knew, she wrote, that Bull wouldn't cheat him; if Bull really cared for her, he'd help him if he got a chance. And it would kill her and her father and mother besides if Martin had to face the disgrace o' not makin' good.

Bull went to bed and dreamt that Martin was up in a pinch, and he

◇ *Big Coveleskie*—Harry Coveleski, at left, in the uniform of the 1917 Detroit Tigers, shaking hands with his brother Stan of the Cleveland Indians. (National Baseball Library, Cooperstown, New York)

was umpirin' behind the plate, and Martin turned round and looked at him just before the ball was pitched, and Bull smiled at him to encourage him, and Martin took an awful wallop at the pill and give it a ride to the fence in right center. That's what Bull dreamt before the second game o' that series. And here's what really come off:

Big Coveleskie and Bush was havin' a whale of a battle. They wasn't ◆◇

◆ *Big Coveleskie*—Harry Coveleski (1886–1950), Detroit's star lefthander, who was winning 22 games in 1916, the third consecutive year he had won over 20 for the Tigers. He was not effective thereafter, and in 1918 closed out a major league career in which he won 81 and lost 57, playing for the Phillies, Reds, and Tigers. His smaller and younger brother, Stan Coveleski, won 214 games for the Indians and three other American League clubs. See Joseph Lawler, "Harry Coveleski," *The Ballplayers*, p. 228.

◇ *Right across the middle it come, as perfect a strike as was ever pitched*—Drawing by M. L. Blumenthal for *The Saturday Evening Post*, June 24, 1916.

nobody scored till the eighth. Cobb got on then, with only one out. So that give Detroit a run. The ninth looked to be all over. Two o' the Ath-a-letics was out. Then somebody got hold o' one and lit on it for three bases, and what was left o' the crowd decided to stick round a w'ile.

Bull says he knowed Martin was comin' up before he ever looked. And he smiled at him when he announced himself as the batter.

Coveleskie come with a fast ball. Martin had to duck to keep from gettin' hit. Coveleskie come with a curve. Martin made a feeble swing and missed it. Jennin's hollered from the bench:

"Run out with the water! The boy's goin' to swoon!"

Another curve ball that broke over, and Martin left it go.

"Strike two!" says Bull.

"It was inside," says Martin.

"You'll never drive in that run with a base on balls," says Bull.

Coveleskie come with a curve that was high and outside. It was the second ball. He come with another curve, in the same spot. It was three and two.

"Give him all you got!" yelled Jennin's. "Get it over there! He's too scared to swing!"

Bull told me that w'ile Coveleskie was gettin' ready for that next pitch he could see Maggie and the old folks in front of him just as plain as if they was there, and a voice kept sayin' to him, "Call it a ball! Call it a ball!"

The ball come—a fast one. Bull knowed what it was and where it was comin', and he bit his tongue to keep from sayin' "Swing!" Right ◇ across the middle it come, as perfect a strike as was ever pitched. And Martin's bat stayed on his shoulder.

"You're out!" says Bull. "It cut the heart!"

The heart o' the plate, and Bull's too, I guess.

Bull met Connie again next day, outside o' the park.

"I've canned your friend Gregory," says Connie.

"Do you know," says Bull. "I come near callin' that last one a ball?"

"If you had," says Connie, "the kid would of been let out anyway, and you'd of fell, in my estimation, from the best umpire in the league to the worst in the world."

Now what does dear little Brother Martin do next? Instead o' goin' back to Montgomery like a man and tryin' to get a fresh start with the club that he'd been borrowed off of, he sets down and writes Maggie that Connie would of kept him only for Bull callin' him out on a ball that was so low and so far outside that the Detroit catcher had to lay down to get it, and that Bull done it because he didn't like him, and if Maggie didn't tie a can to Bull, Martin was through with her and with the old man and old lady too.

Well, the girl wrote back to Bull callin' off the engagement, sayin' how sorry her and her parents was to find out that he would stoop to such meanness and askin' him not to communicate with her no more. And Bull's bull-headed enough so as he wouldn't make a move to square things.

He got the letter from her day before yesterday, just before he left his hotel to come out to the yard. Is it any wonder he didn't say nothin' when I claimed Cady didn't tag me, and went entirely off'n his nut when Cahill called him a crook?

W'ile he was spillin' me the story I got enough into him to make a good sleepin' potion, and then helped him to the hay. The first thing yesterday mornin' I seen Ban and fixed that end of it by repeatin' the romance. But don't never breathe that Ban knows all about it. Bull thinks he's takin' him back because it was his first offense. And he's comin' back; Ban says he's promised to be in there to-morrow.

And right here in my pocket I got somethin' to show him that'll be better news than gettin' back his job. As luck would have it, I was the first guy to get to the park yesterday, and when I blowed into the clubhouse, who was settin' there but young Mr. Gregory himself! He told me his name and wanted to know was they any chance of him gettin' a try-out with us?

"Yes," I says, "they's one chance and you'll get it if you do as I say. Connie couldn't of gave you to the Montgomery club again if we hadn't waived. But I'll fix it for you to join us to-morrow and try your luck again on these conditions: In the first place, you got to go right out now and wire your sister and tell her that the ball you was called out on was right through the middle o' the plate and the best strike you ever seen, and that Connie would of released you anyway, and that if your sister don't wire right back to Bull, in my care, statin' that she's reconsidered and it's still on between she and him, you won't never recognize her as your sister."

"And what if I won't do that?" he says.

"You won't get no chance at a job here," says I, "but you'll get the worst lickin' that was ever gave."

He sent the telegram and I got a night letter this mornin'; addressed to Bull it was, but I read it. I've been tryin' to locate him all day and he's goin' to call up as soon as he gets back to his hotel. Everything's fixed and to-morrow he'll feel so good that he's liable to forget himself and give us somethin' but the worst of it.

As for Martin, if he don't make good with our club it'll be because he can't hit and not because he's too scared to try. I'll have him too scared o' me to be scared of anything else.

The Hold-out

Three people, not countin' myself, think I'm the greatest guy in the ◆ world. One o' them's my first and last wife, another's Mr. Edwards, and the other's Bill Hagedorn.

It'd be hard to pick three that I'd rather have cordial. If a person is livin' with their wife, it makes it kind o' pleasant to have her like you. Mr. Edwards, o' course, is the man I'm workin' for, so it don't hurt me at all to be his hero. And I'm glad to have Bill added to the list, because it means he'll play the bag better for me this year than he's done yet, and with a little pep on first base we're liable to be bad news to George Stallin's, Wilbert Robinson and John J. McGraw. ◆

But listen: If Mr. Edwards ever got hold o' the truth o' the Hagedorn

---

"The Hold-out" was published in *The Saturday Evening Post*, CLXXXIX (March 24, 1917), 8–10, 49–50.

◆ *Three people*—The characters in this story are entirely fictional.

◆ *George Stallin's*—George Tweedy Stallings (1867–1929), manager of the Braves from 1913 to 1920. He had managed Philadelphia in the National League in 1897 and early 1898, Detroit of the American in 1901, and New York of the American in 1909 and 1910. His principal achievement was winning the 1914 pennant with the Braves, to earn him the sobriquet of "The Miracle Man." Stallings' major league playing experience was very limited. He caught four games for Brooklyn in 1890 and played three for the Phillies while managing them. In 20 times at bat, he had two hits. See Norman L. Macht, "George Stallings," *The Ballplayers*, pp. 1034–35.

business, him and I'd be just as clubby as Lord George and the Kaiser. If he didn't drop dead when he found it out, he'd slip me the tinware, contract or no contract, and I wouldn't have the heart to fight it in the courts, because I admit I gave him a raw deal. My only alibi is that I left my feelin's get the best o' me, and that excuse wouldn't be worth a dime with him; they's no excuse that would be, where his pocket-book's concerned, like in this case. He just simply hates money!

The worst of it is that Hagedorn didn't deserve no consideration. I like to see a fella get all that's comin' to him, provided he goes after it in the right way and puts up a real fight. Hagedorn made a hog of himself and was tremblin' all the time he did it. If he was as yellow on the ball field as when he's makin' a play for more dough, I'd take away his uniform and suspend him for life; he wouldn't be no more use to me than a set of adenoids.

He's just as game a ball player, though, as you'll find. The minute he trots out there in the old orchard he's a different guy, afraid o' nothin'. All he's lacked so far is ambish, and I figure he'll show some o' that this year. He'll give me his best out o' gratitude. If he don't, it'll mean his finish on the big time, family or no family.

It's part o' my agreement with Mr. Edwards that I stick on the job all the year round, goin' to the league meetin's with him in winter, helpin' him sign up the boys, and so forth. Well, after we was through last fall, he called me up in the office and begin crabbin' about finances.

"Frank," he says, "we lost $18,000 this season. I pretty near wish I didn't have no ball club."

"You've pretty near got your wish," I says. "If some o' those bushers don't come through next spring, or if we don't swing a couple o' deals between now and then, the clubs that play against us won't even get good practice."

"Bad as we are," he says, "I bet we got the biggest salary list in the big leagues. It looks to me like not only one or two, but several of our men were bein' overpaid."

"Yes, sir," I says; "and on their showin' the last few months some o' them would be overpaid if they drawed a dollar a day."

"Well," he says, "I'm goin' to do some trimmin'. The boys'll kick, I suppose, but I'm dependin' on you to show 'em they deserve cuts."

"That's a nice little job for me," I says. "It's just as easy to convince a ball player that his pay ought to be trimmed as it is to score twelve runs off Alexander."

"I'd just as leave pay good prices for good work," he says, "but I'm not goin' to maintain no pension bureau. These ridic'lous Federal

League contracts have all run out, thank heavens, and from now on my ball club'll be run on a sane basis. Look at Lefty Grant!" he says. "He got $7000 and pitched pretty near eleven full games, winnin' three o' them. And look at Hagedorn! A $6000 contract and no more life in him than a wet rag! What do you suppose ailed him?"

"Federalitis," I says. "He was gettin' soft money in the Federal, with no incentive to win and nobody to try and make him hustle."

"A $6000 salary," says Mr. Edwards, "for a man that hit round .220 and played first base like he was bettin' against us! Maybe we'd better just let loose of him."

"If I was you," I says, "I'd see what the recruits is like before gettin' rid o' Hagedorn. I'll admit he's been loafin', but he's a mighty good ball player when he tries."

"Maybe it'll wake him up to cut him," says he. "I'm goin' to send him a contract for $4000."

"Suit yourself," says I. "He'll holler like an Indian, but if he sees you're in earnest I guess he'll come round."

"He lives here in town," says Mr. Edwards. "I'll have the girl call him up sometime and tell him I want to see him."

So we discussed a few others that was gettin' way more than they earned, and the boss says he wouldn't play no favorites, but would cut 'em all from ten to forty per cent. I knew they'd be plenty o' trouble, but I didn't care a whole lot. I figured that if everybody on the pay roll quit the game and went to work it'd strengthen the team.

Well, Hagedorn accepted Mr. Edwards' invitation to call and I was in the office when Bill come in.

"Mr. Hagedorn," says the boss, "Manager Conley and myself's been talkin' things over and we come to the conclusion that several o' you boys was earnin' less than we paid you. What do you think about it?"

"Well," says Hagedorn, "some o' the boys maybe deserve cuts. But I don't see how I come in on it."

"Why not?" says Mr. Edwards. "The unofficial average gives you a battin' percentage o' .220."

"I can't help what them dam scorers do to me," says Bill. "I never did get fair treatment from the reporters."

"But when you was in the league before," says the boss, "you always hit up round .280, and it's a cinch the scorers didn't cheat you out o' sixty points."

"They'd cheat me out o' my shirt if they had a chance," Bill says. "But even if I did have a bad year with the wood, that ain't no sign I won't do all right next season."

"That's true enough," says Mr. Edwards. "Anybody's liable to have a battin' slump. But Manager Conley and myself wasn't thinkin' about your hittin' alone. We kind o' thought that your work all round was below the standard; that you was sort o' layin' down on the job."

Hagedorn began to whine.

"Mr. Edwards," he says, "you got me entirely wrong. I wouldn't lay down on nobody. I've give you my best every minute, and if I haven't it was because things broke bad for me."

"What things?" I ast him.

"Well," he says, "for one thing, I felt rotten all summer. My legs was bad."

"Well," I says, "you can't expect Mr. Edwards to pay $3000 apiece for bad legs."

"But they're all right now," he says. "I haven't had a bit o' trouble with 'em all fall. And I'm takin' grand care o' myself and next spring I'll be as good as ever."

"Why didn't you tell me about your legs?" I ast him. "I'd of let you lay off. You certainly wasn't helpin' us much."

"I'd of told you only I don't like to quit," he says. "And besides, my legs wasn't the whole trouble."

"What else was it?" I says.

"Well," he says, "the Missus was sick and in the hospital, and I had to pay out a lot o' money and it kept me worried."

"When was she sick?" I ast him.

"Let's see," he says, "it was while we was on our last Eastern trip."

"You never ast me to let you come home," I says.

"No," he says, "I didn't know nothin' at all about it till we got back."

"That's why you worried, I suppose," I says, "and I guess your wife's illness in September was what worried you in June and July."

"She was sick on and off all season," he says.

"I noticed," says I, "that she done most of her sufferin' in a grand-stand seat. Her ailment," I says, "was probably brought on by watchin' you perform."

"She's full o' nerve," he says. "She wouldn't miss a ball game if she was dyin'. And besides, her sickness wasn't all of it."

"Let's hear the whole story at once," I says. "The suspense is fierce."

"Her folks kept botherin' us," says Hagedorn. "They live in Louisville, and they're gettin' old and they wanted that she should come down there and stay with 'em."

"Couldn't they come up here?" I ast him.

"No," he says, "they got their own home and their own friends and everything down there."

"Well," says I, "that'd probably be the square thing for you to do, just pack up and move to Louisville and live with 'em."

"We'd only be there in the winter," he says.

"No," says I, "I'll fix it so's you can be there all the year round."

"What do you mean?" he says.

"I mean that if you don't want to sign at our figures Louisville'd be the ideal spot for you," says I.

"What's your figures?" he ast.

"I'm willin' to give you $4000," says Mr. Edwards.

Hagedorn swelled up.

"If you think I'll take a $2000 cut, you got me wrong," he says.

"All right," says I, "and I hope the Kentucky climate agrees with your legs."

We sent Lefty Grant a contract for $5000 and after a little crabbin' by mail he signed. Joe Marsh stood for a $1000 cut, and Bones McChesney, shaved from $3500 to $3000, refused to sign and got himself sold to Toronto. I didn't cry over losin' him; he'd always been fat from his neck up, and in the last two seasons the epidemic had spread all over his body.

Now it don't often happen that a seventh-place club begins lookin' like a pennant contender between October and February. But that's what come off with us. Our worst weakness last year was at shortstop and third base and back o' the bat. Well, I talked to a lot of Association men durin' the fall, and they told me that I had a second Schalk in this young Stremmle from Indianapolis. And I got swell reports on Berner, the shortstop we drew from Dayton. Both these guys, I was told, were ready. They wouldn't need no more seasonin'.

And then along come the league meetin' in New York, and I happened to catch the St. Louis gang when they were thinkin' about somethin' else, and they traded me Johnny Gould for Hype Corliss and Jack Moran, two guys that I'd kept down in the bull pen all summer so's the bugs couldn't get a good look at 'em. There was my third base hole plugged up and the ball club was bound to be a hundred per cent better, provided Hagedorn signed and give us his best work, or that young Lahey, the first sacker we bought from Davenport, made good. I wasn't worryin' much about him, as I figured right along that Hagedorn would take his $4000 when he seen we were in earnest.

O' course he had a little bit the best of us in the argument—that is, he would of had if he'd knew enough. Him and Lahey was the only candidates for first base, and no matter if he played the position in a hammock, he'd be better than an inexperienced kid from the Three ◆ Eye. Even if he wasn't never worth a nickel over $4000, here was a grand chance for him to hold us up. All he had to do was lay quiet at home, and when it come time for us to go South we'd of looked him up and met his demands. But no, he didn't have the nerve or sense to go at it the right way.

Instead o' keepin' us guessin', what does he do but hunt up excuses to come and hang round the office and try and get a hint o' whether we were goin' to stand pat or back down. I was alone the first time he showed.

"Hello, Bill," I says. "Did you bring your fountain pen?"

"What for?" he says.

"To sign that $4000 contract," says I.

"Oh, no," he says. "I wasn't thinkin' nothin' about the contract. I come up to see if they was any mail for me."

"Not now," I says, "but you may be hearin' from the Louisville club in a few days."

"What would they be writin' me about?" he says.

"Maybe they'll hear about you wantin' to move there," I says, "and they'll probably be askin' you if you'd care to take a job with 'em."

"Well," says Bill, "you won't catch me playin' ball with Louisville."

"Who was you thinkin' about playin' with?" I ast him.

"Nobody," he says. "I've decided to quit."

"That's fine, Bill!" I says. "Sombody left you money?"

"No," he says, "but I got some o' my own saved up."

"How much?" I ast him.

"Close to $2000." says Bill.

"Fine work!" says I. "You must of lived pretty simple to save $2000 in seven years."

"I never skimped," says Bill.

"Well," I says, "I don't know how you managed. But it's nice to feel that you won't never have to skimp again. If you can get six per cent

---

◆ *Three Eye*—The Indiana-Illinois-Iowa League, invariably known as the Three-I League. A Class B minor league operating in secondary Midwestern cities to the west of the Central League, the Three-I was the better known of the two, and usually the stronger. Typical or at least frequent members were Peoria, Moline, Quincy, Decatur, Springfield, Rockford, Rock Island, Davenport, Cedar Rapids, Waterloo, Terre Haute, and Evansville. The league operated from 1901 to 1951, with suspensions for World Wars I and II and the Great Depression.

for your money, that'll mean $120 a year or $10 a month. That puts you on Easy Street. All you'll have to get along without is food, clothes, heat and a place to live."

He paid us another visit Christmas week, thinkin', maybe, that Mr. Edwards would be runnin' over with holiday spirits.

This was a bum guess. The old man's got more relatives than a perch, and when he was through buyin' presents for all o' them he wouldn't of paid a telephone slug for the release o' Ty Cobb.

"No mail yet," I says to Bill when he come in.

"I wasn't expectin' no mail," he says. "I was just wonderin' if I left a pair o' gloves here last time."

"A pair o' tan gloves?" I says.

"Yes," says Hagedorn.

"I didn't see 'em," I says. "I found some gray ones."

"How is everything?" he says.

"Fine!" says I. "It looks like we're goin' to have a regular ball club."

"Well, I hope you do," Bill says.

"Gould's goin' to help us a lot," says I, "and they tell me Stremmle and Berner's both good enough for anybody's team. And then, o' course, we got young Lahey."

"Who's young Lahey?" ast Bill.

"Can't be you never heard of him," I says. "He's the first sacker from Davenport that everybody was after. They say you can't hardly tell him from Hal Chase when he's in action. And he cracked the marble for about .340 last season."

"Hittin' .340 in the sticks and hittin' it up here is two different things," says Hagedorn.

"Not so different," I says. "A bird that can hit .340 anywhere can hit pretty good."

That's right, too. But the truth was that Lahey's figure had been eighty points shy o' what I credited him with. And from what I'd learned from some o' the Three Eye boys, Lahey was the eighth best first baseman in their league.

"Well," says Hagedorn, "if he makes good, you won't have no use for me."

"No," I says, "but I'd hate to see you go back in the bushes."

"Don't worry!" he says. "I'm goin' to stick right here in town."

"And live on your savin's?" I says.

"No," says Bill. "I'm just about signed up to play with the Acmes in the semi-pro league."

"How much are they givin' you?" I ast him.

"Fifty a game, and they only play Sundays," he says.

"Yes," says I, "and they're doin' well if they play twenty games a season. That nets you $1000, and you'll have somethin' like six days a week to spend it in."

"I can work at somethin' durin' the week," he says. "Maybe sell automobiles or somethin'."

"You could do that in the winter, too," I says, "if you didn't waste so much o' your time comin' for your mail and lookin' for your gloves."

"How's Mr. Edwards?" says Bill.

"Fine and dandy!" I says. "Want to see him?"

"What would I want to see him about?" says Bill.

"You might be able to sell him a car," says I. "He's right in the spendin' mood now. His nieces and nephews and Mr. Wilson's peace note has relieved him o' the few hundreds he had left after last season. I wouldn't be surprised if he'd reconsider cuttin' your contract—maybe give you a bonus for the devil of it."

While we was talkin' Mr. Edwards come out from his private office.

"Hello, Hagedorn," he says. "Ready to sign?"

"At my own figure," says Bill.

"That's good," says Mr. Edwards. "Conley and myself was afraid you might accept the cut, and we couldn't hardly afford to keep an extra first baseman at $4000 a year."

"It's best all round," I says. "Bill's goin' to make more dough than we could possibly give him; he's goin' to sell cars durin' the week and play semi-pro ball Sundays. And maybe he can master the barber trade and pick up a few extra hundreds Saturday nights. But even if he don't make a nickel, he's got $2000 hoarded up."

"That's fine!" says the boss. "I like to see thrift in a young man. And it always seems like a pity that so many boys squander their earnin's and have to keep on slavin' as ball players till they're thirty years old and past the prime o' life."

For three or four days early in January they was an epidemic o' lockjaw in Washin'ton, and the market come up enough for Mr. Edwards to take a trip to New Orleans. He left me in charge o' things, and my job consisted o' makin' up stories for the newspaper boys and entertainin' Hagedorn about once a week.

Once he dropped in to find out Joe Marsh's address; it'd of been impossible, o' course, to inquire by telephone. Another time he just happened to be passin', and happened to remember that he was carryin' a letter that his wife had ast him to mail, and wanted to know if I had a stamp.

I entertained him every time with dope on Lahey and what a whale of a man he was goin' to make us. But one day he come up loaded with some real facts about the guy I'd been boostin'.

"I thought you told me Lahey hit .340 with Davenport," he says.

"I did tell you that," says I.

"Well," says Bill, "somebody was stringin' you. I seen the Three Eye records the other day and they give Lahey .262."

"That don't mean nothin'," I says. "The scorers probably had it in for him."

"And he made more boots than any first baseman in the league," says Bill.

"That shows he was hustlin'," I says. "The more ground you cover, the more you're liable to kick 'em round. Besides," I says, "he was so perfect that the scorers probably thought he'd ought to make plays that would be impossible for a common first sacker."

"Another thing," says Hagedorn: "I happened to run acrost Jack Wells that played in the league with him, and he tells me Lahey's a left-hand hitter. Well, Gould's a left-hand hitter and so's young Berner, and you already had two left-hand hitters amongst the regulars. Your club's goin' to be balanced like a stew on a wild broncho. McGraw and them'll left-hand you to death."

"What do you care!" I says.

"It's nothin' to me," says Bill.

"Well, what do you suppose we better do about it?" I ast him.

"If I was you," he says, "I'd try and get myself a first baseman that hits right-handed."

"It's too late to get anybody," says I. "I guess we're just plain up against it. I wisht you hadn't made up your mind to retire."

"I'd play for you," says Bill, "if you'd meet my price."

"That's up to the old man," I says, "but I know he won't back down. He wouldn't give in to one man when he's stood pat on all the rest o' them."

"It won't be just one man," says Bill.

"What do you mean?" I ast him.

"He'll be lucky if he's got anybody when the showdown comes," says Bill. "The fraternity's give orders that nobody's to sign till you hear ◆

◆ *The fraternity*—Baseball players had made several unsuccessful efforts at unionization as a collective defense against the monopsony held by the owners. John Montgomery Ward organized the Brotherhood of Professional Base Ball Players in 1885, but it perished with the failure of its creation, the Players League of

from them, and you won't hear from them till the leagues meets its demands."

"That don't affect our club," I says. "We got every man already signed up except yourself."

"Yes," says Hagedorn, "but signed up or not signed up, they won't report till the fraternity tells 'em to."

"You've been playin' long enough to know better'n that," says I. "If you think any ball player's goin' without his prunes to help out some other ball player, you got even less brains than I figured."

"They'll have to strike if the fraternity says so," says Bill. "They're goin' into the Federation o' Labor and be like any other union. And if they don't strike when they're ordered to they'll be canned out o' the fraternity."

"Well," I says, "suppose you was Ty Cobb, draggin' down a measly $16,000 a year, or whatever he's gettin'. Which would you do if the choice come up, go without the $16,000 or go without the fraternity?"

"I'd certainly stick with the fraternity," says Hagedorn. "If I didn't, I'd be a traitor."

"If I make you out a contract for $6000, will you sign it?" I ast him.

"Sure," he says. "I always told you I'd sign for my price."

"Well, Bill," I says, "I won't give you the contract. I'd hate to think I'd made a traitor out o' you."

"I don't want no contract anyway," says Bill. "I'm through. I'm goin' into business."

"What business?" I says.

"Somethin' pretty good," he says. "I and a friend o' mine's goin' in partners in a garage."

"That's a great idear!" syas I. "You won't have no competition, and it won't cost nothin' to start, and besides that, it's a game you know more about than any other, unless it's dressmakin'."

"My friend knows all about it," says Bill, "and I can pick it up from him."

"You better stick to pickin' up low throws," I says. "It takes years to learn the mechanism of a car when you don't know nothin' to start,

---

(*continued from page 581*)
1890. The Protective Association of Professional Baseball Players, founded in 1900, died quickly. The reference is to the Base Ball Players' Fraternity, formed in 1912. The Federal League's rivalry with Organized Baseball caused a decline in interest in the Fraternity, but it survived until about 1918. See Gerald W. Scully, *The Business of Major League Baseball*, pp. 32–33.

not even what makes the front wheels run. But o' course you won't be the only one in the garage business that has to learn, and so long as it's other people's cars you wreck while you're learnin', why what's the difference!"

"They's good money in a garage," says Bill.'

"I know it, and a whole lot of it's mine," I says. "They's good money in any business like that—smugglin' or counterfeitin' or snatchin' purses. But it must be hell on a man's conscience, even worse'n drawin' $6000 per annum for takin' a six months' nap on the old ball field."

The first thing Mr. Edwards ast me when he got back from the South was what was the latest dope on Hagedorn.

"He's surprised me," I says. "I thought he'd give in long before this. But nothin' doin'."

"What will we do about it?" says the boss.

"Mr. Edwards," I says, "you're the man that's payin' me my money, and it's my business to look out for your interests. If Hagedorn had of kept away from here all winter, if we hadn't heard nothin' from him from the day he first turned down the contract, I'd say give him his $6000. But him comin' round here once a week shows that he needs us as much as we need him, and that he'll stand for the cut if he's got to. Besides, he's showed a mighty poor opinion o' me by expectin' me to believe all that junk about him goin' into business, and so on—stuff that was old in the Noah's Ark League. He couldn't earn a dime a day in anything outside o' baseball. If he had a factory that made shells out o' lake water, he'd be bankrupt in a month. Now they's probably four better first basemen than him in the league, but I doubt if more'n one o' them's drawin' $6000. O' course with him on the ball club it looks like we'd be somewheres up in the race, and we ain't got a chance with a busher playin' the position.

"If it was a case o' givin' him his dough or gettin' along without him, I'd rather see him get the money even if it's a holdup. But if I'm any judge of a ball player, he'll come round here on his hands and knees the day before we start for the Springs, and he'll sign at whatever price you offer him."

"It's a shame," says Mr. Edwards, "when everything else looks so good for us, to have to be worryin' about a man like him, that loafed on us all last summer and that I'd get rid of in a minute if I had somebody in his place. I suppose they's no chance o' tradin' for a first baseman at this stage."

"Oh, yes, they's a chance," I says. "I suppose Matty'd let us have Chase if we'd give up our pitchin' staff and half a dozen infielders

◇ *Schupp*—Lefthander Ferdie Schupp of the Giants in 1913 or 1914. (National Baseball Library, Cooperstown, New York)

and $40,000 or $50,000 in cash. Then we'd have Chase and nothin' with him."

"Maybe young Lahey'll surprise us," says the boss.

"It won't hurt us to hope," I says, "but from what I can learn Bill Doyle was mad at you when he recommended him. And besides," I says, "Lahey's a left-hand hitter, and that'd mean five o' them in the game every day. We'd be a set-up for fellas like Schupp and Smith ◆◇

◆ *Schupp*—Ferdinand Maurice Schupp (1891–1971), a lefthanded pitcher of the Giants about to have his best season, 21–7 in 1917. Schupp pitched for the Giants from 1913 to 1919, the Cardinals until 1921, Brooklyn later in 1921, and the White Sox in 1922, winning 62 and losing 39 in ten seasons. Like several other players, he was unable to regain his effectiveness after his service in World War I. See Alan Asnen, "Ferdie Schupp," *The Ballplayers*, p. 976.

Smith—Sherrod Malone Smith (1891–1949), a lefthander of the Dodgers. After brief trials with the Pirates in 1911 and 1912, Smith pitched for the Dodgers from 1915 until late 1922, and then for the Indians until 1927. In 14 seasons he won 113 and lost 118. See Norman L. Macht, "Sherry Smith," *The Ballplayers*, p. 1016.

◇ *Smith*—Dodgers lefthander Sherry Smith warming up, 1915. (National Baseball Library, Cooperstown, New York)

and Tyler. Take Hagedorn, and he can murder a left-hander even when he ain't hittin' his weight against a regular pitcher."

"Well, all we can do is wait," says Mr. Edwards.

"And I don't think it'll be long," I says.

But when the night come for us to start South, Hagedorn was still a hold-out, though he did show one more sign o' weakenin'. He was down to the station to shake hands with the boys and see us off, and he looked like he was ready to cry. I called him off to one side.

"Would you like to be goin' along, Bill?" I ast him.

"Oh, I don't know," he says.

"Why don't you take your medicine and hop aboard?" I says. "Your missus can pack up your stuff and send it after you."

"I'll go if you say the word," he says.

"You're the one that must do the talkin'," says I.

"Why couldn't I go along without signin'?" he says. "Maybe the old man would meet my figure when he seen how hard I'd work to get in shape."

"No," says I; "this ain't no charity excursion we're runnin'. We pay nobody's fare that ain't signed up and a member o' this ball club. If you want to sign at $4000, they's a contract right there in my grip. If you don't, why you can spend the rest o' the winter countin' snowflakes and cursin' the coal trust."

"Well," he says, "I'll freeze to death before I'll be robbed; starve to death, too, before I'll let old Edwards bull me out o' what's comin' to me."

"I'm sorry, Bill," I says. "But anyway, good luck to you."

"Good luck to you too," says Bill. "You'll need it."

"Oh, I don't know," I says. "I got a hunch that it's goin' to be a great year for everybody in baseball."

"Well," says Hagedorn, "I know some fellas that'll have a great year."

"Who do you mean, Bill?" I ast him.

"All the left-handers that pitches against your ball club," he says.

About half the baseball reporters on our papers know somethin' about the game. The other half's kids that can write cute stories, but don't know a wild pitch from a hit and run sign. This was the half that went on the spring trip with us. The old heads was sent with the Americans, because they'd made a fight for the pennant last year and the public was strong for 'em.

Well, I took advantage of our gang bein' green and made 'em perjure themself to their papers every day. When they'd come to me for the dope, I'd rave to 'em about what a world-beater young Lahey was, and how he'd burn up the league as soon as I'd learned him a few o' the fine points o' first-base play. If they'd been wise they could of told with one look that Mr. Lahey wouldn't do. But they were just kids and they ate it up. I bet if any o' the fellas that had played with Lahey read what I was sayin' about him in the papers they must of thought I was crazy.

My idear, o' course, was to worry Hagedorn. I knew he'd be readin' everything he could find about us, and I didn't want him to get the impression that the ball club was goin' to bust up without him.

I thought Mr. Edwards would have sense enough to get this. But no; he fell just as hard as the reporters. And when he joined us after we'd been at the Springs two weeks, he was all smiles.

"Well," he says, "I been readin' some mighty encouragin' news."

"What news?" I says.

"About Lahey," says he. "I told you he might surprise us."

"He's surprised me in one way," I says. "I'm surprised that he ever had the nerve to come on this trainin' trip. I always thought pretty well o' the Three Eye League till I seen him," I says.

"You're jokin'," says Mr. Edwards. "I've read nothin' but good reports of him."

"I'm responsible for the reports," I says, "but I thought you'd guess that I was fakin' for Hagedorn's benefit."

"Well, if you've fooled Hagedorn, he's got company," says Mr. Edwards. "I thought our troubles was all over."

"Our troubles won't never be over if Hagedorn don't give in," I says.

"But Lahey must be some good, the way he was recommended," says the boss.

"Doyle probably seen him just once," I says, "and that must of been the one good day he had. But even at that, Doyle couldn't of never watched him handle his feet and thought he was a ball player."

"Is it just his feet that's the trouble?" ast Mr. Edwards.

"No," I says, "but they'd be plenty without outside help. We've had infield practice about nine times since we been here, and that means he's got nine hundred self-inflicted spike wounds. And they must of kept first base in a different place down to Davenport. Anyway he can't find it here. And when he does happen to stumble onto it, it's always with the wrong foot. Besides that, every time Gould or Berner makes a low peg Lahey loses a tooth. Gould ast him one day why he didn't wear a mask. But you ought to see him field bunts! If experience counts for anything, he'd ought to be the most accurate thrower in the world, from a sittin' posture."

"How about his hittin'?" the boss ast me.

"He's a consistent hitter," I says. "They's a party from Kansas City stoppin' at the hotel. They come out to every practice and always set in the same place, right back o' the plate, behind the grandstand screen. Well, every ball Lahey's hit so far has made 'em duck."

"Does he act like he had stage fright?" says the boss.

"Not him!" says I. "Nobody but the gamest guy in the world could cut off a few toes every day and come out the next day for more. And nobody without a whole lot o' nerve could keep diggin' after low throws when he knows that they're goin' to uppercut him in the jaw. No, sir! You can't scare Charley!"

"Charley!" says Mr. Edwards. "I thought his name was Mike."

"Gould's nicknamed him Charley," I says, "after Charley Chaplin."

Well, the boss wasn't what you could call tickled to death with my dope on Lahey, but he cheered up a little when I told him about Gould and the rest o' them. Gould was goin' even better than when he was with St. Louis. He was hustlin' like a colt and hittin' everything they throwed up there. And he kept coachin' young Berner like he'd been hired for that job. He put real pep in the infield, and I knew it was tough for him to keep it up when Lahey gummed pretty near every play that was pulled.

Berner cinched his job the first day out. He's the kind of a kid that just won't stay on the bench, as lively and full o' fight as little Bush, at Detroit, or Buck Weaver, or Rabbit Maranville. And Stremmle come up to everything they said about him. Then Joe Marsh seemed to of got over the Federal League and acted five years younger than he is. And our outfield was workin' hard. O' course this young Sheppard showin' up so good helped a lot and made the rest o' them hustle.

I told Mr. Edwards, I says:

"Outside o' first base, I wouldn't trade this ball club for McGraw's. These boys have got more spirit than any team I ever managed. They're the kind that's liable to upset the whole league. If we only just had a good reliable man on that bag, I'd almost guarantee to finish one-two-three."

"And do you still think Hagedorn's goin' to join us?" the boss ast me.

"I certainly do," I says. "I wouldn't be surprised to get a wire from him any day."

But we went along another week without hearin' from Bill. Mr. Edwards kept gettin' more and more nervous. And I guess I was beginnin' to get nervous too.

About the second day o' the third week down there, a letter come to me from Hagedorn's wife. It hit me right in the eye.

Bill, she told me, didn't know she was writin' and would probably kill her if he found it out. She'd been beggin' and beggin' him all winter to take what we offered, and she'd just about had him coaxed when the papers begin printin' the swell reports about Lahey. Those reports had took all the zip out o' Bill. Instead o' frightenin' him into signin' at our figure, they'd convinced him that he wasn't wanted on our club. And Bill was worse than broke. He was over three months behind with the rent and the meat bill and so forth, and coal was a hundred dollars a ton, and they wasn't no coal even at that price, and she was afraid he'd do somethin' desperate. And she thought if I'd just send Bill a wire and tell him that we'd carry him as an extra man, or if I'd try and trade him somewheres where he could make some kind of a salary, he'd be so tickled that he'd come to us or go wherever we sent him at whatever price he could get. And she begged me to not tell anybody that she'd wrote.

Mr. Edwards had just left us to run down to Dallas for a few days.

O' course I wouldn't of let him know about the letter anyway. But him bein' away give me the idear o' keepin' Bill's comin' a secret. I was goin' to surprise him by havin' Bill blow in unexpected, because it was a cinch the old man'd be back before Bill could get there. So I didn't wire Dallas, but just sent a telegram to Bill, sayin', "If you'll sign for $4000, first-base job is yours. Answer."

The answer come the same night. It said all right, that he'd join us the followin' Thursday.

On Wednesday Mr. Edwards come back to the Springs. And that afternoon Charles C. Lahey give the funniest exhibition I ever seen on a ball field. The whole practice was a joke, because Gould and Berner and Marsh and the rest o' them was laughin' so hard they couldn't do nothin'. But the wind-up come near not bein' a joke. It'd of been a tragedy if Lahey wasn't the awkwardest guy in the world.

We was tryin' the double play, first base to second base and back. I hit a ball pretty close to the bag and it took a nice hop, so they wasn't no chance for Charley to boot it. He pegged down to Berner, and then turned round and started lookin' for his own bag. Berner took the throw and sent it back as fast as I ever seen a ball pegged. Well, sir, Lahey found out where first base was by trippin' over it. But just before he tripped he turned his head to look for the throw. If he hadn't tripped and went sprawlin', that ball would of cracked him right in the temple, and if it had, good night! To show you how much Berner had on it, it hit the grandstand on the short hop and made a noise like somewheres in France.

"That'll do, boys!" I hollered to them. "We'll quit. The express rates on caskets between here and Davenport is somethin' fierce."

I walked back to the hotel with Mr. Edwards. I never seen a guy so blue.

"He's impossible," he says.

"Never mind," says I. "He won't be with us long. One o' these days his luck'll desert him and he'll get killed."

"I think we'd better send for Hagedorn," says the boss.

"Oh, no," I says. "He'll show up before long."

"Yes," says Mr. Edwards; "but he'd ought to be here right now to get used to playin' with Gould and Berner. And I ain't so sure he'll show up, neither."

"I'd like to make you a little bet," I says. "I'd like to bet you five that we hear from him before the end o' the week."

"I'lll just take that bet," says Mr. Edwards, "and I'll be glad to pay if I lose."

Well, knowin' him pretty well, I didn't hardly believe that. But I told him the bet was on.

The first train into the Springs from the North is supposed to arrive at nine in the mornin' and it don't hardly ever get in later than 3 P. M. On this Thursday it come at one-thirty. I snuck down alone to meet it, and there was Bill. "Mighty glad to see you, Hagedorn," I says.

"I'm glad to get here," says Bill.

"You don't need to work to-day if you don't want to," says I, "but we want you out there as soon as you feel like it."

"Why, what's happened to this wonderful Lahey?" says Bill.

"Not a thing," I says; "but, as you pointed out, he's a left-hand hitter, and we're overloaded with 'em."

"I suppose you'll play him when they's right-hand pitchin' against us," says Hagedorn.

"No," I says, "I don't believe in switchin' on the infield. Still, you'll have to keep hustlin' to hold him on the bench. He's one o' the most remarkable first sackers in baseball."

"I'm just as good as he is," says Bill.

"You'll have to show me," I says.

"That's just what I'm goin' to do," says Hagedorn.

"And how's everything at home?" I ast him.

"Well, Frank," he says, "it's been a tough winter—the toughest I ever put in. I'm in debt so far that it scares me to think of it."

"Where was that $2000 you had saved?" I says.

"I was just stringin' you about that," says Bill. "I never had a nickel saved. But $2000 is just about what I'm behind."

"Good lord, Bill!" I says to him. "What have you done, bought a limousine?"

"No, sir," he says. "I ain't bought nothin' only clothes and food and not much o' that. But I was way in the hole before, and just this week they've ran up about $200 more on me."

"What for?" I ast him.

"Well, Frank," he says, "the wife presented me with a little boy last Sunday mornin'. If it hadn't been for that, and the way she worried about things, I'd of never been down here to sign for $4000. It was a case of have to, that's all."

I'd left orders for the boys to be out for practice at a quarter to two, and I knew Mr. Edwards would be out there with 'em. I and Bill was pretty near to the hotel by this time, but I stopped him short.

"Bill," I says, "you ain't givin' me no bull like that $2000 fortune, are you?"

"No, Frank," he says, "I'm tellin' you the truth."

"All right, Bill," I says; "I'm takin' your word. They's a northbound local train leavin' here at three bells. You go down and get aboard it and ride to Silver Creek. That's a station about twenty miles up the line. They's a hotel there, and that's about all. You go there and stay till I send for you."

"What's the idear?" he says.

"You'll find out later," I says. "I just tell you now that it's to your interest to do what I say."

"I can't go nowheres," he says. "I've got just forty cents."

"I'll stake you," says I, "and you'll hear from me in three or four days."

"But I want to get out there and see this here Lahey," says Bill. "I want to get busy showin' him up."

"He'll tend to that end of it himself," I says. "But you're on this ball club and I'm manager of it, and if you want to stick on this ball club you'll obey the manager's orders."

So Bill took the local for Silver Creek and I beat it out to the orchard to see that nobody got killed.

I set down with the boss at supper that night.

"Mr. Edwards," I says, "I've changed my mind about Hagedorn."

"What do you mean?" he says.

"I mean that I think he's through with us," I says.

"But good lord!" says the boss. "We can't get along without him."

"Well," says I, "we can get him by givin' him $6000."

Mr. Edwards shook like he had a chill.

"Give in to him now!" he says. "When he's tried to hold us up! And I thought you was so sure he'd come round."

"I did think he would," says I, "but I'm sure now that he won't. He's stuck this long, and he'll stick forever. He's gamer'n I figured."

"But I'd rather lose another $18,000 than let him hold us up," says the boss.

"Well," I says, "that's up to you. But you'll lose the $18,000 all right, and then maybe some, if you don't get him. Because without him on first base we'll be the worst ball club in the league."

Mr. Edwards didn't say nothin' more for maybe five minutes. Then he give up.

"I got a lot o' confidence in you, Frank," he says. "I'll go by what you tell me. If you want to you can wire Hagedorn. Tell him we'll meet his terms, and tell him to get here on the first train."

"I think it's the best thing to do," I says. And I went out and pretended to send Bill a wire.

It takes two days and a half to get to the Springs from home. So I called Bill up at Silver Creek and had him blow into camp on the Sunday train. I met him and tipped him off. He fell all over himself thankin' me and says he was goin' to name the boy Frank. And then he made a request.

"Keep this a secret from my missus," he says. "I want her to think that I got what I was after because I insisted on it. Because she kept tellin' me all winter that I wouldn't never get it and was a sucker to try."

"Don't worry," I says; "I want it to be kept a secret from certain people myself, and I certainly ain't goin' to spill it to no woman."

Mr. Edwards was on the walk in front o' the hotel when I and Bill showed up.

"Well, Hagedorn," he says, "you got what you wanted and I hope you'll try and earn it."

"I'll earn it all right, Mr. Edwards," he says, "and I'm mighty grateful to you for comin' acrost."

The boss turned to me.

"How about our little bet?" he says.

"What bet?" says I.

"You bet me five," he says, "that we'd hear from Hagedorn before the week was over. And this is another week."

"So you want me to pay you that five?" I ast him.

"I certainly do," he says.

Well, I give him the five, and afterwards Bill told me he'd make that up to me as soon as he could. But I can't accept it from him. I'd feel like I was takin' candy from a baby, a baby named Frankie Hagedorn.

The Yellow Kid

The first thing we found out about Crosby was that he couldn't read. ◆ The next thing was that he was scared to death o' women and girls. It was Buck Means that give us the info., and he done it out o' spite.

You see, Buck and Crosby was with the Dallas Club together year before last, and Buck was sore because Crosby got drafted, while Buck was overlooked. And Buck didn't like to see a kid with only one year's experience go up, when Buck himself had been in the sticks four or five seasons and nobody'd paid any attention to him.

Crosby was recommended to us by Jake Atz. Jake wrote up along ◆ in July and ast if we could use the fastest young left-hander he ever seen. So the old man put in a draft and we got him.

Well, Jake was right about the kid's speed. I've faced 'em all, from Rube Waddell down, but I never hit against nobody that could zip 'em through there like Crosby. If he ever beaned a man they'd have to get along afterwards without no head. O' course that wouldn't be no

---

"The Yellow Kid" was published in *The Saturday Evening Post*, CLXXXIX (June 23, 1917), 8–10, 69.

◆ *we*—The team is a fictional version of the White Sox. With the exception of Jake Atz, the minor league characters are fictional.

◆ *Jake Atz*—The story is set during Atz's long managership of Fort Worth, from 1914 to 1929.

hardship to most o' them. It wouldn't affect the work o' nobody on our club.

Our first exhibition game last spring was in Dallas. Buck Means was talkin' to Gilbert and I before the practice.

"How's Crosby comin'?" he ast us.

"I'm glad he's on our club," I says, "so I don't have to hit against him all season."

"He's faster'n Johnson," says Gilbert. "If he was only a little wild with it they'd all be swingin' from the bench."

"They's no doubt about his smoke," says Buck, "but he's got nothin' besides, not even a noodle. He can't even read."

"Can't read!" I says. "Why, he looks brighter'n that."

"Sure!" says Means. "He's a good-lookin' kid. But, from the shoulders up, he's unimproved property."

"Not bein' able to read won't hurt him," I says. "He won't be bothered if the newspaper boys handle him a little rough once in a while."

"But if you got a joker on your club," says Buck, "Crosby'll be pie for him. McGowan, one of our outfielders, made a monkey of him all last year. He'd buy a paper and come and set down somewheres near Crosby and make up stuff that was supposed to be in there, and read it out loud. And he didn't 'read' no compliments, neither, except when it come to Crosby's looks. You see, that's another thing about the poor simp: He's afraid o' skirts. He's so bashful that if they's a girl under ninety stoppin' at the same hotel he'll duck out and buy a meal at his own expense rather'n take a chance o' havin' her look at him in the dinin' room. And McGowan, while pretendin' that the papers was knockin' him as a pitcher, pretended, besides, that they were always printin' how handsome he was and how all the girls was wild about him. And, to make it good, Mac'd write fake love letters to him and he'd get somebody to read 'em, and then good night! He'd lock himself up in his room for a week and never come out, only to get to the ball park. We had him believin' they was a girl in Austin that was crazy to marry him, and he was weak and sick all the time we was there, for the fear she'd call him up or he'd run into her on the street."

Well, when I and Gilbert was alone, I says that maybe we'd better keep this dope to ourself, or somebody might take advantage o' the kid and maybe spoil him as a pitcher. Gilbert was agreeable—that is, he told me he was. But he didn't lose no time spillin' the whole thing to Harry Childs, and he couldn't of picked out a worse one to tell it to.

Harry'd rather kid somebody than hit one on the pick, and him and Joe Jackson hates their base hits just alike.

So as soon as he got a chance he went after Crosby.

We was ridin' to Fort Worth and Childs had a Chicago paper. He flopped down in the seat beside Crosby.

"Well, kid," he says, "do you want to read what the reporters has sent up about you?"

"No," says Crosby. "I ain't interested in no newspaper talk. As long as I give the club the best I got, they can write anything they please."

"Yes," says Childs; "but this is a nice little boost and they's no man can tell me he don't like encouragement."

"But readin' papers on the train always puts my eyes on the bum," says the kid.

"I'll read it to you," says Harry. "I don't think your ears'll be hurt."

So Childs pulled somethin' about like this:

"One o' the most promisin' recruits is Lefty Crosby, that was drafted from the Texas League last fall. Though this boy only had one year's experience in the minors, he already handles himself like a veteran. His speed is terrific and his control a whole lot better than the average young left-hander's.

"Manager Cahill's only fear about him is that the female fans o' Chicago and New York will bother him to death with telephone calls and sweet notes. In appearance, Crosby is a great deal like Francis X. Bushman. It is a certainty that he will take the fair sex by storm, provided he gives them the slightest encouragement."

Crosby was redder'n an undershirt.

"That's bunk!" he says. "Who wrote that?"

"The guy didn't sign his name," says Childs.

"I shouldn't think he would," says Crosby.

"I don't know why not," says Childs. "He was tellin' the truth. A fella as handsome and young-lookin' as you can just about take his pick of any dame in New York or Chi."

"I wasn't thinkin' about gettin' married," says Crosby. "I'm satisfied the way I am."

"Cahill'd rather have you married, though," says Harry. "He figures a man's liable to behave himself better if he's tied down."

"I'll behave all right," says the kid. "I got no bad habits."

"But if they's a beautiful bride for you to support, you'll work harder and improve faster," Childs says.

"I always work as hard as I can," says the kid.

"Maybe you already got a girl here in Texas," says Harry. "Maybe it's some little black-eyed peacherita from acrost the Border."

"I haven't no girl at all, and don't want none," says Crosby. "I don't see why a man can't get along without thinkin' about girls all the while."

"But," says Harry, "the Lord wouldn't of made you so beautiful if he thought you was goin' to be a woman hater."

"I ain't beautiful or nothin' o' the kind," says Crosby, blushin' harder'n ever.

Childs started to tell him he was too modest; but the kid got up and moved away.

In the hotel at Fort Worth, Harry got one o' the telephone girls to call up Crosby's room and tell him she'd love to meet him. He hung up on her. In Oklahoma City, Childs had one o' the local papers print a picture o' Crosby in action. He brought the paper into the dinin' room and flopped down at the same table with the kid.

"Did you see this?" he ast him. "It's pretty fair' but it don't hardly do you justice."

"What do I care!" says Crosby.

"I'd care a whole lot if I was you," says Harry. "If I had your looks I wouldn't allow no picture to be printed that didn't give me a square deal. And you ought to read what it says under it. But maybe it affects your stomach to read while you're eatin'. I'll read it to you."

"I don't care what it says," says Crosby.

"It's only a few words," says Childs. "I don't mind readin' it at all." And he handed him this kind o' stuff: "Above is showed a likeness o' Lefty Crosby, one o' Manager Cahill's recruits from Texas. They expect him to not only break a few strike-out records in the big circuit, but also the hearts of all the girls that gets a good look at him. Crosby promises to be the Adonis o' baseball."

I guess the kid didn't know Adonis from Silk O'Loughlin; but that didn't keep him from blushin' like a beet. Childs leaned over and whispered to him.

"They's a queen over there by the window," he says, "and she's done nothin' only look at you for five minutes. Maybe if I leave you alone she'll come over and introduce herself."

"I don't feel like eatin' no more lunch," says Crosby; and he beat it out o' the room. He hadn't hardly gargled half his soup.

From then on the kid tried to duck Harry all he could. But he didn't have the nerve to offend nobody, and lots o' times Childs'd corner him where he couldn't escape without makin' it too raw.

Crosby's best pal on the club was Joe Martin. Joe's alway the bushers' friend because he don't believe in ridin' 'em. Crosby tried to set with Joe at the same table on the diners and in the hotels, because Martin'd read pretty near the whole bill o' fare out loud and Crosby could pick out what he really wanted to eat. Martin, o' course, done this on purpose, knowin' Crosby couldn't read and was generally always hungry.

It's pretty tough on a kid with a good appetite to not be able to tell what's listed unless somebody reads it off to him.

But Joe couldn't spend all his time makin' things easy for Crosby, and whenever Childs could manage to set with the kid he was meaner to him than a snake. For instance, after we'd had a tough work-out and everybody was starvin', Childs'd pick up the bill and begin crabbin' about how many things had been scratched offen it.

"We're gettin' a fine deal," he'd say. "They's nothin' left only salad and ice cream." Then he'd say to the waiter: "Bring me salad and ice cream."

And Crosby'd have to say that he'd take the same. Childs was willin' to go hungry himself for the sake o' puttin' it over.

The last day we was on the spring trip, Harry bought a rule book and brought it on the train.

"They've certainly made some radical changes this year," he says to Crosby. "A left-handed pitcher can't throw to first base without turnin' round twice before he pegs. And a left-handed pitcher can't throw more'n two curve balls to the same left-handed hitter durin' one time at bat. They're trying to increase the hittin'. And only the first foul counts a strike. And the pitcher and catcher ain't goin' to be allowed to work with signs. And when it's a pitcher's first year in the Big League, he ain't only allowed two strikes up there at bat. That's to hurry the game. And you got to get four men out instead o' three. And you can't pitch nothin' only new balls. The minute a ball's even tipped by a bat, the umps throws it away and gives you a brand-new one. And a pitcher ain't allowed to warm up the day he's goin' to pitch. And a pitcher can't wear a glove. And a pitcher can't wind up unless they's a runner on first or second base. Then he's got to. And if a pitcher's taken out three times in three months, he's automatically released, and either he's got to go to a Class E league or quit playin' ◆ baseball."

◆ *Class E league*—The minor leagues of the time ranged from Class AA to Class

I don't know if Crosby fell for all o' that or not; but, anyway, I got him alone a while later and told him Childs was just kiddin' and the rules was the same as ever. It'd probably been hard enough for him to learn 'em in the first place without ringin' in no long list o' changes for him to try and master.

The train was late pullin' into Chi next mornin' and Harry got one more crack at the kid before we come to Englewood. ◆

"Well, Lefty," he says, "you're goin' to have a real try-out right away. I was talkin' to Cahill and he says he's goin' to start you Friday o' this week."

Crosby looked tickled to death.

"The reason for it," says Childs, "is because Friday is Lady's Day at ◆ our park. The womenfolks all comes in free and the boxes and stand is always full o' them. And the old man wants to get 'em well pleased with the club right from the jump. He figures that if they see you once they'll make their husbands and sweethearts bring 'em every time you pitch."

"I don't know if I'm goin' to be right to pitch Friday or not," says the poor boob. "The old souper felt kind of numb when I worked yesterday."

"On Fridays," says Childs, "the boxes right back of our bench is always saved for showgirls. And the ball players that looks good to them, they always talk to."

"If Friday ain't a nice hot day," says Crosby, "I'm goin' to ask him not to work me. My arm feels rotten."

II

Well, Cahill didn't ask the kid to pitch Friday's game; never had no intention o' doin' it, o' course. But he did start him the followin' Monday, against the Cleveland gang.

(*continued from page 597*)
D. In the entire history of baseball there was one Class E league, the Twin Ports League, which operated only for part of the 1943 season with four teams in the Duluth-Superior area.

◆ *Englewood*—Englewood Union Station on 63rd Street just west of State Street, the stop on the South Side of Chicago for the New York Central, Pennsylvania, Nickel Plate, and Rock Island lines. Less than four miles south of Comiskey Park, it was always attractive to the White Sox and visiting American League teams, especially for departures after games that ran late in the afternoon.

◆ *Friday is Lady's Day at our park*—Both Chicago teams customarily observed Friday as Ladies Day, admitting women at reduced prices.

For five innin's he pitched as pretty a game o' ball as I ever seen and we had 'em licked 3 to 0. Then Childs, who was warmin' the bench, got after him either because he was sore on havin' been took out o' the outfield or just naturally couldn't resist a chance to pull somethin'.

While Cahill was coachin' at first base, Childs called Crosby up to one side o' the shed.

"Did you see her yet?" he ast him.

"See who?" says the kid.

"I guess you know who," says Childs. "They's a peach right behind the middle o' this bench. I noticed her lookin' at you ever since you warmed up. And while you was out there pitchin' last innin', she ast me your name. I told her and she says you was the handsomest man she ever looked at. So then she ast me would I introduce her to you when the game's over."

"I won't have no time," says Crosby.

"But, man," says Harry, "I promised I'd do it."

Just then the innin' was over and we went out. You never seen such a change in a pitcher. He couldn't get one near the plate. He acted like he was scared stiff. He was so wild that he had the ushers duckin'.

Cahill left him in there a few minutes to give him a chance to steady himself. But they wasn't nothin' to do but take him out after he'd walked four o' them without pitchin' a strike. Cahill was ravin' mad.

"Another yellow dog!" he says. "The next time Jake Atz recommends a man to me, I'll wire him at his own expense to take a dose o' bichloride. What do you think o' this stiff? We give him a three-run lead and they can't hit him with a board, and he's only got four innin's to go! And he blows higher'n a kite! Sixteen balls without a strike! And once he pretty near missed the whole grand stand! Go climb in the shower so you'll be clean when you start back for Texas."

Crosby was glad to sneak to the clubhouse and get out o' the park. But I and Martin was suspicious that somethin' had come off, and next time we come in we ast Childs.

"Yes," says Harry, "I suppose it's my fault. But if the poor boob is as simple as that, he'd ought to lose out."

"What did you pull on him?" ast Joe.

"I just told him," says Harry, "that they was a pretty girl settin' right back of our bench that ast to meet him after the game."

"That ain't right, Harry," says Martin. "He looks as good as any left-hander in the league, and we can't afford to spoil him. Just lay offen him. You know he's scared o' women; but that ain't the worst fault in the world, and you got to admit that he didn't look scared o' them Cleveland boys till he blowed up. Leave him alone and he'll win a lot o' ball games for us."

"Why should I leave him alone?" says Harry. "Since they got me settin' on the bench, they's nothin' left for me to do only kid somebody."

"All right," says Joe, "If you won't do it for me I'll put it up to Cahill."

And sure enough, in the clubhouse after the game, Martin told the M. G. R. just what had come off.

"Look here, Childs!" says Cahill. "That'll be enough o' that. I don't care how much fun you have with him offen the field, but when we're playin' a game, lay off! If you don't think I'm in earnest you may soon be takin' a trip to Texas yourself!"

So Childs laid offen him entirely for a while, not even tryin' to pester him when we went on our first trip. But I knew it wouldn't never last. While it did last, though, Crosby done better work than any o' the rest of our pitchers and had the whole league stood on their heads with that fast one o' his.

III

We left Cleveland one evenin', goin' to St. Louis, and the boys started a game o' cards. Childs was in it and Crosby was leanin' over the back of a seat, watchin'. I was settin' in the game, too, right where I could look at Crosby.

Well, Gilbert win three pots in a row, with aces one time, aces up the next time, and the third time he beat Childs with three o' the big bulls.

"Come on, Gil!" says Harry. "Give the aces a chance to roam round the deck once in a while."

"I can't spare 'em, Harry," says Gilbert.

"You put 'em in the deck!" says Childs, just kiddin'.

"You make me put 'em in the deck!" says Gil.

Well, Harry had a gun on his hip, with nothin' in it but blanks, and he pulled it out and laid it on the table in front of him, just for a joke.

But Crosby didn't see the joke. I happened to be lookin' at him when Childs showed the gun. He turned white as a sheet, and I thought for a minute he was goin' to keel over. Then he grabbed the top o' the seat to steady up, and the next thing we knew he was beatin' it for the other end o' the car as fast as he could navigate.

"What's the matter with him now?" says Harry.

"Looks like he objected to the firearms," says Gilbert.

"What the hell ain't he scared of?" says Childs.

"Well," I says, "Ty Cobb for one thing and Bob Veach for another."

"Did he think I'd be monkeyin' with a loaded gat?" says Harry. "I'll have to try him out and see which he likes best, women or artillery."

"Oh, leave him alone!" says I. "As long as he keeps winnin' ball games for us, what's the difference if he's scared o' wild cats or fishworms?"

But Harry'd been good long enough. The next mornin' when we was crossin' the bridge into St. Louis, he finds Crosby in the washroom. Without sayin' nothin', he just simply laid his gun on one o' the sills, pointin' it straight at the kid. And Crosby begin shakin' like a leaf and staggered out o' the room without even waitin' to grab his collar.

Childs told us about it and seemed to think it was the funniest thing ever pulled off. But some o' the rest of us didn't think it was so funny, especially when we had to put Crosby to bed the minute we got to the hotel, and then get along without him all through the series with the Browns.

And Cahill made the remark, so as Childs could hear him, that the next guy that pulled a gun where Crosby was, or left one where he would see it, was through with our ball club for life.

IV

For a while after that, Harry was satisfied to just pull the girl stuff on his victim. He begin writin' fake love letters, like the guy'd done down in the Texas League. Some o' them was wonders. I know, because I read 'em to Crosby myself, he tellin' me that the different handwritin's was so funny that he couldn't make 'em out. But this wasn't much joy for Childs, because you can bet he wasn't never ast to read 'em.

Crosby wouldn't only let me get so far when he'd make me stop, and then he'd take the letters and tear 'em up.

"I wisht all girls would leave me alone," he'd say.

"What have you got against 'em?" I'd say to him.

"Bill," he'd say, "I'd just as lief own up to you. I don't feel comfortable round 'em. I'm just plain bashful. That's what my sister used to tell me. She was the only one I could ever talk to without pretty near faintin'."

"You'd get over that soon enough, if you'd try," I'd tell him. "You won't never know what livin' is till you get married and have a home o' your own. And they's nothin' about girls to be scared of, especially for as nice a lookin' guy as you are. They wouldn't never make fun o' you."

"I ain't afraid o' that," he'd say to me. "I wouldn't mind talkin' to 'em if I thought they'd just laugh and joke with me or talk baseball. But girls is liable to get personal and begin makin' eyes; and if they done that with me, I'd run a mile."

"Wasn't they no girls in the town you come from?"

"Too many o' them," he says. "They was only about two hundred people in the town and half o' them was girls, seemed like to me."

"How'd you get away from 'em?" I says.

"Just by runnin'," he says. "I beat it from home when I was twelve years old and that's why I didn't get no schoolin' to speak of. I joined in with a minin' gang up North, where I was sure they wouldn't be no skirts to bother me."

"You was young to be mixed up with a crowd like that," says I.

"Yes; but they treated me fine," says Crosby. "I'd of been in that game yet only for somethin' happenin'."

"What happened?" I ast.

"Oh, you'd think I was crazy if I told you," he says. "They was too rough for me. I can fight as good as the next guy when it's just usin' your fists. But I can't stand guns. Between you and I, I'm scareder o' them than I am o' girls. It started, I guess, one night when they was a scrap in a saloon. Everybody was lit up and, first thing you know, they had their gats out and was pluggin' away. And the guy that had took care o' me, when I first come to the camp, was shot dead right in front o' my eyes. I got sick at the time, watchin' it, and ever since then I get sick every time I see one o' the damn things."

"You're gunshy and girlshy," I says. "Anything else you're scared of?"

"Yes," he says; "a fast ball that's comin' at my bean. But I guess I got plenty o' company there."

"Well, Lefty," I says, "I can say one thing for you: You're brave enough when it comes to pitchin' against a .400 hitter in a pinch. And that's more than can be said for some o' the rest of our beautiful pitchers."

V

One o' the prettiest girls I ever seen was a telegraph operator at the hotel where we stop at in Detroit. Her name was Mary Lloyd. All the single guys on the ball club was more'n half crazy about her, and even the married ones was never heard objectin' when she give 'em a smile. To see us in that hotel, you'd of thought we was the greatest bunch o' telegram senders in the world.

Harry Childs had probably fell for her stronger than any o' the rest. When he wasn't busy talkin' base hits or kiddin' Crosby, he was tellin' somebody what a pippin she was, like nobody else had suspected it. And I guess he'd sent her enough cards from round the circuit to start a pinochle deck.

"Bill," he'd say to me, "she's the only one I ever met that I felt like I wanted to marry her."

"Go ahead!" I'd tell him. "I'd want to marry her, too, only I kind o' feel my own Missus might make a holler."

"Go ahead!" he'd say. "It's all right to say 'Go ahead'; but every time I start she says 'Back up!' She's worse'n a traffic cop."

"Keep tryin', Harry," I'd say to him. "Maybe she's heard about you bein' the world's champion joker and thinks you're just triflin' with her."

"She does all the jokin' when I'm round," he says. "She makes a regular monkey out o' me."

"Oh, I wouldn't blame that on her!" I says.

Now Mary wasn't no flirt, but she didn't mind bein' admired. She never give one guy more encouragement than another; she didn't play no favorites, or she didn't never let nobody on the club get the idear that she was to be had for the astin'. But she wasn't never too busy to talk to any of us, or to smile back when we smiled at her.

I and Gilbert was standin' there kiddin' with her the first time she seen Crosby. We'd just got in that mornin', and when he come out from breakfast he beat it through the lobby past her desk and out on the front walk.

"Who's that handsome wretch?" she ast us.

"That's the guy that made a sucker out o' Cobb and Veach over home," says Gilbert.

"Maybe if I ast him not to," she says, "he'll leave our team win a game or two this series."

"You got a sweet chance of astin' him anything," says I, "unless you got a megaphone."

"Is he deef?" says Mary.

"When they's girls round he's deef and dumb and blind," I says.

"He must of been disappointed in love," she says.

"Not him," says Gil. "The only time he was ever disappointed was when they postponed the game he was goin' to pitch."

"What's the trouble between him and girls?" says Mary.

"He just naturally don't like 'em—that's all," I says.

"Well," says Mary, "I don't think that's hardly fair to our sex. They ain't so many handsome men in the world that we can afford to have 'em woman haters."

"No," I says; "and they ain't so many good pitchers on our ball club that we can have him scared to death by gettin' a smile from you. So when you happen to run into him, face to face, kindly act like you didn't see him."

"I'm much obliged," she says, "for bein' told that my smile is terrifyin'. I'll keep it to myself after this."

"Not at all," says I. "I'd pretty near rather miss a hit-and-run sign than that smile o' yours. But this kid is just plain bashful; he ain't no woman hater; he's too backward to hate anything. He wants to be left alone—that's all. If a girl looks at him cross-eyed it takes him a week to get so's he can pitch again."

"I believe I'll go right out now," says Mary, "and look at him cross-eyed. You know I ought to be loyal to the Tigers."

"You ought to be loyal to this here beanery," says I; "and if you put him out o' commission, why, we'll just pass up this hotel."

"All right," she says. "I won't pay no attention to him, because I know I'd simply die if you boys stopped somewheres else and gave me a chance to do a little work."

"Has Childs been round yet?" says Gilbert.

"Foolish Question 795!" I says. "He was here even before he went in for his prunes."

"What's the matter with Harry Childs?" she ast us. "Why ain't he playin'?"

"We like to win once in a while," says Gilbert.

"The reason Harry ain't playin'," I says, "is a young outfielder from the Coast, named Patrick."

"Why," says Mary, "Harry told me he was out of it with a Charley Horse."

"Yes," I says; "and a battin' average last year o' .238."

Crosby pitched the first game for us and win 2 to 1 in eleven innin's. He was goin' to wind up the series, but it begin to pour rain at noon o' the last day and the battle was off before we went out to the park. We wasn't startin' home till nine o'clock that night; so we had a lot o' time to kill. Naturally they was a reception all afternoon round Mary's desk. I and Joe Martin happened to be left there alone with her while Childs was gettin' shaved and some o' the others was celebratin'.

"Well," says Mary, "now that they ain't no more chance o' me spoilin' your trip, I think you might bring Mr. Shy round."

"She means the kid," I says to Joe. "I told her all about him."

"Have you seen him?" Joe ast her.

"O' course I seen him," she says.

"What do you think of him?" says Joe.

"Well, gentlemen," she says, "I don't want to hurt the feelin's o' the present company, so I'll just keep still."

"He is a pretty kid," says Martin, "and he's a whole lot better-lookin' since I coaxed him into some decent clothes. But he don't want to meet no girls."

"They's no sense to it," I says. "It wouldn't hurt him a bit to mingle a little with the dames. It'd do him good. And he'd get along O. K. when he found out they wasn't all tryin' to steal him."

"I'll promise not to steal him," says Mary.

"Well, it's up to Joe, here," I says. "He's his best pal."

"I guess he'd come if I ast him," says Martin. "But I don't know if I want to take a chance."

"Oh, come on!" says Mary. "I don't feel comfortable when they's one o' your boys I ain't acquainted with."

"Well," says Joe, "maybe he's up in his room takin' a nap."

"If he is in his room," says I, "that's probably what he's doin'. It's a cinch he ain't readin'."

"Why not?" says Mary.

Joe give me the wink.

"He hates books," I says.

It was just then that the kid come across the lobby, toward the front windows. He looked like he was goin' to cry.

"My! He needs cheerin' up," says Mary. "Do you suppose he's sick?"

"You bet he's sick," says Martin. "He was goin' to give your Tigers another lickin' to-day, and the rain beat him out of it."

"Well, how about callin' him over?" I says.

So Martin went up to him and made the proposition. I could see the poor kid blush and then start like he was goin' to run out in the rain. Then Joe grabbed ahold of his arm and begin arguin' with him. And finally the pair o' them come toward us. Nobody only Joe could of done it.

"Miss Lloyd," says Martin, "this is another o' the boys, Mr. Crosby. He's disappointed about the rain and I thought maybe you could cheer him up."

Mary give him her best smile.

"I'm glad to meet you, Mr. Crosby," she says. "You're the first ball player I ever seen that was disappointed about the rain."

"Except when it didn't fall," I says.

The kid didn't say nothin'; didn't even look at her. I caught him moistenin' his lips, tryin' to get a word out. But he couldn't. He seen her put her hand out to shake, and he finally managed to meet it. But he done it with the one he uses in pitchin'. And then, the minute Martin left go his arm, he backed away, pivoted on a pillar and dashed for the elevator.

"Good night!" says Mary. "Well, of all the rummies!"

"We warned you," says Martin.

"You certainly cheered him up," I says—"all the way up to his room."

"He can stay there, for all o' me," she says. "I won't never try to force my acquaintance on nobody again."

"I bet he's offen me for life," says Joe.

"You ought to be glad if he is," she says.

"But you got to admit he's a handsome brute," says I.

"Yes," says Mary; "and I'd like to scratch his handsome face to pieces."

When we got on the train that night Harry Childs come up to me.

"Bill," he says, "I believe I'm goin' to win out."

"Win out what?" I ast him.

"With Mary," he says. "I took her out to supper. It was the first time she ever let me do it. And she acted like she really was fond o' me."

"Here's luck, Harry!" I says.

I didn't tell him the reason she was so friendly. It was because she'd been stung. And Harry's attentions was salve.

We was in Detroit again the first week in July. Harry took her out to supper or a picture show, or somethin', every night. I never heard her mention Crosby, and I was scared to mention him in front of her.

I did see her try to get even though. She come out from behind her desk one mornin', just as he was walkin' in from outside. She got right in his way, so as he either had to run into her or dodge. And he couldn't help lookin' at her. She looked him right in the eye and didn't speak.

And the kid looked like he was mighty glad of it.

VI

Young Patrick got hurt and Childs was back in the game when we went East in August. Harry was full o' pep.

"I'll show 'em I can hit," he says to me. "I never felt luckier in my life."

"You don't need no luck to hit if you take care o' yourself," I says.

"Don't worry about that," he says. "I got to keep in shape. I'm tryin' to save the coin."

"What for?" I ast him.

"Well, Bill," he says, "I'm kind o' figurin' on gettin' married."

"Nice work, Harry!" I says. "I didn't know you'd gone as far as that."

"They's nothin' settled," he says. "But she's writin' to me, and when we strike Detroit next month I'll make her say yes."

Harry started to paste that pill in Philly. He broke up two games for us there and got seven blows in three days. He was the pepper kid when we got to Washington and he couldn't resist takin' some of it out on Crosby.

They set at lunch together the second day.

"Lefty," he says, "looks like we're goin' to fight Germany. I was down to the White House this mornin' to call on a friend o' mine, a Mr. Wilson, and he says he don't think we can hold out much longer."

"Well," says Crosby, "let 'em fight, as long as they leave us guys out of it."

"Who says they'd leave us out of it?" Harry ast him.

"They'll leave me out of it, all right," says Crosby. "I never shot a gun in my life."

"It ain't guns they want you to shoot. It's Germans," says Childs. "And if the President called for volunteers I bet you'd be one o' the first to go."

"You'd lose your bet," says the kid. "I can't take no chance o' gettin' my left arm shot off."

"Good Lord! That reminds me o' somethin'," says Harry. "I seen in the papers this mornin' that most o' the guns this country's got is left-handed guns. And they'll probably call for all the left-handed men in the United States to handle 'em."

Crosby didn't wait for no desert.

In New York, a couple o' days later, Childs was at him again.

"War's gettin' closer every minute," he says to Crosby.

"The Germans torpedoed the City o' Benton Harbor yesterday and ◆ sunk eleven bootblacks without even givin' 'em a chance to take their stands with 'em. And the Kaiser went fishin' in the mornin' and caught an American sturgeon. The President says if that kind o' thing keeps up he's offen the Kaiser and we'll all have to enlist—that is, all the able-bodied guys."

"That lets me out," says the kid. "My ankles wouldn't hold up a minute if I was to try and march."

"They'd stick you in the calvary and have you ride a motorcycle," says Childs.

"I don't know how," says Crosby; "and, besides, a man couldn't ride no motorcycle acrost the ocean."

"Oh, yes, they could," says Childs, "if the tires was blowed up tight enough. And, anyway, they's lots of us would have to do our fightin' here in this country, to keep the Germans from breakin' up the League."

I went in to breakfast with the kid the mornin' we landed in Boston. I had a paper myself and they was a piece in it sayin' that this country was thinkin' about callin' on all the young men o' nineteen and twenty, to train 'em for war—that is, all the ones that wasn't married. Childs, settin' at the next table, read it and couldn't get over to us fast enough.

"Crosby," he says, "how old are you?"

"Twenty," says the kid.

"You're in tough luck, old boy!" says Childs; and he begin readin' out loud. It was a cinch this time, because the readin' matter was really there.

"Congress," it says, "is considerin' a proposition to start universal military trainin' on account o' the strained relations with Germany and the prospects o' war. The plan is to draft every unmarried man

---

◆ *City of Benton Harbor*—A sidewheel steamer of the Graham & Morton Transportation Co., which plied between Chicago and St. Joseph–Benton Harbor, on the west coast of Michigan's Lower Peninsula. An alternative to the Michigan Central line of the New York Central System between Lardner's hometown of Niles and Chicago was the interurban of the Southern Michigan Railway to St. Joseph and the Graham & Morton Line across the lake. The *City of Benton Harbor*, which had been built by the Craig Shipbuilding Co. at Toledo in 1904, was considered an excellent steamer. Lardner also made reference to her in Jack Keefe's wartime experiences; Keefe refers to a drunken corporal as "all lit up like the City of Benton Harbor" in *Treat 'Em Rough: Letters from Jack the Kaiser Killer* (Indianapolis: The Bobbs-Merrill Co., 1918), p. 81.

in the United States o' the ages o' nineteen and twenty, and make 'em fit for war."

Anyway, it was somethin' like that.

"It looks like your baseball career was pretty near over," Harry says to the kid. "It's a crime too! You've had a great year, and without knowin' nothin' about pitchin' at that. But still, it ain't hard to learn to shoot and duck bullets; and they's a whole lot o' satisfaction in knowin' that you're workin' for the Stars and Stripes."

"When does this business come off?" says Crosby.

"Oh, not for a couple months," says Childs. "They'll probably leave you stick with us through the city series."

Then Childs got up and left us.

"Bill," says Crosby to me, "they ain't kiddin' about this, is they?"

"No, Lefty," I says. "It's there in the paper, all right. But it just says they're thinkin' about it. If I was you I wouldn't start worryin' yet."

"Bill," he says, "before I'll join a army I'll walk out in Lake Michigan till my hat floats."

"Quit frettin' over it," says I. "You won't be able to pitch in this series, and you know we want some o' these games."

"But they're goin' to draft all the twenty-year-olds," he says, "and I just broke into that class. I wisht to the devil I was your age."

"Yes," I says; "or married."

"Married!" says Crosby. "That's right! It's just the single fellas that's gone."

"They ain't nobody gone," says I. "But if you don't quit worryin' you'll be just as good."

Childs spoiled whatever chance the Kid had to quit worryin' by sayin' to him, just before we started the game:

"Well, Lefty, they's one pipe: You'll be the handsomest guy in the army."

Before Crosby was taken out, Harry probably regretted that remark; because the five innin's he pitched our outfielders must of ran back to the fence fifty times.

VII

Joe Martin told me about the kid bracin' him in the hotel that night.

"Joe," Crosby says to him, "I'd kind o' like to get acquainted with a girl."

"Good Lord!" says Joe. "What girl?"

"It don't make no difference," says the kid. "Some girl that ain't married, but might like to be, and ain't liable to want to moon or make eyes or nothin' like that."

"Are you thinkin' o' gettin' married?" Joe ast him.

"Yes; only keep it quiet," says Lefty.

"And do you expect a girl to marry you for your money?" says Joe.

"You know I got no money," Crosby says.

"Well," says Joe. "If you got no money and you want to get married, you got to find a girl that's fond o' you. And a girl that's fond o' you might want to hold hands some time."

"Ain't they no sensible girl that might like me?" says the kid.

"What girls do you know?" Joe ast him.

"Joe," he says, "I ain't met a girl since I was fifteen or sixteen years old."

"Oh, yes, you have," says Joe. "How about that girl you was so nice to in Detroit?"

"Do you mean that girl you introduced me to?" says Crosby.

"Sure!" says Martin. "Mary Lloyd, the telegraph operator."

"Do you think she'd like me?" ast the kid.

"Well," Joe told him, "she ast to meet you, and she certainly was broke up the way you treated her."

"But what kind of a girl is she?" he says. "She ain't too soft?"

"I never caught her at it," says Joe.

"But she's probably sore at me," says Crosby.

"You can apologize to her," says Joe.

"But we won't be in Detroit for ten days," says the kid.

"Write her a letter," says Joe.

"I don't like to write letters," Crosby says. "Joe, will you write her a letter for me?"

"That'd make her sorer than ever," says Martin. "Besides, I don't know what you're tryin' to pull off."

"I'm on the square," says the kid. "If she'll marry me—why, I'll take her."

"That's damn' sweet o' you!" says Joe. "But what's your idear in gettin' married?"

"Never mind, Joe," says the kid. "I just feel like I want to."

"Well," says Joe, "if you want to square it with Mary, and you don't feel like writin' to her, why not send her a night letter?"

"What's that?" says Crosby.

"It's a telegram that goes at night, and you can say about fifty words for fifty cents," Joe told him.

"But I don't know no fifty words to say," says the poor kid.

To make it short, Joe done it for him, either because he was sorry for the kid or because he thought it was a joke or because he ain't none too good friends with Harry Childs. The telegram said that the kid was sorry he'd froze her, that he'd been feelin' tough that afternoon, that he apologized, and would she please forgive him, because he thought a whole lot of her.

The answer come next day, at noon. Mary wired that she'd pay more attention to him if he said all that to her face.

VIII

Harry Childs' lucky spell ended when we stopped over for a game in Cleveland on the way home. He changed his mind at the last minute about makin' a slide to the plate, and they carried him off with a busted leg.

So Harry Childs didn't make the last trip to Detroit.

Young Mr. Crosby did, though he was so scared leavin' Chi that I and Gil and Martin was afraid he'd throw himself offen the train in the night.

The three of us talked it all over.

"He'll fall down, sure!" says Gil. "She'll give him an unmerciful pannin' and he'll faint dead away."

"But suppose he don't," I says. "Suppose he goes through with it and wins. Are we bein' fair to Harry?"

"Why not?" says Martin. "Childs played jokes on him all season. It's pretty near time the kid got back."

"I'm for helpin' him," says Gilbert.

"Me too," says Joe.

"All right, you're on!" I says; and we begin discussin' how to go about it.

We finally fixed it up that we'd get a taxi to come to the hotel at Mary's lunchtime. Then we'd coax 'em into it and slam the doors, and tell the driver to break all the laws o' Michigan.

Because, as Joe said, if we put 'em together where Crosby could get away, he'd get away sure!

They's nothin' more to it. They were back from their ride at one o'clock, both o' them as red as an open switch. But the smile Mary give us was an inch or so wider than we ever got before.

Crosby come blushin' acrost the lobby.

"Well?" we says.

"Well, boys," he says, "it wasn't bad."

"What do you mean—wasn't bad?" says Martin.

"Her," says the kid.

"Not half as bad as one o' them German centipede guns," says I.

"Not half!" says Crosby.

I suppose by this time she's got him through the First Reader.

Lardner Bibliography

Bibliography of General Works on Lardner

Bruccoli, Matthew J., ed. *Ring Around the Bases: The Complete Baseball Stories of Ring Lardner*. New York: Charles Scribner's Sons, 1992.

Bruccoli, Matthew J., and Richard Layman. *Ring W. Lardner: A Descriptive Bibliography*. Pittsburgh: University of Pittsburgh Press, 1976.

Caruthers, Clifford M., ed. *Ring Around Max: The Correspondence of Ring Lardner and Max Perkins*. DeKalb, Ill.: Northern Illinois University Press, 1973.

Clark, Isaac E. "An Analysis of Ring Lardner's American Language, or Who Learnt You Grammar Bud?" Unpublished M.A. thesis, University of Texas, 1944.

Elder, Donald. *Ring Lardner*. Garden City, N.Y.: Doubleday & Co., 1956.

Frakes, James R. "Ring Lardner: A Critical Survey." Unpublished Ph.D. dissertation, University of Pennsylvania, 1953.

Friedrich, Otto. *Ring Lardner*. Minneapolis: University of Minnesota Press, 1965.

Geismar, Maxwell. *Ring Lardner and the Portrait of Folly*. New York: Thomas Y. Crowell Co., 1972.

Keller, Richard D. "The Uncollected 'Busher' Stories of Ring Lardner: A Critical Edition with Introduction." Unpublished Ph.D dissertation, Northern Illinois University, 1972.

Patrick, Walton R. *Ring Lardner*. New York: Twayne Publishers, Inc., 1963.

Seldes, Gilbert. "Editor's Introduction." In *The Portable Ring Lardner*. New York: Viking Press, 1946.

Webb, Howard William, Jr. "Ring Lardner's Conflict and Reconciliation with American Society." Unpublished Ph.D. dissertation, State University of Iowa, 1953.

Yardley, Jonathan. *Ring: A Biography of Ring Lardner*. New York: Random House, 1977.

Index

Index

This index includes all actual persons (and two questionable cases) appearing in the Introduction, the stories, and the footnotes. The principal biographical entry for each person is italicized. Page references do not differentiate between text and notes. Fictional characters, small communities not integral to the plots, and casual references to major cities are not indexed. Teams are listed city name first. For the stories with predominantly fictional characters beginning on page 448, only actual persons and the apparent team on which the story is set are indexed.

The following conventions are used for nonitalicized page references: An "f" after a number indicates a separate reference on the next page, and an "ff" indicates separate references on the next two pages. A continuous discussion over two or more pages is indicated by a span of page numbers, e.g., "pp. 57–58." *Passim* is used for a cluster of references in close but not continuous sequence.

Aaron, Henry, 274, 388
Abbott, Ellis (Mrs. Ring W. Lardner), 5
Abbott, Ruby, 2
Addams, Jane, 8
Akron, Ohio, 34
Alcock, John F. "Scotty," *136*
Alcock, John J. "Johnny," 28
Alexander, Grover Cleveland, 26, 155, 366, *367*, 368, 370f, 377, 383, 390, 442
Altrock, Nicholas, *87–88*, 318
Amarillo, Tex., 53, 56; Panhandlers baseball club, 56
American Association (major league), 35, 37, 158, 312, 492; dissolution of, 507
American Association (minor league), 45, 66, 238

American League: founding of, 34, 39, 507; schedule meetings, 112, 221, 232; near break-up in Mays case, 303–4
American magazine, 18, 23
Ames, Leon K. "Red," *464*
Amherst College, 407
Archer, James P., 222, 223, 338, 342, 349f, 402
Armour & Co., 222, 232
Armour Institute, 2
Atlanta Crackers, Southern Association, 358
Atlantic City, N.J., 309, 311, 326
Atz, Jacob "Jake," 5, *267*, 268, 362, 593, 599
Auden, W. H., 7, 8
Ayers, Yancy W. "Doc," 319

Bagby, James C. J., Jr., 266
Bagby, James C. J., Sr., *266*, 295
Baker, John F. "Home Run," *55–56*, 321, 410–15 *passim*, 420f
Baker Bowl, 368, 370, 436
Ball, Phil, 263
Baltimore, Md.: Terrapins, Federal League, 77, 97, 423, 425; Orioles, National League, 172, 311, 345, 492; Orioles, American League (1901–1902), 172, 405, 493; Orioles, International League, 273, 405, 426; Players League club, 312
Baltimore & Ohio RR, 514
Barnett, Jack, 26–27f, 373–78 *passim*, 393
Barnett, John, 374
Barrow, Edward, 304
Barry, John J. "Jack," *78*, 272, 274, 277, 411, 415, 417, 420f
Baseball: economic organization of, 24, 33–34, 48, 75–76, 98
Base Ball Players Fraternity, 581–82
Baseball Writers' Association of America, 525
Battle Creek club, Southern Michigan Association, 398
Baumgardner, George Washington, 28, 62
Bedford, Ind., 7, 9, 40, 65–75 *passim*, 93f, 100–104 *passim*, 116, 118, 154, 164–68 *passim*, 170, 179–89 *passim*, 201, 208
Belden, Billy, 241
Bender, Charles A. "Chief," 77, 409–21 *passim*
Benton, John C. "Rube," *342*, 401, 464
Benz, Charlotte, 98
Benz, Joseph L. "Blitzen," *55*, *57*, 91, 98, 134, 141, 162f, 180, 197, 207, 222
Berger, Joseph A., *82*, 83, 89
Bescher, Robert H., *412–13*, 417–21 *passim*
Blackburne, Russell A. "Lena," *137*, 139
Black Sox scandal, *see* Chicago White Sox, scandal of 1919; Gandil, Charles A.; World Series, of 1919
Blue Grass League, 374
Bodie, Frank Stephan "Ping," 8, *47*, 51, 66, 69, 78, 86–90 *passim*, 127, 136, 140, 161, 163
Boehling, John Joseph, *141*, 391, 406
Borden, Lizzie, 15
Borton, William B. "Babe," 48
Boston, Mass., 83f, 308, 314, 387, 428; *American*, 5, 432
Boston Braves, 5, 20, 24f, 35, 72, 74, 95, 142, 159, 177, 180, 239, 253, 274, 306, 315, 331, 334, 343, 347, 351–58 *passim*, 369f, 387–88, 391, 399–404 *passim*, 415, 498, 513, 550, 573; story set on team of 1914, 423–47; South End Grounds, 445
Boston Red Sox, 46–49 *passim*, 63–68 *passim*, 78–83 *passim*, 89, 141–50 *passim*, 174, 193, 203, 205, 229, 234, 239, 246, 252, 260–68 *passim*, 275, 278f, 285, 287, 295, 303–4, 307, 314, 316, 368, 432, 498, 550; release of Cicotte to White Sox,

66; sales of players to Yankees, 270–74, 412; championships, 273
Boswell, James, 7, 8
Boyden, Albert A., 18f
Bridwell, Albert H., 222, *343*, 356
Britton, Helen, 424
Brooklyn, N.Y.: Tip-Tops, Federal League, 222, 400, 407, 419; Players League club, 312
Brooklyn Dodgers, 23, 47, 63, 95, 172, 222, 285, 306, 314, 343–50 *passim*, 355, 358, 383f, 388, 400, 405, 427, 429, 492, 519, 573, 584
Brown, Carroll W. "Boardwalk," 409
Brown, Mordecai P. C., 155
Bryan, William Jennings, 433
Bucknell University, 411
Buffalo, N.Y., 33; Electrics, Federal League, 46, 48, 97, 506, 542; Players League club, 307
Burke, James T. "Sunset Jimmy," *297*, 309, 376
Burke, John Patrick "Jack," 376, 398
Burns, George H., *279*
Burns, William T. "Sleepy Bill," 80
Bush, Leslie A. "Bullet Joe," 275, 409, *412*, 416f, 569
Bush, Owen J. "Donie," 26, *66*, 77, 80, 140, 265, 313, 588
Bushman, Francis X., 487, 595
Byrne, Robert M., *440*

Cady, Forrest L. "Hick," 550, *551*, 571
California League, 188
Callahan, James Joseph "Nixey," *43*, 44–51 *passim*, 56, 60, 64–72 *passim*, 76–95 *passim*, 128–40 *passim*, 144–52 *passim*, 160, 162, 229; on world tour, 169–91; replaced as manager of White Sox, 192
Campbell, Arthur Vincent, 333
Camp Grant, Ill., 10
Canadian Pacific Ry., 184
Cantillon, Joseph D., *238*, 476
Canton, Ohio, 34
Capp, Al, 9
Carolina Baseball Association, 487
Carter, Paul W., *339*
Caruso, Enrico, 467, 472
Cather, Theodore P., 425, 430
Central League, 2, 3, 8, 26–27, 29, 35, 44, 48, 54, 66, 222f, 343, 364, 371–75 *passim*, 381, 578; history of, 34
Chance, Frank L., 22, 159, 331, 354, 425
Chaplin, Sir Charles Spencer, 480, 522, 587
Chapman, Raymond J., *82*, 83, 203ff
Chappelle, William H., 354
Chase, Harold H. "Hal," 20, 25, 47, *48*, 80, 96, 98, 138f, 579, 583f
Chattanooga Lookouts, Southern Association, 354, 358
Cheney, Laurance R., *95*, 96, 158, 336, 340, 342, 429
Chicago, Ill., 1f, 112, 377, 387, 394, 444; *Inter-Ocean*, 4; *Examiner*, 4f, 60–61; *Journal*, 5; *Tribune*, 6–7; Surface Lines, 294; *Record-Herald*, 333
Chicago & North Western Ry., 41
Chicago Cubs, 4f, 8, 21, 43, 68, 74, 78, 88, 95, 98, 114, 130, 155, 159, 172, 179, 193, 196, 200f, 222, 282, 297, 306, 311, 315, 365–69 *passim*, 373, 378, 384, 388, 399–402 *passim*, 423, 425, 439, 467, 523; city series with White Sox, 40, 90–96, 152f, 158–63, 170, 404; merger with Whales, 98, 114, 346; Wrigley Field, 196; story set on team of 1913, 331–61; West Side ball park, 348; fictional version of team, 448, 485, 504
Chicago Gunthers, semipro club, 222
Chicago, Rock Island & Pacific RR, 235, 598
Chicago Spauldings, semipro club, 333
Chicago Whales, Federal League,

Chicago Whales (*continued*) 97, 114, 196, 346–47, 400
Chicago White Sox, 4–15 *passim*, 331, 334, 360, 368, 404, 407, 419, 440, 513, 584; scandal of 1919, 9, 15f, 22, 24, 48, 51, 59, 80, 199, 213, 276, 304f, 498; stories set on teams of 1913–1919, 33–327; history of, 34, 37; Comiskey Park, 37f, 62, 254, 258, 277, 294, 598; fictional version of team, 466, 549
Cicotte, Edward V., 15, 17, 22, 25, *65*, 76, 91, 141, 162f, 194, 200, 213, 241, 247f, 256ff, 265, 271, 274, 282, 288, 295, 303–19 *passim*; and Gandil's plot, 314
Cincinnati, Ohio, 317, 372, 377, 386
Cincinnati Reds, 35, 37, 48, 66f, 82, 88, 114, 155, 158, 180, 222, 252, 254, 266, 271, 286–89 *passim*, 295, 306, 336, 342–49 *passim*, 355, 362, 364, 369–72 *passim*, 385, 400–402 *passim*, 412, 427, 438, 464, 569; in 1919 World Series, 315–17, 335; team of 1915, 510–15
City of Benton Harbor, 608
Clark, Isaac E., 12, 169
Clarke, Thomas A., *402*, 514
Cleveland, Ohio, 79–84 *passim*, 97, 298; Rams, 89; Spiders, 297
Cleveland Indians, 40, 54, 58ff, 71, 80, 83, 89, 132–34 *passim*, 141f, 150–55 *passim*, 179, 199–206, 221, 234, 239, 246, 252, 258, 265f, 268, 279, 282, 286f, 292–99 *passim*, 304, 313, 321, 339, 399, 413, 415, 419, 432, 498, 551, 584
Cleveland Naps, 58. *See also* Cleveland Indians
Cobb, Tyrus R., 52, 66–69 *passim*, 73–80 *passim*, 121, 125, 128, 136–40 *passim*, 196, 203, 229, 259, 265, 313, 324, 334, 341, 394, 401, 444, 477, 508, 554, 563, 566, 570, 579, 582, 601, 603; suspension of 1912, 307
Cocreham, Eugene, 425
Cohan, George M., 496
Collins, Edward T., *77–78*, 196, 228, 237, 246, 257, 262, 267, 274, 304, 306, 411–15 *passim*
Collins, John Francis "Shano," *46–47*, 48, 66, 69, 139, 163, 246, 252, 257, 295, 551, 553
Columbia University, 77
Columbus Senators, American Association, 25, 334
Comiskey, Charles A., 8f, 34, *35–36*, 42, 57, 71ff, 96, 99, 103, 112, 114–26 *passim*, 144, 149, 173, 201, 205, 209, 226, 230–34 *passim*, 251, 254, 269, 276, 306f, 313, 425; efforts at building 1917 championship team, 34, 59, 65, 77; relations with Ban Johnson, 37, 39, 304
Connolly, Joseph A., 425
Connolly, Thomas H., *413*, 551
Cook, Albert "Pete," 73
Cooper, Arley Wilbur, *400*
Cornell University, 407
Costain, T. B., 23
Cotton States League, 49
Cottrell, Ensign S., 425
Coumbe, Frederick N. "Fritz," *295*
Coveleski, Harry F., *569*, 570
Coveleski, Stanley A., 569
Crandall, James O. "Doc," 413
Cravath, Clifford C., 159, *368*, 438
Crawford, Samuel E., *67*, 79f, 121, 125, 128, 136, 139, 174, 179, 185, 191, 205, 260, 475, 508, 554; record for triples, 69
Crutcher, Richard L., 425
Cutshaw, George W., *519*

Dale, Emmett E. "Gene," *514*
Dallas club, Texas League, 242, 244, 249f
Danforth, David Charles, 25, 207, 249, 256f, 275, 282, 295
Danville club, Virginia League, 333
Dartmouth College, 356f
Davenport, David W., *267*
Davis, George A., 425

Davis, George S., 5
Davis, Harry R., *415*, 416
Davis, Zachary Taylor, 37
Dayton, Ohio, 3, 393; Central League club, 34, 372, 375; flood, 545–46
Deal, Charles A., 423, 425, 429, 439
DeKamp, C. B., 18
Demaree, Albert W., 409, *415*
Dempsey, William H. "Jack," *297*, 300
Denver & Rio Grande RR, 42
Denver club, Western League, 132, 358
Des Moines club, Western League, 58, 163, 251
Detroit, Mich., 50, 54, 71, 76, 152–57 *passim*, 224, 258f, 264, 286, 288, 296f, 300
Detroit & Cleveland Navigation Co., 79
Detroit Tigers, 17, 52, 54, 60–80 *passim*, 89, 91, 112, 120–30 *passim*, 134–39 *passim*, 147, 174, 194, 200, 206, 213, 222, 248, 256–60 *passim*, 265, 271, 279, 282, 288, 292, 297, 302–27 *passim*, 393, 400, 498, 569, 573
Devore, Joshua D., 425, 430, *438*, 439
Donahue, John Augustus, 5
Donehue, Joseph, 333
Donlin, Michael J. "Turkey Mike," *94*, 187
Dooin, Charles Sebastian "Red," 26–27, *362*, 363–66 *passim*, 370–92 *passim*, 439f, 442
Doran, George H., 558
Dorgan, Thomas Aloysius "Tad," 28, *280*
Dovey, George B., 433
Doyle, John Joseph "Jack," *35*, 39
Doyle, Lawrence J. "Laughing Larry," *179*, 182, 191, 411–20 *passim*
Dryden, Charles, 4, 345, 352
Dubuc, Jean A. "Chauncey," 28, 80
Dugey, Oscar J., 425
Dumont, George H., 199
Dunn, John J. "Jack" or "Dunnie," *405*, 426
Duquesne Brewing Co., 502

Easterly, Theodore H., *64–65*, 98
Eastern League, 93, 339, 346
Eden, David, 333
Ellison, Herbert S. "Babe," *265*
El Paso, Tex., 53
Elston, Charles Curtis "Curt," *332–33*, 334–61 *passim*; singing ability, 345
Empress of Japan, 28, 189–90
Englewood Union Station, Chicago, 598
Erickson, George A., 319
Erie, Pa., 34
Evans, Louis Richard "Steve," 176, 185
Evans, William G., *89*, 137, 139, 159, 203
Evansville, Central League club, 3, 26–27, 86, 372–75
Evers, John J., 222, *331*, 332–58 *passim*, 425, 439

Faber, Urban C. "Red," *162–63*, 178, 182, 201, 207, 237, 242f, 257–58, 305f
Falkenberg, Frederick P. "Cy," 98, *419*
Fall River, Mass., 490
Fanning, Charles "Skeeter," 73
Faust, Charles Victor, *358–59*
Federal League, 21, 23, 46, 48, 65, 77, 88, 115ff, 124, 135–39 *passim*, 148, 162, 176, 178, 196, 206, 263, 315, 335, 342f, 347, 365, 400, 402, 419, 423, 434, 440, 506, 525, 534, 542, 574–75, 582; history of, 97–98
Felsch, Oscar E. "Happy," 207, *251*, 257–58, 263f, 303, 306, 316
Finneran, William, 369
Fittery, Paul C., 26–27, 29, *372–73*

Fitzgerald, F. Scott, 22
Flagstead, Ira J., *260*
Fletcher, Arthur, *419*
Fohl, Leo A. "Lee," *287*, 295
Ford, Edward C. "Whitey," 273
Fort Wayne, Ind., 382; Central League club, 26, 34, 333, 358, 368, 371–76 *passim*
Fort Worth, Tex., 238f; Cats, Texas League, 242, 244, 267f, 399, 593
Fournier, John F. "Jacques," 8, *47*, 86f, 130
Frazee, Harry, 271, 274, 303
Fredericks, Charles Augustus, 40, 122
French Lick Springs, Ind., 167
Fromholtz, Jacob G., 26–27, 29, *372*, 373
Fromme, Arthur H., 409
Fullerton, Hugh S., 4, 7f

Gadski, Johanna, 472
Gaffney, James E., 426
Gainor, Delos C., 68
Gallia, Melvin A. "Bert," *256–57*, 259, 263, 269
Gandil, Charles A. "Chick," 16, 59, 65, 78, *199*, 200, 204f, 213, 254, 257f, 286, 292, 302, 315, 392; and throwing of 1919 World Series, 163, 199, 248, 251, 305, 314; fight with Speaker, 287f
Gardner, William L. "Larry," *267*
Gedeon, Elmer Joseph "Joe," *253–54*, 264
Gehrig, Henry Louis, 253, 271, 289
Gettysburg College, 411
Gibson, George "Moon," *401*
Gibson, Preston, 86
Gilbert, Lawrence W., 425
Gilks, Robert J., 564
Gilmore, James, 97
Gleason, William J. "Kid," 15f, 25, *42–43*, 46–49 *passim*, 60, 65, 68, 76–77f, 83–86 *passim*, 118, 126–38 *passim*, 147–50 *passim*, 160f, 194–201 *passim*, 208, 212f, 449; as White Sox manager, 227–327 *passim*
Good, Wilbur David, *159*, 399
Gotch, Frank A., 561
Gowdy, Henry Morgan "Hank," 425
Grabiner, Harry, 40, 122, 226, 233
Grand Rapids club, Central League, 34
Graney, John Gladstone "Jack," *203*, 204, 287, 295f, 299
Griffith, Clark C., *88*, 212, 234, 282, 510, 558
Griner, Donald D. "Dan," *343*
Groh, Henry K. "Heinie," *315–16*, 401, 513
Grove, Robert M. "Lefty," 405

Hamilton, William R. "Billy," 428
Hand, John, 122
Harper, Harry C., *285*
Harvard University, 142
Hauser, Arnold G., *400*
Hawley, Senator Willis Chatman, 509
Hearn, Bunn, *177*, 178
Hearst's International-Cosmopolitan magazine, 22
Hecht, Ben, 4f
Heeman, Edward C., 8, 168–69
Heilmann, Harry E., 260
Hendricks, John C. "Jack," 358
Henry, John P., *407*
Herrmann, August "Garry," 304, *545*
Herzog, Charles L. "Buck," *513–14*
Hess, Otto C., 425, *432*
Hoblitzell, Richard C. "Hobby," *342*, 401
Hofman, Arthur F. "Solly," 5, 222, 345
Holy Cross, College of the, 78
Hong Kong, 9
Hooper, Harry B., 272, 276f, 550f
Hoppe, William E. "Willie," *450*
Houck, Byron S., 409
Houdini, Harry, 238
Houston club, Texas League, 11, 247
Howard, George E. "Del," *74*, 75

Huggins, Miller J., 304, *427–28*
Humphries, Albert "Bert," *336*
Hutchinson, Duke, 4

Illinois Institute of Technology, 2
Indianapolis, Ind., 339–40; Indians, American Association, 66, 403; Hoosiers, Federal League, 97, 315, 333, 419, 525
International League, 94, 273
Ishpeming, Mich., 398–401 *passim*

Jackson, Joseph J., *59–60*, 65, 83, 133, 196, 207, 257–58, 262, 272–77 *passim*, 296
Jackson, Mich., 49, 467
Jackson, Miss., 49
James, William H. "Big Bill," 257, *498*
James, William L. "Seattle Bill," 402, 425, *498*
Jenkins, Joseph D., *237*, 257, 259
Jennings, Hugh A., *69–70*, 79, 121, 135f, 140, 202, 288, 302–7 *passim*, 312, 320–27 *passim*, 570f
Jersey City club, International League, 94
Johnson, Alexander, 19
Johnson, Byron Bancroft, *39*, 98, 120–26 *passim*, 307, 549, 551, 571; as founder and president of American League, 37, 39; waning of authority of, 39, 304, 306
Johnson, George H. "Chief," *342*
Johnson, Jack, 297
Johnson, Walter Perry, *46*, 76f, 86ff, 141, 150, 155, 199, 207, 238, 242, 282, 365, 391f, 418, 509f, 555, 584; fast ball, 406–8, 555
Johnston, John T., *63*
Johnston, Wheeler R. "Doc," *82*
Judge, Joseph I., *314*

Kalamazoo *Gazette*, 3
Kansas City, Mo., 177, 182; Federal League club, 97, 342, 506
Keeley, James, 6
Kelley, Peter F., *432*, 445
Keough, Hugh E., 6
Kerr, Richard H. "Dickie," 252, 257–58, 260, 305, *306*
Killefer, William L., *370*, 382
Klem, William J., *357*, 358, 402, 512
Knabe, Franz Otto, *423*, 424, 426, 440, 446
Knoll, Charles E. "Punch," 27, *375*, 377, 393
Kopf, William Lorenz "Larry," 286
Kramer, George, 269
Kuhn, Walter C. "Red," 55, 63

Lajoie, Napoleon, *58*, 59, 83, 133
Landis, Kenesaw Mountain, 24, 304
Lange, Frank Herman, 49, 66
Lapp, John W. "Jack," *283*, 284
Lardner, Rex, 3
Lardner, Ringgold Wilmer: removal to New York, 1; early years, 1–6; end of daily sportswriting, 6, 60; later baseball fiction, 22–23; death, 23; relations with Curt Elston, 332
Lardner, Ringgold Wilmer, Jr., 21, 28
Latonia, Ky., 402
Lavender, James S. "Jimmy," *336*
Leach, Thomas W., *96*, 159, 337f, 342, 399
Leddy, Alice, 134
Lee, Guy, 7
Leibold, Harry L. "Nemo," *246*, 257, 292, 296, 316, 322
Lewis, George E. "Duffy," *550*
Liberty magazine, 22
Lillie, Major Gordon W. "Pawnee Bill," 535
Lincoln, Abraham, 15
Little, Mrs. Winifred Laurie, 361
Lobert, John Bernard "Hans," 191
Lord, Harry D., 45, *46*, 56, 66, 68f, 83, 137
Lorimer, George Horace, 7, 18
Los Angeles, Calif., 53f, 73, 126, 128, 179, 181, 405; Angels, Pacific

Los Angeles (*continued*)
Coast League, 41, 50, 54, 67, 412; Dodgers, National League, 45
Louisville club, National League, 365, 388
Lowdermilk, Grover C., 257, *282*, 305
Luderus, Frederick W., *369*, 439
Ludington, Mich., 375, 468
Lueker, Claude, 307
Lusitania, 193
Lynn, Byrd, 257, *276*
Lyons, Theodore A., 163

MacArthur, Charles, 4
McBride, George F., *90*, 408
McCarthy, Joseph V., 425
McClellan, Harvey, 257
McClure's magazine, 18f, 21
McCormack, John, 472
McCormick Harvester Co., 2
MacDonald, Judge Charles, 59
McGinnity, Joseph J., 464
McGraw, John J., 27, *172*, 355f, 358, 375, 395–422 *passim*, 427, 434, 495–96; on Giants–White Sox tour of 1913, 169–91 *passim*
McGraw, Robert E., 304
McInnis, John P. "Jack" or "Stuffy," *142*, 407, 411–16 *passim*, 421
Mack, Connie, 18, 20, 77f, 108, 206, 271, 279, *307*, 309, 325–27, 426, 559, 565, 571f, in 1914 World Series, 395–422 *passim*; in 1916 season, 559, 565–72 *passim*
MacKenzie, Cameron, 18
McMullin, Frederic William, *213*, 214, 257–58
Madison Square Garden, 84
Magee, Lee, *400*
Magee, Sherwood, *368–69*, 378, 438
Mann, Leslie, 425
Maranville, Walter J. V. "Rabbit," *387*, 425, 438f, 588
Marietta, Ohio, 331, 333, 338–39, 358
Marietta College, 33, 39
Maris, Roger, 274
Marlin, Tex., 397
Marquard, Richard W. "Rube," *355*, 356, 409–15 *passim*, 495
Marsans, Armando, *402*
Martin, William L., 425
Mathewson, Christopher, 56, *155*, 355ff, 409–20 *passim*, 434, 464, 495; as manager of Reds, 155, 513, 583; on Giants–White Sox tour of 1913, 173–84 *passim*
Mayer, James Erskine, 17, *311*, 367, 372, 383, 388, 390
Mays, Carl W., 17, 24, 82, 270, *271*, 303–12 *passim*, 318
Mays, Willie H., 388
Maysville, Ky., club, Ohio State League, 339
Memphis Chickasaws, Southern Association, 322, 375
Mencken, H. L., 373
Merkle, Fred, 158, *171–72*, 222, 413f, 420
Metropolitan magazine, 18f
Meyers, John T. "Chief," *357–58*, 414, 523
Michigan Central RR, 2, 319
Milan, Clyde, 69, *88–89*, 213, 392, 406, 557
Milan, Horace, 213
Miller, Ward T. "Windy," *335*, 338
Millsaps College, 321
Milwaukee, Wis., 251; Brewers, American League (1901), 90, 297; Brewers, American Association, 118, 123ff, 133, 138, 228, 243; Western League club, 307
Mineral Wells, Tex., 41, 238–46 *passim*, 250, 550
Minneapolis Millers, American Association, 45, 187, 238, 476
Mitchell, Frederick F., 425
Mobile club, Southern Association, 393
Mollwitz, Frederick A. "Fritz," *513*
Monon Route, 40, 167
Montgomery club, Southern Asso-

ciation, 561f, 564
Moran, John Herbert, 425
Moran, Patrick J., *315*, 316, 365, 367–68, 380–90 *passim*, 438, 504f
Moriarty, George, *68*, 69, 136
Mowrey, Harry H. "Mike," *400–401*
Mullin, George, 98
Murphy, Daniel F., *407*
Murphy, John Edward "Honest Eddie," 257, *407*, 409–20 *passim*
Murray, John J. "Red," *411*, 412–16 *passim*
Musial, Stanley F., 69, 306, 388
Mutrie, James J., 425

Nashville Volunteers, Southern Association, 251, 352, 358, 375, 435
National Baseball Hall of Fame and Museum, Cooperstown, N.Y.: members of, 35, 37, 46, 48, 56, 58f, 63, 77f, 114, 155, 163, 172, 253, 272, 274, 307, 355, 365, 367, 388, 411, 493, 519; players barred from because of 1919 scandal, 48, 59, 65, 271; omissions from, 67, 89, 142, 271, 400
National Commission, 24, 303, 437, *515*
National Football League, 89
National League of Professional Baseball Clubs: establishment of monopsony, 33
Naylor, Roleine Cecil "Rollie," 311
Neary, James B., *433*, 443
Nebraska Wesleyan College, 44
Needham, Thomas J., *334*, 338, 349
Newark club, Federal League, 88, 315, 333, 419, 506–7, 525
New England League, 54, 387
New Orleans Pelicans, Southern Association, 435f
New York, N.Y., 83ff, 112, 151, 307, 314, 431–32
New York Central System, 319, 490, 598
New York Giants, 8, 10, 25, 48, 63, 92, 155, 163, 193, 200, 206f, 215, 271, 306, 312–19 *passim*, 334, 343, 347, 355–62 *passim*, 383, 385; on world tour with White Sox, 8–9, 94, 168–91; in 1913 World Series, 394–422 *passim*, 427, 438, 464, 492, 494, 513, 584
New York Mets, 414
New York Yankees, 39, 47, 49, 55, 63–68 *passim*, 78, 88f, 130, 141, 147, 159, 172, 204, 222, 230, 253, 270, 274, 279–85 *passim*, 289, 297, 304ff, 313, 321, 400, 402, 419, 427, 513, 550; acquisition of players from Red Sox, 271–74, 412
Nickel Plate Road, 598
Nickerson, Herman, 432
Niles, Mich., 1–2; Gas Co., 2; *Daily Sun*, 3
Northwestern League, 178
Norwich University, 142
Noyes, Winfield C. "Wyn," 257

Oakes, Ennis T. "Rebel," *347*, 399f, 510
Oakland, Calif., 42, 50, 199; Oaks, Pacific Coast League, 41, 50f, 73f, 131–32
O'Day, Henry F. "Hank," *158*, 377, 378–79, 384, 399–400ff, 429
Oeschger, Joseph C., 367
Ohio & Pennsylvania League, 34, 89
Ohio State League, 339
Oklahoma City, Okla., 53
Oldfield, Barna E., 292
Oldring, Reuben H., *78*, 405
O'Leary, Charles T., 88, *130*, 222
O'Loughlin, Francis H. "Silk," 199, 596
Omaha club, Western League, 56
O'Neill, Joseph, 122, *309*
Overall, Orval, 345–46

Pacific Coast League, 41, 44, 51, 67, 188, 193, 283, 513
Paskert, George H. "Dode," 26, *370–71*, 504ff

Paso Robles, Calif., 5, 41, 44, 91, 117
Patrick, Walton R., 12, 29
Pearce, George T., *158*, 159, 337
Peckinpaugh, Roger T., *321*
Pennsylvania RR, 598
Perdue, Hubbard E., 5, 25, *351*, 435–44 *passim*
Pere Marquette Ry., 468
Perkins, Maxwell, 29
Perry, Herbert Scott, 306, 311
Pershing, Gen. John J., 14
Phelon, W. A., 334, 339
Philadelphia, Pa., 81, 85, 151, 229f, 302, 308, 312, 326, 380, 382f, 387–94 *passim*
Philadelphia Athletics, 8, 25, 33, 55, 58, 76ff, 82, 86, 141f, 144, 150, 170, 197, 201–6 *passim*, 234, 258, 267, 271, 274f, 279, 292, 297, 307, 309, 325–27, 365, 367, 391, 519; of 1916, 567; story set on team of 1913, 394–422
Philadelphia Phillies, 20, 26, 43, 58, 63, 77, 95f, 142, 159, 206, 257, 306, 311, 315, 331, 336, 345, 347, 399, 405, 415, 419, 426f, 438–42 *passim*, 464, 467, 569, 573; story set on team of 1914, 362–93
Phillips, Wendell, 208
Pickford, Mary, 467
Pierce, George T., *see* Pearce, George T.
Pinkerton, William A., 231
Pipp, Walter C., *289*
Pittsburgh, Pa., 335, 385, 423, 446; club, Federal League, 97, 347, 400, 510
Pittsburgh Pirates, 43, 45, 66, 74, 82, 96, 142, 159, 201, 222, 260, 287, 297, 307, 333, 335, 347, 349, 365, 388, 400f, 407, 412, 419, 423, 427, 440–44 *passim*, 467, 513, 519, 584
Plank, Edward S., 98, 194, 409f, *411*, 412–16 *passim*
Players League, 37, 158, 188, 312, 581
Polo Grounds, 414
Pond, Hy, 27–28, 222–23, 373
Portland, Ore., 359; club, Pacific Coast League, 51, 75
Portsmouth club, Virginia League, 372
Pratt, Derrill B. "Del," *63*, 64
Princeton University, 272
Providence club, Eastern (International) League, 93, 339, 358, 405

Quinn, John Picus, 39, 98

Ragan, Don Carlos Patrick, *306*
Rath, Maurice, 286
Red Book magazine, 19f
Reulbach, Ed, 5
Rhinelander, Wis., 37
Richie, Lewis A. "Lurid Lew," 5, 22, *345*
Richmond club, Virginia League, 367
Rickard, George L. "Tex," 84, *298*
Rigler, Charles "Cy," 26, *343*, 438–41 *passim*, 500, 563
Ringgold, Cadwallader, 2
Risberg, Charles A. "Swede," 213, 254, 257–58, 302
Rixey, Eppa, Jr., 20, 26, *363–65*, 368, 371, 377, 383, 390, 438–41 *passim*, 563
Robinson, Wilbert, *492–93*, 573
Robison, Frank De Haas, 424
Robison, M. Stanley, 424
Rockefeller, John D., 77
Roosevelt, Theodore, 87
Roth, Robert F. "Braggo," 204, 221f, 279
Roush, Edward J., *315–16*
Rowland, Clarence H. "Pants," 28, 43, *192*, 194, 196, 201, 205, 207, 212f, 222, 229; resigns as manager of White Sox, 227–28
Rucker, George Napoleon "Nap," *429*, 493
Rudolph, Richard, 402, 425
Russell, Allen, 304

Russell, Ewell Albert "Reb," *44–45*, 91, 98, 150, 172, 199
Ruth, George H. "Babe," 22, 24, 271, 272–74, 275–91 *passim*, 321, 324, 368; conversion to outfield, 273; transfer to Yankees, 274

Sacramento Solons, Pacific Coast League, 50, 76–77
Saier, Victor S., *159*, 338, 343, 399, 403
St. Joseph, Mo., 53, 57, 175; club, Western Association, 57
St. Louis, Mo., 4, 143, 242, 245, 324, 350, 352, 367, 379, 399, 443; club, Federal League, 97, 263, 267, 335, 343, 402, 411
St. Louis Browns, 37, 48f, 62f, 71, 83, 91, 95, 98, 130, 134, 143, 148, 150, 194, 206, 212, 229, 237, 251–71 *passim*, 275, 282, 287, 296f, 304–9 *passim*, 365, 400, 402, 410ff, 498
St. Louis Cardinals, 47, 63, 68, 130, 176f, 239, 266, 282, 297, 343–47 *passim*, 351, 367, 381ff, 388, 393, 400, 403, 412, 424–28 *passim*, 438, 440, 444, 464, 513f, 584
St. Mary's College, 272
St. Paul, Minn., 34
Sallee, Harry F. "Slim," *347*, 366
San Antonio club, Texas League, 222
San Diego, Calif., 179
San Francisco, Calif., 53, 72–76, 82, 128f, 171, 181f; Seals, Pacific Coast League, 49ff, 74, 130
Saturday Evening Post, 7, 15–23 *passim*
Schaefer, Herman A. "Germany," *87–88*, 176, 186, 188f, 535
Schalk, Raymond W., 50, *63*, 64–69 *passim*, 80, 89, 136, 140, 147, 158, 204f, 241, 253, 257–58, 272, 276f, 288, 290, 302–6 *passim*, 321
Schang, Walter H. "Wally," *271*, 411–20 *passim*
Schmidt, Charles "Boss," 393
Schmidt, Charles J. "Butch," 425, 439
Schneider, Peter J., *513*, 514
Schulte, Frank M. "Wildfire," 5, 8, 25, *96*, 97, 159, 338, 377–78, 399
Schupp, Ferdinand M., *584*
Scott, James "Death Valley," *44*, 56–61 *passim*, 91, 134, 138, 141, 163, 180, 192, 194, 229
Scott, Lewis Everett, *271*, 272
Selee, Frank G., *425*
Shafer, Arthur J. "Tillie," *405*
Shanks, Howard S. "Hank," *89*
Shaw, James A., *282*
Shawkey, James Robert "Bob," 409
Sheckard, Samuel James Tilden, 5, *345*
Sheridan, John F., *188*
Shibe, Ben, 307
Shotton, Burton E., *63*
Sinclair, Harry F., 507
Sioux City club, Western League, 34, 132
Sisler, George H., *253*, 264, 324
Smith, Frank E., 8
Smith, James Carlisle "Red," 425, *429*
Smith, Louis D., 26, 34, *49*
Smith, Sherrod M. "Sherry," *584*, 585
Society for American Baseball Research, 24
Soo Line, 184
Sotheron, Allen S., *266*
South Bend, Ind., 2; Central League club, 3, 34; *Times*, 3, 28, 34, 343; *Tribune*, 3
Southern Association, 89, 188, 266, 332, 354, 358, 366, 393, 442, 561, 564
Southern Michigan Association, 51, 467
Southern Pacific Co., 42
Southwestern College, 249
Southwestern Texas League, 94
Spahn, Warren E., 155, 363, 411
Speaker, Tristam E., 174, 179, 185,

Speaker (*continued*)
191, 196, *203*, 204f, 266, 287f, 295f, 299, 478, 550
Sporting News, 4
Springfield, Ohio, 3, 34
Stallings, George T., 426, *573*
Stanage, Oscar H., *68*, 138
Starrett, Vincent, 336
Steam beer, 53
Steinfeldt, Harry M., 331
Stengel, Charles Dillon "Casey," 23, 172, 347
Stewart, Charles E. "Tuffy," *399*
Stovall, George, 95
Strand, Paul E., 425
Street, Charles E. "Gabby," 86
Strunk, Amos, *274*, 277, 409, 411, 417f
Sullivan, John J. "Lefty," 257
Sullivan, Timothy Paul "Ted," *178*, 428
Sullivan, William J., Sr., *72*, 86, 152
Sunday, William A. "Billy," *467*

Tampa, Fla., 334, 339
Taylor, Bert Leston, 6
Taylor, Luther H. "Dummy," *179*, 283
Terre Haute, Ind., 33, 179; Central League club, 3, 8, 25f, 34f, 39, 49, 115, 376
Terre Haute Brewing Co., 26, 53
Tesreau, Charles Monroe "Jeff," *355–56*, 357, 409, 413, 417, 495
Texas & Pacific Ry., 239
Texas League, 222, 247, 267f, 474
Texas Oklahoma League, 106
Thackeray, William Makepeace, 7, 19
Thorpe, James Francis, *179–80*
Three I League, 375, 578f, 586
Tinker, Joseph B., 98, *114*, 115, 331
Titanic, 15
Tobin, John T. "Jack," *263*, 264, 267
Toledo, Ohio, 297–301 *passim*
Towne, Charles Hanson, 21
Tri-State League, 51
Trollope, Anthony, 24, 29
Turner, Clarence Lamont, *82*
Twin Ports League, 597–98
Tyler, George A., *402*, 425, 434

Union Pacific RR, 41–42
United States Railroad Administration, 308
University of Alabama, 63
University of California, Los Angeles (UCLA), 47
University of Chicago, 77
University of Maryland, 513
University of Michigan, 253
University of Notre Dame, 2, 8
University of Santa Clara, 20, 405
University of Texas, 249
University of Vermont, 267
University of Virginia, 363f
Utica club, New York State League, 374

Valenzuela, Fernando, 45
Vancouver, B.C., 171, 184
Vanderbilt University, 333
Van Haltren, George E. M., 17, *311–12*
Van Loan, Charles, 7
Vaughn, James "Hippo Jim," 92
Veach, Robert H., 17, *67*, 69, 140, 259, 324–25, 601, 603
Veeck, William Louis, Jr., "Bill," 37, 40, 277
Venice club, Pacific Coast League, 53f, 75, 128
Vick, Samuel B., 17, *321*, 322
Virginia League, 333, 346, 372, 374
Visalia, Calif., 51
Vitt, Oscar J., 80
von Kolnitz, Alfred H., *513*

Waddell, George E. "Rube," 108, *365*, 366, 593
Wagner, A. W., 34
Wagner, John Peter "Honus," *388*, 508, 524
Wagner, Joseph B., *513*

Walsh, Edward Augustine, *35*, 43–49 *passim*, 58, 81, 91, 229, 306, 556; singing ability of, 86
Walsh, Martin, 333, *346*
Washington, D.C., 86, 293, 391f; National League club, 307
Washington Senators, 16, 63, 76, 86–90 *passim*, 96, 141, 144, 150, 199–207 *passim*, 214, 234, 238, 246, 253, 257–63 *passim*, 267, 282, 292, 306, 314, 319, 321, 327, 368, 391, 408, 412, 419, 550; effort to acquire Keefe, 212–13
Weatherford, Mineral Wells & North-Western Ry., 239
Weaver, George D. "Buck," 25, *51*, 56, 64, 66, 78–87 *passim*, 96, 137–40 *passim*, 144–45, 159, 171, 239, 241, 246f, 257–58, 265, 285, 299, 588
Wellesley College, 446
Western League, 34, 56, 58, 132, 163, 188, 207, 358
Whaling, Albert J., 425, *439*
Wheat, Zacharia D. "Zack," *519*, 520f
Wheeling, W.Va., 34
Whipple, Amos H., *353*
White, Guy Harris "Doc," 55, 86, 346
Whitted, George B. "Possum," *347*, 425, 430
Wilkinson, Roy H., 257
Willard, Jess, *297*, 298–304 *passim*
Williams, Augustus "Gus," *63*
Williams, Charles G., *346*
Williams, Claude P. "Lefty," 15, 25, 59, 163, 192, 202, *248*, 253, 257–58, 263, 265, 276, 282, 286, 288, 305, 311, 314, 320–21, 498
Williams, Fred "Cy," *399*
Wilson, W. Woodrow, 87, 183f, 193, 208, 234, 512, 565
Wiltse, George L. "Hooks," *177–78*, 180, 187, 191
Withington, Winthrop, 467
Wittenberg College, 413
Wolff, Virginia, 22
Wolfgang, Melford J., *242–43*
Wood, Howard Ellsworth "Smokey Joe," *83*
World Series: of 1911, 409; of 1913, 394–95, 405–22 *passim*; of 1914, 391; of 1915, 273; of 1916, 273; of 1917, 163, 193, 206f, 215, 248; of 1918, 273; of 1919, 163, 199, 248, 286, 306f, 498

Yale University, 20, 83, 431, 438, 446
Young, Denton T. "Cy," *239*, 367
Youngstown, Ohio, 34; *Vindicator*, 89
Yuma, Ariz., 9, 53f

Zanesville, Ohio, 34
Zeider, Rollie H., 48, 557
Zimmerman, Henry "Heinie," 8, *92*, 96, 334–38 *passim*, 399, 403

Library of Congress Cataloging-in-Publication Data

Lardner, Ring, 1885–1933.
[Short stories. Selections]
The annotated baseball stories of Ring W. Lardner, 1914–1919 / edited by George W. Hilton.
p. cm.
Includes bibliographical references and index.
ISBN 0-8047-2405-9 (alk. paper)
1. Baseball stories, American. I. Hilton, George Woodman. II. Title.
PS3523.A7A6 1995
813′.52—dc20 94-28020 CIP

∞ This book is printed on acid-free paper.
It was typeset in 10.5/15 Baskerville by Terry Robinson & Co.
Designed by Kathleen Szawiola